THE WIFE OF
SIR ISAAC HARMAN

&

THE DREAM

THE WIFE OF
SIR ISAAC HARMAN

and

THE DREAM

by

H. G. WELLS

ODHAMS PRESS LIMITED
LONDON, W.C. 2

Printed in Great Britain

THE WIFE OF
SIR ISAAC HARMAN

CONTENTS

CHAPTER ONE

INTRODUCES LADY HARMAN

§ 1

THE motor-car entered a little white gate, came to a porch under a thick wig of jasmine, and stopped. The chauffeur indicated by a movement of the head that this at last was it. A tall young woman with a big soft mouth, great masses of blue-black hair on either side of a broad, low forehead, and eyes of so dark a brown you might have thought them black, drooped forward and surveyed the house with a mixture of keen appreciation and that gentle apprehension which is the shadow of desire in unassuming natures. . . .

The little house with the white-framed windows looked at her with a sleepy wakefulness from under its blinds, and made no sign. Beyond the corner was a glimpse of lawn, a rank of delphiniums, and the sound of a wheel-barrow.

" Clarence ! " the lady called again.

Clarence, with an air of exceeding his duties, decided to hear, descended slowly, and came to the door.

" Very likely—if you were to look for a bell, Clarence . . ."

Clarence regarded the porch with a hostile air, made no secret that he thought it a fool of a porch, seemed on the point of disobedience, and submitted. His gestures suggested a belief that he would next be asked to boil eggs or do the boots. He found a bell and rang it with the needless violence of a man who has no special knowledge of ringing bells. How was *he* to know ? He was a chauffeur. The bell did not so much ring as explode and swamp the place. Sounds of ringing came from all the windows, and even out of the chimneys. It seemed as if once set ringing that bell would never cease. . . .

Clarence went to the bonnet of his machine, and presented his stooping back in a defensive manner against any one who might come out. He wasn't a footman, anyhow. He'd rung that bell all right, and now he must see to his engine.

" He's rung so *loud* ! " said the lady weakly—apparently to God.

The door behind the neat white pillars opened, and a little red-nosed woman, in a cap she had evidently put on without a proper glass, appeared. She surveyed the car and its occupant with disfavour over her also very oblique spectacles.

The lady waved a pink paper to her, a house-agent's order to view. " Is this Black Strands ? " she shouted.

The little woman advanced slowly with her eyes fixed malevolently on the pink paper. She seemed to be stalking it.

" This *is* Black Strands ? " repeated the tall lady, " I

should be so sorry if I disturbed you—if it isn't ; ringing the bell like that—and all. You can't think——— "

" This is Black *Strand*," said the little old woman with a note of deep reproach, and suddenly ceased to look over her glasses and looked through them. She looked no kindlier through them, and her eye seemed much larger. She was now regarding the lady in the car, though with a sustained alertness towards the pink paper. " I suppose," she said, " you've come to see over the place ? "

" If it doesn't disturb any one ; if it is quite convenient——— "

" Mr. Brumley is *hout*," said the little old woman. " And if you got an order to view, you got an order to view."

" If you think I might."

The lady stood up in the car, a tall and graceful figure of doubt and desire and glossy black fur. " I'm sure it looks a very charming house."

" It's *clean*," said the little old woman, " from top to toe. Look as you may."

" I'm sure it is," said the tall lady, and put aside her great fur coat from her lithe, slender, red-clad body. (She was permitted by a sudden civility of Clarence's to descend.) " Why ! the windows," she said, pausing on the step, " are like crystal."

" These very 'ands," said the little old woman, and glanced up at the windows the lady had praised. The little old woman's initial sternness wrinkled and softened as the skin of a windfall does after a day or so upon the ground. She half turned in the doorway and made a sudden vergerlike gesture. " We enter," she said, " by the 'all. . . . Them's Mr. Brumley's 'ats and sticks. Every 'at or cap 'as a stick, and every stick 'as a 'at *or* cap, and on the 'all table is the gloves corresponding. On the right is the door leading to the kitching, on the left is the large droring-room which Mr. Brumley 'as took as 'is study." Her voice fell to lowlier things. " The other door beyond is a small lavatory 'aving a basing for washing 'ands."

" It's a perfectly delightful hall," said the lady. " So low and wide-looking. And everything so bright—and lovely. Those long, Italian pictures ! And how charming that broad outlook upon the garden beyond ! "

" You'll think it charminger when you see the garding," said the little old woman. " It was Mrs. Brumley's especial delight. Much of it—with 'er own 'ands.

" We now enter the droring-room," she proceeded, and flinging open the door to the right was received with an indistinct cry suggestive of the words, " Oh, *damn* it ! " The stout medium-sized gentleman in an artistic green-gray Norfolk suit, from whom the cry proceeded, was kneeling on the floor close to the wide-open window, and he was engaged in lacing up a boot. He had a round, ruddy, rather handsome, amiable face, with a sort of bang of brown hair coming over one temple, and a large silk bow under his chin and a little

towards one ear, such as artists and artistic men of letters affect.
His profile was regular and fine, his eyes expressive, his mouth,
a very passable mouth. His features expressed at first only
the naïve horror of a shy man unveiled.

Intelligent appreciation supervened.

There was a crowded moment of rapid mutual inspection.
The lady's attitude was that of the enthusiastic house-ex-
plorer arrested in full flight, falling swiftly towards apology
and retreat. (It was a frightfully attractive room, too, full
of the brightest colour, and with a big white cast of a statue
—a Venus !—in the window.) She backed over the threshold
again.

" I thought you was out by that window, sir," said the little
old woman intimately, and was nearly shutting the door
between them and all the beginnings of this story.

But the voice of the gentleman arrested and wedged open
the closing door.

" I—— Are you looking at the house ? " he said. " I say !
Just a moment, Mrs. Rabbit."

He came down the length of the room with a slight flicking
noise due to the scandalised excitement of his abandoned
laces. The lady was reminded of her not so very distant school-
days, when it would have been considered a suitable answer
to such a question as his to reply, " No, I am walking down
Piccadilly on my hands." But instead she waved that pink
paper again. " The agents," she said. " Recommended—
specially. So sorry if I intrude. I ought, I know, to have
written first ; but I came on an impulse."

By this time the gentleman in the artistic tie, who had
also the artistic eye for such matters, had discovered that
the lady was young, delightfully slender, either pretty or
beautiful, he could scarcely tell which, and very, very well
dressed. " I am glad," he said, with remarkable decision,
" that I was not out. *I* will show you the house."

" 'Ow *can* you, sir ? " intervened the little old woman.

" Oh ! show a house ! Why not ? "

" The kitchings—you don't understand the range, sir—it's
beyond you. And upstairs. You can't show a lady upstairs."

The gentleman reflected upon these difficulties.

" Well, I'm going to show her all I can show her anyhow.
And after that, Mrs. Rabbit, you shall come in. You needn't
wait."

" I'm thinking," said Mrs. Rabbit, folding stiff little arms
and regarding him sternly. " You won't be much good after
tea, you know, if you don't get your afternoon's exercise."

" Rendez-vous in the kitchen, Mrs. Rabbit," said Mr.
Brumley firmly, and Mrs. Rabbit after a moment of mute
struggle disappeared discontentedly.

" I do not want to be the least bit of a bother," said the
lady. " I'm intruding, I know, without the least bit of notice,

I *do* hope I'm not disturbing you—— " she seemed to make
an effort to stop at that, and failed and added the please
bit. "Do please tell me if I am."

" Not at all," said Mr. Brumley. " I hate my afternoon's
walk as a prisoner hates the treadmill."

" She's such a nice old creature."

" She's been a mother—and several aunts—to us ever since
my wife died. She was the first servant we ever had."

" All this house," he explained to his visitor's questioning
eyes, " was my wife's creation. It was a little featureless
agent's house on the edge of these pinewoods. She saw something in the shape of the rooms—and that central hall. We've
enlarged it, of course. Twice. This was two rooms, that is
why there is a step down in the centre."

" That window and window-seat—— "

" That was her addition," said Mr. Brumley. " All this
room is—replete—with her personality." He hesitated, and
explained further. " When we prepared this house—we
expected to be better off—than we subsequently became—
and she could let herself go. Much is from Holland and Italy."

" And that beautiful old writing-desk with the little single
rose in a glass ! "

" She put it there. She even in a sense put the flower there.
It is renewed of course. By Mrs. Rabbit. She trained Mrs.
Rabbit."

He sighed slightly, apparently at some thought of Mrs.
Rabbit.

" You—you write—— " the lady stopped, and then diverted
a question that she perhaps considered too blunt, " there ? "

" Largely. I am—a sort of author. Perhaps you know my
books. Not very important books—but people sometimes
read them."

The rose-pink of the lady's cheek deepened by a shade.
Within her pretty head, her mind rushed to and fro, saying,
" Brumley ? Brumley ? " Then she had a saving gleam.
" Are you *George* Brumley ? " she asked—" *the* George Brum-
ley ? "

" My name *is* George Brumley," he said, with a proud
modesty. " Perhaps you know my little Euphemia books ?
They are still the most read."

The lady made a faint, dishonest assent-like noise ; and
her rose-pink deepened another shade. But her interlocutor
was not watching her very closely just then.

" Euphemia was my wife," he said, " at least, my wife gave
her to me—a kind of exhalation. *This*—— " his voice fell
with a genuine respect for literary associations—" was Euphemia's home."

" I still," he continued, " go on. I go on writing about
Euphemia. I have to. In this house. With my tradition. . . .
But it is becoming painful—painful. Curiously more painful

now than at the beginning. And I want to go. I want at last to make a break. That is why I am letting or selling the house. . . . There will be no more Euphemia."

His voice fell to silence.

The lady surveyed the long, low, clear room, so cleverly prepared for life, with its white wall, its Dutch clock, its Dutch dresser, its pretty seats about the open fireplace, its cleverly placed bureau, its suntrap at the garden end ; she could feel the rich intention of living in its every arrangement and a sense of uncertainty in things struck home to her. She seemed to see a woman, a woman like hereslf—only very, very much cleverer—flitting about the room and making it. And then this woman had vanished—nowhither. Leaving this gentleman—sadly left—in the care of Mrs. Rabbit.

" And she is dead ? " she said, with a softness in her dark eyes and a fall in her voice that was quite natural and very pretty.

" She died," said Mr. Brumley, " three years and a half ago." He reflected. " Almost exactly."

He paused, and she filled the pause with feeling.

He became suddenly very brave and brisk and business-like. He led the way back into the hall and made explanations. " It is not so much a hall as a hall living-room. We use that end, except when we go out upon the veranda beyond, as our dining-room. The door to the right is the kitchen."

The lady's attention was caught again by the bright, long, eventful pictures that had already pleased her. " They are copies of two of Carpaccio's St. George series in Venice, he said. " We bought them together there. But no doubt you've seen the originals. In a little old place with a custodian and rather dark. One of those corners—so full of that delightful out-of-the-wayishness which is so characteristic, I think, of Venice. I don't know if you found that in Venice ? "

" I've never been abroad," said the lady. " Never. I should love to go. I suppose you and your wife went—ever so much."

He had a transitory wonder that so fine a lady should be untravelled, but his eagerness to display his backgrounds prevented him thinking that out at the time. " Two or three times," he said, " before our little boy came to us. And always returning with something for this place. Look ! " he went on, stepped across an exquisite little brick court to a lawn of soft emerald and turning back upon the house. " That Dellia Robbia plaque we lugged all the way back from Florence with us, and that stone bird-bath is from Siena."

" How bright it is ! " murmured the lady, after a brief still appreciation. " Delightfully bright. As though it would shine even if the sun didn't." And she abandoned herself to the rapture of seeing a house and garden that were, for once, better even than the agent's superlatives. And within her grasp if she chose—within her grasp.

She made the garden melodious with soft appreciative sounds. She had a small voice for her size but quite a charming one, a little live bird of a voice, bright and sweet. It was a clear, unruffled afternoon ; even the unseen wheel-barrow had very sensibly ceased to creak and seemed to be somewhere listening. . . .

Only one trivial matter marred their easy explorations : his boots remained unlaced. No propitious moment came when he could stoop and lace them. He was not a dexterous man with eyelets, and stooping made him grunt and his head swim. He hoped these trailing imperfections went unmarked. He tried subtly to lead this charming lady about and at the same time walk a little behind her. She, on her part, could not determine whether he would be displeased or not if she noticed this slight embarrassment and asked him to set it right. They were quite long leather laces, and they flew about with a sturdy negligence of anything but their own offensive contentment, like a gross man who whistles a vulgar tune as he goes round some ancient church ; flick, flock, they went, and flip, flap, enjoying themselves, and sometimes he trod on one and halted in his steps, and sometimes for a moment she felt her foot tether him. But man is the adaptable animal, and presently they both became more used to these inconveniences and more mechanical in their efforts to avoid them. They treated those laces then exactly as nice people would treat that gross man ; a minimum of polite attention and all the rest pointedly directed away from him. . . .

The garden was full of things that people dream about doing in their gardens and mostly never do. There was a rose garden all blooming in chorus, and with pillar-roses and arches that were not so much growths as overflowing cornucopias of roses, and a neat orchard with shapely trees, white-painted to their exact middles, a stone wall bearing clematis and a clothes-line so gay with Mr. Brumley's blue and white flannel shirts that it seemed an essential part of the design. And then there was a great border of herbaceous perennials backed by delphiniums and monkshood already in flower and budding hollyhocks rising to their duty ; a border that reared its blaze of colour against a hill-slope dark with pines. There was no hedge whatever to this delightful garden. It seemed to go straight into the pinewoods ; only an invisible netting marked its limits and fended off the industrious curiosity of the rabbits.

" This strip of wood is ours right up to the crest," he said, " and from the crest one has a view. One has two views. If you would care—— ? "

The lady made it clear that she was there to see all she could. She radiated her appetite to see. He carried a fur stole for her over his arm and flicked the way up the hill. Flip, flap, flop. She followed demurely.

" This is the only view I care to show you now," he said

at the crest. " There was a better one beyond there. But—
it has been defiled. . . . Those hills ! . . . I knew you would
like them. The space of it ! And yet—— This view—lacks
the shining ponds. There are wonderful distant ponds. After
all, I must show you the other ! But you see there is a high-
road, and the high-road has produced an abomination. Along
here we go. Now. Don't look down, please." His gesture
covered the foreground. " Look right over the nearer things
into the distance. There ! "

The lady regarded the wide view with serene appreciation.
" I don't see," she said, " that it's in any way ruined. It's
perfect."

" You don't see ! Ah ! you look right over. You look high.
I wish I could too. But that screaming board ! I wish the
man's crusts would choke him."

And indeed quite close at hand, where the road curved
about below them, the statement that Staminal Bread, the
True Staff of Life, was sold only by the International Bread
Shops, was flung out with a vigour of yellow and Prussian blue,
that made the landscape tame.

His finger directed her questioning eye.

" Oh ! " said the lady suddenly, as one who is convicted of
a stupidity and coloured slightly.

" In the morning, of course, it is worse. The sun comes
directly on to it. Then really and truly it blots out everything."

The lady stood quite silent for a little time, with her eyes
on the distant ponds. Then he perceived that she was blushing. She turned to her interlocutor as a puzzled pupil might
turn to a teacher.

" It really is very good bread," she said. " They make
it—— Oh ! most carefully. With the germ in. And one has
to tell people."

Her point of view surprised him. He had expected nothing
but a docile sympathy. " But to tell people *here* ! " he said.

" Yes, I suppose one oughtn't to tell them here."

" Man does not live by bread alone."

She gave the faintest assent.

" This is the work of one pushful, shoving creature, a man
named Harman. Imagine him ! Imagine what he must be !
Don't you feel his soul defiling us ?—this summit of a stupendous pile of—dough, thinking of nothing but his miserable,
monstrous profits, seeing nothing in the delight of life, the
beauty of the world but something that attracts attention,
draws eyes, something that gives him his horrible opportunity
of getting ahead of all his poor little competitors and inserting
—*this* ! It's the quintessence of all that is wrong with the
world—squalid, shameless huckstering ! " He flew off at a
tangent. " Four or five years ago they made this landscape
disease—a knight ! "

He looked at her for a sympathetic indignation, and then

suddenly something snapped in his brain and he understood. There was an instant between absolute innocence and absolute knowledge.

"You see," she said, as responsive as though he had cried out sharply at the horror in his mind, "Sir Isaac is my husband. Naturally . . . I ought to have given you my name to begin with. It was silly. . . ."

Mr. Brumley gave one wild glance at the board, but indeed there was not a word to be said in its mitigation. It was the crude advertisement of a crude, pretentious thing crudely sold. "My dear lady !" he said in his largest style, "I am desolated ! But I have said it ! It isn't a pretty board."

A memory of epithets pricked him. "You must forgive— a certain touch of—rhetoric."

He turned about as if to dismiss the board altogether, but she remained with her brows very faintly knit, surveying the cause of his offence.

"It isn't a *pretty* board," she said. "I've wondered at times. . . . It isn't."

"I implore you to forget that outbreak—mere petulance— because, I suppose, of a peculiar liking for that particular view. There are—associations—— "

"I've wondered lately," she continued, holding on to her own thoughts, "what people *did* think of them. And it's curious—to hear—— "

For a moment neither spoke, she surveyed the board and he the tall ease of her pose. And he was thinking she must surely be the most beautiful woman he had ever encountered. The whole country might be covered with boards if it gave us such women as this. He felt the urgent need of some phrase, to pull the situation out of this pit into which it had fallen. He was a little unready, his faculties all, as it were, neglecting his needs and crowding to the windows to stare, and meanwhile she spoke again, with something of the frankness of one who thinks aloud.

"You see," she said, "one *doesn't* hear. One thinks, per- haps—— And there it is. When one marries very young, one is apt to take so much for granted. And afterwards—— "

She was wonderfully expressive in her inexpressiveness, he thought, but found as yet no saving phrase. Her thought continued to drop from her. "One sees them so much that at last one doesn't see them."

She turned away to survey the little house again ; it was visible in bright strips between the red-scarred pine stems. She looked at it chin up, with a still approval—but she was the slenderest loveliness, and with such a dignity !—and she spoke at length as though the board had never existed. "It's a little piece of another world ; so bright and so—perfect."

There was the phantom of a sigh in her voice.

"I think you'll be charmed by our rockery," he said. "It

was one of our particular efforts. Every time we two went abroad we came back with something, saxifrage or house-leek, or some little bulb from the wayside."

" How can you leave it ! "

He was leaving it because it bored him to death. But so intricate is the human mind that it was with perfect sincerity he answered : " It will be a tremendous wrench. . . . I have to go."

" And you've written most of your books here and lived here ! "

The note of sympathy in her voice gave him a sudden suspicion that she imagined his departure due to poverty. Now to be poor as an author is to be unpopular, and he valued his popularity—with the better sort of people. He hastened to explain. " I have to go, because here, you see, here, neither for me nor my little son, is it life. It's a place of memories, a place of accomplished beauty. My son already breaks away—a preparatory school at Margate. Healthier, better, for us to break altogether, I feel, wrench though it may. It's full for us at least—a new tenant would be different, of course—but for *us* it's full of associations we can't alter, can't for the life of us change. Nothing, you see, goes on. And life, you know, *is* change—change, and going on."

He paused impressively in his generalisation.

" But you will want—— You will want to hand it over to —to sympathetic people, of course. People," she faltered, " who will understand."

Mr. Brumley took an immense stride—conversationally. " I am certain there is no one I would more readily see in that house than yourself," he said.

" But——" she protested. " And besides, you don't know me ! "

" One knows some things at once, and I am as sure you would—understand—as if I had known you twenty years. It may seem absurd to you, but when I looked up just now and saw you for the first time, I thought—this, this is the tenant. This is her house. . . . Not a doubt. That is why I did not go for my walk—came round with you."

" You really think you would like us to have that house ? " she said. " *Still ?* "

" No one better," said Mr. Brumley.

" After the board ? "

" After a hundred boards, I let the house to you. . . . "

" My husband, of course, will be the tenant," reflected Lady Harman.

She seemed to brighten again by an effort : " I have always wanted something like this, that wasn't gorgeous, that wasn't mean. I can't *make* things. It isn't every one—can *make* a place. . . . "

§ 2

Mr. Brumley found their subsequent conversation the fullest
realisation of his extremest hopes. Behind his amiable speeches,
which soon grew altogether easy and confident again, a hundred imps of vanity were patting his back for the intuition,
the swift decision that had abandoned his walk so promptly.
In some extraordinary way the incident of the board became
impossible ; it hadn't happened, he felt, or it had happened
differently. Anyhow there was no time to think that over
now. He guided the lady to the two little greenhouses, made
her note the opening glow of the great autumnal border and
brought her to the rock garden. She stooped and loved and
almost kissed the soft healthy cushions of pampered saxifrage ;
she appreciated the cleverness of the moss-bed—where there
were droseras ; she knelt to the gentians ; she had a kindly
word for that bank-holiday corner where London Pride still
belatedly rejoiced ; she cried out at the delicate Alpine poppies
that thrust up between the stones of the rough pavement ; and
so in the most amiable accord they came to the raised seat in
the heart of it all, and sat down and took in the whole effect
of the place, and backing of woods, the lush borders, the neat
lawn, the still neater orchard, the pergola, the nearer delicacies
among the stones, and the gable, the shining white roughcast of the walls, the casement windows, the projecting upper
story, the carefully sought-out old tiles of the roof. And
everything bathed in that caressing sunshine which does not
scorch nor burn but gilds and warms deliciously, that summer
sunshine which only northward islands know.

Recovering from his first astonishment and his first misadventure, Mr. Brumley was soon himself again talkative,
interesting, subtly and gently aggressive. For once one may
use a hackneyed phrase without the slightest exaggeration ;
he was charmed. . . .

He was one of those very natural-minded men with active
imaginations who find women the most interesting things in
a full and interesting universe. He was an entirely good man
and almost professionally on the side of goodness, his pen was
a pillar of the home and he was hostile and even actively
hostile to all those influences that would undermine and change
—anything ; but he did find women attractive. He watched
them and thought about them, he loved to be with them, he
would take great pains to please and interest them, and his
mind was frequently dreaming quite actively of them, of
championing them, saying wonderful and impressive things
to them, having great friendships with them, adoring them
and being adored by them. At times he had to ride this interest on the curb. At times the vigour of its urgencies made
him inconsistent and secretive. . . . Comparatively his own

sex was a matter of indifference to him. Indeed he was a very normal man. Even such abstractions as Goodness and Justice had rich feminine figures in his mind, and when he sat down to write criticism at his desk, that pretty little slut of a Delphic Sibyl presided over his activities.

So that it was a cultivated as well as an attentive eye that studied the movements of Lady Harman, and an experienced ear that weighed the words and cadences of her entirely inadequate and extremely expressive share in their conversation. He had enjoyed the social advantages of a popular and presentable man of letters, and he had met a variety of ladies ; but he had never yet met any one at all like Lady Harman. She was pretty and quite young and fresh ; he doubted if she was as much as four-and-twenty ; she was as simple-mannered as though she was ever so much younger than that, and dignified as though she was ever so much older ; and she had a sort of lustre of wealth about her—— One met it sometimes in young richly married Jewesses, but though she was very dark she wasn't at all of that type ; he was inclined to think she must be Welsh. This manifest spending of great lots of money on the richest, finest, and fluffiest things was the only aspect of her that sustained the parvenu idea ; and it wasn't in any way carried out by her manners, which were as modest and silent and inaggressive as the very best can be. Personally he liked opulence, he responded to countless-guinea furs. . . .

Soon there was a neat little history in his mind that was reasonably near the truth, of a hard-up professional family, fatherless, perhaps, of a mercenary marriage at seventeen or so—and this. . . .

And while Mr. Brumley's observant and speculative faculties were thus active, his voice was busily engaged. With the accumulated artistry of years, he was developing his pose. He did it almost sub-consciously. He flung out hint and impulse, confidence and casual statement with the careless assurance of the accustomed performer, until by nearly imperceptible degrees that finished picture of the two young lovers, happy, artistic, a little Bohemian and one of them doomed to die, making their home together in an atmosphere of sunny gaiety, came into being in her mind. . . .

" It must have been beautiful to have begun life like that," she said in a voice that was a sigh, and it flashed joyfully across Mr. Brumley's mind that this wonderful person could envy his Euphemia.

" Yes," he said, " at least we had our Spring."

" To be together," said the lady, " and—so beautifully poor. . . ."

There is a phase in every relationship when one must generalise if one is to go farther. A certain practice in this kind of talk with ladies blunted the finer sensibilities of Mr. Brumley. At any rate, he was able to produce this sentence without a qualm. " Life," he said, " is sometimes a very extraordinary thing."

Lady Harman reflected upon this statement and then responded with an air of remembered moments : " Isn't it."

" One loses the most precious things," said Mr. Brumley, " and one loses them, and it seems as though one couldn't go on. And one goes on."

" And one finds oneself," said Lady Harman, " without all sorts of precious things—— " And she stopped, transparently realising that she was saying too much.

" There is a sort of vitality about life," said Mr. Brumley, and stopped as if on the verge of profundities.

" I suppose one hopes," said Lady Harman. " And one doesn't think. And things happen."

" Things happen," assented Mr. Brumley.

For a little while their minds rested upon this thought, as chasing butterflies might rest together on a flower.

" And so I am going to leave this," Mr. Brumley resumed. " I am going up there to London for a time with my boy. Then perhaps we may travel—Germany, Italy, perhaps— in his holidays. It is beginning again, I feel, with him. But then, even we two must drift apart. I can't deny him a public school sooner or later. His own road. . . ."

" It will be lonely for you," sympathised the lady.

" I have my work," said Mr. Brumley, with a sort of valiant sadness.

" Yes, I suppose your work——"

She left an eloquent gap.

" There, of course, one's fortunate," said Mr. Brumley.

" I wish," said Lady Harman, with a sudden frankness and a little quickening of her colour, " that I had some work. Something—that was my own."

" But you have— There are social duties. There must be all sorts of things."

" There are—all sorts of things. I suppose I'm ungrateful. I have my children."

" You have children, Lady Harman ! "

" I've *four*."

He was really astonished, " Your *own* ? "

She turned her fawn's eyes on his with a sudden wonder at his meaning. " My own ! " she said, with the faintest tinge of astonished laughter in her voice. " What else could they be ?"

" I thought—— I thought you might have step-children."

" Oh, of course ! No ! I'm their mother—all four of them. They're mine, as far as that goes. Anyhow."

And her eye questioned him again for his intentions.

But his thought ran along its own path. " You see," he said, " there is something about you—so freshly beginning life. So like—Spring."

" You thought I was too young ! I'm nearly six-and-twenty !

But all the same—though, they're mine—*still*—— Why shouldn't a woman have work in the world, Mr. Brumley? —in spite of all that."

" But surely—that's the most beautiful work in the world that any one could possibly have."

Lady Harman reflected. She seemed to hesitate on the verge of some answer and not to say it.

" You see," she said, " it may have been different with you. . . . When one has a lot of nurses, and not very much authority."

She coloured deeply and broke back from the impending revelations.

" No," she said, " I would like some work of my own."

§ 3

At this point their conversation was interrupted by the lady's chauffeur in a manner that struck Mr. Brumley as extraordinary, but which the tall lady evidently regarded as the most natural thing in the world.

Mr. Clarence appeared walking across the lawn towards them, surveying the charms of as obviously a charming garden as one could have, with the disdain and hostility natural to a chauffeur. He did not so much touch his cap as indicate that it was within reach, and that he could if he please touch it. " It's time you were going, my lady," he said. " Sir Isaac will be coming back by the five-twelve, and there'll be a nice to-do if you ain't at home and me at the station and everything in order again."

Manifestly an abnormal expedition.

" Must we start at once, Clarence ? " asked the lady, consulting a bracelet watch. " You surely won't take two hours—— "

" I can give you fifteen minutes more, my lady," said Clarence, " provided I may let her out and take my corners just exactly in my own way."

" And I must give you tea," said Mr. Brumley, rising to his feet. " And there is the kitchen."

" And upstairs ! I'm afraid, Clarence, for this occasion only you must—what is it ?—let her out."

" And no ' Oh, Clarence !' my lady ? "

She ignored that.

" I'll tell Mrs. Rabbit at once," said Mr. Brumley, and started to run and trod in some complicated way on one of his loose laces and was precipitated down the rockery steps. " Oh !" cried the lady. " Mind ! " and clasped her hands.

He made a sound exactly like the word " damnation " as he fell, but he didn't so much get up as bounce up, apparently in the brightest of tempers, and laughed, held out two earthy hands for sympathy with a mock rueful grimace, and went on, earthy-green at the knees and a little more carefully towards

the house. Clarence, having halted to drink deep satisfaction
from this disaster, made his way along a nearly parallel path
towards the kitchen, leaving his lady to follow as she chose
to the house.

" *You'll* take a cup of tea ? " called Mr. Brumley.

" Oh ! *I'll* take a cup all right," said Clarence in the kindly
voice of one who addresses an amusing inferior. . . .

Mrs. Rabbit had already got the tea-things upon out the
cane table in the pretty veranda, and took it ill that she should
be supposed not to have thought of these preparations.

Mr. Brumley disappeared for a few minutes into the house.

He returned with a conscious relief on his face, clean hands,
brushed knees, and his boots securely laced. He found Lady
Harman already pouring out tea.

" You see," she said, to excuse this pleasant enterprise on
her part, " my husband has to be met at the station with the
car. . . . And of course he has no idea——"

She left what it was of which Sir Isaac had no idea to the
groping speculations of Mr. Brumley.

§ 4

That evening Mr. Brumley was quite unable to work. His
mind was full of this beautiful dark lady who had come so
unexpectedly into his world.

Perhaps there are such things as premonitions. At any rate
he had an altogether disproportionate sense of the significance
of the afternoon's adventure—which, after all, was a very small
adventure indeed. A mere talk. His mind refused to leave her,
her black furry slenderness, her dark, trustful eyes, the sweet
firmness of her perfect lips, her appealing simplicity that was
yet somehow compatible with the completest self-possession.
He went over the incident of the board again and again, scrap-
ing his memory for any lurking crumb of detail as a starving
man might scrape an insufficient plate. Her dignity, her
gracious, frank forgiveness ; no queen alive in these days
could have touched her. . . . But it wasn't a mere elaborate
admiration. There was something about her, about the quality
of their meeting.

Most people knew that sort of intimation. This person, it
says, so fine, so brave, so distant still in so many splendid and
impressive qualities, is yet in ways as yet undefined and unexplored, subtly and abundantly—for *you*. It was that made
all her novelty and distinction and high quality and beauty
so dominating among Mr. Brumley's thoughts. Without that
. his interest might have been almost entirely—academic. But
there was woven all through her the hints of an imaginable
alliance, with *us*, with the things that are Brumley, with all
that makes beautiful little cottages and resents advertisements
in lovely places, with us as against something over there
lurking behind that board, something else, something out of

which she came. He vaguely adumbrated what it was out of which she came. A closed narrow life—with horrid vast enviable quantities of money. A life, could one use the word *vulgar* ?—so that Capaccio, Della Robbia, old furniture, a garden unostentatiously perfect, and the atmosphere of *belles-lettres*, seemed things of another more desirable world. (She had never been abroad.) A world, too, that would be so willing, so happy to enfold her, furs, funds, freshness—everything.

And all this was somehow animated by the stirring warmth in the June weather, for spring raised the sap in Mr. Brumley as well as in his trees, had been a restless time for him all his life. This spring particularly had sensitised him, and now a light had shone.

He was so unable to work that for twenty minutes he sat over a pleasant little essay on Shakespeare's garden that by means of a concordance and his natural aptitude he was writing for the book of the National Shakespeare Theatre, without adding a single fancy to its elegant playfulness. Then he decided he needed his afternoon's walk after all, and he took cap and stick and went out, and presently found himself surveying that yellow and blue board and seeing it from an entirely new point of view. . . .

It seemed to him that he hadn't made the best use of his conversational opportunities, and for a time this troubled him. . . .

Toward the twilight he was walking along the path that runs through the heather along the edge of the rusty dark ironstone lake opposite the pinewoods. He spoke his thoughts aloud to the discreet bat that flitted about him. " I wonder," he said, " whether I shall ever set eyes on her again. . . ."

In the small hours when he ought to have been fast asleep he decided she would certainly take the house, and that he would see her again quite a number of times. A long tangle of unavoidable detail for discussion might be improvised by an ingenious man. And the rest of that waking interval passed in such inventions, which became more and more vague and magnificent and familiar as Mr. Brumley lapsed into slumber again. . . .

Next day the garden essay was still neglected, and he wrote a pretty vague little song about an earthly mourner and a fresh presence that set him thinking of the story of Persephone and how she passed in the spring-time up from the shadows again, blessing as she passed. . . .

He pulled himself together about midday, cycled over to Gorshott for lunch at the clubhouse and a round with Horace Toomer in the afternoon, re-read the poem after tea, decided it was poor, tore it up and got himself down to his little fantasy about Shakespeare's Garden for a good two hours before supper. It was a sketch of that fortunate poet (whose definitive immortality is now being assured by an influential committee)

walking round his Stratford garden with his daughter, quoting
himself copiously with an accuracy and inappropriateness that
reflected more credit upon his heart than upon his head,
and saying in addition many distinctively Brumley things.
When Mrs. Rabbit, with a solicitude acquired from the late
Mrs. Brumley, asked him how he had got on with his work
—the sight of verse on his paper had made her anxious—he
could answer quite truthfully, " Like a house afire."

CHAPTER TWO

THE PERSONALITY OF SIR ISAAC HARMAN

§ 1

IT is to be remarked that two facts, usually esteemed as
supremely important in the life of a woman, do not seem
to have affected Mr. Brumley's state of mind nearly so much
as quite trivial personal details about Lady Harman.   The
first of these facts was the existence of the lady's four children,
and the second, Sir Isaac.

Mr. Brumley did not think very much of either of these two
facts ; if he had they would have spoilt the portrait in his
mind ; and when he did think of them it was chiefly to think
how remarkably little they were necessary to that picture's
completeness.

He spent some little time however, trying to recall exactly
what it was she had said about her children. He couldn't now
succeed in reproducing her words, if indeed it had been by
anything so explicit as words that she had conveyed to him
that she didn't feel her children were altogether hers. " Incidental results of the collapse of her girlhood," tried Mr.
Brumley, " when she married Harman."

Expensive nurses, governesses—the best that money without prestige or training could buy.   And then probably a
mother-in-law.   And as for Harman——— ?

There Mr. Brumley's mind desisted for sheer lack of material.
Given this lady and that board and his general impression of
Harman's refreshment and confectionery activity—the data
were insufficient. A commonplace man, no doubt, a tradesman, energetic perhaps and certainly a little brassy, successful
by the chances of that economic revolution which everywhere
replaces the isolated shop by the syndicated enterprise, irrationally conceited about it ; a man perhaps ultimately to be
pitied—with this young goddess finding herself. . . . Mr.
Brumley's mind sat down comfortably to the more congenial
theme of a young goddess finding herself, and it was only very
gradually in the course of several days that the personality
of Sir Isaac began to assume its proper importance in the
scheme of his imaginings.

§ 2

In the afternoon as he went round the links with Horace
Toomer he got some definite light upon Sir Isaac.

His mind was so full of Lady Harman that he couldn't but
talk of her visit. " I've a possible tenant for my cottage," he
said, as he and Toomer, full of the sunny contentment of
English gentlemen who had played a proper game in a proper
manner, strolled back towards the clubhouse. " That man
Harman."

" Not the International Stores and Staminal Bread man.'

" Yes. Odd. Considering my hatred of his board."

" He ought to pay—anyhow," said Toomer. " They say he
has a pretty wife and keeps her shut up."

" She came," said Brumley, neglecting to add the trifling
fact that she had come alone.

" Pretty ? "

" Charming, I thought."

" He's jealous of her. Some one was saying that the chauffeur
has orders not to take her into London—only for trips in the
country. They live in a big, ugly house, I'm told, on Putney
Hill. Did she in any way *look*—as though—— ? "

" Not in the least. If she isn't an absolutely straight young
woman, I've never set eyes on one."

" *He*," said Toomer, " is a disgusting creature."

" Morally ? "

" No, but—generally. Spends his life ruining little trades-
men, for the fun of the thing. He's three parts an invalid with
some obscure kidney disease. Sometimes he spends whole
days in bed, drinking Contrexéville Water and planning the
bankruptcy of decent men. . . . So the party made a knight
of him."

" A party must have funds, Toomer."

" He didn't pay nearly enough. Blapton is an idiot with
the honours. When it isn't Mrs. Blapton. What can you expect
when—— "

(But here Toomer became libellous.)

Toomer was an interesting type. He had a disagreeable
disposition profoundly modified by a public school and
university training. Two antagonistic forces made him. He
was the spirit of scurrility incarnate, that was, as people
say, innate ; and by virtue of those moulding forces he was
doing his best to be an English gentleman. That mysterious
impulse which compels the young male to make objectionable
imputations against seemly lives and to write rare inelegant
words upon clean and decent things burnt almost intolerably
within him, and equally powerful now was the gross craving
he had acquired for personal association with all that is prominent, all that is successful, all that is of good report. He
had found his resultant in the censorious defence of estab-

lished things.   He conducted the *British Critic*, attacking
with a merciless energy all that was new, all that was critical,
all those fresh and noble tentatives that admit of unsavoury
interpretations, and when the urgent Yahoo in him carried
him below the pretentious dignity of his accustomed organ
he would squirt out his bitterness in a little sham facetious
bookstall volume with a bright cover and quaint woodcuts,
in which just as many prominent people as possible were
mentioned by name and a sauce of general absurdity could
be employed to cover and, if need be, excuse particular libels.
So he managed to relieve himself and get along. Harman was
just on the border-line of the class he considered himself free
to revile. Harman was an outsider and aggressive and new,
one of Mrs. Blapton's knights, and of no particular weight
in society ; so far he was fair game ; but he was not so new
as he had been, he was almost through with the running of
the Toomer gauntlet, he had a tremendous lot of money,
and it was with a modified vehemence that the distinguished
journalist and humorist expatiated on his offensiveness to
Mr. Brumley.   He talked in a gentle, rather weary voice,
that came through a moustache like a fringe of light
tobacco.

"Personally, I've little against the man. A wife too young
for him and jealously guarded, but that's all to his credit.
Nowadays. If it wasn't for his blatency in his business. . . .
And the knighthood. . . . I suppose he can't resist taking anything he can get. Bread made by wholesale and distributed like
a newspaper can't, I feel, be the same thing as the loaf of your
honest, old-fashioned baker—each loaf made with individual
attention—out of wholesome English flour—hand-ground—
with a personal touch for each customer.   Still, everything
drifts on to these hugger-mugger large enterprises ; Chicago
spreads over the world. One thing goes after another, tobacco,
tea, bacon, drugs, bookselling. Decent homes destroyed right
and left. Not Harman's affair, I suppose. The girls in his
London tea-shops have, of course, to supplement their wages
by prostitution—probably don't object to that nowadays
considering the novels we have. And his effect on the landscape—— Until they stopped him he was trying very hard
to get Shakespeare's Cliff at Dover. He did for a time have the
Toad Rock at Tunbridge. Still "—something like a sigh escaped
from Toomer—" his private life appears to be almost as blame-
less as anybody's can be. . . . Thanks, no doubt, to his defective health. I made the most careful inquiries when his knighthood was first discussed. Some one has to. Before his marriage
he seems to have lived at home with his mother. At Highbury.
Very quietly and inexpensively."

"Then he's not the conventional vulgarian ? "

"Much more of the Rockfeller type. Bad health, great
concentration, organising power. . . . Applied, of course, to

a narrower range of business . . . I'm glad I'm not a small confectioner in a town he wants to take up."

" He's—hard ? "

" Merciless. Hasn't the beginnings of an idea of fair play. . . . None at all. . . . No human give or take. . . . Are you going to have tea here, or are you walking back now ? "

§ 3

It was fully a week before Mr. Brumley heard anything more of Lady Harman. He began to fear that this shining furry presence would glorify Black Strand no more. Then came a telegram that filled him with the liveliest anticipations. It was worded : " Coming see cottage Saturday afternoon Harman. . . ."

On Saturday morning Mr. Brumley dressed with an apparent ease and unusual care. . . .

He worked rather discursively before lunch. His mind was busy picking up the ends of their previous conversation and going on with them to all sorts of bright knots, bows, and elegant cat's cradling. He planned openings that might give her tempting opportunities, of confidences if she wished to confide, and artless remarks and questions that would make for self-betrayal if she didn't. And he thought of her, he thought of her imaginatively, this secluded rare thing so happily come to him, who was so young, so frank, and fresh, and so unhappily married (he was sure) to a husband at least happily mortal. Yes, dear reader, even on that opening morning Mr. Brumley's imagination, trained very largely upon Victorian literature and *belles-lettres*, leapt forward to the very ending of this story. . . . We, of course, do nothing of the sort, our lot is to follow a more pedestrian route. . . . He lapsed into a vague series of meditations, slower, perhaps, but essentially similar, after his temperate palatable lunch.

He was apprised of the arrival of his visitor by the sudden indignant yaup followed by the general subdued uproar of a motor-car outside the front door, even before Clarence, this time amazingly prompt, assaulted the bell. Then the whole house was like that poem by Edgar Allan Poe, one magnificent texture of clangour.

At the first toot of the horn Mr. Brumley had moved swiftly into the bay, and screened partly by the life-size Venus of Milo that stood in the bay window, and partly by the artistic curtains, surveyed the glittering vehicle. He was first aware of a vast fur coat enclosing a lean, grey-headed, obstinate-looking man with a diabetic complexion who was fumbling with the door of the car and preventing Clarence's assistance. Mr. Brumley was able to remark that the gentleman's nose projected to a sharpened point, and that his thin-lipped mouth was all awry and had a kind of habitual compression, the while that his eyes sought eagerly for the other occupant of the car

She was unaccountably invisible. Could it be that that hood really concealed her ? Could it be . . . ?

The white-faced gentleman descended, relieved himself tediously of the vast fur coat, handed it to Clarence and turned to the house. Reverentially Clarence placed the coat within the automobile and closed the door. Still the protesting mind of Mr. Brumley refused to believe. . . .

He heard the house-door open and Mrs. Rabbit in colloquy with a flat masculine voice. He heard his own name demanded and conceded. Then a silence, not the faintest suggestion of a feminine rustle, and then the sound of Mrs. Rabbit at the door-handle. Conviction stormed the last fastness of the disappointed author's mind.

" Oh, *damn !* " he shouted, with extreme fervour.

He had never imagined it was possible that Sir Isaac could come alone.

§ 4

But the house had to be let, and it had to be let to Sir Isaac Harman. In another moment an amiable though distinguished man of letters was in the hall interviewing the great *entrepreneur*.

The latter gentleman was perhaps three inches shorter than Mr. Brumley, his hair was grey-shot brown, his face clean-shaven, his features had a thin irregularity, and he was dressed in a neat brown suit with a necktie very exactly matching it. " Sir Isaac Harman ? " said Mr. Brumley with a note of gratification.

" That's it," said Sir Isaac. He appeared to be nervous and a little out of breath. " Come," he said, " just to look over it. Just to see it. Probably too small, but if it doesn't put you out—— "

He blew out the skin of his face about his mouth a little.

" Delighted to see you anyhow," said Mr. Brumley, filling the world of unspoken things with singularly lurid curses.

"This. Nice little hall—very," said Sir Isaac. " Pretty, that bit at the end. Many room are there ? "

Mr. Brumley answered inexactly and meditated a desperate resignation of the whole job to Mrs. Rabbit. Then he made an effort and began to explain.

" That clock," said Sir Isaac, interrupting in the dining-room, " is a fake."

Mr. Brumley made silent interrogations.

" Been there myself," said Sir Isaac. " They sell those brass fittings in Ho'bun."

They went upstairs together. When Mr. Brumley wasn't explaining or pointing out, Sir Isaac made a kind of whistling between his clenched teeth. " This bathroom wants refitting anyhow," he said abruptly. " I dare say Lady Harman would like that room with the bay—but it's all—small. It's really

quite pretty ; you've done it cleverly, but—the size of it !
I'd have to throw out a wing. And that, you know, might
spoil the style. That roof—a gardener's cottage ? . . . I
thought it might be. What's this other thing here ? Old barn.
Empty ? That might expand a bit. Couldn't do only just this
anyhow."

He walked in front of Mr. Brumley downstairs and still
emitting that faint whistle led the way into the garden. He
seemed to regard Mr. Brumley merely as a source of answers
to his questions, and a seller in process of preparation for an
offer. It was clear he meant to make an offer. "It's not
the house I should buy if I was alone in this," he said, " but
Lady Harman's taken a fancy somehow. And it might be
adapted." . . .

From first to last Mr. Brumley never said a single word about
Euphemia and the young matrimony and all the other memories
this house enshrined. He felt instinctively that it would not
affect Sir Isaac one way or the other. He tried simply to seem
indifferent to whether Sir Isaac bought the place or not. He
tried to make it appear almost as if houses like this often
happened to him, and interested him only in the most incidental
manner. They had their proper price, he tried to convey, which,
of course, no gentleman would underbid.

In the exquisite garden Sir Isaac said : " One might make a
very pretty little garden of this—if one opened it out a bit."

And of the sunken rock-garden : " That might be dangerous
of a dark night."

" I suppose," he said, indicating the hill of pines behind,
" one could buy or lease some of that. If one wanted to throw
it into the place and open out more.

"From my point of view," he said, " it isn't a house. It's——"
He sought in his mind for an expression—" a Cottage Ornay."

This history declines to record either what Mr. Brumley
said or what he did not say.

Sir Isaac surveyed the house thoughtfully for some moments
from the turf edging of the great herbaceous border.

" How far," he asked, " is it from the nearest railway
station ? . . . "

Mr. Brumley gave details.

" Four miles. And an infrequent service ? Nothing in any
way surburban ? Better to motor into Guildford and get the
express. H'm . . . And what sort of people do we get about
here ? "

" Mildly horsey. That's not bad. No officers about ? . . .
Nothing nearer than Aldershot . . . That's eleven miles, is
it ? H'm, I suppose there aren't any *literary* people about
here, musicians, or that kind of thing, no advanced people of
that sort ? "

" Not when I've gone," said Mr. Brumley, with the faintest
flavour of humour.

Sir Isaac stared at him for a moment with eyes vacantly thoughtful.

" It mightn't be so bad," said Sir Isaac, and whistled a little between his teeth.

Mr. Brumley was suddenly minded to take his visitor to see the view and the effect of his board upon it. But he spoke merely of the view and left Sir Isaac to discover the board or not as he thought fit. As they ascended among the trees, the visitor was manifestly seized by some strange emotion, his face became very white, he gasped and blew for breath, he felt for his face with a nervous hand.

" Four thousand," he said suddenly. " An outside price."

" A minimum," said Mr. Brumley, with a slight quickening of the pulse.

" You won't get three eight," gasped Sir Isaac.

" Not a business man, but my agent tells me—— " panted Mr. Brumley.

" Three eight," said Sir Isaac.

" We're just coming to the view," said Mr. Brumley. " Just coming to the view."

" Practically got to rebuild the house," said Sir Isaac.

" There ! " said Mr. Brumley, and waved an arm widely.

Sir Isaac regarded the prospect with a dissatisfied face. His pallor had given place to a shiny, flushed appearance, his nose, his ears, and his cheeks were pink. He blew his face out, and seemed to be studying the landscape for defects. " This might be built over at any time," he complained.

Mr. Brumley was reassuring.

For a brief interval Sir Isaac's eyes explored the country-side vaguely, then his expression seemed to concentrate and run together to a point. " H'm," he said.

" That board," he remarked, " quite wrong there."

" Well ! " said Mr. Brumley, too surprised for coherent speech.

" Quite," said Sir Isaac Harman. " Don't you see what's the matter ? "

Mr. Brumley refrained from an eloquent response.

" They ought to be," Sir Isaac went on, " white and a sort of green. Like the County Council notices on Hampstead Heath. So as to blend. . . . You see, an ad. that hits too hard is worse than no ad. at all. It leaves a dislike. . . . Advertise-ments ought to blend. It ought to be seen as though all this view were saying it. Not just that board. Now, suppose we had a shade of very light brown, a kind of light khaki—— "

He turned a speculative eye on Mr. Brumley, as if he sought for the effect of this latter suggestion on him.

" If the whole board was invisible—— " said Mr. Brumley.

Sir Isaac considered it. " Just the letters showing," he said. " No—that would be going too far in the other direction."

He made a faint sucking noise with his lips and teeth as he

surveyed the landscape and weighed this important matter. . . .

" Queer how one gets ideas," he said at last, turning away.
" It was my wife told me about that board."

He stopped to survey the house from the exact point of
view his wife had taken nine days before. " I wouldn't give
this place a second thought," said Sir Isaac, "if it wasn't for
Lady Harman."

He confided. " *She* wants a week-end cottage. But *I* don't
see why it *should* be a week-end cottage. I don't see why it
shouldn't be made into a nice little country house. Compact,
of course. By using up that barn."

He inhaled three bars of a tune. " London," he explained,
" doesn't suit Lady Harman."

" Health ? " asked Mr. Brumley, all alert.

" It isn't her health exactly," Sir Isaac dropped out. " You
see—she's a young woman. She gets ideas."

" You know," he continued, " I'd like to have a look at that
barn again. If we develop that—and a sort of corridor across
where the shrubs are—and ran out offices. . . ."

§ 5

Mr. Brumley's mind was still vigorously struggling with
the flaming implications of Sir Isaac's remark that Lady
Harman " got ideas," and Sir Isaac was gently whistling his
way towards an offer of three thousand nine hundred when
they came down out of the pines into the path along the edge
of the herbaceous border. And then Mr. Brumley became aware
of an effect away between the white-stemmed trees towards
the house as if the Cambridge boat-race crew was indulging in a
vigorous scrimmage. Drawing nearer this resolved itself into
the fluent contours of Lady Beach-Mandarin, dressed in sky-
blue and with a black summer straw hat larger than ever and
trimmed effusively with marguerites.

" Here," said Sir Isaac, " can't I get off ? You've got a
friend."

" You must have some tea, said Mr. Brumley, who wanted
to suggest that they should agree to Sir Isaac's figure of three
thousand eight hundred, but not as pounds but guineas. It
seemed to him a suggestion that might prove insidiously
attractive. " It's a charming lady, my friend Lady Beach-
Mandarin. She'll be delighted——"

" I don't think I can," said Sir Isaac. " Not in the habit—
social occasions."

His face expressed a panic terror of this gallant full-rigged
lady ahead of them.

" But you see now," said Mr. Brumley, with a detaining
grip, " it's unavoidable."

And the next moment Sir Isaac was mumbling his apprecia-
tions of the introduction.

I must admit that Lady Beach-Mandarin was almost as much

to meet as one can meet in a single human being, a broad abundant billowing personality with a taste for brims, streamers, pennants, panniers, loose sleeves, sweeping gestures, top notes, and the like that made her altogether less like a woman than an occasion of public rejoicing. Even her large blue eyes projected, her chin and brows and nose all seemed racing up to the front of her as if excited by the clarion notes of her abundant voice, and the pinkness of her complexion was as exuberant as her manners. Exuberance—it was her word. She had evidently been a big, bouncing, bright gaminesque girl at fifteen, and very amusing and very much admired ; she had liked the rôle and she had not so much grown older as suffered enlargement—a very considerable enlargement.

" Ah ! " she cried, " and so I've caught you at home, Mr. Brumley ! And, poor dear, you're at my mercy." And she shook both his hands with both of hers.

That was before Mr. Brumley introduced Sir Isaac, a thing he did so soon as he could get one of his hands loose and wave a surviving digit or so at that gentleman.

" You see, Sir Isaac," she said, taking him in, in the most generous way ; " I and Mr. Brumley are old friends. We knew each other of yore. We have our jokes."

Sir Isaac seemed to feel the need of speech, but got no further than a useful all-round noise.

" And one of them is that when I want him to do the least little thing for me he hides away ! Always. By a sort of instinct. It's such a small thing, Sir Isaac."

Sir Isaac was understood to say vaguely that they always did. But he had become very indistinct.

" Aren't I always at your service ? " protested Mr. Brumley, with a responsive playfulness. " And I don't even know what it is you want."

Lady Beach-Mandarin, addressing herself exclusively to Sir Isaac, began a tale of a Shakespeare Bazaar she was holding in an adjacent village, and how she knew Mr. Brumley (naughty man) meant to refuse to give her autographed copies of his littlest book for the book-stall she was organising. Mr. Brumley confuted her gaily and generously. So discoursing they made their way to the veranda where Lady Harman had so lately " poured."

Sir Isaac was borne along upon the lady's stream of words in a state of mulish reluctance, nodding, saying " Of course," and similar phrases, and wishing he was out of it all with an extreme manifestness. He drank his tea with unmistakable discomfort, and twice inserted into the conversation an entirely irrelevant remark that he had to be going. But Lady Beach-Mandarin had her purposes with him and crushed these quivering tentatives.

Lady Beach-Mandarin had, of course, like everybody else, at that time her own independent movement in the great

national effort to create an official British Theatre upon the
basis of William Shakespeare, and she saw in the as yet un-
enlisted resources of Sir Isaac strong possibilities of reïnforce-
ment of her own particular contribution to the great work.
He was manifestly shy and sulky, and disposed to bolt at the
earliest possible moment, and so she set herself now with
a swift and concentrated combination of fascination and
urgency to commit him to participations. She flattered and
cajoled and bribed. She was convinced that even to be called
upon by Lady Beach-Mandarin is no light privilege for these
new commercial people, and so she made no secret of her
intention of decorating the hall of his large but undistinguished
house in Putney, with her redeeming paste-board. She appealed
to the instances of Venice and Florence to show that " such
men as you, Sir Isaac," who control commerce and industry,
have always been the guardians and patrons of art. And
who more worthy of patronage than William Shakespeare ?
Also she said that men of such enormous wealth as his owed
something to their national tradition. " You have to pay
your footing, Sir Isaac," she said, with impressive vagueness.

" Putting it in round figures," said Sir Isaac, suddenly
and with a white gleam of animosity in his face, the animosity
of a trapped animal at the sight of its captors, " what does
coming on your committee mean, Lady Beach-Mandarin ? "

" It's your name we want," said the lady, " but I'm sure
you'd not be ungenerous. The tribute success owes the arts."

" A hundred ? " he threw out—his ears red.

" Guineas," breathed Lady Beach-Mandarin, with a lofty
sweetness of consent.

He stood up hastily as if to escape further exaction, and
the lady rose too.

" And you'll let me call on Lady Harman," she said honestly
doing her part in the bargain.

" Can't keep the car waiting," was what Brumley could
distinguish in his reply.

" I expect you have a perfectly splendid car, Sir Isaac,"
said Lady Beach-Mandarin, drawing him out. " Quite the
modernest thing."

Sir Isaac replied with the reluctance of an Income Tax
Return that it was a forty-five Rolls-Royce, good, of course,
but nothing amazing.

" We must see it," she said, and turned his retreat into a
procession.

She admired the car, she admired the colour of the car,
she admired the lamps of the car and the door of the car and
the little fittings of the car. She admired the horn. She
admired the twist of the horn. She admired Clarence and the
uniform of Clarence, and she admired and coveted the great
fur coat that he held ready for his employer. (But if she
had it, she said, she would wear the splendid fur outside to

show every little bit of it.) And when the car at last moved forward and tooted—she admired the note—and vanished softly and swiftly through the gates, she was left in the porch with Mr. Brumley still by sheer inertia admiring and envying. She admired Sir Isaac's car number Z 900. (Such an easy one to remember!) Then she stopped abruptly, as one might discover that the water in the bathroom was running to waste and turn it off.

She had a cynicism as exuberant as the rest of her.

" Well," she said, with a contented sigh and an entire flattening of her tone, " I laid it on pretty thick that time. . . . I wonder if he'll send me that hundred guineas, or whether I shall have to remind him of it. . . ." Her manner changed again to that of a gigantic gamin. " I mean to have that money," she said, with bright determination and round eyes. . . .

She reflected, and other thoughts came to her. " Plutocracy," she said, " *is* perfectly detestable, don't you think so, Mr. Brumley ? " . . . And then, " I can't *imagine* how a man who deals in bread and confectionery can manage to go about so completely half-baked."

" He's a very remarkable type," said Mr. Brumley.

He became urgent: " I do hope, dear Lady Beach-Mandarin, you will contrive to call on Lady Harman. She is—in relation to *that*—quite the most interesting woman I have seen."

§ 6

Presently, as they paced the croquet lawn together, the preoccupation of Mr. Brumley's mind drew their conversation back to Lady Harman.

" I wish," he repeated, " you would go and see these people. She's not at all what you might infer from him."

" What could one infer about a wife from a man like that ? Except that she'd have a lot to put up with."

" You know—she's a beautiful person, tall, slender, dark. . . ."

Lady Beach-Mandarin turned her full blue eye upon him.

" *Now !* " she said archly.

" I'm interested in the incongruity."

Lady Beach-Mandarin's reply was silent and singular. She compressed her lips very tightly, fixed her eye firmly on Mr. Brumley's, lifted her finger to the level of her left eyelash, and then shook it at him very deliberately five times. Then, with a little sigh and a sudden and complete restoration of manner she remarked that never in any year before had she seen peonies quite so splendid. " I've a peculiar sympathy with peonies," she said. " They're so exactly my style."

CHAPTER THREE

LADY HARMAN AT HOME

§ 1

EXACTLY three weeks after that first encounter between Lady Beach-Mandarin and Sir Isaac Harman, Mr. Brumley found himself one of a luncheon party at that lady's house in Temperley Square and talking very freely and indiscreetly about the Harmans.

Lady Beach-Mandarin always had her luncheons in a family way at a large round table, so that nobody could get out of her range, and she insisted upon conversation being general, except for her mother, who was impenetrably deaf and the Swiss governess of her only daughter Phyllis who was incomprehensible in any European tongue. The mother was incalculably old and had been a friend of Victor Hugo and Alfred de Musset; she maintained an intermittent monologue about the private lives of those great figures; nobody paid the slightest attention to her but one felt she enriched the table with an undertow of literary associations. A small dark stealthy butler and a convulsive boy with hair (apparently) taking the place of eyes waited. On this occasion Lady Beach-Mandarin had gathered together two cousins, maiden ladies from Perth, wearing valiant hats, Toomer the wit and censor, and Miss Sharsper the novelist (whom Toomer detested), a gentleman named Roper whom she had invited under a misapprehension that he was the Arctic Roper, and Mr. Brumley. She had tried Mr. Roper with questions about penguins, seals, cold, and darkness, icebergs and glaciers, Captain Scott, Doctor Cook, and the shape of the earth, and all in vain, and feeling at last that something was wrong, she demanded abruptly whether Mr. Brumley had sold his house.

" I'm selling it," said Mr. Brumley, " by almost imperceptible degrees."

" He haggles ? "

" Haggles and higgles. He higgles passionately. He goes white and breaks into a cold perspiration. He wants me now to include the gardener's tools—in whatever price we agree upon."

" A rich man like that ought to be easy and generous," said Lady Beach-Mandarin.

" Then he wouldn't be a rich man like that," said Mr. Toomer.

" But doesn't it distress you highly, Mr. Brumley," one of the Perth ladies asked, " to be leaving Euphemia's home to strangers ? The man may go altering it."

" That—that weighs with me very much," said Mr. Brumley,

recalled to his professions. " There I put my trust in Lady
Harman."

" You've seen her again ? " asked Lady Beach-Mandarin.

" Yes. She came with him a few days ago. That couple
interests me more and more. So little akin."

" There's eighteen years between them," said Toomer.

" It's one of those cases," began Mr. Brumley, with a note
of scientific detachment, " where one is really tempted to be
ultra-feminist. It's clear, he uses every advantage. He's her
owner, her keeper, her obstinate, insensitive little tyrant. . . .
And yet there's a sort of effect, as though nothing was decided.
. . . As if she was only growing up."

" They've been married six or seven years," said Toomer.
" She was just eighteen."

" They went over the house together and whenever she
spoke he contradicted her with a sort of vicious playfulness.
Tried to poke clumsy fun at her. Called her ' Lady Harman.'
Only it was quite evident that what she said stuck in his
mind. . . . Very queer—interesting people."

" I wouldn't have any one allowed to marry until they were
five-and-twenty," said Lady Beach-Mandarin.

" Sweet seventeen sometimes contrives to be very marriageable," said the gentleman named Roper.

" Sweet seventeen must contrive to wait," said Lady Beach-
Mandarin. " Sweet fourteen has to—and when I was fourteen
—I was ardent ! There's no earthly objection to a little
harmless flirtation of course. It's the marrying."

" You'd conduce to romance," said Miss Sharsper, " anyhow. Eighteen won't bear restriction and every one would
begin by eloping—illegally."

" I'd put them back," said Lady Beach-Mandarin. " Oh !
remorselessly."

Mr. Roper, who was more and more manifestly not the
Arctic one, remarked that she would " give the girls no end
of an adolescence. . . ."

Mr. Brumley did not attend very closely to the subsequent
conversation. His mind had gone back to Black Strand and
the second visit that Lady Harman, this time under her natural
and proper protection, had paid him. A little thread from
the old lady's discourse drifted by him. She had scented
marriage in the air and she was saying, " Of course they
ought to have let Victor Hugo marry over and over again.
He would have made it all so beautiful. He could throw a
splendour over—over almost anything." Mr. Brumley sank
out of attention altogether. It was so difficult to express his
sense of Lady Harman as a captive, enclosed but unsubdued.
She had been as open and shining as a celandine flower in
the sunshine on that first invasion, but on the second it had
been like overcast weather and her starry petals had been
shut and still. She hadn't been in the least subdued or effaced,

but closed, inaccessible to conversational bees, that astonishing honey of trust and easy friendship had been hidden in a dignified impenetrable reserve. She had had the effect of being not so much specially shut against Mr. Brumley as habitually shut against her husband, as a protection against his continual clumsy, mental interferences. And once when Sir Isaac had made a sudden allusion to price, Mr. Brumley had glanced at her and met her eyes. . . .

" Of course," he said, coming up to the conversational surface again, " a woman like that is bound to fight her way out."

" Queen Mary ! " cried Miss Sharsper. " Fight her way out ! ".

" Queen Mary ! " said Mr. Brumley, " No !—Lady Harman."

" *I* was talking of Queen Mary," said Miss Sharsper.

" And Mr. Brumley was thinking of Lady Harman ! " cried Lady Beach-Mandarin.

" Well," said Mr. Brumley, " I confess I do think about her. She seems to me to be so typical in many ways of—of everything that is weak in the feminine position. As a type —yes, she's perfect."

" I've never seen this lady," said Miss Sharsper. " Is she beautiful ? "

" I've not seen her myself yet," said Lady Beach-Mandarin. " She's Mr. Brumley's particular discovery."

" You haven't called ? " he asked, with a faint reproach.

" But I've been going to—oh ! tremendously. And you revive all my curiosity. Why shouldn't some of us this very afternoon—— ? "

She caught at her own passing idea and held it. " Let's go," she cried. " Let's visit the wife of this ogre, the last of the women in captivity. We'll take the big car and make a party and call *en masse*."

Mr. Toomer protested he had no morbid curiosities.

" But you, Susan ? "

Miss Sharsper declared she would *love* to come. Wasn't it her business to study out-of-the-way types ? Mr. Roper produced a knowing sort of engagement—" I'm provided for already, Lady Beach-Mandarin," he said, and the cousins from Perth had to do some shopping.

" Then we three will be the expedition," said the hostess. " And afterwards if we survive we'll tell you our adventures It's a house on Putney Hill, isn't it, where this Christian maiden, so to speak, is held captive ? I've had her in my mind, but I've always intended to call with Agatha Alimony ; she's so inspiring to down-trodden women."

" Not exactly down-trodden," said Mr. Brumley, " not down-trodden. That's what's so curious about it."

" And what shall we do when we get there ? " cried Lady Beach-Mandarin. " I feel we ought to do something more than

call. Can't we carry her off right away, Mr. Brumley ? I want
to go right in to her and say, ' Look here ! I'm on your side.
Your husband's a tyrant. I'm help and rescue. I'm all that
a woman ought to be—fine and large. Come out from under
that unworthy man's heel ! ' "

" Suppose she isn't at all the sort of person you seem to
think she is," said Miss Sharsper. " And suppose she came ! "

" Suppose she didn't," reflected Mr. Roper.

" I seem to see your flight," said Mr. Toomer. " And the
newspaper placards and headlines. ' Lady Beach-Mandarin
elopes with the wife of an eminent confectioner. She is stopped
at the landing stage by the staff of the Dover branch establishment. Recapture of the fugitive after a hot struggle. Brumley,
the eminent *litterateur*, stunned by a spent bun. . . .' "

" We're all talking great nonsense," said Lady Beach-
Mandarin. " But anyhow, we'll make our call. And *I* know !
—I'll make her accept an invitation to lunch without him."

" If she won't ? " threw out Mr. Roper.

" I *will*," said Lady Beach-Mandarin, with roguish determination. " And if I can't——"

" Not ask him too ! " protested Mr. Brumley.

" Why not get her to come to your Social Friends meeting,"
said Miss Sharsper. . . .

§ 2 .

When Mr. Brumley found himself fairly launched upon this
expedition he had the grace to feel compunction. The Harmans,
he perceived, had inadvertently made him the confidant of
their domestic discords and to betray them to these others
savoured, after all, of treachery.   And besides, much as he
had craved to see Lady Harman again, he now realised he
didn't in the least want to see her in association with the
exuberant volubility of Lady Beach-Mandarin and the hard
professional observation, so remarkably like the ferrule of
an umbrella being poked with a noiseless persistence into one's
eye, of Miss Sharsper. And as he thought these afterthoughts
Lady Beach-Mandarin's chauffeur darted and dodged and
threaded his way with an alacrity that was almost distressing
to Putney.

They ran over the ghost of Swinburne, at the foot of Putney
Hill—or, perhaps, it was only the rhythm of the engine changed
for a moment, and in a couple of minutes more they were
outside the Harman residence. " Here we are ! " said Lady
Beach-Mandarin, more capaciously gaminesque than ever.
" We've done it now."

Mr. Brumley had an impression of a big house in the distended stately-homes-of-England style and very necessarily
and abundantly covered by creepers and then he was assisting
the ladies to descend, and the three of them were waiting
clustered in the ample Victorian doorway.   For some little

interval there came no answer to the bell Mr. Brumley had
rung, but all three of them had a sense of hurried, furtive,
and noiseless readjustments in progress behind the big and
bossy oak door. Then it opened, and a very large egg-shaped
butler with sandy whiskers appeared and looked down himself
at them. There was something paternal about this man, his
professional deference was touched by the sense of ultimate
responsibility. He seemed to consider for a moment whether
he should permit Lady Harman to be in, before he conceded
that she was.

They were ushered through a hall that resembled most of
the halls in the world, it was dominated by a handsome oak
staircase and scarcely gave Miss Sharsper a point, and then
across a creation of the Victorian architect, a massive kind
of conservatory with classical touches—there was an im-
pluvium in the centre and there were arches hung with
manifestly costly Syrian rugs, into a large apartment looking
through four French windows upon a veranda and a large
floriferous garden. At a sideways glance it seemed a very
pleasant place indeed. The room itself was like the rooms
of so many prosperous people nowadays ; it had an effect of
being sedulously and yet irrelevantly over-furnished. It had
none of the large vulgarity that Mr. Brumley would have
considered proper to a wealthy caterer, but it confessed a
complication of " pieces," very carefully authenticated. Some
of them were rather splendid " pieces " ; three big bureaus,
burly and brassy, dominated it ; there was a Queen Anne
cabinet, some exquisite coloured engravings, an ormolu mirror
and a couple of large French vases, that set Miss Sharsper,
who had a keen eye for this traffic, confusedly cataloguing.
And a little incongruously in the midst of this exhibit, stood
Lady Harman, as if she was trying to conceal the fact that
she too was a visitor, in a creamy white dress and dark and
defensive, and yet entirely unabashed.

The great butler gave his large vague impression of Lady
Beach-Mandarin's name, and stood aside and withdrew.

" I've heard so much of you," said Lady Beach-Mandarin,
advancing with hand upraised. " I had to call. Mr. Brumley——"

" Lady Beach-Mandarin met Sir Isaac at Black Strand,"
Mr. Brumley intervened to explain.

Miss Sharsper was, as it were, introduced by default.

" My vividest anticipations outdone," said Lady Beach-
Mandarin, squeezing Lady Harman's fingers with enthusiasm.
" And what a charming garden you have, and what a delightful
situation ! Such air ! And on the very verge of London, high,
on this delightful *literary* hill, and ready at any moment to
swoop in that enviable great car of yours. I suppose you come
a great deal into London, Lady Harman ? "

" No," reflected Lady Harman, " not very much." **She**

seemed to weigh the accuracy of this very carefully. "No," she added in confirmation.

"But you should, you ought to ; it's your duty. You've no right to hide away from us. I was telling Sir Isaac. We look to him, we look to you. You've no right to bury your talents away from us ; you who are rich and young and brilliant and beautiful——

"But if I go on, I shall begin to flatter you," said Lady Beach-Mandarin, with a delicious smile. "I've begun upon Sir Isaac already. I've made him promise a hundred guineas and his name to the Shakespeare Dinners Society—nothing he didn't mention eaten (*you* know) and all the profits to the national movement—and I want your name too. I know you'll let us have your name too. Grant me that, and I'll subside into the ordinariest of callers."

"But surely ; isn't his name enough ? " asked Lady Harman.

"Without yours, it's only half a name ! " cried Lady Beach-Mandarin. "If it were a *business* thing——! " Different, of course. But on my list, I'm like dear old Queen Victoria, you know, the wives must come too."

"In that case," hesitated Lady Harman. . . . "But really, I think Sir Isaac——"

She stopped. And then Mr. Brumley had a psychic experience. It seemed to him as he stood observing Lady Harman with an entirely unnecessary and unpremeditated intentness, that for the briefest interval her attention flashed over Lady Beach-Mandarin's shoulder to the end veranda window ; and following her glance, he saw—and then he did not see—the arrested figure, the white face of Sir Isaac, bearing an expression in which anger and horror were extraordinarily intermingled. If it was Sir Isaac he dodged back with amazing dexterity ; if it was a phantom of the living, it vanished with an air of doing that. Without came the sound of a flower-pot upset and a faint expletive. Mr. Brumley looked very quickly at Lady Beach-Mandarin, who was entirely unconscious of anything but her own uncoiling and enveloping eloquence, and as quickly at Miss Sharsper. But Miss Sharsper was examining a blackish bureau through her glasses as though she were looking for birth-marks, and meant if she could find one to claim the piece as her own long-lost connection. With a mild but gratifying sense of exclusive complicity, Mr. Brumley reverted to Lady Harman's entire self-possession.

"But, dear Lady Harman, it's entirely unnecessary you should consult him—entirely," Lady Beach-Mandarin was saying.

"I'm sure," said Mr. Brumley, with a sense that somehow he had to intervene, "that Sir Isaac would not possibly object. I'm sure that if Lady Harman consults him——"

The sandy-whiskered butler appeared hovering.

"Shall I place the tea-things in the garden, me lady ? " he asked, in the tone of one who knows the answer.

" Oh, *please*, in the garden ! " cried Lady Beach-Mandarin.
" Please ! And how delightful to *have* a garden, a London
garden, in which one *can* have tea. Without being smothered
in blacks. The south-west wind. The dear *English* wind. All
your blacks come to *us*, you know."

She led the way upon the veranda. " Such a wonderful
garden ! The space, the breadth ! Why ! you must have
acres ! "

She surveyed the garden—comprehensively ; her eye rested
for a moment on a distant patch of black that ducked suddenly
into a group of lilacs. " Is dear Sir Isaac at home ? " she
asked.

" He's very uncertain," said Lady Harman, with a quiet
readiness that pleased Mr. Brumley. " Yes, Snagsby, please,
under the big cypress. And tell my mother and sister."

Lady Beach-Mandarin, having paused a moment or so upon
the veranda admiring the garden as a whole, now prepared to
go into details. She gathered her ample skirts together and
advanced into the midst of the large lawn, with very much of
the effect of a fleet of captive balloons dragging their anchors.
Mr. Brumley followed, as it were, in attendance upon her and
Lady Harman. Miss Sharsper, after one last hasty glance at
the room, rather like the last hasty glance of a still unprepared
schoolboy at his book, came behind with her powers of observation strainingly alert.

Mr. Brumley was aware of a brief, mute struggle between the
two ladies of title. It was clear that Lady Harman would have
had them go to the left, to where down a vista of pillar roses a
single large specimen cypress sounded a faint but recognisable
Italian note, and he did his loyal best to support her, but Lady
Beach-Mandarin's attraction to that distant clump of lilac
on the right was equally great and much more powerful.
She flowed, a great and audible tide of socially influential
womanhood across the green spaces of the garden, and drew
the others with her. And it seemed to Mr. Brumley—not that
he believed his eyes—that beyond those lilacs something ran
out, something black that crouched close to the ground and
went very swiftly. It flashed like an arrow across a farther
space of flower-bed, dropped to the ground, became two
agitatedly receding boot soles, and was gone. Had it ever been ?
He glanced at Lady Harman, but she was looking back with
the naïve anxiety of a hostess to her cypress—at Lady Beach-
Mandarin, but she was proliferating compliments and decorative scrolls and flourishes like the engraved frontispiece to a
seventeenth-century book.

" I know I'm inordinately curious," said Lady Beach-
Mandarin, " but gardens are my joy. I want to go into every
corner of this. Peep into everything. And I feel somehow "—
and here she urged a smile on Lady Harman's attention—" that
I shan't begin to know *you*, until I know all your environment."

She turned the flank of the lilacs as she said these words, and advanced in echelon with a stately swiftness upon the laurels beyond.

Lady Harman said there was nothing beyond but sycamores and the fence, but Lady Beach-Mandarin would press on through a narrow path that pierced the laurel hedge, in order, she said, that she might turn back and get the whole effect of the grounds.

And so it was they discovered the mushroom shed.

" A mushroom shed ! " cried Lady Beach-Mandarin. " And if we look in—shall we see hosts and regiments of mushrooms ? I must—I must."

" I *think* it is locked," said Lady Harman.

Mr. Brumley darted forward ; tried the door, and turned quickly. " It's locked," he said, and barred Lady Beach-Mandarin's advance.

" And besides," said Lady Harman, " there's no mushrooms there. They won't come up. It's one of my husband's—annoyances."

Lady Beach-Mandarin had turned round, and now surveyed the house. " What a splendid idea," she cried, " that wistaria ! All mixed with the laburnum ! I don't think I have ever seen such a charming combination of blossoms ! "

The whole movement of the party swept about and faced cypress-ward. Away there the sandy-whiskered butler and a footman and basket-chairs and a tea-table, with a shining white cloth, and two ladies were now grouping themselves. . . .

But the mind of Mr. Brumley gave little heed to these things. His mind was full of a wonder, and the wonder was this, that the mushroom shed had behaved like a living thing. The door of the mushroon shed was not locked, and in that matter he had told a lie. The door of the mushroom shed had been unlocked quite recently, and the key and padlock had been dropped upon the ground. And when he had tried to open the mushroom shed it had first of all yielded to his hand and then it had closed again with great strength—exactly as a living mussel will behave if one takes it unawares. But in addition to this passionate contraction the mushroom shed had sworn in a hoarse whisper and breathed hard, which is more than your mussel can do. . . .

3

Mr. Brumley's interest in Lady Harman was to be almost too crowded by detail before the impulsive call was over. Superposed upon the mystery of the mushroom shed was the vivid illumination of Lady Harman by her mother and sister. They had an effect of having reluctantly become her social inferiors for her own good ; the mother—her name he learnt was Mrs. Sawbridge—had all Lady Harman's tall slenderness, but otherwise resembled her only in the poise of her neck and

an occasional gesture ; she was fair and with a kind of ignoble
and premeditated refinement in her speech and manner. She
was dressed with the restraint of a prolonged and attenuated
widowhood, in a rich and complicatedly quiet dress of mauve
and grey. She was obviously a transitory visitor and not so
much taking the opulence about her and particularly the great
butler for granted as pointedly and persistently ignoring it in
an effort to seem to take it for granted. The sister, on the other
hand, had Lady Harman's pale darkness, but none of her fineness of line. She missed altogether that quality of fineness.
Her darkness was done with a quite perceptible heaviness, her
dignity passed into solidity, and her profile was, with an entire
want of hesitation, handsome. She was evidently the elder by
a space of some years, and she was dressed with severity in
grey.

These two ladies seemed to Mr. Brumley to offer a certain
resistance of spirit to the effusion of Lady Beach-Mandarin,
rather as two small anchored vessels might resist the onset of a
great and foaming tide, but after a time it was clear they
admired her greatly. His attention was, however, a little distracted from them by the fact that he was the sole representative of the more serviceable sex among five women, and so
in duty bound to stand by Lady Harman and assist with
various handings and offerings. The tea equipage was silver
and not only magnificent, but, as certain quick movements of
Miss Sharsper's eyes and nose at its appearance betrayed, very
genuine and old.

Lady Beach-Mandarin having praised the house and garden
all over again to Mrs. Sawbridge, and having praised the
cypress and envied the tea things, resumed her efforts to secure
the immediate establishment of permanent social relations
with Lady Harman. She reverted to the question of the Shakespeare Dinners Society, and now with a kind of large skilfulness
involved Mrs. Sawbridge in her appeal. "Won't *you* come on
our committee ? " said Lady Beach-Mandarin.

Mrs. Sawbridge gave a pinched smile, and said she was only
staying in London for quite a little time, and when pressed,
admitted that there seemed no need whatever for consulting
Sir Isaac upon so obviously foregone a conclusion as Lady
Harman's public adhesion to the great movement.

" I shall put his hundred guineas down to Sir Isaac and Lady
Harman," said Lady Beach-Mandarin, with an air of con
clusion, " and now I want to know, dear Lady Harman, whether
we can't have *you* on our committee of administration. We
want—just one other woman to complete us."

Lady Harman could only parry with doubts of her ability.

" You ought to go on, Ella," said Mrs. Sawbridge suddenly,
speaking for the first time and in a manner richly suggestive of
great principles at stake.

" Ella," thought the curious mind of Mr. Brumley. " And

is that Eleanor, now, or Ellen, or—is there any other name that gives one Ella ? Simply Ella ? "

" But what should I have to do ? " fenced Lady Harman, resisting but obviously attracted.

Lady Beach-Mandarin invented a lengthy paraphrase for prompt acquiescence.

" I shall be chairwoman," she crowned it with. " I can so easily *see you through*, as they say."

" Ella doesn't go out half enough," said Miss Sawbridge suddenly to Miss Sharsper, who was regarding her with furtive intensity—as if she was surreptitiously counting her features.

Miss Sharsper, caught in mid observation, started and collected her mind. " One ought to go out," she said. " Certainly."

" And independently," said Miss Sawbridge with meaning.

" Oh, independently ! " assented Miss Sharsper. It was evident she would now have to watch her chance and begin counting all over again from the beginning.

Mr. Brumley had an impression that Mrs. Sawbridge had said something quite confidential in his ear. He turned perplexed.

" Such charming weather," the lady repeated in the tone of one who doesn't wish so pleasant a little secret to be too generally discussed.

" Never known a better summer," agreed Mr. Brumley.

And then all these minor eddies were submerged in Lady Beach-Mandarin's advance towards her next step, an invitation to lunch. " There," said she, " I'm not Victorian. I always separate husbands and wives—by at least a week. You must come alone."

It was clear to Mr. Brumley that Lady Harman wanted to come alone—and was going to accept, and equally clear that she and her mother and sister regarded this as a very daring thing to do. And when that was settled Lady Beach-Mandarin went on to the altogether easier topic of her Social Friends, a society of smart and influential women ; who devoted a certain fragment of time every week to befriending respectable girls employed in London, in a briskly amiable manner, having them to special teas, having them to special evenings with special light refreshments, knowing their names as far as possible, and asking about their relations, and generally making them feel that Society was being very frank and amiable to them and had an eye on them and meant them well, and was better for them than socialism and radicalism and revolutionary ideas. To this also Lady Harman it seemed was to come. It had an effect to Mr. Brumley's imagination as if the painted scene of that lady's life was suddenly bursting out into open doors—everywhere.

" Many of them are *quite* ladylike," echoed Mrs. Sawbridge suddenly, picking up the whole thing instantly, and speaking

over her teacup in that quasi-confidential tone of hers to Mr.
Brumley.

" Of course they are mostly quite dreadfully sweated," said
Lady Beach-Mandarin. Especially in the confectionery——"
She thought of her position in time. " In the inferior class of
confectioners' establishments," she said, and then hurried on
to : " Of course, when you come to lunch—Agatha Alimony.
I'm most anxious for you and her to meet."

" Is that *the* Agatha Alimony ? " asked Miss Sawbridge
abruptly.

" The one and only," said Lady Beach-Mandarin, flashing a
smile at her. " And what a marvel she is ! I do so want you
to know her, Lady Harman. She'd be a revelation to you. . . ."

Everything had gone wonderfully so far. " And now," said
Lady Beach-Mandarin, thrusting forward a face of almost
exaggerated motherliness and with an unwonted tenderness
suffusing her voice, " show me the chicks."

There was a brief, interrogative pause.

" Your chicks," expanded Lady Beach-Mandarin, on the
verge of crooning. " Your *little* chicks."

" *Oh !* " cried Lady Harman, understanding. " The
children."

" Lucky woman ! " cried Lady Beach-Mandarin. " Yes."

" One hasn't begun to be friends," she added, " until one has
seen—them. . . ."

" So *true*," Mrs. Sawbridge confided to Mr. Brumley, with a
look that almost languished. . . .

" Certainly," said Mr. Brumley, " rather."

He was a little distraught, because he had just seen Sir
Isaac step forward in a crouching attitude from beyond the
edge of the lilacs, peer at the tea-table with a serpent-like
intentness, and then dart back convulsively into cover.

If Lady Beach-Mandarin saw him, Mr. Brumley felt that
anything might happen. . . .

§ 4

Lady Beach-Mandarin always let herself go about children.

It would be unjust to the general richness of Lady Beach-
Mandarin to say that she excelled herself on this occasion. On
all occasions Lady Beach-Mandarin excelled herself. But never
had Mr. Brumley noted quite so vividly Lady Beach-Mandarin's
habitual self-surpassingness. She helped him, he felt, to understand better those stories of great waves that sweep in from the
ocean and swamp islands and devastate whole littorals. She
poured into the Harman nursery and filled every corner of it.
She rose to unprecedented heights therein. It seemed to him
at moments that they ought to make marks on the walls,
like the marks one sees on the houses in the lower valley of the
Maine to record the more memorable floods. " The dears !"

she cried ; " the *little* things ! " before the nursery door was
fairly opened.

(There should have been a line for that at once on the jamb,
just below the lintel.)

The nursery revealed itself as a large, airy, white and green
apartment, entirely free from old furniture, and done rather
in the style of an aesthetically designed hospital, with a tremendously humorous decorative frieze of cocks and puppies, and
very bright-coloured prints on the walls. The dwarfish furniture
was specially designed in green-stained wood, and the floor
was of cork carpet diversified by white furry rugs. The hospital
quality was enhanced by the uniformed and disciplined appearance of the middle-aged and reliable head nurse and her subdued
but intelligent subordinate.

Three sturdy little girls, with a year step between each of
them, stood up to receive Lady Beach-Mandarin's invasion ;
an indeterminate baby sprawled, regardless of its dignity,
on a rug. " Aah ! " cried Lady Beach-Mandarin, advancing
in open order. " Come and be hugged, you dears ! Come and
be hugged ! " Before she knelt down and enveloped their
shrinking little persons Mr. Brumley was able to observe that
they were pretty little things, but not the beautiful children
he could have imagined from Lady Harman. Peeping through
their infantile delicacy, hints all too manifest of Sir Isaac's
characteristically pointed nose gave Mr. Brumley a peculiar—a
eugenic, qualm.

He glanced at Lady Harman, and she was standing over the
ecstasies of her tremendous visitor, polite, attentive—with an
entirely unemotional speculation in her eyes. Miss Sawbridge,
stirred by the great waves of violent philoprogenitive enthusiasm
that circled out from Lady Beach-Mandarin, had caught up
the baby and was hugging it and addressing it in terms of
humorous rapture, and the nurse and her assistant were keeping
respectful but wary eyes upon the handling of their four charges.
Miss Sharsper was taking in the children's characteristics with
a quick expertness. Mrs. Sawbridge stood a little in the background and caught Mr. Brumley's eye and proffered a smile
of sympathetic tolerance. . . .

Mr. Brumley was moved by a ridiculous impulse, which he
just succeeded in suppressing, to say to Mrs. Sawbridge, " Yes,
I admit it looks very well. But the essential point, you know,
is that it isn't so. . . ."

That it wasn't so, indeed, entirely dominated his impression
of that nursery. There was Lady Beach-Mandarin winning
Lady Harman's heart by every rule of the game, rejoicing
effusively in those crowning triumphs of a woman's being, there
was Miss Sawbridge, vociferous in support, and Mrs. Sawbridge
almost offering to join hands in rapturous benediction, and
there was Lady Harman wearing her laurels, not indeed with
indifference, but with a curious detachment. One might

imagine her genuinely anxious to understand why Lady Beach-Mandarin was in such a stupendous ebullition. One might have supposed her a mere cold-hearted intellectual if it wasn't that something in her warm beauty absolutely forbade any such interpretation. There came to Mr. Brumley again a thought that had occurred to him first when Sir Isaac and Lady Harman had come together to Black Strand, which was that life had happened to this woman before she was ready for it, that her mind some years after her body was now coming to womanhood, was teeming with curiosity about all she had hitherto accepted, about Sir Isaac, about her children, and all her circumstances. . . .

There was a recapitulation of the invitations, a renewed offering of outlooks and vistas and Agatha Alimony. " You'll not forget," insisted Lady Beach-Mandarin. " You'll not afterwards throw us over."

" No," said Lady Harman, with that soft determination of hers. " I'll certainly come."

" I'm so sorry, so very sorry, not to have seen Sir Isaac," Lady Beach-Mandarin insisted.

The raid had accomplished its every object and was drifting doorward. For a moment Lady Beach-Mandarin desisted from Lady Harman and threw her whole being into an eddying effort to submerge the already subjugated Mrs. Sawbridge. Miss Sawbridge was behind up the oak staircase explaining Sir Isaac's interest in furniture-buying to Miss Sharsper. Mr. Brumley had his one moment with Lady Harman.

" I gather," he said, and abandoned that sentence.

" I hope," he said, " that you will have my little house down there. I like to think of *you*—walking in my garden."

" I shall love that garden," she said. " But I shall feel unworthy."

" There are a hundred little things I want to tell you—about it."

Then all the others seemed to come into focus again, and with a quick, mutual understanding—Mr. Brumley was certain of its mutuality—they said no more to one another. He was entirely satisfied he had said enough. He had conveyed just everything that was needed to excuse and explain and justify his presence in that company. . . . Upon a big table in the hall he noticed that a silk hat and an umbrella had appeared since their arrival. He glanced at Miss Sharsper, but she was keenly occupied with the table legs. He began to breathe freely again when the partings were over and he could get back into the automobile. " Toot," said the horn, and he made a last grave salutation to the slender white figure on the steps. The great butler stood at the side of the entrance and a step or so below her, with the air of a man who has completed a difficult task. A small, attentive valet hovered out of the shadows behind.

§ 5

(A fragment of the conversation in Lady Beach-Mandarin's returning automobile may be recorded in a parenthesis here).

" But did you see Sir Isaac ? " she cried abruptly.

" Sir Isaac ? " defended the startled Mr. Brumley. " Where ? "

" He was dodging about in the garden all the time."

" Dodging about the garden ! . . . I saw a sort of gardener——"

" I'm sure I saw him," said Lady Beach-Mandarin. " Positive. He hid away in the mushroom shed. The one you found locked."

" But, my *dear* Lady Beach-Mandarin ! " protested Mr. Brumley with the air of one who listens to preposterous suggestions. " What can make you think—— ? "

" Oh, I *know* I saw him," said Lady Beach-Mandarin. " I know. He seemed all over the place. Like a Boy Scout. Didn't you see him too, Susan ? "

Miss Sharsper was roused from deep preoccupation. " What, dear ? " she asked.

" See Sir Isaac ? "

" Sir Isaac ? "

" Dodging about the garden when we went through it."

The novelist reflected. " I didn't notice," she said. " I was busy observing things."

§ 6

Lady Beach-Mandarin's car passed through the open gates and was swallowed up in the dusty stream of traffic down Putney Hill ; the great butler withdrew, the little man-servant vanished, Mrs. Sawbridge and her elder daughter had hovered and now receded from the back of the hall ; Lady Harman remained standing thoughtfully in the large Bulwer-Lyttonesque doorway of her house. Her face expressed a vague expectation. She waited to be addressed from behind.

Then she became aware of the figure of her husband standing before her. He had come out of the laurels in front. His pale face was livid with anger, his hair dishevelled, there was garden mould and greenness upon his knees and upon his extended hands.

She was startled out of her quiet defensiveness. " Why, Isaac ! " she cried. " Where have you been ? "

It enraged him further to be asked so obviously unnecessary a question. He forgot his knightly chivalry.

" What the devil do you mean ? " he cried, " by chasing me all round the garden ? "

" Chasing you ? All round the garden ? "

" You heard me breaking my shins on that infernal flower-

pot you put for me, and out you shot with all your pack
of old women, and chased me round the garden. What do
you mean by it ? "

" I didn't think you were in the garden."

" Any fool could have told I was in the garden. Any fool
might have known I was in the garden. If I wasn't in the
garden, then where the devil was I ? Eh ? Where else could
I be ? Of course I was in the garden, and what you wanted
was to hunt me down and make a fool of me. And look at me !
Look, I say ! Look at my hands ! "

Lady Harman regarded the lord of her being and hesitated
before she answered. She knew what she had to say would
enrage him, but she had come to a point in their relationship
when a husband's good temper is no longer a supreme consideration. " You've had plenty of time to wash them," she
said.

" Yes," he shouted. " And instead I kept 'em to show you.
I stayed out here to see the last of that crew for fear I might
run against 'em in the house. Of all the infernal old women——"

His lips were providentially deprived of speech. He conveyed
his inability to express his estimate of Lady Beach-Mandarin
by a gesture of despair.

" If—if any one calls and I am at home, I have to receive
them," said Lady Harman, after a moment's deliberation.

" Receiving them's one thing. Making a fool of yourself——"
His voice was rising.

" Isaac," said Lady Harman, leaning forward and then in
a low, penetrating whisper, " Snagsby ! "

(It was the name of the great butler.)

" Damn Snagsby ! " hissed Sir Isaac, but dropping his voice
and drawing near to her. What his voice lost in height it
gained in intensity. " What I say is this, Ella, you oughtn't
to have brought that old woman out into the garden at all——"

" She insisted on coming."

" You ought to have snubbed her. You ought to have
done—anything. How the devil was I to get away, once she
was through the veranda ? There I was ! Bagged ! "

" You could have come forward."

" What ! And meet her ! "

" I had to meet her."

Sir Isaac felt that his rage was being fritted away upon
details. " If you hadn't gone fooling about looking at houses,"
he said, and now he stood very close to her and spoke with a
confidential intensity, " you wouldn't have got that holy
terror on our track, see ? And now—here we are ! "

He walked past her into the hall, and the little man-servant
suddenly materialised in the middle of the space and came
forward to brush him obsequiously. Lady Harman regarded
that proceeding for some moments in a preoccupied manner,
and then passed slowly into the classical conservatory. She

felt that in view of her engagements the discussion of Lady Beach-Mandarin was only just beginning.

§ 7

She reopened it herself in the long drawing-room into which they both drifted after Sir Isaac had washed the mould from his hands. She went to a French window, gathered courage, it seemed, by a brief contemplation of the garden, and turned with a little effort.

" I don't agree," she said, " with you about Lady Beach-Mandarin."

Sir Isaac appeared surprised. He had assumed the incident was closed. " *How ?* " he asked compactly.

" I don't agree," said Lady Harman. " She seems friendly and jolly."

" She's a holy terror," said Sir Isaac. " I've seen her twice, Lady Harman."

" A call of that kind," his wife went on, " —when there are cards left and so on—has to be returned."

" You won't," said Sir Isaac.

Lady Harman took a blind-tassel in her hand—she felt she had to hold on to something. " In any case," she said, " I should have to do that."

" In any case ? "

She nodded. " It would be ridiculous not to. We—— It is why we know so few people—because we don't return calls. . . ."

Sir Isaac paused before answering. " We don't *want* to know a lot of people," he said. " And besides—— Why ! anybody could make us go running about all over London calling on them, by just coming and calling on us. No sense in it. She's come and she's gone, and there's an end of it."

" No," said Lady Harman, gripping her tassel more firmly. " I shall have to return that call."

" I tell you, you won't."

" It isn't only a call," said Lady Harman. " You see, I promised to go there to lunch."

" Lunch ! "

" And to go to a meeting with her."

" Go to a meeting ! "

" Of a society called the Social Friends. And something else. Oh ! to go to the committee meetings of her Shakespeare Dinners Movement."

" I've heard of that."

" She said you supported it—or else, of course. . . ."

Sir Isaac restrained himself with difficulty.

" Well," he said at last, " you'd better write and tell her you can't do any of these things ; that's all."

He thrust his hands into his trousers pockets and walked to the French window next to the one in which she stood, with an air of having settled this business completely, and being now free for the tranquil contemplation of horticulture. But Lady Harman had still something to say.

" I am going to *all* these things," she said. " I said I would, and I will."

He didn't seem immediately to hear her. He made the little noise with his teeth that was habitual to him. Then he came towards her. " This is your infernal sister," he said.

Lady Harman reflected. " No," she decided. " It's myself."

" I might have known when we asked her here," said Sir Isaac, with an habitual disregard of her judgments that was beginning to irritate her more and more. " You can't take on all these people. They're not the sort of people we want to know."

" I want to know them," said Lady Harman.

" I don't."

" I find them interesting," Lady Harman said. " And I've promised."

" Well you oughtn't to have promised without consulting me."

Her reply was the material of much subsequent reflection on the part of Sir Isaac. There was something in her manner. . . .

" You see, Isaac," she said, " you kept so out of the way. . . ."

In the pause that followed her words, Mrs. Sawbridge appeared from the garden smiling with a determined amiability, and bearing a great bunch of the best roses (which Sir Isaac hated to have picked) in her hands.

CHAPTER FOUR

THE BEGINNINGS OF LADY HARMAN

§ 1

LADY HARMAN had been married when she was just eighteen.

Mrs. Sawbridge was the widow of a solicitor who had been killed in a railway collision while his affairs, as she put it, were unsettled ; and she had brought up her two daughters in a villa at Penge upon very little money, in a state of genteel protest. Ellen was the younger. She had been a sturdy, dark-eyed, doll-dragging little thing and had then shot up very rapidly. She had gone to a boarding-school at Wimbledon because Mrs. Sawbridge thought the Penge day-school had made Georgina opiniated and unladylike, besides developing her muscular system to an unrefined degree. The Wimbledon school was on less progressive lines, and anyhow Ellen grew taller and more feminine than her sister, and by seventeen was already womanly, dignified and intensely admired by a number of schoolmates and a large circle of their cousins and brothers. She was generally very good and only now and then broke out with a venturesome enterprise that hurt nobody. She got out of a skylight, for example, and perambulated the roof in the moonshine to see how it felt, and did one or two other little things of a similar kind. Otherwise her conduct was admirable and her temper in those days was always contagiously good. That attractiveness which Mr. Brumley felt, was already very manifest, and a little hindered her in the attainment of other distinctions. Most of her lessons were done for her by willing slaves, and they were happy slaves, because she abounded in rewarding kindnesses ; but, on the other hand, the study of English literature and music was almost forced upon her by the zeal of the two visiting professors of these subjects.

And at seventeen, which is the age when girls most despise the boyishness of young men, she met Sir Isaac and filled him with an invincible covetousness. . . .

§ 2

The school at Wimbledon was a large, hushed, faded place, presided over by a lady of hidden motives and great exterior calm named Miss Beeton Clavier. She was handsome without any improper attractiveness, an Associate in Arts of St. Andrews University, and a cousin of Mr. Blenker of the *Old Country Gazette*. She was assisted by several resident mistresses and two very carefully married visiting masters for music and Shakespeare ; and playground and shrubbery and tennis-lawn were all quite effectively hidden from the high-road. The curriculum included Latin grammar—nobody ever got to the reading of books in that formidable tongue—French by an English lady who had been in France, Hanoverian German by an irascible native, the more seemly aspects of English history and literature, arithmetic, algebra, political economy and drawing. There was no hockey played within the precincts, science was taught without the clumsy apparatus or objectionable diagrams that are now so common, and stress was laid upon the carriage of the young ladies and the iniquity of speaking in raised voices. Miss Beeton Clavier deprecated the modern " craze for examinations," and released from such pressure her staff did not so much give courses of lessons as circle in a thorough-looking and patient manner about their subjects. This turn-spit quality was reflected in the school idiom ; one did not learn algebra or Latin or so forth, one *did* algebra, one was *put into* Latin. . . .

The girls went through this system of exercises and occupations, evasively and, as it were, *sotto voce*, making friends, making enemies, making love to one another, following instincts that urged them to find out something about life—in spite of the most earnest discouragement. . . . None of them believed for a moment that the school was preparing them for life. Most of them regarded it as a long, inexplicable passage of blank, gray occupations through which they had to pass. Beyond was the sunshine.

Ellen gathered what came to her. She realised a certain beauty in music in spite of the biographies of great musicians, the technical enthusiasms, and the general professionalism of her teacher; the literature master directed her attention to memoirs, and through these she caught gleams of understanding when the characters of history did for brief intervals cease to be rigidly dignified and institutional like Miss Beeton Clavier, and became human—like schoolfellows. And one little spectacled mistress, who wore art dresses and adorned her class-room with flowers, took a great fancy to her, talked to her with much vagueness and emotion of high aims, and lent her with an impressive furtiveness the works of Emerson and Shelley, and a pamphlet by Bernard Shaw. It was a little difficult to understand what these writers were driving at, they were so dreadfully clever, but it was clear they reflected criticism upon the silences of her mother and the rigidities of Miss Beeton Clavier.

In that suppressed and evasive life beneath the outer forms and procedures of school and home, there came glimmerings of something that seemed charged with the promise of holding everything together, the key, religion. She was attracted to religion, much more attracted than she would confess even to herself, but every circumstance in her training dissuaded her from a free approach. Her mother treated religion with a reverence that was almost indistinguishable from huffiness. She never named the deity, and she did not like the mention of His name; she threw a spell of indelicacy over religious topics that Ellen never thoroughly cast off. She put God among objectionable topics—albeit a sublime one. Miss Beeton Clavier sustained this remarkable suggestion. When she read prayers in school she did so with the balanced impartiality of one who offers no comment. She seemed pained as she read and finished with a sigh. Whatever she intended to convey, she conveyed that even if the divinity was not all He should be, if, indeed, He was a person almost primitive, having neither the restraint nor the self-obliteration of a refined gentlewoman, no word of it should ever pass her lips. And so Ellen as a girl never let her mind go quite easily into this reconciling core of life, and talked of it only very rarely and shyly with a few chosen coevals. It wasn't very profitable talk. They had a guilty feeling, they laughed a little uneasily, they displayed a fatal proclivity to stab the swelling gravity of their souls with some forced and silly jest, and so tumble back to ground again before they rose too high. . . .

Yet great possibilities of faith and devotion stirred already in the girl's heart. She thought little of God by day, but had a strange sense of Him in the starlight; never under the moonlight—that was in no sense divine—but in the stirring darkness of the stars. And it is remarkable that after a course of astronomical enlightenment by a visiting master and descriptions of masses and distances, incredible aching distances, then even more than ever she seemed to feel God among the stars. . . .

A fatal accident to a schoolfellow turned her mind for a time to the dark stillnesses of death. The accident happened away in Wales during the summer holidays ; she saw nothing of it, she only knew of its consequence. Hitherto she had assumed it was the function of girls to grow up and go out from the grey intermediate state of school work into freedoms and realities beyond. Death happened, she was aware, to young people, but not she had thought to the people one knew. This termination came with a shock. The girl was no great personal loss to Ellen, they had belonged to different sets and classes, but the conception of her as lying very, very still for ever, was a haunting one. Ellen felt she did not want to be still for evermore in a confined space, with life and sunshine going on all about her and above her, and it quickened her growing appetite for living to think that she might presently have to be like that. How stifled one would feel !

It couldn't be like that.

She began to speculate about that future life upon which religion insists so much and communicates so little. Was it perhaps in other planets, under those wonderful, many mooned, silver-banded skies ? She perceived more and more a kind of absurdity in the existence all about her. Was all this world a mere make-believe, and would Miss Beeton Clavier and every one about her presently cast aside a veil ? Manifestly there was a veil. She had a very natural disposition to doubt whether the actual circumstances of her life were real. Her mother, for instance, was so lacking in blood and fire, so very like the stiff paper wrapping of something else. But if these things were not real, what was real ? What might she not presently do ? What might she not presently be ? Perhaps death had something to do with that. Was death perhaps no more than the flinging off of grotesque outer garments by the newly-arrived guests at the feast of living ? She had that feeling that there might be a feast of living.

These preoccupations were a jealously guarded secret, but they gave her a quality of slight detachment that added a dreaming dignity to her dark, tall charm.

There were moments of fine, deep excitement that somehow linked themselves in her mind with these thoughts as being set over against the things of every day. These, too, were moments quite different and separate in quality from delight, from the keen appreciation of flowers or sunshine or little vividly living things. Daylight seemed to blind her to them, as they blinded her to starshine. They, too, had a quality of reference to things large and remote, distances, unknown mysteries of light and matter, the thought of mountains, cool, white wildernesses and driving snowstorms, or great periods of time. Such were the luminous transfigurations that would come to her at the evening service in church.

The school used to sit in the gallery over against the organist, and for a year or more Ellen had the place at the corner from which she could look down the hazy candle-lit vista of the nave and see the congregation as ranks and ranks of dim faces and vaguely apprehended clothes, ranks that rose with a peculiar deep and spacious rustle to sing, and sang with a massiveness of effect she knew in no other music. Certain hymns in particular seemed to bear her up and carry her into another larger, more wonderful world : " Light's Abode, Celestial Salem," for example, a world of luminous spiritualised sensuousness. Of such a quality she thought the Heavenly City must surely be, away there and away. But this persuasion differed from those other mystical intimations in its detachment from any sense of the divinity. And remarkably mixed up with it and not yet belonging to it, antagonistic and kindred like a silver dagger stuck through a mystically illuminated parchment, was the angelic figure of a tall fair boy in a surplice who stood out amidst the choir below, and sang, it seemed to her, alone.

She herself on these occasions of exaltation would be far too deeply moved to sing. She was inundated by a swimming sense of boundaries nearly transcended, as though she was upon the threshold of a different life altogether, the real enduring life, and as though if she could only maintain herself long enough in this shimmering exaltation, she would get right over ; things would happen, things that would draw her into that music and magic and prevent her ever returning to everyday life again. There one would walk through music between great candles under eternal stars, hand-in-hand with a tall, white figure. But nothing ever did happen to make her cross that boundary ; the hymn ceased, the " Amen " died away, as if a curtain fell. The congregation subsided. Reluctantly she would sink back into her seat. . . .

But all through the sermon, to which she never gave the slightest attention, her mind would feel mute and stilled, and she used to come out of church silent and preoccupied, returning unwillingly to the commonplaces of life. . . .

§ 3

Ellen met Sir Isaac—in the days before he was Sir Isaac —at the house of a school friend, with whom she was staying at Hythe, and afterwards her mother and sister came down and joined her for a fortnight at a Folkestone boarding-house. Mr. Harman had caught a chill while inspecting his North Wales branches, and had come down with his mother to recuperate. He and his mother occupied a suite of rooms in the most imposing hotel upon the Leas. Ellen's friend's people were partners in a big flour firm and had a pleasant new æsthetic white and green house of roughcast and slates in the pretty country beyond the Hythe golf links, and Ellen's friend's father was deeply anxious to develop amiable arrangements with Mr. Harman. There was much tennis, much croquet, much cycling to the Hythe sea-wall, and bathing from little tents and sitting about in the sunshine, and Mr. Harman had his first automobile with him—they were still something of a novelty in those days—and was urgent to take picnic parties to large lonely places on the downs.

There were only two young men in that circle, one was engaged to Ellen's friend's sister, and the other was bound to a young woman remote in Italy ; neither was strikingly attractive, and both regarded Harman with that awe tempered by undignified furtive derision which wealth and business capacity so often inspire in the young male. At first he was quiet, and simply looked at her, as it seemed any one might look, then she perceived he looked at her intently and continuously, and was persistently close to her and seemed always to be trying to do things to please her and attract her attention. And then, from the general behaviour of the women about her, her mother and Mrs. Harman and her friend's mother and her friend's sister, rather than from any one specific thing they said, it grew upon her consciousness that this important and fabulously wealthy person, who was also, it seemed to her, so modest and quiet and touchingly benevolent, was in love with her.

" Your daughter," said Mrs. Harman repeatedly to Mrs. Sawbridge, " is charming, perfectly charming."

" She's *such* a child," said Mrs. Sawbridge repeatedly in reply.

And she told Ellen's friend's mother apropos of Ellen's friend's engagement that she wanted all her daughters to marry for love, she didn't care what the man had so long as they loved each other, and meanwhile she took the utmost care that Isaac had undisputed access to the girl, was watchfully ready to fend off any one else, made her take everything he offered and praised him quietly and steadily to her. She pointed out how modest and unassuming he was, in spite of the fact that he was " controlling an immense business " and in his own particular trade " a perfect Napoleon."

" For all one sees to the contrary, he might be just a private gentleman. And he feeds thousands and thousands of people. . . ."

" Sooner or later," said Mrs. Harman, " I suppose Isaac will marry. He's been such a good son to me, that I shall feel it dreadfully, and yet, you know, I wish I could see him settled. Then *I* shall settle—in a little house of my own somewhere. Just a little place. I don't believe in coming too much between son and daughter-in-law. . . ."

Harman's natural avidity was tempered by a proper modesty. He thought Ellen so lovely and so infinitely desirable —and indeed she was—that it seemed incredible to him that he could ever get her. And yet he had got most of the things in life he had really and urgently wanted. His doubts gave his love-making an eager, lavish, and pathetic delicacy. He watched her minutely in an agony of appreciation. He felt ready to give or promise anything.

She was greatly flattered by his devotion, and she liked the surprises and presents he heaped upon her extremely. Also she was sorry for him beyond measure. In the deep recesses of her heart was an oleographic ideal of a large, brave young man with blue eyes, a wave in his fair hair, a wonderful tenor voice and—she could not help it, she tried to look away and not think of it—a broad chest. With him she intended to climb mountains. So clearly she could not marry Mr. Harman. And because of that she tried to be very kind indeed to him, and when he faltered that she could not possibly care for him, she reassured him so vaguely as to fill him with wild gusts of hope and herself with a sense of pledges. He told her one day between two sets of tennis—which he played with a certain tricky skill—that he felt that the very highest happiness he could ever attain would be to die at her feet. Presently her pity and her sense of responsibility had become so large and deep that the dream hero with the blue eyes was largely overlaid and hidden by them.

Then, at first a little indirectly and then urgently, and with a voice upon the edge of tears, Harman implored her to marry him. She had never before in the whole course of her life seen a grown-up person on the verge of tears. She felt that the release of such deep fountains as that must be averted at any cost. She felt that for a mere schoolgirl like herself, a backward schoolgirl who had never really mastered quadratics, to cause these immense and tragic distresses was abominable. She was sure her former head-mistress would disapprove very highly of her. " I will make you a queen," said Harman, " I will give all my life to your happiness."

She believed he would.

She refused him for the second time, but with a weakening certainty in a little white summer-house that gave a glimpse of the sea between green and wooded hills. She sat and stared at the sea after he had left her, through a mist of tears ; so pitiful did he seem. He had beaten his poor fists on the stone table, and then caught up her hand, kissed it, and rushed out. . . . She had not dreamt that love could hurt like that.

And all that night—that is to say, for a full hour before her wet eyelashes closed in slumber—she was sleepless with remorse for the misery she was causing him.

The third time when he said with suicidal conviction that he could not live without her, she burst into tears of pity and yielded. And instantly, amazingly, with the famished swiftness of a springing panther, he caught her body into his arms, and kissed her on the lips. . . .

§ 4

They were married with every circumstance of splendour, with very expensive music, and portraits in the illustrated newspapers, and a great glitter of favours and carriages. The bridegroom was most thoughtful and generous about the Sawbridge side of the preparations. Only one thing was a little perplexing. In spite of his impassioned impatience he delayed the wedding. Full of dark hints and a portentous secret, he delayed the wedding for twenty-five whole days, in order that it should follow immediately upon the publication of the birthday honours list. And then they understood.

" You will be Lady Harman," he exulted ; " *Lady* Harman. I would have given double. . . . I have had to back the *Old Country Gazette*, and I don't care a rap. I'd have done anything. I'd have bought the rotten thing outright. . . . Lady Harman ! "

He remained loverlike until the very eve of their marriage. Then suddenly it seemed to her that all the people she cared for in the world were pushing her away from them towards him, giving her up, handing her over. He became—possessive. His abjection changed to pride. She perceived that she was going to be left tremendously alone with him, with an effect, as if she had stepped off a terrace on to what she believed to be land, and had abruptly descended into very deep water. . . .

And while she was still feeling quite surprised by everything and extremely doubtful whether she wanted to go any farther with this business, which was manifestly far more serious, out of all proportion more serious, than anything that had ever happened to her before—and *unpleasant*, abounding, indeed, in crumpling indignities and horrible nervous stresses, it dawned upon her that she was presently to be that strange, grown-up and preoccupied thing, a mother, and that girlhood and youth and vigorous games, mountains and swimming and running and leaping, were over for her, as far as she could see, for ever. . . .

Both the prospective grandmothers became wonderfully kind and helpful and intimate, preparing with gusto and an agreeable sense of delegated responsibility for the child that was to give them all the pride of maternity again and none of its inconveniences.

CHAPTER FIVE

THE WORLD ACCORDING TO SIR ISAAC

§ I

HER marriage had carried Ellen out of the narrow world of home and school into another that had seemed at first vastly larger, if only on account of its freedom from the perpetual achievement of small economies. Hitherto the urgent necessity of these had filled life with irksome precautions, and clipped the wings of every dream. This new life into which Sir Isaac led her by the hand promised not only that release but more light, more colour, more movement, more people. There was to be, at any rate, so much in the way of rewards and compensation for her pity of him.

She found the establishment at Putney ready for her. Sir Isaac had not consulted her about it, it had been his secret, he had prepared it for her with meticulous care as a surprise. They returned from a honeymoon in Skye, in which the attentions of Sir Isaac and the comforts of a first-class hotel had obscured a marvellous background of sombre mountain and wide stretches of shining sea. Sir Isaac had been very fond and insistent and inseparable, and she was doing her best to conceal a strange, distressful jangling of her nerves, which she now feared might presently dispose her to scream. Sir Isaac had been goodness itself, but how she craved now for solitude ! She was under the impression now that they were going to his mother's house in Highbury. Then she thought he would have to go away to business for part of the day at any rate, and she could creep into some corner and begin to think of all that had happened to her in these short summer months.

They were met at Euston by his motor-car. " *Home*," said Sir Isaac, with a little gleam of excitement, when the more immediate luggage was aboard.

As they hummed through the West-End afternoon, Ellen became aware that he was whistling through his teeth. It was his invariable indication of mental activity, and her attention came drifting back from her idle contemplation of the shoppers and strollers of Piccadilly to link this already alarming symptom with the perplexing fact that they were manifestly travelling west.

" But this," she said presently, " is Knightsbridge."

" Goes to Kensington," he replied, with attempted indifference.

" But your mother doesn't live this way."

" *We* do," said Sir Isaac, shining at every point of his face.

" But," she halted. " Isaac !—where are we going ? "

" Home," he said.

" You've not taken a house ? "

" Bought it."

" But—it won't be ready ! "

" I've seen to that."

" Servants ! " she cried in dismay.

" That's all right." His face broke into an excited smile. His little eyes danced and shone. " Everything," he said.

" But the servants ! " she said.

" You'll see," he said. " There's a butler—and everything.

" A butler ! " He could now no longer restrain himself. " I was weeks," he said, " getting it ready. Weeks and weeks. . . . It's a house. . . . I'd had my eye on it before ever I met you. It's a real *good* house, Elly. . . ."

The fortunate girl-wife went on through Brompton to Walham Green with a stunned feeling. So women have felt in tumbrils. A nightmare of butlers, a galaxy of possible butlers, filled her soul.

No one was quite so big and formidable as Snagsby, towering up to receive her, upon the steps of the home her husband was so amazingly giving her.

The reader has already been privileged to see something of this house in the company of Lady Beach-Mandarin. At the top of the steps stood Mrs. Crumble, the new and highly recommended cook-housekeeper in her best black silk, flounced and expanded, and behind her peeped several neat maids in caps and aprons. A little valet-like under-butler appeared and tried to balance Snagsby by hovering two steps above him on the opposite side of the Victorian mediæval porch.

Assisted officiously by Snagsby, and amidst the deferential unhelpful gestures of the under-butler, Sir Isaac handed his wife out of the car. " Everything all right, Snagsby ? " he asked brusquely if a little breathless.

" Everything in order, Sir Isaac."

" And here—this is her ladyship."

" I 'ope her ladyship 'ad a pleasent journey to 'er new 'ome. I'm sure if I may presume, Sir Isaac, we shall all be very glad to serve her ladyship."

(Like all well-trained English servants, Snagsby always dropped as many h's as he could when conversing with his superiors. He did this as a mark of respect and to prevent social confusion, just as he was always careful to wear a slightly misfitting dress coat and fold his trousers so that they creased at the sides and had a wide, flat effect in front.)

Lady Harman bowed a little shyly to his good wishes, and was then led up to Mrs. Crumble, in a stiff black silk, who curtseyed with a submissive amiability to her new mistress. " I'm sure, me lady," she said, " I'm sure——"

There was a little pause. " Here they are, you see, right and ready," said Sir Isaac, and then, with an inspiration, " Got any tea for us, Snagsby ? "

Snagsby, addressing his mistress, inquired if he should serve tea in the garden or the drawing-room, and Sir Isaac decided for the garden.

" There's another hall beyond this," he said, and took his wife's arm, leaving Mrs. Crumble still bowing amiably before the hall table. And every time she bowed she rustled richly. . . .

" It's quite a big garden," said Sir Isaac.

§ 2

And so the woman who had been a girl three weeks ago, this tall, dark-eyed, slightly perplexed and very young-looking lady, was introduced to the home that had been made for her. She went about it with an alarmed sense of strange responsibilities, not in the least feeling that anything was being given to her. And Sir Isaac led her from point to point full of the pride and joy of new possession—for it was his first own house as well as hers—rejoicing over it, and exacting gratitude.

" It's all right, isn't it ? " he asked, looking up at her.

" It's wonderful. I'd no idea."

" See," he said, indicating a great brass bowl of perennial sunflowers on the landing, " your favourite flower ! "

" My favourite flower ? "

" You said it was—in that book. Perennial sunflower."

She was perplexed, and then remembered.

She understood now why he had said downstairs, when she had glanced at a big photographic enlargement of a portrait of Doctor Barnardo, " your favourite hero in real life."

He had brought her at Hythe, one day, a popular Victorian device, a confession album, in which she had had to write down on a neat, rose-tinted page, her favourite author, her favourite flower, her favourite colour, her favourite hero in real life, her " pet aversion," and quite a number of such particulars of her subjective existence. She had filled this page in a haphazard manner late one night, and she was disconcerted to find how thoroughly her careless replies had come home to roost. She had put down " pink " as her favourite colour, because the page she was writing upon suggested it, and the paper of the room was pale pink, the curtains strong pink, with a pattern of paler pink and tied with large pink bows, and the lamp shades, the bedspread, the pillow-cases, the carpet, the chairs, .the very crockery—everything but the omnipresent perennial sunflowers—was pink. Confronted with this realisation, she understood that pink was the least agreeable of all possible hues for a bedroom. She perceived she had to live now in a chromatic range between rather underdone mutton and salmon. She had said that her favourite musical composers were Bach and Beethoven ; she really meant it, and a bust of Beethoven materialised that statement, but she had made Doctor Barnardo her favourite hero in real life because his name also began with a B, and she had heard some one say somewhere that he was a very good man. The predominance of George Eliot's pensive rather than delightful countenance in her bedroom and the array of all that lady's works in a lusciously tooled pink leather, was due to her equally reckless choice of a favourite author. She had said, too, that Nelson was her favourite historical character, but Sir Isaac, with a delicate jealousy, had preferred to have this heroic but regrettable immoral personality represented in his home only by an engraving of the Battle of Copenhagen. . . .

She stood surveying this room, and her husband watched her eagerly. She was, he felt, impressed at last ! . . .

Certainly she had never seen such a bedroom in her life. By comparison even with the largest of the hotel apartments they had occupied, it was vast ; it had writing-tables and a dainty bookcase and a blushing sofa, and dressing-tables and a bureau and a rose-red screen, and three large windows. Her thoughts went back to the narrow little bedroom at Penge with which she had hitherto been so entirely content. Her own few little books, a photograph or so—they'd never dare to come here, even if she dared to bring them.

" Here," said Sir Isaac, flinging open a white door, " is your dressing-room."

She was chiefly aware of a huge white bath standing on a marble slab under a window of crinkled pink-stained glass, and of a wide space of tiled floor with white fur rugs.

" And here," he said, opening a panel that was covered by wall-paper, " is *my* door."

" Yes," he said, to the question in her eyes, " that's my room. You got this one—for your own. It's how people do now. People of our position. . . . There's no lock."

He shut the door slowly again and surveyed the splendours he had made with infinite satisfaction.

" All right ? " he said, " isn't it ? " . . . He turned to the pearl for which the casket was made, and slipped an arm about her waist. His arm tightened.

" Got a kiss for me, Elly ? " he whispered.

At this moment, a gong almost worthy of Snagsby summoned them to tea. It came booming in to them with a vast, officious arrogance that brooked no denial. It made one understand the imperatives of the last trump, albeit with a greater dignity. . . . There was a little awkward pause.

" I'm so dirty and trainy," she said, disengaging herself from his arm. " And we ought to go to tea."

§ 3

The same exceptional aptitude of Sir Isaac for detailed administration that had relieved his wife from the need of furnishing and arranging a home, made the birth of her children and the organisation of her nursery an almost detached affair for her. Sir Isaac went about in a preoccupied way, whistling between his teeth and planning with expert advice the equipment of an ideal nursery, and her mother and his mother became as it were, voluminous clouds of uncommunicative wisdom and precaution. In addition, the conversation of Miss Crump, the extremely skilled and costly nurse, who arrived a full Advent before the child, fresh from the birth of a viscount, did much to generalise whatever had remained individual of this thing that was happening. With so much intelligence focussed, there seemed to Lady Harman no particular reason why she should not do her best to think as little as possible about the impending affair, which meant for her, she now understood quite clearly, more and more discomfort, culminating in an agony. The summer promised to be warm, and Sir Isaac took a furnished house for the great event in the hills behind Torquay. The maternal instinct is not a magic thing, it has to be evoked and developed, and I decline to believe it is indicative of any peculiar unwomanliness in Lady Harman that when at last she beheld her newly-born daughter in the hands of the experts, she moaned druggishly, " Oh ! please take it away. Oh ! Take it—away. Anywhere—anywhere."

It was very red and wrinkled and aged-looking and, except when it opened its mouth to cry, extraordinarily like its father. This resemblance disappeared—along with a crop of darkish red hair—in the course of a day or two, but it left a lurking dislike to its proximity in her mind long after it had become an entirely infantile and engaging baby.

§ 4

Those early years of their marriage were the happiest period of Sir Isaac's life.

He seemed to have everything that man could desire. He was still only just forty at his marriage ; he had made for himself a position altogether dominant in the world of confectionery and popular refreshment, he had won a title, he had a home after his own heart, a beautiful young wife, and presently delightful children in his own image, and it was only after some years of contentment and serenity, and with a certain incredulity that he discovered that something in his wife, something almost in the nature of discontent with her lot, was undermining and threatening all the comfort and beauty of his life.

Sir Isaac was one of those men whom modern England delights to honour, a man of unpretentious acquisitiveness, devoted to business, and distracted by no æsthetic or intellectual interests. He was the only son of his mother, the widow of a bankrupt steam-miller, and he had been a delicate child to rear. He left Mr. Gambard's college at Ealing after passing the second-class examination of the College of Preceptors at the age of sixteen, to go into a tea-office as clerk without a salary, a post he presently abandoned for a clerkship in the office of a large refreshment catering firm. He attracted the attention of his employers by suggesting various administrative economies, and he was already drawing a salary of two hundred and fifty pounds a year when he was twenty-one. Many young men would have rested satisfied with so rapid an advancement, and would have devoted themselves to the amusements that are now considered so permissible to youth, but young Harman was made of sterner stuff, and it only spurred him to further efforts. He contrived to save a considerable proportion of his salary for some years, and at the age of twenty-seven he started, in association with a firm of flour millers, the International Bread and Cake Stores, which spread rapidly over the country. They were not in any sense of the word " International," but in a search for inflated and inflating adjectives this word attracted him most, and the success of the enterprise justified his choice. Originally conceived as a syndicated system of baker's shops running a specially gritty and nutritious line of bread, the Staminal Bread, in addition to the ordinary descriptions, it rapidly developed a catering side, and, in a little time, there were few centres of clerkly employment in London or the Midlands where an International could not be found supplying the midday scone or poached egg, washed down by a cup of tea, or coffee, or lemonade. It meant hard work for Isaac Harman. It drew lines on his cheeks, sharpened his always rather pointed nose to an extreme efficiency, greyed his hair, and gave an acquired firmness to his rather retreating mouth. All his time was given to the details of this development ; always he was inspecting premises, selecting and dismissing managers, making codes of rules and fines for his growing army of employees, organising and reorganising his central offices and his central bakeries, hunting up cheaper and cheaper supplies of eggs and flour, and milk and ham, devising advertisements and agency developments. He had something of an artist's passion in these things ; he went about, a little bent and peaky, calculating and planning and hissing through his teeth, and feeling not only that he was getting on, but that he was getting on in the most exemplary way. Manifestly, anybody in his line of business who wanted to be leisurely, or to be generous, who possessed any broader interests than the shop, who troubled to think about the nation or the race or any of the deeper mysteries of life, was bound to go down before him. He dealt privately with every appetite—until his marriage no human being could have suspected him of any appetite but business—he disposed of every distracting impulse with unobtrusive decision ; and even his political inclination towards Radicalism sprang chiefly from an irritation with the legal advantages of landlordism natural to a man who is frequently leasing shops.

At school Sir Isaac had not been a particularly prominent figure ; his disposition at cricket to block and to bowl " sneaks "

and "twisters" under-arm had raised his average rather than
his reputation ; he had evaded fights and dramatic situations,
and protected himself upon occasions of unavoidable violence
by punching with his white knuckles held in a peculiar and
vicious manner. He had always been a little insensitive to
those graces of style, in action if not in art, which appeal so
strongly to the commoner sort of English mind ; he played
first for safety, and that assured, for the uttermost advantage.
These tendencies became more marked with maturity. When
he took up tennis for his health's sake, he developed at once
an ungracious service that had to be killed like vermin ; he
developed an instinct for the deadest ball available, and his
returns close up to the net were like assassinations. Indeed,
he was inherently incapable of any vision beyond the express
prohibitions and permissions of the rules of the games he
played, or beyond the laws and institutions under which he
lived. His idea of generosity was the undocumented and
unqualified purchase of a person by payments made in the
form of a gift.

And this being the quality of Sir Isaac's mind, it followed
that his interpretations of the relationship of marriage were
simple and strict. A woman, he knew, had to be wooed to be
won, but when she was won, she was won. He did not understand wooing after that was settled. There was the bargain
and her surrender. He, on his side, had to keep her, dress her,
be kind to her, give her the appearances of pride and authority,
and in return he had his rights and his privileges and undefined powers of control. That, you know, by the existing
rules is the reality of marriage, where there are no settlements
and no private property of the wife's. That is to say, it is the
reality of marriage in ninety-nine cases out of the hundred.
And it would have shocked Sir Isaac extremely, and, as a
matter of fact, it did shock him, for any one to suggest the
slightest revision of so entirely advantageous an arrangement.
He was confident of his good intentions, and resolved to the
best of his ability to make his wife the happiest of living
creatures, subject only to reasonable acquiescences and general
good behaviour.

Never before had he cared for anything so much as he did
for her—not even for the International Bread and Cake
Stores. He gloated upon her. She distracted him from business.
He resolved from the outset to surround her with every luxury
and permit her no desire that he had not already anticipated.
Even her mother and Georgina, whom he thought extremely
unnecessary persons, were frequent visitors to his house. His
solicitude for her was so great that she found it difficult even
to see her doctor except in his presence. And he bought her
a pearl necklace that cost six hundred pounds. He was, in
fact, one of those complete husbands who grow rare in these
decadent days.

The social circle to which Sir Isaac introduced his wife was not a very extensive one. The business misadventures of his father had naturally deprived his mother of most of her friends ; he had made only acquaintances at school, and his subsequent concentration upon business had permitted very few intimacies. Renewed prosperity had produced a certain revival of cousins, but Mrs. Harman, established in a pleasant house at Highbury, had received their attentions with a well merited stiffness. His chief associates were his various business allies, and these and their wives and families formed the nucleus of the new world to which Ellen was gradually and temperately introduced. There were a few local callers, but Putney is now too deeply merged with London for this practice of the countryside to have any great effect upon a new-comer's visiting circle.

Perhaps Mr. Charterson might claim to be Sir Isaac's chief friend at the time of that gentleman's marriage. Transactions in sugar had brought them together originally. He was Sir Isaac's best man, and the new knight entertained a feeling of something very like admiration for him. Moreover, Mr. Charterson had very large ears, more particularly was the left one large, extraordinarily large and projecting upper teeth, which he sought vainly to hide beneath an extravagant moustache, and a harsh voice, characteristics that did much to allay the anxieties natural to a newly-married man. Mr. Charterson was, moreover, adequately married to a large, attentive, enterprising, swarthy wife, and possessed a splendid house in Belgravia. Not quite so self-made as Sir Isaac, he was still sufficiently self-made to take a very keen interest in his own social advancement and in social advancement generally, and it was through him that Sir Isaac's attention had been first directed to those developing relations with politics that arise as a business grows to greatness. " I'm for Parliament," said Charterson. " Sugar's in politics, and I'm after it. You'd better come, too, Harman. Those chaps up there, they'll play jiggery-pokery with sugar if we aren't careful. And it won't be only sugar, Harman ! "

Pressed to expand this latter sentence, he pointed out to his friend that " any amount of interfering with employment " was in the air—" any amount."

" And besides," said Mr. Charterson, " men like us have a stake in the country, Harman. We're getting biggish people. We ought to do our share. I don't see the fun of leaving everything to the landlords and the lawyers. Men of our sort have got to make ourselves felt. We want a business government. Of course—one pays. So long as I get a voice in calling the tune, I don't mind paying the piper a bit. There's going to be a lot of interference with trade. All this social legislation. And there's what you were saying the other day about these leases. . . ."

" I'm not much of a talker," said Harman.   " I don't see
myself gassing in the House."

" Oh ! I don't mean going into Parliament," said Charterson.
" That's for some of us, perhaps. . . . But come into the
party, make yourself felt. . . ."

Under Charterson's stimulation it was that Harman
joined the National Liberal Club, and presently went on to
the climax, and through him he came to know something
of that inner traffic of arrangements and bargains which
does so much to keep a great historical party together and
maintain its vitality. For a time he was largely overshadowed
by the sturdy Radicalism of Charterson, but presently as he
understood this interesting game better, he embarked upon
a line of his own. Charterson wanted a seat, and presently he
got it ; his maiden speech on the sugar bounties won a compli-
ment from Mr. Evesham ; and Harman, who would have
piloted a monoplane sooner than address the House, decided
to be one of those silent influences that work outside our
national assembly. He came to the help of an embarrassed
Liberal weekly, and then in a Fleet Street crisis, undertook
the larger share of backing the *Old Country Gazette*, that
important social and intellectual party organ. His knighthood
followed almost automatically.

Such political developments introduced a second element
into the intermittent social relations of the Harman household.
Before his knighthood and marriage Sir Isaac had participated
in various public banquets and private parties and little
dinners in the vaults of the House and elsewhere, arising out
of his political intentions, and with the appearance of a Lady
Harman there came a certain urgency on the part of those
who maintain in a state of hectic dullness the social activities
of the great Liberal party. Horatio Blenker, Sir Isaac's editor,
showed a disposition to be socially very helpful, and after
Mrs. Blenker had called in a state of worldly instructiveness,
there was a little dinner at the Blenkers' to introduce young
Lady Harman to the great political world. It was the first
dinner-party of her life, and she found it dazzling rather
than really agreeable.

She felt very slender and young, and rather unclothed about
the arms and neck, in spite of the six hundred pound pearl
necklace that had been given to her just as she stood before
the mirror in her white-and-gold dinner dress ready to start.
She had to look down at that dress ever and again and at her
shining arms to remind herself that she wasn't still in schoolgirl clothes, and it seemed to her there was not another woman
in the room who was not fairly entitled to send her off to bed
at any moment. She had been a little nervous about the
details of the dinner, but there was nothing strange or difficult
but caviare, and in that case she waited for some one else
to begin. The Chartersons were there, which was very re-

assuring, and the abundant flowers on the table were a sort of protection. The man on her right was very nice, gently voluble, and evidently quite deaf, so that she had merely to make kind, respectful faces at him. He talked to her most of the time, and described the peasant costumes in Marken and Walcheren. And Mr. Blenker, with a fine appreciation of Sir Isaac's watchful temperament and his own magnetism, spoke to her three times and never looked at her once all through the entertainment.

A few weeks later they went to dinner at the Chartersons', and then she gave a dinner, which was arranged very skilfully by Sir Isaac and Snagsby and the cook-housekeeper, with a little outside help, and then came a big party reception at Lady Barleypound's, a multitudinous miscellaneous assembly in which the obviously wealthy rubbed shoulders with the obviously virtuous and the not quite so obviously clever. It was a great orgy of standing about and seeing the various Blenkers and the Cramptons, and the Weston Massinghays, and the Daytons, and Mrs. Millingham, with her quivering lorgnette and her last tame genius, and Lewis, and indeed all the tapirs and tadpoles of Liberalism, being tremendously active and influential and important throughout the evening. The house struck Ellen as being very splendid, the great staircase particularly so, and never before had she seen a great multitude of people in evening dress. Lady Barleypound in the golden parlour at the head of the stairs, shook hands automatically, lost, it would seem, in some amiable dream, Mrs. Blapton and a daughter rustled across the gathering in a hasty, vindictive manner, and vanished, and a number of handsome, glittering, dark-eyed, splendidly-dressed women kept together in groups, and were tremendously but occultly amused. The various Blenkers seemed everywhere, Horatio in particular, with his large fluent person and his luminous tenor, was like a shop-walker taking customers to the departments : one felt he was weaving all these immiscibles together into one great, wise, Liberal purpose, and that he deserved quite wonderful things from the party ; he even introduced five or six people to Lady Harman, looking sternly over her head and restraining his charm as he did so on account of Sir Isaac's feelings. The people he brought up to her were not very interesting people, she thought, but then that was perhaps due to her own dreadful ignorance of politics. . . .

Lady Harman ceased even to dip into the vortex of London society after March, and in June she went with her mother and a skilled nurse to that beautiful furnished house Sir Isaac had found near Torquay, in preparation for the birth of their first little daughter.

§ 5

It seemed to her husband that it was both unreasonable and ungrateful of her to become a tearful young woman after their union, and for a phase of some months she certainly was a tearful young woman, but his mother made it clear to him that this was quite a correct and permissible phase for her, as she was, and so he expressed his impatience with temperance, and presently she was able to pull herself together and begin to readjust herself to a universe that had seemed for a time almost too shattered for endurance. She resumed the process of growing-up that her marriage had for a time so vividly interrupted, and if her school-days were truncated and the college phase omitted, she had, at any rate, a very considerable amount of fundamental experience to replace these now customary completions.

Three little girls she brought into the world in the first three years of her married life, then, after a brief interval of indifferent health, she had a fourth girl baby, of a physique quite obviously inferior to its predecessors, and then, after— and perhaps as a consequence of—much whispered conversation of the two mothers-in-law, protests and tactful explanation on the part of the elderly and trustworthy family doctor and remarks of an extraordinary breadth (and made at table, too, almost before the door had closed on Snagsby !) from Ellen's elder sister, there came a less reproductive phase. . . .

But by that time Lady Harman had acquired the habit of reading and the habit of thinking over what she read, and from that it is an easy step to thinking over oneself and the circumstances of one's own life. The one thing trains for the other.

Now the chief circumstance in the life of Lady Harman was Sir Isaac. Indeed, as she grew to a clear consciousness of herself and her position, it seemed to her he was not so much a circumstance as a circumvallation. There wasn't a direction in which she could turn without immediately running up against him. He had taken possession of her extremely. And from her first resignation to this as an inevitable fact, she had come, she hardly knew how, to a renewed disposition to regard this large and various universe beyond him and outside of him, with something of the same slight adventurousness she had felt before he so comprehensively happened to her. After her first phase of despair she had really done her best to honour the bargain she had rather unwittingly made, and to love and to devote herself and be a loyal and happy wife to this clutching, hard-breathing little man who had got her, and it was the insatiable excesses of his demands quite as much as any outer influence that made her realise the impossibility of such a concentration.

His was a supremely acquisitive and possessive character,

so that he insulted her utmost subjugations by an obtrusive
suspicion and jealousy, he was jealous of her childish worship
of her dead father, jealous of her disposition to go to church,
jealous of the poet Wordsworth, because she liked to read
his sonnets, jealous because she loved great music, jealous
when she wanted to go out; if she seemed passionless, and
she seemed more and more passionless, he was jealous, and
the slightest gleam of any warmth of temperament filled him
with a vile and furious dread of dishonouring possibilities.
And the utmost resolution to believe in him could not hide
from her for ever the fact that his love manifested itself almost
wholly as a parade of ownership and a desire, without kindliness, without any self-forgetfulness.   All his devotion, his
self-abjection, had been the mere qualms of a craving, the
flush of eager courtship.   Do as she would to overcome these
realisations, forces within her stronger than herself, primordial
forces with the welfare of all life in their keeping, cried out
upon the meanness of his face, the ugly pointed nose, and
the thin compressed lips, the weak neck, the clammy hands,
the ungainly, nervous gestures, the tuneless whistling between
the clenched teeth.   He would not let her forget a single detail.
Whenever she tried to look at any created thing, he thrust
himself, like one of his own open-air advertisements, athwart
the attraction.

As she grew up to an achieved womanhood—and it was
even a physical growing-up, for she added more than an
inch of stature after her marriage—her life became more
and more consciously like a fencing match in which her vision
flashed over his head and under his arms and this side of
him and that, while with a toiling industry he fought to
intercept it.   And from the complete acceptance of her matrimonial submission, she passed on by almost insensible degrees
towards a conception of her life as a struggle, that seemed
at first entirely lonely and unsupported, to exist—*against*
him.

In every novel, as in every picture, there must be an immense simplification, and so I tell the story of Lady Harman's
changing attitude without any of those tangled leapings-
forward or harkings-back, those moods and counter-moods
and relapses which made up the necessary course of her mind.
But sometimes she was here and sometimes she was there,
sometimes quite back to the beginning, an obedient scrupulously loyal and up-looking young wife, sometimes a wife
concealing the humiliation of an unhappy choice in a spurious
satisfaction and affection.   And mixed up with widening
spaces of criticism and dissatisfaction and hostility there were,
you must understand, moments of real liking for this outrageous
little man, and streaks of an absurd maternal tenderness for
him.   They had been too close together to avoid that.   She
had a woman's affection of ownership too, and disliked to

see him despised or bettered or untidy ; even those ridiculous muddy hands had given her a twinge of solicitude. . . .

And all the while she was trying to see the universe also, the great background of their two little lives, and to think what it might mean for her over and above their too obliterating relationship.

§ 6

It would be like counting the bacteria of an infection to trace how ideas of insubordination came drifting into Sir Isaac's paradise. The epidemic is in the air. There is no Tempter nowadays, no definite apple. The disturbing force has grown subtler, blows in now like a draught, creeps and gathers like the dust—a disseminated serpent. Sir Isaac brought home this young, beautiful, and rather crumpled and astonished Eve, and by all his standards he was entitled to be happy ever afterwards. He knew of one danger, but against that he was very watchful. Never once, for six long years, did she have a private duologue with another male. But Mudie and Sir Jesse Boot sent parcels to the house unchecked, the newspaper drifted in not even censored ; the nurses who guided Ellen through the essential incidents of a feminine career talked of something called a " movement." And there was Georgina. . . .

The thing they wanted they called the Vote, but that demand so hollow, so eyeless, had all the terrifying effect of a mask. Behind that mask was a formless, invincible discontent with the lot of womanhood. It wanted—it was not clear what it wanted, but whatever it wanted, all the domestic instincts of mankind were against admitting there was anything it could want. That remarkable agitation had already worked up to the thunderous pitch, there had been demonstrations at public meetings, scenes in the Ladies' Gallery, and something like rioting in Parliament Square, before ever it occurred to Sir Isaac that this was a disturbance that touched his home. He had supposed suffragettes were ladies of all too certain an age, with red noses and spectacles and a masculine style of costume, who wished to be hugged by policemen. He said as much rather knowingly and wickedly to Charterson. He could not understand any woman not coveting the privileges of Lady Harman. And then one day, while Georgina and her mother were visiting them, as he was looking over the letters at the breakfast table, according to his custom before giving them out, he discovered two identical newspaper packets addressed to his wife and his sister-in-law, and upon them were these words, printed very plainly, " Votes for Women."

" Good Lord ! " he cried. " What's this ? It oughtn't to be allowed." And he pitched the papers at the wastepaper basket under the sideboard.

"I'll thank you," said Georgia, "not to throw away our *Votes for Women*. We subscribe to that."

"Eh?" cried Sir Isaac.

"We're subscribers. Snagsby, just give us those papers." (A difficult moment for Snagsby.) He picked up the papers and looked at Sir Isaac.

"Put 'em down there," said Sir Isaac, waving to the sideboard, and then in an ensuing silence handed two letters of no importance to his mother-in-law. His face was pale, and he was breathless. Snagsby, with an obvious tactfulness, retired.

Sir Isaac watched the door close.

His remark pointedly ignored Georgina.

"What you been thinking about, Elly," he asked, "subscribing to *that* thing?"

"I wanted to read it."

"But you don't hold with all that rubbish——"

"*Rubbish!*" said Georgina, helping herself to marmalade.

"Well, rot, then, if you like," said Sir Isaac, unamiably and panting.

With that, as Snagsby afterwards put it—for the battle raged so fiercely as to go on even when he presently returned to the room—"the fat was in the fire." The Harman breakfast-table was caught up into the great controversy, with heat and fury like a tree that is overtaken by a forest fire. It burnt for weeks, and smouldered still when the first white heats had abated. I will not record the arguments of either side, they were abominably bad, and you have heard them all, time after time ; I do not think that whatever side you have taken in this matter you would find much to please you in Sir Isaac's goadings or Georgina's repartees. Sir Isaac would ask if women were prepared to go as soldiers, and Georgina would inquire how many years of service he had done, or horrify her mother by manifest allusion to the agonies and dangers of maternity—things like that. It gave a new interest to breakfast for Snagsby ; and the peculiarly ladylike qualities of Mrs. Sawbridge, a gift for silent, pallid stiffness, a disposition, tactful but unsuccessful, to "change the subject," an air of being about to leave the room in disdain had never shone with such baleful splendour. Our interest here is rather with the effect of these remarkable disputes, which echoed in Sir Isaac's private talk long after Georgina had gone again, upon Lady Harman. He could not leave this topic of feminine emancipation alone, once it had been set going, and though Ellen would always preface her remarks by, "Of course Georgina goes too far," he worried her slowly into a series of definite, insurgent positions. Sir Isaac's attacks on Georgina certainly brought out a good deal of absurdity in her positions, and Georgina at times left Sir Isaac without a leg to stand on, and the net result of their disputes, as of most human controversies, was not conviction for the hearer, but release. Her mind escaped between them and went exploring for itself through the great gaps they had made in the simple, obedient assumptions of her girlhood. That question originally put in Paradise, " Why shouldn't we ? " came into her mind and stayed there. It is a question that marks a definite stage in the departure from innocence. Things that had seemed opaque and immutable appeared translucent and questionable. She began to read more and more in order to learn things and get a light upon things, and less and less to pass the time. Ideas came to her that seemed at first strange altogether and then grotesquely justifiable, and then crept to a sort of acceptance by familiarity. And a disturbing intermittent sense of a general responsibility increased and increased in her.

You will understand this sense of responsibility which was growing up in Lady Harman's mind if you have felt it yourself, but if you have not then you may find it a little difficult to understand. You see it comes, when it comes at all, out of a phase of disillusionment. All children, I suppose, begin by taking for granted the rightness of things in general, the soundness of accepted standards, and many people are at least so happy that they never really grow out of this assumption. They go to the grave with an unbroken confidence that somewhere behind all the immediate injustices and disorders of life, behind the antics of politics, the rigidities of institutions, the pressure of custom and the vagaries of law, there is wisdom and purpose and adequate provision, they never lose that faith in the human household they acquired amongst the directed securities of home. But for more of us and more there comes a dissolution of these assurances ; there comes illumination as the day comes into a candle-lit, uncurtained room. The warm lights that once rounded off our world so completely are betrayed for what they are, smoky and guttering candles. Beyond what once seemed a casket of dutiful security is now a limitless and indifferent universe. Ours is a wisdom or there is no wisdom; ours is the decision or there is no decision. That burden is upon each of us in the measure of our capacity. The talent has been given us and we may not bury it.

§ 7

And as we reckon up the disturbing influences that were stirring Lady Harman out of that life of acquiescences to which women are perhaps even more naturally disposed than men, we may pick out the conversation of Susan Burnet as something a little apart from the others, as something with a peculiar barbed pointedness of its own that was yet in other respects very representative of a multitude of nudges and nips and pricks and indications that life was giving Lady Harman's awaking mind. Susan Burnet was a woman who came to renovate and generally do up the Putney curtains and furniture

and loose covers every spring ; she was Mrs. Crumble's discovery, she was sturdy and short, and she had open blue
eyes and an engaging simplicity of manner that attracted Lady
Harman from the outset. She was stuck away in one of the
spare bedrooms, and there she was available for any one, so
long, she explained, as they didn't fluster her when she was
cutting out, with a flow of conversation that not even a mouth
full of pins seemed to interrupt. And Lady Harman would go
and watch Susan Burnet by the hour together, and think what
an enviably independent young woman she was, and listen
with interest and something between horror and admiration
to the various impressions of life she had gathered during a
hardy and adventurous career.

Their earlier conversations were about Susan Burnet's business and the general condition of things in that world of up-
holsterers' young women in which Susan had lived until she
perceived the possibilities of a " connection," and set up for
herself. And the condition of things in that world, as Susan
described it, brought home to Lady Harman just how sheltered
and limited her own upbringing had been. " It isn't right,"
said Susan, " the way they send girls out with fellers into
empty houses. Naturally the men get persecuting them. They
don't seem hardly able to help it, some of them, and I will say
this for them, that a lot of the girls go more than half way
with them, leading them on. Still, there's a sort of man won't
leave you alone. One I used to be sent out with, and a married
man too, he was, oh !—he used to give me a time. Why, I've
bit his hands before now, bit hard, before he'd leave go of me.
It's my opinion the married men are worse than the single.
Bolder they are. I pushed him over a scuttle once, and he hit
his head against a bookcase. I was fair frightened of him.
' You little devil,' he says ; ' I'll be even with you yet. . . .'
Oh ! I've been called worse things than that. . . . Of course,
a respectable girl gets through with it, but it's trying, and to
some it's a sort of temptation. . . ."

" I should have thought," reflected Lady Harman, " you
could have told some one."

" It's queer," said Susan ; " but it never seemed to me the
sort of thing a girl ought to go telling. It's a kind of private
thing. And besides, it isn't exactly easy to tell. . . . I suppose
the firm didn't want to be worried by complaints and disputes
about that sort of thing. And it isn't always easy to say just
which of the two is to blame."

" But how old are the girls they send out ? " asked Lady
Harman.

" Some's as young as seventeen or eighteen. It all depends
on the sort of work that's wanted to be done. . . ."

" Of course, a lot of them have to marry. . . ."

This lurid little picture of vivid happenings in unoccupied
houses and particularly of the prim, industrious, capable Susan

Burnet, biting aggressive wrists, stuck in Lady Harman's imagination. She seemed to be looking into hitherto unsuspected pits of simple and violent living just beneath her feet. Susan told some upholsteress love tales, real love tales, with a warmth and honesty of passion in them that seemed at once dreadful and fine to Lady Harman's underfed imagination. Under encouragement Susan expanded the picture, beyond these mere glimpses of workshop and piece-work and furtive lust. It appeared that she was practically the head of her family ; there was a mother who had specialised in ill-health, a sister of defective ability who stayed at home, a brother in South Africa who was very good and sent home money, and three younger sisters growing up. And father—she evaded the subject of father at first. Then presently Lady Harman had some glimpses of an earlier phase in Susan Burnet's life " before any of us were earning money." Father appeared as a kindly, ineffectual, insolvent figure struggling to conduct a baker's and confectioner's business in Walthamstow, mother was already specialising, there were various brothers and sisters being born and dying.

" How many were there of you altogether ? " asked Lady Harman.

" Thirteen there was. Father always used to laugh and say he'd had a fair baker's dozen. There was Luke to begin with——"

Susan began to count on her fingers and recite braces of Scriptural names.

She could only make up her tale to twelve. She became perplexed. Then she remembered. " Of course ! " she cried : " there was Nicodemus. He was still-born. I *always* forget Nicodemus, poor little chap ! But he came—was it sixth or seventh ?—seventh after Anna."

She gave some glimpses of her father, and then there was a collapse of which she fought shy. Lady Harman was too delicate to press her to talk of that.

But one day in the afternoon Susan's tongue ran.

She was telling how first she went to work before she was twelve.

" But I thought the board schools——" said Lady Harman.

" I had to go before the committee," said Susan. " I had to go before the committee and ask to be let go to work. There they was, sitting round a table in a great big room, and they was as kind as anything, one old gentleman with a great white beard, he was as kind as could be. ' Don't you be frightened, my dear,' he says. ' You tell us why you want to go out working.' ' Well,' I says, ' *somebody's* got to earn something,' and that made them laugh in a sort of fatherly way, and after that there wasn't any difficulty. You see, it was after father's inquest, and everybody was disposed to be kind to us. ' Pity they can't all go instead of this educational tommy rot,' the old gentleman says. 'You learn to work, my dear'—and I did. . . ."

She paused.

"Father's inquest?" said Lady Harman.

Susan seemed to brace herself to the occasion. "Father," she said, "was drowned. I know—I hadn't told you that before. He was drowned in the Lea. It's always been a distress and humiliation to us there had to be an inquest. And they threw out things. . . . It's why we moved to Haggerston. It's the worst that ever happened to us in all our lives. Far worse. Worse than having the things sold or the children with scarlet fever, and having to burn everything. . . . I don't like to talk about it. I can't help it, but I don't. . . .

"I don't know why I talk to you as I do, Lady Harman, but I don't seem to mind talking to you. I don't suppose I've opened my mouth to any one about it, not for years—except to one dear friend I've got—her who persuaded me to be a church member. But what I've always said and what I will always say is this, that I don't believe any evil of father, I don't believe, I won't ever believe he took his life. I won't even believe he was in drink. I don't know how he got in the river, but I'm certain it wasn't so. He was a weak man, was father, I've never denied he was a weak man. But a harder working man than he was never lived. He worried, any one would have worried, seeing the worries he had. The shop wasn't paying as it was ; often we never tasted meat for weeks together, and then there came one of these Internationals, giving overweight and underselling. . . ."

"One of these Internationals?"

"Yes, I don't suppose you've ever heard of them. They're in the poorer neighbourhoods chiefly. They sell teas and things mostly now, but they began as bakers' shops, and what they did was to come into a place and undersell until all the old shops were ruined and shut up. That was what they tried to do, and father hadn't no more chance amongst them than a mouse in a trap. . . . It was just like being run over. All the trade that stayed with us after a bit was bad debts. You can't blame people, I suppose, for going where they get more and pay less, and it wasn't till we'd all gone right away to Haggerston that they altered things and put the prices up again. Of course father lost heart, and all that. He didn't know what to do, he'd sunk all he had in the shop ; he just sat and moped about. Really—he was pitiful. He wasn't able to sleep ; he used to get up at nights and go about downstairs. Mother says she found him once sweeping out the bakehouse at two o'clock in the morning. He got it into his head that getting up like that would help him. But I don't believe and I won't believe he wouldn't have seen it through if he could. Not to my dying day will I believe that. . . ."

Lady Harman reflected. "But couldn't he have got work again—as a baker?"

" It's hard, after you've had a shop. You see, all the younger men've come on. They know the new ways. And a man who's had a shop and failed, he's lost heart. And these stores setting up make everything drivinger. They do things a d'fferent way. They make it harder for every one."

Both Lady Harman and Susan Burnet reflected in silence for a few seconds upon the International Stores. The sewing woman was the first to speak.

" Things like that," she said, " didn't ought to be. One shop didn't ought to be allowed to set out to ruin another. It isn't fair trading, it's a sort of murder. It oughtn't to be allowed. How was father to know ? . . ."

" There's got to be competition," said Lady Harman.

" I don't call that competition," said Susan Burnet.

" But—I suppose they give people cheaper bread."

" They do for a time. Then when they've killed you they do what they like. . . . Luke—he's one of those who'll say anything—well, he used to say it was a regular monopoly. But it's hard on people who've set out to live honest and respectable and bring up a family plain and decent to be pushed out of the way like that."

" I suppose it is," said Lady Harman.

" What was father to *do* ? " said Susan, and turned to Sir Isaac's arm-chair, from which this discourse had distracted her.

And then suddenly, in a voice thick with rage, she burst out : " And then Alice must needs go and take their money. That's what sticks in *my* throat."

Still on her knees, she faced about to Lady Harman.

" Alice goes into one of their Ho'burn branches as a waitress, do what I could to prevent her. It makes one mad to think of it. Time after time I've said to her, ' Alice,' I've said, ' sooner than touch their dirty money I'd starve in the street.' And she goes ! She says it's all nonsense of me to bear a spite. Laughs at me ! ' Alice,' I told her, ' it's a wonder the spirit of poor father don't rise up against you.' And she laughs. Calls that bearing a spite. . . . Of course she was little when it happened. She can't remember, not as I remember. . . ."

Lady Harman reflected for a time. " I suppose you don't know," she began, addressing Susan's industrious back ; " you don't know who—owns these International Stores ? "

" I suppose it's some company," said Susan. " I don't see that it lets them off—being in a company."

§ 8

We have done much in the last few years to destroy the severe limitations of Victorian delicacy, and all of us, from princesses and prime-ministers' wives downward, talk of topics that would have been considered quite gravely improper in the nineteenth century. Nevertheless, some topics have, if anything, become more indelicate than they were, and this is especially true of the discussion of income, of any discussion that tends, however remotely, to inquire, Who is it at the base of everything who really pays in blood and muscle and involuntary submissions for *your* freedom and magnificence ? This, indeed, is almost the ultimate surviving indecency. So that it was with considerable private shame and discomfort that Lady Harman pursued even in her privacy the train of thought that Susan Burnet had set going. It had been conveyed into her mind long ago, and it had settled down there and grown into a sort of security, that the International Bread and Cake Stores were a very important contribution to progress, and that Sir Isaac, outside the gates of his home, was a very useful and beneficial personage, and richly meriting a baronetcy. She hadn't particularly analysed this persuasion, but she supposed him engaged in a kind of daily repetition, but upon modern scientific lines, of the miracle of the loaves and fishes, feeding a great multitude that would otherwise have gone hungry. She knew, too, from the advertisements that flowered about her path through life, that this bread in question was exceptionally clean and hygienic ; whole front pages of the *Daily Messenger*, headed the " Fauna of Small Bakehouses," and adorned with a bordering of *Blatta orientalis*, the common cockroach, had taught her that, and she knew that Sir Isaac's passion for purity had also led to the *Old Country Gazette's* spirited and successful campaign for a non-party measure securing additional bakehouse regulation and inspection. And her impression had been that the growing and developing refreshment side of the concern was almost a public charity ; Sir Isaac gave, he said, a larger, heavier scone, a bigger pat of butter, a more elegant teapot, ham more finely cut, and less questionable pork-pies than any other system of syndicated teashops. She supposed that whenever he sat late at night going over schemes and papers, or when he went off for days together to Cardiff, or Glasgow, or Dublin, or such-like centres, or when he became preoccupied at dinner and whistled thoughtfully through his teeth, he was planning to increase the amount or diminish the cost of tea and cocoa-drenched farinaceous food in the stomachs of that section of our national adolescence which goes out daily into the streets of our great cities to be fed. And she knew his vans and catering were indispensable to the British army upon its manœuvres. . . .

Now the smashing up of the Burnet family by the International Stores was disagreeably not in the picture of these suppositions. And the remarkable thing is that this one little tragedy wouldn't for a moment allow itself to be regarded as an exceptional accident in an otherwise fair vast development. It remained obstinately a specimen—of the other side of the great syndication.

It was just as if she had been doubting subconsciously all along. . . . In the silence of the night she lay awake and tried to make herself believe that the Burnet case was just a unique overlooked disaster, that it needed only to come to Sir Isaac's attention to be met by the fullest reparation. . . .

After all she did not bring it to Sir Isaac's attention.

But one morning, while this phase of new doubts was still lively in her mind, Sir Isaac told her he was going down to Brighton, and then along the coast road in a car to Portsmouth, to pay a few surprise visits, and see how the machine was working. He would be away a night, an unusual breach in his habits.

" Are you thinking of any new branches, Isaac ? "

" I may have a look at Arundel."

" Isaac." She paused to frame her question carefully. " I suppose there are some shops at Arundel now ? "

" I've got to see to that."

" If you open—— I suppose the old shops get hurt. What becomes of the people if they do get hurt ? "

" That's *their* look-out," said Sir Isaac.

" Isn't it bad for them ? "

" Progress is progress, Elly."

" It *is* bad for them. I suppose—— Wouldn't it be sometimes kinder if you took over the old shop—made a sort of partner of him, or something ? "

Sir Isaac shook his head. " I want younger men," he said. " You can't get a move on the older hands."

" But, then, it's rather bad—— I suppose these little men you shut up—some of them must have families."

" You're theorising a bit this morning, Elly," said Sir Isaac, looking up over his coffee cup.

" I've been thinking—about these little people."

" Some one's been talking to you about my shops," said Sir Isaac, and stuck out an index finger. " If that's Georgina——"

" It isn't Georgina," said Lady Harman, but she had it very clear in her mind that she must not say who it was.

" You can't make a business without squeezing somebody," said Sir Isaac. " It's easy enough to make a row about any concern that grows a bit. Some people would like to have every business tied down to a maximum turnover, and so much a year profit. I dare say you've been hearing of these articles in the *London Lion*. Pretty stuff it is, too. This fuss about the little shopkeepers ; that's a new racket. I've had all that row about the waitresses before, and the yarn about the Normandy eggs, and all that, but I don't see that you need go reading it against me, and bringing it up at the breakfast-table. A business is a business, it isn't a charity, and I'd like to know where you and I would be if we didn't run the concern on business lines. . . . Why, that *London Lion* fellow came to me with the first two of those articles before the thing began. I could have had the whole thing stopped if I liked, if I'd chosen to take the back page of his beastly cover. That shows the stuff the whole thing is made of. That shows you. Why!—he's just a blackmailer, that's what he is. Much he cares for my waitresses if he can get the dibs. Little shopkeepers, indeed ! I know 'em ! Nice martyrs they are ! There isn't one wouldn't *skin* all the others if he got half a chance. . . ."

Sir Isaac gave way to an extraordinary fit of nagging anger. He got up and stood upon the hearthrug to deliver his soul the better. It was an altogether unexpected and illuminating outbreak. He was flushed with guilt. The more angry and eloquent he became, the more profoundly thoughtful grew the attentive lady at the head of his table. . . .

When at last Sir Isaac had gone off in the car to Victoria, Lady Harman rang for Snagsby. " Isn't there a paper," she asked, " called the *London Lion* ? "

" It isn't one I think your ladyship would like," said Snagsby, gently but firmly.

" I know. But I want to see it. I want copies of all the issues in which there have been articles upon the International Stores ? "

" They're thoroughly volgar, me lady," said Snagsby, with a large, dissuasive smile.

" I want you to go out into London and get them now."

Snagsby hesitated and went. Within five minutes he re-appeared with a handful of buff-covered papers.

" There 'appened to be copies in the pantry, me lady," he said. " We can't imagine 'ow they got there ; some one must have brought them in, but 'ere they are, quite at your service, me lady.'' He paused for a discreet moment. Something indescribably confidential came into his manner. " I doubt if Sir Isaac will quite like to 'ave them left about, me lady—after you done with them.''

She was in a mood of discovery. She sat in the room that was all furnished in pink (her favourite colour), and read a bitter, malicious, coarsely written and yet insidiously credible account of her husband's business methods. Something within herself seemed to answer, " But didn't you know this all along?'' That large conviction that her wealth and position were but the culmination of a great and honourable social service, a conviction that had been her tacit comfort during much dis-tasteful loyalty seemed to shrivel and fade. No doubt the writer was a thwarted blackmailer ; even her unaccustomed mind could distinguish a twang of some such vicious quality in his sentences ; but that did not alter the realities he ex-hibited and exaggerated. There was a description of how Sir Isaac pounced on his managers that was manifestly derived from a manager he had dismissed. It was dreadfully like him. Convincingly like him. There was a statement of the wages he paid his girl assistants, and long extracts from his code of rules and schedules of fines. . . .

When she put down the paper she was suddenly afflicted by a vivid vision of Susan Burnet's father, losing heart and not knowing what to do. She had an unreasonable feeling that Susan Burnet's father must have been a small, kindly, furry, bunnyish, little man. Of course there had to be progress and the survival of the fittest. She found herself weighing what she imagined Susan Burnet's father to be like, against the ferrety face, stooping shoulders, and scheming whistle of Sir Isaac.

There were times now when she saw her husband with an extreme distinctness.

§ 9

As this cold and bracing realisation that all was not right with her position, with Sir Isaac's business procedure, and the world generally, took possession of Lady Harman's thoughts there came also with it and arising out of it quite a series of new moods and dispositions. At times she was very full of the desire " to do something," something that would, as it were, satisfy and assuage this growing uneasiness of responsibility in her mind. At times her consuming wish was not to assuage but escape from this urgency. It worried her and made her feel helpless, and she wanted, beyond anything else, to get back to that child's world where all experiences are adventurous and everything is finally right. She felt, I think, that it was a little unfair to her that this something within her should be calling upon her to take all sorts of things gravely— hadn't she been a good wife and brought four children into the world. . . . ?

I am setting down here as clearly as possible what wasn't by any means clear in Lady Harman's mind. I am giving you, side by side, phases that never came side by side in her thoughts, but which followed and ousted and obliterated one another. She had moods of triviality. She had moods of magnificence. She had moods of intense secret hostility to her urgent little husband, and moods of genial tolerance for everything there was in her life. She had moods, and don't we all have moods ? —of scepticism and cynicism, much profounder than the conventions and limitations of novel-writing permit us to tell here. And for hardly any of these moods had she terms and recognitions. . . .

It isn't a natural thing to keep on worrying about the morality of one's material prosperity. These are proclivities superinduced by modern conditions of the conscience. There is a natural resistance in every healthy human being to such distressful heart-searchings. Strong instincts battled in Lady Harman against this intermittent sense of responsibility that was beginning to worry her. An immense lot of her was for simply running away from these troublesome considerations, for covering herself up from them, for distraction.

And about this time she happened upon *Elizabeth and her German Garden*, and was very greatly delighted and stimulated by that little sister of Montaigne. She was charmed by the book's fresh gaiety, by its gallant resolve to set off all the good things there are in this world, the sunshine and flowers and laughter, against the limitations and thwartings and disappointments of life. For a time it seemed to her that these brave consolations were solutions, and she was stirred by an imitative passion. How stupid had she not been to let life and Sir Isaac overcome her ! She felt that she must make herself like Elizabeth, exactly like Elizabeth ; she tried forthwith, and a certain difficulty she found, a certain deadness, she ascribed to the square modernity of her house and something in the Putney air. The house was too large, it dominated the garden and controlled her. She felt she must get away to some place that was chiefly exterior, in the sunshine, far from towns and struggling, straining, angry and despairing humanity, from syndicated shops and all the embarrassing challenges of life. Somehow there it would be possible to keep Sir Isaac at arm's length ; and the ghost of Susan Burnet's father could be left behind to haunt the square rooms of the London house. And there she would live, horticultural, bookish, whimsical, witty, defiant, happily careless.

And it was this particular conception of evasion that had set her careering about the countryside in her car, looking for conceivable houses of refuge from this dark novelty of social and personal care, and that had driven her into the low, long room of Black Strand and the presence of Mr. Brumley.

Of what ensued and the appearance and influence of Lady Beach-Mandarin, and how it led among other things to a lunch invitation from that lady the reader has already been informed.

CHAPTER SIX

THE ADVENTUROUS AFTERNOON

§ 1

You will perhaps remember that before I fell into this extensive digression about Lady Harman's upbringing, we had got to the entry of Mrs. Sawbridge into the house bearing a plunder of Sir Isaac's best roses. She interrupted a conversation of some importance. Those roses at this point are still unwithered and fragrant, and moreover they are arranged according to Mrs. Sawbridge's ideas of elegance abou Sir Isaac's home. . . . And Sir Isaac, when that conversatio could be renewed, categorically forbade Lady Harman to go to Lady Beach-Mandarin's lunch, and Lady Harman went to Lady Beach-Mandarin's lunch.

She had some peculiar difficulties in getting to that lunch.

It is necessary to tell certain particulars. They are particulars that will distress the delicacy of Mrs. Sawbridge unspeakably, if ever she chances to read this book. But a story has to be told. You see, Sir Isaac Harman had never considered it advisable to give his wife a private allowance. Whatever she wished to have, he maintained, she could have. The bill would afterwards be paid by his cheque on the first day of the month following the receipt of the bill. He found a generous pleasure in writing these cheques, and Lady Harman was magnificently housed, fed, and adorned. Moreover, whenever she chose to ask for money he gave her money, usually double of what she demanded—and often a kiss or so into the bargain. But after he had forbidden her to go to Lady Beach-Mandarin's, so grave an estrangement ensued that she could not ask him for money. A door closed between them. And the crisis had come at an unfortunate moment. She possessed the sum of five shillings and eightpence.

She perceived quite early that this shortness of money would greatly embarrass the rebellion she contemplated. She was exceptionally ignorant of most worldly things, but she knew there was never yet a campaign without a war chest. She felt entitled to money. . . .

She planned several times to make a demand for replenishment with a haughty dignity ; the haughty dignity was easy enough to achieve, but the demand was not. A sensitive dread of her mother's sympathetic curiosity barred all thoughts of borrowing in that direction—she and her mother " never discussed money matters." She did not want to get Georgina into further trouble. And besides, Georgina was in Devonshire.

Even to get to Lady Beach-Mandarin's became difficult under these circumstances. She knew that Clarence, though he would take her into the country quite freely, had been instructed, on account of Sir Isaac's expressed dread of any accident happening to her while alone, not to plunge with her into the vortex of London traffic. Only under direct orders from Sir Isaac would Clarence take her down Putney Hill ; though she might go up and away—to anywhere. She knew nothing of pawnshops or any associated methods of getting cash advances, and the possibility of using the telephone to hire an automobile never occurred to her. But she was fully resolved to go. She had one advantage in the fact that Sir Isaac didn't know the precise date of the disputed engagement. When that arrived she spent a restless morning, and dressed herself at last with great care. She instructed Peters, her maid, who participated in these preparations with a mild astonishment, that she was going out to lunch, asked her to inform Mrs.

Sawbridge of the fact, and, outwardly serene, made a bolt for it down the staircase and across the hall. The great butler appeared ; she had never observed how like a large note of interrogation his forward contours could be.

"I shall be out to lunch, Snagsby," she said, and went past him into the sunshine.

She left a discreetly astonished Snagsby behind her.

(" Now, where are we going out to lunch ? " said Snagsby presently to Peters.

" I've never known her so particular with her clothes," said the maid.

" Never before—not in the same way ; it's something new and special to this affair," Snagsby reflected, " I wonder now, if Sir Isaac. . . . "

" One can't help observing things," said the maid, after a pause. " Mute though we be.")

Lady Harman had the whole five and eightpence with her. She had managed to keep it intact in her jewel case, declaring she had no change when any small demands were made on her.

With an exhilaration so great that she wanted sorely to laugh aloud, she walked out through her big open gates and into the general publicity of Putney Hill. Why had she not done as much years ago ? How long she had been working up to this obvious thing ! She hadn't been out in such complete possession of herself since she had been a schoolgirl. She held up a beautifully gloved hand to a private motor-car going downhill, and then to an engaged taxi going up, and then with a slightly dashed feeling, picked up her skirt and walked observantly downhill. Her reason dispelled a transitory impression that these two vehicles were on Sir Isaac's side against her.

There was quite a nice taxi on the rank at the bottom of the hill. The driver, a pleasant-looking young man in a white cap, seemed to have been waiting for her in particular ; he met her timid invitation half-way, and came across the road to her and jumped down and opened the door. He took her instructions as though they were after his own heart, and right in front of her as she sat was a kind of tin cornucopia full of artificial flowers that seemed like a particular attention to her. His fare was two and eightpence, and she gave him four shillings. He seemed quite gratified by her largesse, his manner implied he had always thought as much of her, from first to last their relations had been those of sunny content-ment, and it was only as she ascended the steps of Lady Beach-Mandarin's portico, that it occurred to her that she now had insufficient money for an automobile to take her home. But there were railways and buses and all sorts of possibilities ; the day was an adventure ; and she entered the drawing-room with a brow that was beautifully unruffled.

She wanted to laugh still ; it animated her eyes and lips with the pleasantest little stir you can imagine.

"A—a—a—a—a—h !" cried Lady Beach-Mandarin in a high note, and threw out—it had an effect of being quite a number of arms—as though she was one of those brass Indian goddesses one sees.

Lady Harman felt taken in at once to all that capacious bosom involved and contained. . . .

§ 2

It was quite an amusing lunch. But any lunch would have been amusing to Lady Harman in the excitement of her first act of deliberate disobedience. She had never been out to lunch alone in all her life before ; she experienced a kind of scared happiness, she felt like some one at Lourdes who has just thrown away crutches. She was seated between a pink young man with an eyeglass, whose place was labelled "Bertie Trevor" and who was otherwise unexplained, and Mr. Brumley. She was quite glad to see Mr. Brumley again, and no doubt her eyes showed it. She had hoped to see him. Miss Sharsper was sitting nearly opposite to her, a real live novelist, pecking observations out of life as a hen pecks seeds amidst scenery, and next beyond was a large-headed, inattentive, fluffy person who was Mr. Keystone, the well-known critic. And there was Agatha Alimony under a rustling vast hat of green-black cock's feathers next to Sir Markham Crosby, with whom she had been having an abusive controversy in the *Times*, and to whom quite elaborately she wouldn't speak, and there was Lady Viping with her lorgnette, and Adolphus Blenker, Horatio's younger and, if possible, more gentlemanly brother —Horatio of the *Old Country Gazette* that is—sole reminder that there was such a person as Sir Isaac in the world. Lady Beach-Mandarin's mother, and the Swiss governess, and the tall but retarded daughter, Phyllis, completed the party. The reception was lively and cheering ; Lady Beach-Mandarin enfolded her guests in generosities and kept them all astir like a sea-swell under a squadron, and she introduced Lady Harman to Miss Alimony by public proclamation right across the room, because there were two lavish tables of bric-à-brac, a marble bust of old Beach-Mandarin, and most of the rest of the party in the way. And at the table conversation was like throwing bread, you never knew whom you might hit, or who might hit you. (But Lady Beach-Mandarin produced an effect of throwing whole loaves.) Bertie Trevor was one of those dancing young men who talk to a woman as though they were giving a dog biscuits, and mostly it was Mr. Brumley who did such talking as reached Lady Harman's ear.

Mr. Brumley was in very good form that day. He had contrived to remind her of all their Black Strand talk while they were still eating *Petites Bouchées à la Reine*. "Have

you found that work yet ? " he asked, and carried her mind
to the core of her situation. Then they were snatched up into
a general discussion of bazaars. Sir Markham spoke of a great
bazaar that was to be held on behalf of one of the many
Shakespeare Theatre movements that were then so prevalent.
Was Lady Beach-Mandarin implicated ? Was any one ? He
told of novel features in contemplation. He generalised about
bazaars and, with an air of having forgotten the presence of
Miss Alimony, glanced at the Suffrage Bazaar—it was a season
of bazaars. He thought poorly of the Suffrage Bazaar. The
hostess intervened promptly with anecdotes of her own cynical
daring as a bazaar-seller, Miss Sharsper offered fragments of
a reminiscence about signing one of her own books for a
bookstall, Blenker told a well-known bazaar anecdote brightly
and well, and the impending skirmish was averted.

While the bazaar talk still whacked to and fro about the
table, Mr. Brumley got at Lady Harman's ear again. " Rather
tantalising these meetings at table," he said. " It's like trying
to talk while you swim in a rough sea. . . . "

Then Lady Beach-Mandarin intervened with demands for
support for her own particular bazaar project, and they were
eating salad before there was a chance of another word between
them. " I must confess that when I want to talk to people
I like to get them alone," said Mr. Brumley, and gave form
to thoughts that were already on the verge of crystallisation
in her own mind. She had been recalling that she had liked
his voice before, noting something very kindly and thoughtful
and brotherly about his right profile, and thinking how much
an hour's talk with him would help to clear up her ideas.

" But it's so difficult to get one alone," said Lady Harman,
and suddenly an idea of the utmost daring and impropriety
flashed into her mind. She was on the verge of speaking it
forthwith, and then didn't, she met something in his eye that
answered her own, and then Lady Beach-Mandarin was
foaming over them like a dam-burst over an American town.

" What do *you* think, Mr. Brumley ? " demanded Lady
Beach-Mandarin.

" ? "

" About Sir Markham's newspaper symposium. They asked
him what allowance he gave his wife. Sent a prepaid reply
telegram."

" But he hasn't got a wife ! "

" They don't stick at a little thing like that," said Sir
Markham grimly.

" I think a husband and wife ought to have everything
in common, like the early Christians," said Lady Beach-
Mandarin.   " *We* always did," and so got the discussion
afloat again off the sandbank of Mr. Brumley's inattention.

It was quite a good discussion, and Lady Harman contributed an exceptionally alert and intelligent silence.   Sir

Markham distrusted Lady Beach-Mandarin's communism, and thought that anyhow it wouldn't do for a financier or business man. He favoured an allowance. " So did Sir Joshua," said the widow Viping. This roused Agatha Alimony. " Allowance indeed ! " she cried. " Is a wife to be on no better footing than a daughter ? The whole question of a wife's financial autonomy needs reconsidering. . . . "

Adolphus Blenker became learned and lucid upon pin-money and dowry, and the customs of savage tribes, and Mr. Brumley helped with corroboration. . . .

Mr. Brumley managed to say just one other thing to Lady Harman before the lunch was over. It struck her for a moment as being irrelevant. " The gardens at Hampton Court," he said, " are delightful just now. Have you seen them ? Autumnal fires. All the September perennials lifting their spears in their last great chorus. It's the *Götterdämmerung* of the year."

She was going out of the room before she appreciated his possible intention.

Lady Beach-Mandarin delegated Sir Markham to preside over the men's cigars, and bounced and slapped her four ladies upstairs to the drawing-room. Her mother disappeared, and so did Phyllis and the governess. Lady Harman heard a large aside to Lady Viping : " Isn't she perfectly lovely ? " glanced to discover the lorgnette in appreciative action, and then found herself drifting into a secluded window-seat and a duologue with Miss Agatha Alimony. Miss Alimony was one of that large and increasing number of dusky, grey-eyed ladies who go through life with an air of darkly incomprehensible significance. She led off Lady Harman as though she took her away to reveal unheard-of mysteries, and her voice was a contralto undertone that she emphasised in some inexplicable way by the magnetic use of her eyes. Her hat of cock's feathers which rustled like familiar spirits, greatly augmented the profundity of her effect. As she spoke she glanced guardedly at the other ladies at the end of the room, and from first to last she seemed undecided in her own mind whether she was a conspirator or a prophetess. She had heard of Lady Harman before, she had been longing impatiently to talk to her all through the lunch. " You are just what we want," said Agatha.

" What who want ? " asked Lady Harman, struggling against the hypnotic influence of her interlocutor.

" *We*," said Miss Agatha, " the Cause. The G.S.W.S.

" We want just such people as you," she repeated, and began in panting rhetorical sentences to urge the militant cause.

For her it was manifestly a struggle against " the men." Miss Alimony had no doubts of her sex. It had nothing to learn, nothing to be forgiven, it was compact of obscured and persecuted marvels, it needed only revelation. " They

know nothing," she said of the antagonist males, bringing
deep notes out of the melodious caverns of her voice ; " they
know *nothing* of the deeper secrets of woman's nature." Her
discourse of a general feminine insurrection fell in very closely
with the spirit of Lady Harman's private revolt. " We want
the Vote," said Agatha, " and we want the Vote because the
Vote means autonomy. And then———— "

She paused voluminously. She had already used that word
" autonomy " at the lunch table, and it came to her hearer
to supply a long-felt want. Now she poured meanings into it,
and Lady Harman with each addition realised more clearly
that it was still a roomy sack for more. " A woman should
be absolute mistress of herself," said Miss Alimony, " absolute
mistress of her person. She should be free to develop———— "

Germinating phrases these were in Lady Harman's ear.

She wanted to know about the Suffrage movement from
some one less generously impatient than Georgina, for Georgina
always lost her temper about it, and to put it fairly, *ranted* ;
this, at any rate, was serene and confident, and she asked
tentative, ill-formed questions, and felt her way among Miss
Alimony's profundities. She had her doubts, her instinctive
doubts about this campaign of violence, she doubted its
wisdom, she doubted its rightness, and she perceived, but
she found it difficult to express her perception, that Miss
Alimony wasn't so much answering her objections as trying
to swamp her with exalted emotion. And if there was any
flaw whatever in her attention to Miss Alimony's stirring talk,
it was because she was keeping a little look-out in the tail
of her eye for the reappearance of the men, and more particularly for the reappearance of Mr. Brumley, with whom she
had a peculiar feeling of uncompleted relations. And at last
the men came, and she caught his glance and saw that her
feeling was reciprocated.

She was presently torn from Agatha, who gasped with pain
at the parting and pursued her with a sedulous gaze as a
doctor might watch an injected patient, she parted with Lady
Beach-Mandarin with a vast splash of enthusiasm and mutual
invitations, and Lady Viping came and pressed her to come
to dinner and rapped her elbow with her lorgnette to emphasise her invitation. And Lady Harman, after a still moment
for reflection, athwart which the word autonomy flickered,
accepted this invitation also.

§ 3

Mr. Brumley hovered for a few moments in the hall conversing with Lady Beach-Mandarin's butler, whom he had
known for some years and helped about a small investment,
and who was now being abjectly polite and grateful to him
for his attention. It gave Mr. Brumley a nice feudal feeling
to establish and maintain such relationships. The furry-eyed

boy fumbled with the sticks and umbrellas in the background, and wondered if he too would ever climb to these levels of respectful gilt-tipped friendliness. Mr. Brumley hovered the more readily because he knew Lady Harman was with the looking-glass in the little parlour behind the dining-room on her way to the outer world. At last she emerged. It was instantly manifest to Mr. Brumley that she had expected to find him there. She smiled frankly at him, with the faintest admission of complicity in her smile.

" Taxi, milady ? " said the butler.

She seemed to reflect. " No, I will walk." She hesitated over a glove button. " Mr. Brumley, is there a Tube station near here ? "

" Not two minutes. But can't I perhaps take you in a taxi ? "

" I'd rather walk."

" I will show you—— "

He found himself most agreeably walking off with her.

Still more agreeable things were to follow for Mr. Brumley. She appeared to meditate upon a sudden idea. She disregarded some conversational opening of his that he forgot in the instant. " Mr. Brumley," she said, " I didn't intend to go directly home."

" I'm altogether at your service," said Mr. Brumley.

" At least," said Lady Harman, with that careful truthfulness of hers, " it occurred to me during lunch that I wouldn't go directly home."

Mr. Brumley reined in an imagination that threatened to bolt with him.

" I want," said Lady Harman, " to go to Kensington Gardens, I think. This can't be far from Kensington Gardens —and I want to sit there on a green chair and—meditate— and afterwards I want to find a tube railway or something that will take me back to Putney. There is really no need for me to go directly home. . . . It's very stupid of me, but I don't know my way about London as a rational creature should do. So will you take me and put me in a green chair and— tell me how, afterwards, I can find the Tube and get home. Do you mind ? "

" All my time, so long as you want it, is at your service," said Mr. Brumley with convincing earnestness. " And it's not five minutes to the gardens. And afterwards a taxi-cab—— "

" No," said Lady Harman, mindful of her one-and-eight-pence, " I prefer a tube. But that we can talk about later. You're sure, Mr. Brumley, I'm not invading your time ? "

" I wish you could see into my mind," said Mr. Brumley.

She became almost barefaced. " It is so true," she said, " that at lunch one can't really talk to any one. And I've so wanted to talk to you. Ever since we met before."

Mr. Brumley conveyed an unfeigned delight.

" Since then," said Lady Harman, " I've read your *Euphemia* books." Then, after a little unskilful pause, " again." Then she blushed, and added, " I *had* read one of them, you know, before."

" Exactly," he said, with an infinite helpfulness.

" And you seem so sympathetic, so understanding. I feel that all sorts of things that are muddled in my mind would come clear if I could have a really good talk. To you. . . ."

They were now through the gates approaching the Albert Memorial. Mr. Brumley was filled with an idea so desirable that it made him fear to suggest it.

" Of course we can talk very comfortably here," he said, " under these great trees. But I do so wish—— Have you seen those great borders at Hampton Court ? The whole place is glowing, and in such sunshine as this—— A taxi—will take us there under the hour. If you are free until half-past five."

Why shouldn't she ?

The proposal seemed so outrageous to all the world of Lady Harman, that in her present mood she felt it was her duty, in the cause of womanhood, to nerve herself and accept it. . . .

" I mustn't be later than half-past five."

" We could snatch a glimpse of it all and be back before then."

" In that case——It would be very agreeable."

(*Why shouldn't she ?* It would, no doubt, make Sir Isaac furiously angry—if he heard of it. But it was the sort of thing other women of her class did ; didn't all the novels testify ? She had a perfect right——

And besides, Mr. Brumley was so entirely harmless.)

§ 4

It had been Lady Harman's clear intention to have a luminous and illuminating discussion of the peculiar difficulties and perplexities of her position with Mr. Brumley. Since their first encounter, this idea had grown up in her mind. She was one of those women who turn instinctively to men and away from women for counsel. There was to her perception something wise and kindly and reassuring in him ; she felt that he had lived and suffered and understood, and that he was ready to help other people to live, his heart she knew from his published works was buried with his dead Euphemia, and he seemed as near a thing to a brother and a friend as she was ever likely to meet. She wanted to tell him all this, and then to broach her teeming and tangled difficulties, about her own permissible freedoms, about her social responsibilities, about Sir Isaac's business. But now, as their taxi dodged through the traffic of Kensington High Street and went on its way past Olympia and so out westwards, she found it extremely difficult to fix her mind upon the large propositions with which it had been her intention to open. Do as she would to feel that this was a momentous occasion, she could not suppress, she could not ignore an obstinate and entirely undignified persuasion that she was having a tremendous lark. The passing vehicles, various motors, omnibuses, vans, carriages, the thronging pedestrians, the shops and houses, were all so distractingly interesting that at last she had to put it fairly to herself whether she hadn't better resign herself to the sensations of the present and reserve that sustained discussion for an interval she foresaw as inevitable on some comfortable seat under great trees at Hampton Court. You cannot talk well and penetratingly about fundamental things when you are in a not too well-hung taxi which is racing to get ahead of a vast red motor-omnibus.

With a certain discretion, Mr. Brumley had instructed the chauffeur to cross the river, not at Putney but at Hammersmith, and so they went by Barnes station and up a still almost rural lane into Richmond Park, and there suddenly they were among big trees and bracken and red deer, and it might have been a hundred miles from London streets. Mr. Brumley directed the driver to make a detour that gave them quite all the best of the park.

The mind of Mr. Brumley was also agreeably excited and dispersed on this occasion. It was an occasion of which he had been dreaming very frequently of late, he had invented quite remarkable dialogues during those dreams, and now he too was conversationally inadequate and with a similar feeling of unexpected adventures. He was now no more ready to go to the roots of things than Lady Harman. He talked on the way down chiefly of the route they were following, of the changes in the London traffic due to motor traction, and of the charm and amenity of Richmond Park. And it was only after they had arrived at Hampton Court and dismissed the taxi and spent some time upon the borders, that they came at last to a seat under a grove beside a long piece of water bearing water lilies, and sat down and made a beginning with the good talk. Then indeed she tried to gather together the heads of her perplexity, and Mr. Brumley did his best to do justice to the confidence she reposed in him. . . .

It wasn't at all the conversation he had dreamt of ; it was halting, it was inconclusive, it was full of a vague dissatisfaction.

The roots of this dissatisfaction lay perhaps more than anything else in her inattention to him—how shall I say it ?—as *Him*. Hints have been conveyed to the reader already that for Mr. Brumley the universe was largely a setting, a tangle, a maze, a quest enshrining at the heart of it and adumbrating everywhere, a mystical Her, and his experience of this world had pointed him very definitely to the conclusion that for that large other half of mankind which is woman, the quality of things was reciprocal and centred, for all the appearances and pretences of other interests, in—Him. And he was disposed to believe that the other things in life, not merely the pomp and glories, but the faiths and ambitions and devotions, were all demonstrably little more than posings and dressings of this great duality. A large part of his own interests and of the interests of the women he knew best, was the sustained and in some cases recurrent discovery and elaboration of lights and glimpses of Him or Her as the case might be, in various definite individuals ; and it was a surprise to him, it perplexed him, to find that this lovely person, so beautifully equipped for those mutual researches which constituted, he felt, the heart of life, was yet completely in her manner unaware of this primary sincerity and looking quite simply, as it were, over him and through him at such things as the ethics of the baking, confectionery and refreshment trade and the limits of individual responsibility in these matters. The conclusion that she was " unawakened " was inevitable.

The dream of " awakening " this sleeping beauty associated itself in a logical sequence with his interpretations. I do not say that such thoughts were clear in Mr. Brumley's mind, they were not, but into this shape the forms of his thoughts fell. Such things dimly felt below the clear level of consciousness were in him. And they gave his attempt to take up and answer the question that perplexed her, something of the quality of an attempt to clothe and serve hidden purposes. It could not but be evident to him that the effort of Lady Harman to free herself a little from her husband's circumvallation and to disentangle herself a little from the realities of his commercial life. might lead to such a liberation as would leave her like a nascent element ready to recombine. And it was entirely in the vein of this drift of thought in him that he should resolve upon an assiduous proximity against that moment of release and awakening. . . .

I do not do Mr. Brumley as the human lover justice if I lead you to suppose that he plotted thus clearly and calculatingly. Yet all this was in his mind. All this was in Mr. Brumley, but it wasn't Mr. Brumley. Presented with it as a portrait of his mind, he would have denied it indignantly—and, knowing it was there, have grown a little flushed in his denials. Quite equally in his mind was a simple desire to please her, to do what she wished, to help her because she wanted help. And a quite keen desire to be clean and honest about her and everything connected with her, for his own sake as well as for her sake—for the sake of the relationship. . . .

So you have Mr. Brumley on the green seat under the great trees at Hampton Court, in his neat London clothes, his quite becoming silk-hat, above his neatly handsome and intelligent profile, with his gloves in his hand and one arm over

the seat back, going now very earnestly and thoughtfully into
the question of the social benefit of the International Bread
and Cake Stores, and whether it was possible for her to " do
anything " to repair any wrongs that might have arisen out
of that organisation, and you will understand why there is a
little flush in his cheek and why his sentences are a trifle disconnected and tentative, and why his eye wanders now to the
soft raven tresses about Lady Harman's ear, now to the sweet
movement of her speaking lips, and now to the gracious droop
of her pose as she sits forward, elbow upon crossed knee and
chin on glove, and jabs her parasol at the ground in her unaccustomed efforts to explain and discuss the difficulties of
her position.

And you will understand too why it is that he doesn't deal
with the question before him so simply and impartially as he
seems to do. Obscuring this extremely interesting problem
of a woman growing to man-like sense of responsibility in her
social consequences, is the dramatic proclivity that makes him
see all this merely as something which must necessarily weaken
Lady Harman's loyalty and qualify her submission to Sir
Isaac, that makes him want to utilise it and develop it in that
direction. . . .

§ 5

Moreover, so complex is the thought of man, there was also
another stream of mental activity flowing in the darker recesses
of Mr. Brumley's mind. Unobtrusively he was trying to count
the money in his pockets and make certain estimates.

It had been his intention to replenish his sovereign purse
that afternoon at his club, and he was only reminded of this
abandoned plan when he paid off his taxi at the gates of Hampton Court. The fare was nine and tenpence, and the only piece
of gold he had was a half-sovereign. But there was a handful
of loose silver in his trouser pocket, and so the fare and tip
were manageable. " Will you be going back, sir ? " asked the
driver.

And Mr. Brumley reflected too briefly and committed a
fatal error. " No," he said, with his mind upon that loose
silver. " We shall go back by train."

Now it is the custom with taxi-cabs that take people to
such outlying and remote places as Hampton Court, to be
paid off and to wait loyally until their original passengers
return. Thereby the little machine is restrained from ticking
out twopences which should go in the main to the absent
proprietor, and a feeling of mutuality is established between
the driver and his fare. But of course this cab being released
presently found another passenger and went away. . . .

I have written in vain if I have not conveyed to you that
Mr. Brumley was a gentleman of great and cultivated delicacy.

that he liked the seemly and handsome side of things, and dreaded the appearance of any flaw upon his prosperity as only a man trained in an English public school can do. It was intolerable to think of any hitch in this happy excursion which was to establish, he knew not what, confidence between himself and Lady Harman. From first to last he felt it had to go with an air—and what was the first-class fare from Hampton Court to Putney—which latter station he believed was on the line from Hampton Court to London—and could one possibly pretend it was unnecessary to have tea? And so, while Lady Harman talked about her husband's business —" our business " she called it—and shrank from ever saying anything more about the more intimate question she had most in mind, the limits to a wife's obedience, Mr. Brumley listened with these financial solicitudes showing through his expression and giving it a quality of intensity that she found remarkably reassuring. And once or twice they made him miss points in her remarks that forced him back upon that very inferior substitute for the apt answer, a judicious " Um."

(It would be quite impossible to go without tea, he decided. He himself wanted tea quite badly. He would think better when he had had some tea. . . .)

The crisis came at tea. They had tea at the inn upon the green that struck Mr. Brumley as being most likely to be cheap and which he pretended to choose for some trivial charm about the windows. And it wasn't cheap, and when at last Mr. Brumley was faced by the little slip of the bill and could draw his money from his pocket and look at it, he knew the worst, and the worst was worse than he had expected. The bill was five shillings. (Should he dispute it? Too ugly altogether, a dispute with a probably ironical waiter!) and the money in his hand amounted to four shillings and sixpence.

He acted surprise with the waiter's eye upon him. (Should he ask for credit? They might be frightfully disagreeable in such a Cockney resort as this.) " Tut, tut," said Mr. Brumley, and then—a little late for it—resorted to and discovered the emptiness of his sovereign purse. He realised that this was out of the picture at this stage, felt his ears and nose and cheeks grow hot and pink. The waiter's colleague across the room became interested in the proceedings.

" I had no idea," said Mr. Brumley, which was a premeditated falsehood.

" Is anything the matter? " asked Lady Harman, with a sisterly interest.

" My dear Lady Harman. I find myself—— Ridiculous position. Might I borrow half a sovereign? "

He felt sure that the two waiters exchanged glances. He looked at them—a mistake again—and got hotter.

" Oh! " said Lady Harman, and regarded him with frank amusement in her eyes. The thing struck her at first in the

light of a joke. " I've only got one-and-eightpence. I didn't
expect—— "

She blushed as beautifully as ever. Then she produced a
small but plutocratic-looking purse and handed it to him.

" Most remarkable—inconvenient," said Mr. Brumley, opening the precious thing and extracting a shilling. " That will do,"
he said, and dismissed the waiter with a tip of sixpence. Then,
with the open purse still in his hand, he spent much of his
remaining strength trying to look amused and unembarrassed,
feeling all the time that with his flushed face and in view of
all the circumstances of the case he must be really looking
very silly and fluffy.

" It's really most inconvenient," he remarked.

" I never thought of the—of this. It was silly of me," said
Lady Harman.

" Oh, no ! Oh, dear, no ! The silliness, I can assure you, is
all mine. I can't tell you how entirely apologetic—— Ridiculous fix. And after I had persuaded you to come here."

" Still, we were able to pay," she consoled him.

" But you have to get home ! "

She hadn't, so far, thought of that. It brought Sir Isaac
suddenly into the picture. " By half-past five," she said,
with just the faintest flavour of interrogation.

Mr. Brumley looked at his watch. It was ten minutes to
five.

" Waiter," he said, " how do the trains run from here to
Putney ? "

" I don't *think*, sir, that we have any trains from here to
Putney—— "

An A.B.C. Railway Guide was found, and Mr. Brumley
learnt for the first time that Putney and Hampton Court are
upon two distinct and separate and, as far as he could judge
by the time-table, mutually hostile branches of the South
Western Railway, and that at the earliest they could not
get to Putney before six o'clock.

Mr. Brumley was extremely disconcerted. He perceived
that he ought to have kept his taxi. It amounted almost to
a debt of honour to deliver this lady secure and untarnished
at her house within the next hour. But this reflection did not
in the least degree assist him to carry it out, and, as a matter
of fact, Mr. Brumley became flurried and did not carry it out.
He was not used to being without money, it unnerved him,
and he gave way to a kind of hectic *savoir faire*. He demanded
a taxi of the waiter. He tried to evolve a taxi by will-power
alone. He went out with Lady Harman and back towards the
gates of Hampton Court to look for taxis. Then it occurred
to him that they might be losing the 5.25 up. So they hurried
over the bridge to the station.

He had a vague notion that he would be able to get tickets
on credit at the booking-office if he presented his visiting card.

But the clerk in charge seemed to find something uncongenial in his proposal. He did not seem to like what he saw of Mr. Brumley through his little square window, and Mr. Brumley found something slighting and unpleasant in his manner. It was one of those little temperamental jars which happen to men of delicate sensibilities, and Mr. Brumley tried to be reassuringly overbearing in his manner, and then lost his temper, and was threatening, and so wasted precious moments what time Lady Harman waited on the platform, with a certain shadow of doubt falling upon her confidence in him, and watched the five-twenty-five gather itself together and start Londonward. Mr. Brumley came out of the ticket-office resolved to travel without tickets and carry things through with a high hand just as it became impossible to do so by that train, and then I regret to say he returned for some further haughty passages with the ticket-clerk upon the duty of public servants to point out such oversights as his, that led to repartee and did nothing to help Lady Harman on her homeward way.

Then he discovered a current time-table, and learnt that now even were all the ticket difficulties overridden he could not get Lady Harman to Putney before twenty minutes past seven, so completely is the South Western Railway not organised for conveying people from Hampton Court to Putney. He explained this as well as he could to Lady Harman, and then led her out of the station in another last desperate search for a taxi.

" We can always come back for that next train," he said. " It doesn't go for half an hour."

" I cannot blame myself sufficiently," he said for the eighth or ninth time. . . .

It was already well past a quarter to six before Mr. Brumley bethought himself of the London County Council tramcars that run from the palace gates. Along these an ample four-pennyworth was surely possible, and at the end would be taxis—— There *must* be taxis. The tram took them—but oh ! how slowly it seemed !—to Hammersmith by a devious route, through interminable roads and streets, and long before they reached that spot twilight had passed into darkness, and all the streets and shops were flowering into light, and the sense of night and lateness was very strong. After they were seated in the tram a certain interval of silence came between them, and then Lady Harman laughed and Mr. Brumley laughed—there was no longer any need for him to be energetic and fussy—and they began to have that feeling of adventurous amusement which comes on the farther side of desperation. But beneath the temporary elation Lady Harman was a prey to grave anxieties, and Mr. Brumley could not help thinking he had made a tremendous ass of himself in that ticket-clerk dispute. . . .

At Hammersmith they got out, two quite penniless travellers, and after some anxious moments found a taxi. It took them to Putney Hill. Lady Harman descended at the outer gates of her home and walked up the drive in the darkness, while Mr. Brumley went on to his club and solvency again. It was five minutes past eight when he entered the hall of his club. . . .

§ 6

It had been Lady Harman's original intention to come home before four, to have tea with her mother and to inform her husband when he returned from the city of her entirely dignified and correct disobedience to his absurd prohibitions. Then he would have bullied at a disadvantage, she would have announced her intention of dining with Lady Viping and making the various calls and expeditions for which she had arranged, and all would have gone well. But you see how far accident and a spirit of enterprise may take a lady from so worthy a plan, and when at last she returned to the Victorian baronial home in Putney, it was very nearly eight, and the house blazed with crisis from pantry to nursery. Even the three little girls, who were accustomed to be kissed good-night by their "boofer muvver," were still awake and—catching the subtle influence of the atmosphere of dismay about them—in tears. The very under-housemaids were saying : "Where *ever* can her ladyship 'ave got to ? "

Sir Isaac had come home that day at an unusually early hour and with a peculiar pinched expression that filled even Snagsby with apprehensive alertness. Sir Isaac had, in fact, returned in a state of quite unwonted venom. He had come home early because he wished to vent it upon Ellen, and her absence filled him with something of that sensation one has when one puts out a foot for the floor and instead a step drops one down—it seems abysmally.

"But where's she gone, Snagsby ? "

"Her ladyship *said* to lunch, Sir Isaac," said Snagsby.

"Good gracious ! Where ? "

"Her ladyship didn't *say*, Sir Isaac."

"But where ? Where the devil—— ? "

"I have—'ave no means whatever of knowing, Sir Isaac."

He had a defensive inspiration.

"Perhaps Mrs. Sawbridge, Sir Isaac. . . ."

Mrs. Sawbridge was enjoying the sunshine upon the lawn. She sat in the most comfortable garden chair, held a white sunshade overhead, had the last new novel by Mrs. Humphry Ward upon her lap, and was engaged in trying not to wonder where her daughter might be. She beheld with a distinct blenching of the spirit, Sir Isaac advancing towards her. She wondered more than ever where Ellen might be.

"Here ! " cried her son-in-law. "Where's Ellen gone ? "

Mrs. Sawbridge, with an affected off-handedness, was sure she hadn't the faintest idea.

"Then you *ought* to have," said Isaac. "She ought to be at home."

Mrs. Sawbridge's only reply was to bridle slightly.

"Where's she got to? Where's she gone? Haven't you any idea at all?"

"I was not favoured by Ellen's confidence," said Mrs. Sawbridge.

"But you *ought* to know," cried Sir Isaac. "She's your daughter. Don't you know anything of *either* of your daughters? I suppose you don't care where they are, either of them, or what mischief they're up to. Here's a man—comes home early to his tea—and no wife! After hearing all I've done at the club."

Mrs. Sawbridge stood up in order to be more dignified than a seated position permitted.

"It is scarcely my business, Sir Isaac," she said, "to know of the movements of your wife."

"Nor Georgina's apparently either. Good God! I'd have given a hundred pounds that this shouldn't have happened!"

"If you must speak to me, Sir Isaac, will you please kindly refrain from—from the deity—— "

"Oh! shut it!" said Sir Isaac, blazing up to violent rudeness. "Why! Don't you know, haven't you an idea? The infernal foolery! Those tickets. She got those women—— Look here, if you go walking away with your nose in the air before I've done—— Look here, Mrs. Sawbridge, you listen to me—— Georgina. I'm speaking of Georgina."

The lady was walking now swiftly and stiffly towards the house, her face very pale and drawn, and Sir Isaac hurrying beside her in a white fury of expostulation. "I tell you," he cried, "Georgina—— "

There was something maddeningly incurious about her. He couldn't understand why she didn't even pause to hear what Georgina had done and what he had to say about it. A person so wrapped up in her personal and private dignity makes a man want to throw stones. Perhaps she knew of Georgina's misdeeds. Perhaps she sympathised. . . .

A sense of the house windows checked his pursuit of her ear. "Then go," he said to her retreating back. "*Go!* I don't care if you go for good. I don't care if you go altogether. If *you* hadn't had the upbringing of these two girls—— "

She was manifestly out of earshot and in full yet almost queenly flight for the house. He wanted to say things about her. *To* some one. He was already saying things to the garden generally. What does one marry a wife for? His mind came round to Ellen again. Where had she got to? Even if she had gone out to lunch, it was time she was back. He went to his study and rang for Snagsby.

"Lady Harman back yet?" he asked grimly.

"No, Sir Isaac."

" Why isn't she back ? "

Snagsby did his best. " Perhaps, Sir Isaac, her ladyship has experienced—'as hexperienced a naxident."

Sir Isaac stared at that idea for a moment. Then he thought, " Some one would have telephoned." " No," he said, " she's out. That's where she is. And I suppose I can wait here, as well as I can, until she chooses to come home. Degenerate foolish nonsense. . . . ! "

He whistled between his teeth like an escape of steam. Snagsby, after the due pause of attentiveness, bowed respectfully and withdrew. . . .

He had barely time to give a brief outline of the interview to the pantry before a violent ringing summoned him again. Sir Isaac wished to speak to Peters, Lady Harman's maid. He wanted to know where Lady Harman had gone ; this being impossible, he wanted to know where Lady Harman had seemed to be going.

" Her ladyship *seemed* to be going out to lunch, Sir Isaac," said Peters, her meek face irradiated by helpful intelligence.

" Oh, *get* out ! " said Sir Isaac. " *Get* out ! "

" Yes, Sir Isaac," said Peters, and obeyed. . . .

" He's in a rare bait about her," said Peters to Snagsby downstairs.

" I'm inclined to think her ladyship will catch it pretty hot," said Snagsby.

" He can't *know* anything," said Peters.

" What about ? " said Snagsby.

" Oh, *I* don't know," said Peters. " Don't ask *me* about her. . . ."

About ten minutes later Sir Isaac was heard to break a little china figure of the goddess Kwannon, that had stood upon his study mantel-shelf. The fragments were found afterwards in the fireplace. . . .

The desire for self-expression may become overwhelming. After Sir Isaac had talked to himself about Georgina and Lady Harman for some time in his study, he was seized with a great longing to pour some of this spirited stuff into the entirely unsympathetic ear of Mrs. Sawbridge. So he went about the house and garden looking for her, and being at last obliged to inquire about her, learnt from a scared, defensive housemaid whom he cornered suddenly in the conservatory, that she had retired to her own room. He went and rapped at her door, but after one muffled " Who's that ? " he could get no further response.

" I want to tell you about Georgina," he said.

He tried the handle but the discreet lady within had turned the key upon her dignity.

" I want," he shouted, " to tell you about Georgina. . . . GEORGINA ! Oh, *damn* ! "

Silence.

Tea awaited him downstairs. He hovered about the drawing room, making noises between his teeth.

"Snagsby," said Sir Isaac, "just tell Mrs. Sawbridge I shall be obliged if she will come down to tea."

"Mrs. Sawbridge 'as a 'ead ache, Sir Isaac," said Snagsby, with extreme blandness. "She asked me to acquaint you. She 'as ordered tea in 'er own apartment."

For a moment Sir Isaac was baffled. Then he had an inspiration. "Just get me the *Times*, Snagsby," he said.

He took the paper and unfolded it until a particular paragraph was thrown into extreme prominence. This he lined about with his fountain pen and wrote about it with a quivering hand, "These women's tickets were got by Georgina under false pretences from me." He handed the paper thus prepared back to Snagsby. "Just take this paper to Mrs. Sawbridge," he said, "and ask her what she thinks of it ?"

But Mrs. Sawbridge tacitly declined this proposal for a correspondence *via* Snagsby.

§ 7

There was no excuse for Georgina.

Georgina had obtained tickets from Sir Isaac for the great party reception at Barleypound House, under the shallow pretext that she wanted them for "two spinsters from the country," for whose good behaviour she would answer, and she had handed them over to that organisation of disorder which swayed her mind. The historical outrage upon Mr. Blapton was the consequence.

Two desperate and misguided emissaries had gone to the great reception, dressed and behaving as much as possible like helpful Liberal women ; they had made their way towards the brilliant group of leading Liberals, of which Mr. Blapton was the centre, assuming an almost Whig-like expression and bearing to mask the fires within, and had then suddenly accosted him. It was one of those great occasions when the rank and file of the popular party is privileged to look upon Court dress. The ministers and great people had come on from Buckingham Palace in their lace and legs. Scarlet and feathers, splendid trains and mysterious ribbons and stars, gave an agreeable intimation of all that it means to be in office to the dazzled wives and daughters of the party stalwarts and fired the ambition of innumerable earnest but earnestly competitive young men. It opened the eyes of the Labour leaders to the higher possibilities of Parliament. And then suddenly came a stir, a rush, a cry of "Tear off his epaulettes ! " and outrage was afoot. And two quite nice-looking women !

It is unhappily not necessary to describe the scene that followed. Mr. Blapton made a brave fight for his epaulettes, fighting chiefly with his cocked hat, which was bent double in the struggle. Mrs. Blapton gave all the assistance true

womanliness could offer, and, in fact, she boxed the ears of
one of his assailants very soundly. The intruders were rescued
in an extremely torn and draggled condition from the indignant
statesmen who had fallen upon them by tardy but decisive
police. . . .

Such scenes sprinkle the recent history of England with
green and purple patches, and the interest of this particular
one for us is only because of Georgina's share in it. That was
brought home to Sir Isaac, very suddenly and disagreeably,
while he was lunching at the Climax Club with Sir Robert
Charterson. A man named Gobbin, an art critic or something
of that sort, one of those flimsy, literary people, who mar
the solid worth of so many great clubs, a man with a lot of
hair and the sort of loose tie that so often seems to be less of
a tie than a detachment from all decent restraints, told him.
Charterson was holding forth upon the outrage.

" That won't suit Sir Isaac, Sir Robert," said Gobbin,
presuming on his proximity.

Sir Isaac tried to give him the sort of look one gives to an
unsatisfactory clerk.

" They went there with Sir Isaac's tickets," said Gobbin.]

" They *never*—— ! "

" Horatio Blenker was looking for you in the hall. Haven't
you seen him ? After all the care they took. The poor man's
almost in tears."

" They never had tickets of mine ! " cried Sir Isaac, stoutly
and indignantly.

And then the thought of Georgina came like a blow upon
his heart. . . .

In his flurry he went on denying. . . .

The subsequent conversation in the smoking-room was as
red-eared and disagreeable for Sir Isaac as any conversation
could be. " But how *could* such a thing have happened ? "
he asked in a voice that sounded bleached to him. " How
could such a thing have come about ? " Their eyes were dreadful. Did they guess. Could they guess ? Conscience within
him was going up and down shouting out, " Georgina, your
sister-in-law, Georgina," so loudly that he felt the whole
smoking-room must be hearing it. . . .

§ 8

As Lady Harman came up through the darkness of the
drive to her home, she was already regretting very deeply
that she had not been content to talk to Mr. Brumley in
Kensington Gardens instead of accepting his picturesque
suggestion of Hampton Court. There was an unpleasant,
waif-like feeling about this return. She was reminded of
pictures published in the interests of Doctor Barnardo's
philanthropies—Dr. Barnardo, her favourite hero in real
life—in which wistful little outcasts creep longingly towards

brightly lit but otherwise respectable homes. It wasn't at all the sort of feeling she would have chosen if she had had a choice of feelings. She was tired and dusty, and as she came into the hall the bright light was blinding. Snagsby took her wrap. "Sir Isaac, me lady, 'as been inquiring for your lady-ship," he communicated.

Sir Isaac appeared on the staircase.

"Good gracious, Elly ! " he shouted. "Where you been ? "

Lady Harman decided against an immediate reply. "I shall be ready for dinner in half an hour," she told Snagsby, and went past him to the stairs.

Sir Isaac awaited her. "Where you been ? " he repeated, as she came up to him.

A housemaid on the staircase and the second nursemaid on the nursery landing above shared Sir Isaac's eagerness to hear her answer. But they did not hear her answer, for Lady Harman, with a movement that was all too reminiscent of her mother's in the garden, swept past him towards the door of her own room. He followed her and shut the door on the thwarted listeners.

"Here ! " he said, with a connubial absence of restraint. "Where the devil you been ? What the deuce do you think you've been getting up to ? "

She had been calculating her answers since the moment she had realised that she was to return home at a disadvantage. (It is not my business to blame her for a certain disingenuous-ness ; it is my business simply to record it.) "I went out to lunch at Lady Beach-Mandarin's," she said. "I told you I meant to."

"Lunch ! " he cried. "Why, it's eight ! "

"I met—some people. I met Agatha Alimony. I have a perfect right to go out to lunch—— "

"You met a nice crew, I'll bet. But that don't account for your being out to eight ? With all the confounded household doing as it pleases ! "

"I went on—to see the borders at Hampton Court."

"With *her* ? "

"*Yes*," said Lady Harman. . . .

It wasn't what she had meant to happen. It was an in-glorious declension from her contemplated pose of dignified assertion. She was impelled to do her utmost to get away from this lie she had uttered at once, to eliminate Agatha from the argument by an emphatic generalisation. "I've a perfect right," she said, suddenly nearly breathless, "to go to Hampton Court with any one I please, talk about anything I like, and stay there as long as I think fit."

He squeezed his thin lips together for a silent moment, and then retorted, "You've got nothing of the sort, nothing of the sort. You've got to do your duty like everybody else in the world, and your duty is to be in this house controlling

it—and not gossiping about London, just where any silly
fancy takes you."

" I don't think that *is* my duty," said Lady Harman, after
a slight pause to collect her forces.

" Of *course* it's your duty. You know it's your duty. You
know perfectly well. It's only these rotten, silly, degenerate,
decadent fools who've got ideas into you—— " The sentence
staggered under its load of adjectives like a camel under the
last straw and collapsed. " *See ?* " he said.

Lady Harman knitted her brows.

" I do my duty," she began.

But Sir Isaac was now resolved upon eloquence. His mind
was full with the accumulations of an extremely long and
bitter afternoon, and urgent to discharge. He began to answer
her, and then a passion of rage flooded him. Suddenly he
wanted to shout and use abusive expressions, and it seemed
to him there was nothing to prevent his shouting and using
abusive expressions. So he did. " Call this your duty," he
said, " gadding about with some infernal old suffragette—— "

He paused to gather force. He had never quite let himself
go to his wife before ; he had never before quite let himself
go to any one. He had always been in every crisis just a little
too timid to let himself go. But a wife is privileged. He
sought strength, and found it in words from which he had
hitherto abstained. It was not a discourse to which print
could do justice ; it flickered from issue to issue. He touched
upon Georgina, upon the stiffness of Mrs. Sawbridge's manner,
upon the neurotic weakness of Georgina's unmarried state,
upon the general decay of feminine virtue in the community,
upon the laxity of modern literature, upon the dependent
state of Lady Harman, upon the unfairness of their relations,
which gave her every luxury while he spent his days in arduous
toil, upon the shame and annoyance in the eyes of his servants
that her unexplained absence had caused him.

He emphasised his speech by gestures. He thrust out one
rather large, ill-shaped hand at her with two vibrating fingers
extended. His ears became red, his nose red, his eyes seemed
red, and all about these points his face was wrathful white.
His hair rose up into stiff, scared, listening ends. He had his
rights, he had some *little* claim to consideration, surely, he
might be just nobody, but he wasn't going to stand this much
anyhow. He gave her fair warning. What was she, what did
she know of the world into which she wanted to rush ? He
lapsed into views of Lady Beach-Mandarin—unfavourable
views. I wish Lady Beach-Mandarin could have heard him. . . .

Ever and again Lady Harman sought to speak. This incessant voice confused and baffled her ; she had a just, attentive mind at bottom, and down there was a most weakening
feeling that there must indeed be some misdeed in her to
evoke so impassioned a storm. She had a curious and dis-

concerting sense of responsibility for his dancing exasperation, she felt she was to blame for it, just as years ago she had felt she was to blame for his tears when he had urged her so desperately to marry him. Some irrational instinct made her want to allay him. It is the supreme feminine weakness, that wish to allay. But she was also clinging desperately to her resolution to proclaim her other forthcoming engagements. Her will hung on to that as a man hangs on to a mountain path in a thunderburst. She stood gripping her dressing-table, and ever and again trying to speak. But whenever she did so Sir Isaac lifted a hand and cried almost threateningly : " You hear me out, Elly ! You hear me out ! " and went on a little faster. . . .

(Limburger in his curious *Sexuelle Unterschiede der Seele*, points out as a probably universal distinction between the sexes, that when a man scolds a woman, if only he scolds loudly enough and long enough, conviction of sin is aroused, while in the reverse case the result is merely a murderous impulse. This he further says is not understood by women, who hope by scolding to produce the similar effect upon men that they themselves would experience. The passage is illustrated by figures of ducking stools and followed by some carefully analysed statistics of connubial crime in Berlin in the years 1901–2. But in this matter let the student compare the achievement of Paulina in *The Winter's Tale* and reflect upon his own life. And, moreover, it is difficult to estimate how far the twinges of conscience that Lady Harman was feeling were not due to an entirely different cause, the falsification of her position by the lie she had just told Sir Isaac.)

And presently upon this noisy scene in the great pink bedroom, with Sir Isaac walking about and standing and turning and gesticulating, and Lady Harman clinging on to her dressing-table, and painfully divided between her new connections, her sense of guilty deception, and the deep instinctive responsibilities of a woman's nature, came, like one of those rows of dots that are now so frequent and so helpful in the art of fiction, the surging, deep, assuaging note of Snagsby's gong : Boooooooom. Boom. Booooooom. . . .

" Damn it ! " cried Sir Isaac, smiting at the air with both fists clenched, and speaking as though this was Ellen's crowning misdeed, " and we aren't even dressed for dinner ! "

§ 9

Dinner had something of the stiffness of court ceremonial.

Mrs. Sawbridge, perhaps erring on the side of discretion, had consumed a little soup and a wing of chicken in her own room. Sir Isaac was down first, and his wife found him grimly astride before the great dining-room fire awaiting her. She had had her dark hair dressed with extreme simplicity, and had slipped on a blue velvet tea-gown, but she had been delayed by a visit to the nursery, where the children were now flushed and uneasily asleep.

Husband and wife took their places at the genuine Sheraton dining-table—one of the very best pieces Sir Isaac had ever picked up—and were waited on with a hushed, scared dexterity by Snagsby and the footman.

Lady Harman and her husband exchanged no remarks during the meal ; Sir Isaac was a little noisy with his soup, as became a man who controls honest indignation, and once he complained briefly in a slightly hoarse voice to Snagsby about the state of one of the rolls. Between the courses he leant back in his chair and made faint sounds with his teeth. These were the only breach of the velvety quiet. Lady Harman was surprised to discover herself hungry, but she ate with thoughtful dignity and gave her mind to the attempted digestion of the confusing interview she had just been through.

It was a very indigestible interview.

On the whole, her heart hardened again. With nourishment and silence her spirit recovered a little from its abasement, and her resolution to assert her freedom to go hither and thither, and think as she chose, renewed itself. She tried to plan some way of making her declaration so that she would not again be overwhelmed by a torrent of response. Should she speak to him at the end of dinner ? Should she speak to him while Snagsby was in the room ? But he might behave badly even with Snagsby in the room, and she could not bear to think of him behaving badly to her in the presence of Snagsby. She glanced at him over the genuine old silver bowl of roses in the middle of the table—all the roses were good *new* sorts—and tried to estimate how he might behave under various methods of declaration.

The dinner followed its appointed ritual to the dessert. Came the wine and Snagsby placed the cigars and a little silver lamp beside his master.

She rose slowly with a speech upon her lips. Sir Isaac remained seated, looking up at her with a mitigated fury in his little red-brown eyes.

The speech receded from her lips again.

" I think," she said, after a strained pause, " I will go and see how mother is now."

" She's only shamming," said Sir Isaac belatedly to her back, as she went out of the room.

She found her mother in a wrap before her fire and made her dutiful inquiries.

" It's only quite a *slight* headache," Mrs. Sawbridge confessed. " But Isaac was so upset about Georgina and about " —she flinched—" about—everything, that I thought it better to be out of the way."

" What exactly has Georgina done ? "

" It's in the paper, dear. On the table there."

Ellen studied the *Times*.

" Georgina got them the tickets," Mrs. Sawbridge explained.
" I wish she hadn't. It was so—so unnecessary of her."

There was a little pause as Lady Harman read. She put
down the paper and asked her mother if she could do anything
for her.

" I—I suppose it's all right, dear, now ? " Mrs. Sawbridge
asked.

" Quite," said her daughter. " You're sure I can do nothing
for you, mummy ? "

" I'm kept so in the dark about things."

" It's quite all right now, mummy."

" He went on—dreadfully."

" It was annoying—of Georgina."

" It makes my position so difficult. I do wish he wouldn't
want to speak to me—about all these things. . . . Georgina
treats me like a perfect nonentity, and then he comes——
It's so inconsiderate. Starting disputes. Do you know, dear,
I really think—if I were to go for a little time to Bournemouth—— ? "

Her daughter seemed to find something attractive in the
idea. She came to the hearthrug and regarded her mother
with maternal eyes.

" Don't you *worry* about things, mummy," she said.

" Mrs. Bleckhorn told me of such a nice quiet boarding-
house, almost looking on the sea. . . . One would be safe
from insult there. You know—— " her voice broke for a
moment, " he was insulting, he *meant* to be insulting. I'm
—upset. I've been thinking over it ever since."

§ 10

Lady Harman came out upon the landing. She felt absolutely
without backing in the world. (If only she hadn't told a lie !)
Then, with an effort she directed her course downstairs to
the dining-room.

(The lie had been necessary. It was only a detail. It mustn't
blind her to the real issue.)

She entered softly and found her husband standing before
the fire plunged in gloomy thoughts. Upon the marble mantel-
shelf behind him was a little glass ; he had been sipping port
in spite of the express prohibition of his doctor, and the wine
had reddened the veins of his eyes and variegated the normal
pallor of his countenance with little flushed areas. " Hel-lo,"
he said, looking up suddenly as she closed the door behind
her.

For a moment there was something in their two expressions
like that on the faces of men about to box.

" I want you to understand," she said, and then : " The
way you behaved—— "

There was an uncontrollable break in her voice. She had

a dreadful feeling that she might be going to cry. She made a great effort to be cold and clear.

" I don't think you have a right—just because I am your wife—to control every moment of my time. In fact, you haven't. And I have a right to make engagements. . . . I want you to know I am going to an afternoon meeting at Lady Beach-Mandarin's. Next week. And I have promised to go to Miss Alimony's to tea."

" Go on," he encouraged grimly.

" I am going to Lady Viping's to dinner too ; she asked me and I accepted. Later."

She stopped.

He seemed to deliberate. Then suddenly he thrust out a face of pinched determination.

" You *won't*, my lady," he said. " You bet your life you won't. *No !* So *now*, then ! "

And then gripping his hands more tightly behind him, he made a step towards her.

" You're losing your bearings, Lady Harman," he said, speaking with much intensity in a low, earnest voice. " You don't seem to be remembering where you are. You come and you tell me you're going to do this and that. Don't you know, Lady Harman, that it's your wifely duty to obey, to do as I say, to behave as I wish." He brought out a lean index finger to emphasise his remarks. " And I am going to make you do it ! " he said.

" I've a perfect right," she repeated.

He went on, regardless of her words. " What do you think you can do, Lady Harman ? You're going to all these places —how ? Not in *my* motor-car, not with *my* money. You've not a thing that isn't mine, that *I* haven't given you. And if you're going to have a lot of friends I haven't got, where're they coming to see you ? Not in *my* house ? I'll chuck 'em out if I find 'em. I won't have 'em: I'll turn 'em out. See ? "

" I'm not a slave."

" You're a wife—and a wife's got to do what her husband wishes. You can't have two heads on a horse. And in *this* horse—this house, I mean, the head's—*me !* "

" I'm not a slave, and I won't be a slave."

" You're a wife, and you'll stick to the bargain you made when you married me. I'm ready in reason to give you anything you want—if you do your duty as a wife should. Why ! —I spoil you. But this going about on your own, this highty-flighty go-as-you-please—no man on earth who's worth calling a man will stand it. I'm not going to begin to stand it. . . . You try it on. You try it, Lady Harman. . . . You'll come to your senses soon enough. See ? You start trying it on now—straight away. We'll make an experiment. We'll watch how it goes. Only don't expect me to give you any money, don't expect me to help your struggling family, don't expect me to alter my arrangements because of you. Let's keep apart for a bit, and you go your way and I'll go mine. And we'll see who's sick of it first, we'll see who wants to cry off."

" I came down here," said Lady Harman, " to give you a reasonable notice——— "

" And you found *I* could reason too," interrupted Sir Isaac in a kind of miniature shout, " you found I could reason too ! "

" You think——— Reason ! I *won't*," said Lady Harman, and found herself in tears. By an enormous effort she re-covered something of her dignity and withdrew. He made no effort to open the door, but stood a little hunchbacked and with a sense of rhetorical victory surveying her retreat.

§ 11

After Lady Harman's maid had left her that night, she sat for some time in a low, easy-chair before her fire, trying at first to collect together into one situation all the events of the day and then lapsing into that state of mind which is not so much thinking as resting in the attitude of thought. Presently, in a vaguely conceived future, she would go to bed. She was stunned by the immense dimensions of the row her simple act of defiance had evoked.

And then came an incredible incident, so incredible that next day she still had great difficulty in deciding whether it was an actuality or a dream. She heard a little very familiar sound. It was the last sound she would have expected to hear, and she turned sharply when she heard it. The paper-covered door in the wall of her husband's apartment opened softly, paused, opened some more, and his little undignified head appeared. His hair was already tumbled from his pillow.

He regarded her steadfastly for some moments with an expression between shame and curiosity and smouldering rage, and then allowed his body, clad now in purple-striped pyjamas, to follow his head into her room. He advanced guiltily.

" Elly," he whispered. " Elly ! "

She caught her dressing-gown about her and stood up.

" What is it, Isaac," she asked, feeling curiously abashed at this invasion.

" Elly," he said, still in that furtive undertone. " *Make it up !* "

" I want my freedom," she said, after a little pause.

" Don't be *silly*, Elly," he whispered in a tone of remon-strance and advancing slowly towards her. " Make it up. Chuck all these ideas."

She shook her head.

" We've got to get along together. You can't go going about just anywhere. We've got—we've got to be reason-able."

He halted, three paces away from her. His eyes weren't sorrowful eyes, or friendly eyes ; they were just shiftily eager eyes. " Look here," he said. " It's all nonsense. . . . Elly, old girl ; let's—let's make it up."

She looked at him, and it dawned upon her that she had always imagined herself to be afraid of him and that indeed she wasn't. She shook her head obstinately.

" It isn't reasonable," he said. " Here, we've been the happiest of people—— Anything in reason I'll let you have." He paused with an effect of making an offer.

" I want my autonomy," she said.

" Autonomy ! " he echoed. " Autonomy ! What's autonomy ? Autonomy ! "

This strange word seemed first to hold him in distressful suspense and then to infuriate him.

" I come in here to make it up," he said, with a voice charged with griefs, " after all you've done, and you go and you talk of autonomy ! "

His feelings passed beyond words. An extremity of viciousness flashed into his face. He gave vent to a snarl of exasperation, " Ya-ap ! " he said, he raised his clenched fists and seemed on the verge of assault, and then with a gesture between fury and despair, he wheeled about and the purple-striped pyjamas danced in passionate retreat from her room.

" Autonomy ! . . . "

A slam, a noise of assaulted furniture, and then silence.

Lady Harman stood for some moments regarding the paper-covered door that had closed behind him. Then she bared her white forearm and pinched it—hard.

It wasn't a dream ! This thing had happened.

§ 12

At a quarter to three in the morning, Lady Harman was surprised to find herself wide awake. It was exactly a quarter to three when she touched the stud of the ingenious little silver apparatus upon the table beside her bed which reflected a luminous clock-face upon the ceiling. And her mind was no longer resting in the attitude of thought, but extraordinarily active. It was active, but as she presently began to realise it was not progressing. It was spinning violently round and round the frenzied figure of a little man in purple-striped pyjamas retreating from her presence, whirling away from her like something blown before a gale. That seemed to her to symbolise the completeness of the breach the day had made between her husband and herself.

She felt as a statesman might feel who had inadvertently —while conducting some trivial negotiations—declared war.

She was profoundly alarmed. She perceived ahead of her abundant possibilities of disagreeable things. And she wasn't by any means as convinced of the righteousness of her cause as a happy warrior should be. She had a natural disposition towards truthfulness, and it worried her mind that while she was struggling to assert her right to these common social freedoms she should be tacitly admitting a kind of justice in her husband's objections by concealing the fact that her afternoon's companion was a man. She tried not to recognise the existence of a doubt, but deep down in her mind there did indeed lurk a weakening uncertainty about the right of a woman to free conversation with any man but her own. Her reason disowned that uncertainty with scorn. But it wouldn't go away for all her reason. She went about in her mind doing her utmost to cut that doubt dead. . . .

She tried to go back to the beginning and think it all out. And as she was not used to thinking things out, the effort took the form of an imaginary explanation to Mr. Brumley of the difficulties of her position. She framed phrases. " You see, Mr. Brumley," she imagined herself to be saying, " I want to do my duty as a wife, I have to do my duty as a wife. But it's so hard to say just where duty leaves off and being a mere slave begins. I cannot believe that *blind* obedience is any woman's duty. A woman's needs—autonomy." Then her mind went off for a time to a wrestle with the exact meaning of autonomy, an issue that had not arisen hitherto in her mind. . . . And as she planned out such elucidations, there grew more and more distinct in her mind a kind of idealised Mr. Brumley, very grave, very attentive, wonderfully understanding, saying illuminating, helpful, tonic things, that made everything clear, everything almost easy. She wanted some one of that quality so badly. The night would have been unendurable if she could not have imagined Mr. Brumley of that quality. And imagining him of that quality her heart yearned for him. She felt that she had been terribly inexpressive that afternoon, she had shirked points, misstated points, and yet he had been marvellously understanding. Ever and again his words had seemed to pierce right through what she had been saying to what she had been thinking. And she recalled with peculiar comfort a kind of abstracted, calculating look that had come at times into his eyes, as though his thoughts were going ever so much deeper and ever so much further than her blundering questionings could possibly have taken them. He weighed every word, he had a guarded way of saying " Um. . . ."

Her thoughts came back to the dancing little figure in purple-striped pyjamas. She had a scared sense of irrevocable breaches. What would he do to-morrow ? What should she do to-morrow? Would he speak to her at breakfast, or should she speak first to him ? . . . She wished she had some money. If she could have foreseen all this she would have got some money before she began. . . .

So her mind went on round and round and the dawn was breaking before she slept again.

§ 13

Mr. Brumley, also, slept little that night. He was wakefully mournful, recalling each ungraceful incident of the afternoon's failure in turn, and more particularly his dispute with the ticket-clerk, and thinking over all the things he might have done—if only he hadn't done the things he had done. He had made an atrocious mess of things. He felt he had hopelessly shattered the fair fabric of impressions of him that Lady Harman had been building up, that image of a wise, humane, capable man, to whom a woman would gladly turn ; he had been flurried, he had been incompetent, he had been ridiculously incompetent, and it seemed to him that life was a string of desolating inadequacies, and that he would never smile again.

The probable reception of Lady Harman by her husband never came within his imaginative scope. Nor did the problems of social responsibility that Lady Harman had been trying to put to him exercise him very greatly. The personal disillusionment was too strong for that.

About half-past four a faint ray of comfort came with the consideration that after all a certain practical incapacity is part of the ensemble of a literary artist, and then he found himself wondering what flowers of wisdom Montaigne might not have culled from such a day's experience ; he began an imitative essay in his head, and he fell asleep upon this at last at about ten minutes past five in the morning.

There were better things than this in the composition of Mr. Brumley, we shall have to go deep into these reserves before we have done with him, but when he had so recently barked the shins of his self-esteem they had no chance at all.

CHAPTER SEVEN

LADY HARMAN LEARNS ABOUT HERSELF

§ I

So it was that the great and long incubated quarrel between Lady Harman and her husband broke into active hostilities.

In spite of my ill-concealed bias in favour of Lady Harman, I have to confess that she began this conflict rashly, planlessly, with no equipment and no definite end. Particularly I would emphasise that she had no definite end. She had wanted merely to establish a right to go out by herself occasionally, exercise a certain choice of friends, take on, in fact, the privileges of a grown-up person, and in asserting that she had never anticipated that the participation of the household would be invoked, or that a general breach might open between herself and her husband. It had seemed just a definite little point at issue, but at Sir Isaac's angry touch a dozen other matters that had seemed safely remote, matters she had never yet quite properly thought about, had been drawn into controversy. It was not only that he drew in things from outside ; he evoked things within herself. She discovered she was disposed to fight not simply to establish certain liberties for herself but also—which had certainly not been in her mind before—to keep her husband away from herself. Something latent in the situation had surprised her with this effect. It had arisen out of the quarrel like a sharpshooter out of an ambuscade. Her right to go out alone had now only the value of a mere pretext for far more extensive independence. The ultimate extent of these independences, she still dared not contemplate.

She was more than a little scared. She wasn't prepared for so wide a revision of her life as this involved. She wasn't at all sure of the rightfulness of her position. Her conception of the marriage contract at that time was liberal towards her husband. After all, didn't she owe obedience ? Didn't she owe him a subordinate co-operation ? Didn't she, in fact, owe him the whole marriage service contract ? When she thought of the figure of him in his purple-striped pyjamas dancing in a paroxysm of exasperation, that sense of responsibility which was one of her innate characteristics reproached her. She had a curious persuasion that she must be dreadfully to blame for provoking so ridiculous, so extravagant an outbreak. . . .

§ 2

She heard him getting up tumultuously, and when she came down—after a brief interview with her mother, who was still keeping her room—she found him sitting at the breakfast-table eating toast and marmalade in a greedy, malignant manner. The tentative propitiations of his proposal to make things up had entirely disappeared, he was evidently in a far profounder rage with her than he had been overnight. Snagsby, too, that seemly domestic barometer, looked extraordinarily hushed and grave. She made a greeting-like noise, and Sir Isaac scrunched " morning " up amongst a crowded, fierce mouthful of toast. She helped herself to tea and bacon, and looking up presently discovered his eye fixed upon her with an expression of ferocious hatred. . . .

He went off in the big car, she supposed to London, about ten, and she helped her mother to pack and depart by a train a little after midday. She made a clumsy excuse for not giving that crisp little trifle of financial assistance she was accustomed to, and Mrs. Sawbridge was anxiously tactful about the dis-appointment. They paid a visit of inspection and farewell to the nursery before the departure. Then Lady Harman was left until lunch to resume her meditation upon this unprecedented breach that had opened between her husband and herself.

She was presently moved to write a little note to Lady Beach-Mandarin expressing her intention of attending a meeting of the Social Friends, and asking whether the date was the following Wednesday or Thursday. She found three penny stamps in the bureau at which she wrote, and this served to remind her of her penniless condition. She spent some time thinking out the possible consequences of that. How, after all, was she going to do things, with not a penny in the world to do them with ?

Lady Harman was not only instinctively truthful, but also almost morbidly honourable. In other words, she was simple-minded. The idea of a community of goods between husband and wife had never established itself in her mind, she took all Sir Isaac's presents in the spirit in which he gave them, presents, she felt they were on trust, and so it was that with a six-hundred-pound pearl necklace, a diamond tiara, bracelets, lockets, rings, chains, and pendants of the most costly kind—there had been a particularly beautiful bracelet when Millicent was born, a necklace on account of Florence, a fan painted by Charles Conder for Annette, and a richly splendid set of old Spanish jewellery—yellow sapphires set in gold—to express Sir Isaac's gratitude for the baby—with all sorts of purses, bags, boxes, trinkets, and garments, with a bedroom and morning-room rich in admirable loot, and with endless trades-people willing to give her credit, it didn't, for some time, occur to her that there was any possible means of getting pocket-money except by direct demand from Sir Isaac. She surveyed her balance of two penny stamps and even about these she felt a certain lack of negotiable facility.

She thought, indeed, that she might, perhaps, borrow money, but there again her paralysing honesty made her recoil from the prospect of uncertain repayment. And besides, from whom could she borrow ? . . .

It was on the evening of the second day that a chance remark from Peters turned her mind to the extensive possibilities of liquidation that lay close at hand. She was discussing her dinner dress with Peters, she wanted something very plain and high and unattractive, and Peters, who disapproved of this tendency and was all for female wiles and propitiations, fell into an admiration of the pearl necklace. She thought, per-haps, by so doing she might induce Lady Harman to wear it, and if she wore it Sir Isaac might be a little propitiated, and if Sir Isaac was a little propitiated it would be much more com-fortable for Snagsby and herself and every one. She was reminded of a story of a lady who sold one and substituted imitation pearls, no one the wiser, and she told this to her mistress out of sheer garrulousness. " But if no one found out," said Lady Harman, " how do you know ? "

" Not till her death, me lady, said Peters, blushing, " when all things are revealed. Her husband, they say, made it a present of to another lady and the other lady, me lady, had it valued. . . ."

Once the idea had got into Lady Harman's head it stayed there very obstinately. She surveyed the things on the table before her with a slightly lifted eyebrow. At first she thought the idea of disposing of them an entirely dishonourable idea, and if she couldn't get it out of her head again at least she made it stand in a corner. And while it stood in a corner she began putting a price for the first time in her life first upon this coruscating object and then that. Then somehow she found herself thinking more and more whether among all these glittering possessions there wasn't something that she might fairly regard as absolutely her own. There were, for example, her engagement ring, and, still more debatable, certain other pre-nuptial trinkets Sir Isaac had given her. Then there were things given her on her successive birthdays. A birthday present of all presents is surely one's very own ? But selling is an extreme exercise of ownership. Since those early schooldays when she had carried on an unprofitable traffic in stamps, she had never sold anything—unless we are to reckon that for once and for all she had sold herself.

Concurrently with these insidious speculations Lady Harman found herself trying to imagine how one sold jewels. She tried to sound Peters by taking up the story of the necklace again. But Peters was uninforming. " But where," asked Lady Harman, " could such a thing be done ? "

" There are places, me lady," said Peters.

" But where ? "

" In the West End, me lady. The West End is full of places —for things of that sort. There's scarcely anything you can't do there, me lady—if only you know how."

That was really all that Peters could impart.

" How *does* one sell jewels ? " Lady Harman became so interested in this side of her perplexities that she did a little lose sight of those subtler problems of integrity that had at first engaged her. Do jewellers buy jewels as well as sell them ? And then it came into her head that there were such things as pawnshops. By the time she had thought about pawnshops and tried to imagine one, her original complete veto upon any idea of selling had got lost to sight altogether. Instead, there was a growing conviction that if ever she sold anything it would be a certain sapphire and diamond ring which she didn't like and never wore that Sir Isaac had given her as a birthday present two years ago. But of course she would never dream of selling anything ; at the utmost she need but pawn. She reflected and decided that, on the whole, it would be wiser not to ask Peters how one pawned. It occurred to her to consult the *Encyclopædia Britannica* on the subject, but though she learnt that the Chinese pawnshops must not charge more than three per cent. per annum, that King Edward the Third pawned his jewels in 1338, and that Father Bernardino di Feltre, who set up pawnshops in Assisi and Padua and Pavia, was afterward canonised, she failed to get any very clear idea of the exact ritual of the process. And then suddenly she remembered that she knew a finished expert in pawnshop work in the person of Susan Burnet. Susan could tell her everything. She found some curtains in the study that needed replacement, consulted Mrs. Crumble, and, with a view to economising her own resources, made that lady send off an urgent letter to Susan, bidding her come forthwith.

§ 3

It has been said that Fate is a plagiarist. Lady Harman's fate, at any rate, at this juncture behaved like a benevolent plagiarist, who was also a little old-fashioned. This phase of speechless hostility was complicated by the fact that two of the children fell ill, or at least seemed for a couple of days to be falling ill. But all the rules of British sentiment, this ought to have brought about a headlong reconciliation at the tumbled bedside. It did nothing of the sort ; it merely wove fresh perplexities into the tangled skein of her thoughts.

On the day after her participation in that forbidden lunch Millicent, her eldest daughter, was discovered with a temperature of a hundred and one, and then Annette, the third, followed suit with a hundred. This carried Lady Harman post haste to the nursery, where, to a unprecedented degree, she took command. Latterly she had begun to mistrust the physique of her children, and to doubt whether the trained efficiency of Mrs. Harblow the nurse wasn't becoming a little blunted at the edges by continual use. And the tremendous quarrel she had afoot made her keenly resolved not to let anything go wrong in the nursery and less disposed than she usually was to leave things to her husband's servants. She interviewed the doctor herself, arranged for the isolation of two flushed and cross little girls, saw to the toys and amusements, which she discovered had become a little flattened and disused by the servants' imperatives of tidying up and putting away, and spent the greater part of the next two days between the night and day nurseries.

She was a little surprised to find how readily she did this and how easily the once entirely authoritative Mrs. Harblow submitted. It was much the same surprise that growing young people feel when they reach some shelf that has hitherto been inaccessible. The crisis soon passed. At his first visit the doctor was a little doubtful whether the Harman nursery wasn't under the sway of measles, which were then raging in a particularly virulent form in London ; the next day he inclined to the view that the trouble was merely a feverish cold, and before night this second view was justified by the disappearance of the " temperatures " and a complete return to normal conditions.

But as for that hushed reconciliation in the fevered presence of the almost sacrificial offspring, it didn't happen. Sir Isaac merely thrust aside the stiff silences behind which he masked his rage to remark : " This is what happens when wimmen go gadding about ! "

That much and glaring eyes and compressed lips and emphasising fingers and then he had gone again.

Indeed rather than healing their widening breach this crisis did much to spread it into strange new regions. It brought Lady Harman to the very verge of realising how much of instinct and how much of duty held her the servant of the children she had brought into the world, and how little there mingled with that any of those factors of pride and admiration that go to the making of heroic maternal love. She knew what is expected of a mother, the exalted and lyrical devotion, and it was with something approaching terror that she perceived that certain things in these children of hers she *hated*. It was her business, she knew, to love them blindly ; she lay awake at night in infinite dismay realising she did nothing of the sort. Their weakness held her more than anything else, the invincible pathos of their little limbs in discomfort, so that she was ready to die she felt to give them ease. But so she would have been held, she was assured, by the little children of anybody if they had fallen with sufficient helplessness into her care.

Just how much she didn't really like her children she presently realised, when in the feeble irascibility of their sickness they fell quarrelling. They became—horrid. Millicent and Annette being imprisoned in their beds, it seemed good to Florence when she came back from the morning's walk, to annex and hide a selection of their best toys. She didn't take them and play with them, she hid them with an industrious earnestness in a box window-seat that was regarded as peculiarly hers, staggering with armfuls across the nursery floor. Then Millicent by some equally mysterious agency divined what was afoot and set up a clamour for a valued set of doll's furniture, which immediately provoked a similar outcry from little Annette for her Teddy Bear. Followed woe and uproar. The invalids insisted upon having every single toy they possessed brought in and put upon their beds ; Florence was first disingenuous, and then surrendered her loot with passionate howlings. The Teddy Bear was rescued from baby after a violent struggle in which one furry hind leg was nearly twisted off. It jars upon the philoprogenitive sentiment of our time to tell of these things, and still more to record that all four, stirred by possessive passion to the profoundest depths of their beings, betrayed to an unprecedented degree in their little sharp noses, their flushed faces, their earnest eyes, their dutiful likeness to Sir Isaac. He peeped from under Millicent's daintily knitted brows and gestured with Florence's dimpled fists. It was as if God had tried to make him into four cherubim, and as if in spite of everything he was working through.

Lady Harman toiled to pacify these disorders, gently, attentively, and with a faint dismay in her dark eyes. She bribed and entreated and marvelled at mental textures so unlike her own. Baby was squared with a brand new Teddy Bear, a rare sort, a white one, which Snagsby went and purchased in the Putney High Street and brought home in his arms, conferring such a lustre upon the deed that the lower orders, the very street-boys, watched him with reverence as he passed. Annette went to sleep amidst a discomfort of small treasures, and woke stormily when Mrs. Harblow tried to remove some of the spikier ones. And Lady Harman went back to her large pink bedroom and meditated for a long time upon these things, and tried to remember whether in her own less crowded childhood with Georgina, either of them had been quite so inhumanly hard and grasping as these feverish little mites in her nursery. She tried to think she had been, she tried to think that all children were such little distressed lumps of embittered individuality, and she did what she could to overcome the queer feeling that this particular clutch of offspring had been foisted upon her and weren't at all the children she could now imagine and desire—gentle children, sweet spirited children. . . .

§ 4

Susan Burnet arrived in a gusty mood and brought new matter for Lady Harman's ever broadening consideration of the wifely position. Susan, led by a newspaper placard, had discovered Sir Isaac's relations to the International Bread and Cake Stores.

" At first I thought I wouldn't come," said Susan. " I really did. I couldn't hardly believe it. And then I thought, " it isn't *her*. It can't be *her* ! " But I'd never have dreamt before that I could have been brought to set foot in the house of the man who drove poor father to ruin and despair. . . . You've been so kind to me. . . . "

Susan's simple, right-down mind stopped for a moment with something very like a sob, baffled by the contradictions of the situation.

" So I came," she said, with a forced bright smile.

" I'm glad you came," said Lady Harman. " I wanted to see you. And you know, Susan, I know very little—very little indeed—of Sir Isaac's business."

" I quite believe it, my lady. I've never for one moment thought *you*—— I don't know how to say it, my lady."

" And indeed I'm not," said Lady Harman, taking it as said.

" I knew you weren't," said Susan, relieved to be so understood.

And the two women looked perplexedly at one another over the neglected curtains Susan had come to " see to," and shyness just snatched back Lady Harman from her impulse to give Susan a sisterly kiss. Nevertheless, Susan, who was full of wise intuitions, felt that kiss that was never given, and in the remote world of unacted deeds returned it with effusion.

" But it's hard," said Susan, " to find one's own second sister mixed up in a strike, and that's what it's come to last week. They've struck, all the International waitresses have struck, and last night in Piccadilly they were standing on the kerb and picketing and her among them. With a crowd cheering. . . . And me ready to give my right hand to keep that girl respectable ! "

And with a volubility that was at once tumultuous and effective, Susan sketched in the broad outlines of the crisis that threatened the dividends and popularity of the International Bread and Cake Stores. The unsatisfied demands of that bright journalistic enterprise, *The London Lion*, lay near the roots of the trouble. *The London Lion* had stirred it up. But it was only too evident that *The London Lion* had merely given a voice and form and cohesion to long smouldering discontents.

Susan's account of the matter had that impartiality which comes from intellectual incoherence, she hadn't so much a judgment upon the whole as a warring mosaic of judgments. It was talking upon post-impressionist lines, talking in the manner of Picasso. She had the firmest conviction that to strike against employment, however ill-paid or badly conditioned, was a disgraceful combination of folly, ingratitude, and general wickedness, and she had an equally strong persuasion that the treatment of the employees of the International Bread and Cake Stores was such as no reasonably spirited person ought to stand. She blamed her sister extremely and sympathised with her profoundly, and she put it all down in turn to *The London Lion*, to Sir Isaac, and to a small, round-faced person called Babs Wheeler, who appeared to be the strike leader and seemed always to be standing on tables in the branches, or clambering up to the lions in Trafalgar Square, or being cheered in the streets.

But there could be no mistaking the quality of Sir Isaac's " International " organisation as Susan's dabs of speech shaped it out. It was, indeed, what we all of us see everywhere about us, the work of the base, energetic mind, raw and untrained, in possession of the keen instruments of civilisation, the peasant mind allied and blended with the Ghetto mind, grasping and acquisitive, clever as a Norman peasant or a Jew pedlar is clever, and beyond that outrageously stupid and ugly. It was a new view and yet the old familiar view of her husband, but now she saw him not as little eager eyes, a sharp nose, gaunt gestures, and a leaden complexion, but as shops and stores and rules and cash registers, and harsh advertisements and a driving, merciless hurry to get—to get anything and everything, money, monopoly, power, prominence, whatever any other human being seemed to admire or seemed to find desirable, a lust rather than a living soul. Now that her eyes were at last opened, Lady Harman who had seen too little heretofore now saw too much; she saw all that she had not seen, with an excess of vision, monstrous, caricatured. Susan had already dabbed in the disaster of Sir Isaac's unorganised competitors going to the wall—for charity or the state to neglect or bandage as it might chance—the figure of that poor little "Father," moping hopelessly before his "accident" symbolised that; and now she gave in vivid splotches of allusion, glimpses of the business machine that had replaced those shattered enterprises and carried Sir Isaac to the squalid glory of a Liberal honours list—the carefully balanced antagonisms and jealousies of the girls and the manageresses, those manageresses who had been obliged to invest little bunches of savings as guarantees, and who had to account for every crumb and particle of food stock that came to the branch, and the hunt for cases and inefficiency by the inspectors, who had somehow to justify a salary of two hundred a year, not to mention a percentage of the fines they inflicted.

"There's all that business of the margarine," said Susan. "Every branch gets its butter under weight—the water squeezes out—and every branch has overweight margarine. Of course the rules say that mixing's forbidden, and if they get caught they go, but they got to pay-in for that butter, and it's setting a snare for their feet. People who've never thought to cheat, when they get it like that, day after day, they cheat, my lady. . . . And the girls get left food for rations. There's always trouble, it's against what the rules say, but they get it. Of course it's against the rules, but what can a manageress do ?—if the waste doesn't fall on them, it falls on her. She's tied there with her savings. . . . Such driving, my lady, it's against the very spirit of God. It makes scoffers point. It makes people despise law and order. There's Luke, he gets bitterer and bitterer ; he says that it's in the Word we mustn't muzzle the ox that treadeth out the corn, but these Stores, he says, they'd muzzle the ox and keep it hungry, and make it work a little machine, he says, whenever it put down its head in the hope of finding a scrap. . . ."

So Susan, bright-eyed, flushed and voluble, pleading the cause of that vague greatness in humanity that would love, that would loiter, that would think, that would, if it could, give us art, delight, and beauty, that turns blindly and stumblingly towards joy, towards intervals, towards the mysterious things of the spirit, against all this sordid strenuousness, this driving, destructive association of hard-fisted peasant soul and Ghetto greed, this fool's " efficiency," that rules our world to-day.

Then Susan lunged for a time at the waitress life her sister led. " She has 'er 'ome with us, but some—they haven't homes.

" They made a fuss about all this White Slave Traffic," said Susan, " but if ever there were white slaves it's the girls who work for a living and keep themselves respectable. And nobody wants to make an example of the men who get rich out of *them*. . . ."

And after some hearsay about the pressure in the bake-houses and the accidents to the vanmen, who worked on a speeding-up system, that Sir Isaac had adopted from an American business specialist, Susan's mental discharge poured out into the particulars of the waitresses' strike, and her sister's share in that. " She *would* go into it," said Susan, " she let herself be drawn in. I asked her never to take the place. Better service, I said, a thousand times. I begged her, I could have begged her on my bended knees. . . ."

The immediate cause of the strike, it seemed, was the exceptional disagreeableness of one of the London district managers. " He takes advantage of his position," repeated Susan, with face aflame, and Lady Harman was already too wise about Susan's possibilities to urge her towards particulars. . . .

Now, as Lady Harman listened to all this confused, effective picturing of the great catering business which was the other side of her husband and which she had taken on trust so long, she had in her heart a quite unreasonable feeling of shame that she should listen at all, a shyness, as though she was prying, as though this really did not concern her. She knew she had to listen, and still she felt beyond her proper jurisdiction. It is against instinct, it is with an enormous reluctance that women are bringing their quick emotions, their flashing, unstable intelligences, their essential romanticism, their inevitable, profound generosity into the world of politics and business. If only they could continue believing that all that side of life is grave and wise and admirably managed for them they would. It is not in a day or a generation that we shall unspecialise women. It is a wrench nearly as violent as birth for them to face out into the bleak realisation that the man who goes out for them into business, into affairs, and returns so comfortably loaded with housings and wrappings and trappings and toys, isn't, as a matter of fact, engaged in benign creativeness while he is getting these desirable things.

§ 5

Lady Harman's mind was so greatly exercised by Susan Burnet's voluminous confidences that it was only when she returned to her own morning room that she recalled the pawning problem. She went back to Sir Isaac's study and found Susan with all her measurements taken and on the very edge of departure.

" Oh, Susan ! " she said.

She found the matter a little difficult to broach. Susan remained in an attitude of respectful expectation.

" I wanted to ask you," said Lady Harman, and then broke off to shut the door. Susan's interest increased.

" You know, Susan," said Lady Harman, with an air of talking about commonplace things, " Sir Isaac is very rich and—of course—very generous. . . . But sometimes one feels, one wants a little money of one's own."

" I think I can understand that, my lady," said Susan.

" I knew you would," said Lady Harman, and then with a brightness that was slightly forced, " I can't always get money of my own. It's difficult—sometimes."

And then blushing vividly : " I've got lots of *things*. . . . Susan, have you ever pawned anything ? "

And so she broached it.

" Not since I got fairly into work," said Susan ; " I wouldn't have it. But when I was little we were always pawning things. Why ! we've pawned kettles ! . . . "

She flashed three reminiscences.

Meanwhile Lady Harman produced a little glittering object and held it between finger and thumb. " If I went into a pawnshop near here," she said, " it would seem so odd. . . . This ring, Susan, must be worth thirty or forty pounds. And it seems so silly when I have it that I should really be wanting money. . . . "

Susan displayed a peculiar reluctance to handle the ring. " I've never," she said, " pawned anything valuable—not valuable like that. Suppose—suppose they wanted to know how I had come by it.

" It's more than Alice earns in a year," she said. " It's——" she eyed the glittering treasure ; " it's a queer thing for me to have."

A certain embarrassment arose between them. Lady Harman's need of money became more apparent. " I'll do it for you," said Susan, " indeed I'll do it. But—— There's one thing—— "

Her face flushed hotly. " It isn't that I want to make difficulties. But people in our position—we aren't like people in your position. It's awkward sometimes to explain things. You've got a good character, but people don't know it. You can't be too careful. It isn't sufficient—just to be honest. If I take that—— If you were just to give me a little note—in your handwriting—on your paper—just asking me—— I don't suppose I need show it to any one. . . . "

" I'll write the note," said Lady Harman. A new set of

uncomfortable ideas was dawning upon her. " But Susan——
You don't mean that any one, any one who's really honest
—might get into trouble ? "

" You can't be too careful," said Susan, manifestly resolved not to give our highly civilised state half a chance with
her.

§ 6

The problem of Sir Isaac and just what he was doing and
what he thought he was doing and what he meant to do increased in importance in Lady Harman's mind as the days
passed by. He had an air of being malignantly up to something, and she could not imagine what this something could
be. He spoke to her very little, but he looked at her a great
deal. He had more and more of the quality of a premeditated
imminent explosion. . . .

One morning she was standing quite still in the drawing-
room, thinking over this now almost oppressive problem of
why the situation did not develop further with him when
she became aware of a thin, flat, unusual book upon the small
side table near the great arm-chair at the side of the fire. He
had been reading that overnight, and it lay obliquely—it
might almost have been left out for her.

She picked it up. It was *The Taming of the Shrew* in that
excellent folio edition of Henley's which makes each play a
comfortable thin book apart. A curiosity to learn what it
was had drawn her husband to English literature made her
turn over the pages. *The Taming of the Shrew* was a play she
knew very slightly. For the Harmans, though deeply implicated like most other rich and striving people in plans for
honouring the immortal William, like most other people found
scanty leisure to read him.

As she turned over the pages, a pencil mark caught her
eye. Thence words were underlined and further accentuated
by a deeply scored line in the margin.

> " But for my bonny Kate, she must with me.
> Nay ; look not big, nor stamp, nor stare, nor fret ;
> I will be master of what is mine own :
> She is my goods, my chattels ; she is my house,
> She is my household stuff, my field, my barn,
> My horse, my ox, my ass, my anything :
> And here she stands, touch her whoever dare ;
> I'll bring mine action on the proudest He,
> That stops my way in Padua."

With a slightly heightened colour Lady Harman read on,
and presently found another page slashed with Sir Isaac's
approval. . . .

Her face became thoughtful. Did he mean to attempt

—Petruchio ? He could never dare. There were servants, there were the people one met, the world. . . . He would never dare. . . .

What a strange play it was ! Shakespeare, of course, was wonderfully wise, the crown of English wisdom, the culminating English mind—or else one might almost find something a little stupid and clumsy. . . . Did women nowadays really feel like these Elizabethan wives who talked—like girls, very forward girls indeed, but girls of sixteen ? . . .

She read the culminating speech of Katharina, and now she had so forgotten Sir Isaac she scarcely noted the pencil line that endorsed the immortal words.

" Thy husband is thy Lord, thy Life, they Keeper,
   Thy Head, thy Sovereign ; one who cares for thee,
   And for thy maintenance commits his body
   To painful labour both by sea and land,
   To watch the night in storms, the day in cold,
   Whilst thou liest warm at home, secure and safe ;
   And craves no other tribute at thy hands
   But love, fair looks, and true obedience ;
   Too little payment for so great a debt.
   Such duty as the Subject owes the Prince,
   Even such a woman oweth to her husband ;
   And when she is forward, peevish, sullen, sour,
   And not obedient to his honest will,
   What is she but a foul, contending Rebel
   And graceless traitor to her loving Lord ?
   I am ashamed that women are so simple
   To offer war, where they should kneel for peace ;
   .   .   .   .
   My mind has been as big as one of yours,
   My heart as great ; my reason, haply, more,
   To bandy word for word and frown for frown.
   But now I see our lances are but straws ;
   Our strength is weak, our weakness past compare,
   Seemind that most which we indeed least are. . . . "

She wasn't indignant. Something in these lines took hold of her protesting imagination.

She knew that so she could have spoken of a man.

But that man—she apprehended him as vaguely as an Anglican bishop apprehends God. He was obscured altogether by the shadows ; he had only one known characteristic, that he was totally unlike Sir Isaac. And the play was false, she felt, in giving this speech to a broken woman. Such things are not said by broken women. Broken women do no more than cheat and lie. But so a woman might speak out of her unconquered wilfulness, as a queen might give her lover a kingdom out of the fullness of her heart.

§ 7

The evening after his wife had had this glimpse into Sir
Isaac's mental processes he telephoned that Charterson and
Horatio Blenker were coming home to dinner with him.
Neither Lady Charterson nor Mrs. Blenker were to be present ;
it was to be a business conversation and not a social occasion,
and Lady Harman he desired, should wear her black and gold,
with just a touch of crimson in her hair. Charterson wanted a
word or two with the flexible Horatio on sugar at the London
docks, and Sir Isaac had some vague ideas that a turn might
be given to the public judgment upon the waitresses' strike,
by a couple of Horatio's thoughtful, yet gentlemanly, articles.
And in addition, Charterson seemed to have something else
upon his mind ; he did not tell as much to Sir Isaac, but he
was weighing the possibilities of securing a controlling share
in the *Daily Spirit*, which simply didn't know at present where
it was upon the sugar business, and of installing Horatio's
brother, Adolphus, as its editor. He wanted to form some
idea from Horatio of what Adolphus might expect before he
approached Adolphus.

Lady Harman wore the touch of crimson in her hair as her
husband had desired, and the table was decorated simply
with a big silver bowl of crimson roses. A slight shade of
apprehension in Sir Isaac's face changed to approval at the
sight of her obedience. After all, perhaps she was beginning
to see the common sense of her position.

Charterson struck her as looking larger, but then whenever
she saw him he struck her as looking larger. He enveloped
her hand in a large amiable paw for a minute and asked after
the children with gusto. The large teeth beneath his discursive
moustache gave him the effect of a perennial smile, to which
his asymmetrical ears added a touch of waggery. He always
betrayed a fatherly feeling towards her, as became a man who
was married to a handsome wife old enough to be her mother.
Even when he asked about the children, he did it with something of the amused knowingness of assured seniority, as if,
indeed, he knew all sorts of things about the children that she
couldn't as yet even begin to imagine. And though he confined his serious conversation to the two other men, he would
ever and again show himself mindful of her and throw her
some friendly inquiry, some quizzically puzzling remark.
Blenker, as usual, treated her as if she were an only very indistinctly visible presence to whom an effusive yet inattentive
politeness was due. He was clearly nervous almost to the pitch
of jumpiness. He knew he was to be spoken to about the
sugar business directly he saw Charterson, and he hated being
spoken to about the sugar business. He had his code of honour.
Of course, one has to make concessions to one's proprietors,
but he could not help feeling that if only they would consent

to see his really quite obvious gentlemanliness more clearly it would be better for the paper, better for the party, better for them, far better for himself. He wasn't altogether a fool about that sugar ; he knew how things lay. They ought to trust him more. His nervousness betrayed itself in many little ways. He crumbled his bread constantly, until, thanks to Snagsby's assiduous replacement, he had made quite a pile of crumbs, he dropped his glasses in the soup—a fine occasion for Snagsby's *sang-froid*—and he forgot not to use a fish knife with the fish as Lady Grove directs, and tried, when he dis-covered his error, to replace it furtively on the table-cloth. Moreover, he kept on patting the glasses on his nose—after Snagsby had whisked his soup plate away, rescued, wiped, and returned them to him—until that feature glowed modestly at such excesses of attention, and the soup and sauces and things bothered his fine blond moustache unusually. So that Mr. Blenker what with the glasses, the napkin, the food, and the things seemed as restless as a young sparrow. Lady Harman did her duties as hostess in the quiet key of her sombre dress, and until the conversation drew her out into un-expected questionings, she answered rather than talked, and she did not look at her husband once throughout the meal.

At first the talk was very largely Charterson. He had no intention of coming to business with Blenker until Lady Harman had given place to the port and the man's nerves were steadier. He spoke of this and that in the large, dis-cursive way men use in clubs, and it was past the fish before the conversation settled down upon the topic of business organi-sation, and Sir Isaac, a little warmed by champagne, came out of the uneasily apprehensive taciturnity into which he had fallen in the presence of his wife. Horatio Blenker was keenly interested in the idealisation of commercial syndication, he had been greatly stirred by a book of Mr. Gerald Stanley Lee's called *Inspired Millionaires*, which set out to show just what magnificent airs rich men might give themselves, and he had done his best to catch its tone and to find *Inspired Million-aires* in Sir Isaac and Charterson, and to bring it to their notice and to the notice of the readers of the *Old Country Gazette*. He felt that if only Sir Isaac and Charterson would see getting rich as a great creative act it would raise their tone, and his tone, and the tone of the *Old Country Gazette* tremendously. It wouldn't, of course, materially alter the methods or policy of the paper, but it would make them all feel nobler, and Blenker was of that finer clay that does honestly want to feel nobler. He hated pessimism and all that criticism and self-examination that makes weak men pessimistic, he wanted to help weak men and be helped himself, he was all for that school of optimism that would have each dunghill was a well upholstered throne, and his nervous, starry contributions to the talk were like patches of water ranunculuses trying to flower in the overflow of a sewer.

Because you know it is idle to pretend that the talk of Charterson and Sir Isaac wasn't a heavy flow of base ideas ; they hadn't even the wit to sham very much about their social significance. They cared no more for the growth, the stamina, the spirit of the people whose lives they dominated than a rat cares for the stability of the house it gnaws. They *wanted* a broken-spirited people. They were in such relations wilfully and offensively stupid, and I do not see why we people who read and write books should pay this stupidity merely because it is prevalent even the mild tribute of an ironical civility. Charterson talked of the gathering trouble that might lead to a strike of the transport workers in London docks, and what he had to say, he said—he repeated it several times —was, " *Let* them strike. We're ready. The sooner they strike the better. Devonport's a man, and this time we'll *beat* 'em. . . .'"

He expanded generally on strikes. " It's a question practically whether we are to manage our own businesses or whether we're to have them managed for us. *Managed*, I say ! . . .''

" They know nothing, of course, of the details of organisation," said Blenker, shining with intelligence and looking quickly first to the right and then to the left. " Nothing."

Sir Isaac broke out into confirmatory matter. There was an idea in his head that this talk might open his wife's eyes to some sense of the magnitude of his commercial life, to the wonder of its scale and quality. He compared notes with Charterson upon a speeding-up system for delivery vans invented by an American specialist, and it made Blenker flush with admiration and turn, as if for sympathy, to Lady Harman to realise how a modification in a tail-board might mean a yearly saving in wages of many thousand pounds. " The sort of thing they don't understand," he said. And then Sir Isaac told of some of his own little devices. He had recently taken to having the returns of percentage increase and decrease from his various districts printed on post cards and circulated monthly among the district managers, post cards endorsed with such stimulating comments in red type as " Well done, Cardiff ! " or " What ails Portsmouth ? "—the results had been amazingly good ; " neck and neck work," he said, " everywhere ''—and thence they passed to the question of confidential reports and surprise inspectors. Thereby they came to the rights and wrongs of the waitress strike.

And then it was that Lady Harman began to take a share in the conversation.

" She interjected a question. " Yes," she said suddenly, and her interruption was so unexpected that all three men turned their eyes to her. " But how much do the girls get a week ? "

" I thought," she said, to some confused explanations

by Blenker and Charterson, " that gratuities were forbidden."

Blenker further explained that most of the girls of the class Sir Isaac was careful to employ lived at home. Their income was " supplementary."

" But what happens to the others who don't live at home, Mr. Blenker ? " she asked.

" Very small minority," said Mr. Blenker, reassuring himself about his glasses.

" But what do they do ? "

Charterson couldn't imagine whether she was going on in this way out of sheer ignorance or not.

" Sometimes their fines make big unexpected holes in their week's pay," she said.

Sir Isaac made some indistinct remark about " utter nonsense."

" It seems to me to be driving them straight upon the streets."

The phrase was Susan's. Its full significance wasn't at that time very clear to Lady Harman, and it was only when she had uttered it that she realised from Horatio Blenker's convulsive start just what a blow she had delivered at that table. His glasses came off again. He caught them and thrust them back, he seemed to be holding his nose on, holding his face on, preserving those carefully arranged features of himself from hideous revelations ; his free hand made weak movements with his dinner napkin. He seemed to be holding it in reserve against the ultimate failure of his face. Charterson surveyed her through an immense pause, open-mouthed ; then he turned his large, now frozen, amiability upon his host. " These are awful questions," he gasped, " rather beyond us, don't you think ? " and then magnificently : " Harman, things are looking pretty queer in the Far East again. I'm told there are chances—of revolution—even in Pekin. . . . "

Lady Harman became aware of Snagsby's arm and his steady, well-trained breathing beside her as, tenderly almost, but with a regretful disapproval, he removed her plate. . . .

§ 8

If Lady Harman had failed to remark at the time the deep impression her words had made upon her hearers, she would have learnt it later from the extraordinary wrath in which Sir Isaac, as soon as his guests had departed, visited her. He was so angry he broke the seal of silence he had set upon his lips. He came raging into the pink bedroom through the paper-covered door, as if they were back upon their old intimate footing. He brought a flavour of cigars and manly refreshment with him, his shirt front was a little splashed and crumpled, and his white face was variegated with flushed patches.

" What ever d'you mean," he cried, " by making a fool of

me in front of those fellers ? . . . What's my business got to do with you ? "

Lady Harman was too unready for a reply.

" I ask you what's my business got to do with you ? It's *my* affair, *my* side. You got no more right to go shoving your spoke into that than—anything. See ? What do *you* know of the rights and wrongs of business ? How can *you* tell what's right and what isn't right ? And the things you came out with —the things you came out with ! Why, Charterson—after you'd gone, Charterson said, she doesn't know, she can't know what she's talking about ! A decent woman ! a *lady* ! talking of driving girls on the street. You ought to be ashamed of yourself ! You aren't fit to show your face. . . . It's these damned .papers and pamphlets, all this blear-eyed stuff, these decadent novels and things putting narsty thoughts, *narsty*, *dirty* thoughts into decent women's heads. It ought to be rammed back down their throats, it ought to be put a stop to ! "

Sir Isaac suddenly gave way to woe. " What have I *done* ? " he cried, " what have I done ? Here's everything going so well ! We might be the happiest of couples ! We're rich, we got everything we want. . . . And then you go harbouring these ideas, fooling about with rotten people, taking up with Socialism—Yes, I tell you—Socialism ! "

His moment of pathos ended. " NO ! " he shouted in an enormous voice.

He became white and grim. He emphasised his next words with a shaken finger.

" It's got to end, my lady. It's going to end sooner than you expect. That's all ! . . . "

He paused at the papered door. He had a popular craving for a vivid curtain, and this he felt was just a little too mild.

" It's going to end," he repeated, and then with great violence, with almost alcoholic violence, with the round eyes and shouting voice and shaken fist and blaspheming violence, of a sordid, thrifty peasant enraged, " it's going to end a damned sight sooner than you expect."

CHAPTER EIGHT

SIR ISAAC AS PETRUCHIO

§ I

TWICE had Sir Isaac come near to betraying the rapid and extensive preparations for the subjugation of his wife, that he hid behind his silences. He hoped that their estrangement might be healed by a certain display of strength and decision. He still refused to let himself believe that all this trouble that had arisen between them, this sullen insistence upon unbecoming freedoms of intercourse and movement, this questioning spirit and a gaucherie of manner that might almost be mistaken for an aversion from his person, were due to any essential evil in her nature ; he clung almost passionately to the alternative that she was the victim of those gathering forces of discontent, of that interpretation which can only be described as decadent and that veracity which can only be called immodest, that darken the intellectual skies of our time, a sweet thing he held her still though touched by corruption, a prey to " idees," " idees " imparted from the poisoned mind of her sister, imbibed from the carelessly edited columns of newspapers, from all too laxly censored plays, from " blear-eyed " books—how he thanked the Archbishop of York for that clever, expressive epithet !—from the careless talk of rashly admitted guests, from the very atmosphere of London. And it had grown clearer and clearer to him that his duty to himself and the world and her was to remove her to a purer, simpler air, beyond the range of these infections, to isolate her and tranquillise her, and so win her back again to that acquiescence, that entirely hopeless submissiveness that had made her so sweet and dear a companion for him in the earlier years of their married life. Long before Lady Beach-Mandarin's crucial luncheon, his deliberate, foreseeing mind had been planning such a retreat, Black Strand, even at his first visit, had appeared to him in the light of a great opportunity, and the crisis of their quarrel did but release that same torrential energy which had carried him to a position of Napoleonic predominance in the world of baking, light catering, and confectionery, into the channels of a scheme already very definitely formed in his mind.

His first proceeding after the long hours of sleepless passion that had followed his wife's Hampton Court escapade, had been to place himself in communication with Mr. Brumley. He learnt at Mr. Brumley's club that that gentleman had slept there overnight and had started but a quarter of an hour before, back to Black Strand. Sir Isaac, in hot pursuit and gathering force and assistance in mid flight, reached Black Strand by midday.

It was with a certain twinge of the conscience that Mr. Brumley perceived his visitor, but it speedily became clear that Sir Isaac had no knowledge of the guilty circumstances of the day before. He had come to buy Black Strand—incontinently, that was all. He was going, it became clear at once, to buy it with all its fittings and furnishings as it stood —lock, stock, and barrel. Mr. Brumley, concealing that wild elation, that sense of a joyous rebirth, that only the liquidation of nearly all one's possessions can give, was firm but not excessive. Sir Isaac haggled as a wave breaks and then gave in, and presently they were making a memorandum upon the pretty writing-desk beneath the traditional rose Euphemia had established there when Mr. Brumley was young and already successful.

This done, and it was done in less than fifteen minutes, Sir Isaac produced a rather crumpled young architect from the motor-car as a conjurer might produce a rabbit from a hat, a builder from Aleham appeared astonishingly in a dog-cart—he had been summoned by telegram—and Sir Isaac began there and then to discuss alterations, enlargements, and, more particularly, with a view to his nursery require-ments, the conversion of the empty barn into a nursery wing and its connection with the house by a corridor across the shrubbery.

" It will take you three months," said the builder from Aleham. " And the worst time of the year coming."

" It won't take three weeks—if I have to bring down a young army from London to do it," said Sir Isaac.

" But such a thing as plastering—— "

" We won't have plastering."

" There's canvas and paper, of course," said the young architect.

" There's canvas and paper," said Sir Isaac. " And those new patent building units, so far as the corridor goes. I've seen the ads."

" We can whitewash 'em. They won't show much," said the young architect.

" Oh, if you do things in *that* way," said the builder from Aleham, with bitter resignation. . . .

§ 2

The morning dawned at last when the surprise was ripe. It was four days after Susan's visit, and she was due again on the morrow with the money that would enable her employer to go to Lady Viping's now imminent dinner. Lady Harman had had to cut the Social Friends' meeting altogether, but the day before the surprise Agatha Alimony had come to tea in her jobbed car, and they had gone together to the committee meeting of the Shakespeare Dinner Society. Sir Isaac had ignored that defiance, and it was an unusually confident and quite unsuspicious woman who descended in a warm October sunshine to the surprise. In the breakfast-room she discovered an awe-stricken Snagsby standing with his plate-basket before her husband, and her husband wearing strange, unusual tweeds and gaiters—buttoned gaiters, and standing astraddle —unusually astraddle, on the hearthrug.

" That's enough, Snagsby," said Sir Isaac, at her entrance. " Bring it all."

She met Snagsby's eye, and it was portentous.

Latterly Snagsby's eye had lost the assurance of his former days. She had noted it before, she noted it now more than ever · as though he was losing confidence, as though he was beginning to doubt, as though the world he had once seemed to rule grew insecure beneath his feet. For a moment she met his eye ; it might have been a warning he conveyed, it might have been an appeal for sympathy, and then he had gone. She looked at the table. Sir Isaac had breakfasted acutely.

In silence, among the wreckage, and with a certain wonder growing, Lady Harman attended to her needs.

Sir Isaac cleared his throat.

She became aware that he had spoken. " What did you say, Isaac ? " she asked, looking up. He seemed to have widened his straddle almost dangerously, and he spoke with a certain conscious forcefulness.

" We're going to move out of this house, Elly," he said. " We're going down into the country right away."

She sat back in her chair and regarded his pinched and determined visage.

" What do you mean ? " she asked.

" I've bought that house of Brumley's—Black Strand. We're going to move down there—*now*. I've told the servants. . . . When you've done your breakfast you'd better get Peters to pack your things. The big car's going to be ready at half-past ten."

Lady Harman reflected.

" To-morrow evening," she said, " I was going out to dinner at Lady Viping's."

" Not my affair—seemingly," said Sir Isaac, with irony. " Well, the car's going to be ready at half-past ten."

" But that dinner—— ! "

" We'll think about it when the time comes."

Husband and wife regarded each other.

" I've had about enough of London," said Sir Isaac. " So we're going to shift the scenery. See ? "

Lady Harman felt that one might adduce good arguments against this course, if only one knew of them.

Sir Isaac had a bright idea. He rang.

" Snagsby," he said, " just tell Peters to pack up Lady Harman's things. . . . "

" *Well !* " said Lady Harman, as the door closed on Snagsby. Her mind was full of confused protest, but she had again that entirely feminine and demoralising conviction that if she tried to express it she would weep or stumble into some such emotional disaster. If now she went upstairs and told Peters *not* to pack—— !

Sir Isaac walked slowly to the window, and stood for a time staring out into the garden.

Extraordinary bumpings began overhead in Sir Isaac's room. No doubt somebody was packing something. . . .

Lady Harman realised with a deepening humiliation that she dared not dispute before the servants, and that he could. " But the children—— " she said at last.

" I've told Mrs. Harblow," he said, over his shoulder.
" Told her it was a bit of a surprise." He turned, with a
momentary lapse into something like humour. " You see,"
he said, " it *is* a bit of a surprise."

" But what are you going to do with this house ? "

" Lock it all up for a bit. . . . I don't see any sense in
living where we aren't happy. Perhaps down there we shall
manage better. . . . "

It emerged from the confusion of Lady Harman's mind
that perhaps she had better go to the nursery, and see how
things were getting on there. Sir Isaac watched her departure
with a slightly dubious eye, made little noises with his teeth
for a time, and then went towards the telephone.

In the hall she found two strange young men in green aprons
assisting the under-butler to remove the hats and overcoats
and such-like personal material into a motor-van outside.
She heard two of the housemaids scurrying upstairs. " 'Arf
an hour," said one, " isn't what I call a proper time to pack
a box in."

In the nursery the children were disputing furiously what
toys were to be taken into the country.

Lady Harman was a very greatly astonished woman. The
surprise had been entirely successful.

§ 3

It has been said, I think, by Limburger, in his already cited
work, that nothing so excites and prevails with women as
rapid and extensive violence, sparing and yet centring upon
herself, and certainly it has to be recorded that, so far from
being merely indignant, and otherwise a helplessly pathetic
spectacle, Lady Harman found, though perhaps she did not
go quite so far as to admit to herself that she found, this
vehement flight from the social, moral, and intellectual con-
taminations of London an experience not merely stimulating
but entertaining. It lifted her delicate eyebrows. Something,
it may have been a sense of her own comparative immobility
amid this sudden extraordinary bustle of her home, put it
into her head that so it was long ago that Lot must have
bundled together his removable domesticities.

She made one attempt at protest. " Isaac," she said, " isn't
all this rather ridiculous—— "

" Don't speak to me ! " he answered, waving her off. " Don't
speak to me ! You should have spoken before, Elly. *Now*
—things are happening."

The image of Black Strand, as, after all, a very pleasant
place indeed returned to her. She adjudicated upon the
nursery difficulties, and then went in a dream-like state of
mind to preside over her own more personal packing. She
found Peters exercising all that indecisive helplessness which
is characteristic of ladies' maids the whole world over.

It was from Peters she learnt that the entire household, men and maids together, was to be hurled into Surrey. " Aren't they all rather surprised ?" asked Lady Harman.

" Yes, m'm," said Peters on her knees, " but of course if the drains is wrong the sooner we all go the better."

(So that was what he had told them.)

A vibration and a noise of purring machinery outside drew the lady to the window, and she discovered that at least four of the large motor-vans from the International Stores were to co-operate in the trek. There they were waiting, massive and uniform. And then she saw Snagsby in his alpaca jacket *running* towards the house from the gates. Of course he was running only very slightly indeed, but still he was running, and the expression of distress upon his face convinced her that he was being urged to unusual and indeed unsuitable tasks under the immediate personal supervision of Sir Isaac. . . . Then from round the corner appeared the under-butler, or at least the legs of him going very fast, under a pile of shirt boxes and things belonging to Sir Isaac. He dumped them into the nearest van and heaved a deep sigh, and returned houseward after a remorseful glance at the windows.

A violent outcry from baby, who, with more than her customary violence was making her customary morning protest against being clad, recalled Lady Harman from the contemplation of these exterior activities. . . .

The journey to Black Strand was not accomplished without misadventure ; there was a puncture near Farnham, and as Clarence with a leisurely assurance entertained himself with the Stepney, they were passed first by the second car with the nursery contingent, which went by in a shrill chorus, crying, " *We-e-e* shall get there first, *We-e-e* shall get there first," and then by a large hired car all agog with housemaids and Mrs. Crumble, and with Snagsby, as round and distressed as the full moon, and the under-butler, cramped and keen beside the driver. There followed the leading International Stores car, and then the Stepney was on and they could hasten in pursuit. . . .

And at last they came to Black Strand, and when they saw Black Strand it seemed to Lady Harman that the place had blown out a huge inflamed red cheek, and lost its pleasant balance altogether. " *Oh !* " she cried.

It was the old barn flushed by the strain of adaptation to a new use, its comfortable old wall ruptured by half a dozen brilliant new windows, a light red chimney stack at one end. From it a vividly artistic corridor ran to the house, and the rest of the shrubbery was all trampled and littered with sheds, bricks, poles, and material generally. Black Strand had left the hands of the dilettante school and was in the grip of those vigorous moulding forces that are shaping our civilisation to-day.

The jasmine wig over the porch had suffered a strenuous clipping ; the door might have just come out of prison.   In the hall the Carpaccio copies still glowed, but there were dust sheets over most of the furniture, and a plumber was moving his things out with that eleventh-hour reluctance so characteristic of plumbers. Mrs. Rabbit, a little tearful, and dressed for departure very respectably in black, was giving the youngest and least experienced housemaid a faithful history of Mr. Brumley's earlier period.   "'Appy we all was," said Mrs. Rabbit, " as birds in a nest."

Through the windows two of the Putney gardeners were busy replacing Mr. Brumley's doubtful roses by recognised sorts, the *right* sorts. . . .

" I've been doing all I can to make it ready for you," said Sir Isaac at his wife's ear, bringing a curious reminiscence of the first home-coming to Putney into her mind.

§ 4

" And now," said Sir Isaac, with evident premeditation and a certain deliberate amiability, " now we got down here, now we got away a bit from all those London things, with nobody to cut in between us, me and you can have a bit of a talk, Elly, and see what it's all about."

They had lunched together in the little hall dining-room— the children had had a noisily cheerful picnic in the kitchen with Mrs. Harblow, and now Lady Harman was standing at the window surveying the ravages of rose replacement.

She turned towards him " Yes," she said.   " I think—I think we can't go on like this."

" *I* can't," said Sir Isaac, " anyhow."

He too came and stared at the rose planting.

" If we were to go up there—among the pine woods "— he pointed with his head at the dark background of Euphemia's herbaceous borders—" we shouldn't hear quite so much of this hammering. . . . "

Husband and wife walked slowly in the afternoon sunlight across the still beautiful garden. Each was gravely aware of an embarrassed incapacity for the task they had set themselves. They were going to talk things over. Never in their lives had they really talked to each other clearly and honestly about anything. Indeed it is scarcely too much to say that neither had ever talked about anything to any one. She was too young, her mind was now growing up in her and feeling its way to conscious expression, and he had never before wanted to express himself. He did now want to express himself. For behind his rant and fury Sir Isaac had been thinking very hard indeed during the last three weeks about his life and her life, and their relations ; he had never thought so much about anything except his business economics. So far, he had either

joked at her, talked " silly " to her, made, as they say, " remarks," or vociferated. That had been the sum of their mental
intercourse, as indeed it is the sum of the intercourse of most
married couples. His attempt to state his case to her had so
far always flared into rhetorical outbreaks. But he was discontented with these rhetorical outbreaks. His dispositions
to fall into them made him rather like a nervous sepia that
cannot keep its ink sac quiet while it is sitting for its portrait.
In the earnestness of his attempt at self-display, he vanished
in his own outpourings.

He wanted now to reason with her simply and persuasively.
He wanted to say quietly impressive and convincing things
in a low tone of voice and make her abandon every possible
view except his view. He walked now slowly meditating the
task before him, making a faint, thoughtful noise with his
teeth, his head sunken in the collar of the motor overcoat he
wore because of a slight cold he had caught. And he had to
be careful about colds because of his constitutional defect.
She too felt she had much to say. Much too she had in her
mind that she couldn't say, because this strange quarrel had
opened unanticipated things for her ; she had found and
considered repugnances in her nature she had never dared to
glance at hitherto. . . .

Sir Isaac began rather haltingly when they had reached a
sandy, ant-infested path that ran slantingly up among the
trees. He affected a certain perplexity. He said he did not
understand what it was his wife was " after," what she " thought
she was doing " in " making all this trouble " ; he wanted to
know just what it was she wanted, how she thought they ought
to live, just what she considered his rights were as her husband,
and just what she considered were her duties as his wife—if,
that is, she considered she had any duties. To these inquiries
Lady Harman made no definite reply ; their estrangement
instead of clearing her mind had on the whole perplexed it
more, by making her realise the height and depth and extent
of her possible separation from him. She replied, therefore,
with an unsatisfactory vagueness ; she said she wanted to
feel that she possessed herself, that she was no longer a child,
that she thought she had a right to read what she chose, see
what people she liked, go out a little by herself, have a certain
independence—she hesitated, " have a certain definite allowance of my own."

" Have I ever refused you money ? " cried Sir Isaac, protesting.

" It isn't that," said Lady Harman ; it's the feeling—— "

" The feeling of being able to—defy—anything I say," said
Sir Isaac, with a note of bitterness. " As if I didn't understand ! "

It was beyond Lady Harman's powers to express just how
that wasn't the precise statement of the case.

Sir Isaac, reverting to his tone of almost elaborate reasonableness, expanded his view that it was impossible for husband and wife to have two different sets of friends ;—let alone every other consideration, he explained, it wasn't convenient for them not to be about together, and as for reading or thinking what she chose he had never made any objection to anything, unless it was " decadent rot " that any decent man would object to his womanfolk seeing, rot she couldn't understand the drift of—fortunately. Blear-eyed humbug. . . . He checked himself on the verge of an almost archiepiscopal outbreak in order to be patiently reasonable again. He was prepared to concede that it would be very nice if Lady Harman could be a good wife and also an entirely independent person, very nice, but the point was—his tone verged on the ironical —that she couldn't be two entirely different people at the same time.

" But you have your friends," she said, " you go away alone—— "

" That's different," said Sir Isaac, with a momentary note of annoyance. " It's business. It isn't that I want to."

Lady Harman had a feeling that they were neither of them gaining any ground. She blamed herself for her lack of lucidity. She began again, taking up the matter at a fresh point. She said that her life at present wasn't full, that it was only half a life, that it was just home and marriage and nothing else ; he had his business, he went out into the world, he had politics, and—" all sorts of things " ; she hadn't these interests ; she had nothing in place of them——

Sir Isaac closed this opening rather abruptly by telling her that she should count herself lucky she hadn't, and again the conversation was suspended for a time.

" But I want to know about these things," she said.

Sir Isaac took that musingly.

" There's things go on," she said ; " outside home. There's social work, there's interests—— Am I never to take any part—in that ? "

Sir Isaac still reflected.

" There's one thing," he said at last, " I want to know. We'd better have it out—*now*."

But he hesitated for a time.

" Elly ! " he blundered, " you aren't—you aren't getting somehow—not fond of me ? "

She made no immediate reply.

" Look here ! " he said in an altered voice. " Elly ! there isn't something below all this ? There isn't something been going on that I don't know ? "

Her eyes, with a certain terror in their depths, questioned him.

" Something," he said, and his face was deadly white— " *Some other man, Elly ?* "

She was suddenly crimson, a flaming indignation.

" Isaac ! " she said, " what do you *mean* ? How can you *ask* such a thing ? "

" If it's that ! " said Sir Isaac, his face suddenly full of malignant force, " I'll—— But I'd *kill* you. . . ."

" If it isn't that," he went on, searching his mind ; " why should a woman get restless ? Why should she want to go away from her husband, go meeting other people, go gadding about ? If a woman's satisfied, she's satisfied. She doesn't harbour fancies. . . . All this grumbling and unrest. Natural for your sister, but why should you ? You've got everything a woman needs, husband, children, a perfectly splendid home, clothes, good jewels, and plenty of them, respect ! Why should you want to go out after things ? It's mere spoilt-childishness. Of course you want to wander out—and if there isn't a man——"

He caught her wrist suddenly. " There isn't a man ? " he demanded.

" Isaac ! " she protested in horror.

" Then there'll be one. You think I'm a fool, you think I don't know anything all these literary and society people know. I *do* know. I know that a man and a woman have got to stick together, and if you go straying—you may think you're straying after the moon or social work, or anything—but there's a strange man waiting round the corner for every woman, and a strange woman for every man. Think *I've* had no temptations ? . . . Oh ! I *know*, I *know*. What's life or anything, but that ? and it's just because we've not gone on having more children, just because we listened to all those fools who said you were overdoing it, that all this fretting and grumbling began. We've got on to the wrong track, Elly, and we've got to get back to plain, wholesome ways of living. See ? That's what I've come down here for, and what I mean to do. We've got to save ourselves. I've been too—too modern and all that. I'm going to be a husband as a husband should. I'm going to protect you from these idees—protect you from your own self. . . . And that's about where we stand, Elly, as I make it out."

He paused with the effect of having delivered himself of a long, premeditated thing.

Lady Harman essayed to speak. But she found that directly she set herself to speak she sobbed and began weeping. She choked for a moment. Then she determined she would go on, and if she must cry, she must cry. She couldn't let a disposition to tears seal her in silence for ever.

" It isn't," she said, " what I expected—of life. It isn't——"

" It's what life is," Sir Isaac cut in.

" When I think," she sobbed, " of what I've lost——"

" *Lost !* " cried Sir Isaac. " Lost ! Oh, come now, Elly, I like that. What !—*lost*. Hang it ! You got to look facts in

the face. You can't deny—— Marrying like this—you made a
jolly good thing of it."

" But the beautiful things, the noble things ! "

" *What's* beautiful ? " cried Sir Isaac in protesting scorn.
" *What's* noble ?   ROT ! Doing your duty if you like, and
being sensible, that's noble and beautiful, but not fretting
about and running yourself into danger.   You've got to have
a sense of humour, Elly, in this life——" He created a quotation. " As you make your bed—so shall you lie."

For an interval neither of them spoke. They crested the
hill, and came into view of that advertisement board she had
first seen in Mr. Brumley's company.   She halted, and he
went a step farther and halted too.   He recalled his ideas about
the board. He had meant to have them all altered, but other
things had driven it from his mind. . . .

" Then you mean to imprison me here," said Lady Harman
to his back. He turned about.

" It isn't much like a prison. I'm asking you to stay here—
and be what a wife *should* be."

" I'm to have no money."

" That's—that depends entirely on yourself. You know
that well enough."

She looked at him gravely.

" I won't stand it," she said at last, with a gentle deliberation.

She spoke so softly that he doubted his hearing. " *What ?* "
he asked sharply.

" I won't stand it," she repeated. " No."

" But—what can you do ? "

" I don't know," she said, after a moment of grave consideration.

For some moments his mind hunted among possibilities.

" It's me that's standing it," he said. He came closely up
to her. He seemed on the verge of rhetoric. He pressed his
thin white lips together. " Standing it ! when we might be so
happy," he snapped, and shrugged his shoulders and turned
with an expression of mournful resolution towards the house
again. She followed slowly.

He felt that he had done all that a patient and reasonable
husband could do. *Now*—things must take their course.

§ 5

The imprisonment of Lady Harman at Black Strand lasted
just one day short of a fortnight.

For all that time except for such interludes as the urgent
needs of the strike demanded, Sir Isaac devoted himself to
the siege. He did all he could to make her realise how re-
strainedly he used the powers the law vests in a husband, how
little he forced upon her the facts of marital authority and
wifely duty. At times he sulked, at times he affected a cold

dignity, and at times a virile anger swayed him at her unsub-
missive silences. He gave her little peace in that struggle, a
struggle that came to the edge of physical conflict. There
were moments when it seemed to her that nothing remained
but that good old-fashioned connubial institution, the tussle
for the upper hand, when with a feminine horror she felt
violence shouldering her shoulder or contracting ready to grip
her wrist. Against violence she doubted her strength, was
filled with a desolating sense of yielding nerve and domitable
muscle. But just short of violence Sir Isaac's spirit failed him.
He would glower and bluster, half threaten, and retreat. It
might come to that at last, but at present it had not come to
that.

She could not understand why she had neither message nor
sign from Susan Burnet, but she hid that anxiety and disappointment under her general dignity.

She spent as much time with the children as she could, and
until Sir Isaac locked up the piano she played, and was surprised to find far more in Chopin than she had ever suspected
in the days when she had acquired a passable dexterity of
execution. She found, indeed, the most curious things in
Chopin, emotional phrases, that stirred and perplexed and
yet pleased her. . . .

The weather was very fine and open that year. A golden
sunshine from October passed on into November, and Lady
Harman spent many of these days amidst the pretty things
the builder from Aleham had been too hurried to desecrate,
dump, burn upon, and flatten into indistinguishable mire,
after the established custom of builders in gardens since the
world began. She would sit in the rockery, where she had sat
with Mr. Brumley, and recall that momentous conversation,
and she would wander up the pinewood slopes behind, and she
would spend long, musing intervals among Euphemia's perennials, thinking sometimes, and sometimes not so much thinking
as feeling the warm tendernesses of nature and the perplexing
difficulties of human life. With an amused amazement Lady
Harman reflected as she walked about the pretty borders and
the little patches of lawn and orchard, that in this very place
she was to have realised an imitation of the immortal " Elizabeth," and have been wise, witty, gay, defiant, gallant, and
entirely successful with her " Man of Wrath." Evidently
there was some temperamental difference, or something in her
situation, that altered the values of the affair. It was clearly
a different sort of man for one thing. She didn't feel a bit gay,
and her profound and deepening indignation with the alternative to this stagnation was tainted by a sense of weakness and
incapacity.

She came very near surrender several times. There were
afternoons of belated, ripened warmth, a kind of summer that
had been long in the bottle, with a certain lassitude in the air

and a blue haze among the trees, that made her feel the folly of all resistances to fate.   Why, after all, shouldn't she take life as she found it, that is to say, as Sir Isaac was prepared to give it to her ?   He wasn't really so bad, she told herself. The children—their noses were certainly a little sharp, but there might be worse children. The next might take after herself more. Who was she to turn upon her appointed life and declare it wasn't good enough ?   Whatever happened, the world was still full of generous and beautiful things—trees, flowers, sunset and sunrise, music and mist and morning dew. . . . And as for this matter of the sweated workers, the harshness of the business, the ungracious competition, suppose if, instead of fighting her husband with her weak powers, she persuaded him.   She tried to imagine just exactly how he might be persuaded. . . .

She looked up and discovered with an extraordinary amazement, Mr. Brumley with eager gestures and a flushed and excited visage hurrying towards her across the croquet lawn.

§ 6

Lady Viping's dinner-party had been kept waiting exactly thirty-five minutes for Lady Harman. Sir Isaac, with a certain excess of zeal, had intercepted the hasty note his wife had written to account for her probable absence. The party was to have centred entirely upon Lady Harman, it consisted either of people who knew her already, or of people who were to have been specially privileged to know her, and Lady Viping telephoned twice to Putney before she abandoned hope.   " It's disconnected," she said, returning in despair from her second struggle with the great public service.   " They can't get a reply."

" It's that little wretch," said Lady Beach-Mandarin. " He hasn't let her come. *I* know him."

" It's like losing a front tooth," said Lady Viping, surveying her table as she entered the dining-room.

" But surely—she would have written," said Mr. Brumley, troubled and disappointed, regarding an aching gap to the left of his chair, a gap upon which a pathetic little card bearing Lady Harman's name still lay obliquely.

Naturally the talk tended to centre upon the Harmans. And naturally Lady Beach-Mandarin was very bold and outspoken, and called Sir Isaac quite a number of vivid things. She also aired her views of the marriage of the future which involved a very stringent treatment of husbands indeed. " Half his property and half his income," said Lady Beach-mandarin, " paid into her separate banking account."

" But," protested Mr. Brumley, " would men marry under those conditions ? "

" Men will marry anyhow," said Lady Beach-Mandarin, " under *any* conditions."

" Exactly Sir Joshua's opinion, said Lady Viping.

All the ladies at the table concurred, and only one cheerful bachelor barrister dissented. The other men became gloomy, and betrayed a distaste for this general question. Even Mr. Brumley felt a curious faint terror, and had for a moment a glimpse of the possibilities that might lie behind the Vote. Lady Beach-Mandarin went bouncing back to the particular instance. At present, she said, witness Lady Harman, women were slaves, pampered slaves, if you will, but slaves. As things were now, there was nothing to keep a man from locking up his wife, opening all her letters, dressing her in sackcloth, separating her from her children. Most men, of course, didn't do such things, they were amenable to public opinion, but Sir Isaac was a jealous little Ogre. He was a gnome who carried off a princess. . . .

She threw out projects for assailing the Ogre. She would descend to-morrow morning upon the Putney house, a living flamboyant writ of Habeas Corpus. Mr Brumley, who had been putting two and two together, was abruptly moved to tell of the sale of Black Strand. " They may be there," she said.

" He's carried her off," cried Lady Beach-Mandarin on a top note. " It might be the eighteenth century for all he cares. But if it's Black Strand—I'll go to Black Strand. . . . "

But she had to talk about it for a week before she actually made her raid, and then, with an instinctive need for an audience she took with her a certain Miss Garradice, one of those mute, emotional, nervous spinsters, who drift detachedly, with quick, sudden movements, glittering eyeglasses, and a pent-up, imminent look, about our social system. There is something about this type of womanhood—it is hard to say— almost as though they were the bottled souls of departed buccaneers grown somehow virginal. She came with Lady Beach-Mandarin quietly, almost humorously, and yet it was as if the pirate glittered dimly visible through the polished glass of her erect exterior.

" Here we are ! " said Lady Beach-Mandarin, staring astonished at the once familiar porch. " Now for it ! "

She descended and assailed the bells herself, and Miss Garradice stood beside her with the light of combat in her eyes and glasses and cheeks.

" Shall I offer to take her for a drive ? "

" Let's," said Miss Garradice in an enthusiastic whisper. " Right away ! For ever."

" I will," said Lady Beach-Mandarin, and nodded desperately.

She was on the point of ringing again when Snagsby appeared. He stood with a large obstructiveness in the doorway. " Lady 'Arman, my lady," he said, with a well-trained deliberation, " is not a tome."

" Not at home ? " queried Lady Beach-Mandarin.

" Not a tome, my lady," repeated Snagsby invincibly.

" But—when will she be at home ? "

" I can't say, my lady."

" Is Sir Isaac—— ? "

" Sir Isaac, my lady, is not a tome. Nobody is a tome, my lady."

" But we've come from London ! " said Lady Beach-Mandarin.

" I'm very sorry, my lady."

" You see, I want my friend to see this house and garden."

Snagsby was visibly disconcerted. " I 'ave no instructions, my lady," he tried.

" Oh, but Lady Harman would never object—— "

Snagsby's confusion increased. He seemed to be wanting to keep his face to the visitors and at the same time glance over his shoulder. " I will," he considered, " I will inquire, my lady." He backed a little, and seemed inclined to close the door upon them. Lady Beach-Mandarin was too quick for him. She got herself well into the open doorway. "And of whom are you going to inquire ? "

A large distress betrayed itself in Snagsby's eye. " The 'ousekeeper," he attempted. " It falls to the 'ousekeeper, my lady."

Lady Beach-Mandarin turned her face to Miss Garradice shining in support. " Stuff and nonsense," she said, " of course we shall come in." And with a wonderful movement that was at once powerful and perfectly lady-like, this intrepid woman—" butted " is not the word—collided herself with Snagsby and hurled him backward into the hall. Miss Garradice followed closely behind and at once extended herself in open order on Lady Beach-Mandarin's right. " Go and inquire," said Lady Beach-Mandarin, with a sweeping gesture of her arm. " Go and inquire."

For a moment Snagsby surveyed the invasion with horror, and then fled precipitately into the recesses of the house.

" Of *course* they're at home ! " said Lady Beach-Mandarin. " Fancy that—that—that *navigable*—trying to shut the door on us ! "

For a moment the two brightly excited ladies surveyed each other, and then Lady Beach-Mandarin, with a quickness of movement wonderful in one so abundant, began to open first one and then another of the various doors that opened into the long hall-living-room. At a peculiar little cry from Miss Garradice she turned from a contemplation of the long low study in which so much of the Euphemia books had been written, to discover Sir Isaac behind her, closely followed by an agonised Snagsby.

" A-a-a-h ! " she cried, with both hands extended, " and so you've come in, Sir Isaac ! That's perfectly delightfu

This is my friend Miss Garradice, who's *dying* to see anything you've left of poor Euphemia's garden. And *how* is dear Lady Harman ? "

For some crucial moments Sir Isaac was unable to speak, and regarded his visitors with an expression that was unpretendingly criminal.

Then he found speech. " You can't," he said. " It—can't be managed." He shook his head ; his lips were whitely compressed.

" But all the way from London, Sir Isaac ! "

" Lady Harman's ill," lied Sir Isaac. " She mustn't be disturbed. Everything has to be kept quiet. See ? Not even shouting. Not even ordinarily raised voices. A voice like yours—might kill her. That's why Snagsby here said we were not at home. We aren't at home—not to any one."

Lady Beach-Mandarin was baffled.

" Snagsby," said Sir Isaac, " open that door."

" But can't I see her—just for a moment ? "

Sir Isaac's malignity had softened a little at the prospect of victory. " Absolutely impossible," he said. " Everything disturbs her, every tiny thing. You—— You'd be certain to."

Lady Beach-Mandarin looked at her companion, and it was manifest that she was at the end of her resources. Miss Garradice, after the fashion of highly strung spinsters, suddenly felt disappointed in her leader. It wasn't, her silence intimated, for her to offer suggestions.

The ladies were defeated. When at last that stiff interval ended their dresses rustled doorward, and Sir Isaac broke out into the civilities of a victor. . . .

It was only when they were a mile away from Black Strand that fluent speech returned to Lady Beach-Mandarin. " The little—Crippen," she said. " He's got her locked up in some cellar. . . . Horrid little face he has ! He looked like a rat at bay."

" I think perhaps if we'd done *differently*," said Miss Garradice, in a tone of critical irresponsibility.

" I'll write to her. That's what I'll do," said Lady Beach-Mandarin, contemplating her next step. " I'm really—concerned. And didn't you feel—something sinister. That butler-man's expression—a kind of round horror."

That very evening she told it all—it was almost the trial trip of the story—to Mr. Brumley. . . .

Sir Isaac watched their departure furtively from the study window, and then ran out to the garden. He went right through into the pine woods beyond and presently, far away up the slopes, he saw his wife loitering down towards him, a gracious white tallness touched by a ray of sunlight—and without a suspicion of how nearly rescue had come to her.

§ 7

So you see under what excitement Mr. Brumley came down to Black Strand.

Luck was with him at first, and he forced the defence with ridiculous ease.

" Lady Harman, sir, is not a tome," said Snagsby.

" Ah ! " said Mr. Brumley, with all the assurance of a former proprietor, " then I'll just have a look round the garden," and was through the green door in the wall and round the barn end before Snagsby's mind could function. That unfortunate man went as far as the green door in pursuit, and then with a gesture of despair retreated to the pantry and began cleaning all his silver to calm his agonised spirit. He could pretend, perhaps, that Mr. Brumley had never rung at the front door at all. If not——

Moreover Mr. Brumley had the good fortune to find Lady Harman quite unattended and pensive upon the little seat that Euphemia had placed for the better seeing of her herbaceous borders.

" Lady Harman ! " he said rather breathlessly, taking both her hands with an unwonted assurance, and then sitting down beside her, " I am so glad to see you. I came down to see you—to see if I couldn't be of any service to you."

" It's so kind of you to come," she said, and her dark eyes said as much or more. She glanced round, and he too glanced round for Sir Isaac.

" You see," he said. " I don't know. . . . I don't want to be impertinent. . . . But I feel—if I can be of any service to you. . . . I feel perhaps you want help here. I don't want to seem to be taking advantage of a situation. Or making unwarrantable assumptions. But I want to assure you—I would willingly die—if only I could do anything. . . . Ever since I first saw you."

He said all this in a distracted way, with his eyes going about the garden for the possible apparition of Sir Isaac, and all the time his sense of possible observers made him assume an attitude as though he was engaged in the smallest of small talk. Her colour quickened at the import of his words, and emotion, very rich and abundant emotion, its various factors not altogether untouched, perhaps, by the spirit of laughter, lit her eyes. She doubted a little what he was saying, and yet she had anticipated that somehow, some day, in quite other circumstances, Mr. Brumley might break into some such strain.

" You see," he went on, with a quality of appeal in his eyes, " there's so little time to say things—without possible interruption. I feel you are in difficulties, and I want to make you understand—— We—— Every beautiful woman, I suppose, has a sort of right to a certain sort of man. I want

to tell you—I'm not really presuming to make love to you
—but I want to tell you I am altogether yours, altogether
at your service. I've had sleepless nights. All this time I've
been thinking about you. I'm quite clear, I haven't a doubt,
I'll do anything for you, without reward, without return, I'll
be your devoted brother, anything, if only you'll make use
of me. . . ."

Her colour quickened. She looked around and still no
one appeared. "It's so kind of you to come like this," she
said. "You say things—— But I *have* felt that you wanted
to be brotherly. . . ."

"Whatever I *can* be," assured Mr. Brumley.

"My situation here," she said, her dark frankness of gaze
meeting his troubled eyes. "It's so strange and difficult.
I don't know what to do. I don't know—what I *want* to do. . . ."

"In London," said Mr. Brumley, "they think—they say
—you have been taken off—brought down here—to a sort of
captivity."

"I *have*," admitted Lady Harman, with a note of recalled
astonishment in her voice.

"If I can help you to escape——! "

"But where can I escape ? "

And one must admit that it is a little difficult to indicate
a correct refuge for a lady who finds her home intolerable.
Of course there was Mrs. Sawbridge, but Lady Harman felt
that her mother's disposition to lock herself into her bedroom
at the slightest provocation made her a weak support for
a defensive fight, and in addition that boarding-house at
Bournemouth did not attract her. Yet what other wall in
all the world was there for Lady Harman to set her back
against ? During the last few days Mr. Brumley's mind had
been busy with the details of impassioned elopements conducted in the most exalted spirit, but now in the actual
presence of the lady these projects did in the most remarkable
manner vanish.

"Couldn't you," he said at last, "go somewhere ? " And
then with an air of being meticulously explicit. "I mean,
isn't there somewhere, where you might safely go ? "

(And in his dreams he had been crossing high passes with her ;
he had halted suddenly and stayed her mule. In his dream,
because he was a man of letters and a poet, it was always
a mule, never a *train de luxe.* "Look," he had said, "below
there—*Italy !*—the country you have never seen before.")

"There's nowhere," she answered.

"No *where* ? " asked Mr. Brumley, "and how ? " with
the tone and something of the gesture of one who racks his
mind. "If you only trust yourself to me—— Oh ! Lady
Harman, if I dared ask it——"

He became aware of Sir Isaac walking across the lawn
towards them. . . .

The two men greeted each other with a reasonable cordiality
" I wanted to see how you were getting on down here," said
Mr. Brumley, " and whether there was anything I could do
for you."

" We're getting on all right," said Sir Isaac, with no manifest
glow of gratitude.

" You've altered the old barn—tremendously."

" Come and see it," said Sir Isaac. " It's a wing."

Mr. Brumley remained seated. " It was the first thing that
struck me, Lady Harman. This evidence of Sir Isaac's energy.'

" Come and look over it," Sir Isaac persisted.

Mr. Brumley and Lady Harman rose together.

" One's enough to show him that," said Sir Isaac.

" I was telling Lady Harman how much we missed her at
Lady Viping's, Sir Isaac."

" It was on account of the drains," Sir Isaac explained.
" You can't—it's foolhardy to stay a day when the drains
are wrong, dinners or no dinners."

" You know *I* was extremely sorry not to come to Lady
Viping's. I hope you'll tell her. I wrote."

But Mr. Brumley didn't remember clearly enough to make
any use of that.

" Everybody naturally *is* sorry on an occasion of that
sort," said Sir Isaac. " But you come and see what we've
done in that barn. In three weeks. They couldn't have got
it together in three months ten years ago. It's—system."

Mr. Brumley still tried to cling to Lady Harman. " Have
you been interested in this building ? " he asked.

" I still don't understand the system of the corridor," she
said, rising a little belatedly to the occasion. " I *will* come."

Sir Isaac regarded her for a moment with a dubious expression and then began to explain the new method of building
with large prepared units and shaped pieces of reinforced
concrete instead of separate bricks that Messrs. Prothero and
Cuthbertson had organised, and which had enabled him to
create this artistic corridor so simply. It was a rather uncomfortable three-cornered conversation, Sir Isaac addressed his
exposition exclusively to Mr. Brumley, and Mr. Brumley made
repeated ineffectual attempts to bring Lady Harman, and
Lady Harman made repeated ineffectual attempts to bring
herself into a position in the conversation.

Their eyes met, the glow of Mr. Brumley's declarations
remained with them, but neither dared risk any phrase that
might arouse Sir Isaac's suspicions or escape his acuteness.
And when they had gone through the new additions pretty
thoroughly—the plumbers were still busy with the barn bathroom—Sir Isaac asked Mr. Brumley if there was anything
more he would like to see. In the slight pause that ensued
Lady Harman suggested tea. But tea gave them no opportunity of resuming their interrupted conversation, and as

Sir Isaac's invincible determination to shadow his visitor until he was well off the premises became more and more unmistakable—he made it quite ungraciously unmistakable,—Mr. Brumley's inventiveness failed. One thing came to him suddenly, but it led to nothing of any service to him.

"But I heard you were dangerously ill, Lady Harman!" he cried. "Lady Beach-Mandarin called here——"

"But when?" asked Lady Harman, astonished over the tea-things.

"But you *know* she called!" said Mr. Brumley, and looked in affected reproach at Sir Isaac.

"I've not been ill at all!"

"Sir Isaac told her."

"Told her I was ill!"

"Dangerously ill. That you couldn't bear to be disturbed."

"But *when*, Mr. Brumley?"

"Three days ago."

They both looked at Sir Isaac, who was sitting on the music-stool and eating a piece of tea-cake with a preoccupied air. He swallowed and then spoke thoughtfully in a tone of detached observation. Nothing but a slight reddening of the eyes betrayed any unusual feeling in him.

"It's my opinion," he said, "that that old lady—Lady Beach-Mandarin, I mean—doesn't know what she's saying half the time. She says—oh! remarkable things. Saying *that*, for example!"

"But did she call on me?"

"She called. I'm surprised you didn't hear. And she was all in a flurry for going on. . . . Did you come down, Mr. Brumley, to see if Lady Harman was ill?"

"That weighed with me."

"Well—you see she isn't," said Sir Isaac, and brushed a stray crumb from his coat. . . .

Mr. Brumley was at last impelled gateward and Sir Isaac saw him as far as the high-road.

"Good-bye!" cried Mr. Brumley, with excessive amiability.

Sir Isaac, with soundless lips, made a good-bye like gesture.

"And now," said Sir Isaac to himself, with extreme bitterness, "now to see about getting a dog."

"Bull mastiff?" said Sir Isaac, developing his idea as he went back to Lady Harman. "Or perhaps a thoroughly vicious collie?"

"How did that chap get in?" he demanded. "What had he got to say to you?"

"He came in—to look at the garden," said Lady Harman. "And of course he wanted to know if I had been well—because of Lady Viping's party. And I suppose because of what you told Lady Beach-Mandarin."

Sir Isaac grunted doubtfully. He thought of Snagsby and

of all the instructions he had given Snagsby. He turned about and went off swiftly and earnestly to find Snagsby. . . .

Snagsby lied. But Sir Isaac was able to tell from the agitated way in which he was cleaning his perfectly clean silver at that unseasonable hour that the wretched man was lving.

§ 8

Quite a number of words came to the lips of Mr. Brumley as he went unwillingly along the pleasant country road that led from Black Strand to the railway station. But the word he ultimately said showed how strongly the habits of the gentlemanly *littérateur* prevailed in him. It was the one inevitable word for his mood—" Baffled ! "

Close upon its utterance came the weak irritation of the impotent man. " What the *devil* ? " cried Mr. Brumley. Some critical spirit within him asked him urgently why he was going to the station, what he thought he was doing, what he thought he had done, and what he thought he was going to do. To all of which questions Mr. Brumley perceived he had no adequate reply.

Earlier in the day he had been inspired by a vague yet splendid dream of large, masterful liberations achieved. He had intended to be very disinterested, very noble, very firm, and so far as Sir Isaac was concerned, a trifle overbearing. You know now what he said and did. " Of course if we could have talked for a little longer," he said. From the stormy dissatisfaction of his retreat this one small idea crystallised, that he had not talked enough without disturbance to Lady Harman. The thing he had to do was to talk to her some more. To go on with what he had been saying. That thought arrested his steps. On that hypothesis there was no reason whatever why he should go on to the station and London. Instead— He stopped short, saw a convenient gate ahead, went to it, seated himself upon its topmost rail, and attempted a calm survey of the situation. He had somehow to continue that conversation with Lady Harman.

Was it impossible to do that by going back to the front door of Black Strand ? His instinct was against that course. He knew that if he went back now openly he would see nobody but Sir Isaac or his butler. He must therefore not go back openly. He must go round now and into the pine-woods at the back of Black Strand ; thence he must watch the garden and find his opportunity of speaking to the imprisoned lady. There was something at once attractively romantic and repellantly youthful about this course of action. Mr. Brumley looked at his watch, then he surveyed the blue, clear sky overhead, with just one warm tinted wisp of cloud. It would be dark in an hour, and it was probable that Lady Harman had already gone indoors for the day. Might it be possible after dark to approach the house ? No one surely knew the garden so well as he.

Of course this sort of thing is always going on in romances ; in the stories of that last great survivor of the Stevensonian tradition, H. B. Marriott Watson, the heroes are always creeping through woods, tapping at windows, and scaling house-walls, but Mr. Brumley, as he sat on his gate, became very sensible of his own extreme inexperience in such adventures. And yet anything seemed in his present mood better than going back to London.

Suppose he tried his luck !

He knew, of course, the lie of the land about Black Strand very well indeed, and his harmless literary social standing gave him a certain freedom of trespass. He dropped from his gate on the inner side, and taking a bridle path through a pine-wood was presently out upon the moorland behind his former home. He struck the high-road that led past the Staminal Bread Board and was just about to clamber over the barbed wire on his left and make his way through the trees to the crest that commanded the Black Strand garden when he perceived a man in a velveteen coat and gaiters strolling towards him. He decided not to leave the road until he was free from observation. The man was a stranger, an almost conventional game-keeper, and he endorsed Mr. Brumley's remark upon the charmingness of the day with guarded want of enthusiasm. Mr. Brumley went on for some few minutes, then halted, assured himself that the stranger was well out of sight, and returned at once towards the point where high-roads were to be left and adventure begun. But he was still some yards away when he became aware of that velveteen-coated figure approaching again. " Damn ! " said Mr. Brumley, and slacked his eager paces. This time he expressed a view that the weather was extremely mild. " Very," said the man in velveteen, with a certain lack of respect in his manner.

It was no good turning back again. Mr. Brumley went on slowly, affected to botanise, watched the man out of sight, and immediately made a dash for the pinewoods, taking the barbed wire in a manner extremely detrimental to his left trouser leg. He made his way obliquely up through the trees to the crest from which he had so often surveyed the shining ponds of Aleham. Then he paused to peer back for that gamekeeper—whom he supposed, in spite of reason, to be stalking him—to recover his breath, and to consider his further plans. The sunset was very fine that night, a great red sun was sinking towards acutely outlined hill-crests, the lower, nearer distances were veiled in lavender mists, and three of the ponds shone like the fragments of a shattered pink topaz. But Mr. Brumley had no eye for landscape. . . .

About two hours after nightfall Mr. Brumley reached the railway station. His trousers and the elbow of his coat bore witness to a second transit of the barbed-wire fence in the darkness, he had manifestly walked into a boggy place, and had some difficulty in recovering firm ground and he had also been sliding in a recumbent position down a bank of moist ferruginous sand. Moreover, he had cut the palm of his left hand. There was a new, strange stationmaster who regarded him without that respect to which he had grown accustomed. He received the information that the winter train service had been altered, and that he would have to wait forty-five minutes for the next train to London with the resignation of a man already chastened by misfortune and fatigue. He went into the waiting-room and after a vain search for the poker—the new stationmaster evidently kept it in a different place—sat down in front of an irritatingly dull fire banked up with slack, and nursed his damaged hand and meditated on his future plans.

His plans were still exactly in the state in which they had been when Sir Isaac parted from him at the gate of Black Strand. They remained in the same state for two whole days. Throughout all that distressing period his general intention of some magnificent intervention on behalf of Lady Harman remained unchanged, it produced a number of moving visions of flights at incredible speeds in (recklessly hired) motor-cars of colossal power—most of the purchase money for Black Strand was still uninvested at his bank—of impassioned interviews with various people, of a divorce court with a hardened judge congratulating the manifestly quite formal co-respondent on the moral beauty of his behaviour, but it evolved no sort of concrete practicable detail upon which any kind of action might be taken. And during this period of indecision Mr. Brumley was hunted through London by a feverish unrest. When he was in his little flat in Pont Street he was urged to go to his club, when he got to his club he was urged to go anywhere else, he called on the most improbable people, and as soon as possible fled forth again, he even went to the British Museum and ordered out a lot of books on matrimonial law. Long before that great machine had disgorged them for him he absconded, and this neglected, this widowed pile of volumes still standing to his account only came back to his mind in the middle of the night suddenly and disturbingly while he was trying to remember the exact words he had used in his brief conversation with Lady Harman. . . .

§ 9

Two days after Mr. Brumley's visit, Susan Burnet reached Black Strand. She, too, had been baffled for a while. For some week or more she couldn't discover the whereabouts of Lady Harman, and lived in the profoundest perplexity. She had brought back her curtains to the Putney house in a large but luggable bundle, they were all made and ready to put up, and she found the place closed and locked, in the charge of a caretaker whose primary duty it was to answer no questions. It needed several days of thought and amazement, and a vast amount of " I wonder," and " I just would like to know," before it occurred to Susan that if she wrote to Lady Harman at the Putney address the letter might be forwarded. And even then she almost wrecked the entire enterprise by mentioning the money, and it was by a quite exceptional inspiration that she thought after all it was wiser not to say that, but to state that she had finished the curtains and done everything (under-lined) that Lady Harman had desired. Sir Isaac read it and tossed it over to his wife. "Make her send her bill," he remarked.

Whereupon Lady Harman set Mrs. Crumble in motion to bring Susan down to Black Strand. This wasn't quite easy because, as Mrs. Crumble pointed out, they hadn't the slightest use for Susan's curtains there, and Lady Harman had to find the morning light quite intolerable in her bedroom—she always slept with window wide open and curtains drawn back—to create a suitable demand for Susan's services. But at last Susan came, too humbly invisible for Sir Isaac's attention, and directly she found Lady Harman alone in the room with her, she produced a pawn ticket and twenty pounds. "I 'ad to give all sorts of particulars," she said. "It was a job. But I did it. . . ."

The day was big with opportunity, for Sir Isaac had been unable to conceal the fact that he had to spend the morning in London. He had gone up in the big car, and his wife was alone, and so, with Susan upstairs still deftly measuring for totally unnecessary hangings, Lady Harman was able to add a fur stole and a muff and some gloves to her tweed gardening costume, walk unchallenged into the garden and from the garden into the wood and up the hillside and over the crest and down to the high-road and past that great advertisement of Staminal Bread, and so for four palpitating miles, to the railway station and the outer world.

She had the good fortune to find a train imminent—the twelve-seventeen. She took a first-class ticket for London and got into a compartment with another woman, because she felt it would be safer.

§ 10

Lady Harman reached Miss Alimony's flat at half-past three in the afternoon. She had lunched rather belatedly and un-comfortably in the Waterloo Refreshment Room, and she had found out that Miss Alimony was at home through the tele-phone. "I want to see you urgently," she said, and Miss Alimony received her in that spirit. She was hatless, but she had a great cloud of dark fuzzy hair above the gray profundity of her eyes, and she wore an artistic tea-gown that, in spite of a certain looseness at neck and sleeve, emphasised the fine lines of her admirable figure. Her flat was furnished chiefly with books and rich oriental hangings, and vast cushions and great bowls of scented flowers. On the mantel-shelf was the crystal that amused her lighter moments, and above it hung a circular allegory by Florence Swinstead, very rich in colour, the Awakening of Woman, in a heavy gold frame. Miss Alimony conducted her guest to an armchair, knelt flexibly on the hearthrug before her, took up a small and elegant poker with a brass handle and a spear-shaped service end of iron and poked the fire.

The service end came out from the handle and fell into the grate. " It always does that," said Miss Alimony charmingly. " But never mind." She warmed both hands at the blaze. " Tell me all about it," she said softly.

Lady Harman felt she would rather have been told all about it. But perhaps that would follow.

" You see," she said, " I find—— My married life——"

She halted. It *was* very difficult to tell.

" Every one," said Agatha, giving a fine firelit profile, and remaining gravely thoughtful through a little pause.

" Do you mind," she asked abruptly, " if I smoke ? "

When she had completed her effect with a delicately flavoured cigarette, she encouraged Lady Harman to proceed.

This Lady Harman did in a manner do. She said her husband left her no freedom of mind or movement, gave her no possession of herself, wanted to control her reading and thinking. " He insists——" she said.

" Yes," said Miss Agatha, sternly blowing aside her cigarette smoke. " They all insist."

" He insists," said Lady Harman, " on seeing all my letters, choosing all my friends. I have no control over my house or my servants, no money except what he gives me."

" In fact you are property."

" I'm simply property."

" A harem of one. And all *that* is within the provisions of the law ! "

" How any woman can marry ! " said Miss Agatha, after a little interval. " I sometimes think that is where the true strike of the sex ought to begin. If none of us married ! If we said, all of us, ' No—definitely—we refuse this bargain ! It is a man-made contract. We have had no voice in it. We decline.' Perhaps it will come to that. And I knew that you, you with that quiet, beautiful penetration in your eyes, would come to see it like that. The first task, after the vote is won, will be the revision of that contract. The very first task of our women statesmen. . . ."

She ceased and revived her smouldering cigarette, and mused, blinking through the smoke. She seemed for a time almost lost to the presence of her guest in a great daydream of woman-statecraft.

" And so," she said, " you've come, as they all come—to join us."

" *Well*," said Lady Harman in a tone that made Agatha turn eyes of surprise upon her.

"Of course," continued Lady Harman, "I suppose—I shall join you ; but, as a matter of fact, you see, what I've done to-day has been to come right away. . . . You see, I am still in my garden tweeds. . . . There it was down there, a sort of stalemate. . . ."

Agatha sat up on her heels.

"But, my dear ! " she said, "you don't mean you've run away ? "

"Yes—I've run away."

"But—run away ! "

"I sold a ring and got some money, and here I am ! "

"But—what are you going to do ? "

"I don't know. I thought you, perhaps—might advise."

"But—a man like your husband ! He'll pursue you ! "

"If he knows where I am, he will," said Lady Harman.

"He'll make a scandal. My dear ! are you wise ? Tell me, tell me exactly, why have you run away ? I didn't understand at all—that you had run away."

"Because," began Lady Harman, and flushed hotly. "It was impossible," she said.

Miss Alimony regarded her deeply. "I wonder," she said.

"I feel," said Lady Harman, "if I stayed, if I gave in—— I mean, after—after I had once—rebelled. Then I should just be—a wife—ruled, ordered——"

"It wasn't your place to give in," said Miss Alimony, and added one of those parliament touches that creep more and more into feminine phraseology ; "I agree to that—nemine contradicente. But—I wonder. . . ."

She began a second cigarette, and thought in profile again.

"I think, perhaps, I haven't explained, clearly, how things are," said Lady Harman, and commenced a rather more explicit statement of her case. She felt she had not conveyed and she wanted to convey to Miss Alimony that her rebellion was not simply a desire for personal freedom and autonomy, that she desired these things because she was becoming more and more aware of large affairs outside her home life in which she ought to be not simply interested but concerned, that she had been not merely watching the workings of the business that made her wealthy, but reading books about socialism, about social welfare that had stirred her profoundly. . . .

"But he won't even allow me to know of such things," she said. . . .

Miss Alimony listened a little abstractedly.

Suddenly she interrupted. "Tell me," she said, "one thing. . . . I confess," she explained, "I've no business to ask. But if I'm to advise—— If my advice is to be worth anything . . ."

"Yes ? " asked Lady Harman.

"Is there—— Is there some one else ? "

"Some one else ? " Lady Harman was crimson.

" On *your* side ! "

" Some one else on my side? "

" I mean—some one. A man, perhaps ? Some man that you care for ? More than you do for your husband ? . . ."

" *I can't imagine,*" whispered Lady Harman, " *anything*——" And left her sentence unfinished. Her breath had gone. Her indignation was profound.

" Then I can't understand why you should find it so important to come away."

Lady Harman could offer no elucidation.

" You see," said Miss Alimony, with an air of expert knowledge, " our case against our opponents is just exactly their great case against us. They say to us when we ask for the Vote, ' the Woman's Place is the Home.' ' Precisely,' we answer, ' the Woman's Place *is* the Home. *Give* us our Homes ! ' Now *your* place is your home—with your children. That's where you have to fight your battle. Running away—for you it's simply running away."

" But—— If I stay I shall be beaten." Lady Harman surveyed her hostess with a certain dismay. " Do you understand, Agatha ? I *can't* go back."

" But, my dear ! What else can you do ? What had you thought ? "

" You see," said Lady Harman, after a little struggle with that childish quality in her nerves that might, if it wasn't controlled, make her eyes brim. " You see, I didn't expect you quite to take this view. I thought, perhaps, you might be disposed—— If I could have stayed with you here, only for a little time, I could have got some work or something——"

" It's so dreadful," said Miss Alimony, sitting far back with the relaxation of infinite regrets. " It's dreadful."

" Of course, if you don't see it as I do——"

" I can't," said Miss Alimony. " I can't."

She turned suddenly upon her visitor and grasped her knees with her shapely hands. " Oh, let me implore you ! Don't run away. Please, for my sake, for all our sakes, for the sake of Womanhood, don't run away ! Stay at your post. You mustn't run away. You must *not*. If you do, you admit everything. Everything. You must fight in your home. It's *your* home. That is the great principle you must grasp—it's not his. It's there your duty lies. And there are your children —*your* children, your little ones ! Think, if you go—there may be a fearful fuss—proceedings. Lawyers—a search. Very probably he will take all sorts of proceedings. It will be a matrimonial case. How can I be associated with that ? We mustn't mix up Women's Freedom with Matrimonial Cases. Impossible ! We *dare* not ! A woman leaving her husband ! Think of the weapon it gives our enemies. If once other things complicate the Vote—the Vote is lost. After

all our self-denial, after all our sacrifices. . . . You see !
Don't you *see* ? . . ."

"*Fight !*" she summarised, after an eloquent interval.

"You mean," said Lady Harman—"You think I ought to
go back."

Miss Alimony paused to get her full effect. "*Yes,*" she
said in a profound whisper, and endorsed it, "Oh, so much
so !—yes."

"Now ? "

"Instantly."

For an interval neither lady spoke. It was the visitor at
last who broke the tension.

"Do you think," she asked in a small voice and with the
hesitation of one whom no refusal can surprise, "you could
give me a cup of tea ? "

Miss Alimony rose with a sigh and a slow unfolding rustle.
"I forgot," she said. "My little maid is out."

Lady Harman, left alone, sat for a time staring at the
fire with her eyes rather wide and her eyebrows raised as
though she mutely confided to it her infinite astonishment.
This was the last thing she had expected. She would have
to go to some hotel. Can a woman stay alone at a hotel ?
Her heart sank. Inflexible forces seemed to be pointing her
back to home—and Sir Isaac. He would be a very triumphant
Sir Isaac, and she'd not have much heart left in her. . . . "I *won't*
go back," she whispered to herself. "Whatever happens,
I *won't* go back. . . ."

Then she became aware of the evening newspaper Miss
Alimony had been reading. The headline, "Suffrage raid
on Regent Street," caught her eye. A queer little idea came
into her head. It grew with tremendous rapidity. She put
out a hand and took up the paper and read.

She had plenty of time to read because her hostess not
only got the tea herself, but went, during that process, to her
bedroom and put on one of those hats that have contributed
so much to remove the stigma of dowdiness from the suffrage
cause, as an outward and visible sign that she was presently
ceasing to be at home. . . .

Lady Harman found an odd fact in the report before her.
"One of the most difficult things to buy at the present time
in the West End of London," it ran, "is a hammer. . . ."

Then a little further : "The magistrate said it was impossible to make discriminations in this affair. All the de-
fendants must have a month's imprisonment. . . ."

When Miss Alimony returned Lady Harman put down
the paper almost guiltily.

Afterwards Miss Alimony recalled that guilty start, and
the still more guilty start that had happened, when presently
she went out of the room again and returned with a lamp,
for the winter twilight was upon them. Afterwards, too,

she was to learn what had become of the service end of her small poker, the little iron club, which she missed almost as soon as Lady Harman had gone. . . .

Lady Harman had taken that grubby but convenient little instrument and hidden it in her muff, and she had gone straight out of Miss Alimony's flat to the Post Office at the corner of Jago Street, and there, with one simple, effective impact, had smashed a ground-glass window, the property of His Majesty King George the Fifth. And having done so, she had called the attention of a youthful policeman, fresh from Yorkshire, to her offence, and after a slight struggle with his incredulity and a visit to the window in question, had escorted him to the South Hampsmith police-station, and had there made him charge her. And on the way she explained to him with a new-found lucidity why it was that woman should have votes.

And all this she did from the moment of percussion onward, in a mood of exaltation entirely strange to her, but, as she was astonished to find, by no means disagreeable. She found afterwards that she only remembered very indistinctly her selection of the window and her preparations for the fatal blow, but that the effect of the actual breakage remained extraordinarily vivid upon her memory. She saw with extreme distinctness both as it was before and after the breakage, first as a rather irregular gray surface, shining in the oblique light of a street lamp, and giving pale, phantom reflections of things in the street, and then as it was after her blow. It was all visual impression in her memory ; she could not re-collect afterwards if there had been any noise at all. Where there had been nothing but a milky dinginess a thin-armed, irregular star had flashed into being, and a large triangular piece at its centre, after what seemed an interminable indecision, had slid, first covertly downward, and then fallen forward at her feet and shivered into a hundred fragments. . . .

Lady Harman realised that a tremendous thing had been done—irrevocably. She stared at her achievement open mouthed. The creative lump of iron dropped from her hand. She had a momentary doubt whether she had really wanted to break that window at all ; and then she understood that this business had to be seen through, and seen through with neatness and dignity ; and that wisp of regret vanished absolutely in her concentration upon these immediate needs.

§ 11

Some day, when the arts of the writer and illustrator are more closely blended than they are to-day, it will be possible to tell of all that followed this blow, with an approach to its actual effect. Here there should stand a page showing simply and plainly the lower half of the window of the Jago Street Post Office, a dark, rather grimy pane, reflecting the light of a street lamp—and *broken*. Below the pane would come a band of evilly painted woodwork, a corner of letter-box, a foot or so of brickwork, and then the pavement with a dropped lump of iron. That would be the sole content of this page, and the next page would be the same, but very slightly fainter, and across it would be printed a dim sentence or so of explanation. The page following that would show the same picture again, but now several lines of type would be visible, and then, as one turned over the smashed window would fade a little, and the printed narrative, still darkened and dominated by it, would nevertheless resume. One would read on how Lady Harman returned to convince the incredulous young Yorkshireman of her feat, how a man with a barrow-load of bananas volunteered comments, and how she went in custody, but with the extremest dignity, to the police-station. Then, with some difficulty, because that imposed picture would still prevail over the letterpress, and because it would be in small type, one would learn how she was bailed out by Lady Beach-Mandarin, who was clearly the woman she ought to have gone to in the first place, and who gave up a dinner with a duchess to entertain her, and how Sir Isaac, being too torn by his feelings to come near her, spent the evening in a frantic attempt to keep the whole business out of the papers. He could not manage it. The magistrate was friendly next morning, but inelegant in his friendly expedients ; he remanded Lady Harman until her mental condition could be inquired into, but among her fellow-defendants—there had been quite an epidemic of window-smashing that evening—Lady Harman shone pre-eminently sane. She said she had broken this window because she was assured that nothing would convince people of the great dissatisfaction of women with their conditions except such desperate acts, and when she was reminded of her four daughters she said it was precisely the thought of how they too would grow up to womanhood that had made her strike her blow. The statements were rather the outcome of her evening with Lady Beach-Mandarin than her own unaided discoveries, but she had honestly assimilated them, and she expressed them with a certain simple dignity.

Sir Isaac made a pathetic appearance before the court, and Lady Harman was shocked to see how worn he was with distress at her scandalous behaviour. He looked a broken man. That curious sense of personal responsibility, which had slumbered throughout the Black Strand struggle, came back to her in a flood, and she had to grip the edge of the dock tightly to maintain her self-control. Unaccustomed as he was to public speaking, Sir Isaac said in a low, sorrow-laden voice, he had provided himself with a written statement dissociating himself from the views his wife's rash action might seem to imply, and expressing his own opinions upon women's suffrage and the relations of the sexes generally, with especial reference to contemporary literature. He had been writing it most of the night. He was not, however, permitted to read this, and he then made an unstudied appeal for the consideration and mercy of the court. He said Lady Harman had always been a good mother and a faithful wife ; she had been influenced by misleading people, and bad books and publications, the true significance of which she did not understand, and if only the court would regard this first offence leniently, he was ready to take his wife away and give any guarantee that might be specified that it should not recur. The magistrate was sympathetic and kindly, but he pointed out that this window-breaking had to be stamped out, and that it could only be stamped out by refusing any such exception as Sir Isaac desired. And so Sir Isaac left the court widowed for a month, a married man without a wife, and terribly distressed.

All this and more one might tell in detail, and how she went to her cell, and the long tedium of her imprisonment, and how deeply Snagsby felt the disgrace, and how Miss Alimony claimed her as a convert to the magic of her persuasions, and many such matters—there is no real restraint upon a novelist fully resolved to be English and Gothic and unclassical, except obscure and inexplicable instincts. But these obscure and inexplicable instincts are at times imperative, and on this occasion they insist that here must come a break, a pause, in the presence of this radiating gap in the Postmaster-General's glass, and the phenomenon of this gentle and beautiful lady, the mother of four children, grasping in her gloved hand, and with a certain amateurishness, a lumpish poker-end of iron.

We make the pause by ending the chapter here and by resuming the story at a fresh point—with an account of various curious phases in the mental development of Mr. Brumley.

CHAPTER NINE

MR. BRUMLEY IS TROUBLED BY DIFFICULT IDEAS

§ 1

THEN, as that picture of a post-office pane, smashed and with a large hole knocked clean through it, fades at last upon the reader's consciousness, let another and a kindred spectacle replace it. It is the carefully cleaned and cherished window of Mr. Brumley's mind, square and tidy and, as it were, " frosted " against an excess of light, and in that also we have now to record the most jagged and all devastating fractures.

Little did Mr. Brumley reckon when first he looked up from his laces at Black Strand, how completely that pretty young woman in the dark furs was destined to shatter all the assumptions that had served his life.

But you have already had occasion to remark a change in Mr. Brumley's bearing and attitude that carries him far from the kindly and humorous conservatism of his earlier work. You have shared Lady Harman's astonishment at the ardour of his few stolen words in the garden, an astonishment that not only grew but flowered in the silences of her captivity, and you know something of the romantic impulses, more at least than she did, that gave his appearance at the little local railway station so belated and so disreputable a flavour. In the chilly ill-flavoured solitude of her prison cell and with a mind quickened by meagre and distasteful fare, Lady Harman had ample leisure to reflect upon many things, she had already fully acquainted herself with the greater proportion of Mr. Brumley's published works, and she found the utmost difficulty in reconciling the flushed, impassioned quality of his few words of appeal, with the moral assumptions of his published opinions. On the whole, she was inclined to think that her memory had a little distorted what he had said. In this, however, she was mistaken ; Mr. Brumley had really been proposing an elopement, and he was now entirely preoccupied with the idea of rescuing, obtaining, and possessing Lady Harman for himself as soon as the law released her.

One may doubt whether this extensive change from a humorous conservatism to a primitive and dangerous romanticism is to be ascribed entirely to the personal charm, great as it no doubt was, of Lady Harman ; rather did her tall, soft, dark presence come to release a long accumulating store of discontent and unrest beneath the polished surfaces of Mr. Brumley's mind. Things had been stirring in him for some time ; the later Euphemia books had lacked much of the freshness of their precursors, and he had found it increasingly hard, he knew now why, to keep up the lightness, the geniality, the friendly badinage of successful and accepted things, the sunny disregard of the grim and unamiable aspects of existence, that were the essential merits of that optimistic period of our literature in which Mr. Brumley had begun his career. With every justification in the world Mr. Brumley had set out to be an optimist, even in the *Granta* his work had been distinguished by its gay yet steadfast superficiality, and his early success, his rapid popularity, had done much to turn this early disposition into a professional attitude. He had determined that for all his life he would write for comfortable, untroubled people in the character of a lightspirited, comfortable, untroubled person, and that each year should have its book of connubial humour, its travel in pic-

turesque places, its fun and its sunshine, like roses budding
in succession on a stem. He did his utmost to conceal from
himself the melancholy realisation that the third and the
fourth roses were far less wonderful than the first and the
second, and that by continuing the descending series a rose
might be attained at last that was almost unattractive, but
he was already beginning to suspect that he was getting less
animated and a little irritable when Euphemia very gently
and gracefully but very firmly and rather enigmatically died,
and after an interval of tender and tenderly expressed regrets
he found himself, in spite of the most strenuous efforts to
keep bright and kindly and optimistic in the best style, dull
and getting duller—he could disguise the thing no longer.
And he weighed more.   Six—eight—eleven pounds more.
He took a flat in London, dined and lunched out lightly but
frequently, sought the sympathetic friendship of several
charming ladies, and involved himself deeply in the affairs of
the Academic Committee. Indeed, he made a quite valiant
struggle to feel that optimism was just where it always had
been and everything all right and very bright with him and
with the world about him. He did not go under without a
struggle. But as Max Beerbohm's caricature—the 1908 one
I mean—brought out all too plainly, there was in his very
animation something of the alert liveliness of the hunted man.
Do what he would, he had a terrible irrational feeling that
things, as yet scarce imagined things, were after him and would
have him. Even as he makes his point, even as he gesticulates
airily, with his rather distinctively North European nose
Beerbohmically enlarged, and his sensitive nostril in the air,
he seems to be looking at something he does not want to look
at, something conceivably pursuing, out of the corner of his eye.

The thing that was assailing Mr. Brumley and making his
old-established humour and tenderness seem dull and opaque
and giving this new, uneasy quality to his expression was, of
course, precisely the thing that Sir Isaac meant when he
talked about "idees" and their disturbing influence upon all
the once assured tranquillities and predominances of Putney
life. It was criticism breaking bounds.

As a basis and substance for the tissue of whimsically expressed happiness and confident appreciation of the good things
of life, which Mr. Brumley had set before himself as his agreeable—and it was to be hoped popular and profitable—life-task
certain assumptions had been necessary. They were assumptions
he had been very willing to make and which were being made
in the most exemplary way by the writers who were succeeding
all about him at the commencement of his career. And these
assumptions had had such an air then of being quite trustworthy, as being certain to wash and wear ! Already nowadays it is difficult to get them stated ; they have become
incredible while still too near to justify the incredibility that

attaches to history. It was assumed, for example, that in the institutions, customs, and culture of the middle Victorian period, humanity had, so far as the broad lines of things are concerned, achieved its goal. There were, of course, still bad men and women—individually—and classes one had to recognise as " lower," but all the main things were right, general ideas were right ; the law was right, institutions were right, Consols and British Railway Debentures were right and were going to keep right for ever. The Abolition of Slavery in America had been the last great act which had inaugurated this millennium. Except for individual instances the tragic intensities of life were over now and done with ; there was no more need for heroes and martyrs ; for the generality of humanity the phase of genial comedy had begun. There might be improvements and refinements ahead, but social, political, and economic arrangement were now in the main outlines settled for good and all ; nothing better was possible, and it was the agreeable task of the artist and the man of letters to assist and celebrate this establishment. There was to be much editing of Shakespeare and Charles Lamb, much delightful humour and costume romance, and an academy of refined fine writers would presently establish belles lettres on the reputable official basis, write *finis* to creative force, and undertake the task of stereotyping the language. Literature was to have its once terrible ferments reduced to the quality of a helpful pepsin. Ideas were dead—or domesticated. The last wild idea, in an impoverished and pitiful condition, had been hunted down and killed in the mobbing of *The Woman Who Did*. For a little time the world did actually watch a phase of English writing that dared nothing, penetrated nothing, suppressed everything, and aspired at most to Charm, creep like a transitory patch of sunlight across a storm-rent universe. And vanish. . . .

At no time was it a perfectly easy task to pretend that the crazy makeshifts of our legal and political systems, the staggering accidents of economic relationship, the festering disorder of contemporary philosophy and religious teaching, the cruel and stupid bed of King Og that is our last word in sexual adjustment, really constituted a noble and enduring sanity, and it became less and less so with the acute disillusionments that arose out of the Boer War. The first decade of the twentieth century was for the English a decade of badly sprained optimism. Our empire was nearly beaten by a handful of farmers amidst the jeering contempt of the whole world—and we felt it acutely for several years. We began to question ourselves. Mr. Brumley found his gay but entirely respectable irresponsibility harder and harder to keep up as that decade wore on. And close upon the South African trouble came that extraordinary new discontent of women with a woman's lot which we have been observing as it reached and troubled the life of Lady Harman. Women who had hitherto so passively made the bulk of that reading public which sustained Mr. Brumley and his kind—they wanted something else !

And behind and beneath these immediately disconcerting things still more sinister hintings and questionings were beginning to pluck at contentment. In 1899 nobody would have dreamt of asking and in 1909 even Mr. Brumley was asking, " Are things going on much longer ? " A hundred little incidents conspired to suggest that a Christianity that had, to put it mildly, shirked the Darwinian challenge, had no longer the palliating influence demanded of a national religion, and that down there in the deep levels of labour where they built railways to carry Mr. Brumley's food and earn him dividends, where they made engines and instruments and textiles and drains for his little needs, there was a new, less bounded discontent, a grimmer spirit, something that one tried in vain to believe was only the work of " agitators," something that was to be pacified no longer by the thin pretences of liberalism, something that might lead ultimately— optimism scarcely dared to ask whither. . . .

Mr. Brumley did his best to resist the influence of these darkening ideas. He tried to keep it up that everything was going well and that most of these shadows and complaints were the mischief of a few incurably restless personalities. He tried to keep it up that to belong to the working class was a thoroughly jolly thing—for those who were used to it. He declared that all who wanted to alter our laws or our ideas about property or our methods of production were envious and base, and all who wanted any change between the sexes, foolish or vicious. He tried to go on disposing of socialists, agitators, feminists, women's suffragists, educationists, and every sort of reformer with a good-humoured contempt. And he found an increasing difficulty in keeping his contempt sufficiently good-humoured. Instead of laughing down at folly and failure, he had moments when he felt that he was rather laughing up—a little wryly at monstrous things impending. And since ideas are things of atmosphere and the spirit, insidious wolves of the soul, they crept up to him and gnawed the insides out of him even as he posed as their manful antagonist.

Insensibly Mr. Brumley moved with his times. It is the necessary first phase in the break-up of any system of unsound assumptions that a number of its votaries should presently set about padding its cutting corners and relieving the harsh pressure of its injustices by exuberances of humour and sentimentality. Mr. Brumley became charitable and romantic— orthodox still but charitable and romantic. He was all for smashing with the generalisation, but now in the particular instance he was more and more for forgiveness. One finds creeping into the later Euphemia books a Bret-Harte-like doctrine that a great number of bad women are really good and a persuasion in the " Raffles " key that a large proportion of criminals are really very picturesque and admirable fellows. One wonders how far Mr. Brumley's less ostensible life was softening in harmony with this exterior change, this tender twilight of principle. He wouldn't as yet face the sterner fact that most people who are condemned by society, whether they are condemned justly or not, are by the very gregariousness of man's nature debased, and that a law or custom that stamps you as bad makes you bad. A great state should have high and humane and considerate laws nobly planned, nobly administered, and needing none of the shabby little qualifications *sotto voce*. To find goodness in the sinner and justification in the outcast is to condemn the law, but as yet Mr. Brumley's heart failed where his intelligence pointed towards that conclusion. He hadn't the courage to revise his assumptions about right and wrong to that extent ; he just allowed them to get soft and sloppy. He waded, where there should be firm ground. He waded toward wallowing. This is a perilous way of living, and the sad little end of Euphemia, flushed and coughing, left him no doubt in many ways still more exposed to the temptations of the sentimental byway and the emotional gloss. Happily this is a book about Lady Harman and not an exhaustive monograph upon Mr. Brumley. We will at least leave him the refuge of a few shadows.

Occasionally he would write an important signed review for the *Twentieth Century* or the *Hebdomadal Review*, and on one such occasion he took in hand several studies of contemporary conditions by various " New Witnesses," " Young Liberals," *New Age* rebels, and associated insurgent authors. He intended to be rather kindly with them, rather disillusioned, quite sympathetic but essentially conventional and conservative and sane. He sat at a little desk near the drooping Venus, under the benediction of Euphemia's posthumous rose, and turned over the pages of one of the least familiar of the group. The stuff was written with a crude force that at times became almost distinguished, but with a bitterness that he felt he must reprove. And suddenly he came upon a passionate tirade against the present period. It made him nibble softly with his lips at the top of his fountain pen as he read.

" We live," said the writer, " in a second Byzantine age, in one of those multitudinous accumulations of secondary interests, of secondary activities and conventions and colossal intricate insignificances, that lie like dust heaps in the path of the historian. The true history of such periods is written in bank books and cheque counterfoils, and burnt to save individual reputations ; it sneaks along under a thousand pretences, it finds its mole-like food and safety in the dirt ; its outer forms remain for posterity, a huge debris of unfathomable riddles."

"H'm!" said Mr. Brumley. "He slings it out. And what's this?"

"A civilisation arrested and decayed, waiting through long, inglorious ages of unscheduled crime, unchallenged social injustice, senseless luxury, mercenary politics and universal vulgarity and weakness, for the long overdue scavenging of the Turk."

"I wonder where the children pick up such language," whispered Mr. Brumley, with a smile.

But presently he had pushed the book away and was thinking over this novel and unpleasant idea that perhaps after all his age didn't matter as some ages have mattered and as he had hitherto always supposed it did matter. Byzantine, with the gold of life stolen and the swans changed to geese? Of course always there had been a certain qualification upon heroes, even Cæsar had needed a wreath, but, at any rate, the age of Cæsar had mattered. Kings, no doubt, might be more kingly and the issues of life plainer and nobler, but this had been true of every age. He tried to weigh values against values, our past against our present, temperately and sanely. Our art might perhaps be keener for beauty than it seemed to be, but still—it flourished. And our science at least was wonderful—wonderful. There certainly this young detractor of existing things went astray. What was there in Byzantium to parallel with the electric light, the electric tram, wireless telegraphy, aseptic surgery? Of course this about "unchallenged social injustice" was nonsense. Rant. Why! we were challenging social injustice at every general election—plainly and openly. And crime! What could the man mean about unscheduled crime? Mere words! There was, of course, a good deal of luxury, but not *wicked* luxury, and to compare our high-minded and constructive politics with the mere conflict of unscrupulous adventurers about that semi-oriental throne! It was nonsense!

"This young man must be spanked," said Mr. Brumley, and, throwing aside an open illustrated paper in which a full-length portrait of Sir Edward Carson faced a picture of the king and queen in their robes sitting side by side under a canopy at the Coronation Durbar, he prepared himself to write in an extremely salutary manner about the follies of the younger generation, and incidentally to justify his period and his professional contentment.

§ 2

One is reminded of those houses into which the white ants have eaten their way; outwardly still fair and solid, they crumble at the touch of a hand. And now you will begin to understand those changes of bearing that so perplexed Lady Harman, that sudden insurgence of flushed, half-furtive passion in the garden, through the thin pretences of a liberal friendship. His hollow honour had been gripped, and had given way.

He had begun so well. At first Lady Harman had occupied his mind in the properest way. She was another man's wife, and sacred—according to all honourable standards, and what he wanted was merely to see more of her, talk to her, interest her in himself, share whatever was available outside her connubial obligations—and think as little of Sir Isaac as possible.

How quickly the imaginative temperament of Mr. Brumley enlarged that to include a critical hostility to Sir Isaac, we have already recorded. Lady Harman was no longer simply a charming, suppressed young wife, crying out for attentive development ; she became an ill-treated, beautiful woman—misunderstood. Still scrupulously respecting his own standards, Mr. Brumley embarked upon the dangerous business of inventing just how Sir Isaac might be outraging them, and once his imagination had started to hunt in that field, it speedily brought in enough matter for a fine state of moral indignation, a white heat of not altogether justifiable chivalry. Assisted by Lady Beach-Mandarin Mr. Brumley had soon converted the little millionaire into a matrimonial ogre to keep an anxious lover very painfully awake at nights. Because by that time and quite insensibly he had become an anxious lover—with all gaps in the thread of realities that would have made him that, quite generously filled up from the world of reverie.

Moral indignation is jealousy with a halo. It is the peculiar snare of the perplexed orthodox, and soon Mr. Brumley was in a state of nearly unendurable moral indignation with Sir Isaac for a hundred exaggerations of what he was and of what conceivably he might have done to his silent yet manifestly unsuitably mated wife. And now that romantic streak which is, as I have said, the first certain symptom of decay in a system of moral assumptions began to show itself in Mr. Brumley's thoughts and conversation. " A marriage like that," said Mr. Brumley to Lady Beach-Mandarin, " isn't a marriage. It flouts the true ideal of marriage. It's slavery—following a kidnapping. . . ."

But this is a wide step from the happy optimism of the Cambridge days. What becomes of the sanctity of marriage and the institution of the family when respectable gentlemen talk of something called " true marriage," as non-existent in relation to a lady who is already the mother of four children ? I record this lapsing of Mr. Brumley into romanticism without either sympathy or mitigation. The children, it presently became apparent, were not " true " children. " Forced upon her," said Mr. Brumley. " It makes one ill to think of it ! " It certainly very nearly made him ill. And as if these exercises in distinction had inflamed his conscience, Mr. Brumley wrote two articles in the *Hebdomadal* denouncing impure literature, decadence, immorality, various recent scandalous instances, and the suffragettes, declaring that woman's place was the home, and that " in a pure and exalted monogamy lies the sole unitary basis for a civilised state." The most remarkable thing about this article is an omission. That Sir Isaac's monogamy with any other instances that might be akin to it was not pure and exalted, and that it needed—shall we call it readjustment ? is a view that in this article Mr. Brumley conspicuously doesn't display. It's as if for a moment, pen in hand, he had eddied back to his old absolute positions. . . .

In a very little while Mr. Brumley and Lady Beach-Mandarin had almost persuaded each other that Sir Isaac was applying physical torture to his proudly silent wife, and Mr. Brumley was no longer dreaming and glancing at but steadily facing the possibility of a pure minded and handsomely done elopement to " free " Lady Harman, that would be followed in due course by a marriage, a " true marriage " on a level understanding far above any ordinary respectable wedding, amidst universal sympathy and admiration and the presence of all the very best people. In these anticipations he did rather remarkably overlook the absence of any sign of participation on the part of Lady Harman in his own impassioned personal feelings, and he overlooked still more remarkably as possible objections to his line of conduct, Millicent, Florence, Annette, and Baby. These omissions no doubt simplified but also greatly falsified his outlook.

This proposal that all the best people shall applaud the higher rightness that was to be revealed in his projected elopement, is in the very essence of the romantic attitude. All other people are still to remain under the law. There is to be nothing revolutionary. But with exceptional persons under exceptional conditions——

Mr. Brumley stated his case over and over again to his utmost satisfaction, and always at great moral altitudes and with a kind of transcendent orthodoxy. The more difficult any aspect of the affair appeared from the orthodox standpoint the more valiantly Mr. Brumley soared ; if it came to his living with Lady Harman for a time before they could be properly married amidst picturesque foreign scenery in a little *casa* by the side of a stream, then the water in that stream was to be quite the purest water conceivable and the scenery and associations as morally faultless as a view that had passed the exacting requirements of Mr. John Ruskin. And Mr. Brumley was very clear in his mind that what he proposed to do was entirely different in quality even if it was similar in form from anything that any one else had ever done who had ever before made a scandal or appeared in the divorce court. This is always the way in such cases—always. The scandal was to be a noble scandal, a proud scandal, one of those instances of heroical love that turn misdemeanours—admittedly misdemeanours—into edifying marvels.

This was the state of mind to which Mr. Brumley had attained when he made his ineffectual raid upon Black Strand,

and you will remark about it, if you are interested in the changes
in people's ideas that are going on to-day, that although he was
prepared to make the most extensive glosses in this particular
instance upon the commonly accepted rules of what is right
and proper, he was not for a moment prepared to accord the
terrible gift of an independent responsibility to Lady Harman.
In that direction lay regions that Mr. Brumley had still to
explore. Lady Harman he considered was married wrongly
and disastrously, and this he held to be essentially the fault
of Sir Isaac—with perhaps some slight blame attaching to
Lady Harman's mother. The only path of escape he could
conceive as yet for Lady Harman lay through the chivalry of
some other man. That a woman could possibly rebel against
one man without the sympathy and moral maintenance of
another was still outside the range of Mr. Brumley's understanding. It is still outside the range of most men's understandings—and of a great many women's. If he generalised at
all from these persuasions it was in the direction that in the
interests of " true marriage " there should be greater facilities
for divorce and also a kind of respectableisation of divorce.
Then these " false marriages " might be rectified without
suffering. The reasons for divorce he felt should be extended
to include things not generally reprehensible, and chivalrous
people coming into court should be protected from the indelicate publicity of free reporting. . . .

§ 3

Mr. Brumley was still contemplating rather inconclusively
the possibility of a long and intimate talk leading up to and
preparing for an elopement with Lady Harman, when he read
of her Jago Street escapade and of her impending appearance
at the South Hampsmith police court. He was astonished.
The more he contemplated the thing the greater became his
astonishment.

Even at the first impact he realised that the line she had taken
wasn't quite in the picture with the line he had proposed for
her. He felt—left out. He felt as though a door had slammed
between himself and affairs to which he had supposed himself
essential. He could not understand why she had done this
thing instead of coming straight to his flat and making use of all
that chivalrous service she surely knew was at her disposal.
This self-reliance, this direct dealing with the world, seemed
to him, even in the height of his concern, unwomanly, a deeper
injury to his own abandoned assumptions than any he had
contemplated. He felt it needed explanation, and he hurried
to secure an elbowed unsavoury corner in the back of the court
in order to hear her defence. He had to wait through long stuffy
spaces of time before she appeared. There were half a dozen
other window-smashers—plain or at least untidy-looking
young women. The magistrate told them they were silly, and

the soul of Mr. Brumley acquiesced. One tried to make a speech, and it was such a poor speech—squeaky. . . .

When at last Lady Harman entered the box—the strangest place it seemed for her—he tried to emerge from the jostling crowd about him into visibility, to catch her eye, to give her the support of his devoted presence. Twice, at least, she glanced in his direction, but gave no sign of seeing him. He was surprised that she could look without fear or detestation, indeed once with a gesture of solicitude, at Sir Isaac. She was astonishingly serene. There seemed to be just the faintest shadow of a smile about her lips as the stipendiary explained the impossibility of giving her anything less than a month. An uneasy object like the smashed remains of a colossal box of bon-bons that was riding out a gale, down in the middle of the court, turned round at last completely and revealed itself as the hat of Lady Beach-Mandarin, but though Mr. Brumley waved his hand he could not even make that lady aware of his presence. A powerful, rude, criminal-looking man who stood in front of him and smelt grossly of stables, would not give him a fair chance of showing himself, and developed a strong personal hostility to him on account of his alleged " shoving about." It would not, he felt, be of the slightest help to Lady Harman for him to involve himself in a personal struggle with a powerful and powerfully flavoured criminal.

It was all very dreadful.

After the proceedings were over and Lady Harman had been led away into captivity, he went out and took a taxi in an agitated distraught manner to Lady Beach-Mandarin's house.

" She meant," said Lady Beach-Mandarin, " to have a month's holiday from him and think things out. And she's got it."

Perhaps that was it. Mr. Brumley could not tell, and he spent some days in that state of perplexity which, like the weariness that heralds a cold, marks so often the onset of a new series of ideas. . . .

Why hadn't she come to him ? Had he, after all, rather overloaded his memory of her real self with imaginative accessories ? Had she really understood what he had been saying to her in the garden ? Afterwards, when he had met her eyes, as he and she went over the new wing with Sir Isaac, she had so manifestly—and, when one came to think of it, so tranquilly—seemed to understand. . . .

It was such an extraordinary thing to go smashing a window like that—when there he was at hand ready to help her. She knew her address ? Did she ? For a moment Mr. Brumley cherished that wild surmise. Was that perhaps it ? But surely she could have looked in the Telephone Directory or *Who's Who*. . . .

But if that was the truth of the matter she would have

looked and behaved differently in court—quite differently.
She would have been looking for him. She would have seen
him. . . .

It was queer too to recall what she had said in court about
her daughters. . . .

Could it be, he had a frightful qualm, that after all—he
wasn't the man ? How little he knew of her really. . . .

" This wretched agitation," said Mr. Brumley, trying to
flounder away anyhow from these disconcerting riddles ; " it
seems to unbalance them all."

But he found it impossible to believe that Lady Harman was
seriously unbalanced.

§ 4

And if Mr. Brumley's system of romantically distorted moral
assumptions was shattered by Lady Harman's impersonal
blow at a post-office window when all the rules seemed to
require her to fly from the oppression of one man to the
chivalry of another, what words can convey the devastating
effect upon him of her conduct after her release ? To that
crisis he had been looking forward continually ; to record
the variety of his expectations would fill a large volume, but
throughout them all prevailed one general idea, that when
she came out of prison her struggle with her husband would
be resumed, and that this would give Mr. Brumley such extraordinary opportunities of displaying his devotion that her
response, which he was now beginning to suspect might be
more reluctant than his earlier dreams had assumed, was
ultimately inevitable. In all these dreams and meditations
that response figured as the crown. He had to win and possess
Lady Harman. The idea had taken hold of his busy yet
rather pointless life, had become his directing object. He
was full of schemes for presently arresting and captivating·
her imagination. He was already convinced that she cared
for him ; he had to inflame interest and fan liking into the
fire of passion. And with a mind so occupied, Mr. Brumley
wrote this and that, and went about his affairs. He spent two
days and a night at Margate visiting his son at his preparatory
school, and he found much material for musing in the question
of just how the high romantic affairs ahead of him would
affect this delicately intelligent boy. For a time perhaps
he might misjudge his father. . . . He spent a week-end
with Lady Viping, and stayed on until Wednesday, and then
he came back to London. His plans were still unformed
when the day came for Lady Harman's release, and indeed
beyond an idea that he would have her met at the prison
gates by an enormous bunch of snowy-white and crimson
chrysanthemums, he had nothing really concrete at all in his
mind.

She had, however, been released stealthily a day before

her time, and this is what she had done. She had asked that
—of all improbable people !—Sir Isaac's mother should meet
her, the biggest car had come to the prison gates, and she
had gone straight down with Mrs. Harman to her husband
—who had taken a chill and was in bed drinking Contrexéville
water—at Black Strand.

As these facts shaped themselves in answer to the blanched
inquiries of Mr. Brumley, his amazement grew. He began
to realise that there must have been a correspondence during
her incarceration, that all sorts of things had been happening
while he had been dreaming, and when he went round to
Lady Beach-Mandarin, who was just packing up to be the
life and soul of a winter-sports party at a nice non-Lunnite
hotel at Lenzerheide, he learnt particulars that chilled him to
the marrow. "They've made it up," said Lady Beach-
Mandarin.

" But how ? " gasped Mr. Brumley, with his soul in infinite
distress. " But how ? "

" The ogre, it seems, has come to see that bullying won't
do. He's given in tremendously. He's let her have her way
with the waitress strike, and she's going to have an allowance
of her own and all kinds of things. It's settled. It's his mother
and that man Charterson talked him over. You know—his
mother came to me—as her friend. For advice. Wanted to
find out what sort of things we might have been putting in
her head. She said so. A curious old thing—vulgar, but—
wise. I liked her. He's her darling—and she just knows what
he is. . . . He doesn't like it, but he's taken his dose. The
thought of her going to prison again—— ! He's let her do
anything rather than that. . . ."

" And she's gone to him ! "

" Naturally," said Lady Beach-Mandarin, with what he felt
to be deliberate brutality. Surely she must have understood——

" But the waitress strike—what has it got to do with the
waitress strike ? "

" She cared—tremendously."

" *Did* she ? "

" Tremendously. And they all go back and the system of
inspection is being altered, and he's even forgiven Babs Wheeler.
It made him ill to do it, but he did."

" And she's gone back to him."

" Like Godiva," said Lady Beach-Mandarin, with that
sweeping allusiveness that was part of her complicated charm.

§ 5

For three days Mr. Brumley was so staggered by these
things that it did not occur to him that it was quite possible
for him to see Lady Harman for himself, and find out just
how things stood. He remained in London with an imagination
dazed. And as it was the Christmas season and as George

Edmund in a rather expectant holiday state had now come up from Margate, Mr. Brumley went in succession to the Hippodrome, to *Peter Pan*, and to an exhibition at Olympia, assisted at an afternoon display of the kinemacolor at La Scala Theatre, visited Hamley's, and lunched George Edmund once at the Criterion and twice at the Climax Club, while thinking of nothing in all the world but the incalculable strangeness of women. George Edmund thought him a very passive, leadable parent indeed, less querulous about money matters, and altogether much improved. The glitter and colour of these various entertainments reflected themselves upon the surface of that deep flood of meditation, hook-armed, wooden-legged pirates, intelligent elephants, ingenious but extremely expensive toys, flickering processions, comic turns, snatches of popular music, and George Edmund's way of eating an orange, pictured themselves on his mind confusedly without in any way deflecting its course. Then on the fourth day he roused himself, gave George Edmund ten shillings to get himself a cutlet at the Café Royal, and do the cinematographs round and about the West End, and so released reached Aleham in time for a temperate lunch. He chartered the Aleham car to take him to Black Strand, and arrived there about a quarter-past three, in a great effort to feel himself a matter-of-course visitor.

It ought to be possible to record that Mr. Brumley's mind was full of the intensest sense of Lady Harman during that journey and of nothing else, but, as a matter of fact, his mind was now curiously detached and reflective, the tensions and expectation of the past month and the astonishment of the last few days had worked themselves out and left him, as it were, the passive instrument of the purpose of his more impassioned moods. This distressed lover approached Black Strand in a condition of philosophical lassitude.

The road from Aleham to Black Strand is a picturesque old English road, needlessly winding and badly graded, wriggling across a heathy wilderness with occasional pine woods. Something in that familiar landscape—for his life had run through it since first he and Euphemia on a tandem bicycle and altogether very young had sought their ideal home in the south of England—set his mind swinging and generalising. How freshly youthful he and Euphemia had been when first he came along that road, how crude, how full of happy expectations of success ; it had been as bright and it was now as completely gone as the sunsets they had seen together.

How great a thing life is ! How much greater than any single romance, or any individual affection ! Since those days he had grown, he had succeeded, he had suffered in a reasonable way, of course, still he could recall with a kind of satisfaction tears and deep, week-long moods of hopeless melancholy—and he had changed. And now dominating this landscape, filling him with new emotions and desires and perplexing intimations of ignorance and limitations he had never suspected in his youth, was this second figure of a woman. She was different from Euphemia. With Euphemia everything had been so simple and easy; until that slight fading, that fatigue of entire success and satisfaction, of the concluding years. He and Euphemia had always kept it up that they had no thought in the world except for one another. . . . Yet if that had been true, why hadn't he died when she did. He hadn't died—with remarkable elasticity. Clearly in his case there had been these unexplored, unsuspected hinterlands of possibility towards which Lady Harman seemed now to be directing him. It came to him that afternoon as an entirely fresh thought that there might also have been something in Euphemia beyond their simple, so charmingly treated relationship. He began to recall moments when Euphemia had said perplexing little things, had looked at him with an expression that was unexpected, had been—difficult. . . .

I write of Mr. Brumley to tell you things about him, and not to explain him. It may be that the appetite for thorough good talks with people grows upon one, but, at any rate, it did occur to Mr. Brumley on his way to talk to Lady Harman, it occurred to him as a thing distressingly irrevocable that he could now never have a thorough good talk with Euphemia about certain neglected things between them. It would have helped him so much. . . .

His eyes rested as he thought of these things upon the familiar purple hill crests, patched that afternoon with the lingering traces of a recent snowstorm, the heather slopes, the dark, mysterious woods, the patches of vivid green where a damp and marshy meadow or so broke the moorland surface. To-day, in spite of the sun, there was a bright blue-white line of frost to the northward of every hedge and bank, the trees were dripping down the white edgings of the morning into the pine-needle mud at their feet; he had seen it so like this before; years hence he might see it all like this again; all this great breezy countryside had taken upon itself a quality of endurance, as though it would still be real and essential in his mind when Lady Harman had altogether passed again. It would be real when he himself had passed away, and in other costumes and other vehicles fresh Euphemias and new crude George Brumleys would come along, feeling in the ultimate bright new wisdom of youth that it was all for them —a subservient scenery, when really it was entirely indifferent in its careless permanence to all their hopes and fancies. . . .

§ 6

Mr. Brumley's thoughts on the permanence of landscape and the mutability of human affairs were more than a little dashed when he came within sight of Black Strand, and perceived that once cosily beautiful little home slipped and extended, its shrubbery wrecked and the old barn now pierced with windows and adorned—for its new chimneys were not working very well—by several efficient novelties in chimney cowls. Up the slopes behind Sir Isaac had extended his boundaries, and had been felling trees and levelling a couple of tennis courts for next summer.

Something was being done to the porch, and the jasmine had been cleared away altogether. Mr. Brumley could not quite understand what was in progress ; Sir Isaac, he learnt afterwards, had found a wonderful bargain in a real genuine Georgian portal of great dignity and simplicity in Aleham, and he was going to improve Black Strand by transferring it thither—with the utmost precaution and every piece numbered—from its original situation. Mr. Brumley stood among the preparatory debris of this and rang a quietly resolute electric bell, which was answered no longer by Mrs. Rabbit but by the ample presence of Snagsby.

Snagsby in that doorway had something of the preposterous effect of a very large face beneath a very small hat. He had, to Mr. Brumley's eye, a restored look, as though his self-confidence had been thoroughly done up since their last encounter. Bygones were bygones. Mr. Brumley was admitted as one is admitted to any normal home. He was shown into the little study-drawing-room with the stepped floor, which had been so largely the scene of his life with Euphemia, and he was left there for the better part of a quarter of an hour before his hostess appeared.

The room had been changed very little. Euphemia's solitary rose had gone, and instead there were several bowls of beaten silver scattered about, each filled with great chrysanthemums from London. Sir Isaac's jackdaw acquisitiveness had also overcrowded the corner beyond the fireplace with a very fine and genuine Queen Anne cabinet ; there were a novel by Elizabeth Robins and two or three feminist and socialist works lying on the table, which would certainly not have been visible, though they might have been in the house, during the Brumley régime. Otherwise things were very much as they always had been.

A room like this, thought Mr. Brumley among much other mental driftage, is like a heart—so long as it exists it must be furnished and tenanted. No matter what has been, however bright and sweet and tender, the spaces still cry aloud to be filled again. The very essence of life is its insatiability. How complete all this had seemed in the moment when first he and Euphemia had arranged it. And indeed how complete life had seemed altogether at seven-and-twenty. Every year since then he had been learning—or, at any rate, unlearning. Until at last he was beginning to realise he had still every-thing to learn. . . .

The door opened and the tall dark figure of Lady Harman stood for a moment in the doorway before she stepped down into the room.

She had always the same effect upon him, the effect of being suddenly remembered. When he was away from her he was always sure that she was a beautiful woman, and when he saw her again he was always astonished to see how little he had borne her beauty in mind. For a moment they regarded one another silently. Then she closed the door behind her and came towards him.

All Mr. Brumley's philosophising had vanished at the sight of her. His spirit was reborn within him. He thought of her and of his effect upon her, vividly, and of nothing else in the world.

She was paler, he thought, beneath her dusky hair, a little thinner and graver. . . .

There was something in her manner as she advanced towards him that told him he mattered to her, that his coming there was something that moved her imagination as well as his own. With an almost impulsive movement she held out both her hands to him, and with an inspiration as sudden he took them and kissed them. When he had done so he was ashamed of his temerity; he looked up to meet in her dark eyes the scared shyness of a fallow deer. She suddenly remembered to withdraw her hands, and it became manifest to both of them that the incident must never have happened. She went to the window, stood almost awkwardly for a moment looking out of it, then turned. She put her hands on the back of the chair and stood holding it.

" I knew you would come to see me," she said.

" I've been very anxious about you," he said, and on that their minds rested through a little silence.

" You see," he explained, " I didn't know what was happening to you. Or what you were doing."

" After asking your advice," she said.

" Exactly."

" I don't know why I broke that window. Except I think that I wanted to get away."

" But why didn't you come to me ? "

" I didn't know where you were. And besides—— I didn't somehow want to come to you."

" But wasn't it wretched in prison ? Wasn't it miserably cold ? I used to think of you of nights in some wretched, ill-aired cell. . . . You. . . ."

" It *was* cold," she admitted. " But it was very good for me. It was quiet. The first few days seemed endless ; then they began to go by quickly. Quite quickly at last. And I came to think. In the day there was a little stool where one sat. I used to sit on that and brood, and try to think things out—all sorts of things I've never had the chance to think about before."

" Yes," said Mr. Brumley.

" All this," she said.

" And it has brought you back here ! " he said, with something of the tone of one who has a right to inquire, with some flavour too of reproach.

" You see," she said after a little pause, " during that time it was possible to come to understandings. Neither I nor my husband had understood the other. In that interval it was possible—to explain.

" Yes. You see, Mr. Brumley, we—we both misunderstood. It was just because of that and because I had no one who seemed able to advise me that I turned to you. A novelist always seems so wise in these things. He seems to know so many lives. One can talk to you as one can scarcely talk to any one ; you are a sort of doctor—in these matters. And it was necessary—that my husband should realise that I had grown up and that I should have time to think just how one's duty and one's—freedom have to be fitted together. . . . And my husband is ill. He has been ill, rather short of breath—the doctor thinks it is asthma—for some time, and all the agitation of this business has upset him and made him worse. He is upstairs now—asleep. Of course if I had thought I should make him ill I could never have done any of this. But it's done now and here I am, Mr. Brumley, back in my place. With all sorts of things changed. Put right. . . ."

" I see," said Mr. Brumley stupidly.

Her speech was like the falling of an opaque curtain upon some romantic spectacle. She stood there, almost defensively behind her chair as she made it. There was a quality of premeditation in her words, yet something in her voice and bearing made him feel that she knew just how it covered up and extinguished his dreams and impulses. He heard her out and then suddenly his spirit rebelled against her decision. " No ! " he cried.

She waited for him to go on.

" You see," he said, " I thought that it was just that you wanted to get away—— That this life was intolerable—— That you were — forgive me if I seem to be going beyond —going beyond what I ought to be thinking about you. Only, why should I pretend ? I care, I care for you tremendously. And it seemed to me that you didn't love your husband, that you were enslaved and miserable. I would have done anything to help you—anything in the world, Lady Harman. I know —it may sound ridiculous—there have been times when I would have faced death to feel you were happy and free. I thought all that, I felt all that—and then—then you come back here. You seem not to have minded. As though I had misunderstood. . . ."

He paused, and his face was alive with an unwonted sincerity. His self-consciousness had for a moment fallen from him.

" I know," she said, " it *was* like that. I knew you cared. That is why I have so wanted to talk to you. It looked like that. . . ."

She pressed her lips together in that old familiar hunt for words and phrases.

" I didn't understand, Mr. Brumley, all there was in my husband or all there was in myself. I just saw his hardness and his—his hardness in business. It's become so different now. You see, I forgot he has bad health. He's ill ; I suppose he was getting ill then. Instead of explaining himself—he was—excited and—unwise. And now——"

" Now I suppose he has—explained," said Mr. Brumley slowly and with infinite distaste. " Lady Harman, *what* has he explained ? "

" It isn't so much that he has explained, Mr. Brumley," said Lady Harman, " as that things have explained themselves."

" But how, Lady Harman ? How ? "

" I mean about my being a mere girl, almost a child when I married him. Naturally he wanted to take charge of everything and leave nothing to me. And quite as naturally he didn't notice that now I am a woman, grown up altogether. And it's been necessary to do things. And naturally, Mr. Brumley, they shocked and upset him. But he sees now so clearly, he wrote to me, such a fair letter—an unusual letter—quite different from when he talks—it surprised me, telling me he wanted me to feel free, that he meant to make me—to arrange things that is, so that I should feel free and more able to go about as I pleased. It was a *generous* letter, Mr. Brumley. Generous about all sorts of affairs that there had been between us. He said things, quite kind things, not like the things he has ever said before——"

She stopped short and then began again.

" You know, Mr. Brumley, it's so hard to tell things without telling other things that somehow are difficult to tell. Yet if I don't tell you them, you won't know them, and then you won't be able to understand in the least how things are with us."

Her eyes appealed to him.

" Tell me," he said, " whatever you think fit."

" When one has been afraid of any one and felt they were ever so much stronger and cruel and hard than one is, and one suddenly finds they aren't, it alters everything."

He nodded, watching her.

Her voice fell nearly to a whisper. " Mr. Brumley," she said, " when I came back to him—you know he was in bed here—instead of scolding me—he *cried*. He cried like a vexed child. He put his face into the pillow—just misery. . . . I'd never seen him cry—at least only once—long ago. . . ."

Mr. Brumley looked at her flushed and tender face, and it seemed to him that indeed he could die for her quite easily.

" I saw how hard I had been," she said. " In prison I'd thought of that, I'd thought women mustn't be hard, whatever happens to them. And when I saw him like that I knew at once how true that was. . . . He begged me to be a good wife to him. No !—he just said, ' Be a wife to me,' not even a good wife—and then he cried. . . ."

For a moment or so Mr. Brumley didn't respond. " I see," he said at last. " Yes."

" And there were the children—such helpless little things. In prison I worried about them. I thought of things for them. I've come to feel—they are left too much to nurses and strangers. . . . And then you see he has agreed to nearly everything I had wanted. It wasn't only the personal things— I was anxious about those silly girls—the strikers. I didn't want them to be badly treated. It distressed me to think of them. I don't think you know how it distressed me. And he— he gave way upon all that. He says I may talk to him about the business, about the way we do our business—the kindness of it, I mean. And this is why I am back here. Where else *could* I be ? "

" No," said Mr. Brumley, still with the utmost reluctance. " I see. Only——"

He paused, downcast, and she waited for him to speak.

" Only it isn't what I expected, Lady Harman. I didn't think that matters could be settled by such arrangements. It's sane, I know, it's comfortable and kindly. But I thought—oh ! I thought of different things, quite different things from all this. I thought of you who are so beautiful caught in a loveless, passionless world. I thought of the things there might be for you, the beautiful and wonderful things of which you are deprived. . . . Never mind what I thought ! Never mind ! You've made your choice. But I thought that you didn't love, that you couldn't love—this man. It seemed to me that you felt too—that to live as you are doing—with him—was a pro- fanity. Something—I'd give everything I have, everything I am to save you from. Because I care. . . . I misunder- stood you. I suppose you can—do what you are doing."

He jumped to his feet as he spoke, and walked three paces away and turned to utter his last sentences. She too stood up.

" Mr. Brumley," she said weakly, " I don't understand. What do you mean ? I have to do what I am doing. He—he is my husband."

He made a gesture of impatience. " Do you understand nothing of love ? " he cried.

She pressed her lips together and remained still and silent, dark against the casement window.

There came a sound of tapping from the room above. Three taps and again three taps.

Lady Harman made a little gesture as though she would put this sound aside.

"Love," she said at last. "It comes to some people. It happens. It happens to young people. . . . But when one is married——"

Her voice fell almost to a whisper. "One must not think of it," she said. "One must think of one's husband and one's duty. Life cannot begin again, Mr. Brumley."

The taps were repeated, a little more urgently.

"That is my husband," she said.

She hesitated through a little pause. "Mr. Brumley," she said, "I want friendship so badly, I want some one to be my friend. I don't want to think of things—disturbing things—things I have lost—things that are spoilt. *That*—that which you spoke of ; what has it to do with me ? "

She interrupted him as he was about to speak.

" Be my friend. Don't talk to me of impossible things. Love ! Mr. Brumley, what has a married woman to do with love ? I never think of it. I never read of it. I want to do my duty. I want to do my duty by him and by my children and by all the people I am bound to. I want to help people, weak people, people who suffer. I want to help him to help them. I want to stop being an idle, useless, spending woman. . . ."

She made a little gesture of appeal with her hands.

"Oh ! " he sighed, and then, "You know if I can help you—— Rather than distress you——"

Her manner changed. It became confidential and urgent.

"Mr. Brumley," she said, "I must go up to my husband. He will be impatient. And when I tell him you are here he will want to see you. . . . You will come up and see him ? "

Mr. Brumley sought to convey the struggle within him by his pose.

"I will do what you wish, Lady Harman," he said, with an almost theatrical sigh.

He closed the door after her and was alone in his former study once more. He walked slowly to his old writing-desk and sat down in his familiar seat. Presently he heard her footfalls across the room above. Mr. Brumley's mind under the stress of the unfamiliar and unexpected was now lapsing rapidly towards the theatrical. " My *God* ! " said Mr. Brumley.

He addressed that friendly, memorable room in tones that mingled amazement and wrong. "He is her husband ! " he said, and then ; "The power of words ! " . . .

§ 7

It seemed to Mr. Brumley's now entirely disordered mind that Sir Isaac, propped up with cushions upon a sofa in the upstairs sitting-room, white-faced, wary, and very short of breath, was like proprietorship enthroned. Everything about him referred deferentially to him. Even his wife dropped at once into the position of a beautiful satellite. His illness, he assured his visitor with a thin-lipped emphasis, was " quite temporary, quite the sort of thing that might happen to any one." He had had a queer little benumbing of one leg, " just a trifle of nerve fag did it," and the slight asthma that came and went in his life had taken advantage of his condition to come again with a little beyond its usual aggressiveness. " Elly is going to take me off to Marienbad next week or the week after," he said. " I shall have a cure and she'll have a treat, and we shall come back as fit as fiddles." The incidents of the past month were to be put on a facetious footing, it appeared. " It's a mercy they didn't crop her hair," he said, à propos of nothing, and with an air of dry humour. No further allusion was made to Lady Harman's incarceration.

He was dressed in a llama wool bedroom suit, and his resting leg was covered by a very splendid and beautiful fur rug. All Euphemia's best and gayest cushions sustained his back. The furniture had been completely rearranged for his comfort and convenience. Close to his hand was a little table with carefully selected remedies and aids and helps and stimulants, and the latest and best of the light fiction of the day was tossed about between the table, the couch, and the floor. At the foot of the couch Euphemia's bedroom writing-table had been placed, and over this there were scattered traces of the stenographer who had assisted him to wipe off the day's correspondence. Three black cylinders and other appliances in the corner witnessed that his slight difficulty in breathing could be relieved by oxygen, and his eyes were regaled by a great abundance of London flowers at every available point in the room. Of course there were grapes, fabulous looking grapes.

Everything conspired to give Sir Isaac and his ownership the centre of the picture. Mr. Brumley had been brought up-stairs to him, and the tea-table, with scarcely a reference to any one else, was arranged by Snagsby conveniently to his hand. And Sir Isaac himself had a confidence—the assurance of a man who has been shaken and has recovered. Whatever tears he had ever shed had served their purpose and were forgotten. " Elly " was his and the house was his and everything about him was his—he laid his hand upon her once when she came near him, his possessiveness was so gross—and the strained suspicion of his last meeting with Mr. Brumley was replaced now by a sage and wizened triumph over anticipated and arrested dangers.

Their party was joined by Sir Isaac's mother, and the sight of her sturdy, swarthy, and rather dignified presence flashed the thought into Mr. Brumley's mind that Sir Isaac's father must have been a very blond and very nosey person indeed. She was homely and practical, and contributed very usefully to a conversation that remained a trifle fragmentary and faintly uncomfortable to the end.

Mr. Brumley avoided as much as he could looking at Lady Harman, because he knew Sir Isaac was alert for that, but he was acutely aware of her presence dispensing the tea and moving about the room, being a good wife. It was his first impression of Lady Harman as a good wife, and he disliked the spectacle extremely. The conversation hovered chiefly about Marienbad, drifted away and came back again. Mrs. Harman made several confidences that provoked the betrayal of a strain of irritability in Sir Isaac's condition. "We're all looking forward to this Marienbad expedition," she said. "I do hope it will turn out well. Neither of them have ever been abroad before—and there's the difficulty of the languages."

"Ow," snarled Sir Isaac, with a glance at his mother that was almost vicious and a lapse into Cockney intonations and phrases that witnessed how her presence recalled his youth. "It'll *go* all right, mother. *You* needn't fret."

"Of course they'll have a courier to see to their things, and go train de luxe and all that," Mrs. Harman explained with a certain gusto. "But still, it's an adventure, with him not well, and both, as I say, more like children than grown-up people."

Sir Isaac intervened with a crushing clumsiness to divert this strain of explanation, with questions about the quality of the soil in the wood where the ground was to be cleared and levelled for his tennis lawn.

Mr. Brumley did his best to behave as a man of the world should. He made intelligent replies about the sand, he threw out obvious but serviceable advice upon travel on the Continent of Europe, and he tried not to think that this was the way of living into which the sweetest, tenderest, most beautiful woman in the world had been trapped. He avoided looking at her until he felt it was becoming conspicuous, a negative stare. Why had she come back again ? Fragmentary phrases she had used downstairs came drifting through his mind. " I never think of it. I never read of it." And she so made for beautiful love and a beautiful life ! He recalled Lady Beach-Mandarin's absurdly apt, absurdly inept, " like Godiva," and was suddenly impelled to raise the question of those strikers.

" Your trouble with your waitresses is over, Sir Isaac."

Sir Isaac finished a cup of tea audibly and glanced at his wife. " I never meant to be hard on them," he said, putting down his cup. " Never. The trouble blew up suddenly. One can't be all over a big business everywhere all at once, more particularly if one is worried about other things. As soon as I had time to look into it I put things right. There was mis-understandings on both sides."

He glanced up again at Lady Harman. (She was standing behind Mr. Brumley so that he could not see her, but—did their eyes meet ?)

" As soon as we are back from Marienbad," Sir Isaac volunteered, " Lady Harman and I are going into all that business thoroughly."

Mr. Brumley concealed his intense aversion for this association under a tone of intelligent interest. " Into—I don't quite understand—what business ? "

" Women employees in London—hostels—all that kind of thing. Bit more sensible than suffragetting, eh, Elly ? "

" Very interesting," said Mr. Brumley, with a hollow cordiality, " very."

" Done on business lines, mind you," said Sir Isaac, looking suddenly very sharp and keen ; " done on proper business lines, there's no end of a change possible. And it's a perfectly legitimate outgrowth from such popular catering as ours. It interests me."

He made a little whistling noise with his teeth at the end of this speech.

" I didn't know Lady Harman was disposed to take up such things," he said. " Or I'd have gone into them before."

" He's going into them now," said Mrs. Harman, " heart and soul. Why ! we have to take his temperature over it, to see he doesn't work himself up into a fever." Her manner became reasonable and confidential. She spoke to Mr. Brumley as if her son was slightly deaf. " It's better than his fretting," she said. . . .

§ 8

Mr. Brumley returned to London in a state of extreme mental and emotional unrest. The sight of Lady Harman had restored all his passion for her, the all too manifest fact that she was receding beyond his reach stirred him with unavailing impulses towards some impossible extremity of effort. She had filled his mind so much that he could not endure the thought of living without hope of her. But what hope was there of her ? And he was jealous, detestably jealous, so jealous that in that direction he did not dare to let his mind go. He sawed at the bit and brought it back, or he would have had to writhe about the carriage. His thoughts ran furiously all over the place to avoid that pit. And now he found himself flashing at moments into wild and hopeless rebellion against the institution of marriage of which he had hitherto sought always to be the dignified and smiling champion against the innovator, the over-critical, and the young. He had never rebelled before. He was so astonished at the violence of his own objection that he lapsed from defiance to an incredulous examination of his own novel attitude. " It's not *true* marriage I object to," he told himself. " It's this marriage like a rat-trap, alluring and scarcely unavoidable, so that in we all go, and then with no escape—unless you tear yourself to rags. No escape. . . ."

It came to him that there was at least one way out for Lady Harman : *Sir Isaac might die !* . . .

He pulled himself up presently, astonished and dismayed at the activities of his own imagination. Among other things, he had wondered if by any chance Lady Harman had ever allowed her mind to travel in this same post-mortem direction. At times surely the thing must have shone upon her as a possibility, a hope. From that he had branched off to a more general speculation. How many people were there in the world, nice people, kind people, moral and delicate-minded people, to whom the death of another person means release from that inflexible barrier—possibilities of secretly desired happiness, the realisation of crushed and forbidden dreams ? He had a vision of human society, like the vision of a night landscape seen suddenly in a lightning flash, as of people caught by couples in traps and quietly hoping for one another's deaths. " Good Heavens ! " said Mr Brumley, " what are we coming to," and got up in his railway compartment—he had it to himself—and walked up and down its narrow limits until a jolt over a point made him suddenly sit down again. " Most marriages are happy," said Mr. Brumley, like a man who has fallen into a river and scrambles back to safety. " One mustn't judge by the exceptional cases. . . .

" Though, of course, there are—a good many—exceptional cases. . . ."

He folded his arms, crossed his legs, frowned and reasoned with himself—resolved to dismiss post-mortem speculations—absolutely.

He was not going to quarrel with the institution of marriage. That was going too far. He had never been able to see the beginnings of reason in sexual anarchy—never. It is against the very order of things. Man is a marrying animal just as much as he was a fire-making animal ; he goes in pairs like mantel ornaments ; it is as natural for him to marry and to exact and keep good faith—if need be with a savage jealousy, as it is for him to have lobes to his ears and hair under his armpits. These things jar with the dream perhaps ; the gods on painted ceilings have no such ties, acting beautifully by their very nature ; and here on the floor of the world one had them and one had to make the best of them. . . . Are we making the best of them ? Mr. Brumley was off again. That last thought opened the way to speculative wildernesses, and into these Mr. Brumley went wandering with a novel desperate enterprise to find a kind of marriage that would suit him.

He began to reform the marriage laws. He did his utmost not to think especially of Lady Harman and himself while he was doing so. He would just take up the whole question and deal with it in a temperate, reasonable way. It was so necessary to be reasonable and temperate in this question—and not to think of death as a solution. Marriages to begin with were too easy to make and too difficult to break ; countless girls—Lady Harman was only a type—were married long before

they could know the beginnings of their own minds. We
wanted to delay marriage—until the middle twenties, say.
Why not ? Or, if by the infirmities of humanity, one must
have marriage before then, there ought to be some especial
opportunity of rescinding it later. (Lady Harman ought to
have been able to rescind her marriage.) What ought to be the
marriageable age in a civilised community ? When the mind
was settled into its general system of opinions, Mr. Brumley
thought, and then lapsed into a speculation whether the mind
didn't keep changing and developing all through life ; Lady
Harman's was certainly still doing so. . . . This pointed to
logical consequences of an undesirable sort. . . .

(Some little mind-slide occurred just at this point, and he
found himself thinking that perhaps Sir Isaac might last for
years and years, might even outlive a wife exhausted by
nursing. And anyhow to wait for death ! To leave the thing
one loved in the embrace of the moribund !)

He wrenched his thoughts back as quickly as possible to a
disinterested reform of the marriage laws. What had he
decided so far ? Only for more deliberation and a riper age
in marrying. Surely that should appeal even to the most
orthodox. But that alone would not eliminate mistakes and
deceptions altogether. (Sir Isaac's skin had a peculiar, unhealthy look.) There ought, in addition, to be the widest
facilities for divorce possible. Mr. Brumley tried to draw up
a schedule in his head of the grounds for divorce that a really
civilised community would entertain. But there are practical
difficulties. Marriage is not simply a sexual union, it is an
economic one of a peculiarly inseparable sort—and there are
the children. And jealousy ! Of course, so far as economics
went, a kind of marriage settlement might meet most of the
difficulties, and as for the children, Mr. Brumley was no
longer in that mood of enthusiastic devotion to children that
had made the birth of George Edmund so tremendous an
event. Children, alone, afforded no reason for indissoluble
lifelong union. Face the thing frankly. How long was it
absolutely necessary for people to keep a home together for
their children ? The prosperous classes, the best classes in
the community, packed the little creatures off to school at
the age of nine or ten. One might overdo—we were overdoing in our writing nowadays this—philoprogenitive enthusiasm. . . .

He found himself thinking of George Meredith's idea of ten-
year marriages. . . .

His mind recoiled to Sir Isaac's pillowed-up possession.
What flimsy stuff all this talk of altered marriage was ! These
things did not even touch the essentials of the matter. He
thought of Sir Isaac's thin lips and wary, knowing eyes.
What possible divorce law could the wit of man devise that
would release a desired woman from that—grip ? Marriage

was covetousness made law. As well ask such a man to sell all his goods and give to the poor, as expect the Sir Isaacs of this world to relax the matrimonial subjugation of the wife. Our social order is built on jealousy, sustained by jealousy, and those brave schemes we evolve in our studies for the release of women from ownership—and for that matter for the release of men too—they will not stand the dusty heat of the market-place for a moment, they wilt under the first fierce breath of reality. Marriage and property are the twin children of man's individualistic nature ; only on these terms can he be drawn into societies. . . .

Mr. Brumley found his little scheme for novelties in mar-riage and divorce lying dead, and for the most part stillborn in his mind ; himself in despair. To set to work to alter marriage in any essential point was, he realised, as if an ant should start to climb a thousand feet of cliff. This great institution rose upon his imagination like some insurmountable sierra, blue and sombre, between himself and the life of Lady Harman and all that he desired. There might be a certain amount of tinkering with matrimonial law in the next few years, of petty tinkering that would abolish a few pretences and give ease to a few amiable people, but if he were to come back to life a thousand years hence he felt he would still find the ancient, gigantic barrier, crossed perhaps by a dangerous road, pierced perhaps by a narrow tunnel or so, but in all its great essentials the same, between himself and Lady Harman. It wasn't that it was rational, it wasn't that it was justifiable, but it was one with the blood in one's veins and the rain-cloud in the sky, a necessity in the nature of present things. Before mankind emerged from the valley of these restraints— if ever they did emerge—thousands of generations must follow one another, there must be tens of thousands of years of struggle and thought and trial, in the teeth of prevalent habit and opinion—and primordial instincts. A new hu-manity. . . .

His heart sank to hopelessness.

Meanwhile ? Meanwhile we had to live our lives.

He began to see a certain justification for the hidden cults that run beneath the fair appearances of life, those social secrecies by which people—how could one put it ?—people who do not agree with established institutions, people, at any rate not merely egoistic and jealous as the crowd is egoistic and jealous, hide and help one another to mitigate the inflexible austerities of the great unreason.

Yes, Mr. Brumley had got to a phrase of that quality for the undiscriminating imperatives of the fundamental social institution. You see how a particular situation may undermine the assumptions of a mind originally devoted to uncritical acceptances. He still insisted it was a necessary great un-reason, absolutely necessary—for the mass of people, a part

of them, a natural expression of them, but he could imagine
the possibility—of " understandings." . . . Mr. Brumley was
very vague about those understandings, those mysteries of the
exalted that were to filch happiness from the destroying grasp
of the crude and jealous. He had to be vague. For secret
and noble are ideas like oil and water ; you may fling them
together with all the force of your will, but in a little while
they will separate again.

For a time this dream of an impossible secrecy was uppermost in Mr. Brumley's meditations. It came into his head
with the effect of a discovery that always among the un-
climbable barriers of this supreme institution there had been
—caves. He had been reading Anatole France recently and
the lady of *Le Lys Rouge* came into his thoughts. There was
something in common between Lady Harman and the Countess
Martin, they were tall and dark and dignified, and Lady
Harman was one of those rare women who could have carried
the magnificent name of Thérèse. And there in the setting of
Paris and Florence was a whole microcosm of love, real but
illicit, carried out, as it were, secretly and tactfully, beneath
the great shadow of the cliff. But he found it difficult to
imagine Lady Harman in that. Or Sir Isaac playing Count
Martin's part. . . .

How different were those Frenchwomen, with their afternoons vacant except for love, their detachment, their lovers,
those secret, convenient, romantically furnished flats, that
compact explicit business of *l'amour !* He had indeed some
moments of regret that Lady Harman wouldn't go into that
picture. She was different—if only in her simplicity. There
was something about these others that put them whole worlds
apart from her, who was held so tethered from all furtive
adventure by her filmy tentacles of responsibility, her ties
and strands of relationship, her essential delicacy. That
momentary vision of Ellen as the Countess Martin broke up
into absurdities directly he looked at it fully and steadfastly.
From thinking of the two women as similar types he passed
into thinking of them as opposites ; Thérèse, hard, clear,
sensuous, secretive, trained by a brilliant tradition in the
technique of connubial betrayal, was the very antithesis of
Ellen's vague but invincible veracity and openness. Not for
nothing had Anatole France made his heroine the daughter of
a grasping financial adventurer. . . .

Of course the cave is a part of the mountain. . . .

His mind drifted away to still more general speculations,
and always he was trying not to see the figure of Sir Isaac,
grimly and yet meanly resolute—in possession. Always too,
like some open-mouthed yokel at a fair, who knows nothing
of the insult chalked upon his back, he disregarded how he
himself coveted and desired and would, if he could, have
gripped. He forgot his own watchful attention to Euphemia

in the past, nor did he think what he might have been if Lady Harman had been his wife. It needed the chill veràcities of the small hours to bring him to that. He thought now of crude egotism as having Sir Isaac's hands and Sir Isaac's eyes and Sir Isaac's position. He forgot any egotism he himself was betraying.

All the paths of enlightenment he thought of, led to Lady Harman.

§ 9

That evening George Edmund, who had come home with his mind aglitter with cinematograph impressions, found his father a patient but inattentive listener. For indeed Mr. Brumley was not listening at all ; he was thinking and thinking. He made noises like " Ah ! " and " Um," at George Edmund, and patted the boy's shoulder kindly and repeated words unintelligently, such as " Red Indians, eh ! " or " Came out of the water backwards ! My eye ! "

Sometimes he made what George Edmund regarded as quite footling comments. Still George Edmund had to tell some one, and there was no one else to tell. So George Edmund went on talking and Mr. Brumley went on thinking.

§ 10

Mr. Brumley could not sleep at all until it was nearly five. His intelligence seemed to be making up at last for years of speculative restraint. In a world for the most part given up to slumber Mr. Brumley may be imagined as clambering hand over fist in the silences, feverishly and wonderfully overtaking his age. In the morning he got up pallid and he shaved badly, but he was a generation ahead of his own Euphemia series, and the school of charm and quiet humour and of letting things slide with a kind of elegant donnishness had lost him for ever. . . .

And among all sorts of things that had come to him in that vast gulf of nocturnal thinking was some vivid self-examination. At last he got to that. He had been dragged down to very elemental things indeed by the manifest completeness of Lady Harman's return to her husband. He had had at last to look at himself starkly for the male he was, to go beneath the gentlemanly airs, the refined and elegant virilities of his habitual poses. Either this thing was un-endurable—there were certainly moments when it came near to being unendurable—or it was not. On the whole and excepting mere momentary paroxysms, it was not, and so he had to recognise, and he did recognise, with the greatest amazement that there could be something else besides sexual attraction and manœuvring and possession between a beautiful woman and a man like himself. He loved Lady Harman, he loved her, he now began to realise just how much, and she could defeat him and reject him as a conceivable lover, turn that aside as a thing impossible, shame him as the romantic school would count shame, and still command him with her confident eyes and her friendly, extended hands. He admitted he suffered, let us rather say he claimed to suffer, the heated torments of a passionate nature, but he perceived like fresh air and sunrise coming by blind updrawn and opened window into a fœtid chamber, that also he loved her with a clean and bodiless love, was anxious to help her, was anxious now—it was a new thing—to understand her, to reassure her, to give unrequited what once he had sought rather to seem to give in view of an imagined exchange.

He perceived too, in these still hours, how little he had understood her hitherto. He had been blinded—obsessed. He had been seeing her and himself and the whole world far too much as a display of the eternal dualism of sex, the incessant pursuit. Now with his sexual imaginings newly humbled and hopeless, with a realisation of her own tremendous minimisation of that fundamental of romance, he began to see all that there was in her personality and their possible relations outside that. He saw how gravely and deeply serious was her fine philanthropy, how honest and simple and impersonal her desire for knowledge and understandings. There is the brain of her at least, he thought, far out of Sir Isaac's reach. She wasn't abased by her surrenders, their simplicity exalted her, showed her innocent and himself a flushed and congested soul. He perceived now, with the astonishment of a man newly awakened, just how the great obsession of sex had dominated him—for how many years ? Since his early undergraduate days. Had he anything to put beside her own fine detachment ? Had he ever since his manhood touched philosophy, touched a social question, thought of anything human, thought of art, or literature or belief, without a glancing reference of the whole question to the uses of this eternal hunt ? During that time had he ever talked to a girl or woman with an unembarrassed sincerity ? He stripped his pretences bare ; the answer was no. His very refinements had been no more than indicative fig-leaves. His conservatism and morality had been a mere dalliance with interests that too brutal a simplicity might have exhausted prematurely. And, indeed, hadn't the whole period of literature that had produced him been, in its straining purity and refinement, as it were one glowing, one illuminated fig-leaf, a vast conspiracy to keep certain matters always in mind by conspicuously covering them away ? But this wonderful woman—it seemed —she hadn't them in mind ! She shamed him if only by her trustful unsuspiciousness of the ancient selfish game of him and her that he had been so ardently playing. . . . He idolised and worshipped this clean blindness. He abased himself before it.

"No," cried Mr. Brumley, suddenly in the silence of the night, "I will rise again. I will rise again by love out of these morasses. . . . She shall be my goddess, and by virtue of her I will end this incessant, irrational craving for women. . . . I will be her friend and her faithful friend."

He lay still for a time, and then he said in a whisper very humbly: "*God help me.*"

He set himself in those still hours which are so endless and so profitable to men in their middle years to think how he might make himself the perfect lover instead of a mere plotter for desire, and how he might purge himself from covetousness and possessiveness and learn to serve.

And if very speedily his initial sincerity was tinged again with egotism, and if he drowsed at last into a portrait of himself as beautifully and admirably self-sacrificial, you must not sneer too readily at him, for so God has made the soul of Mr. Brumley and otherwise it could not do.

CHAPTER TEN

LADY HARMAN COMES OUT

§ 1

THE treaty between Lady Harman and her husband which was to be her Great Charter, the constitutional basis of her freedoms throughout the rest of her married life, had many practical defects. The chief of these was that it was largely undocumented; it had been made piecemeal, in various ways, at different times, and for the most part indirectly through diverse intermediaries. Charterson had introduced large vaguenesses by simply displaying more of his teeth at crucial moments, Mrs. Harman had conveyed things by hugging and weeping that were afterwards discovered to be indistinct; Sir Isaac, writing from a bed of sickness, had frequently been totally illegible. One cannot therefore detail the clauses of this agreement or give its provisions with any great precision; one can simply intimate the kind of understanding that had had an air of being arrived at. The working interpretations were still to come.

Before anything else it was manifestly conceded by Lady Harman that she would not run away again, and still more manifest that she undertook to break no more windows or do anything that might lead to a second police court scandal. And she was to be a true and faithful wife and comfort, as a wife should be, to Sir Isaac. In return for that consideration and to ensure its continuance, Sir Isaac came great distances from his former assumption of a matrimonial absolutism. She was to be granted all sorts of small autonomies—the word autonomy was carefully avoided throughout but its spirit was omnipresent.

She was, in particular, to have a banking account for her dress and personal expenditure into which Sir Isaac would cause to be paid a hundred pounds monthly, and it was to be private to herself alone until he chose to go through the cashed cheques and counterfoils. She was to be free to come and go as she saw fit, subject to a punctual appearance at meals, the comfort and dignity of Sir Isaac, and such specific engagements as she might make with him. She might have her own friends, but there the contract became a little misty ; a time was to come when Sir Isaac was to betray a conviction that the only proper friends that a woman can have are women. There were also non-corroborated assurances as to the privacy of her correspondence. The second Rolls-Royce car was to be entirely at her service, and Clarence was to be immediately supplemented by a new and more deferential man, and as soon as possible assisted to another situation and replaced. She was to have a voice in the further furnishing of Black Strand and in the arrangement of its gardens. She was to read what she chose and think what she liked within her head without too minute or suspicious an examination by Sir Isaac, and short of flat contradiction at his own table, she was to be free to express her own opinions in any manner becoming a lady. But more particularly if she found her ideas infringing upon the management or influence of the International Bread and Cake Stores, she was to convey her objections and ideas in the first instance privately and confidentially to Sir Isaac.

Upon this point he displayed a remarkable and creditable sensitiveness. His pride in that organisation was, if possible, greater than his original pride in his wife, and probably nothing in all the jarring of their relationship had hurt him more than her accessibility to hostile criticism and the dinner-table conversation with Charterson and Blenker that had betrayed this fact. He began to talk about it directly she returned to him. His protestations and explanations were copious and heartfelt. It was perhaps the chief discovery made by Lady Harman at this period of reconstruction that her husband's business side was not to be explained completely as a highly energetic and elaborate avarice. He was no doubt acquisitive and retentive and mean-spirited, but these were merely the ugly aspects of a disposition that involved many other factors. He was also incurably a schemer. He liked to fit things together, to dovetail arrangements to devise economies, to spread ingeniously into new fields ; he had a love of organisation and contrivance as disinterested as an artist's love for the possibilities of his medium. He would rather have made a profit of ten per cent. out of a subtly

planned shop than thirty by an unforeseen accident. He
wouldn't have cheated to get money for the world. He knew
he was better at figuring out expenditures and receipts than
most people, and he was as touchy about his reputation for
this kind of cleverness as any poet or painter for his fame.
Now that he had awakened to the idea that his wife was
capable of looking into and possibly even understanding his
business, he was passionately anxious to show her just how
wonderfully he had done it all, and when he perceived she was
in her large, unskilled, helpless way intensely concerned for
all the vast multitude of incompetent or partially competent
young women who floundered about in badly paid employment
in our great cities, he grasped at once at the opportunity of
recovering her lost interest and respect by doing some brilliant
feats of contrivance in that direction. Why shouldn't he ?
He had long observed with a certain envy the admirable
advertisement such firms as Lever and Cadbury and Bur-
roughs & Wellcome gained from their ostentatiously able and
generous treatment of their workpeople, and it seemed to him
conceivable that in the end it might not be at all detrimental
to his prosperity to put his hands to this long neglected piece
of social work. The Babs Wheeler business had been a real
injury in every way to the International Bread and Cake
Stores, and even if he didn't ultimately go to all the lengths
his wife seemed to contemplate, he was resolved, at any rate,
that an affair of that kind should not occur again. The expedition to Marienbad took with it a secretary who was also a
stenographer. A particularly smart young inspector and
Graper, the staff manager, had brisk four-day holidays once or
twice for consultation purposes ; Sir Isaac's rabbit-like architect was in attendance for a week, and the Harmans returned
to Putney with the first vivid greens of late March—for the
Putney Hill house was to be reopened and Black Strand
reserved now for week-end and summer use—with plans
already drawn out for four residential hostels in London,
primarily for the girl waitresses of the International Stores
who might have no homes or homes at an inconvenient
distance, and, secondarily, if any vacant accommodation
remained over, for any other employed young woman of the
same class. . . .

§ 2

Lady Harman came back to England from the pine-woods
and bright order and regimen and foreign novelty of their
Bohemian Kur-Ort, in a state of renewed perplexity. Already
that undocumented Magna Charta was manifestly not working
upon the lines she had anticipated. The glosses Sir Isaac put
upon it were extensive and remarkable and invariably in the
direction of restricting her liberties and resuming controls she
had supposed abandoned.

Marienbad had done wonders for him ; his slight limp had disappeared, his nervous energy was all restored ; except for a certain increase in his natural irritability and occasional panting fits, he seemed as well as he had ever been. At the end of their time at the Kur he was even going for walks. Once he went half-way up the Podhorn on foot. And with every increment in his strength his aggressiveness increased, his recognition of her new freedoms was less cordial, and her sense of contrition and responsibility diminished. Moreover, as the scheme of those hostels, which had played so large a part in her conception of their reconciliation, grew more and more definite, she perceived more and more that it was not certainly that fine and humanising thing she had presumed it would be. She began to feel more and more that it might be merely an extension of Harman methods to cheap boarding-houses for young people. But, faced with a mass of detailed concrete projects and invited to suggest modifications, she was able to realise for the first time how vague, how ignorant and incompetent, her wishes had been, how much she had to understand and how much she had to discover before she could meet Sir Isaac with his " I'm doing it all for you, Elly. If you don't like it, you tell me what you don't like and I'll alter it. But just vague doubting ! One can't do anything with vague doubting."

She felt that once back in England, out of this picturesque, toylike German world, she would be able to grasp realities again and deal with these things. She wanted advice, she wanted to hear what people said of her ideas. She would also, she imagined, begin to avail herself of those conceded liberties which their isolation together abroad and her husband's constant need of her presence had so far prevented her from tasting. She had an idea that Susan Burnet might prove suggestive about the hostels.

And, moreover, if now and then she could have a good talk with some one understanding and intelligent, some one she could trust, some one who cared enough for her to think with her and for her. . . .

§ 3

We have traced thus far the emergence of Lady Harman from that state of dutiful subjection and social irresponsibility which was the lot of woman in the past to that limited, ill-defined and quite unsecured freedom which is her present condition. And now we have to give an outline of the ideas of herself and her uses and what she had to do, which were forming themselves in her mind. She had made a determination of herself, which carried her along the lines of her natural predisposition, to duty, to service. There she displayed that acceptance of responsibility which is so much more often a eminine than a masculine habit of thinking. But she brought to the achievement of this determination a discriminating integrity of mind that is more frequently masculine than feminine. She wanted to know clearly what she was undertaking and how far its consequences would reach and how it was related to other things.

Her confused reading during the last few years, and her own observation and such leakages of fact into her life as the talk of Susan Burnet, had all contributed to her realisation that the world was full of needless discomfort and hardships and failure, due to great, imperfectly apprehended injustices and maladjustments in the social system, and recently it had been borne in upon her, upon the barbed point of the *London Lion* and the quick tongue of Susan, that if any particular class of people was more answerable than any other for these evils, it was the people of leisure and freedom like herself, who had time to think, and the directing, organising people like her husband, who had power to change. She was called upon to do something, at times the call became urgent, and she could not feel any assurance which it was of the many vague and conflicting suggestions that came drifting to her that she had to do. Her idea of hostels for the International waitresses had been wrung out of her prematurely during her earlier discussions with her husband. She did not feel that it was anything more than a partial remedy for a special evil. She wanted something more general than that, something comprehensive enough to answer completely so wide a question as " What ought I to be doing with all my life ? " In the honest simplicity of her nature she wanted to find an answer to that. Out of the confusion of voices about us she hoped to be able to disentangle directions for her life. Already she had been reading voraciously ; while she was still at Marienbad she had written to Mr. Brumley, and he had sent her books and papers, advanced and radical in many cases, that she might know, " What are people thinking ? "

Many phrases from her earlier discussions with Sir Isaac stuck in her mind in a curiously stimulating way and came back to her as she read. She recalled him, for instance, with his face white and his eyes red and his flat hand sawing at her, saying : " I dessay I'm all wrong, I dessay I don't know anything about anything, and all those chaps you read, Bernud Shaw, and Gosworthy, and all the rest of them are wonderfully clever ; but you tell me, Elly, what they say we've got to do ! You tell me that. You go and ask some of those chaps just what they want a man like me to do. . . . They'll ask me to endow a theatre or run a club for novelists or advertise the lot of them in the windows of my International Stores or something. And that's about all it comes to. You go and see if I'm not right. They grumble and they grumble ; I don't say there's not a lot to grumble at, but give me something they'll back themselves for all they're worth as good to get done. . . .

That's where I don't agree with all these idees. They're wind, Elly, weak wind at that."

It is distressing to record how difficult it was for Lady Harman to form even the beginnings of a disproof of that. Her life through all this second phase of mitigated autonomy was an intermittent pilgrimage in search of that disproof. She could not believe that things as they were, this mass of hardships, cruelties, insufficiencies, and heartburnings were the ultimate wisdom and possibility of human life, yet when she went from them to the projects that would replace or change them she seemed to pass from things of overwhelming solidity to matters more thin and flimsy than the twittering of sparrows on the gutter. So soon as she returned to London she started upon her search for a solution ; she supplemented Mr. Brumley's hunt for books with her own efforts, she went to meetings—sometimes Sir Isaac took her, once or twice she was escorted by Mr. Brumley, and presently her grave interest and her personal charm had gathered about her a circle of companionable friends. She tried to talk to people, and made great efforts to hear people who seemed authoritative and wise and leaderlike, talking.

There were many interruptions to this research, but she persevered. Quite early she had an illness that ended in a miscarriage, an accident for which she was by no means inconsolable, and before she had completely recovered from that Sir Isaac fell ill again, the first of a series of relapses that necessitated further foreign travel—always in elaborately comfortable trains with maid, courier, valet, and secretary, to some warm and indolent southward place. And few people knew how uncertain her liberties were. Sir Isaac was the victim of an increasing irritability, at times he had irrational outbursts of distrust that would culminate in passionate outbreaks and scenes that were truncated by an almost suffocating breathlessness. On several occasions he was on the verge of quarrelling violently with her visitors, and he would suddenly oblige her to break engagements, pour abuse upon her, and bring matters back to the very verge of her first revolt. And then he would break her down by pitiful appeals. The cylinders of oxygen would be resorted to, and he would emerge from the crisis rather rueful, tamed, and quiet for the time.

He was her chief disturbance. Her children were healthy children, and fell in with the routines of governess and tutor that their wealth provided. She saw them often, she noted their increasing resemblance to their father, she did her best to soften the natural secretiveness and aggressiveness of their manners, she watched their teachers and intervened whenever the influences about them seemed to her to need intervention, she dressed them and gave them presents and tried to believe she loved them, and as Sir Isaac's illness increased she took a larger and larger share in the direction of the household. . . .

Through all these occupations and interruptions and im-
mediacies she went trying to comprehend and at times almost
believing she comprehended life, and then the whole spectacle
of this modern world of which she was a part would seem to
break up again into a multitude of warring and discordant
fragments having no conceivable common aim or solution.
Those moments of unifying faith and confidence, that glowed
so bravely and never endured, were at once tantalising and
sustaining.   She could never believe but that ultimately she
would not grasp and hold—something. . . .

Many people met her and liked her, and sought to know
more of her ; Lady Beach-Mandarin and Lady Viping were
happy to be her social sponsors, the Blenkers and the Chartersons met her out and woke up cautiously to this new possibility ;
her emergence was rapid in spite of the various delays and
interruptions I have mentioned, and she was soon in a position
to realise just how little one meets when one meets a number òf
people and how little one hears when one has much conversation.   Her mind was presently crowded with confused impressions of pleasant men evading her agreeably and making
out of her gravities an opportunity for bright sayings, and of
women being vaguely solemn and quite indefinite.

She went into the circle of movements, was tried over by
Mrs. Hubert Plessington, she questioned this and that pro-
moter of constructive schemes, and instead of mental meat
she was asked to come upon committees and sounded for
subscriptions. On several occasions, escorted by Mr. Brumley—
some instinct made her conceal or minimise his share in these
expeditions to her husband—she went as inconspicuously as
possible to the backs of public meetings in which she understood
great questions were being discussed or great changes inaugurated.   Some public figures she even followed up for a time,
distrusting her first impressions.

She became familiar with the manners and bearing of our
platform class, with the solemn dummy-like chairman or
chairwoman, saying a few words, the alert secretary or organiser,
the prominent figures sitting with an air of grave responsibility,
generously acting an intelligent attention to others until the
moment came for them themselves to deliver. Then with an
ill-concealed relief some would come to the footlights, some
leap up in their places with a tenoring eagerness, some would be
facetious, and some speak with neuralgic effort, some were
impertinent, some propitiatory, some dull, but all were—
disappointing, disappointing. God was not in any of them. A
platform is no setting for the shy processes of an honest human
mind—we are all strained to artificiality in the excessive glare
of attention that beats upon us there. One does not exhibit
opinions at a meeting, one acts them, the very truth must
rouge its cheeks and blacken its eyebrows to tell, and to Lady
Harman it was the acting chiefly and the make up that was

visible. They didn't grip her, they didn't lift her, they failed to convince her even of their own belief in what they supported.

§ 4

But occasionally among the multitude of conversations that gave her nothing, there would come some talk that illuminated and for the time almost reconciled her to the effort and the loss of time and distraction her social expeditions involved. One evening at one of Lady Tarvrille's carelessly compiled parties she encountered Edgar Wilkins, the novelist, and got the most suggestive glimpses of his attitude towards himself and towards the world of intellectual ferment to which he belonged. She had been taken down by an amiable but entirely uninteresting permanent official, who, when the time came, turned his stereotyped talk over to the other side of him with a quite mechanical indifference, and she was left for a little while in silence until Wilkins had disengaged himself.

He was a flushed man with untidy hair, and he opened at once with an appeal to her sympathies.

" Oh ! bother ! " he said. " I say—I've eaten that mutton. I didn't notice. One eats too much at these affairs. One doesn't notice at the time and then afterwards one finds out."

She was a little surprised at his gambit and could think of nothing but a kindly murmur.

" Detestable thing," he said ; " my body."

" But surely not," she tried and felt as she said it that was a trifle bold.

" You're all right," he said, making her aware he saw her. " But I've this thing that wheezes and fattens at the slightest excuse and—it encumbers me—bothers me to take exercise. . . . But I can hardly expect you to be interested in my troubles, can I ? "

He made an all too manifest attempt to read her name on the slip of card that lay before her among the flowers, and as manifestly succeeded. " We people who write and paint, and all that sort of thing, are a breed of insatiable egotists, Lady Harman. With the least excuse. Don't you think so ? "

" Not—not exceptionally," she said.

" Exceptionally," he insisted.

" It isn't my impression," she said. " You're—franker."

" But some one was telling me—you've been taking impressions of us lately. I mean all of us people who go flapping ideas about in the air. Somebody—was it Lady Beach-Mandarin ? —was saying you'd come out looking for intellectual heroes —and found Bernard Shaw. . . . But what could you have expected ? "

" I've been trying to find out and understand what people are thinking. I want ideas."

" It's disheartening, isn't it ? "

" It's—perplexing sometimes."

" You go to meetings and try to get to the bottom of movements, and you want to meet and know the people who write
the wonderful things ? Get at the wonderful core of it ? "

" One feels there are things going on."

" Great, illuminating things."

" Well—yes."

" And when you see those great thinkers and teachers and
guides and brave spirits and high brows generally——"

He laughed, and stopped just in time on the very verge of
taking pheasant.

" Oh, take it away," he cried sharply.

" We've all been through that illusion, Lady Harman," he
went on.

" But I don't like to think—— Aren't great men, after all—
great ? "

" In their ways, in their places—Yes. But not if you go up
to them and look at them. Not at the dinner table, not in their
beds. . . . What a time of disillusionment you must have had !

" You see, Lady Harman," he said, leaning back from his
empty plate, inclining himself confidentially to her ear and
speaking in a privy tone ; " it's in the very nature of things
that we—if I may put myself into the list—we ideologists,
should be rather exceptionally loose and untrustworthy and
disappointing men. Rotters—to speak plain contemporary
English. If you come to think of it, it has to be so."

" But——" she protested.

He met her eye firmly. " It has to be."

" Why ? "

" The very qualities that make literature entertaining,
vigorous, inspiring, revealing, wonderful, beautiful, and—all
that sort of thing, make its producers—if you will forgive the
word again—rotters."

She smiled, and lifted her eyebrows protestingly.

" Sensitive nervous tissue," he said, with a finger up to
emphasise his words. " Quick responsiveness to stimulus, a
vivid, almost uncontrollable, expressiveness ; that's what you
want in your literary man."

" Yes," said Lady Harman, following cautiously. " Yes, I
suppose it is."

" Can you suppose for a moment that these things conduce
to self-control, to reserve, to consistency, to any of the qualities
of a trustworthy man ? . . . Of course you can't. And so we
aren't trustworthy, we *aren't* consistent. Our virtues are our
vices. . . . *My* life," said Mr. Wilkins still more confidentially,
" won't bear examination. But that's by the way. It need not
concern us now."

" But Mr. Brumley ? " she asked, on the spur of the moment.

" I am not talking of him," said Wilkins, with careless
cruelty. " He's restrained. I mean the really imaginative
people, the people with vision, the people who let themselves

go. You see now why they are rotten, why they must be
rotten. (No ! No ! take it away. I'm talking.) I feel so strongly
about this, about the natural and necessary disreputableness
of everybody who produces reputable writing—and for the
matter of that, art generally—that I set my face steadily
against all these attempts that keep on cropping up to make
figures of us. We aren't figures, Lady Harman ; it isn't our
line. Of all the detestable aspects of the Victorian period
surely that disposition to make figures of its artists and literary
men was the most detestable. Respectable figures—examples
to the young. The suppressions, the coverings up that had to
go on, the white-washing of Dickens—who was more than a
bit of a rip, you know, the concealment of Thackeray's
mistresses. Did you know he had mistresses ? Oh, rather !
And so on. It's like that bust of Jove—or Bacchus, was it ?—
they pass off as Plato, who probably looked like any other
literary grub. That's why I won't have anything to do with
these academic developments that my friend Brumley—do
you know him, by the way ?—goes in for. He's the third man
down—— You *do* know him. And he's giving up the Academic
Committee, is he ? I'm glad he's seen it at last. What *is* the
good of trying to have an academy and all that, and put us in
uniform and make out we are somebodies, and respectable
enough to be shaken hands with by George and Mary, when,
as a matter of fact, we are, by our very nature, a collection of
miscellaneous scandals—— We *must* be. Bacon, Shakespeare,
Byron, Shelley—all the stars. . . . No, Johnson wasn't a star,
he was a character by Boswell. . . . Oh ! great things come out
of us, no doubt, our arts are the vehicles of wonder and hope,
the world is dead without these things we produce, but that's
no reason why—why the mushroom-bed should follow the
mushrooms into the soup, is it ? Perfectly fair image. (No,
take it away.)"

He paused, and then jumped in again as she was on the point
of speaking.

"And you see even if our temperaments didn't lead in-
evitably to our—dipping rather, we should still have to—*dip*.
Asking a writer or a poet to be seemly and academic, and so on,
is like asking an eminent surgeon to be stringently decent.
It's—you see, it's incompatible. Now, a king, or a butler, or a
family solicitor—if you like."

He paused again.

Lady Harman had been following him with an attentive
reluctance.

"But what are we to do," she asked, "we people who are
puzzled by life, who want guidance and ideas and—help, if—if
all the people we look to for ideas are—— ? "

"Bad characters."

"Well—it's your theory, you know—bad characters ? "

Wilkins answered with the air of one who carefully disentangles a complex but quite solvable problem. " It doesn't follow," he said, " that because a man is a bad character he's not to be trusted in matters where character—as we commonly use the word—doesn't come in. These sensitives, these—would you mind if I were to call myself an Æolian harp ?—these Æolian harps ; they can't help responding to the winds of heaven. Well—listen to them. Don't follow them, don't worship them, don't even honour them, but listen to them. Don't let any one stop them from saying and painting and writing and singing what they want to. Freedom, canvas, and attention, those are the proper honours for the artist, the poet, and the philosopher. Listen to the noise they make, watch the stuff they produce, and presently you will find certain things among the multitude of things that are said and shown and put out and published, something—light in *your* darkness—a writer for you, something for you. Nobody can have a greater contempt for artists and writers and poets and philosophers than I, oh ! a squalid crew they are, mean, jealous, pugnacious, disgraceful in love, *disgraceful*—but out of it all comes the greatest, serenest thing, the mind of the world, Literature. Nasty little midges, yes—but fireflies—carrying light for the darkness. . . . "

His face was suddenly lit by enthusiasm, and she wondered that she could have thought it rather heavy and commonplace. He stopped abruptly and glanced beyond her at her other neighbour, who seemed on the verge of turning to them again. " If I go on," he said, with a voice suddenly dropped, " I shall talk loud."

" You know," said Lady Harman, in a halty undertone, " you—you are too hard upon—upon clever people, but it is true. I mean it is true in a way. . . . "

" Go on, I understand exactly what you are saying."

" I mean, there *are* ideas. It's just that, that is so—so—— I mean they seem never to be just there and always to be present."

" Like God. Never in the flesh—now. A spirit everywhere. You think exactly as I do, Lady Harman. It is just that. This is a great time, so great that there is no chance for great men. Every chance for great work. And we're doing it. There is a wind—blowing out of heaven. And when beautiful people like yourself come into things—— "

" I try to understand," she said. " I want to understand. I want—I want not to miss life."

He was on the verge of saying something further, and then his eyes wandered down the table and he stopped short.

He ended his talk as he had begun it with " Bother ! Lady Tarvrille, Lady Harman, is trying to catch your eye."

Lady Harman turned her face to her hostess and answered her smile. Wilkins caught at his chair and stood up.

" It would have been jolly to have talked some more," he said.

" I hope we shall."

" Well ! " said Wilkins, with a sudden hardness in his eyes,
and she was swept away from him.

She found no chance of talking to him upstairs, Sir Isaac
came for her early ; but she went in hope of another meeting.

It did not come. For a time that expectation gave dinners
and luncheon parties a quite appreciable attraction. Then she
told Agatha Alimony. " I've never met him but that once,"
she said.

" One doesn't meet him now," said Agatha darkly.

" But why ? "

Deep significance came into Miss Alimony's eyes. " My
dear," she whispered, and glanced about them. " Don't you
know ? "

Lady Harman was a radiant innocence.

And then Miss Alimony began in impressible undertones,
with awful omissions like pits of darkness, and with such
richly embroidered details as serious spinsters enjoy, adding,
indeed, two quite new things that came to her mind as the
tale unfolded, and, naming no names and giving no chances
of verification or reply, handed on the fearful and at that time
extremely popular story of the awful wickedness of Wilkins the
author.

Upon reflection Lady Harman perceived that this explained
all sorts of things in their conversation and particularly the
flash of hardness at the end.

Even then, things must have been hanging over him. . . .

§ 5

And while Lady Harman was making these meritorious and
industrious attempts to grasp the significance of life and to
get some clear idea of her social duty, the developments of
those Hostels she had started—she now felt so prematurely
—was going on. There were times when she tried not to think
of them, turned her back on them, fled from them, and times
when they and what she ought to do about them and what
they ought to be and what they ought not to be, filled her
mind to the exclusion of every other topic. Rigorously and
persistently Sir Isaac insisted they were hers, asked her counsel,
demanded her appreciation, presented as it were his recurring
bill for them.

Five of them were being built, not four but five. There was
to be one, the largest, in a conspicuous position in Bloomsbury
near the British Museum, one in a conspicuous position looking
out upon Parliament Hill, one conspicuously placed upon the
Waterloo Road near St. George's Circus, one at Sydenham,
and one in the Kensington Road which was designed to catch
the eye of people going to and fro to the various exhibitions
at Olympia.

In Sir Isaac's study at Putney there was a huge and rather

splendid-looking morocco portfolio on a stand, and this portfolio bore in excellent gold lettering the words, International
Bread and Cake Hostels.   It was her husband's peculiar
pleasure after dinner to take her to turn over this with him ;
he would sit pencil in hand, while she, poised at his request
upon the arm of his chair, would endorse a multitude of
admirable modifications and suggestions.   These hostels were
to be done—indeed they were being done—by Sir Isaac's
tame architect, and the interlacing yellow and mauve tiles,
and the Doulton ware mouldings that were already familiar
to the public as the uniform of the Stores, were to be used upon
the façades of the new institutions.   They were to be boldly
labelled

INTERNATIONAL HOSTELS

right across the front.

The plans revealed in every case a site depth as great as
the frontage, and the utmost ingenuity had been used to
utilise as much space as possible.   " Every room we get in,"
said Sir Isaac, " adds one to the denominator in the cost ; "
and carried his wife back to her schooldays.   At last she had
found sense in fractions.   There was to be a series of convenient and spacious rooms on the ground floor, a refectory,
which might be cleared and used for meetings—" dances,"
said Lady Harman.   " Hardly the sort of thing we want 'em
to get up to," said Sir Isaac—various offices, the matron's
apartments—" We ought to begin thinking about matrons,"
said Sir Isaac ;—a bureau, a reading-room, and a library—
" We can pick good serious stuff for them," said Sir Isaac,
" instead of their filling their heads with trash "—one or two
work-rooms with tables for cutting out and sewing ; this
last was an idea of Susan Burnet's.   Upstairs there was to
be a beehive of bedrooms, floor above floor, and each floor
as low as the building regulations permitted.   There were to
be long dormitories with cubicles at three-and-sixpence a
week—make your own beds—and separate rooms at prices
ranging from four-and-sixpence to seven-and-sixpence.   Every
three cubicles and every bedroom had lavatory basins with
hot and cold water ; there were pull-out drawers under the
beds and a built-in chest of drawers, a hanging cupboard, a
looking-glass, and a radiator in each cubicle, and each floor
had a box-room.   It was ship-shape.

" A girl can get this cubicle for three-and-six a week," said
Sir Isaac, tapping the drawing before him with his pencil.
" She can get her breakfast with a bit of bacon or a sausage
for two shillings a week, and she can get her high tea, with
cold meat, good potted salmon, shrimp paste, jam and cetera,
for three-and-six a week.   Say her bus fares and lunch out mean
another four shillings.   That means she can get along on about

twelve-and-six a week. comfortable. read the papers, have a
book out of the library. . . . There's nothing like it to be got
now for twice the money. The sort of thing they have now is
one room, dingy, badly fitted, extra for coals. . . .

"That's the answer to your problem, Elly," he said. "There
we are. Every girl who doesn't live at home can live here—
with a matron to keep her eye on her. . . . And properly
run, Elly, properly run the thing's going to pay two or three
per cent.—let alone the advertisement for the Stores. . . .

"We can easily make these Hostels obligatory on all our
girls who don't live at their homes," he said. "That ought
to keep them off the streets, if anything can. I don't see how
even Miss Babs Wheeler can have the face to strike against
that.

"And then we can arrange with some of the big firms,
drapers' shops and all that sort of thing near each hostel to
take over most of our other cubicle space. A lot of them—
overflow.

"Of course we'll have to make sure the girls get in at night."
He reached out for a ground floor plan of the Bloomsbury
establishment which was to be the first built. "If," he said,
"we were to have a sort of porter's lodge with a book—and
make 'em ring a bell after eleven say—just here. . . ."

He took out a silver pencil case and got to work.

Lady Harman's expression as she leant over him, became
thoughtful.

There were points about this project that gave her the
greatest misgivings ; that matron, keeping her eye on the
girls, that carefully selected library, the porter's bell, these
casual allusions to "discipline" that set her thinking of scraps
of the Babs Wheeler controversy. There was a regularity, an
austerity about this project that chilled her, she hardly knew
why. Her own vague intentions had been an amiable, hospi-
table, agreeably cheap establishment to which the homeless
feminine employees in London could resort freely and cheerfully, and it was only very slowly that she perceived that her
husband was by no means convinced of the spontaneity of
their coming. He seemed always glancing at methods for
compelling them to come in and oppressions when that com-
pulsion had succeeded. There had already hovered over several
of these anticipatory evenings, his very manifest intention to
have very carefully planned "Rules." She felt there lay
ahead of them much possibility for divergence of opinion
about these "Rules." She foresaw a certain narrowness and
hardness. She herself had made her fight against the characteristics of Sir Isaac and—perhaps she was lacking in that
aristocratic feeling which comes so naturally to most successful
middle-class people in England—she could not believe that
what she had found bad and suffocating for herself could be
agreeable and helpful for her poorer sisters.

It occurred to her to try the effect of the scheme upon
Susan Burnet. Susan had such a knack of seeing things from
unexpected angles. She contrived certain operations upon the
study blinds, and then broached the business to Susan casually
in the course of an inquiry into the welfare of the Burnet
family.

Susan was evidently prejudiced against the idea.

" Yes," said Susan after various explanations and exhibitions, " but where's the home in it ? "

" The whole thing is a home."

" Barracks *I* call it," said Susan. " Nobody ever felt at
home in a room coloured up like that—and no curtains, nor
valances, nor toilet covers, nor anywhere where a girl can
hang a photograph or anything. What girl's going to feel
at home in a strange place like that ? "

" They ought to be able to hang up photographs," said
Lady Harman, making a mental note of it.

" And of course there'll be all sorts of Rules."

" *Some* rules."

" Homes, real homes don't have Rules. And I dare say—
Fines."

" No, there shan't be any fines," said Lady Harman quickly.
" I'll see to that."

" You got to back up rules somehow—once you got 'em,"
said Susan. " And when you get a crowd, and no father and
mother, and no proper family feeling, I suppose there's got to
be Rules."

Lady Harman pointed out various advantages of the project.

" I'm not saying it isn't cheap and healthy and social,"
said Susan, " and if it isn't too strict I expect you'll get plenty
of girls to come to it, but at the best it's an Institution, Lady
Harman. It's going to be an Institution. That's what it's
going to be."

She held the front elevation of the Bloomsbury Hostel in
her hand and reflected.

" Of course, for my part, I'd rather lodge with nice struggling
believing Christian people anywhere than go into a place like
that. It's the feeling of freedom, of being yourself and on your
own. Even if the water wasn't laid on and I had to fetch it
myself. . . . If girls were paid properly there wouldn't be any
need of such places, none at all. It's the poverty makes 'em
what they are. . . . And after all, somebody's got to lose the
lodgers if this place gets them. Suppose this sort of thing
grows up all over the place, it'll just be the story of the little
baker and little grocer and all those people over again. Why
in London there are thousands of people who just keep a home
together by letting two or three rooms or boarding some one
—and it stands to reason, they'll have to take less or lose the
lodgers if this kind of thing's going to be done. Nobody isn't
going to build a Hostel for them."

" No," said Lady Harman, " I never thought of them."

" Lots of 'em haven't anything in the world but their bits of furniture and their lease and their they are stuck and tied. There's Aunt Hannah, Father's sister, she's like that. Sleeps in the basement and works and slaves, and often I've had to lend her ten shillings to pay the rent with, through her not being full. This sort of place isn't going to do much good to her."

Lady Harman surveyed the plan rather blankly. " I suppose it isn't."

" And then if you manage this sort of place easy and attrac- tive, it's going to draw girls away from their homes. There's girls like Alice who'd do anything to get a bit of extra money to put on their backs and seem to think of nothing but chatter- ing and laughing and going about. Such a place like this would be fine fun for Alice ; in when she liked and out when she liked, and none of us to ask her questions. She'd be just the sort to go, and Mother who's had the upbringing of her, how's she to make up for Alice's ten shillings what she pays in every week ? There's lots like Alice. She's not bad isn't Alice, she's a good girl and a good-hearted girl ; I will say that for her, but she's shallow, say what you like she's shallow, she's got no thought and she's wild for pleasure, and sometimes it seems to me that that's as bad as being bad for all the good it does to any one else in the world, and so I tell her. But of course she hasn't seen things as I've seen them and doesn't feel as I do about all these things. . . ."

Thus Susan.

Her discourse so puzzled Lady Harman that she bethought herself of Mr. Brumley and called in his only too readily accorded advice. She asked him to tea on a day when she knew unofficially that Sir Isaac would be away, she showed him the plans and sketched their probable development. Then with that charming confidence of hers in his knowledge and ability she put her doubts and fears before him. What did he really think of these places ? What did he think of Susan Burnet's idea of ruined lodging-house keepers ? " I used to think our stores were good things," she said. " Is this likely to be a good thing at all ? "

Mr. Brumley said " Um " a great number of times and realised that he was a humbug. He fenced with her and affected sagacity for a time and suddenly he threw down his defences and confessed he knew as little of the business as she did. " But I see it is a complex question and—it's an interesting one too. May I inquire into it for you ? I think I might be able to hunt up a few particulars. . . . "

He went away in a glow of resolution.

Georgina was about the only intimate who regarded the new development without misgiving.

" You think you're going to do all sorts of things with

these Hostels, Ella," she said, " but as a matter of fact they're bound to become just exactly what we've always wanted."

" And what may that be ? " asked Mrs. Sawbridge over her macramé work.

" Strongholds for a garrison of suffragettes," said Georgina with the light of the Great Insane Movement in her eyes and a ringing note in her voice. " Fort Chabrols for women."

§ 6

For some months in a negative and occasionally almost negligent fashion Mr. Brumley had been living up to his impassioned resolve to be an unselfish lover of Lady Harman. He had been rather at loose ends intellectually, deprived of his old assumptions and habitual attitudes and rather chaotic in the matter of his new convictions. He had given most of his productive hours to the writing of a novel which was to be an entire departure from the Euphemia tradition. The more he got on with this, the more clearly he realised that it was essentially insignificant. When he re-read what he had written he was surprised by crudities where he had intended sincerities and rhetoric where the scheme had demanded passion. What was the matter with him ? He was stirred that Lady Harman should send for him, and his inability to deal with her perplexities deepened his realisation of the ignorance and superficiality he had so long masked even from himself beneath the tricks and pretensions of a gay scepticism. He went away fully resolved to grapple with the entire Hostel question, and he put the patched and tortured manuscript of the new novel aside with a certain satisfaction to do this.

The more he reflected upon the nature of this study he proposed for himself the more it attracted him. It was some such reality as this he had been wanting. He could presently doubt whether he would ever go back to his novel-writing again, or at least to the sort of novel-writing he had been doing hitherto. To invent stories to save middle-aged prosperous middle-class people from the distresses of thinking, is surely no work for a self-respecting man. Stevenson in the very deeps of that dishonourable traffic had realised as much and likened himself to a *fille de joie*, and Haggard, of the same school and period, had abandoned blood and thunder at the climax of his success for the honest study of agricultural conditions. The newer successes were turning out work, less and less conventional and agreeable and more and more stiffened with facts and sincerities. . . . He would show Lady Harman that a certain debonair quality he had always affected, wasn't incompatible with a powerful grasp of general conditions. . . . And she wanted this done. Suppose he did it in a way that made him necessary to her. Suppose he did it very well.

He set to work, and understanding as you do a certain quality of the chameleon in Mr. Brumley's moral nature, you will understand that he worked through a considerable variety of moods. Sometimes he worked with disinterested passion and sometimes he was greatly sustained by this thought that here was something that would weave him in with the gravities of her life and give him perhaps a new inlet to intimacy. And presently a third thing came to his help, and that was the discovery that the questions arising out of this attempt to realise the importance of those Hostels, were in themselves very fascinating questions for an intelligent person.

Because before you have done with the business of the modern employee, you must, if you are an intelligent person, have taken a view of the whole vast process of social reorganisation that began with the development of factory labour and big towns, and which is even now scarcely advanced enough for us to see its general trend. For a time Mr. Brumley did not realise the magnitude of the thing he was looking at ; when he did, theories sprouted in his mind like mushrooms and he babbled with mental excitement. He came in a state of the utmost lucidity to explain his theories to Lady Harman, and they struck that lady at the time as being the most illuminating suggestions she had ever encountered. They threw an appearance of order, of process, over a world of trade and employment and competition that had hitherto seemed too complex and mysterious for any understanding.

" You see," said Mr. Brumley—they had met that day in Kensington Gardens and they were sitting side by side upon green chairs near the frozen writhings of Physical Energy— " You see, if I may lecture a little, putting the thing as simply as possible, the world has been filling up new spaces ever since the discovery of America ; all the period from then to about 1870, let us say, was a period of rapid increase of population in response to new opportunities of living and new fullnesses of life in every direction. During that time, four hundred years of it roughly, there was a huge development of family life ; to marry and rear a quite considerable family became the chief business of everybody, celibacy grew rare, monasteries and nunneries which had abounded vanished like things dissolving in a flood and even the priests became Protestant against celibacy and took unto themselves wives and had large families. The natural checks upon increase, famine and pestilence, were lifted by more systematised communication and by scientific discovery ; and altogether and as a consequence the world now has probably three or four times the human population it ever carried before. Everywhere in that period the family prevailed again, the prospering multiplying household ; it was a return to the family, to the reproductive social grouping of early barbaric life, and naturally all the thought of the modern world which has emerged since the fifteenth century falls into this form. So I see it, Lady Harman. The generation of our grandfathers in the opening nineteenth century had two shaping ideas, two forms of thought, the family and progress, not realising that that very progress which had suddenly reopened the doors of opportunity for the family that had revived the ancient injunction to increase and multiply and replenish the earth, might presently close that door again and declare the world was filled. But that is what is happening now. The doors close. That immense swarming and multiplying of little people is over, and the forces of social organisation have been coming into play now, more and more for a century and a half, to produce new wholesale ways of doing things, new great organisations, organisations that invade the autonomous family more and more, and are perhaps destined ultimately to destroy it altogether and supersede it. At least it is so I make my reading of history in these matters."

" Yes," said Lady Harman, with knitted brows, " Yes," and wondered privately whether it would be possible to get from that opening to the matter of her Hostels before it was time for her to return for Sir Isaac's tea.

Mr. Brumley continued to talk with his eyes fixed as it were upon his thoughts. " These things, Lady Harman, go on at different paces in different regions. I will not trouble you with a discussion of that, or of emigration, or of any of the details of the vast proliferation that preceded the present phase. Suffice it, that now all the tendency is back towards restraints upon increase, to an increasing celibacy, to a fall in the birth-rate and in the average size of families, to—to a release of women from an entire devotion to a numerous offspring, and so at last to the supercession of those little family units that for four centuries have made up the substance of social life and determined nearly all our moral and sentimental attitudes. The autonomy of the family is being steadily destroyed, and it is being replaced by the autonomy of the individual in relation to some syndicated economic effort."

" I think," said Lady Harman slowly, arresting him by a gesture, " if you could make that about autonomy a little clearer. . . . "

Mr. Brumley did. He went on to point out with the lucidity of a University Extension lecturer what he meant by these singular phrases. She listened intelligently but with effort. He was much too intent upon getting the thing expressed to his own satisfaction to notice any absurdity in his preoccupation with these theories about the population of the world in the face of her immediate practical difficulties. He declared that the onset of this new phase in human life, the modern phase, wherein there was apparently to be no more " proliferating," but instead a settling down of population towards a stable equilibrium, became apparent first with the expropriation of the English peasantry and the birth of the factory system

and machine production. " Since that time one can trace a
steady substitution of wholesale and collective methods for
household and family methods. It has gone far with us now.
Instead of the woman drawing water from a well, the pipes
and taps of the water company. Instead of the home-made
rushlight, the electric lamp. Instead of home-spun, ready-
made clothes. Instead of home-brewed, the brewer's cask.
Instead of home-baked, first the little baker and then, clean
and punctual, the International Bread and Cake Stores.
Instead of the child learning at its mother's knee, the compulsory elementary school. Flats take the place of separate
houses. Instead of the little holding, the big farm, and instead
of the children working at home, the factory. Everywhere
synthesis. Everywhere the little independent proprietor gives
place to the company and the company to the trust. You
follow all this, Lady Harman ? "

" Go on," she said, encouraged by that transitory glimpse of
the Stores in his discourse.

" Now London—and England generally—had its period
of expansion and got on to the beginnings at least of this
period of synthesis that is following it, sooner than any other
country in the world ; and because it was the first to reach
the new stage it developed the characteristics of the new
stage with a stronger flavour of the old than did such later
growths of civilisation as New York or Bombay or Berlin.
That is why London and our British big cities generally are
congestions of little houses, little homes, while the newer great
cities run to apartments and flats. We hadn't grasped the
logical consequences of what we were in for so completely
as the people abroad did who caught it later, and that is why,
as we began to develop our new floating population of mainly
celibate employees and childless people, they had mostly to go
into lodgings, they went into the homes that were intended
for families as accessories to the family, and they were able
to go in because the families were no longer so numerous as
they used to be. London is still largely a city of landladies
and lodgings, and in no other part of the world is there so big
a population of lodgers. And this business of your Hostels
is nothing more nor less than the beginning of the end of that.
Just as the great refreshment caterers have mopped up the
ancient multitude of coffee-houses and squalid little special
feeding arrangements of the days of Tittlebat Titmouse and
Dick Swiveller, so now your Hostels are going to mop up
the lodging-house system of London. Of course there are
other and kindred movements. Naturally. The Y.W.C.A.,
the Y.M.C.A., the London Girls' Club Union, and so forth
are all doing kindred work."

" But what, Mr. Brumley, what is to become of the landladies ? " asked Lady Harman.

Mr. Brumley was checked in mid theory.

" I hadn't thought of the landladies," he said, after a short pause.

" They worry me," said Lady Harman.

" Um," said Mr. Brumley, thrown out.

" Do you know the other day I went into Chelsea, where there are whole streets of lodgings, and—I suppose it was wrong of me, but I went and pretended to be looking for rooms for a girl clerk I knew, and I saw—Oh ! no end of rooms. And such poor old women, such dingy, worked-out, broken old women, with a kind of fearful sharpness, so eager, so dreadfully eager to get that girl clerk who didn't exist. . . . "

She looked at him with an expression of pained inquiry.

" That," said Mr. Brumley, " that I think is a question, so to speak, for the social ambulance. If perhaps I might go on—— That particular difficulty we might consider later. I think I was talking of the general synthesis."

" Yes," said Lady Harman. " And what is it exactly that is to take the place of these isolated little homes and these dreary little lodgings ? Here are we, my husband and I, rushing in with this new thing, just as he rushed in with his stores thirty years ago and overset little bakers and confectioners and refreshment dealers by the hundred. Some of them—poor dears—they—— I don't like to think. And it wasn't a good thing he made after all—only a hard sort of thing. He made all those shops of his—with the girls who strike and say they are sweated and driven. . . . And now here we are making a kind of barrack place for people to live in ! "

She expressed the rest of her ideas with a gesture of the hands.

" I admit the process has its dangers," said Mr. Brumley. " It's like the supersession of the small holdings by the *latifundia* in Italy. But that's just where our great opportunity comes in. These synthetic phases have occurred before in the world's history and their history is a history of lost opportunities. . . . But need ours be ? "

She had a feeling as though something had slipped through her fingers.

" I feel," she said, " that it is more important to me than anything else in life, that these Hostels, anyhow, which are springing so rapidly from a chance suggestion of mine, shouldn't be lost opportunities."

" Exactly," said Mr. Brumley, with the gesture of one who recovers a thread. " That is just what I am driving at."

The fingers of his extended hand felt in the warm afternoon air for a moment, and then he said " Ah ! " in a tone of recovery while she waited respectfully for the resumed thread.

" You see," he said, " I regard this process of synthesis, this substitution of wholesale and collective methods for homely and individual ones as, under existing conditions,

inevitable — inevitable. It's the phase we live in, it's to
this we have to adapt ourselves. It is as little under your
control or mine as the movement of the sun through the
zodiac. Practically, that is. And what we have to do is not,
I think, to sigh for lost homes and the age of gold and spade
husbandry, and pigs and hens in the home, and so on, but
to make this new synthetic life tolerable for the mass of men
and women, hopeful for the mass of men and women, a thing
developing and ascending. That's where your Hostels come
in, Lady Harman ; that's where they're so important. They're
a pioneer movement. If they succeed — and things in Sir
Isaac's hands have a way of succeeding at any rate to the
paying point — then there'll be a headlong rush of imitations,
imitating your good features, imitating your bad features,
deepening a groove. . . . You see my point ? "

"Yes," she said. " It makes me—more afraid than ever."

" But hopeful," said Mr. Brumley, presuming to lay his
hand for an instant on her arm. " It's big enough to be inspiring."

" But I'm afraid," she said.

" It's laying down the lines of a new social life—no less.
And what makes it so strange, so typical, too, of the way
social forces work nowadays, is that your husband, who has
all the instinctive insistence upon every right and restriction
of the family relation in his private life, who is narrowly,
passionately *for* the home in his own case, who hates all books
and discussion that seem to touch it, should in his business
activities be striking this tremendous new blow at the ancient
organisation. For that, you see, is what it amounts to."

" Yes," said Lady Harman slowly. " Yes. Of course, he
doesn't know. . . . "

Mr. Brumley was silent for a little while. " You see," he
resumed, " at the worst this new social life may become a
sort of slavery in barracks ; at the best—it might become
something very wonderful. My mind's been busy now for
days thinking just how wonderful the new life might be.
Instead of the old bickering, crowded family home, a new
home of comrades. . . . "

He made another pause, and his thoughts ran off upon a
fresh track.

" In looking up all these things I came upon a queer little
literature of pamphlets and so forth, dealing with the case of
the shop assistants. They have a great grievance in what they
call the living-in system. The employers herd them in dormitories over the shops, and usually feed them by gaslight
in the basements ; they fine them and keep an almost intolerable grip upon them ; make them go to bed at half-past
ten, make them go to church on Sundays—all sorts of petty
tyrannies. The assistants are passionately against this, but
they've got no power to strike. Where could they go if they

struck ? Into the street. Only people who live out and have homes of their own to sulk in *can* strike. Naturally, therefore, as a preliminary to any other improvement in the shop assistant's life, these young people want to live out. Practically that's an impossible demand at present, because they couldn't get lodgings and live out with any decency at all on what it costs their employers to lodge and feed them *in*. Well, here you see a curious possibility for your Hostels. You open the prospect of a living-out system for shop assistants. But just in the degree in which you choose to interfere with them, regulate them, bully and deal with them wholesale through their employers, do you make the new living-out method approximate to the living-in. *That's* a curious side development, isn't it ? "

Lady Harman appreciated that.

" That's only the beginning of the business. There's something more these Hostels might touch. . . . "

Mr. Brumley gathered himself together for the new aspect. " There's marriage," he said.

" One of the most interesting and unsatisfactory aspects of the life of the employee to-day—and you know the employee is now in the majority in the adult population—is this. You see, we hold them celibate. We hold them celibate for a longer and longer period ; the average age at marriage rises steadily ; and so long as they remain celibate we are prepared with some sort of ideas about the future development of their social life, clubs, hostels, living-in, and so forth. But at present we haven't any ideas at all about the adaptation of the natural pairing instinct to the new state of affairs. Ultimately the employee marries ; they hold out as long as they possibly can, but ultimately they have to. They have to, even in the face of an economic system that holds out no prospects of anything but insecurity and an increasing chance of trouble and disaster to the employee's family group. What happens is that they drop back into a distressful, crippled, insecure imitation of the old family life as one had it in what I might call the multiplying periods of history. They start a home— they dream of a cottage, but they drift to a lodging, and usually it isn't the best sort of lodging, for landladies hate wives and the other lodgers detest babies. Often the young couple doesn't have babies. You see, they are more intelligent than peasants, and intelligence and fecundity vary reciprocally," said Mr. Brumley.

" You mean ? " interrupted Lady Harman softly.

" There is a world-wide fall in the birthrate. People don't have the families they did."

" Yes," said Lady Harman. " I understand now."

" And the more prosperous or the more sanguine take these suburban little houses, these hutches that make such places as Hendon nightmares of monotony, or go into ridiculous jerry-built sham cottages in some Garden Suburb, where each young wife does her own housework and pretends to like it. They have a sort of happiness for a time, I suppose ; the woman stops all outside work, the man, very much handicapped, goes on competing against single men. Then—nothing more happens. Except difficulties. The world goes dull and grey for them. They look about for a lodger, perhaps. Have you read Gissing's *Paying Guest* ? . . ."

" I suppose," said Lady Harman, " I suppose it is like that. One tries not to think it is so."

" One needn't let oneself believe that dullness is unhappiness," said Mr. Brumley. " I don't want to paint things sadder than they are. But it's not a fine life, it's not a full life, that life in a Neo-Malthusian suburban hutch."

" Neo—— ? " asked Lady Harman.

" A mere phrase," said Mr. Brumley hastily. " The extraordinary thing is that, until you set me looking into these things with your questions, I've always taken this sort of thing for granted, as though it couldn't be otherwise. Now I seem to see it with a kind of freshness. I'm astounded at the muddle of it, the waste and aimlessness of it. And here again it is, Lady Harman, that I think your opportunity comes in. With these Hostels as they might be projected now, you seem to have the possibility of a modernised, more collective and civilised family life than the old close congestion of the single home, and I see no reason at all why you shouldn't carry that collective life on to the married stage. As things are now these little communities don't go beyond the pairing—and out they drift to find the homestead they will never possess. What has been borne in upon me more and more forcibly as I have gone through your—your nest of problems, is the idea that the new social—association, that has so extensively replaced the old family group, might be carried on right through life, that it might work in with all sorts of other discontents and bad adjustments. . . . The life of the women in these little childless or one-or-two-child homes is more unsatisfactory even than the man's."

Mr. Brumley's face flushed with enthusiasm, and he wagged a finger to emphasise his words. " Why not make Hostels, Lady Harman, for married couples ? Why not try that experiment so many people have talked about of the conjoint kitchen and refectory, the conjoint nursery, the collective social life, so that the children who are single children or at best children in small families of two or three, may have the advantages of playfellows, and the young mothers still, if they choose, continue to have a social existence and go on with their professional or business work ? That's the next step your Hostels might take. . . . Incidentally you see this opens a way to a life of relative freedom for the woman who is married. . . . I don't know if you have read Mrs. Stetson. .

Yes, Charlotte Perkins Gilman Stetson. . . . Yes, *Woman and Economics*, that's the book.

" I know," Mr. Brumley went on, " I seem to be opening out your project like a concertina, but I want you to see just how my thoughts have been going about all this. I want you to realise I haven't been idle during these last few weeks. I know it's a far cry from what the Hostels are to all these new ideas of what they might begin to be, I know the difficulties in your way—all sorts of difficulties. But when I think just how you stand at the very centre of the moulding forces in these changes. . . . "

He dropped into an eloquent silence.

Lady Harman looked thoughtfully at the sunlight under the trees.

" You think," she said, " that it comes to as much as all this."

" More," said Mr. Brumley.

" I was frightened before. *Now*—— You make me feel as though some one had put the wheel of a motor-car in my hand, started it, and told me to steer. . . . "

§ 7

Lady Harman went home from that talk in a taxi, and on the way she passed the building operations in the Kensington Road. A few weeks ago it had been a mere dusty field of operation for the house-wreckers ; now its walls were already rising to the second story. She realised how swiftly nowadays the search for wisdom can be outstripped by reinforced concrete.

§ 8

It was only by slow degrees and rather in the absence of a more commanding interest than through any invincible quality in their appeal to her mind that these Hostels became in the next three years the grave occupation of Lady Harman's thoughts and energies. She yielded to them reluctantly. For a long time she wanted to look over them and past them and discover something—she did not know what—something high and domineering to which it would be easy to give herself. It was difficult to give herself to the Hostels. In that Mr. Brumley, actuated by a mixture of more or less admirable motives, did his best to assist her. These Hostels alone he thought could give them something upon which they could meet, give them a common interest and him a method of service and companionship. It threw the qualities of duty and justification over their more or less furtive meetings, their little expeditions together, their quiet frequent association.

Together they made studies of the Girls' Clubs which are

scattered about London, supplementary homes that have in
such places as Walworth and Soho worked small miracles of
civilisation. These institutions appealed to a lower social
level than the one their Hostels were to touch, but they had
been organised by capable and understanding minds, and
Lady Harman found in one or two of their evening dances
and in the lunch she shared one morning with a row of cheerful
young factory girls from Soho just that quality of concrete
realisation for which her mind hungered. Then Mr. Brumley
took her once or twice for evening walks, just when the stream
of workers is going home ; he battled his way with her along
the footpath of Charing Cross Railway Bridge from the Waterloo side, they swam in the mild evening sunshine of September
against a trampling torrent of bobbing heads, and afterwards
they had tea together in one of the International Stores near
the Strand, where Mr. Brumley made an unsuccessful attempt
to draw out the waitress on the subject of Babs Wheeler and
the recent strike. The young woman might have talked freely
to a man alone, or freely to Lady Harman alone, but the
combination of the two made her shy. The bridge experience
led to several other expeditions, to see home-going on the
tube, at the big railway termini, on the train—and once they
followed up the process to Streatham, and saw how the people
pour out of the train at last and scatter—until at last they
are just isolated individuals running up steps, diving into
basements. And then it occurred to Mr. Brumley that he knew
some one who would take them over " Gerrard," that huge
telephone exchange, and there Lady Harman saw how the
National Telephone Company, as it was in those days, had
a care for its staff, the pleasant club rooms, the rest room,
and stood in that queer rendezvous of messages, where the
" Hello " girl sits all day, wearing a strange metallic apparatus
over ear and mouth, watching small lights that wink signifi-
cantly at her, and perpetually pulling out and slipping in
and releasing little flexible strings that seem to have a resilient
volition of their own. They hunted out Mrs. Barnet and heard
her ideas about conjoint homes for spinsters in the Garden
Suburb. And then they went over a Training College for
elementary teachers and visited the Post Office, and then
came back to more unobtrusive contemplation, from the
customer's little table, of the ministering personalities of the
International Stores.

There were times when all these things seen, seemed to
fall into an entirely explicable system under Mr. Brumley's
exposition, when they seemed to be giving, and most generously
giving, the clearest indications of what kind of thing the
Hostels had to be, and at times when this all vanished again
and her mind became confused and perplexed. She tried to
express just what it was she missed to Mr. Brumley. " One
doesn't," she said, " see all of them, and what one sees isn't

what we have to do with. I mean we see them dressed up and respectable and busy, and then they go home and the door shuts. It's the home that we are going to alter and replace— and what is it like ? " Mr. Brumley took her for walks in Highbury and the newer parts of Hendon and over to Clapham. " I want to go inside those doors," she said.

" That's just what they won't let you do," said Mr. Brumley. " Nobody visits but relations—and prospective relations, and the only other social intercourse is over the garden wall. Perhaps I can find books—— "

He got her novels by Edwin Pugh and Pett Ridge and Frank Swinnerton and George Gissing. They didn't seem to be attractive homes. And it seemed remarkable to her that no woman had ever given the woman's view of the small London home from the inside. . . .

She overcame her own finer scruples and invaded the Burnet household. Apart from fresh aspects of Susan's character in the capacity of a hostess, she gained little light from that. She had never felt so completely outside a home in her life as she did when she was in the Burnets' parlour. The very table-cloth on which the tea was spread had an air of being new and protective of familiar things ; the tea was manifestly quite unlike their customary tea, it was no more intimate than the confectioner's shop window from which it mostly came ; the whole room was full of the muffled cries of things hastily covered up and specially put away. Vivid oblongs on the faded wallpaper betrayed even a rearrangement of the pictures. Susan's mother was a little dingy woman, wearing a very smart new cap to the best of her ability ; she had an air of having been severely shaken up and admonished, and her general bearing confessed only too plainly how shattered those preparations had left her. She watched her capable daughter for cues. Susan's sisters displayed a disposition to keep their backs against something and at the earliest opportunity to get into the passage and leave Susan and her tremendous visitor alone but within earshot. They started convulsively when they were addressed, and insisted on " your ladyship." Susan had told them not to but they would. When they supposed themselves to be unobserved, they gave themselves up to the impassioned inspection of Lady Harman's costume. Luke had fled into the street, and in spite of various messages conveyed to him by the youngest sister he refused to enter until Lady Harman had gone again and was well out of the way. And Susan was no longer garrulous and at her ease ; she had no pins in her mouth, and that perhaps hampered her speech ; she presided flushed and bright-eyed in a state of infectious nervous tension. Her politeness was awful. Never in all her life had Lady Harman felt her own lack of real conversational power so acutely. She couldn't think of a thing that mightn't be construed as an impertinence and that

didn't remind her of district visiting.   Yet perhaps she succeeded better than she supposed.

"What a family you have had ! " she said to Mrs. Burnet.
" I have four little girls, and I find them as much as we can
manage."

"They're young yet, my ladyship," said Mrs. Burnet,
" and they aren't always the blessings they seem to be.   It's
the rearing's the difficulty."

"They're all such healthy-looking—people."

" I wish we could get hold of Luke, my ladyship, and show
you '*im*.   He's that sturdy.   And yet when 'e was a little
feller—— "

She was launched for a time on those details that were
always so dear to the mothers of the past order of things.
Her little spate of reminiscences was the only interlude of
naturalness in an afternoon of painfully constrained behaviour. . . .

Lady Harman returned a trifle shamefacedly from this
abortive dip into realities to Mr. Brumley's speculative
assurance.

§ 9

While Lady Harman was slowly accustoming her mind to
this idea that the development of those Hostels was her
appointed career in life, so far as a wife may have a career
outside her connubial duties, and while she was getting insensibly to believe in Mr. Brumley's theory of their exemplary
social importance, the Hostels themselves, with a haste that
she felt constantly was premature, were achieving a concrete
existence.   They were developing upon lines that here and
there disregarded Mr. Brumley's ideas very widely ; they
gained in practicality what perhaps they lost in social value,
through the entirely indirect relations between Mr. Brumley
on the one hand and Sir Isaac on the other.   For Sir Isaac
manifestly did not consider and would have been altogether
indisposed to consider Mr. Brumley as entitled to plan or
suggest anything of the slightest importance in this affair,
and whatever of Mr. Brumley reached that gentleman reached
him in a very carefully transmitted form as Lady Harman's
own unaided idea.   Sir Isaac had sound Victorian ideas about
the place of literature in life.   If any one had suggested to him
that literature could supply ideas to practical men he would
have had a choking fit, and he regarded Mr. Brumley's sedulous
attentions to these hostel schemes with feelings, the kindlier
elements of whose admixture was a belief that ultimately he
would write some elegant and respectful approval of the
established undertaking.

The entire admixture of Sir Isaac's feelings towards Mr.
Brumley was by no means kindly.   He disliked any man to
come near Lady Harman, any man at all ; he had a faint

uneasiness even about waiters and hotel porters and the clergy. Of course he had agreed she should have friends of her own, and he couldn't very well rescind that without something definite to go upon. But still this persistent follower kept him uneasy. He kept this uneasiness within bounds by reassuring himself upon the point of Lady Harman's virtuous obedience, and so reassured he was able to temper his distrust with a certain contempt. The man was in love with his wife ; that was manifest enough, and dangled after her. . . . Let him dangle. What after all did he get for it ? . . .

But occasionally he broke through this complacency, betrayed a fitful ingenious jealousy, interfered so that she missed appointments and had to break engagements. He was now more and more a being of pathological moods. The subtle changes of secretion that were hardening his arteries, tightening his breath and poisoning his blood, reflected themselves upon his spirit in an uncertainty of temper and exasperating fatigues and led to startling outbreaks. Then for a time he would readjust himself, become in his manner reasonable again, become accessible.

He was the medium through which this vision that was growing up in her mind of a reorganised social life had to translate itself, as much as it could ever translate itself, into reality. He called these hostels her hostels, made her the approver of all he did, but he kept every particle of control in his own hands. All her ideas and desires had to be realised by him. And his attitudes varied with his moods ; sometimes he was keenly interested in the work of organisation, and then he terrified her by his bias towards acute economies ; sometimes he was resentful at the burden of the whole thing, sometimes he seemed to scent Brumley or at least some moral influence behind her mind, and met her suggestions with a bitter resentment as though any suggestion must needs be a disloyalty to him. There was a remarkable outbreak upon her first tentative proposal that the hostel system might ultimately be extended to married couples.

He heard her with lips pressing tighter and tighter together until they were yellow white and creased with a hundred wicked little horizontal creases. Then he interrupted her with silent gesticulations. Then words came.

" I never did, Elly," he said. " I never did. Reely—there are times when you ain't rational. Married couples who're assistants in shops and places ! "

For a little while he sought some adequate expression of his point of view.

" Nice thing to go keeping a place for these chaps to have their cheap bits of skirt in," he said at last.

Then further : " If a man wants a girl let him work himself up until he can keep her. Married couples indeed ! "

He began to expand the possibilities of the case with a quite

unusual vividness. " Double beds in each cubicle, I suppose,"
he said, and played for a time about this fancy. . . . " Well,
to hear such an idea from you of all people, Elly. I never
did."

He couldn't leave it alone. He had to go on to the bitter
end with the vision she had evoked in his mind. He was
jealous, passionately jealous, it was only too manifest, of the
possible happinesses of these young people. He was possessed
by that instinctive hatred for the realised love of others which
lies at the base of so much of our moral legislation. The bare
thought—whole corridors of bridal chambers !—made his face
white and his hands quiver. *His* young men and young women!
The fires of a hundred Vigilance Committees blazed suddenly
in his reddened eyes. He might have been a concentrated
society for preventing the rapid multiplication of the unfit.
The idea of facilitating early marriages was manifestly shameful to him, a disgraceful service to render, a job for Pandarus.
What was she thinking of ? Elly of all people ! Elly who
had been as innocent as driven snow before Georgina came
interfering !

It ended in a fit of abuse and a panting seizure, and for a
day or so he was too ill to resume the discussion, to do more
than indicate a disgusted aloofness. . . .

And then it may be the obscure chemicals at work within
him changed their phase of reaction. At any rate he mended,
became gentler, was more loving to his wife than he had
been for some time, and astonished her by saying that if she
wanted Hostels for married couples, it wasn't perhaps so
entirely unreasonable. Selected cases, he stipulated, it would
have to be, and above a certain age limit, sober people. " It
might even be a check on immorality," he said, " properly
managed. . . ."

But that was as far as his acquiescence went and Lady
Harman was destined to be a widow before she saw the founda-
tion of any Hostel for young married couples in London.

§ 10

The reinforced concrete rose steadily amidst Lady Harman's
questionings and Mr. Brumley's speculations. The Harmans
returned from a recuperative visit to Kissingen, to which Sir
Isaac had gone because of a suspicion that his Marienbad
specialist had failed to cure him completely in order to get
him back again, to find the first of the five hostels nearly ripe
for its opening. There had to be a manageress and a staff
organised, and neither Lady Harman nor Mr. Brumley were
prepared for that sort of business. A number of abler people,
however, had become aware of the opportunities of the new
development ; and Mrs. Hubert Plessington, that busy publi-
cist, got the Harmans to a helpful little dinner, before Lady
Harman had the slightest suspicion of the needs that were

now so urgent. There shone a neat compact widow, a Mrs. Pembrose, who had buried her husband some eighteen months ago after studying social questions with him with great éclat for ten happy years, and she had done settlement work and Girls' Club work and had perhaps more power of organisation —given a suitable director to provide for her lack of creativeness, Mrs. Plessington told Sir Isaac, than any other woman in London. Afterwards Sir Isaac had an opportunity of talking to her ; he discussed the suffrage movement with her, and was pleased to find her views remarkably sympathetic with his own. She was, he declared, a sensible woman, anxious to hear a man out and capable, it was evident, of a detachment from feminist particularism rare in her sex at the present time. Lady Harman had seen less of the lady that evening, she was chiefly struck by her pallor, by a kind of animated silence about her, and by the deep impression her capabilities had made on Mr. Plessington, who had hitherto seemed to her to be altogether too overworked in admiring his wife to perceive the points of any other human being. Afterwards Lady Harman was surprised to hear from one or two quite separate people that Mrs. Pembrose was the only possible person to act as general director of the new hostels. Lady Beach-Mandarin was so enthusiastic in the matter that she made a special call. " You've known her a long time ? " said Lady Harman.

" Long enough to see what a chance she is ! " said Lady Beach-Mandarin.

Lady Harman perceived equivocation. " Now how long is that really ? " she said.

" Count not in years, nor yet in moments on a dial," said Lady Beach-Mandarin, with a fine air of quotation. " I'm thinking of her quiet strength of character. Mrs. Plessington brought her round to see me the other afternoon."

" Did she talk to you ? "

" I saw, my dear, I saw."

A vague aversion from Mrs. Pembrose was in some mysterious way strengthened in Lady Harman by this extraordinary convergence of testimony. When Sir Isaac mentioned the lady with a kind of forced casualness at breakfast as the only conceivable person for the work of initiation and organisation that lay before them, Lady Harman determined to see more of her. With a quickened subtlety she asked her to tea. " I have heard so much of your knowledge of social questions, and I want you to advise me about my work," she wrote, and then scribbled a note to Mr. Brumley to call and help her judgments.

Mrs. Pembrose appeared dressed in dove colour, with a neat bonnetesque straw hat to match. She had a pale slightly freckled complexion, little hard blue-grey eyes, with that sort of nose which redeems a squarish shape by a certain delicacy of structure ; her chin was long and protruding, and

her voice had a wooden resonance and a ghost of a lisp. Her
talk had a false consecutiveness due to the frequent use of the
word " Yes." Her bearing was erect and her manner guardedly
alert.

From the first she betrayed a conviction that Mr. Brumley
was incidental and unnecessary and that her real interest lay
with Sir Isaac. She might almost have been in possession of
special information upon that point.

" Yes," she said, " I'm rather specially *up* in this sort of
question. I worked side by side with my poor Frederick all
his life, we were collaborators, and this question of the urban
distributive employee was one of his special studies. Yes, he
would have been tremendously interested in Sir Isaac's project."

" You know what we are doing ? "

" Every one is interested in Sir Isaac's enterprise. Naturally.
Yes, I think I have a fairly good idea of what you mean to do.
It's a great experiment."

" You think it is likely to answer ? " said Mr. Brumley.

" In Sir Isaac's hands it is *very* likely to answer," said Mrs.
Pembrose with her eye steadily on Lady Harman.

There was a little pause. " Yes, now you wrote of difficulties
and drawing upon my experience. Of course just now I'm
quite at Sir Isaac's disposal."

Lady Harman found herself thrust perforce into the rôle of
her husband's spokeswoman. She asked Mrs. Pembrose if she
knew the exact nature of the experiment they contemplated.

Mrs. Pembrose hadn't a doubt she knew. Of course for a
long time and more especially in the Metropolis where the
distances were so great and increasing so rapidly, there had
been a gathering of feeling not only in the catering trade, but
in very many factory industries against the daily journey to
employment and home again. It was irksome and wasteful to
every one concerned, there was a great loss in control, later
hours of beginning, uncertain service. " Yes, my husband
calculated the hours lost in London every week, hours that
are neither work nor play, mere tiresome stuffy journeying.
It made an enormous sum. It worked out at hundreds of
working lives per week." Sir Isaac's project was to abolish
all that, to bring his staff into line with the drapers and grocers
who kept their assistants on the living-in system. . . .

" I thought people objected to the living-in system," said
Mr. Brumley.

" There's an agitation against it on the part of a small
Trade Union of Shop Assistants," said Mrs. Pembrose. " But
they have no real alternative to propose."

" And this isn't Living In," said Mr. Brumley.

' Yes, I think you'll find it is," said Mrs. Pembrose with a
nice little expert smile.

" Living-in isn't *quite* what we want," said Lady Harman

slowly and with knitted brows, seeking a method of saying just what the difference was to be.

" Yes, not perhaps in the strictest sense," said Mrs. Pembrose giving her no chance, and went on to make fine distinctions. Strictly speaking, living-in meant sleeping over the shop and eating underneath it, and this hostel idea was an affair of a separate house and of occupants who would be assistants from a number of shops. " Yes, collectivism, if you like," said Mrs. Pembrose. But the word collectivism, she assured them, wouldn't frighten her, she was a collectivist, a socialist, as her husband had always been. The day was past when socialist could be used as a term of reproach. " Yes, instead of the individual employer of labour, we already begin to have the collective employer of labour, with a labour bureau—and so on. We share them. We no longer compete for them. It's the keynote of the time."

Mr. Brumley followed this with a lifted eyebrow. He was still new to these modern developments of collectivist ideas, this socialism of the employer.

The whole thing Mrs. Pembrose declared was a step forward in civilisation, it was a step in the organisation and discipline of labour. Of course the unruly and the insubordinate would cry out. But the benefits were plain enough, space, light, baths, association, reasonable recreations, opportunities for improvement—— "

" But freedom ? " said Mr. Brumley.

Mrs. Pembrose inclined her head a little on one side, looked at him this time and smiled the expert smile again. " If you knew as much as I do of the difficulties of social work," she said, " you wouldn't be very much in love with freedom."

" But—it's the very substance of the soul ! "

" You must permit me to differ," said Mrs. Pembrose, and for weeks afterwards Mr. Brumley was still seeking a proper polite retort to that difficult counterstroke. It was such a featureless reply. It was like having your nose punched suddenly by a man without a face.

They descended to a more particular treatment of the problems ahead. Mrs. Pembrose quoted certain precedents from the Girls' Club Union.

" The people Lady Harman contemplates—entertaining," said Mr. Brumley, " are of a slightly more self-respecting type than those young women."

" It's largely veneer," said Mrs. Pembrose. . . .

" Detestable little wretch," said Mr. Brumley when at last she had departed. He was very uncomfortable. " She's just the quintessence of all one fears and dreads about these new developments, she's perfect—in that way—self-confident, arrogant, instinctively aggressive, with a tremendous class contempt. There's a multitude of such people about who hate the employed classes, who *want* to see them broken in and

subjugated. I suppose that kind of thing is in humanity.
Every boy's school has louts of that kind, who love to torment
fags for their own good, who spring upon a chance smut on
the face of a little boy to scrub him painfully, who have a kind
of lust to dominate under the pretence of improving. I remember—— But never mind that now. Keep that woman out of
things or your hostels work for the devil."

" Yes," said Lady Harman. " Certainly she shall not——
No."

But there she reckoned without her husband.

" I've settled it," he said to her at dinner two nights later.

" What ? "

" Mrs. Pembrose."

" You've not made her—— ? "

" Yes, I have. And I think we're very lucky to get her."

" But—Isaac ! I don't want her ! "

" You should have told me that before, Elly. I've made an
agreement."

She suddenly wanted to cry. " But—— You said I should
manage these Hostels myself."

" So you shall, Elly. But we must have somebody. When
we go abroad and all that and for all the sort of business stuff
and looking after things that you can't do. We've *got* to have
her. She's the only thing going of her sort."

" But—I don't like her."

" Well," cried Sir Isaac, " why in goodness couldn't you
tell me that before, Elly ? I've been and engaged her."

She sat pale-faced staring at him with wide open eyes in
which tears of acute disappointment were shining. She did
not dare another word because of her trick of weeping.

" It's all right, Elly," said Sir Isaac. " How touchy you are
Anything you want about these Hostels of yours, you've only
got to tell me and it's done."

§ 11

Lady Harman was still in a state of amazement at the
altered prospects of her hostels when the day arrived for the
formal opening of the first of these in Bloomsbury. They
made a little public ceremony of it in spite of her reluctance,
and Mr. Brumley had to witness things from out of the general
crowd and realise just how completely he wasn't in it, in spite
of all his efforts. Mrs. Pembrose was modestly conspicuous,
like the unexpected in all human schemes. There were several
reporters present, and Horatio Blenker, who was going to
make a loyal leader about it, to be followed by one or two
special articles for the *Old Country Gazette*.

Horatio had procured Mrs. Blapton for the opening after
some ineffectual angling for the Princess Adeline, and the
thing was done at half-past three in the afternoon. In the
bright early July sunshine outside the new building there was

a crimson carpet down on the pavement and an awning above
it, there was a great display of dog-daisies at the windows and
on the steps leading up to the locked portals, an increasing
number of invited people lurked shyly in the ground-floor
rooms ready to come out by the back way and cluster expec-
tantly when Mrs. Blapton arrived, Graper the staff manager
and two assistants in dazzling silk hats seemed everywhere,
the rabbit-like architect had tried to look doggish in a huge
black silk tie and only looked more like a rabbit than ever,
and there was a steady driftage of small boys and girls, nurses
with perambulators, cab touts, airing grandfathers and similar
unemployed people towards the promise of the awning, the
carpet and the flowers. The square building in all its bravery
of Doulton ware and yellow and mauve tiles and its great gilt
inscription

INTERNATIONAL HOSTELS

above the windows of the second story seemed typical of all
those modern forces that are now invading and dispelling the
ancient peace of Bloomsbury.

Mrs. Blapton appeared only five minutes late, escorted by
Bertie Trevor and her husband's spare secretary. Graper
became so active at the sight of her that he seemed more like
some beast out of the Apocalypse with seven hands and ten
hats than a normal human being ; he marshalled the significant
figures into their places, the door was unlocked without serious
difficulty, and Lady Harman found herself in the main corridor
beside Mr. Trevor and a little behind Mrs. Blapton, engaged
in being shown over the new creation. Sir Isaac (driven by
Graper at his elbow) was in immediate attendance on the
great political lady, and Mrs. Pembrose, already with an air of
proprietorship, explained glibly on her other hand. Close
behind Lady Harman came Lady Beach-Mandarin, expanding
like an appreciative gas in a fine endeavour to nestle happily
into the whole big place, and with her were Mrs. Hubert
Plessington and Mr. Pope, one of those odd people who are
called publicists because one must call them something, and
who take chairs and political sides and are vice-presidents of
everything and organise philanthropies, write letters to the
papers, and cannot let the occasion pass without saying a few
words and generally prevent the institutions of this country
from falling out of human attention. He was a little abstracted
in his manner, every now and then his lips moved as he imagined a fresh turn to some classic platitude ; any one who
knew him might have foretold the speech into which he presently broke. He did this in the refectory where there was a
convenient step up at the end. Beginning with the customary
confession of incontinence, " could not let the occasion pass,"
he declared that he would not detain them long, but he felt
that every one there would agree with him that they shared

that day in no slight occasion, no mean enterprise, that here was one of the most promising, one of the most momentous, nay ! he would go further and add with due deference to them all, one of the most pregnant of social experiments in modern social work. In the past he had himself—if he might for a moment allow a personal note to creep into his observations, he himself had not been unconnected with industrial development.—(Querulous voice, " Who the devil is that ? " and whispered explanations on the part of Horatio Blenker : " Pope—very good man—East Purblow Experiment—Payment in Kind instead of Wages—Yes "). . . .

Lady Harman ceased to listen to Mr. Pope's strained but not unhappy tenor. She had heard him before, and she had heard his like endlessly. He was the larger moiety of every public meeting she had ever attended. She had ceased even to marvel at the dull self-satisfaction that possessed him. To-day her capacity for marvelling was entirely taken up by the details of this extraordinary reality which had sprung from her dream of simple, kindly, beautiful homes for distressed and overworked young women ; nothing in the whole of life had been so amazing since that lurid occasion when she had been the agonised vehicle for the entry of Miss Millicent Harman upon this terrestrial scene. It was all so entirely what she could never have thought possible. A few words from other speakers followed, Mrs. Blapton, with the young secretary at hand to prompt, said something, and Sir Isaac was poked forwards to say, " Thank you very much. It's all my wife's doing, really. . . . Oh dash it ! Thank you very much." It had the effect of being the last vestige of some more elaborate piece of eloquence that had suddenly disintegrated in his mind.

" And now, Elly," he said, as their landaulette took them home, " you're beginning to have your hostels."

" Then they *are* my hostels ? " she asked abruptly.

" Didn't I say they were ? " The satisfaction of his face was qualified by that fatigued irritability that nowadays always followed any exertion or excitement.

" If I want things done ? If I want things altered ? "

" Of course you may, of course you may. What's the matter with you, Elly ? What's been putting ideers into your head. You got to have a directress to the thing ; you must have a woman of education who knows a bit about things to look after the matrons and so on. Very likely she isn't everything you want. She's the only one we could get, and I don't see—— Here I go and work hard for a year and more getting these things together to please you, and then suddenly you don't like 'em. There's a lot of the spoilt child in you, Elly— first and last. There they are. . . . "

They were silent for the rest of the journey to Putney, both eing filled with incommunicable things.

§ 12

And now Lady Harman began to share the trouble of all those who let their minds pass out of the circle of their immediate affections with any other desire save interest and pleasure. Assisted in this unhappy development by the sedulous suggestions of Mr. Brumley she had begun to offend against the most sacred law in our sensible British code, she was beginning to take herself and her hostels seriously, and think that it mattered how she worked for them and what they became. She tried to give all the attention her children's upbringing, her husband's ailments, and the general demands of her household left free, to this complex, elusive, puzzling and worrying matter. Instead of thinking that these hostels were just old hostels and that you start them and put in a Mrs. Pembrose and feel very benevolent and happy and go away, she had come to realise partly by dint of her own conscientious thinking and partly through Mr. Brumley's strenuous resolve that she should not take Sir Isaac's gift horse without the most exhaustive examination of its quality, but this new work, like most new things in human life, was capable not only of admirable but of altogether detestable consequences, and that it rested with her far more than with any other human being to realise the former and avoid the latter. And directly one has got to this critical pose towards things, just as one ceases to be content with things anyhow and to want them precisely somehow, one begins to realise just how intractable, confused and disingenuous are human affairs. Mr. Brumley had made himself see how inevitable these big wholesale ways of doing things, these organisations and close social co-operations, have become unless there is to be a social disintegration and set back, and he had also brought himself and her to realise how easily they may develop into a new servitude, how high and difficult is the way towards methods of association that will ensure freedom and permit people to live fine individual lives. Every step towards organisation raises a crop of vices peculiar to itself, fresh developments of the egotism and greed and vanity of those into whose hands there falls control, fresh instances of that hostile pedantry which seems so natural to officials and managers, insurgencies and obstinacies and suspicions on the part of every one. The poor lady had supposed that when one's intentions were obviously benevolent every one helped. She only faced the realities of this task that she had not so much set for herself as had happened to her, after dreadful phases of disillusionment and dismay.

" These hostels," said Mr. Brumley in his most prophetic mood, " can be made free, fine things—or not—just as all the world of men we are living in, could be made a free, fine world. And it's our place to see they are that. It's just by being generous and giving ourselves, helping without enslaving, and giving without exacting gratitude, planning and protecting with infinite care, that we bring that world nearer. . . . Since I've known you I've come to know such things are possible. . . ."

The Bloomsbury hostel started upon its career with an embarrassing difficulty. The young women of the International Stores Refreshment Departments for whom these institutions were primarily intended displayed what looked extremely like a concerted indisposition to come in. They had been circularised and informed that henceforth, to ensure the " good social tone " of the staff, all girls not living at home with their parents or close relations would be expected to reside in the new hostels. There followed an attractive account of the advantages of the new establishment. In drawing up this circular with the advice of Mrs. Pembrose, Sir Isaac had overlooked the fact that his management was very imperfectly informed just where the girls did live, and that after its issue it was very improbable that it would be possible to find out this very necessary fact. But the girls seemed to be unware of this ignorance at headquarters, Miss Babs Wheeler was beginning to feel a little bored by good behaviour and crave for those dramatic cessations at the lunch hour, those speeches, with cheers, from a table top, those interviews with reporters, those flushed and eager councils of war and all the rest, of that good old crisis feeling that had previously ended so happily. Mr. Graper came to his proprietor headlong, Mrs. Pembrose was summoned and together they contemplated the lamentable possibility of this great social benefit they had done the world being discredited at the outset by a strike of the proposed beneficiaries. Sir Isaac fell into a state of vindictiveness and was with difficulty restrained by Mr. Graper from immediately concluding the negotiations that were pending with three great Oxford Street firms that would have given over the hostels to their employees and closed them against the International girls for ever.

Even Mrs. Pembrose couldn't follow Sir Isaac in that, and remarked : " As I understand it, the whole intention was to provide proper housing for our own people first and foremost."

" And haven't we provided it, *damn* them ? " said Sir Isaac in white desperation. . . .

It was Lady Harman who steered the newly launched institutions through these first entanglements. It was her first important advantage in the struggle that had hitherto been going relentlessly against her. She now displayed her peculiar gift, a gift that is indeed unhappily all too rare among philanthropists, the gift of not being able to classify the people with whom she was dealing, but of continuing to regard them as a multitude of individualised souls as distinct and considerable as herself. That makes no doubt for slowness and " inefficiency " and complexity in organisation, but it does make for understandings. And now, through a little talk with Susan Burnet about her sister's attitude upon the dispute, she was able to take the whole situation in the flank.

Like many people who are not easily clear, Lady Harman when she was clear acted with very considerable decision, which was perhaps none the less effective because of the large softnesses of her manner.

She surprised Sir Isaac by coming of her own accord into his study, where with an altogether novel disfavour he sat contemplating the detailed plans for the Sydenham Hostel.
" I think I've found out what the trouble is," she said.

" What trouble ? "

" About my hostel."

" How do you know ? "

" I've been finding out what the girls are saying."

" They'd say anything."

" I don't think they're clever enough for that," said Lady Harman after consideration. She recovered her thread. " You see, Isaac, they've been frightened by the Rules. I didn't know you had printed a set of Rules."

" One must *have* rules, Elly."

" In the background," she decided. " But you see these Rules—were made conspicuous. They were printed in two colours on wall cards just exactly like that list of rules and scale of fines you had to withdraw—— "

" I know," said Sir Isaac shortly.

" It reminded the girls. And that circular that seems to threaten them if they don't give up their lodgings and come in. And the way the front is got up to look just exactly like one of the refreshment-room branches—it makes them feel it will be unhomelike, and that there will be a kind of repetition in the evening of all the discipline and regulations they have to put up with during the day."

" Have to put up with ! " murmured Sir Isaac.

" I wish that had been thought of sooner. If we had made the places look a little more ordinary and called them Osborne House or something a little old-fashioned like that, something with a touch of the Old Queen about it and all that kind of thing."

" We can't go to the expense of taking down all those big gilt letters just to please the fancies of Miss Babs Wheeler."

" It's too late now to do that, perhaps. But we could do something, I think, to remove the suspicions. . . . I want, Isaac—— I think—— " She pulled herself together to announce her determination. " I think if I were to go to the girls and meet a delegation of them, and just talk to them plainly about what we mean by this hostel."

" *You* can't go making speeches."

" It would just be talking to them."

" It's such a Come Down," said Sir Isaac, after a momentary contemplation of the possibility.

For some time they talked without getting very far from these positions they had assumed. At last Sir Isaac shifted back upon his expert. " Can't we talk about it to Mrs. Pembrose ? She knows more about this sort of business than we do."

" I'm not going to talk to Mrs. Pembrose," said Lady Harman, after a little interval. Some unusual quality in her quiet voice made Sir Isaac lift his eyes to her face for a moment.

So one Saturday afternoon, Lady Harman had a meeting with a roomful of recalcitrant girls at the Regent Street Refreshment Branch, which looked very odd to her with grey cotton wrappers over everything and its blinds down, and for the first time she came face to face with the people for whom almost in spite of herself she was working. It was a meeting summoned by the International Branch of the National Union of Waitresses and Miss Babs Wheeler and Mr. Graper were, so to speak, the north and south poles of the little group upon the improvised platform from which Lady Harman was to talk to the gathering. She would have liked the support of Mr. Brumley, but she couldn't contrive any unostentatious way of bringing him into the business without putting it upon a footing that would have involved the appearance of Sir Isaac and Mrs. Pembrose and—everybody. And essentially it wasn't to be everybody. It was to be a little talk.

Lady Harman rather liked the appearance of Miss Babs Wheeler, and met more than an answering approval in that insurbordinate young woman's eye. Miss Wheeler was a minute swaggering person, much akimbo, with a little round blue-eyed innocent face that shone with delight at the lark of living. Her three companions who were in the lobby with her to receive and usher in Lady Harman seemed just as young, but they were relatively unilluminated except by their manifest devotion to their leader. They displayed rather than concealed their opinion of her as a " dear " and a " fair wonder." And the meeting generally it seemed to her was a gathering of very human young women, rather restless, then agog to see her and her clothes, and then somehow allayed by her appearance and quite amiably attentive to what she had to say. A majority were young girls dressed with the cheap smartness of the suburbs, the rest were for the most part older and dingier, and here and there were dotted young ladies of a remarkable and questionable smartness. In the front row, full of shy recognitions and a little disguised by an unfamiliar hat, was Susan's sister Alice.

As Lady Harman had made up her mind that she was not going to deliver a speech she felt no diffidence in speaking. She was far too intent on her message to be embarrassed by any thought of the effect she was producing. She talked as she might have talked in one of her easier moods to Mr.

Brumley. And as she talked it happened that Miss Babs Wheeler and quite a number of the other girls present watched her face and fell in love with her.

She began with her habitual prelude. " You see," she said, and stopped and began again. She wanted to tell them and with a clumsy simplicity she told them how these hostels had arisen out of her desire that they should have something better than the uncomfortable lodgings in which they lived. They weren't a business enterprise, but they weren't any sort of charity. " And I wanted them to be the sort of place in which you would feel quite free. I hadn't any sort of intention of having you interfered with. I hate being interfered with myself and I understand just as well as any one can that you don't like it either. I wanted these Hostels to be the sort of place that you might perhaps after a time almost manage and run for yourselves. You might have a committee or something. . . . Only you know it isn't always easy to do as one wants. Things don't always go in this world as one wants them to go—particularly if one isn't clever." She lost herself for a moment at that point, and then went on to say she didn't like the new rules. They had been drawn up in a hurry and she had only read them after they were printed. All sorts of things in them——

She seemed to be losing her theme again, and Mr. Graper handed her the offending card, a big varnished wall placard, with eyelets and tape complete. She glanced at it. For example, she said, it wasn't her idea to have fines. (Great and long continued applause.) There was something she had always disliked about fines. (Renewed applause.) But these rules could easily be torn up. And as she said this and as the meeting broke into acquiescence again it occurred to her that there was the card of rules in her hands, and nothing could be simpler than to tear it up there and then. It resisted her for a moment, she compressed her lips and then she had it in halves. This tearing was so satisfactory to her that she tore it again and then again. As she tore it, she had a pleasant irrational feeling that she was tearing Mrs. Pembrose. Mr. Graper's face betrayed his shocked feelings, and the meeting which had become charged with a strong desire to show how entirely it approved of her, made a crowning attempt at applause. They hammered umbrellas on the floor, they clapped hands, they rattled chairs, and gave a shrill cheer. A chair was broken.

" I wish," said Lady Harman when that storm had abated, " you'd come and look at the Hostel. Couldn't you come next Saturday afternoon. We could have a stand-up tea and you could see the place and then afterwards your committee and I—and my husband—could make out a real set of rules. . . ."

She went on for some little time longer, she appealed to them with all the strength of her honest purpose to help her to make this possible good thing a real good thing, not to

suspect, not to be hard on her—" and my husband "—not
to make a difficult thing impossible, it was so easy to do that,
and when she finished she was in the happiest possession of
her meeting. They came thronging round her with flushed
faces and bright eyes, they wanted to come near her, wanted
to touch her, wanted to assure her that for her they were
quite prepared to live in any kind of place. For her. " You
come and talk to us, Lady Harman," said one ; " *we'll* show
you."

" Nobody hasn't told us, Lady Harman, how these Hostels
were *yours*."

" You come and talk to us again, Lady Harman." . . .

They didn't wait for the following Saturday. On Monday
morning Mrs. Pembrose received thirty-seven applications to
take up rooms.

§ 13

For the next few years it was to be a matter of recurrent
heart-searching for Lady Harman whether she had been profoundly wise or extremely foolish in tearing up that card of
projected rules. At the time it seemed the most natural and
obvious little action imaginable ; it was long before she realised
just how symbolical and determining a few movements of the
hand and wrist can be. It fixed her line not so much for herself
as for others. It put her definitely, much more definitely than
her convictions warranted, on the side of freedom against
discipline. For indeed her convictions, like most of our convictions, kept along a tortuous watershed between these two.
It is only a few rare extravagant spirits who are wholly for
the warp or wholly for the woof of human affairs.

The girls applauded and loved her. At one stroke she had
acquired the terrible liability of partisans. They made her
their champion and sanction ; she was responsible for an endless succession of difficulties that flowered out of their interpretations of her act. These Hostels that had seemed passing
out of her control, suddenly turned back upon her and took
possession of her.

And they were never simple difficulties. Right and wrong
refused to unravel for her ; each side of every issue seemed to
be so often in suicidal competition with its antagonist for the
inferior case. If the forces of order and discipline showed
themselves perennially harsh and narrow, it did not blind her
perplexed eyes to the fact that the girls were frequently
extremely naughty. She wished very often, she did so wish—
they wouldn't be. They set out with a kind of eagerness for
conflict.

Their very loyalty to her expressed itself not so much in
any sustained attempt to make the hostels successful as in
cheering inconveniently, in embarrassing declarations of a
preference, in an ingenious and systematic rudeness to any

one suspected of imperfect devotion to her. The first comers into the Hostels were much more like the swelling inrush of a tide than, as Mrs. Pembrose would have preferred, like something laid on through a pipe, and when this lady wanted to go on with the old rules until Sir Isaac had approved of the new, the new arrivals went into the cutting-out room and manifested. Lady Harman had to be telephoned for to allay the manifestation.

And then arose questions of deportment, trivial in themselves, but of the gravest moment for the welfare of the hostels. There was a phrase about " noisy or improper conduct " in the revised rules. Few people would suspect a corridor, ten feet wide and two hundred feet long as a temptation to impropriety, but Mrs. Pembrose found it was so. The effect of the corridors upon undisciplined girls quite unaccustomed to corridors was for a time most undesirable. For example they were moved to *run* along them violently. They ran races along them, when they overtook they jostled, when they were overtaken they squealed. The average velocity in the corridors of the lady occupants of the Bloomsbury Hostel during the first fortnight of its existence was seven miles an hour. Was that violence ? Was that impropriety ? The building was all steel construction, but one *heard* even in the Head Matron's room. And then there was the effect of the rows and rows of windows opening out upon the square. The square had some pleasant old trees, and it was attractive to look down into their upper branches, where the sparrows mobbed and chattered perpetually, and over them at the chimneys and turrets and sky signs of the London world. The girls looked. So far they were certainly within their rights. But they did not look modestly, they did not look discreetly. They looked out of wide-open windows, they even sat perilously and protrudingly on the window sills conversing across the façade from window to window, attracting attention, and once to Mrs. Pembrose's certain knowledge a man in the street joined in. It was on a Sunday morning, too, a Bloomsbury Sunday morning !

But graver things were to rouse the preventive prohibitionist in the soul of Mrs. Pembrose. There was the visiting of one another's rooms and cubicles. Most of these young people had never possessed or dreamt of possessing a pretty and presentable apartment to themselves, and the first effect of this was to produce a decorative outbreak, a vigorous framing of photographs and hammering of nails ("dust-gathering litter "—*Mrs. Pembrose*) and then—visiting. They visited at all hours and in all costumes ; they sat in groups of three or four, one on the chair and the rest on the bed, conversing into late hours—entirely uncensored conversations too often accompanied by laughter. When Mrs. Pembrose took this to Lady Harman she found her extraordinarily blind to the conceivable evils of this free intercourse. " But, Lady Harman ! " said

Mrs. Pembrose, with a note of horror, " some of them—kiss each other ! "

" But if they're fond of each other," said Lady Harman. " I'm sure I don't see—— "

And when the floor matrons were instructed to make little surprise visits up and down the corridors the girls who occupied rooms took to locking their doors—and Lady Harman seemed inclined to sustain their right to do that. The floor matrons did what they could to exercise authority, one or two were former department manageresses, two were ex-elementary teachers, crowded out by younger and more certificated rivals, one, and the most trustworthy one, Mrs. Pembrose found, was an ex-wardress from Holloway. The natural result of these secret talkings and conferrings in the rooms became apparent presently in some mild ragging and in the con-coction of petty campaigns of annoyance designed to soften the manners of the more authoritative floor matrons. Here again were perplexing difficulties. If a particular floor matron has a clear commanding note in her voice, is it or is it not " violent and improper " to say " Haw ! " in clear commanding tones whenever you suppose her to be within earshot ? As for the door-locking, Mrs. Pembrose settled that by carrying off all the keys.

Complaints and incidents drifted towards definite scenes and " situations." Both sides in this continuing conflict of dispositions were so definite, so intolerant, to the mind of the lady with the perplexed dark eyes who mediated. Her reason was so much with the matrons ; her sympathies so much with the girls. She did not like the assured brevity of Mrs. Pem-brose's judgments and decisions ; she had an instinctive perception of the truth that all compact judgments upon human beings are unjust judgments. The human spirit is but poorly adapted either to rule or to be ruled, and the honesty of all the efforts of Mrs. Pembrose and her staffs—for soon the hostels at Sydenham and West Kensington were open—were marred not merely by arrogance but by an irrita-bility, a real hostility to complexities and difficulties and resisters and troublesome characters. And it did not help the staff to a triumphant achievement of its duties that the girls had an exaggerated perception that Lady Harman's heart was on their side.

And presently the phrase " weeding out " crept into the talk of Mrs. Pembrose. Some of the girls were being marked as ringleaders, foci of mischief, characters it was desirable to " get rid of." Confronted with it Lady Harman perceived she was absolutely opposed to this idea of getting rid of any one—unless it was Mrs. Pembrose. She liked her various people ; she had no desire for a whittled success with a picked remnant of subdued and deferential employees. She put that

Mr. Brumley and Mr. Brumley was indignant and eloquent

in his concurrence. A certain Mary Trunk, a dark young woman
with a belief that it became her to have a sweet disorder in
her hair, and a large blonde girl named Lucy Baxandall seemed
to be the chief among the bad influences of the Bloomsbury
hostel, and they took it upon themselves to appeal to Lady
Harman against Mrs. Pembrose. They couldn't, they complained, " do a Thing right for her. . . . "

So the tangle grew.

Presently Lady Harman had to go to the Riviera with
Sir Isaac, and when she came back Mary Trunk and Lucy
Baxandall had vanished from both the International Hostel
and the International Stores. She tried to find out why, and
she was confronted by inadequate replies and enigmatical
silences. " They decided to go," said Mrs. Pembrose, and
dropped " fortunately " after that statement. She disavowed
any exact knowledge of their motives. But she feared the
worst. Susan Burnet was uninforming. Whatever had happened
had failed to reach Alice Burnet's ears. Lady Harman could
not very well hold a commission of inquiry into the matter,
but she had an uneasy sense of a hidden campaign of dis-
lodgment. And about the corridors and cubicles and club
rooms there was she thought a difference, a discretion, a
flavour of subjugation. . . .

CHAPTER ELEVEN

THE LAST CRISIS

§ 1

IT would be quite easy for any one with the knack of reserve
to go on from this point with a history of Lady Harman
that would present her as practically a pure philanthropist.
For from these beginnings she was destined to proceed to
more and more knowledge and understanding and clear
purpose and capable work in this interesting process of collective regrouping, this process which may even at last justify
Mr. Brumley's courageous interpretations and prove to be an
early experiment in the beginning of a new social order. Perhaps some day there will be an official biography, another
addition to the inscrutable records of British public lives,
in which all these things will be set out with tact and dignity.
Horatio Blenker or Adolphus Blenker may survive to be
entrusted with this congenial task. She will be represented
as a tall inanimate person pursuing one clear benevolent
purpose in life from her very beginning, and Sir Isaac and her
relations with Sir Isaac will be rescued from reality. The
book will be illustrated by a number of carefully posed photo-
grapher's photographs of her, studies of the Putney house
and perhaps an unappetising woodcut of her early home at

Penge. The aim of all British biography is to conceal. A great
deal of what we have already told will certainly not figure in
any such biography, and still more certainly will the things
we have yet to tell be missing.

Lady Harman was indeed only by the force of circumstances
and intermittently a pure philanthropist, and it is with the
intercalary passages of less exalted humanity that we are
here chiefly concerned. At times no doubt she did really come
near to filling and fitting and becoming identical with that
figure of the pure philanthropist which was her world-ward
face, but for the most part that earnest and dignified figure
concealed more or less extensive spaces of nothingness, while
the errant soul of the woman within strayed into less exalted
ways of thinking.

There were times when she was almost sure of herself—
Mrs. Hubert Plessington could scarcely have been surer of
herself, and times when the whole magnificent project of
constructing a new urban social life out of those difficult
hostels, a collective urban life that should be liberal and free,
broke into grimacing pieces and was the most foolish of experiments. Her struggles with Mrs. Pembrose thereupon
assumed a quality of mere bickering, and she could even doubt
whether Mrs. Pembrose wasn't justified in her attitude and
wiser by her very want of generosity. She felt then something
childish in the whole undertaking that otherwise escaped her,
she was convicted of an absurd self-importance, she discovered
herself an ignorant woman availing herself of her husband's
power and wealth to attempt presumptuous experiments. In
these moods of disillusionment, her mind went adrift and was
driven to and fro from discontent to discontent ; she would
find herself taking soundings and seeking an anchorage upon
the strangest most unfamiliar shoals. And in her relations
and conflicts with her husband there was a smouldering shame
for her submissions to him that needed only a phase of fatigue
to become acute. So long as she believed in her hostels and
her mission that might be endured, but forced back upon her
more personal life its hideousness stood unclothed. Mr. Brumley could sometimes reassure her by a rhetorical effort upon
the score of her hostels, but most of her more intimate and
inner life was not, for very plain reasons, to be shown to
him. He was full of the intention of generous self-denials,
but she had long since come to measure the limits of his self-
denial. . . .

Mr. Brumley was a friend in whom smouldered a love,
capable she knew quite clearly of tormented and tormenting
jealousies. It would be difficult to tell, and she certainly
could never have told how far she knew of this by instinct,
how far it came out of rapid intuitions from things seen and
heard. But she understood that she dared not let a single
breath of encouragement, a hint of physical confidence, reach

that banked-up glow. A sentinel discretion in her brain was always on the watch for that danger, and that restraint, that added deliberate inexpressiveness, kept them most apart, when most her spirit cried out for companionship.

The common quality of all these moods of lassitude was a desolating loneliness. She had at times a need that almost overwhelmed her to be intimate, to be comforted and taken up out of the bleak harsh disappointments and stresses of her customary life. At times after Sir Isaac had either been too unloving or too loving, or when the girls or the matrons had achieved some new tangle of mutual unreasonableness, or when her faith failed, she would lie in the darkness of her own room with her soul crying out for—how can one put it ?— the touch of other soul-stuff. And perhaps it was the constant drift of Mr. Brumley's talk, the little suggestions that fell drop by drop into her mind from his, that disposed her to believe that this aching sense of solitude in the void was to be assuaged by love, by some marvel of close exaltation that one might reach through a lover. She had told Mr. Brumley long ago that she would never let herself think of love, she still maintained to him that attitude of resolute aloofness, but almost without noting what she did, she was tampering now in her solitude with the seals of that locked chamber. She became secretly curious about love. Perhaps there was something in it of which she knew nothing. She found herself drawn towards poetry, found a new attraction in romance ; more and more did she dally with the idea that there was some unknown beauty in the world, something to which her eyes might presently open, something deeper and sweeter than anything she had ever known, close at hand, something to put all the world into proportion for her.

In a little while she no longer merely tampered with these seals, for quite silently the door had opened and she was craning in. This love it seemed to her might after all be so strange a thing that it goes unsuspected and yet fills the whole world of a human soul. An odd grotesque passage in a novel by Wilkins gave her that idea. He compared love to electricity, of all things in the world ; that throbbing life amidst the atoms that we now draw upon for light, warmth, connection, the satisfaction of a thousand wants and the cure of a thousand ills. There it is and always has been in the life of man, and yet until a century ago it worked unsuspected, was known only for a disregarded oddity of amber, a crackling in frost-dry hair and thunder. . . .

And then she remembered how Mr. Brumley had once broken into a panegyric of love. " It makes life a different thing. It is like the home-coming of something lost. All this dispersed perplexing world *centres*. Think what true love means ; to live always in the mind of another and to have that other living always in your mind. . . . Only there can be no restraints, no reserves, no admission of prior rights. One must feel *safe* of one's welcome and freedoms. . . ."

Wasn't it worth the risk of almost any breach of boundaries to get to such a light as that ? . . .

She hid these musings from every human being, she was so shy with them, she hid them almost from herself. Rarely did they have their way with her and when they did, presently she would accuse herself of slackness and dismiss them and urge herself to fresh practicalities in her work. But her work was not always at hand, Sir Isaac's frequent relapses took her abroad to places where she found herself in the midst of beautiful scenery with little to do and little to distract her from these questionings. Then such thoughts would inundate her.

This feeling of the unsatisfactoriness of life, of incompleteness and solitariness, was not of that fixed sort that definitely indicates its demand. Under its oppression she tried the idea of love, but she also tried certain other ideas. Very often this vague appeal had the quality of a person, sometimes a person shrouded in night, a soundless whisper, the unseen lover who came to Psyche in the darkness. And sometimes that person became more distinct, less mystic and more companionable. Perhaps because imaginations have a way of following the line of least resistance, it took upon itself something of the form, something of the voice and bearing of Mr. Brumley. She recoiled from her own thoughts when she discovered herself wondering what manner of lover Mr. Brumley might make—if suddenly she lowered her defences, freed his suffocating pleading, took him to herself.

In my anxiety to draw Mr. Brumley as he was, I have perhaps a little neglected to show him as Lady Harman saw him. We have employed the inconsiderate verisimilitude of a novelist repudiating romance in his portrayal ; towards her he kept a better face. He was at least a very honest lover, and there was little disingenuousness in the flow of fine mental attitudes that met her ; the thought and presence of her made him fine ; as soon could he have turned his shady side towards the sun. And she was very ready and eager to credit him with generous qualities. We of his club and circle, a little assisted perhaps by Max Beerbohm's diabolical index finger, may have found and been not unwilling to find his face chiefly expressive of a kind of empty alertness ; but when it was turned to her its quite pleasantly modelled features glowed and it was transfigured. So far as she was concerned, with Sir Isaac as foil, he was real enough and good enough for her. And by the virtue of that unlovely contrast even a certain ineffectiveness —became infinite delicacy. . . .

The thought of Mr. Brumley in that relation and to that extent of clearness came but rarely into her consciousness, and when it did it was almost immediately dismissed again.

It was the most fugitive of proffered consolations. And it is to be remarked that it made its most successful apparitions when Mr. Brumley was far away, and by some weeks or months of separation a little blurred and forgotten. . . .

And sometimes this unrest of her spirit, this unhappiness turned her in quite another direction as it seemed, and she had thoughts of religion. With a deepened shame she would go seeking into that other, that greater indelicacy, from which her upbringing had divorced her mind. She would even secretly pray. Greatly daring, she fled on several occasions from her visitation of the hostels or slipped out of her home, and evading Mr. Brumley, went once to the Brompton Oratory, once or twice to the Westminster Cathedral, and then having discovered Saint Paul's to Saint Paul's in search of this nameless need. It was a need that no plain and ugly little place of worship would satisfy. It was a need that demanded choir and organ. She went to Saint Paul's haphazard when her mood and opportunity chanced together, and there in the afternoons she found a wonder of great music and chanting voices, and she would kneel looking up into those divine shadows and perfect archings and feel for a time assuaged, wonderfully assuaged. Sometimes, there, she seemed to be upon the very verge of grasping that hidden reality which makes all things plain. Sometimes it seemed to her that this very indulgence was the hidden reality.

She could never be sure in her mind whether these secret worshippings helped or hampered her in her daily living. They helped her to a certain disregard of annoyances and indignities and so far they were good, but they also helped towards a more general indifference. She might have told these last experiences to Mr. Brumley if she had not felt them to be indescribable. They could not be half told. They had to be told completely or they were altogether untellable. So she hid them, and at once accepted and distrusted the consolation they brought her, and went on with the duties and philanthropies that she had chosen as her task in the world.

§ 2

One day in Lent—it was nearly three years after the opening of the first hostel—she went to Saint Paul's.

She was in a mood of great discouragement ; the struggle between Mrs. Pembrose and the Bloomsbury girls had suddenly reopened in an acute form, and Sir Isaac, who was sickening again after a period of better health, had become strangely restless and irritable and hostile to her. He had thwarted her unusually, and taken the side of the matrons in a conflict in which Susan Burnet's sister Alice was now distinguished as the chief of the malcontents. The new trouble seemed to Lady Harman to be traceable in one direction to that ardent

Unionist, Miss Babs Wheeler, under the spell of whose round-faced, blue-eyed, distraught personality Alice had altogether fallen. Miss Babs Wheeler was fighting for the Union ; she herself lived at Highbury with her Mother, and Alice was her chosen instrument in the hostels. The Union had always been a little against the ladylike instincts of many of the waitresses ; they felt strikes were vulgar and impaired their social standing, and this feeling had been greatly strengthened by irruptions of large contingents of shop assistants from various department stores. The Bloomsbury Hostel in particular now accommodated a hundred refined and elegant hands—they ought rather to have been called figures—from the great Oxford Street costume house of Eustace and Mills, young people with a tall sweeping movement and an elevation of chin that had become nearly instinctive, and a silent yet evident intention to find the International girls " low " at the slightest provocation. It is only too easy for poor humanity under the irritation of that tacit superiority to respond with just the provocation anticipated. What one must regretfully speak of as the vulgar section of the International girls had already put itself in the wrong by a number of aggressive acts before the case came to Lady Harman's attention. Mrs. Pembrose seized the occasion for weeding on a courageous scale, and Miss Alice Burnet and three of her dearest friends were invited to vacate their rooms " pending re-decoration."

With only too much plausibility the threatened young women interpreted this as an expulsion, and declined to remove their boxes and personal belongings. Miss Babs Wheeler thereupon entered the Bloomsbury Hostels and in the teeth of three express prohibitions from Mrs. Pembrose went a little up the staircase and addressed a confused meeting in the central hall. There was loud and continuous cheering for Lady Harman at intervals during this incident. Thereupon Mrs. Pembrose demanded sweeping dismissals, not only from the Hostels but the shops as an alternative to her resignation, and Lady Harman found herself more perplexed than ever. . . .

Georgina Sawbridge had contrived to mingle herself in an entirely characteristic way in these troubles by listening for a brief period to an abstract of her sister's perplexities, then demanding to be made Director-General of the whole affair, refusing to believe this simple step impossible and retiring in great dudgeon to begin a series of letters of even more than sisterly bitterness. And Mr. Brumley when consulted had become dangerously sentimental. Under these circumstances, Lady Harman's visit to Saint Paul's had much of the quality of a flight.

It was with an unwonted sense of refuge that she came from the sombre stress and roar of London without into the large hushed spaces of the cathedral. The door closed behind her—and all things changed. Here was meaning, coherence, unity

Herei nstead of a pelting confusion of movements and motives was a quiet concentration upon the little focus of light about the choir, the gentle, complete dominance of a voice intoning. She slipped along the aisle and into the nave and made her way to a seat. How good this was ! Outside she had felt large, awkwardly responsible, accessible to missiles—a distressed, conspicuous thing ; within this living peace she suddenly became no more than one of a tranquil, hushed community of small black-clad Lenten people ; she found a chair and knelt and felt she vanished even from her own conciousness. . . .

How beautiful was this place ! She looked up presently at the great shadowy arcs far above her, so easy, so gracious that it seemed they had not so much been built by men as shaped by circling flights of angels. The service, a little cluster-ing advance of voices unsustained by any organ, mingled in her mind with the many-pointed glow of candles. And then into this great dome of worship and beauty, like a bed of voices breaking into flower, like a springtime breeze of sound, came Allegri's Miserere. . . .

Her spirit clung to this mood of refuge. It seemed as though the disorderly, pugnacious, misunderstanding universe had opened and shown her luminous mysteries. She had a sense of penetration. All that conflict, that jar of purposes and motives, was merely superficial ; she had left it behind her. For a time she had no sense of effort in keeping hold of this, only of attainment, she drifted happily upon the sweet sustain-ing sounds, and then—then the music ceased. She came back into herself. Close to her a seated man stirred and sighed. She tried to get back her hold upon that revelation, but it had gone. Inexorably, opaque, impenetrable doors closed softly on her moment of vision. . . .

All about her was the stir of departure.

She walked out slowly into the cold March daylight, to the leaden greys, the hurrying black shapes, the chaotic afternoon traffic of London. She paused on the steps, still but half reawakened. A passing omnibus obtruded the familiar inscrip-tion, " International Stores for Staminal Bread."

She turned like one who remembers, to where her chauffeur stood waiting.

§ 3

As her motor-car, with a swift smoothness, carried her along the Embankment towards the lattice bar of Charing Cross bridge and the remoter towers of the Houses of Parliament, grey now and unsubstantial against the bright western sky, her mind came back slowly to her particular issues of life. But they were no longer the big, exasperatingly important things that had seemed to hold her life by a hundred painful hooks before she went into the cathedral. They were small still under this dome of evening, small even by the measure

of the grey buildings to the right of her and the warm lit
river to her left, by the measure of the clustering dark barges,
the teeming trams, the streaming crowds of people, the note
of the human process that sounds so loud there. She felt small
even to herself, for the touch of beauty saves us from our own
personalities, makes gods of us to our own littleness.   She
passed under the railway bridge at Charing Cross, watched
the square cluster of Westminster's pinnacles rise above her
until they were out of sight overhead, ran up the little incline
and round into Parliament Square, and was presently out
on the riverside embankment again with the great chimneys
of Chelsea smoking athwart the evening gold.   And thence
with a sudden effect of skies shut and curtains drawn she came
by devious ways to the Fulham Road and the crowding traffic
of Putney Bridge and Putney High Street and so home.

Snagsby, assisted by a new under-butler, a lean, white-
faced young man with red hair, received her ceremoniously
and hovered serviceably about her. On the hall table lay three
or four visiting cards of no importance, some circulars, and
two letters. She threw the circulars into the basket placed
for them and opened her first letter. It was from Georgina ;
it was on several sheets and it began, " I still cannot believe
that you refuse to give me the opportunity the director-
generalship of your hostels means to me. It is not as if you
yourself had either the time or the abilities necessary for them
yourself ; you haven't, and there is something almost dog-in-
the-manger-ish to my mind in the way in which you will
not give me my chance, the chance I have always been longing
for——"

At this point Lady Harman put down this letter for subsequent perusal and took its companion, which was addressed
in an unfamiliar hand. It was from Alice Burnet, and it was
written in that sprawling hand and diffused style natural to
a not very well educated person with a complicated story to
tell in a state of unusual emotion. But the gist was in the
first few sentences, which announced that Alice had been
evicted from the hostel. " I found my things on the pavement," wrote Alice.

Lady Harman became aware of Snagsby still hovering at
hand.

" Mrs. Pembrose, my lady, came here this afternoon," he
said, when he had secured her attention.

" Came here."

" She asked for you, my lady, and when I told her you
were not at 'ome, she asked if she might see Sir Isaac."

" And did she ? "

" Sir Isaac saw her, my lady. They 'ad tea in the study."

" I wish I had been at home to see her," said Lady Harman,
after a brief interval of reflection.

She took her two letters and turned to the staircase. They

were still in her hand when presently she came into her husband's study. " I don't want a light," he said, as she put out her hand to the electric switch. His voice had a note of discontent, but he was sitting in the arm-chair against the window, so that she could not see his features.

" How are you feeling this afternoon ? " she asked.

" I'm feeling all right," he answered testily. He seemed to dislike inquiries after his health almost as much as he disliked neglect.

She came and stood by him and looked out from the dusk of the room into the garden darkening under a red-barred sky. " There is fresh trouble between Mrs. Pembrose and the girls," she said.

" She's been telling me about it."

" She's been here ? "

" Pretty nearly an hour," said Sir Isaac.

Lady Harman tried to imagine that hour's interview on the spur of the moment and failed. She came to her immediate business. " I think," she said, " that she has been—high-handed. . . ."

" You would," said Sir Isaac after an interval.

His tone was hostile, so hostile that it startled her.

" Don't you ? "

He shook his head. " My idees and your idees—or anyhow the idees you've got hold of—somewhere—somehow——   I don't know where you *get* your ideas.   We haven't got the same idees, anyhow. You got to keep order in these places —anyhow. . . ."

She perceived that she was in face of a prepared position. " I don't think," she threw out, " that she does keep order. She represses—and irritates. She gets an idea that certain girls are against her. . . ."

" And you get an idea she's against certain girls. . . ."

" Practically she expels them. She has in fact just turned one out into the street."

" You got to expel 'em. You got to. You can't run these places on sugar and water. There's a sort of girl, a sort of man, who makes trouble. There's a sort makes strikes, makes mischief, gets up grievances. You got to get rid of 'em somehow. You got to be practical somewhere. You can't go running these places on a lot of littry idees and all that. It's no good."

The phrase " littry idees " held Lady Harman's attention for a moment. But she could not follow it up to its implications, because she wanted to get on with the issue she had in hand.

" I want to be consulted about these expulsions. Girl after girl has been sent away——"

Sir Isaac's silhouette was obstinate.

" She knows her business," he said.

He seemed to feel the need of a justification.   " They shouldn't make trouble."

On that they rested for a little while in silence. She began to realise with a gathering emotion that this matter was far more crucial than she had supposed. She had been thinking only of the reinstatement of Alice Burnet, she hadn't yet estimated just what that overriding of Mrs. Pembrose might involve.

" I don't want to have any girl go until I have looked into her case. It's—— It's vital."

" She says she can't run the show unless she has some power."

Neither spoke for some seconds. She had the feeling of hopeless vexation that might come to a child that has wandered into a trap. " I thought," she began. " These hostels——"

She stopped short.

Sir Isaac's hand tightened on the arm of his chair. " I started 'em to please you," he said. " I didn't start 'em to please your friends."

She turned her eyes quickly to his grey up-looking face.

" I didn't start them for you and that chap Brumley to play about with," he amplified. " And now you know about it, Elly."

The thing had found her unprepared. " As if—— " she said at last.

" As if ! " he mocked.

She stood quite still staring blankly at this unmanageable situation. He lifted one hand and dropped it again with a dead impact on the arm of his chair. " I got the things," he said, " and there they are. Anyhow—they got to be run in a proper way."

She made no immediate answer. She was seeking desperately for phrases that escaped her. " Do you think," she began at last. " Do you really think—— ? "

He stared out of the window. He answered in tones of excessive reasonableness : " I didn't start these hostels to be run by you and your—friend." He gave the sentence the quality of an ultimatum, an irreducible minimum.

" He's my friend," she explained, " only—because he does work—for the hostels."

Sir Isaac seemed for a moment to attempt to consider that. Then he relapsed upon his predetermined attitude. " God ! " he exclaimed, " but I been a fool ! "

She decided that that must be ignored.

" I care more for those hostels than I care for anything—anything else in the world," she told him. " I want them to work—I want them to succeed. . . . And then—— "

He listened in sceptical silence.

" Mr. Brumley is nothing to me but a helper. He—— How can you imagine, Isaac—— ? *I !* How can you dare ? To suggest—— ! "

" Very well," said Sir Isaac and reflected and made his old

familiar sound with his teeth. " Run the hostels without him, Elly," he propounded. " Then I'll believe."

She perceived that suddenly she was faced by a test, or a bargain. In the background of her mind the figure of Mr. Brumley, as she had seen him last, in brown and with a tie rather to one side, protested vainly. She did what she could for him on the spur of the moment. " But," she said, " he's so helpful. He's so—harmless."

" That's as may be," said Sir Isaac and breathed heavily.

" How can one suddenly turn on a friend ? "

" I don't see that you ever wanted a friend," said Sir Isaac.

" He's been so good. It isn't reasonable, Isaac. When any one has—slaved."

" I don't say he isn't a good sort of chap," said Sir Isaac, with that same note of almost superhuman rationality, " only —he isn't going to run my hostels."

" But what do you mean, Isaac ? "

" I mean you got to choose."

He waited as if he expected her to speak and then went on.

" What it comes to is this, Elly, I'm about sick of that chap. I'm sick of him." He paused for a moment because his breath was short. " If you don't go on with the hostels he's—Phew—got to mizzle. *Then*—I don't mind—if you want that girl Burnet brought back in triumph . . . It'll make Mrs. Pembrose chuck the whole blessed show, you know, but I say—I don't mind. . . . Only in that case, I don't want to see or hear—or hear about—Phew—or hear about your Mr. Brumley again. And I don't want you to, either. . . . I'm being pretty reasonable and pretty patient over this, with people—people—talking right and left. Still,—there's a limit. . . . You've been going on—if I didn't know you were an innocent—in a way . . . I don't want to talk about that. There you are, Elly."

It seemed to her that she had always expected this to happen. But however much she had expected it to happen she was still quite unprepared with any course of action. She wanted with an equal want of limitation to keep both Mr. Brumley and her hostels.

" But, Isaac," she said. " What do you suspect ? What do you think ? This friendship has been going on—— How can I end it suddenly ? "

" Don't you be too innocent, Elly. You know and I know perfectly well what there is between men and women. I don't make out I know—anything I don't know. I don't pretend you are anything but straight. Only—— "

He suddenly gave way to his irritation. His self-control vanished. " Damn it ! " he cried, and his panting breath quickened ; " the thing's got to end. As if I didn't understand ! As if I didn't understand ! "

She would have protested again but his voice held her. " It's got to end. It's got to end. Of course you haven't done anything, of course you don't know anything or think of anything. . . . Only here I am ill. . . . *You* wouldn't be sorry if I got worse. . . . *You* can wait; you can. . . . All right ! All right ! And there you stand, irritating me—arguing. You know—it chokes me. . . . Got to end, I tell you. . . . Got to end. . . ."

He beat at the arms of his chair and then put a hand to his throat.

" Go away," he cried to her. " Go to hell ! "

§ 4

I cannot tell whether the reader is a person of swift decisions or one of the newer race of doubters ; if he be the latter he will better understand how Lady Harman did in the next two days make up her mind definitely and conclusively to two entirely opposed lines of action. She decided that her relations with Mr. Brumley, innocent as they were, must cease in the interests of the hostels and her struggle with Mrs. Pembrose, and she decided with quite equal certainty that her husband's sudden veto upon these relations was an intolerable tyranny that must be resisted with passionate indignation. Also she was surprised to find how difficult it was now to think of parting from Mr. Brumley. She made her way to these precarious conclusions and on from whichever it was to the other through a jungle of conflicting considerations and feelings. When she thought of Mrs. Pembrose and more particularly of the probable share of Mrs. Pembrose in her husband's objection to Mr. Brumley her indignation kindled. She perceived Mrs. Pembrose as a purely evil personality, as a spirit of espionage, distrust, calculated treachery and malignant intervention, as all that is evil in rule and officialism, and a vast wave of responsibility for all those difficult and feeble and likeable young women who elbowed and giggled and misunderstood and blundered and tried to live happily under the commanding stresses of Mrs. Pembrose's austerity carried her away. She had her duty to do to them and it overrode every other duty. If a certain separation from Mr. Brumley's assiduous aid was demanded, was it too great a sacrifice ? And no sooner was that settled than the whole question reopened with her indignant demand why any one at any price had the right to prohibit a friendship that she had so conscientiously kept innocent. If she gave way to this outrageous restriction to-day, what fresh limitations might not Sir Isaac impose to-morrow ? And now, she was so embarrassed in her struggle by his health. She could not go to him and have things out with him, she could not directly defy him, because that might mean a suffocating seizure for him. . . .

It was entirely illogical, no doubt, but extremely natural for

Lady Harman to decide that she must communicate her
decision, whichever one it was, to Mr. Brumley in a personal
interview. She wrote to him and arranged to meet and talk
to him in Kew Gardens, and with a feeling of discretion went
thither not in the automobile but in a taxi-cab. And so delicately now were her two irrevocable decisions balanced in her
mind that twice on her way to Kew she swayed over from one
to the other.

Arrived at the gardens she found herself quite disinclined to
begin the announcement of either decision. She was quite
exceptionally glad to see Mr. Brumley ; he was dressed in a
new suit of lighter brown that became him very well indeed,
the day was warm and bright, a day of scyllas and daffodils
and snow-upon-the-mountains and green-powdered trees and
frank sunshine—and the warmth of her feelings for her friend
merged indistinguishably with the springtime stir and glow.
They walked across the bright turf together in a state of un-
justifiable happiness, purring little admirations at the ingenious
elegance of creation at its best as gardeners set it out for our
edification, and the whole tenor of Lady Harman's mind was
to make this occasion an escape from the particular business
that had brought her thither.

" We'll look for daffodils away there towards the river under
the trees," said Mr. Brumley, and it seemed preposterous not
to enjoy those daffodils at least before she broached the great
issue between an irresistible force and an immovable post,
that occupied her mental background.

Mr. Brumley was quite at his best that afternoon. He was
happy, gay, and deferential ; he made her realise by his every
tone and movement that if he had his choice of the whole
world that afternoon and all its inhabitants and everything,
there was no other place in which he would be, no other companion, no other occupation than this he had. He talked of
spring and flowers, quoted poets and added the treasures of
a well-stored mind to the amenities of the day. " It's good to
take a holiday at times," he said, and after that it was more
difficult than ever to talk about the trouble of the hostels.

She was able to do this at last while they were having tea
in the little pavilion near the pagoda. It was the old pavilion,
the one that Miss Alimony's suffragettes were afterwards to
burn down in order to demonstrate the relentless logic of
women. They did it in the same eventful week when Miss
Alimony was, she declared, so nearly carried off by White Slave
Traders (disguised as nurses, but, fortunately for her, smelling
of brandy) from the Brixton Temperance Bazaar. But in those
simpler days the pavilion still existed ; it was tended by
agreeable waiters whose evening dress was mitigated by
cheerful little straw hats, and an enormous multitude of valiant
and smutty Cockney sparrows chirped and squeaked and
begged and fluttered and fought, venturing to the very tables

and feet of the visitors. And here, a little sobered from their first elation by much walking about and the presence of jam and watercress, Mr. Brumley and Lady Harman could think again of the work they were doing for the reconstitution of society upon collective lines.

She began to tell him of the conflict between Mrs. Pembrose and Alice Burnet that threatened the latter with extinction. She found it more convenient to talk at first as though the strands of decision were still all in her hands ; afterwards she could go on to the peculiar complication of the situation through the unexpected weakening of her position in relation to Mrs. Pembrose. She described the particular of the new trouble, the perplexing issue between the " ladylike," for which as a feminine idea there was so much to be said on the one hand and the " genial," which was also an admirable quality, on the other. " You see," she said, " it's very rude to cough at people and make noises, but then it's so difficult to explain to the others that it's equally rude to go past people and pretend not to see or hear them. Girls of that sort always seem so much more underbred when they are trying to be superior than when they are not ; they get so stiff and—exasperating. And this keeping out of the Union because it isn't genteel, it's the very essence of the trouble with all these employees. We've discussed that so often. Those drapers' girls seem full of such cold, selfish, base, pretentious notions ; much more full even than our refreshment girls. And then as if it wasn't all difficult enough comes Mrs. Pembrose and her wardresses doing all sorts of hard, clumsy things, and one can't tell them just how little they are qualified to judge good behaviour. Their one idea of discipline is to speak to people as if they were servants and to be distant and crushing. And long before one can do anything come trouble and tart replies and reports of " gross impertinence " and expulsion. We keep on expelling girls. This is the fourth time girls have had to go. What is to become of them ? I know this Burnet girl quite well as you know. She's just a human, kindly little woman. . . . She'll feet disgraced. . . . How can I let a thing like that occur ? "

She spread her hands apart over the tea things.

Mr. Brumley held his chin in his hand and said " Um " and looked judicial, and admired Lady Harman very much, and tried to grasp the whole trouble and wring out a solution. He made some admirable generalisations about the development of a new social feeling in response to changed conditions, but apart from a remark that Mrs. Pembrose was all organisation and no psychology, and quite the wrong person for her position, he said nothing in the slightest degree contributory to the particular drama under consideration. From that utterance, however, Lady Harman would no doubt have gone on to the slow, tentative but finally conclusive statement of the new difficulty that had arisen out of her husband's jealousy and to the discussion of the more fundamental decisions it forced upon her, if a peculiar blight had not fallen upon their conversation and robbed it at last of even an appearance of ease.

This blight crept upon their minds. . . . It began first with Mr. Brumley.

Mr. Brumley was rarely free from self-consciousness. Whenever he was in a restaurant or any such place of assembly, then whatever he did or whatever he said he had a kind of surplus attention, a quickening of the ears, a wandering of the eyes, to the groups and individuals round about him. And while he had seemed entirely occupied with Lady Harman, he had nevertheless been aware from the outset that a dingy and inappropriate-looking man in a bowler hat and a ready-made suit of grey, was listening to their conversation from an adjacent table.

This man had entered the pavilion oddly. He had seemed to dodge in and hesitate. Then he had chosen his table rather deliberately—and he kept looking, and trying not to seem to look.

That was not all. Mr. Brumley's expression was overcast by the effort to recall something. He sat elbows on table and leant forward towards Lady Harman and at the blossom-laden trees outside the pavilion and trifled with two fingers on his lips and spoke between them in a voice that was speculative and confidential and muffled and mysterious. " Where have I seen our friend to the left before ? "

She had been aware of his distraction for some time.

She glanced at the man and found nothing remarkable in him. She tried to go on with her explanations.

Mr. Brumley appeared attentive and then he said again : " But where have I seen him ? "

And from that point their talk was blighted ; the heart seemed to go out of her. Mr. Brumley she felt was no longer taking in what she was saying. At the time she couldn't in any way share his preoccupation. But what had been difficult before became hopeless and she could no longer feel that even presently she would be able to make him understand the peculiar alternatives before her. They drifted back by the great conservatory and the ornamental water, aripple with ducks and swans, to the gates where his taxi waited.

Even then it occurred to her that she ought to tell him something of the new situation. But now their time was running out, she would have to be concise, and what wife could ever say abruptly and offhand that frequent fact, " Oh, by the by, my husband is jealous of you ? " Then she had an impulse to tell him simply, without any explanation at all, that for a time he must not meet her. And while she gathered herself together for that, his preoccupations intervened again.

He stood up in the open taxi-cab and looked back.
" That chap," he said, " is following us."

§ 5

The effect of this futile interview upon Lady Harman was
remarkable. She took to herself an absurd conviction that this
inconclusiveness had been an achievement. Confronted by a
dilemma, she had chosen neither horn and assumed an attitude
of inoffensive defiance. Springs in England vary greatly in their
character ; some are easterly and quarrelsome, some are north-
westerly and wetly disastrous, a bleak invasion from the ocean ;
some are but the broken beginnings of what are not so much
years as stretches of meteorological indecision. This particular
spring was essentially a south-westerly spring, good and friendly,
showery but in the lightest way, and so softly reassuring as to
be gently hilarious. It was a spring to get into the blood of any
one ; it gave Lady Harman the feeling that Mrs. Pembrose
would certainly be dealt with properly and without unreasonable delay by Heaven, and that meanwhile it was well to take
the good things of existence as cheerfully as possible. The
good things she took were very innocent things. Feeling
unusually well and enjoying great draughts of spring air and
sunshine were the chief. And she took them only for three
brief days. She carried the children down to Black Strand to
see her daffodils, and her daffodils surpassed expectation.
There was a delirium of blackthorn in the new wild garden she
had annexed from the woods and a close carpet of encouraged
wild primroses. Even the Putney garden was full of happy
surprises. The afternoon following her visit to Black Strand
was so warm that she had tea with her family in great gaiety
on the lawn under the cedar. Her offspring were unusually
sweet that day, they had new blue cotton sunbonnets, and
Baby and Annette at least succeeded in being pretty. And
Millicent, under the new Swiss governess, had acquired, it
seemed quite suddenly, a glib colloquial French that somehow
reconciled one to the extreme thinness and shapelessness of her
legs.

Then an amazing new fact broke into this gleam of irrational
contentment, a shattering new fact. She found she was being
watched. She discovered that dingy man in the grey suit
following her.

The thing came upon her one afternoon. She was starting
out for a talk with Georgina. She felt so well, so confident
of the world that it was intolerable to think of Georgina
harbouring resentment ; she resolved she would go and have
things out with her and make it clear just how impossible it
was to impose a Director-General upon her husband. She
became aware of the man in grey as she walked down Putney
Hill.

She recognised him at once. He was at the corner of Redfern

Road and still unaware of her existence. He was leaning
against the wall with the habituated pose of one who is
frequently obliged to lean against walls for long periods of
time, and he was conversing in an elucidatory manner with the
elderly crossing-sweeper who still braves the motor-cars at that
point. He became aware of her emergence with a start, he
ceased to lean and became observant.

He was one of those men whose face suggests the word
" muzzle," with an erect combative nose and a forward slant
of the body from the rather inturned feet. He wore an observant bowler hat a little too small for him, and there was something about the tail of his jacket—as though he had been
docked.

She passed at a stride to the acceptance of Mr. Brumley's
hitherto incredible suspicion. Her pulses quickened. It came
into her head to see how far this man would go in following
her. She went on demurely down the hill leaving him quite
unaware that she had seen him.

She was amazed, and after her first belief incredulous again.
Could Isaac be going mad ? At the corner she satisfied herself
of the grey man's proximity and hailed a taxi-cab. The man
in grey came nosing across to listen to her directions and hear
where she was going.

" Please drive up the hill until I tell you," she said, " slowly "
—and had the satisfaction, if one may call it a satisfaction, of
seeing the grey man dive towards the taxi-cab rank. Then
she gave herself up to hasty scheming.

She turned her taxi-cab abruptly when she was certain of
being followed, went back into London, turned again and
made for Westridge's great stores in Oxford Street. The grey
man ticked up twopences in pursuit. All along the Brompton
Road he pursued her with his nose like the jib of a ship.

She was excited and interested, and not nearly so shocked
as she ought to have been. It didn't somehow jar as it ought
to have jarred with her idea of Sir Isaac. Watched by a
detective ! This then was the completion of the conditional
freedom she had won by smashing that window. She might
have known. . . .

She was astonished and indignant, but not nearly so entirely
indignant as a noble heroine should have been. She was
certainly not nearly so queenly as Mrs. Sawbridge would have
shown herself under such circumstances. It may have been due
to some plebeian strain in her father's blood that over and
above her proper indignation she was extremely interested.
She wanted to know what manner of man it was whose nose
was just appearing above the window edge of the taxi-cab
behind. In her inexperienced inattention she had never yet
thought it was possible that men could be hired to follow
women.

She sat a little forward, thinking.

How far would he follow her and was it possible to shake him off ? Or are such followers so expert that once upon a scent, they are like the Indian hunting dog, inevitable. She must see.

She paid off her taxi at Westridge's and, with the skill of her sex, observed him by the window reflection, counting the many doors of the establishment. Would he try to watch them all ? There were also some round the corner. No, he was going to follow her in. She had a sudden desire, an unreasonable desire, to see that man among baby-linen. It was in her power for a time to wreathe him with incongruous objects. This was the sort of fancy a woman must control. . . .

He stalked her with an unreal *sang-froid*. He ambushed behind a display of infants' socks. Driven to buy by a saleswoman he appeared to be demanding improbable varieties of infants' socks.

Are these watchers and trackers sometimes driven to buying things in shops ? If so, strange items must figure in accounts of expenses. If he bought those socks, would they appear in Sir Isaac's bill ? She felt a sudden craving for the sight of Sir Isaac's Private Detective Account. And as for the articles themselves, what became of them ? She knew her husband well enough to feel sure that if he paid for anything he would insist upon having it. But where—where did he keep them ? . . .

But now the man's back was turned ; he was no doubt improvising paternity and an extreme fastidiousness in baby's footwear—— Now for it !—through departments of deepening indelicacy to the lift !

But he had considered that possibility of embarrassment ; he got round by some other way, he was just in time to hear the lift gate clash upon a calmly preoccupied lady, who still seemed as unaware of his existence as the sky.

He was running upstairs, when she descended again, without getting out ; he stopped at the sight of her shooting past him, their eyes met and there was something appealing in his. He was very moist and his bowler was flagging. He had evidently started out in the morning with misconceptions about the weather. And it was clear he felt he had blundered in coming into Westridge's. Before she could get a taxi he was on the pavement behind her, hot but pursuing.

She sought in her mind for corner shops, with doors on this street and that. She exercised him upon Peter Robinson's and Debenham and Freebody's and then started for the monument. But on her way to the monument she thought of the moving staircase at Harrod's. If she went up and down on this, she wanted to know what he would do, would he run up and down the fixed flight ? He did. Several times. And then she bethought herself of the Piccadilly tube ; he got in at Brompton Road and got out at Down Street and then got in again and went to South Kensington, and he darted in and out of adjacent

carriages and got into lifts by curious retrograde movements,
being apparently under the erroneous impression that his back
was less characteristic than his face.

By this time he was evidently no longer unaware of her
intelligent interest in his movements. It was clear too that he
had received a false impression that she wanted to shake him
off and that all the sleuth in him was aroused. He was dishevelled and breathing hard and getting a little close and coarse
in his pursuit, but he was sticking to it with a puckered intensi-
fied resolution. He came up into the South Kensington air
open-mouthed and sniffing curiously, but invincible.

She discovered suddenly that she did not like him at all, and
that she wanted to go home.

She took a taxi, and then away in the wilds of the Fulham
Road she had her crowning idea. She stopped the cab at a
dingy little furniture shop, paid the driver exorbitantly and
instructed him to go right back to South Kensington station,
buy her an evening paper and return for her. The pursuer
drew up thirty yards away, fell into her trap, paid off his cab
and feigned to be interested by a small window full of penny
toys, cheap chocolate, and cocoanut ice. She bought herself
a brass door weight, paid for it hastily and posted herself just
within the furniture-shop door.

Then you see her cab returned suddenly and she got in at
once and left him stranded.

He made a desperate effort to get a motor omnibus. She saw
him rushing across the traffic gesticulating. Then he collided
with a boy with a basket on a bicycle—not so far as she could
see injuriously, they seemed to leap at once into a crowd and
an argument, and then he was hidden from her by a bend in the
road.

§ 6

For a little while her mind was full of fragments of speculation about this man. Was he a married man ? Was he very
much away from home ? What did he earn ? Were there ever
disputes about his expenses ? . . .

She must ask Isaac. For she was determined to go home and
challenge her husband. She felt buoyed up by indignation and
the consciousness of innocence. . . .

And then she felt an odd little doubt whether her innocence
was quite so manifest as she supposed ?

That doubt grew to uncomfortable proportions.

For two years she had been meeting Mr. Brumley as con-
fidently as though they had been invisible beings, and now
she had to rack her brains for just what might be mistaken,
what might be misconstrued. There was nothing, she told
herself, nothing, it was all as open as the day, and still her
mind groped about for some forgotten circumstance, something
gone almost out of memory that would bear misinterpre-

tation. . . . How should she begin ? " Isaac," she would
say, " I am being followed about London." Suppose he denied
his complicity ! How could he deny his complicity ?

The cab ran in through the gates of her home and stopped
at the door. Snagsby came hurrying down the steps with a
face of consternation. " Sir Isaac, my lady, has come home in a
very sad state indeed."

Beyond Snagsby in the hall she came upon a lost-looking
round-eyed Florence.

" Daddy's ill again," said Florence.

" You run to the nursery," said Lady Harman.

" I thought I might help," said Florence. " I don't want to
play with the others."

" No, run away to the nursery."

" I want to see the ossygen let out," said Florence petulantly
to her mother's unsympathetic back. " I *never* see the ossygen
let out. Mum—my ! . . ."

Lady Harman found her husband on the couch in his bedroom. He was propped up in a sitting position with every
available cushion and pillow. His coat and waistcoat and
collar had been taken off and his shirt and vest torn open.
The nearest doctor, Almsworth, was in attendance, but oxygen
had not arrived, and Sir Isaac with an expression of bitter
malignity upon his face was fighting desperately for breath.
If anything his malignity deepened at the sight of his wife.
" Damned climate," he gasped. " Wouldn't have come back—
except for *your* foolery."

It seemed to help him to say that. He took a deep in-
halation, pressed his lips tightly together, and nodded at her to
confirm his words.

" If he's fanciful," said Almsworth. " If in any way your
presence irritates him——"

" Let her stay," said Sir Isaac. " It—pleases her. . . ."

Almsworth's colleague entered with the long-desired oxygen
cylinder.

§ 7

And now every other interest in life was dominated and
every other issue postponed by the immense urgencies of Sir
Isaac's illness. It had entered upon a new phase. It was
manifest that he could no longer live in England, that he must
go to some warm and kindly climate. There and with due
precautions and observances Almsworth assured Lady Harman
he might survive for many years—" an invalid, of course, but a
capable one."

For some time the business of the International Stores had
been preparing itself for this withdrawal. Sir Isaac had been
entrusting his managers with increased responsibility and
making things ready for the flotation of a company that would
take the whole network of enterprises off his hands. Charterson

was associated with him in this, and everything was sufficiently definite to be managed from any Continental resort to which his doctors chose to send him. They chose to send him to Santa Margherita, on the Ligurian coast, near Rapallo and Porto Fino.

It was old Bergener of Marienbad who chose this place. Sir Isaac had wanted to go to Marienbad, his first resort abroad ; he had a lively and indeed an exaggerated memory of his Kur there ; his growing disposition to distrust had turned him against his London specialist, and he had caused Lady Harman to send gigantic telegrams of inquiry to old Bergener before he would be content. But Bergener would not have him at Marienbad ; it wasn't the place, it was the wrong time of year, there was the very thing for them at the Regency Hotel at Santa Margherita, an entire dépendance in a beautiful garden right on the sea, admirably furnished and adapted in every way to Sir Isaac's peculiar needs. There, declared Doctor Bergener, with a proper attendant, due precaution, occasional oxygen, and no excitement, he would live indefinitely—that is to say, eight or ten years. And attracted by the eight or ten years, which was three more than the London specialist offered, Sir Isaac finally gave in and consented to be taken to Santa Margherita.

He was to go as soon as possible, and he went in a special train and with an immense elaboration of attendance and comforts. They took with them a young doctor their specialist at Marienbad had recommended, a bright young Bavarian, with a perfectly square blonde head, an incurable frock coat, the manners of the less kindly type of hotel-porter and luggage which apparently consisted entirely of apparatus, an arsenal of strange-shaped shining black cases. He joined them in London, and went right through with them. From Genoa, at his request, they obtained the services of a trained nurse, an amiable, fluent-shaped woman who knew only Italian and German. For reasons that he declined to give, but which apparently had something to do with the suffrage agitation, he would have nothing to do with an English trained nurse. They had also a stenographer and typist for Sir Isaac's correspondence, and Lady Harman had a secretary, a young lady with glasses named Summersley Satchell, who obviously reserved opinions of a harshly intellectual kind, and had previously been in the service of the late Lady Mary Justin. She established un-friendly relations with the young doctor at an early date by attempting, he said, to learn German from him. Then there was a maid for Lady Harman, an assistant maid, and a valet-attendant for Sir Isaac. The rest of the service in the dépend-ance was supplied by the hotel management.

It took some weeks to assemble this expedition and transport it to its place of exile. Arrangements had to be made for closing the Putney house and establishing the children with

Mrs. Harman at Black Strand.   There was an exceptional amount of packing up to do, for this time Lady Harman felt she was not coming back—it might be for years.   They were going out to warmth and sunlight for the rest of Sir Isaac's life.

He was entering upon the last phase in the slow disorganisation of his secretions and the progressive hardening of his arterial tissues that had become his essential history.   His appearance had altered much in the last few months ; he had become visibly smaller, his face in particular had become sharp and little-featured.   It was more and more necessary for him to sit up in order to breathe with comfort, he slept sitting up ; and his senses were affected, he complained of strange tastes in his food, quarrelled with the cook, and had fits of sickness.   Sometimes, latterly, he had complained of strange sounds, like air whistling in water-pipes, he said, that had no existence outside his ears.   Moreover, he was steadily more irritable and more suspicious, and less able to control himself when angry.   A long-hidden vein of vile and abusive language, hidden, perhaps, since the days of Mr. Gambard's college at Ealing, came to the surface. . . .

For some days after his seizure Lady Harman was glad to find in the stress of his necessities an excuse for disregarding altogether the crisis in the hostels and the perplexing problem of her relations to Mr. Brumley.   She wrote two brief notes to the latter gentleman breaking appointments and pleading pressure of business.   Then, at first during intervals of sleeplessness at night, and presently during the day, the danger and ugliness of her outlook began to trouble her.   She was still, she perceived, being watched, but whether that was because her husband had failed to change whatever orders he had given, or because he was still keeping himself minutely informed of her movements, she could not tell.   She was now constantly with him, and except for small spiteful outbreaks and occasional intervals of still and silent malignity, he tolerated and utilised her attentions.   It was clear his jealousy of her rankled, a jealousy that made him even resentful at her health and ready to complain of any brightness of eye or vigour of movement.   They had drifted far apart from the possibility of any real discussion of the hostels since that talk in the twilight study.   To re-open that now or to complain of the shadowing pursuer who dogged her steps abroad would have been to precipitate Mr. Brumley's dismissal.

Even at the cost of letting things drift at the hostels for a time, she wished to avoid that question.   She would not see him, but she would not shut the door upon him.   So far as the detective was concerned, she could avoid discussion by pretending to be unaware of his existence, and as for the hostels— the hostels each day were left until the morrow.

She had learnt many things since the days of her first rebellion, and she knew now that this matter of the man friend

and nothing else in the world is the central issue in the emancipation of women. The difficulty of him is latent in every other
restriction of which women complain. The complete emancipation of women will come with the complete emancipation of
humanity from jealousy—and no sooner. All other emancipa-
tions are shams until a woman may go about as freely with
this man as with that, and nothing remains for emancipation
when she can. In the innocence of her first revolt this question
of friendship had seemed to Lady Harman the simplest, most
reasonable of minor concessions, but that was simply because
Mr. Brumley hadn't in those days been talking of love to her,
nor she been peeping through that once locked door. Now she
perceived how entirely Sir Isaac was by his standards justified.

And after all that was recognised she remained indisposed
to give up Mr. Brumley.

Yet her sense of evil things happening in the hostels was a
deepening distress. It troubled her so much that she took the
disagreeable step of asking Mrs. Pembrose to meet her at the
Bloomsbury Hostel and talk out the expulsions. She found
that lady alertly defensive, entrenched behind expert knowledge and pretension generally. Her little blue eyes seemed
harder than ever, the metallic resonance in her voice more
marked, the lisp stronger. " Of course, Lady Harman, if you
were to have some practical experience of control——" and
" Three times I have given these girls every opportunity—
every opportunity."

" It seems so hard to drive these girls out," repeated Lady
Harman. " They're such human creatures."

" You have to think of the ones who remain. You must—
think of the Institution as a Whole."

" I wonder," said Lady Harman, peering down into profundities for a moment. Below the great truth glimmered and
vanished that Institutions were made for man and not man for
Institutions.

" You see," she went on, rather to herself than to Mrs
Pembrose, " we shall be away now for a long time."

Mrs. Pembrose betrayed no excesses of grief.

" It's no good for me to interfere and then leave everything. . . ."

" That way spells utter disorganisation," said Mrs. Pembrose.

" But I wish something could be done to lessen the harshness
—to save the pride—of such a girl as Alice Burnet. Practically
you tell her she isn't fit to associate with—the other girls."

" She's had her choice and warning after warning."

" I dare say she's—stiff. Oh !—she's difficult. But—being
expelled is bitter."

" I've not *expelled* her—technically."

" She thinks she's expelled. . . ."

" You'd rather perhaps, Lady Harman, that *I* was expelled."

The dark lady lifted her eyes to the little bridling figure in front of her for a moment and dropped them again. She had had an unspeakable thought, that Mrs. Pembrose wasn't a gentlewoman, and that this sort of thing was a business for the gentle and for nobody else in the world. " I'm only anxious not to hurt any one if I can help it," said Lady Harman.

She went on with her attempt to find some way of compromise with Mrs. Pembrose that should save the spirit of the new malcontents. She was much too concerned on account of the things that lay ahead of them to care for her own pride with Mrs. Pembrose. But that good lady had all the meagre inflexibilities of her class and at last Lady Harman ceased.

She came out into the great hall of the handsome staircase, ushered by Mrs. Pembrose as a guest is ushered by a host. She looked at the spacious proportion of the architecture and thought of the hopes and imaginations she had allowed to centre upon this place. It was to have been a glowing home of happy people, and over it all brooded the chill stillness of rules and regulations and methodical suppressions and tactful discouragement. It was an Institution, it had the empty orderliness of an Institution, Mrs. Pembrose had just called it an Institution, and so Susan Burnet had prophesied it would become five years or more ago. It was a dream subjugated to reality.

So it seemed to Lady Harman must all dreams be subjugated to reality, and the tossing spring greenery of the square, the sunshine, the tumult of sparrows and the confused sound of distant traffic, framed as it was in the hard dark outline of the entrance door, was as near as the promise of joy could ever come to her. " Caught and spoilt," that seemed to be the very essential of her life ; just as it was of these Hostels, all the hopes, the imaginings, the sweet large anticipations, the generosities, and stirring warm desires. . . .

Perhaps Lady Harman had been a little overworking with her preparations for exile. Because as these unhappy thoughts passed through her mind she realised that she was likely to weep. It was extremely undesirable that Mrs. Pembrose should see her weeping.

But Mrs. Pembrose did see her weeping, saw her dark eyes swimming with uncontrollable tears, watched her walk past her and out, without a word or a gesture of farewell.

A kind of perplexity came upon the soul of Mrs. Pembrose. She watched the tall figure descend to her car and enter it and dispose itself gracefully and depart. . . .

" Hysterical," whispered Mrs. Pembrose at last and was greatly comforted.

" Childish," said Mrs. Pembrose sipping further consolation for an unwonted spiritual discomfort.

" Besides," said Mrs. Pembrose, " what else can one do ? "

§ 8

Sir Isaac was greatly fatigued by his long journey to Santa
Margherita in spite of every expensive precaution to relieve
him ; but as soon as the effect of that wore off, his recovery
under the system Bergener had prescribed, was for a time
remarkable. In a little while he was out of bed again and in an
arm-chair. Then the young doctor began to talk of drives.
They had no car with them, so he went into Genoa and spent an
energetic day securing the sweetest running automobile he
could find and having it refitted for Sir Isaac's peculiar needs.
In this they made a number of excursions through the hot
beauty of the Italian afternoons, eastward to Genoa, westward
to Sestri and northward to Montallegro. Then they went up
to the summit of the Monte de Porto Fino and Sir Isaac descended and walked about and looked at the view and praised
Bergener. After that he was encouraged to visit the gracious
old monastery that overhangs the road to Porto Fino.

At first Lady Harman did her duty of control and association
with an apathetic resignation. This had to go on—for eight
or ten years. Then her imagination began to stir again. There
came a friendly letter from Mr. Brumley and she answered
with a description of the colour of the sea and the charm and
wonder of its tideless shore. The three elder children wrote
queer little letters and she answered them. She went into
Rapallo and got herself a carriageful of Tauchnitz books. . . .

That visit to the monastery on the Porto Fino road was like
a pleasant little glimpse into the brighter realities of the Middle
Ages. The place, which is used as a home of rest for convalescent
Carthusians, chanced to be quite empty and deserted ; the
Bavarian rang a jangling bell again and again and at last
gained the attention of an old gardener working in the vineyard
above, an unkempt, unshaven, ungainly creature dressed in
scarce decent rags of brown, who was yet courteous-minded
and, albeit crack-voiced, with his yellow-fanged mouth full of
gracious polysyllables. He hobbled off to get a key and returned
through the still heat of the cobbled yard outside the monastery
gates, and took them into cool airy rooms and showed them
clean and simple cells in shady corridors, and a delightful
orangery, and led them to a beautiful terrace that looked out
upon the glowing quivering sea. And he became very anxious
to tell them something about " Francesco ;" they could not understand him until the doctor caught " Battaglia " and " Pavia "
and had an inspiration. Francis the First, he explained in
clumsy but understandable English, slept here, when he was a
prisoner of the Emperor and all was lost but honour. They
looked at the slender pillars and graceful arching about them.

" Chust as it was now," the young doctor said, his imagination touched for a moment by mere unscientific things. . . .

They returned to their dépendance in a state of mutual

contentment, Sir Isaac scarcely tired, and Lady Harman ran
upstairs to change her dusty dress for a fresher muslin, while
he went upon the doctor's arm to the balcony where tea was
to be served to them.

She came down to find her world revolutionised.

On the table in the balcony the letters had been lying convenient to his chair and he—it may be without troubling to
read the address, had seized the uppermost and torn it open.

He was holding that letter now a little crumpled in his hand.

She had walked close up to the table before she realised the
change. The little eyes that met hers were afire with hatred,
his lips were white and pressed together, his nostrils were
dilated in his struggle for breath. " I knew it," he gasped.

She clung to her dignity though she felt suddenly weak
within. " That letter," she said, " was addressed to me."

There was a gleam of derision in his eyes.

" Look at it ! " he said, and flung it towards her.

" My private letter ! "

" Look at it ! " he repeated.

" What right have you to open my letter ? "

" Friendship ! " he said. " Harmless friendship ! Look
what your—friend says ! "

" Whatever there was in my letter——"

" Oh ! " cried Sir Isaac. " Don't come *that* over me ! Don't
you try it ! Oooh ! phew ! " He struggled for breath for a
time. " He's so harmless. He's so helpful. He—— Read it,
you——"

He hesitated and then hurled a strange word at her.

She glanced at the letter on the table, but made no movement
to touch it. Then she saw that her husband's face was reddening
and that his arm waved helplessly. His eyes, deprived abruptly
of all the fury of conflict, implored assistance.

She darted to the French window that opened into the
dining-room from the balcony. " Doctor Greve ! " she cried.
" Doctor Greve ! "

Behind her the patient was making distressful sounds.
" Doctor Greve," she screamed, and from above she heard the
Bavarian shouting and then the noise of his coming down the
stairs.

He shouted some direction in German as he ran past her.
By an inspiration she guessed he wanted the nurse.

Miss Summersley Satchell appeared in the doorway and
became helpful.

Then every one in the house seemed to be converging upon
the balcony.

It was an hour before Sir Isaac was in bed and sufficiently
allayed for her to go to her own room. Then she thought
of Mr. Brumley's letter, and recovered it from the table on
the balcony where it had been left in the tumult of her husband's
seizure.

It was twilight and the lights were on. She stood under one of them and read with two moths circling about her. . . .

Mr. Brumley had had a mood of impassioned declaration. He had alluded to his " last moments of happiness at Kew." He said he would rather kiss the hem of her garment than be the " lord of any other woman's life."

It was all so understandable—looked at in the proper light. It was all so impossible to explain. And why had she let it happen ? Why had she let it happen ?

§ 9

The young doctor was a little puzzled and rather offended by Sir Isaac's relapse. He seemed to consider it incorrect and was on the whole disposed to blame Lady Harman. He might have had such a seizure, the young doctor said, later, but not now. He would be thrown back for some weeks, then he would begin to mend again, and then whatever he said, whatever he did, Lady Harman must do nothing to contradict him. For a whole day Sir Isaac lay inert, in a cold sweat. He consented once to attempt eating, but sickness overcame him. He seemed so ill that all the young doctor's reassurances could not convince Lady Harman that he would recover. Then suddenly towards evening his arrested vitality was flowing again, the young doctor ceased to be anxious for his own assertions, the patient could sit up against a pile of pillows and breathe and attend to affairs. There was only one affair he really seemed anxious to attend to. His first thought when he realised his returning strength was of his wife. But the young doctor would not let him talk that night.

Next morning he seemed still stronger. He was restless and at last demanded Lady Harman again.

This time the young doctor transmitted the message.

She came to him forthwith and found him, white-faced and unfamiliar-looking, his hands gripping the quilt and his eyes burning with hatred.

" You thought I'd forgotten," was his greeting.

" Don't argue," signalled the doctor from the end of Sir Isaac's bed.

" I've been thinking it out," said Sir Isaac. " When you were thinking I was too ill to think. . . . I know better now."

He sucked in his lips and then went on. " You've got to send for old Crappen," he said. " I'm going to alter things. I had a plan. But that would have been letting you off too easy. See ? So—you send for old Crappen."

" What do you mean to do ? "

" Never you mind, my lady, never you mind. You send for old Crappen."

She waited for a moment. " Is that all you want me to do ? "

" I'm going to make it all right about those Hostels. Don't
you fear. You and your Hostels! You shan't *touch* those
Hostels ever again. Ever. Mrs. Pembrose go! Why! You
ain't worthy to touch the heel of her shoe! Mrs. Pembrose!"

He gathered together all his forces and suddenly expelled
with rousing force the word he had already applied to her on
the day of the intercepted letter.

He found it seemed great satisfaction in the sound and
taste of it. He repeated it thrice. " Zut," cried the doctor,
" Sssh!"

Then Sir Isaac intimated his sense that calm was imperative. " You send for Crappen," he said with a quiet earnestness.

She had become now so used to terms of infamy during the
last year or so, so accustomed to forgive them as part of his
suffering, that she seemed not to hear the insult.

" Do you want him at once? " she asked. " Shall I telegraph? "

" Want him at once! " He dropped his voice to a whisper.
" Yes, you fool—yes. Telegraph. (Phew.) Telegraph. . . .
I mustn't get angry, you know. You—telegraph."

He became suddenly still. But his eyes were active with
hate.

She glanced at the doctor, then moved to the door.

" I will send a telegram," she said, and left him still malignant.

She closed the door softly and walked down the long cool
passage towards her own room. . . .

§ 10

She had to be patient. She had to be patient. This sort
of thing had to go on from crisis to crisis. It might go on for
years. She could see no remedy and no escape.

What else was there to do but be patient? It was all amazing
unjust, but to be a married woman she was beginning to understand is to be outside justice. It is autocracy. She had once
imagined otherwise, and most of her life had been the slow
unlearning of that initial error. She had imagined that the
hostels were hers simply because he had put it in that way.
They had never been anything but his, and now it was manifest he would do what he liked with his own. The law takes
no cognisance of the unwritten terms of a domestic reconciliation.

She sat down at the writing-table the hotel management
had improvised for her.

She rested her chin on her hand and tried to think out her
position. But what was there to think out, seeing that nature
and law and custom have conspired together to put women
altogether under the power of jealous and acquisitive men?

She drew the telegram form towards her.

She was going to write a telegram that she knew would bring Crappen headlong—to disinherit her absolutely. And —it suddenly struck her—her husband had trusted her to write it. She was going to do what he had trusted her to do. . . . But it was absurd.

She sat making patterns of little dots with her pencil point upon the telegram form, and there was a faint smile of amusement upon her lips.

It was absurd—and everything was absurd. What more was to be said or thought about it ? This was the lot of woman. She had made her struggle, rebelled her little bit of rebellion. Most other women no doubt had done as much. It made no difference in the long run.

But it was hard to give up the hostels. She had been foolish of course, but she had not let them make her feel *real*. And she wasn't real. She was a wife—just *this*. . . .

She sighed and bestirred herself and began to write.

Then abruptly she stopped writing.

For three years her excuse for standing—everything, had been these hostels. If now the hostels were to be wrenched out of her hands, if at her husband's death she was to be stripped of every possession and left a helpless dependant on her own children, if for all her good behaviour she was to be insulted by his frantic suspicions as long as he lived and then disgraced by his posthumous mistrust ; was there any reason why she should go on standing anything any more ? Away there in England was Mr. Brumley, *her* man, ready with service and devotion. . . .

It was a profoundly comforting thing to think of him there as hers. He was hers. He'd given so much and on the whole so well. If at last she were to go to him. . . .

Yet when she came to imagine the reality of the step that was in her mind, it took upon itself a chill and forbidding strangeness. It was like stepping out of a familiar house into empty space. What could it be like ? To take some odd trunks with her, meet him somewhere, travel, travel through the evening, travel past nightfall ? The bleak strangeness of that going out never to return !

Her imagination could give her no figure of Mr. Brumley as intimate, as habitual. She could as easily imagine his skeleton. He remained in all this queer speculation something friendly, something incidental, more than a trifle disembodied, entirely devoted of course in that hovering way— but hovering. . . .

And she wanted to be free. It wasn't Mr. Brumley she wanted ; he was but a means—if indeed he was a means—to an end. The person she wanted, the person she had always wanted—was *herself*. Could Mr. Brumley give her that ? Would Mr. Brumley give her that. Was it conceivable he would carry sacrifice to such a pitch as that ? . . .

And what nonsense was this dream ! Here was her husband
needing her. And the children, whose inherent ungainliness,
whose ungracious spirits demanded a perpetual palliation of
culture and instilled deportment. What honest over-nurse
was there for him or helper and guide and friend for them,
if she withdrew ? There was something undignified in a flight
for mere happiness. There was something vindictive in flight
from mere insult. To go, because she was disinherited, because
her hostels were shattered.—No ! And in short—she couldn't
do it. . . .

If Sir Isaac wanted to disinherit her he must disinherit
her. If he wanted to go on seizing and reading her letters,
then he could. There was nothing in the whole scheme of
things to stop him if he did not want to stop himself, nothing
at all. She was caught. This was the lot of women. She was
a *wife*. What else in honour was there but to be a wife up to
the hilt ? . . .

She finished writing her telegram.

§ 11

Suddenly came a running in the passage outside, a rap at
the door and the nurse entered, scared, voluble in Italian, but
with gestures that translated her.

Lady Harman rose, realised the gravity and urgency of the
moment and hurried with her along the passage. " Est-il
mauvais ? " the poor lady attempted, " Est-il——"

Oh ! what words are there for " taken worse " ?

The woman attempted English and failed. She resorted
to her native Italian and exclaimed about the " povero signore."
She conveyed a sense of pitiful extremities. Could it be that
he was in pain again ? What was it ? What was it ? Ten
minutes ago he had been so grimly angry.

At the door of the sick-room the nurse laid a warning hand
on the arm of Lady Harman and made an apprehensive
gesture. They entered almost noiselessly.

The Bavarian doctor turned his face from the bed at their
entrance. He was bending over Sir Isaac. He held up one
hand as if to arrest them ; his other was engaged with his
patient. " No," he said. His attention went back to the
sick man, and he remained very still in that position, leaving
Lady Harman to note for the first time how broad and flat he
was both between his shoulders and between his ears. Then
his face came round slowly, he relinquished something heavy,
stood up, held up a hand. " Zu spät," he whispered, as though
he too was surprised. He sought in his mind for English and
then found his phrase : " He has gone ! "

" Gone ? "

" In one instant."

" Dead ? "

" So. In one instant."

On the bed lay Sir Isaac. His hand was thrust out as though he grasped at some invisible thing. His open eyes stared hard at his wife, and as she met his eyes he snored noisily in his nose and throat.

She looked from the doctor to the nurse. It seemed to her that both these people must be mad. Never had she seen anything less like death. " But he's not dead ! " she protested, still standing in the middle of the room.

" It iss chust the air in his throat," the doctor said. " He went—so ! In one instant as I was helping him."

He waited to see some symptom of feminine weakness. There was a quality in his bearing—as though this event did him credit.

" But—Isaac ! "

It was astounding. The noise in his throat ceased. But he still stared at her. And then the nurse made a kind of assault upon Lady Harman, caught her—even if she didn't fall. It was no doubt the proper formula to collapse. Or to fling oneself upon the deceased. Lady Harman resisted this assistance, disentangled herself and remained amazed ; the nurse a little disconcerted but still ready behind her.

" But," said Lady Harman slowly, not advancing and pointing incredulously at the unwinking stare that met her own, " is he dead ? Is he really dead ? Like that ? "

The doctor's gesture to the nurse betrayed his sense of the fine quick scene this want of confidence had ruined. Under no circumstances in life did English people really seem to know how to behave or what was expected of them. He answered with something bordering upon irony. " Madam," he said, with a slight bow, " he is *really* det."

" But—like *that* ! " cried Lady Harman.

" Like that," repeated the doctor.

She went three steps nearer and stopped, open-eyed, wonderstruck, her lips compressed.

§ 12

For a time astonishment overwhelmed her mind. She did not think of Sir Isaac, she did not think of herself, her whole being was filled by this marvel of death and cessation. Like *that* ! '

Death !

Never before had she seen it. She had expected an extreme dignity, an almost ceremonial sinking back, a slow ebbing, but this was like a shot from a bow. It stunned her. And for some time she remained stunned, while the doctor and her secretary and the hotel people did all that they deemed seemly on this great occasion. She let them send her into another room ; she watched with detached indifference a post-mortem consultation in whispers with a doctor from Rapallo. Then came a great closing of shutters. The nurse and her maid hovered about her, ready to assist her when the sorrowing began. But she had no sorrow. The long moments lengthened out, and he was still dead and she was still only amazement. It seemed part of the extraordinary, the perennial surprisingness of Sir Isaac that he should end in this way. Dead ! She didn't feel for some hours that he had in any way ended. He had died with such emphasis that she felt now that he was capable of anything. What mightn't he do next ? When she heard movements in the chamber of death it seemed to her that of all the people there, most probably it was he who made them. She would not have been amazed if he had suddenly appeared in the doorway of her room, anger-white and his hand quiveringly extended, spluttering some complaint.

He might have cried : " Here I am dead ! And it's *you*, damn you—it's *you* ! "

It was after distinct efforts, after repeated visits to the room in which he lay, that she began to realise that death was death, that death goes on, that there was no more any Sir Isaac, but only a still body he had left behind, that was being moulded now into a stiff image of peace.

Then for a time she roused herself to some control of their proceedings. The doctor came to Lady Harman to ask her about the meals for the day, the hotel manager was in entanglements of tactful consideration, and then the nurse came for instructions upon some trivial matter. They had done what usage prescribes, and now, in the absence of other direction, they appealed to her wishes. She remarked that every one was going on tiptoe and speaking in undertones. . . .

She realised duties. What does one have to do when one's husband is dead ? People would have to be told. She would begin by sending off telegrams to various people, to his mother, to her own, to his lawyer. She remembered she had already written a telegram—that very morning to Crappen. Should she still let the lawyer come out. He was her lawyer now. Perhaps he had better come, but instead of that telegram which still lay upon the desk, she would wire the news of the death to him. . . .

Does one send to the papers ? How does one send to the papers ?

She took Miss Summersley Satchell, who was hovering outside in the sunshine on the balcony, into her room, and sat pale and businesslike and very careful about details, while Miss Summersley Satchell offered practical advice and took notes and wrote telegrams and letters. . . .

There came a hush over everything as the day crept towards noon, and the widowed woman sat in her own room with an inactive mind, watching thin bars of sunlight burn their slow way across the floor. He was dead. It was going on now more steadfastly than ever. He was keeping dead. He was dead at last for good and her married life was over, that life that had always seemed the only possible life, and this stunning incident, this thing that was like the blinding of eyes or the bursting of eardrums, was to be the beginning of strange new experiences.

She was afraid at first at their possible strangeness. And then, you know, in spite of a weak protesting compunction she began to feel glad. . . .

She would not admit to herself that she was glad, that she was anything but a woman stunned, she maintained her still despondent attitude as long as she could, but gladness broke upon her soul as the day breaks, and a sense of release swam up to the horizons of her mind and rose upon her, flooding every ripple of her being, as the sun rises over water in a clear sky. Presently she could sit there no longer, she had to stand up. She walked to the closed Venetians to look out upon the world, and checked herself upon the very verge of flinging them open. He was dead and it was all over for ever. Of course !—it was all over ! Her marriage was finished and done. Miss Satchell came to summon her to lunch. Throughout that meal Lady Harman maintained a sombre bearing, and listened with attention to the young doctor's comments on the manner of Sir Isaac's going. And then—it was impossible to go back to her room.

"My head aches," she said, "I must go down and sit by the sea ;" and her maid, a little shocked, brought her not only her sunshade, but needless wraps—as though a new-made widow must necessarily be very sensitive to the air. She would not let her maid come with her, she went down to the beach alone. She sat on some rocks near the very edge of the transparent water, and fought her gladness for a time, and presently yielded to it. He was dead. One thought filled her mind, for a while so filled her mind that no other thought it seemed could follow it, it had an effect of being final ; it so filled her mind that it filled the whole world ; the broad sapphire distances of the sea, the lapping waves amidst the rocks at her feet, the blazing sun, the dark headland of Porto Fino and a small sailing boat that hung beyond came all within it like things enclosed within a golden globe. She forgot all the days of nursing and discomfort and pity behind her, all the duties and ceremonies before her, forgot all the details and circumstances of life in this one luminous realisation. She was free at last. She was a free woman.

Never more would he make a sound or lift a finger against her life, never more would he contradict her or flout her ; never more would he come peeping through that papered panel between his room and hers, never more could hateful and humiliating demands be made upon her as his right ; no more strange distresses of the body nor raw discomfort of the nerves could trouble her—for ever. And no more detectives, no more suspicions, no more accusations. That last blow he had meant to aim was frozen before it could strike her. And she would have the Hostels in her hands, secure and undisputed, she could deal as she liked with Mrs. Pembrose, take such advisers as she pleased. . . . She was free.

She found herself planning the regeneration of those difficult and disputed hostels, plans that were all coloured by the sun and sky of Italy. The manacles had gone ; her hands were free. She would make this her supreme occupation. She had learnt her lesson now, she felt, she knew something of the mingling of control and affectionate regard that was needed to weld the warring uneasy units of her new community. And she could do it, now as she was and unencumbered, she knew this power was in her. When everything seemed lost to her, suddenly it was all back in her hands. . . .

She discovered the golden serenity of her mind with a sudden astonishment and horror. She was amazed and shocked that she should be glad. She struggled against it and sought to subdue her spirit to a becoming grief. One should be sorrowful at death in any case, one should be grieved. She tried to think of Sir Isaac with affection, to recall touching generosities, to remember kind things and tender and sweet things, and she could not do so. Nothing would come back but the white intensities of his face, nothing but his hatred, his suspicion and his pitiless mean mastery. From which she was freed.

She could not feel sorry. She did her utmost to feel sorry ; presently when she went back into the dépendance, she had to check her feet to a regretful pace ; she dreaded the eyes of the hotel visitors she passed in the garden lest they should detect the liberation of her soul. But the hotel visitors being English were for the most part too preoccupied with manifestations of a sympathy that should be at once heart-felt and quite unobtrusive, and altogether in the best possible taste, to have any attention free for the soul of Lady Harman.

The sense of her freedom came and went like the sunlight of a day in spring, though she attempted her utmost to remain overcast. After dinner that night she was invaded by a vision of the great open years before her, at first hopeful but growing at last to fear and a wild restlessness, so that in defiance of possible hotel opinion, she wandered out into the moonlight and remained for a long time standing by the boat landing, dreaming, recovering, drinking in the white serenities of sea and sky. There was no hurry now. She might stay there as long as she chose. She need account for herself to no one ; she was free. She might go where she pleased, do what she pleased, there was no urgency any more. . . .

There was Mr. Brumley. Mr. Brumley made a very little figure at first in the great prospect before her. . . . Then he grew larger in her thoughts. She recalled his devotions, his services, his self-control. It was good to have one understanding friend in this great limitless world. . . .

She would have to keep that friendship. . . .

But the glorious thing was freedom, to live untrammelled. . . .

Through the stillness a little breeze came stirring, and she awoke out of her dream and turned and faced the shuttered dépendance. A solitary dim light was showing on the veranda. All the rest of the building was a shapeless mass of grey. The long pale front of the hotel seen through a grove of orange trees was lit now at every other window with people going to bed. Beyond, a black hill-side clambered up to the edge of the sky.

Far away out of the darknesses a man with a clear, strong voice was singing to a tinkling accompaniment.

In the black orange trees swam and drifted a score of fire-flies, and there was a distant clamour of nightingales when presently the unseen voice had done.

§ 13

When she was in her room again she began to think of Sir Isaac and more particularly of that last fixed stare of his. . . .

She was impelled to go and see him, to see for herself that he was peaceful and no longer a figure of astonishment. She went slowly along the corridor and very softly into his room —it remained, she felt, his room. They had put candles about him, and the outline of his face, showing dimly through the linen that veiled it, was like the face of one who sleeps very peacefully. Very gently she uncovered it.

He was not simply still, he was immensely still. He was more still and white than the moonlight outside, remoter than moon or stars. . . . She stood surveying him.

He looked small and pinched and as though he had been very tired. Life was over for him, altogether over. Never had she seen anything that seemed so finished. Once, when she was a girl, she had thought that death might be but the opening of a door upon a more generous feast of living than this cramped world could give, but now she knew, she saw, that death can be death.

Life was over. She felt she had never before realised the meaning of death. That beautiful night outside, and all the beautiful nights and days that were still to come, and all the sweet and wonderful things of God's world could be nothing to him now for ever. There was no dream in him that could ever live again, there was no desire, no hope in him.

And had he ever had his desire or his hope, or felt the intensities of life?

There was this beauty she had been discovering in the last few years, this mystery of love—all that had been hidden from him.

She began to realise something sorrowful and pitiful in his quality, in his hardness, his narrowness, his bickering suspicions, his malignant refusals of all things generous and beautiful. He made her feel, as sometimes the children made her feel, the infinite pity of perversity and resistance to the bounties and kindliness of life.

The shadow of sorrow for him came to her at last.

Yet how obstinate he looked, the little frozen white thing that had been Sir Isaac Harman! And satisfied, wilfully satisfied ; his lips were compressed and his mouth a little drawn in at the corners as if he would not betray any other feeling than content with the bargain he had made with life. She did not touch him ; not for the world would she ever touch that cold waxen thing that had so lately clasped her life, but she stood for a long time by the side of his quiet, immersed in the wonder of death. . . .

He had been such a hard little man, such a pursuing little man, so unreasonable and difficult a master, and now—he was such a poor shrunken little man for all his obstinacy! She had never realised before that he was pitiful. . . . Had she perhaps feared him too much, disliked him too much to deal fairly with him ? Could she have helped him ? Was there anything she could have done that she had not done ? Might she not at least have saved him his suspicion ? Behind his rages, perhaps he had been wretched.

Could any one else have helped him ? If perhaps some one had loved him more than she had ever pretended to do——

How strange that she should be so intimately in this room —and still so alien—so alien that she could feel nothing but detached wonder at his infinite loss ! . . . *Alien*—that was what she had always been, a captured alien in this man's household—a girl he had taken. Had he ever suspected how alien ? The true mourner, poor woman ! was even now, in charge of Cook's couriers and interpreters, coming by express from London, to see with her own eyes this last still phase of the son she had borne into the world and watched and sought to serve. She was his nearest ; she indeed was the only near thing there had ever been in his life. Once at least he must have loved her ? And even she had not been very near. No one had ever been very near his calculating, suspicious heart. Had he ever said or thought any really sweet or tender thing —even about her? He had been generous to her in money matters, of course—but out of a vast abundance. . . .

How good it was to have a friend ! How good it was to have even one single friend ! . . .

At the thought of his mother Lady Harman's mind began to drift slowly from this stiff culmination of life before her. Presently she replaced the white cloth upon his face and turned slowly away. Her imagination had taken up the question of how that poor old lady was to be met, how was she to be consoled, what was to be said to her. . . .

She began to plan arrangements. The room ought to be filled with flowers ; Mrs. Harman would expect flowers, large heavy white flowers, in great abundance. That would have to be seen to soon. One might get them in Rapallo. And afterwards—they would have to take him to England, and have a fine, great funeral, with every black circumstance his wealth and his position demanded. Mrs. Harman would need that, and so it must be done. Cabinet Ministers must follow him, members of Parliament, all Blenkerdom feeling self-consciously and, as far as possible, deeply, the Chartersons by way of friends, unfamiliar blood relations, a vast retinue of employees. . . .

How could one take him ? Would he have to be embalmed ? Embalming !—what a strange complement of death ! She averted herself a little more from the quiet figure on the bed, and could not turn to it again. They might come here and do all sorts of things to it, mysterious, evil seeming things with knives and drugs. . . .

She must not think of that. She must learn exactly what Mrs. Harman thought and desired. Her own apathy with regard to her husband had given way completely now to a desire to anticipate and meet Mrs. Harman's every conceivable wish.

CHAPTER TWELVE

LOVE AND A SERIOUS LADY

§ 1

THE news of Sir Isaac's death came quite unexpectedly to Mr. Brumley. He was at the Climax Club, and rather bored ; he had had some tea and dry toast in the magazine room, and had been through the weeklies, and it was a particularly uninteresting week. Then he came down into the hall, looked idly at the latest bulletins upon the board, and read that " Sir Isaac Harman died suddenly this morning at Sta. Margherita, in Ligure, whither he had gone for rest and change."

He went on mechanically reading down the bulletin, leaving something of himself behind him that did not read on. Then he returned to that remarkable item and re-read it, and picked up that lost element of his being again.

He had awaited this event for so long, thought of it so often in such a great variety of relationships, dreamt of it, hoped for it, prayed for it, and tried not to think of it, that now it came to him in reality it seemed to have no substance or significance whatever. He had exhausted the fact before it happened. Since first he had thought of it there had passed four long years, and in that time he had seen it from every

aspect, exhausted every possibility. It had become a theoretical
possibility, the basis of continually less confident, continually
more unsubstantial day dreams. Constantly he had tried not
to think of it, tried to assure himself of Sir Isaac's invalid
immortality. And here it was!

The line above it concerned an overdue ship, the line below
resumed a speech by Mr. Lloyd George. " He would challenge
the honourable member to repeat his accusations—— "

Mr. Brumley stood quite still before the mauve-coloured
print letters for some time, then went slowly across the hall
into the breakfast-room, sat down in a chair by the fire-place,
and fell into a kind of featureless thinking. Sir Isaac was
dead, his wife was free, and the long waiting that had become
a habit was at an end.

He had anticipated a wild elation, and for a while he was
only sensible of change, a profound change. . . .

He began to feel glad that he had waited, that she had
insisted upon patience, that there had been no disaster, no
scandal between them. Now everything was clear for them.
He had served his apprenticeship. They would be able to
marry, and have no quarrel with the world.

He sat with his mind forming images of the prospect before
him, images that were at first feeble and vague, and then,
though still in a silly way, more concrete and definite. At first
they were quite petty anticipations, of how he would have
to tell people of his approaching marriage, of how he would
break it to George Edmund that a new mother impended.
He mused for some time upon the details of that. Should
he take her down to George Edmund's school, and let the
boy fall in love with her—he would certainly fall in love with
her—before anything definite was said, or should he first go
down alone and break the news? Each method had its own
attractive possibilities of drama.

Then Mr. Brumley began to think of the letter he must
write Lady Harman—a difficult letter. One does not rejoice
at death. Already Mr. Brumley was beginning to feel a generous pity for the man he had done his utmost not to detest
for so long. Poor Sir Isaac had lived like a blind thing in the
sunlight, gathering and gathering, when the pride and pleasure
of life is to administer and spend. . . . Mr. Brumley fell wondering just how she could be feeling now about her dead husband.
She might be in a phase of quite real sorrow. Probably the last
illness had tired and strained her. So that his letter would
have to be very fine and tender and soothing, free from all
harshness, free from any gladness—yet it would be hard not
to let a little of his vast relief peep out. Always hitherto,
except for one or two such passionate lapses as that which
had precipitated the situation at Santa Margherita, his epis-
tolary manner had been formal, his matter intellectual and
philanthropic, for he had always known that no letter was

absolutely safe from Sir Isaac's insatiable research. Should he still be formal, still write to "Dear Lady Harman," or suddenly break into a new warmth ? Half an hour later he was sitting in the writing-room, with some few flakes of torn paper on the carpet between his feet and the partially filled wastepaper basket, still meditating upon this difficult issue of the address.

The letter he achieved at last began, "My dear Lady," and went on to, "I do not know how to begin this letter— perhaps you will find it almost as difficult to receive. . . ."

In the small hours he woke to one of his habitual revulsions. Was that, he asked himself, the sort of letter a lover should write to the beloved on her release, on the sudden, long prayed-for opening of a way to her, on the end of her shameful servitude and his humiliations ? He began to recall the cold and stilted sentences of that difficult composition. The gentility of it ! All his life he had been a prey to gentility, had cast himself free from it, only to relapse again in such fashion as this. Would he never be human and passionate and sincere ? Of course he was glad, and she ought to be glad, that Sir Isaac, their enemy and their prison, was dead ; it was for them to rejoice together. He turned out of bed at last, when he could lie still under these self-accusations no longer, and wrapped himself in his warm dressing-gown and began to write. He wrote in pencil. His fountain-pen was as usual on his night-table, but pencil seemed the better medium, and he wrote a warm and glowing love-letter that was brought to an end at last by an almost passionate fit of sneezing. He could find no envelopes in his bedroom Davenport, and so he left that honest scrawl under a paper-weight, and went back to bed greatly comforted. He re-read it in the morning with emotion, and some slight misgivings that grew after he had despatched it. He went to lunch at his club contemplating a third letter that should be sane and fine and sweet, and that should rectify the confusing effect of those two previous efforts. He wrote this letter later in the afternoon.

The days seemed very long before the answer to his first letter came to him, and in that interval two more—aspects went to her. Her reply was very brief, and written in the large, firm, still girlishly clear hand that distinguished her.

" I was so glad of your letter. My life is so strange here, a kind of hushed life. The nights are extraordinarily beautiful, the moon very large, and the little leaves on the trees sharp and black. We are coming back to England, and the funeral will be from our Putney house."

That was all, but it gave Mr. Brumley an impression of her that was exceedingly vivid and close. He thought of her,

shadowy and dusky in the moonlight until his soul swam
with love for her ; he had to get up and walk about ; he
whispered her name very softly to himself several times ; he
groaned gently, and at last he went to his little desk and wrote
to her his sixth letter—quite a beautiful letter. He told her
that he loved her, that he had always loved her since their
first moment of meeting, and he tried to express just the wave
of tenderness that inundated him at the thought of her away
there in Italy. Once, he said, he had dreamt that he would
be the first to take her to Italy. Perhaps some day they would
yet be in Italy together.

§ 2

It was only by insensible degrees that doubt crept into Mr.
Brumley's assurances. He did not observe at once that none
of the brief letters she wrote him responded to his second, the
impassioned outbreak in pencil. And it seemed only in keeping
with the modest reserves of womanhood that she should be
restrained—she always had been restrained.

She asked him not to see her at once when she returned to
England ; she wanted, she said, " to see how things are,"
and that fell in very well with a certain delicacy in himself.
The unburied body of Sir Isaac—it was now provisionally
embalmed—was, through some inexplicable subtlety in his
mind, a far greater barrier than the living man had ever been,
and he wanted it out of the way. And everything settled.
Then, indeed, they might meet.

Meanwhile he had a curious little private conflict of his
own. He was trying not to think, day and night he was trying
not to think, that Lady Harman was now a very rich woman.
Yet some portions of his brain, and he had never suspected
himself of such lawless regions, persisted in the most vulgar
and outrageous suggestions, suggestions that made his soul
blush ; schemes, for example, of splendid foreign travel, of
hotel staffs bowing, of a yacht in the Mediterranean, of motor-
cars, of a palatial flat in London, of a box at the opera, of
artists patronised, of—most horrible !—a baronetcy. . . . The
more authentic parts of Mr. Brumley cowered from and sought
to escape these squalid dreams of magnificences. It shocked
and terrified him to find such things could come out in him.
He was like some pest-stricken patient, amazedly contemplating his first symptom. His better part denied, repudiated.
Of course he would never touch, never even propose—or hint.
. . . It was an aspect he had never once contemplated before
Sir Isaac died. He could on his honour, and after searching
his heart, say that. Yet in Pall Mall one afternoon, suddenly,
he caught himself with a thought in his head so gross, so smug,
that he uttered a faint cry and quickened his steps. . . . Benevolent stepfather !

These distresses begot a hope. Perhaps, after all, probably,

there would be some settlement. . . . She might not be rich,
not so very rich. . . . She might be tied up. . . .

He perceived in that lay his hope of salvation. Otherwise
—oh, pitiful soul !—things were possible in him ; he saw only
too clearly what dreadful things were possible.

If only she were disinherited, if only he might take her,
stripped of all these possessions that even in such glancing
anticipations begot—this horrid indigestion of the imagination !

But then—the Hostels ? . . .

There he stumbled against an invincible riddle !

There was something dreadful about the way in which these
considerations blotted out the essential fact of separations
abolished, barriers lowered, the way to an honourable love
made plain and open. . . .

The day of the funeral came at last, and Mr. Brumley tried
not to think of it, paternally, at Margate. He fled from Sir
Isaac's ultimate withdrawal. Blenker's obituary notice in the
Old Country Gazette was a masterpiece of tactful eulogy, ostentatiously loyal, yet extremely not unmindful of the widowed
proprietor, and of all the possible changes of ownership looming
ahead. Mr. Brumley, reading it in the Londonward train, was
greatly reminded of the Hostels. That was a riddle he didn't
begin to solve. Of course, it was imperative the Hostels should
continue—imperative. Now they might run them together,
openly, side by side. But then with such temptations to
hitherto inconceivable vulgarities. And again, insidiously,
those visions returned of two figures, manifestly opulent,
grouped about a big motor-car or standing together under a
large subservient archway. . . .

There was a long letter from her at his flat, a long and
amazing letter. It was so folded that his eye first caught the
writing on the third page ; "*never marry again. It is so clear
that our work needs all my time and all my means.*" His eyebrows
rose, his expression became consternation ; his hands trembled
a little as he turned the letter over to read it though. It was
a deliberate letter. It began :—

"*Dear Mr. Brumley,—I could never have imagined how much
there is to do after we are dead, and before we can be buried.*"

"Yes," said Mr. Brumley ; " but what does this *mean* ? "

"*There are so many surprises———*"

"It isn't clear."

"*In ourselves and the things about us.*"

"Of course, he would have made some complicated settlement. I might have known."

"*It is the strangest thing in the world to be a widow, much
stranger than any one could ever have supposed, to have no one
to control one, no one to think of as coming before one, no one to
answer to, to be free to plan one's life for oneself———*"

He stood with the letter in his hand after he had read it through, perplexed.

"I can't stand this," he said. " I want to know."

He went to his desk and wrote :—

"*My dear, I want you to marry me.*"

What more was to be said ? He hesitated with this brief challenge in his hand, was minded to telegraph it, and thought of James's novel, *In the Cage.* Telegraph operators are only human after all. He determined upon a special messenger and rang up his quarter valet—he shared service in his flat—to despatch it.

The messenger boy got back from Putney that evening about half-past eight. He brought a reply in pencil.

"*My dear Friend,*" she wrote.   "*You have been so good to me, so helpful. But I do not think that is possible. Forgive me. I want so badly to think, and here I cannot think. I have never been able to think here. I am going down to Black Strand, and in a day or so I will write and we will talk. Be patient with me.*"

She signed her name " *Ellen* " ; always before she had been " E. H."

" Yes," cried Mr. Brumley, " but I want to know ! "

He fretted for an hour and went to the telephone.

Something was wrong with the telephone, it buzzed and went faint, and it would seem that at her end she was embarrassed. " I want to come to you now," he said. " Impossible," was the clearest word in her reply. Should he go in a state of virile resolution, force her hesitation as a man should ? She might be involved there with Mrs. Harman, with all sorts of relatives and strange people. . . .

In the end he did not go.

§ 3

He sat at his lunch alone next day at one of the little tables men choose when they shun company. But to the right of him was the table of the politicians, Adolphus Blenker and Pope of the East Purblow Experiment, and Sir Piper Nicolls, and Munk, the editor of the *Daily Rectification*, sage men all, deep in those mysterious manipulations and wire-pullings by which the Liberal party organisation was even then preparing for itself unusual distrust and dislike, and Horatio Blenker was tenoring away after his manner about a case of right and conscience, " Blenking like Winking " was how a silent member had put it once to Brumley in a gust of hostile criticism. " Practically if she marries again, she is a pauper," struck on Brumley's ears.

" Of course," said Mr. Brumley, and stopped eating.

" I don't know if you remember the particulars of the Astor case," began Munk. . . .

Never had Mr. Brumley come so frankly to eavesdropping. But he heard no more of Lady Harman. Munk had to quote the rights and wrongs of various American wills, and then Mr. Pope seized his opportunity. " At East Purblow," he went on, " in quite a number of instances we had to envisage this problem of the widow—— "

Mr. Brumley pushed back his plate and strolled towards the desk.

It was exactly what he might have expected, what indeed had been at the back of his mind all along, and on the whole he was glad. Naturally she hesitated ; naturally she wanted time to think, and as naturally it was impossible for her to tell him what it was she was thinking about.

They would marry. They must marry. Love has claims supreme over all other claims, and he felt no doubt that for her his comparative poverty of two thousand a year would mean infinitely more happiness than she had ever known or could know with Sir Isaac's wealth. She was reluctant, of course, to become dependent upon him until he made it clear to her what infinite pleasure it would be for him to supply her needs. Should he write to her forthwith ? He outlined a letter in his mind, a very fine and generous letter, good phrases came, and then he reflected that it would be difficult to explain to her just how he had learnt of her peculiar situation. It would be far more seemly to wait either for a public announcement or for some intimation from her.

And then he began to realise that this meant the end of all their work at the Hostels. In his first satisfaction at escaping that possible great motor-car and all the superfluities of Sir Isaac's accumulation, he had forgotten that side of the business. . . .

When one came to think it over, the Hostels did complicate the problem. It was ingenious of Sir Isaac. . . .

It was infernally ingenious of Sir Isaac. . . .

He could not remain in the club for fear that somebody might presently come talking to him and interrupt his train of thought. He went out into the streets.

These Hostels upset everything.

What he had supposed to be a way of escape was really the mouth of a net.

Whichever way they turned Sir Isaac crippled them. . . .

§ 4

Mr. Brumley grew so angry that presently even the strangers in the street annoyed him. He turned his face homeward. He hated dilemmas ; he wanted always to deny them, to thrust them aside, to take impossible third courses.

" For three years," shouted Mr. Brumley, free at last in his

study to give way to his rage, " for three years I've been
making her care for these things. And then—and then—they
turn against me ! "

A violent, incredibly undignified wrath against the dead
man seized him. He threw books about the room. He cried
out vile insults and mingled words of an unfortunate common-
ness with others of extreme rarity. He wanted to go off to
Kensal Green and hammer at the grave there and tell the
departed knight exactly what he thought of him. Then
presently he became calmer, he lit a pipe, picked up the books
from the floor, and meditated revenges upon Sir Isaac's
memory. I deplore my task of recording these ungracious
moments in Mr. Brumley's love history. I deplore the ease
with which men pass from loving and serving women to an
almost canine fight for them. It is the ugliest essential of
romance. There is indeed much in the human heart that I
deplore. But Mr. Brumley was exasperated by disappointment. He was sore, he was raw. Driven by an intolerable
desire to explore every possibility of the situation, full indeed
of an unholy vindictiveness, he went off next morning with
strange questions to Maxwell Hartington.

He put the case as a general case.

" Lady Harman ? " said Maxwell Hartington.

" No, not particularly Lady Harman. A general principle.
What are people—what are women tied up in such a way
to do ? "

Precedents were quoted and possibilities weighed. Mr.
Brumley was flushed, vague but persistent.

" Suppose," he said, " that they love each other passionately—and their work, whatever it may be, almost as passionately. Is there no way—— ? "

" He'll have a *dum casta* clause right enough," said Maxwell
Hartington.

" *Dum*——? *Dum casta !* But, oh ! anyhow *that's* out of
the question—absolutely," said Mr. Brumley.

" Of course," said Maxwell Hartington, leaning back in his
chair and rubbing the ball of his thumb into one eye. " Of
course—nobody ever enforces these *dum casta* clauses. There
isn't any one to enforce them. Ever."—He paused and then
went on, speaking apparently to the array of black tin boxes
in the dingy fixtures before him. " Who's going to watch you ?
That's what I always ask in these cases. Unless the lady goes
and does things right under the noses of these trustees they
aren't going to bother. Even Sir Isaac I suppose hasn't provided funds for a private detective. Eh ? You said something?"

" Nothing," said Mr. Brumley.

" Well, why should they start a perfectly rotten action like
that," continued Maxwell Hartington, now addressing himself
very earnestly to his client, " when they've only got to keep
quiet and do their job and be comfortable. In these matters,

Brumley, as in most matters affecting the relations of men
and women, people can do absolutely what they like nowadays,
absolutely, unless there's some one about ready to make a row.
Then they can't do anything. It hardly matters if they don't
do anything. A row's a row and damned disgraceful. If there
isn't a row, nothing's disgraceful. Of course all these laws and
regulations and institutions and arrangements are just ways
of putting people at the mercy of blackmailers and jealous and
violent persons. One's only got to be a lawyer for a bit to
realise that. Still that's not *our* business. That's psychology.
If there aren't any jealous and violent persons about, well,
then no ordinary decent person is going to worry what you
do. No decent person ever does. So far as I can gather the
only barbarian in this case is the testator—now in Kensal
Green. With additional precautions I suppose in the way of
an artistic but thoroughly massive monument presently to be
added——"

" He'd—turn in his grave."

" Let him. No trustees are obliged to take action on *that*.
I don't suppose they'd know if he did. I've never known a
trustee bother yet about post-mortem movements of any
sort. If they did, we'd all be having Prayers for the Dead.
Fancy having to consider the subsequent reflections of the
testator ! "

" Well anyhow," said Mr. Brumley, after a little pause,
" such a breach, such a proceeding is out of the question—
absolutely out of the question. It's unthinkable."

" Then why did you come here to ask me about it ? " demanded Maxwell Hartington, beginning to rub the other eye
in an audible and unpleasant manner.

§ 5

When at last Mr. Brumley was face to face with Lady
Harman again, a vast mephitic disorderly creation of anticipations, intentions, resolves, suspicions, provisional hypotheses,
urgencies, vindications, and wild and whirling stuff generally
vanished out of his mind. There beside the raised seat in the
midst of the little rock garden where they had talked together
five years before, she stood waiting for him, this tall simple
woman he had always adored since their first encounter, a
little strange and shy now in her dead black uniform of widowhood, but with her honest eyes greeting him, her friendly
hands held out to him. He would have kissed them but for
the restraining presence of Snagsby, who had brought him
to her ; as it was, it seemed to him that the phantom of a kiss
passed like a breath between them. He held her hands for a
moment and relinquished them.

" It is so good to see you," he said, and they sat down side
by side. " I am very glad to see you again."

Then for a little while they sat in silence.

Mr. Brumley had imagined and rehearsed this meeting in many different moods. Now he found none of his premeditated phrases served him, and it was the lady who undertook the difficult opening.

" I could not see you before," she began. " I did not want to see any one." She sought to explain. " I was strange. Even to myself. Suddenly—— " She came to the point. " To find oneself free. . . . Mr. Brumley—*it was wonderful !* "

He did not interrupt her, and presently she went on again.

" You see," she said, " I have become a human being— owning myself. I had never thought what this change would be to me. . . . It has been—— It has been—like being born, when one hadn't realised before that one wasn't born. . . . Now—now I can act. I can do this and that. I used to feel as though I was on strings—with somebody able to pull. . . . There is no one now able to pull at me, no one able to thwart me. . . ."

Her dark eyes looked among the trees, and Mr. Brumley watched her profile.

" It has been like falling out of a prison from which one never hoped to escape. I feel like a moth that has just come out of its case—you know how they come out, wet and weak but—released. For a time I feel I can do nothing but sit in the sun."

" It's queer," she repeated, " how one tries to feel differently from what one really feels, how one tries to feel as one supposes people expect one to feel. At first I hardly dared look at myself. . . . I thought I ought to be sorrowful and helpless. . . . I am not in the least sorrowful or helpless. . . ."

" But," said Mr. Brumley, " are you so free ? "

" Yes."

" Altogether ? "

" As free now—as a man."

" But—people are saying in London—— Something about a will——"

Her lips closed. Her brows and eyes became troubled. She seemed to gather herself together for an effort and spoke at length, without looking at him. " Mr. Brumley," she said, " before I knew anything of the will—— On the very evening when Isaac died—— I knew—I would never marry again. Never."

Mr. Brumley did not stir. He remained regarding her with a mournful expression.

" I was sure of it then," she said, " I knew nothing about the will. I want you to understand that—clearly."

She said no more. The still pause lengthened. She forced herself to meet his eyes.

" I thought," he said after a silent scrutiny, and left her to imagine what he had thought. . . .

" But," he urged to her protracted silence, " you *care* ? "

She turned her face away. She looked at the hand lying idly upon her crape-covered knee. " You are my dearest friend," she said very softly. " You are almost my only friend. But—— I can never go into marriage any more. . . ."

" My dear," he said, " the marriage you have known——"

" No," she said. " No sort of marriage."

Mr. Brumley heaved a profound sigh.

" Before I had been a widow twenty-four hours, I began to realise that I was an escaped woman. It wasn't the particular marriage. . . . It was any marriage. . . . All we women are tied. Most of us are willing to be tied perhaps, but only as people are willing to be tied to lifebelts in a wreck—from fear from drowning. And now, I am just one of the free women, like the women who can earn large incomes, or the women who happen to own property. I've paid my penalties and my service is over. . . . I knew, of course, that you would ask me this. It isn't that I don't care for you, that I don't love your company and your help—and the love and the kindness. . . ."

" Only," he said, " although it is the one thing I desire, although it is the one return you can make me—— But whatever I have done—I have done willingly. . . ."

" My dear ! " cried Mr. Brumley, breaking out abruptly at a fresh point, " I want you to marry me. I want you to be mine, to be my dear close companion, the care of my life, the beauty in my life. . . . I can't frame sentences, my dear. You know, you know. . . . Since first I saw you, talked to you in this very garden. . . ."

" I don't forget a thing," she answered. " It has been my life as well as yours. Only—— "

The grip of her hand tightened on the back of their seat. She seemed to be examining her thumb intently. Her voice sank to a whisper. " I won't marry you," she said.

§ 6

Mr. Brumley leant back, then he bent forward in a desperate attitude with his hands and arms thrust between his knees, then suddenly he recovered, stood up and then knelt with one knee upon the seat. " What are you going to do with me then?" he asked.

" I want you to go on being my friend."

" I can't."

" You can't ? "

" No—I've *hoped*."

And then with something almost querulous in his voice, he repeated, " My dear, I want you to marry me and I want now nothing else in the world."

She was silent for a moment. " Mr. Brumley," she said,

looking up at him, " have you no thought for our Hostels ? "

Mr. Brumley as I have said hated dilemmas. He started to
his feet, a man stung. He stood in front of her and quivered
extended hands at her. " What do such things matter," he
cried, " when a man is in love ? "

She shrank a little from him. " But," she asked, " haven't
they always mattered ? "

" Yes," he expostulated ; " but these Hostels, these Hostels.
. . . We've started them—isn't that good enough ? We've set
them going. . . ."

" Do you know," she asked, " what would happen to the
hostels if I were to marry ? "

" They would go on," he said.

" They would go to a committee. Named. It would include Mrs. Pembrose. . . . Don't you see what would happen ?
He understood the case so well. . . ."

Mr. Brumley seemed suddenly shrunken. " He understood
too well," he said.

He looked down at her soft eyes, at her drooping gracious
form, and it seemed to him that indeed she was made for
love and that it was unendurable that she should be content
to think of friendship and freedom as the ultimate purposes
of her life. . . .

§ 7

Presently these two were walking in the pine-woods beyond
the garden and Mr. Brumley was discoursing lamentably of
love, this great glory that was denied them.

The shade of perplexity deepened in her dark eyes as she
listened. Ever and again she seemed about to speak and then
checked herself and let him talk on.

He spoke of the closeness of love and the deep excitement
of love and how it filled the soul with pride and the world
with wonder, and of the universal right of men and women
to love. He told of his dreams and his patience, and of the
stormy hopes that would not be suppressed when he heard
that Sir Isaac was dead. And as he pictured to himself the
lost delights at which he hinted, as he called back those covert
expectations, he forgot that she had declared herself resolved
upon freedom at any cost, and his rage against Sir Isaac,
who had possessed and wasted all that he would have cherished
so tenderly, grew to nearly uncontrollable proportions. " Here
was your life," he said, " your beautiful life opening and full
—full of such dear seeds of delight and wonder, calling for
love, ready for love, and there came this *Clutch*, this Clutch
that embodied all the narrow meanness of existence, and
gripped and crumpled you and spoilt you. . . . For I tell you,
my dear, you don't know ; you don't begin to know. . . ."

He disregarded her shy eyes, giving way to his gathered
wrath.

"And he conquers! This little monster of meanness, he conquers to the end—his dead hand, his dead desires, out of the grave they hold you! Always, always, it is *Clutch* that conquers; the master of life! I was a fool to dream, a fool to hope. I forgot. I thought only of you and I—that perhaps you and I——"

He did not heed her little sound of protest. He went on to a bitter denunciation of the rule of jealousy in the world, forgetting that the sufferer under that rule in this case was his own consuming jealousy. That was life. Life was jealousy. It was all made up of fierce graspings, fierce suspicions, fierce resentments; men preyed upon one another even as the beasts they came from; reason made its crushed way through their conflict, crippled and wounded by their blows at one another. The best men, the wisest, the best of mankind, the stars of human wisdom, were but half ineffectual angels carried on the shoulders and guided by the steps of beasts. One might dream of a better world of men, of civilisations and wisdom latent in our passion-strained minds, of calms and courage and great heroical conquests that might come, but they lay tens of thousands of years away and we had to live, we had to die, no more than a herd of beasts tormented by gleams of knowledge we could never possess, of happiness for which we had no soul. He grew more and more eloquent as these thoughts sprang and grew in his mind.

"Of course I am absurd," he cried. "All men are absurd. Man is the absurd animal. We have parted from primordial motives—lust and hate and hunger and fear, and from all the tragic greatness of uncontrollable fate, and we, we've got nothing to replace them. We are comic—comic! Ours is the stage of comedy in life's history, half lit and blinded—and we fumble. As absurd as a kitten with its poor little head in a bag. There's your soul of man! Mewing. We're all at it, the poets, the teachers. How can any one hope to escape? Why should I escape? What am I that I should expect to be anything but a thwarted lover, a man mocked by his own attempts at service? Why should I expect to discover beauty and think that it won't be snatched away from me? All my life is comic—the story of this—this last absurdity could it make anything but a comic history? and yet within me my heart is weeping tears. The farther one has gone, the deeper one wallows in the comic marsh. I am one of the newer kind of men, one of those men who cannot sit and hug their credit and their honour and their possessions and be content. I have seen the light of better things than that, and because of my vision, because of my vision and for no other reason, I am the most ridiculous of men. Always I have tried to go out from myself to the world and give. Those early books of mine, those meretricious books in which I pretended all was so well with the world—I did them because I wanted

to give happiness and contentment and to be happy in the
giving. And all the watchers and the grippers, the strong
silent men and the calculating possessors of things, the masters
of the world, they grinned at me. How I lied to please ! But
I tell you for all their grinning, in my very prostitution, there
was a better spirit than theirs in their successes. If I had to
live over again—— "

He left that hypothesis uncompleted.

" And now," he said, with a curious contrast between his
voice and the exaltation of his sentiments, " now that I am
to be your tormented, your emasculated lover to the very
end of things, emasculated by laws I hate and customs I hate
and vile foresights that I despise—— "

He paused, his thread lost for a moment.

" Because," he said, " I'm going to do it. I'm going to do
what I can. I'm going to be as you wish me to be, to help
you, to serve you. . . . If you can't come to meet me, I'll
meet you. I can't help but love you, I can't do without you.
Never in my life have I subscribed willingly to the idea of
renunciation. I've hated renunciation. But if there is no
other course but renunciation, renunciation let it be. I'm
bitter about this, bitter to the bottom of my soul, but at least
I'll have you know I love you. Anyhow. . . . "

His voice broke. There were tears in his eyes.

And on the very crest of these magnificent capitulations
his soul rebelled. He turned about so swiftly, that for a
sentence or so she did not realise the nature of his change.
Her mind remained glowing with her distressed acceptance of
his magnificent nobility.

" I can't," he said.

He flung off his surrenders as a savage might fling off a
garment.

" When I think of his children," he said.

" When I think of the world filled by his children, the
children you have borne him—and I—forbidden almost to
touch your hand ! "

And flying into a passion Mr. Brumley shouted " No ! "

" Not even to touch your hand ! "

" I won't do it," he assured her. " I won't do it. If I cannot
be your lover—I will go away. I will never see you again. I
will do anything—anything, rather than suffer this degradation.
I will go abroad. I will go to strange places. I will aviate. I
will kill myself—or anything, but I won't endure this. I won't.
You see, you ask too much, you demand more than flesh and
blood can stand. I've done my best to bring myself to it and
I can't. I won't have that—that—— "

He waved his trembling fingers in the air. He was absolutely
unable to find an epithet pointed enough and bitter enough to
stab into the memory of the departed knight. He thought of
him as marble, enthroned at Kensal Green, with a false dignity,

a false serenity, and intolerable triumph. He wanted something, some monosyllable to expound and strip all that, some lung-filling, sky-splitting monosyllable that one could shout. His failure increased his exasperation.

" I won't have him grinning at me," he said at last. " And so, it's one thing or the other. There's no other choice. But I know your choice. I see your choice. It's good-bye—and why—why shouldn't I go now ? "

He waved his arms about. He was pitifully ridiculous. His face puckered as an ill-treated little boy's might do. This time it wasn't just the pathetic twinge that had broken his voice before ; he found himself to his own amazement on the verge of loud, undignified, childish weeping. He was weeping passionately and noisily ; he was over the edge of it, and it was too late to snatch himself back. The shame which could not constrain him, overcame him. A preposterous upward gesture of the hands expressed his despair. And abruptly this unhappy man of letters turned from her and fled, the most grief-routed of creatures, whooping and sobbing along a narrow pathway through the trees.

§ 8

He left behind him an exceedingly distressed and astonished lady. She had stood with her eyes opening wider and wider at this culminating exhibition.

" But, Mr. Brumley ! " she had cried at last. " Mr. Brumley ! "

He did not seem to hear her. And now he was running and stumbling along very fast through the trees, so that in a few minutes he would be out of sight. Dismay came with the thought that he might presently go out of sight altogether.

For a moment she seemed to hesitate. Then with a swift decision and a firm large grasp of the hand, she gathered up her black skirts and set off after him along the narrow path. She ran. She ran lightly, with a soft rythmic fluttering of white and black. The long crêpe bands she wore in Sir Isaac's honour streamed out behind her.

" But Mr. Brumley," she panted unheard. " Mis-ter Brumley ! "

He went from her fast, faster than she could follow, amidst the sun-dappled pine stems, and as he went he made noises between bellowing and soliloquy, heedless of any pursuit. All she could hear was a heart-wringing but inexpressive " Wa, wa, wooh, wa, woo," that burst from him ever and again. Through a more open space among the trees she fancied she was gaining upon him, and then as the pines came together again and were mingled with young spruces, she perceived that he drew away from her more and more. And he went round a curve and was hidden, and then visible again much farther off: and then hidden——

She attempted one last cry to him, but her breath failed her, and she dropped her pace to a panting walk.

Surely he would not go thus into the high-road ! It was unendurable to think of him rushing out into the high-road— blind with sorrow—it might be into the very bonnet of a passing automobile.

She passed beyond the pines and scanned the path ahead as far as the stile. Then she saw him, lying where he had flung himself, face downward among the bluebells.

" Oh ! " she whispered to herself, and put one hand to her heart and drew nearer.

She was flooded now with that passion of responsibility, with that wild irrational charity which pours out of the secret depths of a woman's stirred being.

She came up to him so lightly as to be noiseless. He did not move, and for a moment she remained looking at him.

" Then she said once more, and very gently—

" Mr. Brumley "

He started, listened for a second, turned over, sat up and stared at her. His face was flushed and his hair extremely ruffled. And a slight moisture recalled his weeping.

" Mr. Brumley," she repeated, and suddenly there were tears of honest vexation in her voice and eyes. " You *know* I cannot do without you."

He rose to his knees, and never, it seemed to him, had she looked so beautiful. She was a little out of breath, her dusky hair was disordered, and there was an unwonted expression in her eyes, a strange mingling of indignation and tenderness. For a moment they stared unaffectedly at each other, each making discoveries.

" Oh ! " he sighed at last ; " whatever you please, my dear. Whatever you please. I'm going to do as you wish, if you wish it, and be your friend and forget all this "—he waved an arm—" loving."

There were signs of a recrudescence of grief, and, inarticulate as ever, she sank to her knees close beside him.

" Let us sit quietly among these hyacinths," said Mr. Brumley. " And then afterwards we will go back to the house and talk . . . talk about our Hostels."

He sat back and she remained kneeling.

" Of course," he said, " I'm yours—to do just as you will with. And we'll work—— I've been a bit of a stupid brute. We'll work. For all those people. It will be—oh ! a big work, quite a big work. Big enough for us to thank God for. Only——"

The sight of her panting lips had filled him with a wild desire, that set every nerve a quivering, and yet for all that had a kind of moderation, a reasonableness. It was a sisterly thing he had in mind. He felt that if this one desire could be satisfied, then honour would be satisfied, that he would cease grudging Sir Isaac—anything. . . .

But for some moments he could not force himself to speak of this desire, so great was his fear of a refusal.

" There's one thing," he said, and all his being seemed aquiver.

He looked hard at the trampled bluebells about their feet. " Never once," he went on, " never once. In all these years —have we two even—once—kissed. . . . It is such a little thing. . . . So much. . . ."

He stopped breathless. He could say no more because of the beating of his heart. And he dared not look at her face. . . .

There was a swift, soft rustling as she moved. . . ."

She crouched down upon him, and taking his shoulder in her hand, upset him neatly backwards, and, doing nothing by halves, had kissed the astonished Mr. Brumley full upon the mouth.

THE DREAM

CONTENTS

Part One
How Harry Mortimer Smith was made

Part Two
The Loves and Death of Harry Mortimer Smith

Part One
How Harry Mortimer Smith was Made

CHAPTER ONE

THE EXCURSION

§ 1

SARNAC had worked almost continuously for the better part of a year upon some very subtle chemical reactions of the nervous cells of the sympathetic system. His first inquiries had led to the opening out of fresh and surprising possibilities, and these again had lured him on to still broader and more fascinating prospects. He worked perhaps too closely ; he found his hope and curiosity unimpaired, but there was less delicacy of touch in his manipulation, and he was thinking less quickly and accurately. He needed a holiday. He had come to the end of a chapter in his work and wished to brace himself for a new beginning. Sunray had long hoped to be away with him ; she, too, was at a phase in her work when interruption was possible, and so the two went off together to wander among the lakes and mountains.

Their companionship was at a very delightful stage. Their close relationship and their friendship were of old standing, so that they were quite at their ease with one another, yet they were not too familiar to have lost the keen edge of their interest in each other's proceedings. Sunray was very much in love with Sarnac and glad, and Sarnac was always happy and pleasantly exalted when Sunray was near him. Sunray was the richer-hearted and cleverer lover. They talked of everything in the world but Sarnac's work, because that had to rest and grow fresh again. Of her own work Sunray talked abundantly. She had been making stories and pictures of happiness and sorrow in the past ages of the world, and she was full of curious speculations about the ways in which the ancestral mind has thought and felt.

They played with boats upon the great lake for some days, they sailed and paddled and drew up their canoe among the sweet-scented rushes of the islands and bathed and swam. They went from one guest-house to another upon the water and met many interesting and refreshing people. In one house an old man of ninety-eight was staying : he was amusing his declining years by making statuettes of the greatest beauty and humour ; it was wonderful to see the clay take shape in his hands. Moreover, he had a method of cooking the lake-fish that was very appetising, and he made a great dish of them so that every one who was dining in the place could have some. And there was a musician who made Sunray talk about the days gone by, and afterwards he played music with his own hands on a clavier to express the ancient feelings of men. He played one piece that was, he explained, two thousand years old ; it was by a man named Chopin, and it was called the " Revolutionary Étude." Sunray could not have believed a piano capable of such passionate resentment. After that he played grotesque and angry battle-music and crude marching tunes from those half-forgotten times, and then he invented wrathful and passionate music of his own.

Sunray sat under a golden lantern and listened to the musician and watched his nimble hands, but Sarnac was more deeply moved. He had not heard very much music in his life, and this player seemed to open shutters upon deep and dark and violent things that had long been closed to mankind. Sarnac sat, cheek on hand, his elbow on the parapet of the garden-wall, looking across the steely blue of the lake at the darkling night sky at the lower end. The sky had been starry, but a monstrous crescent of clouds like a hand that closes was now gathering all the stars into its fist of darkness. Perhaps there would be rain to-morrow. The lanterns hung still, except that ever and again a little shiver of the air set them swaying. Now and then a great white moth would come fluttering out of the night and beat about among the lanterns for a time and pass away. Presently it would return again or another moth like it would come. Sometimes there would be three or four of these transitory phantoms ; they seemed to be the only insects abroad that night.

A faint ripple below drew his attention to the light of a boat, a round yellow light like a glowing orange, which came gliding close up to the terrace wall out of the blue of the night. There was the sound of a paddle being shipped and a diminishing drip of water, but the people in the boat sat still and listened until the musician had done altogether. Then they came up the steps to the terrace and asked the master of the guest-house for rooms for the night. They had dined at a place farther up the lake.

Four people came by this boat. Two were brother and sister, dark handsome people of Southern origin, and the others were fair women, one blue-eyed and one with hazel eyes, who were clearly very much attached to the brother and sister. They came and talked about the music and then of a climbing expedition they had promised themselves in the great mountains above the lakes. The brother and sister were named Radiant and Starlight, and their work in life, they explained, was to educate animals ; it was a business for which they had an almost instinctive skill. The two fair girls, Willow and Firefly, were electricians. During the last few days Sunray had been looking ever and again at the glittering snowfields and desiring them ; there was always a magic call for her in snowy mountains. She joined very eagerly in the mountain-talk, and it was presently suggested that she and Sarnac should accompany these new acquaintances up

to the peaks they had in mind. But before they went on
to the mountains, she and Sarnac wanted to visit some ancient
remains that had recently been excavated in a valley that
came down to the lake from the East. The four newcomers
were interested in what she told them about these ruins, and
altered their own plans to go with her and Sarnac to see them.
Then afterwards all six would go into the mountains.

§ 2

These ruins were rather more than two thousand years old.
There were the remains of a small old town, a railway-
station of some importance, and a railway-tunnel which
came right through the mountains. The tunnel had collapsed,
but the excavators had worked along it and found several
wrecked trains in it which had evidently been packed with
soldiers and refugees. The remains of these people, much
disturbed by rats and other vermin, lay about in the trains
and upon the railway-tracks. The tunnel had apparently been
blocked by explosives and these train-loads of people entombed.
Afterwards the town itself and all its inhabitants had been
destroyed by poison-gas, but what sort of poison-gas it was
the investigators had still to decide. It had had an unusual
pickling effect, so that many of the bodies were not so much
skeletons as mummies ; and there were books, papers, papier-
mâché objects or the like in a fair state of preservation in
many of the houses. Even cheap cotton goods were preserved,
though they had lost all their colour. For some time after
the great catastrophe this part of the world must have remained
practically uninhabited. A landslide had presently blocked
the lower valley and banked back the valley waters so as to
submerge the town and cover it with a fine silt and seal up
the tunnel very completely. Now the barrier had been cut
through and the valley drained again, and all these evidences
of one of the characteristic disasters of the last war period
in man's history had been brought back to the light once
more.

The six holiday-makers found the visit to this place a very
vivid experience, almost too vivid for their contentment.
On Sarnac's tired mind it made a particularly deep impression. The material collected from the town had been arranged
in a long museum gallery of steel and glass. There were many
almost complete bodies ; one invalid old woman, embalmed
by the gas, had been replaced in the bed from which the
waters had floated her, and there was a shrivelled little baby
put back again in its cradle. The sheets and quilts were
bleached and browned, but it was quite easy to see what
they had once been like. The people had been taken by surprise,
it seemed, while the midday meal was in preparation ; the
tables must have been set in many of the houses ; and now,
after a score of centuries beneath mud and weeds and fishes,

the antiquaries had disinterred and reassembled these old machine-made cloths and plated implements upon the tables. There were great stores of such pitiful discoloured litter from the vanished life of the past.

The holiday-makers did not go far into the tunnel ; the suggestion of things there was too horrible for their mood, and Sarnac stumbled over a rail and cut his hand upon the jagged edge of a broken railway-carriage window. The wound pained him later, and did not heal so quickly as it should have done. It was as if some poison had got into it. It kept him awake in the night.

For the rest of the day the talk was all of the terrible days of the last wars in the world and the dreadfulness of life in that age. It seemed to Firefly and Starlight that existence must have been almost unendurable, a tissue of hate, terror, want and discomfort, from the cradle to the grave. But Radiant argued that people then were perhaps no less happy and no happier than himself ; that for every one in every age there was a normal state, and that any exaltation of hope or sensation above that was happiness and any depression below it misery. It did not matter where the normal came. " They went to great intensities in both directions," he said. There was more darkness in their lives and more pain, but not more unhappiness. Sunray was inclined to agree with him.

But Willow objected to Radiant's psychology. She said that there could be permanently depressed states in an unhealthy body or in a life lived under restraint. There could be generally miserable creatures just as there could be generally happy creatures.

" Of course," interjected Sarnac, " given a standard outside themselves."

" But why did they make such wars ? " cried Firefly. " Why did they do such horrible things to one another ? They were people like ourselves."

" No better," said Radiant, " and no worse. So far as their natural quality went. It is not a hundred generations ago."

" Their skulls were as big and well shaped."

" Those poor creatures in the tunnel ! " said Sarnac. " Those poor wretches caught in the tunnel ! But every one in that age must have felt caught in a tunnel."

After a time a storm overtook them and interrupted their conversation. They were going up over a low pass to a guest house at the head of the lake, and it was near the crest of the pass that the storm burst. The lightning was tremendous and a pine-tree was struck not a hundred yards away. They cheered the sight. They were all exhilarated by the elemental clatter and uproar ; the rain was like a whip on their bare, strong bodies and the wind came in gusts that held them staggering and laughing, breathlessly unable to move forward. They had doubts and difficulties with the path ; for a time they

lost touch with the blazes upon the trees and rocks. Followed
a steady torrent of rain, through which they splashed and
stumbled down the foaming rocky pathway to their resting-
place. They arrived wet as from a swim and glowing ; but
Sarnac, who had come behind the others with Sunray, was
tired and cold. The master of this guest-house drew his shutters
and made a great fire for them with pine-knots and pine-cones
while he prepared a hot meal.

After a while they began to talk of the excavated town
again and of the shrivelled bodies lying away there under
the electric light of the still glass-walled museum, indifferent
for evermore to the sunshine and thunderstorms of life without.

" Did they ever laugh as we do ? " asked Willow. " For
sheer happiness of living ? "

Sarnac said very little. He sat close up to the fire, pitching
pine-cones into it and watching them flare and crackle. Presently he got up, confessed himself tired, and went away to
his bed.

§ 3

It rained hard all through the night and until nearly midday, and then the weather cleared. In the afternoon the
little party pushed on up the valley towards the mountains
they designed to climb, but they went at a leisurely pace,
giving a day and a half to what was properly only one day's
easy walking. The rain had refreshed everything in the upper
valley and called out a great multitude of flowers.

The next day was golden and serene.

In the early afternoon they came to a plateau and meadows
of asphodel, and there they sat down to eat the provisions
they had brought with them. They were only two hours'
climb from the mountain-house in which they were to pass
the night, and there was no need to press on. Sarnac was
lazy ; he confessed to a desire for sleep ; in the night he had
been feverish and disturbed by dreams of men entombed in
tunnels and killed by poison-gas. The others were amused
that any one should want to sleep in the daylight, but Sunray
said she would watch over him. She found a place for him
on the sward, and Sarnac laid down beside her and went to
sleep with his cheek against her side as suddenly and trustfully
as a child goes to sleep. She sat up—as a child's nurse might
do—enjoining silence on the others by gestures.

" After this he will be well again," laughed Radiant, and
he and Firefly stole off in one direction, while Willow and
Starlight went off in another to climb a rocky headland near
at hand, from which they thought they might get a very
wide and perhaps a very beautiful view of the lakes below.

For some time Sarnac lay quite still in his sleep and then
he began to twitch and stir. Sunray bent down attentively
with her warm face close to his. He was quiet again for a time

and then he moved and muttered, but she could not distinguish any words. Then he rolled away from her and threw his arms about and said : " I can't stand it. I can't endure it. Nothing can alter it now. You're unclean and spoiled." She took him gently and drew him into a comfortable attitude again, just as a nurse might do. " Dear," he whispered, and in his sleep reached out for her hand. . . .

When the others came back he had just awakened.

He was sitting up with a sleepy expression and Sunray was kneeling beside him with her hand on his shoulder. " Wake up ! " she said.

He looked at her as if he did not know her and then with puzzled eyes at Radiant. " Then there *is* another life ! " he said at last.

" Sarnac ! " cried Sunray, shaking him. " Don't you know me ? "

He passed a hand over his face. " Yes," he said slowly. " Your name is Sunray. I seem to remember. Sunray . . . Not Hetty—— No. Though you are very like Hetty. Queer ! And mine—mine is Sarnac.

" Of course ! I am Sarnac." He laughed at Willow. " But I thought I was Harry Mortimer Smith," he said. " I did indeed. A moment ago I *was* Henry Mortimer Smith. . . . Henry Mortimer Smith."

He looked about him. " Mountains," he said, " sunshine, white narcissus. Of course, we walked up here this very morning. Sunray splashed me at a waterfall. . . . I remember it perfectly. . . . And yet I was in bed—shot. I was in bed. . . . A dream ? . . . Then I have had a dream, a whole lifetime, two thousand years ago ! "

" What do you mean ? " said Sunray.

" A lifetime—childhood, boyhood, manhood. And death. He killed me. Poor rat !—he killed me ! "

" A dream ? "

" A dream—but a very vivid dream. The realest of dreams. If it *was* a dream. . . . I can answer all your questions now, Sunray. I have lived through a whole life in that old world. I know. . . .

" It is as though that life was still the real one and this only a dream. . . . I was in a bed. Five minutes ago I was in bed. I was dying. . . . The doctor said : ' He is going.' And I heard the rustle of my wife coming across the room. . . . "

" Your *wife* ! " cried Sunray.

" Yes—my wife—Milly."

Sunray looked at Willow with raised eyebrows and a helpless expression.

Sarnac stared at her, dreamily puzzled. " Milly," he repeated very faintly. " She was by the window."

For some moments no one spoke.

Radiant stood with his arm on Firefly's shoulder.

" Tell us about it, Sarnac. Was it hard to die ? "

" I seemed to sink down and down into quiet—and then I woke up here."

" Tell us now, while it is still so real to you."

" Have we not planned to reach the mountain-house before nightfall ? " said Willow, glancing at the sun.

" There is a little guest-house here, within five minutes' walk of us," said Firefly.

Radiant sat down beside Sarnac. " Tell us your dream, now. If it fades out presently or if it is uninteresting we can go on ; but if it is entertaining, we can hear it out and sleep down here to-night. It is a very pleasant place here, and there is a loveliness about those mauve-coloured crags across the gorge, a faint mistiness in their folds, that I could go on looking at for a week without impatience. Tell us your dream, Sarnac."

He shook his friend. " Wake up, Sarnac ! "

Sarnac rubbed his eyes. " It is so queer a story. And there will be so much to explain."

He took thought for a while.

" It will be a long story."

" Naturally, if it is a whole life."

" First let me get some cream and fruit from the guest-house for us all," said Firefly, " and let Sarnac tell us his dream. Five minutes, Sarnac, and I will be back here."

" I will come with you," said Radiant, hurrying after her.

This that follows is the story Sarnac told.

CHAPTER TWO

THE BEGINNING OF THE DREAM

§ 1

THIS dream of mine began," he said, " as all our lives begin, in fragments, in a number of disconnected impressions. I remember myself lying on a sofa, a sofa covered with a curious sort of hard, shiny material with a red and black pattern on it, and I was screaming, but I do not know why I screamed. I discovered my father standing in the doorway of the room looking at me. He looked very dreadful ; he was partially undressed in trousers and a flannel shirt and his fair hair was an unbrushed shock ; he was shaving and his chin was covered with lather. He was angry because I was screaming. I suppose I stopped screaming, but I am not sure. And I remember kneeling upon the same hard red and black sofa beside my mother and looking out of the window—the sofa used to stand with its back to the window-sill—at the rain falling on the roadway outside. The window-sill smelled faintly of paint ; soft bad paint that had blistered in the sun. It was a violent storm of rain and the road was an ill-made road of a yellowish sandy clay. It was covered with muddy water and the storming rainfall made a multitude of flashing bubbles, that drove along before the wind and burst and gave place to others.

" ' Look at 'em, dearie,' said my mother. ' Like sojers.'

" I think I was still very young when that happened, but I was not so young that I had not often seen soldiers with their helmets and bayonets marching by."

" That," said Radiant, " was some time before the Great War then, and the Social Collapse."

" Some time before," said Sarnac. He considered. " Twenty-one years before. This house in which I was born was less than two miles from the great military camp of the British at Low-cliff in England, and Lowcliff railway station was only a few hundred yards away. ' Sojers ' were the most conspicuous objects in my world outside my home. They were more brightly coloured than other people. My mother used to wheel me out for air every day in a thing called a perambulator, and whenever there were soldiers to be seen she used to say : ' Oh ! PRITTY sojers ! '

" ' Sojers ' must have been one of my earliest words. I used to point my little wool-encased finger—for they wrapped up children tremendously in those days and I wore even gloves— and I would say : ' Sosher.'

" Let me try and describe to you what sort of home this was of mine and what manner of people my father and mother were. Such homes and houses and places have long since vanished from the world, not many relics of them have been kept, and though you have probably learned most of the facts concerning them, I doubt if you can fully realise the feel and the reality of the things I found about me. The name of the place was Cherry Gardens ; it was about two miles from the sea at Sandbourne, one way lay the town of Cliffstone from which steamboats crossed the sea to France, and the other way lay Lowcliff and its rows and rows of ugly red brick bar-racks and its great drilling plain, and behind us inland was a sort of plateau covered with raw new roads of loose pebbles— you cannot imagine such roads !—and vegetable-gardens and houses new-built or building, and then a line of hills, not very high but steep and green and bare, the downs. The Downs made a graceful skyline that bounded my world to the north as the sapphire line of the sea bounded it to the south, and they were almost the only purely beautiful things in that world. All the rest was touched and made painful by human confusion. When I was a very little boy I used to wonder what lay behind those downs, but I never went up them to see until I was seven or eight years old."

" This was before the days of aeroplanes ? " asked Radiant.

" They came into the world when I was eleven or twelve. I saw the first that ever crossed the Channel between the mainland of Europe and England. That was considered a very wonderful thing indeed. (" It *was* a wonderful thing," said Sunray.) I went with a lot of other boys, and we edged through a crowd that stood and stared at the quaint old machine ; it was like a big canvas grasshopper with outspread wings ; in a field—somewhere beyond Cliffstone. It was being guarded, and the people were kept away from it by stakes and a string.

" I find it hard to describe to you what sort of places Cherry Gardens and Cliffstone were like—even though we have just visited the ruins of Domodossola. Domodossola was a sprawling, aimless town enough, but these sprawled far more and looked with a far emptier aimlessness into the face of God. You see in the thirty or forty years before my birth there had been a period of comparative prosperity and productivity in human affairs. It was not of course in those days the result of any statesmanship or forethought ; it just happened,— as now and then in the course of a rain-torrent there comes a pool of level water between the rapids. But the money and credit system was working fairly well ; there was much trade and intercourse, no extensive pestilences, exceptionally helpful seasons, and a few very widespread wars. As a result of this conspiracy of favourable conditions there was a perceptible rise in the standards of life of the common people, but for the most part it was discounted by a huge increase of population. As our schoolbooks say, ' In those days Man was his own Locust.' Later in my life I was to hear furtive whispers of a forbidden topic called Birth Control, but in the days of my childhood the whole population of the world, with very few exceptions, was in a state of complete and carefully protected ignorance about the elementary facts of human life and happiness. The surroundings of my childhood were dominated by an unforeseen and uncontrollable proliferation. Cheap proliferation was my scenery, my drama, my atmosphere."

" But they had teachers and priests and doctors and rulers to tell them better," said Willow.

" Not to tell them better," said Sarnac. " These guides and pilots of life were wonderful people. They abounded, and guided no one. So far from teaching men and women to control births or avoid diseases or work generously together, they rather prevented such teaching. This place called Cherry Gardens had mostly come into existence in the fifty years before my birth. It had grown from a minute hamlet into what we used to call an ' urban district.' In that old world in which there was neither freedom nor direction, the land was divided up into patches of all sorts and sizes and owned by people who did what they liked with it, subject to a few vexatious and unhelpful restrictions. And in Cherry Gardens, a sort of men called speculative builders bought pieces of land,

—often quite unsuitable land, and built houses for the swarming increase of population that had otherwise nowhere to go.
There was no plan about this building. One speculative builder
built here and another there, and each built as cheaply as
possible and sold or let what he had built for as much as
possible. Some of the houses they built in rows and some
stood detached, each with a little patch of private garden—
garden they called it, though it was either a muddle or a
waste—fenced in to keep people out."

" Why did they keep people out ? "

" They liked to keep people out. It was a satisfaction for
them. They were not secret gardens. People might look over
the fence if they chose. And each house had its own kitchen
where food was cooked—there was no public eating-place in
Cherry Gardens—and each, its separate store of household
gear. In most houses there was a man who went out to work
and earn a living—they didn't so much live in those days as
earn a living—and came home to eat and sleep, and there was
a woman, his wife, who did all the services, food and cleaning
and everything, and also she bore children, a lot of unpremeditated children—because she didn't know any better. She was
too busy to look after them well, and many of them died.
Most days she cooked a dinner. She cooked it. . . . It *was*
cooking ! "

Sarnac paused—his brows knit. " Cooking ! Well, well.
That's over, anyhow," he said.

Radiant laughed cheerfully.

" Almost every one suffered from indigestion. The newspapers were full of advertisements of cures," said Sarnac, still
darkly retrospective.

" I never thought of that aspect of life in the old world,"
said Sunray.

" It was—fundamental," said Sarnac. " It was a world, in
every way, out of health.

" Every morning, except on the Sunday, after the man had
gone off to his day's toil and the children had been got up
and dressed and those who were old enough sent off to school,
the woman of the house tidied up a bit and then came the
question of getting in food. For this private cooking of hers.
Every day except Sunday a number of men with little pony-
carts or with barrows they pushed in front of them, bearing
meat and fish and vegetables and fruit, all of it exposed to
the weather and any dirt that might be blowing about, came
bawling along the roads of Cherry Gardens, shouting the sort
of food they were selling. My memory goes back to that red-
and-black sofa by the front window and I am a child once
again. There was a particularly splendid fish-hawker. What
a voice he had ! I used to try to reproduce his splendid noises
in my piping childish cries : ' Mackroo-E-y'are Macroo !
Fine Macroo ! Thee a Sheen. Mac-*roo* ! '

The housewives would come out from their domestic mysteries to buy or haggle and, as the saying went, ' pass the time of day ' with their neighbours. But everything they wanted was not to be got from the hawkers, and that was where my father came in. He kept a little shop. He was what was called a greengrocer ; he sold fruits and vegetables, such poor fruits and vegetables as men had then learned to grow—and also he sold coals and paraffin (which people burned in their lamps) and chocolate and ginger-beer and other things that were necessary to the barbaric housekeeping of the time. He also sold cut-flowers and flowers in pots, and seeds and sticks and string and weed killer for the little gardens. His shop stood in a row with a lot of other shops ; the row was like a row of the ordinary houses with the lower rooms taken out and replaced by the shop, and he ' made his living ' and ours by buying his goods as cheaply as he could and getting as much as he could for them. It was a very poor living because there were several other able-bodied men in Cherry Gardens who were also greengrocers, and if he took too much profit then his customers would go away and buy from these competitors and he would get no profit at all.

" I and my brother and sisters—for my mother had been unable to avoid having six babies and four of us were alive—lived by and in and round about this shop. In the summer we were chiefly out of doors or in the room above the shop ; but in the cold weather it cost too much trouble and money to have a fire in that room—all Cherry Gardens was heated by open coal fires—and we went down into a dark underground kitchen where my mother, poor dear ! cooked according to her lights."

" You were troglodytes ! " said Willow.

" Practically. We always ate in that down-stairs room. In the summer we were sunburned and ruddy, but in the winter, because of this—inhumation, we became white and rather thin. I had an elder brother who was monstrous in my childish memory ; he was twelve years older than I ; and I had two sisters, Fanny and Prudence. My elder brother Ernest went out to work, and then he went away to London and I saw very little of him until I too went to London. I was the youngest of the lot ; and when I was nine years old, my father, taking courage, turned my mother's perambulator into a little push-cart for delivering sacks of coals and suchlike goods.

" Fanny, my elder sister, was a very pretty girl, with a white face from which her brown hair went back in graceful, natural waves and curls, and she had very dark blue eyes. Prudence was also white but of a duller whiteness, and her eyes were grey. She would tease me and interfere with me, but Fanny was either negligent or gracefully kind to me and I adored her. I do not, strangely enough, remember my mother's appearance at all distinctly, though she was, of course, the dominant fact of my childish life. She was too familiar, I suppose, for the sort of attention that leaves a picture on the mind.

"I learned to speak from my family and chiefly from my mother. None of us spoke well; our common idioms were poor and bad, we mispronounced many words, and long words we avoided as something dangerous and pretentious. I had very few toys: a tin railway-engine I remember, some metal soldiers, and an insufficient supply of wooden building-bricks. There was no special place for me to play, and if I laid out my toys on the living-room table, a meal was sure to descend and sweep them away. I remember a great longing to play with the things in the shop, and especially with the bundles of firewood and some fire-kindlers that were most seductively shaped like wheels, but my father discouraged such ambitions. He did not like to have me about the shop until I was old enough to help, and the indoor part of most of my days was spent in the room above it or in the underground room below it. After the shop was closed it became a very cold, cavernous, dark place to a little boy's imagination; there were dreadful shadows in which terrible things might lurk, and even holding fast to my mother's hand on my way to bed, I was filled with fear to traverse it. It had always a faint, unpleasant smell, a smell of decaying vegetation varying with the particular fruit or vegetable that was most affected, and a constant element of paraffin. But on Sundays when it was closed all day the shop was different, no longer darkly threatening but very very still. I would be taken through it on my way to church or Sunday-school. (Yes—I will tell you about church and Sunday-school in a minute.) When I saw my mother lying dead—she died when I was close upon sixteen —I was instantly reminded of the Sunday shop. . . .

"Such, my dear Sunray, was the home in which I found myself. I seemed to have been there since my beginning. It was the deepest dream I have ever had. I had forgotten even you."

§ 2

"And how was this casually begotten infant prepared for the business of life?" asked Radiant. "Was he sent away to a Garden?"

"There were no Children's Gardens such as we know them, in that world," said Sarnac. "There was a place of assembly called an elementary school. Thither I was taken, twice daily, by my sister Prudence, after I was six years old.

"And here again I find it hard to convey to you what the reality was like. Our histories tell you of the beginning of general education in that distant time and of the bitter jealousy felt by the old priesthoods and privileged people for the new sort of teachers, but they give you no real picture of the ill-equipped and understaffed schoolhouses and of the gallant work of the underpaid and ill-trained men and women who did the first rough popular teaching. There was in particular a gaunt dark man with a cough who took the older boys, and a little freckled woman of thirty or so who fought with the lower children, and, I see now, they were holy saints. His name I forget, but the little woman was called Miss Merrick. They had to handle enormous classes, and they did most of their teaching by voice and gesture and chalk upon a black-board. Their equipment was miserable. The only materials of which there was enough to go round were a stock of dirty reading-books, Bibles, hymn-books, and a lot of slabs of slate in frames on which we wrote with slate pencils to economise paper. Drawing materials we had practically none ; most of us never learned to draw. Yes. Lots of sane adults in that old world never learned to draw even a box. There was nothing to count with in that school and no geometrical models. There were hardly any pictures except a shiny one of Queen Victoria and a sheet of animals, and there were very yellow wall-maps of Europe and Asia twenty years out of date. We learned the elements of mathematics by recitation. We used to stand in rows, chanting a wonderful chant called our Tables:

> " ' *Twi*-swun-two.
> *Twi*-stewer four.
> *Twi*-sfree'r six.
> *Twi*-sfour'rate.'

" We used to sing—in unison—religious hymns for the most part. The school had a second-hand piano to guide our howlings. There had been a great fuss in Cliffstone and Cherry Gardens when this piano was bought. They called it a luxury, and pampering the working-classes."

" Pampering the working-classes ! " Firefly repeated. " I suppose it's all right. But I'm rather at sea."

" I can't explain everything," said Sarnac. " The fact remains that England grudged its own children the shabbiest education, and so for the matter of fact did every other country. They saw things differently in those days. They were still in the competitive cave. America, which was a much richer country than England, as wealth went, then, had if possible meaner and shabbier schools for her common people. . . . My dear ! it *was* so. I'm telling you a story, not explaining the universe. . . . And naturally, in spite of the strenuous efforts of such valiant souls as Miss Merrick, we children learned little and we learned it very badly. Most of my mem-ories of school are memories of boredom. We sat on wooden forms at long worn wooden desks, rows and rows of us—I can see again all the little heads in front of me—and far away was Miss Merrick with a pointer trying to interest us in the Rivers of England :—

"Ty.   Wear.   Teasumber."

"Is that what they used to call swearing?" asked Willow.
"No. Only Jogriphy. And History was:—

"Wi-yum the Conqueror.   Tessisstysiss.
Wi-yum Ruefiss.   Ten eighty-seven."

"What did it mean?"
"To us children?   Very much what it means to you—
gibberish. The hours, those interminable hours of childhood
in school! How they dragged! Did I say I lived a life in my
dream?   In school I lived eternities. Naturally we sought
such amusement as was possible. One thing was to give your
next-door neighbour a pinch or a punch and say, 'Pass it on.'
And we played furtive games with marbles. It is rather
amusing to recall that I learned to count, to add and subtract
and so forth, by playing marbles in spite of discipline."
"But was that the best your Miss Merrick and your saint
with the cough could do?" asked Radiant.
"Oh! *they* couldn't help themselves. They were in a
machine, and there were periodic Inspectors and examinations
to see that they were kept in it."
"But," said Sunray, "that Incantation about 'Wi-yum
the Conqueror' and the rest of it. It meant something? At
the back of it, lost to sight perhaps, there was some rational
or semi-rational idea?"
"Perhaps," reflected Sarnac. "But I never detected it."
"They called it history," said Firefly helpfully.
"They did," Sarnac admitted. "Yes, I think they were
trying to interest the children of the land in the doings of the
Kings and Queens of England, probably as dull a string of
monarchs as the world has ever seen. If they rose to interest
at times it was through a certain violence; there was one
delightful Henry VIII. with such a craving for love and such
a tender conscience about the sanctity of marriage that he
always murdered one wife before he took another. And there
was one Alfred who burned some cakes—I never knew why.
In some way it embarrassed the Danes, his enemies."
"But was that all the history they taught you?" cried
Sunray.
"Queen Elizabeth of England wore a ruff and James the
First of England and Scotland kissed his men favourites."
"But history!"
Sarnac laughed. "It *is* odd. I see that—now that I am
awake again. But indeed that was all they taught us."
"Did they tell you nothing of the beginnings of life and
the ends of life, of its endless delights and possibilities?"
Sarnac shook his head.
"Not at school," said Starlight, who evidently knew her
books; "they did that at church. Sarnac forgets the churches.

It was, you must remember, an age of intense religious activity.
There were places of worship everywhere. One whole day in
every seven was given up to the Destinies of Man and the study
of God's Purpose. The worker ceased from his toil. From end
to end of the land the air was full of the sound of church-bells
and of congregations singing. Wasn't there a certain beauty in
that, Sarnac ? ''

Sarnac reflected and smiled. " It wasn't quite like that,"
he said. " Our histories, in that matter, need a little revision."

" But one sees the churches and chapels in the old photographs and cinema pictures. And we still have many of their
cathedrals. And some of those are quite beautiful.''

" And they have all had to be shored up and under-pinned
and tied together with steel," said Sunray, " because they were
either so carelessly or so faithlessly built. And anyhow, these
were not built in Sarnac's time."

" Mortimer Smith's time," Sarnac corrected.

" They were built hundreds of years earlier than that."

§ 3

" You must not judge the religion of an age by its temples
and churches," said Sarnac. " An unhealthy body may have
many things in it that it cannot clear away, and the weaker
it is the less it can prevent abnormal and unserviceable growths.
. . . Which sometimes may be in themselves quite bright and
beautiful growths.

" But let me describe to you the religious life of my home
and upbringing. There was a sort of State Church in England,
but it had lost most of its official standing in regard to the
community as a whole ; it has two buildings in Cherry Gardens
—one an old one dating from the hamlet days with a square
tower and rather small as churches went, and the other new
and spacious with a spire. In addition there were the chapels
of two other Christian communities, the Congregationalists
and the Primitive Methodists, and also one belonging to the
old Roman Catholic communion. Each professed to present
the only true form of Christianity and each maintained a
minister, except the larger Church of England place, which
had two, the vicar and the curate. You might suppose that,
like the museums of history and the Temples of Vision we set
before our young people, these places would display in the
most moving and beautiful forms possible the history of our
race and the great adventure of life in which we are all engaged,
they would remind us of our brotherhood and lift us out of
selfish thoughts. . . . But let me tell you how I saw it :—

" I don't remember my first religious instruction. Very
early I must have learned to say a rhymed prayer to—

> " ' Gentle Jesus, meek and mild,
>   Look on me, a little child.'

" And also another prayer about ' Trespassing ' which I thought referred to going into fields or woods where there was no public footpath, and which began with the entirely incomprehensible words, ' Our Father Charting Heaven, Haloed B thy Name.' Also one asked for one's ' daily bread ' and that God's Kingdom should come. I learned these two prayers from my mother at an incredibly early age, and said them every night and sometimes in the morning. She held these words in far too great reverence to explain them, and when I wanted to ask for my ' daily bread and butter,' she scolded me bitterly. I also wanted to ask what would happen to good Queen Victoria when God's Kingdom came, but I never mustered courage to ask my mother that. I had a curious idea that there could be a marriage, but that nobody had thought of that solution. This must have been very early in my life, because Victoria the Good died when I was five, during the course of a long, faraway, and now almost-forgotten struggle called the Boer War.

" These infantile perplexities deepened and then gave way to a kind of self-protective apathy when I was old enough to go to church and Sunday-school.

" Sunday morning was by far the most strenuous part of all the week for my mother. We had all had a sort of bath overnight in the underground kitchen, except my father and mother, who I don't think ever washed all over—I don't know for certain—and on Sunday morning we rose rather later than usual and put on our ' clean things ' and our best clothes. (Everybody in those days wore a frightful lot of clothes. You see, they were all so unhealthy they could not stand the least exposure to wet or cold.) Breakfast was a hurried and undistinguished meal on the way to greater things. Then we had to sit about, keeping out of harm's way, avoiding all crumpling or dirt, and pretending to be interested in one of the ten or twelve books our home possessed, until church time. Mother prepared the Sunday meal, almost always a joint of meat in a baking-dish which my elder sister took into the baker's next door but one to be cooked while we worshipped. Father rose later than any one and appeared strangely transformed in a collar, dickey and cuffs and a black coat and his hair smoothed down and parted. Usually some unforeseen delay arose ; one of my sisters had a hole in her stocking, or my boots wouldn't button and nobody could find the button-hook, or a prayer-book was mislaid. This engendered an atmosphere of flurry. There were anxious moments when the church-bell ceased to ring and began a monotonous ' tolling-in.'

" ' Oh ! we shall be late *again* ! ' said my mother. ' We shall be late *again*.'

" ' I'll go on with Prue ! ' my father would say.

" ' Me too ! ' said Fanny.

" ' Not till you've found that button-'ook, Miss Huzzy,' my mother would cry. ' For well I know you've 'ad it.'

" Fanny would shrug her shoulders.

" ' Why 'e carn't 'ave lace-up shoes to 'is feet like any other kid, I *carn't* understand,' my father would remark unhelpfully.

" My mother, ashen white with flurry, would wince and say, ' Lace-up shoes *is* age ! Let alone that 'e'd break the laces.'

" ' What's that on the chiffoneer ? ' Fanny would ask abruptly.

" ' Ah ! Naturally you know.'

" ' Naturally I use my eyes.'

" ' Tcha ! Got your answer ready ! Oh, you *wicked* girl ! '

" Fanny would shrug her shoulders again and stare out of the window. There was more trouble afoot than a mislaid button-hook between her and my mother. Overnight ' Miss Huzzy ' had been abroad long after twilight, a terrible thing from a mother's point of view, as I will make plain to you later.

" My mother, breathing hard, would button my boots in a punitive manner and then off we would go, Prue hanging on to father ahead, Fanny a little apart and scornful, and I trying to wriggle my little white-cotton-gloved hand out of my mother's earnest grip.

" We had what was called a ' sitting ' at church, a long seat with some hassocks and a kind of little praying-ledge at the back of the seat in front. We filed into our sitting and knelt and rose up, and were ready for the function known as morning service."

§ 4

" And this service again was a strange thing. We read about these churches and their services in our histories and we simplify and idealise the picture ; we take everything in the account, as we used to say in that old world, at its face value. We think that the people understood and believed completely the curious creeds of those old-world religions ; that they worshipped with a simple ardour ; that they had in their hearts a secret system of comforts and illusions which some of us even now try to recover. But life is always more complicated than any account or representation if it can be. The human mind in those days was always complicating and overlaying its ideas, forgetting primary in secondary considerations, substituting repetition and habit for purposive acts, and forgetting and losing its initial intentions. Life has grown simpler for men as the ages have passed because it has grown clearer. We were more complicated in our lives then because we were more confused. And so we sat in our pews on Sunday, in a state of conforming inattention, not really thinking out what we were doing, feeling rather than knowing significances and with our thoughts wandering like water from a leaky vessel. We watched the people about us furtively and minutely and we were acutely aware that they watched us. We stood up, we half knelt, we sat, as the ritual of the service required us to do. I can still recall quite vividly the long complex rustle of the congregation as it sat down or rose up in straggling unison.

"This morning service was a mixture of prayers and recitations by the priests—vicar and curate we called them—and responses by the congregation, chants, rhymed hymns, the reading of passages from the Hebrew-Christian Bible, and at last a discourse. Except for this discourse all the service followed a prescribed course set out in a prayer-book. We hopped from one page of the prayer-book to another, and ' finding your place ' was a terrible mental exercise for a small boy with a sedulous mother on one side and Prue on the other.

"The service began lugubriously and generally it was lugubrious. We were all miserable sinners, there was no health in us ; we expressed our mild surprise that our Diety did not resort to violent measures against us. There was a long part called the Litany in which the priest repeated with considerable gusto every possible human misfortune, war, pestilence, famine, and so on, and the congregation interjected at intervals, ' Good Lord deliver us ! ' although you might have thought that these were things within the purview of our international and health and food administrators rather than matters for the Supreme Being. Then the officiating priest went on to a series of prayers for the Queen, the rulers of the State, heretics, unfortunate people, travellers, and the harvest, all of which I concluded were being dangerously neglected by Divine Providence, and the congregation reinforced the priest's efforts by salvos of ' We beseech Thee to hear us, Good Lord.' The hymns were of very variable quality, but the greater part were effusive praises of our Maker, with frequent false rhymes and bad quantities. We thanked Heaven for our ' blessings,' and that without a thought of irony. Yet you would imagine that a Deity of Infinite Power might easily have excused our gratitude for the precarious little coal and greengrocery business in Cherry Gardens and all my mother's toil and anxieties and my father's worries.

"The general effect of this service beneath its surface adulation of the worshipped God, was to blame Him thoroughly and completely for every human misfortune and to deny the responsibility of mankind for its current muddle and wretchedness. Throughout the land and throughout most of the world, Sunday after Sunday, by chant and hymn and prayer and gesture, it was being dinned into the minds of young people, whenever for a moment the service broke through the surface of their protective instinctive inattention, that mankind was worthless and hopeless, the helpless plaything of a moody, impulsive, vain, and irresistible Being. This rain of suggestion came between their minds and the Sun of Life ; it hid the Wonderful from them ; it robbed them of access to the Spirit of Courage. But so alien was this doctrine of abasement from the heart of man, that for the most part the congregation sat or stood or knelt in rows in its pews repeating responses and singing mechanically, with its minds distracted to a thousand distant more congenial things, watching the deportment of its neighbours, scheming about business or pleasure, wandering in reverie.

" There would come at times into this service, sometimes but not always, parts of another service, the Communion Service. This was the reduced remainder of that Catholic Mass of which we have all learned in our histories. As you know, the world of Christianity was still struggling, nineteen hundred years after Christianity had begun, to get rid of the obsession of a mystical blood sacrifice, to forget a traditional killing of a God-man, that was as old as agriculture and the first beginnings of human settlement. The English State Church was so much a thing of compromise and tradition that in the two churches it had in Cherry Gardens the teaching upon this issue was diametrically opposed ; one, the new and showy one, St. Jude's, was devoted to an exaggeration of the importance of the Communion, called it the Mass, called the table on which it was celebrated the Altar, called the Rev. Mr. Snapes the Priest, and generally emphasised the ancient pagan interpretation, while the other, the little old church of St. Osyth, called its priest a Minister, its altar the Lord's Table, and the Communion the Lord's Supper, denied all its mystical importance, and made it merely a memorial of the life and death of the Master. These age-long controversies between the immemorial temple-worship of our race and the new life of intellectual and spiritual freedom that had then been dawning in the world for three or four centuries were far above my poor little head as I fretted and ' behaved myself ' in our sitting. To my youthful mind the Communion Service meant nothing more than a long addition to the normal tediums of worship. In those days I had a pathetic belief in the magic of prayer, and oblivious of the unflattering implications of my request I would whisper throughout the opening prayers and recitations of the morning : ' Pray God there *won't* be a Communion Service. Pray God there *won't* be a Communion Service.'

" Then would come the sermon, the original composition of the Rev. Mr. Snapes, and the only thing in the whole service that was not set and prescribed and that had not been repeated a thousand times before.

" Mr. Snapes was a youngish pinkish man with pinkish golden hair and a clean-shaven face ; he had small chubby features like a cluster of *champignons*, an expression of beatific self-satisfaction, and a plump voice. He had a way of throwing

back the ample white sleeve of his surplice when he turned
the pages of his manuscript, a sort of upthrow of the posed
white hand, that aroused in me one of the inexplicable detes-
tations of childhood. I used to hate this gesture, watch for
its coming and squirm when it came.

"The sermons were so much above my head that I cannot
now tell what any of them were about. He would talk of
things like the 'Comfort of the Blessed Eucharist' and the
'Tradition of the Fathers of the Church.' He would discourse
too of what he called the Feasts of the Church, though a collec-
tion-plate was the nearest approach to feasting we saw. He
made much of Advent and Epiphany and Whitsuntide, and
he had a certain form of transition to modern considerations,
'And we too, dear Brethren in these latter days have our
Advents and our Epiphanies.' Then he would pass to King
Edward's proposed visit to Lowcliff or to the recent dispute
about the Bishop of Natal or the Bishop of Zanzibar. You
cannot imagine how remote it was from anything of moment
in our normal lives.

"And then suddenly, when a small boy was losing all hope
of this smooth voice ever ceasing, came a little pause and then
the blessed words of release : 'And now to God the Father,
God the Son——'

"It was over ! There was a stir throughout the church.
We roused ourselves, we stood up. Then we knelt for a brief
moment of apparent prayer and then we scrabbled for hats,
coats, and umbrellas, and so out into the open-air, a great
pattering of feet upon the pavement, dispersing this way and
that, stiff greetings of acquaintances, Prue to the baker's for
the Sunday dinner and the rest of us straight home.

"Usually there were delightful brown potatoes under the
Sunday joint and perhaps there would be a fruit-pie also.
But in the spring came rhubarb, which I hated. It was held
to be particularly good for me, and I was always compelled
to eat exceptionally large helpings of rhubarb tart.

"In the afternoon there was Sunday-school or else 'Children's Service,' and, relieved of the presence of our parents,
we three children went to the school-house or to the church
again to receive instruction in the peculiarities of our faith.
In the Sunday-school untrained and unqualified people whom
we knew in the week-days as shop assistants and an auctioneer's
clerk and an old hairy deaf gentleman named Spendilow,
collected us in classes and discoursed to us on the ambiguous
lives and doings of King David of Israel and of Abraham,
Isaac, and Jacob and the misbehaviour of Queen Jezebel and
the like topics. And we sang easy hymns in unison. At times
our teachers spoke of the Master of Mankind, but they spoke
without understanding ; they spoke of him as a sort of trickster
who worked miracles and achieved jail delivery from the tomb.
And so had 'saved' us—in spite of the manifest fact that we

were anything but saved. The teaching of the Master was, you know, buried under these tales of Resurrection and Miracles for two thousand years. He was a light shining in the darkness and the darkness knew it not. And of the great past of life, of the races of men and their slow growth in knowledge, of fears and dark superstitions and the dawning victories of truth, of the conquest and sublimation of human passions through the ages, of the divinity of research and discovery, of the latent splendour of our bodies and senses, and the present dangers and possibilities amidst which the continually more crowded masses of our race were then blundering so tragically and yet with such bright gleams of hope and promise, we heard no talk at all. We were given no intimation that there was so much as a human community with a common soul and an ultimate common destiny. It would have been scandalous and terrifying to those Sunday-school teachers to have heard any such things spoken about in Sunday-school.

" And mind you," said Sarnac, " there was no better preparation for life in all the world then than the sort of thing I was getting. The older church of St. Osyth was in the hands of the Rev. Thomas Benderton, who dispersed a dwindling congregation by bellowing sermons full of the threat of hell. He had scared my mother to the church of St. Jude by his frequent mention of the devil, and the chief topic of his discourse was the sin of idolatry ; he treated it always with especial reference to the robes adopted by Mr. Snapes when he celebrated Holy Communion and to something obscure that he did with small quantities of bread and wine upon his Communion-table.

" Of what the Congregationalists and the Primitive Methodists did and taught in their places of resort, their chapels and Sunday-schools, I do not know very exactly, because my mother would have been filled with a passion of religious terror if ever I had gone near those assemblies. But I know that their procedure was only a plainer version of our church experiences with still less of the Mass and still more of the devil. The Primitive Methodists, I know, laid their chief stress upon the belief that the greater portion of mankind, when once they had done with the privations and miseries of this life, would be tortured exquisitely for ever and ever in hell. I got this very clearly because a Primitive Methodist boy a little older than myself conveyed his anxieties to me one day when we had gone for a walk into Cliffstone.

" He was a bent sort of boy with a sniff and he wore a long white woollen comforter ; there hasn't been such a figure in the world now for hundreds of years. We walked along the promenade that followed the cliff edge, by the band-stand and by the people lounging in deck-chairs. There were swarms of people in their queer holiday clothes, and

behind, rows of the pallid grey houses in which they lodged.
And my companion bore his testimony. ' Mr. Molesly 'e says
that the Day of Judgment might come any minute—come
in fire and glory before ever we get to the end of these Leas.
And all them people'd be tried.' . . .

" ' Jest as they are ? '

" ' Jest as they are. That woman there with the dog and
that fat man asleep in 'is chair and—the policeman.'

" He paused, a little astonished at the Hebraic daring of
his thoughts. ' The policeman,' he repeated. ' They'd be
weighed and found wanting, and devils would come and torture them. Torture that policeman. Burn him and cut him
about. And everybody. Horrible, horrible torture. . . . '

" I had never heard the doctrines of Christianity applied
with such particularity before. I was dismayed.

" ' I sh'd 'ide,' I said.

" ' 'E'd see you. 'E'd see you and tell the devils,' said my
little friend. ' 'E sees the wicked thoughts in us now.' " . . .

" But did people really believe such stuff as that ? " cried
Sunray.

" As far as they believed anything," said Sarnac. " I admit
it was frightful, but so it was. Do you realise what cramped
distorted minds grew up under such teaching in our under-
nourished, infected bodies ? "

" Few people could have really believed so grotesque a
fairy-tale as hell," said Radiant.

" More people believed than you would think," said Sarnac.
" Few people, of course, held it actively for long—or they
would have gone mad—but it was in the background of a
lot of minds. And the others ? The effect of this false story
about the world upon the majority of minds was a sort of
passive rejection. They did not deny, but they refused to
incorporate the idea with the rest of their thoughts. A kind
of dead place, a *scar*, was made just where there ought to
have been a sense of human destiny, a vision of life beyond
the immediate individual life. . . .

" I find it hard to express the state of mind into which
one grew. The minds of the young had been outraged by
these teachings ; they were no longer capable of complete
mental growth, a possibility had been destroyed. Perhaps
we never did really take into ourselves and believe that
grotesque fairy-tale, as you call it, about hell, but because
of what it had done to our minds we grew up without a living
faith and without a purpose. The nucleus of our religious
being was this suppressed fear of hell. Few of us ever had it
out fairly into the light of day. It was considered to be bad
taste to speak of any such things, or indeed of any of the
primaries of life, either by way of belief or denial. You might
allude circuitously. Or joke. Most of the graver advances
in life were made under a mask of facetiousness.

" Mentally that world in the days of Mortimer Smith was a world astray. It was astray like a lost dog and with no idea of direction. It is true that the men of that time were very like the men of this time—in their possibilities—but they were unhealthy in mind as well as body, they were adrift and incoherent. Walking as we do in the light, and by comparison simply and directly, their confusion, the tortuous perplexity of their thoughts and conduct is almost inconceivable to us. There is no sort of mental existence left in our world now, to which it can be compared."

§ 5

" I think I mentioned the line of hills, the Downs that bounded the world of my upbringing to the north. What lay beyond them was a matter for wonder and speculation to me long before I was able to clamber to their crests. In summer-time the sun set behind them to the north-west, often in a glow of gold and splendour, and I remember that among my fancies was a belief that the Day of Judgment was over there and that Celestial City to which Mr. Snapes would some day lead us—in procession, of course, and with a banner.

" My first ascent of this childhood's boundary must have occurred when I was eight or nine. I do not remember with whom I went or any other particulars, but I have a very acute memory of my disappointment at looking down a long, very gentle slope and seeing nothing but fields and hedges and groups of large sheep feeding. What I had expected to find I cannot now remember. I seem to have noted only the foreground then, and it must have been after many such excursions that I began to realise the variegated spaciousness of the country to the north. The view indeed went very far ; on a clear day we saw blue hills nearly twenty miles away ; there were woodlands and parklands, brown ridges of plough-land that became golden ridges of corn in summer-time, village churches amidst clustering greenery, and the gleaming of ponds and lakes. Southward the horizon lifted as the Downs were ascended and the breadth of the sea-belt increased. It was my father drew my attention to that, on the first occasion of our crossing the Downs together.

" ' Go as 'igh as you like, 'Arry,' he said, ' and the sea goes up as 'igh. There it is, you see—level with us and we ever so 'igh above Cherry Gardens. And yet it don't *drown'd* Cherry Gardens ! And why don't it drown'd Cherry Gardens seeing that it might ? Tell me that, 'Arry.'

" I couldn't.

" ' Providence,' said my father triumphantly. ' Providence does it. 'Olds back the sea, Thus Far. And over there, see 'ow plain it is ! is France.'

" I saw France and it was exceptionally plain.

' ' Sometimes you see France and sometimes you don't,'

said my father. ' There's a lesson in that too, my boy, for those who care to take it.'

" It had always been the custom of my father to go out after tea on Sundays, summer and winter alike, and walk right over the Downs to Chessing Hanger, six miles and more away. He went, I knew, to see my Uncle John, Uncle John Julip, my mother's brother, who was gardener to Lord Bramble of Chessing Hanger Park. But it was only when he began to take me with him that I realised that these walks had any other motive than fraternal (in law) affection and the natural desire of a pent-up shopkeeper for exercise. But from the first journey on I knew that the clue to these expeditions lay in the burdens with which we returned to Cherry Gardens. Always there was supper in the cosy little gardener's cottage, and always as we departed we picked up an unobtrusive load of flowers, fruit, or vegetables, celery, peas, aubergines, mushrooms, or what not, and returned through the dusk or moonlight or darkness or drizzle as the season and the weather might determine to the little shop. And sometimes my father would be silent or whistle softly and sometimes he would improve our journey with a discourse on the wonders of nature, the beauty of goodness, and the beneficence of Providence to man.

" He talked of the moon one moonlight night. ' Look at it, 'Arry,' he said—' a dead world. Like a skull it is, up there, stripped of its soul which is its flesh so to speak and all its trees, which, if you take me, were its 'air and its whiskers —stripped and dead for ever and ever. Dry as a bone. And every one who lived there gone too. Dust and ashes and gone.'

" ' Where they gone, farver ? ' I would ask.

" ' Gorn to their judgment,' he would explain with gusto. ' Kings and greengroshers, all the lot of 'em, tried and made sheep and goats of, and gone to their bliss or their sufferings, 'Arry. According to their iniquities. Weighed and found wanting.'

" Long pause.

" ' It's a pity,' he said.

" ' What is, farver ? ''

" ' Pity it's over. It 'ud be something to look at, them running about up there. Friendly-like it 'ud be. But that's questioning the ways of Providence, that is. I suppose we'd be always staring up and falling over things. . . . You never see a thing in this world, 'Arry, that you think isn't right but what when you come to think it out it isn't wiser than you knew. Providence is as deep as 'E is I and you can't get be'ind 'im. And don't go banging them pears against your side, my boy ; they'm Wi'yums, and they won't like it.'

" About the curious habits of animals and the ways and migrations of birds my father would also talk very freely.

" ' Me and you, 'Arry, we walk by the light of reason. We 'ave reasonable minds given us to do it with. But animals and birds and worms and things, they live by Instink ; they jus' feel they 'ave to do this or that and they do it. It's Instink keeps the whale in the sea and the bird in the air ; but we go where our legs carry us as reason 'as directed. You can't ask an animal Why did you do this ? or Why did you do that ?—you just '*it*' it ; but a man you ask and 'e 'as to answer, being a reasonable creature. That's why we 'as jails and punishment and are answerable for our sins, 'Arry. Every sin we 'as to answer for, great or small. But an animal don't 'ave to answer. It's innocent. You '*it*' it or else you leave it be. . . .'

" My father thought for a time. ' Except for dogs and some *old* cats,' he said. He mused among his memories for a time. ' I've known some *sinful* cats, 'Arry,' he said.

" He would enlarge on the wonders of instinct.

" He would explain how swallows and starlings and storks and suchlike birds were driven by instincts thousands of miles, getting drowned on the way and dashed to pieces against lighthouses. ' Else they'd freeze and starve where they was, 'Arry,' said my father. And every bird knew by instinct what sort of nest it had to build, no one ever showing it or telling it. Kangaroos carried their young in pouches by instinct, but man being a reasonable creature made perambulators. Chickens ran about by instinct directly they were born ; not like human children, who had to be carried and taken care of until reason came. And jolly lucky that was for the chicken, ' For 'ow a 'en would carry them,' said my father, ' I *carn't* imagine.'

" I remember that I put my father into a difficulty by asking him why Providence had not given birds an instinct against beating themselves against light-houses and moths against the gas-jet and the candle-flame. For in the room over the shop on a summer's night it was quite unpleasant to read a book because of the disabled flies and moths that fell scorched upon its pages. ' It's to teach 'em some lessons,' said my father at last. ' But what it's to teach them, 'Arry I don't rightly know.'

" And sometimes he would talk, with illustrative stories, of ill-gotten gold never staying with the getter, and sometimes he would talk about murders—for there were still many murders in the world—and how they always came out, ' hide them as you may.' And always he was ready to point out the goodness and wisdom, the cleverness, forethought, ingenuity, and kindliness of Providence in the most earnest and flattering manner.

" With such high discourse did we enliven our long trudges between Cherry Gardens and Chessing Hanger, and my father's tone was always so exalted that with a real shock I presently came to realise that every Sunday evening we were in plain English stealing and receiving stolen produce from Lord Bramble's gardens. Indeed, I cannot imagine how we should have got along without that weekly raid. Our little home at Cherry Gardens was largely supported by my father's share in the profits of these transactions. When the produce was too good and costly for Cherry Gardens' needs, he would take it down to Cliffstone and sell it to a friend there who had a fashionable trade."

Sarnac paused.

"Go on," said Radiant. "You are making us believe in your story. It sounds more and more as if you had been there. It is so circumstantial. Who was this Lord Bramble? I have always been curious about Lords."

§ 6

"Let me tell my story in my own way," said Sarnac. "If I answer questions I shall get lost. You are all ready to ask a hundred questions already about things I have mentioned and points familiar to me but incomprehensible to you because our world has forgotten them, and if I weaken towards you you will trail me away and away further and further from my father and my Uncle Julip. We shall just talk about manners and customs and about philosophy and history. I want to tell my story."

"Go on with your story," said Sunray.

"This Uncle John Julip of mine, although he was my mother's brother, was a cynical, opinionated man. He was very short and fatter than was usual among gardeners. He had a smooth white face and a wise self-satisfied smile. To begin with, I saw him only on Sundays and in white shirt-sleeves and a large straw hat. He made disparaging remarks about my physique and about the air of Cherry Gardens every time he saw me. His wife had been a dissenter of some sort and had become a churchwoman under protest. She too was white-faced and her health was bad. She complained of pains. But my Uncle John Julip disparaged her pains because he said they were not in a reasonable place. There was stomachache and backache and heartburn and the wind, but her pains were neither here nor there; they were therefore pains of the imagination and had no claim upon our sympathy.

"When I was nearly thirteen years old my father and uncle began planning for me to go over to the Chessing Hanger gardens and be an under-gardener. This was a project I disliked very greatly; not only did I find my uncle unattractive, but I thought weeding and digging and most of the exercises of a garden extremely tiring and boring. I had taken very kindly to reading—I like languages—I had inherited something of my father's loquaciousness, and I had won a special prize for an essay in my school. This had fired the most unreasonable ambitions in me—to write, to write in newspapers, possibly even to write books. At Cliffstone was what was called a public library to which the householders of Cliffstone had access and from which members of their families could borrow books—during holidays I would be changing my book almost every day—but at Chessing Hanger there were no books at all. My sister Fanny encouraged me in my reading ; she too was a voracious reader of novels, and she shared my dislike of the idea that I should become a gardener.

"In those days, you must understand, no attempt was made to gauge the natural capacity of a child. Human beings were expected to be grateful for any opportunity of ' getting a living.' Parents bundled their children into any employment that came handy, and so most people followed occupations that were misfits, that did not give full scope for such natural gifts as they possessed and which commonly cramped or crippled them. This in itself diffused a vague discontent throughout the community, and inflicted upon the great majority of people strains and restraints and suppressions that ate away their possibility of positive happiness. Most youngsters as they grew up, girls as well as boys, experienced a sudden tragic curtailment of freedom and discovered themselves forced into some unchosen specific drudgery from which it was very difficult to escape. One summer holiday came, when, instead of enjoying delightful long days of play and book-devouring in Cliffstone, as I had hitherto done, I was sent off over the hills to stay with Uncle John Julip, and ' see how I got on ' with him. I still remember the burning disgust, the sense of immolation with which I lugged my little valise up the hills and over the Downs to the gardens.

"This Lord Bramble, Radiant, was one of the landlords who were so important during the reigns of the Hanoverian Kings up to the time of Queen Victoria the Good. They owned large areas of England as private property ; they could do what they liked with it. In the days of Victoria the Good and her immediate predecessors these landlords who had ruled the Empire through the House of Lords made a losing fight for predominance against the new industrialists, men who employed great masses of people for their private gain in the iron and steel industries, cotton and wool, beer and shipping, and these again gave way to a rather different type who developed advertisement and a political and financial use of newspapers and new methods of finance. The old land-holding families had to adapt themselves to the new powers or be pushed aside. Lord Bramble was one of those pushed aside, an indignant, old-fashioned, impoverished landowner. He was in a slough of debts. His estates covered many square miles ; he owned farms and woodlands, a great white uncomfortable house, far too roomy for his shrunken means, and two square miles of park. The park was greatly neglected, it was covered with groups of old trees infested and rotten with fungus ; rabbits and moles abounded, and thistles and nettles. There were no young trees there at all. The fences and gates were badly patched ; and here and there ran degenerating roads. But boards threatening trespassers abounded, and notices saying ' NO THOROUGHFARE.' For it was the dearest privilege of the British landlord to restrict the free movements of ordinary people, and Lord Bramble guarded his wilderness with devotion. Great areas of good land in England in those days were in a similar state of picturesquely secluded dilapidation."

"Those were the lands where they did the shooting," said Radiant.

"How did you know ? "

"I have seen a picture. They stood in a line along the edge of a copse, with brown-leaved trees and a faint smell of decay and a touch of autumnal dampness in the air, and they shot lead pellets at birds."

"They did. And the beaters—I was pressed into that service one or twice—drove the birds, the pheasants, towards them. Shooting-parties used to come to Chessing Hanger, and the shooting used to go on day after day. It was done with tremendous solemnity."

"But why ? " asked Willow.

"Yes," said Radiant. "Why did men do it ? "

"I don't know," said Sarnac. "All I know is that at certain seasons of the year the great majority of the gentlemen of England who were supposed to be the leaders and intelligence of the land, who were understood to guide its destinies and control its future, went out into the woods or on the moors to massacre birds of various sorts with guns, birds bred specially at great expense for the purpose of this slaughter. These noble sportsmen were marshalled by gamekeepers : they stood in rows, the landscape was animated with the popping of their guns. The highest in the land participated gravely in this national function and popped with distinction. The men of this class were in truth at just that level above imbecility where the banging of a gun and the thrill of seeing a bird swirl and drop is inexhaustibly amusing. They never tired of it. The bang of the gun seems to have been essential to the sublimity of the sensations of these sportsmen. It wasn't mere killing, because in that case these people could also have assisted in killing the sheep and oxen and pigs required by the butchers, but this sport they left to men of an inferior social class. Shooting birds on the wing was the essential idea. When Lord Bramble was not killing pheasants or grouse he shot in the south of France at perplexed pigeons with clipped wings just let out of traps. Or he hunted—not real animal-hunting, not a fair fight with bear or tiger or elephant in a jungle, but the chasing of foxes—small stinking red animals about the size of water-spaniels which were sedulously kept from extinction for this purpose of hunting ; they were hunted across cultivated land and the hunters rode behind a pack of dogs. Lord Bramble dressed himself up with extreme care in a red jacket and breeches of pigskin to do this. For the rest of his time the good man played a card game called bridge, so limited and mechanical that any one nowadays would be able to read out the results and exact probabilities of every deal directly he saw his cards. There were four sets of thirteen cards each. But Lord Bramble, who had never learned properly to count up to thirteen, found it full of dramatic surprises and wonderful sensations. A large part of his time was spent in going from race-course to race-course ; they raced a specially flimsy breed of horses in those days. There again he dressed with care. In the illustrated papers in the public library I would see photographs of Lord Bramble, with a silk hat—a top hat, *you* know—cocked very much on one side ' in the Paddock ' or ' snapped with a lady-friend.' There was much betting and knowingness about this horse-racing. His Lordship dined with comparative intelligence, erring only a little on the excessive side with the port. People still smoked in those days, and Lord Bramble would consume three or four cigars a day. Pipes he thought plebeian and cigarettes effeminate. He could read a newspaper but not a book, being incapable of sustained attention ; after dinner in town he commonly went to a theatre or music-hall where women could be seen, more or less undraped. The clothing of that time filled such people as Lord Bramble with a coy covetousness for nakedness. The normal beauty of the human body was a secret and a mystery, and half the art and decoration of Chessing Hanger House played stimulatingly with the forbidden vision.

" In that past existence of mine I took the way of life of Lord Bramble as a matter of course, but now that I recall it I begin to see the enormous absurdity of these assassins of frightened birds, these supporters of horses and ostlers, these peepers at feminine thighs and shoulder-blades. Their women sympathised with their gunmanship, called their horses ' the dears,' cultivated dwarfed and crippled breeds of pet dogs, and yielded the peeps expected of them.

" Such was the life of the aristocratic sort of people in those days. They set the tone of what was considered a hard, bright, healthy life. The rest of the community admired them greatly and imitated them to the best of its ability. The tenant farmer, if he could not shoot pheasants, shot rabbits, and if he could not bet twenty-pound notes at the fashionable race-meeting at Goodwood, put his half-crown upon his fancy at the Cliffstone races on Byford Downs—with his hat cocked over one eye as much like Lord Bramble and King Edward as possible.

" Great multitudes of people there were whose lives were

shaped completely by the habits and traditions of these leaders. There was my Uncle John Julip for example. His father had been a gardener and his grandfather before him, and almost all his feminine ancestry and his aunts and cousins were, as the phrase went, ' in service.' None of the people round and about the down-stairs of Chessing Hanger had natural manners ; all were dealing in some more or less plausible imitation of some real lady or gentleman. My Uncle John Julip found his ideal in a certain notorious Sir John ffrench-Cuthbertson. He sought similar hats and adopted similar attitudes.

" He bet heavily in imitation of his model, but he bet less fortunately. This my aunt resented, but she found great comfort in the way in which his clothing and gestures understudied Sir John.

" ' If only he'd been *born* a gentleman,' said my aunt, ' everything 'ud a-been all right. 'E's a natural sportsman ; 'e eats 'is 'eart out in the gardens.'

" He certainly did not work his heart out. I do not remember ever seeing him dig or carry or wheel a barrow. My memory of him in the garden is of one who stood, one hand gripping a hoe as if it were a riding-whip under the tail of his coat, and the other gesticulating or pointing out what had to be done.

" To my father and myself he was always consciously aristocratic, bearing himself in the grand manner. This he did, although my father was a third as tall again as he was and far more abundantly intelligent. He always called my father ' Smith.'

" ' What are you going to do with that boy, Smith ? ' he would ask. ' Seems to me, wants feedin' up and open-air.'

" My father, who secretly shared the general view that my Uncle John under happier stars would have made a very fine gentleman, always tried, as he expressed it, ' to keep his end up ' by calling my uncle ' John.' He would answer. ' Carn't say as I've rightly settled that, John. 'E's a regular bookworm nowadays, say what you like to him.'

" ' Books ! ' said my Uncle John Julip with a concentrated scorn of books that was essentially English. ' You can't get anything out of books that 'asn't been put into them. It stands to reason. There's nothing in books that didn't come out of the sile. Books is flattened flowers at the best, as 'is Lordship said at dinner only the other night.'

" My father was much struck by the idea. " That's what I tell 'im,' he said—inexactly.

" ' Besides, who's going to put anything into a book that's worth knowing ? ' said my uncle. ' It's like expecting these here tipsters in the papers to give away something worth keeping to theirselves. Not it ! '

" ' 'Arf the time,' my father agreed, ' I expect they're telling you lies in these books of yours and larfing at you. All the same,' he reflected with an abrupt lapse from speculation to reverence, ' there's One Book, John.'

" He had remembered the Bible.

" ' I wasn't speaking of that, Smith,' said my uncle sharply. ' Sufficient unto the day—— I mean, that's Sunday Stuff.'

" I hated my days of trial in the gardens. Once or twice during that unpleasant month I was sent with messages up to the kitchen and once to the pantry of the great house. There I said something unfortunate for my uncle, something that was to wipe out all possibility of a gardener's career for me.

" The butler, Mr. Petterton, was also a secondary aristocrat, but in a larger and quite different manner from that of my uncle. He towered up and looked down the slopes of himself, his many chins were pink and stabbed by his collar, and his hair was yellow and very shiny. I had to deliver into his hands a basket of cucumbers and a bunch of blue flowers called borage used in the mixing of summer drinks. He was standing at a table talking respectfully to a foxy little man in tweeds who was eating bread and cheese and drinking beer ; this I was to learn later was Lord Bramble's agent. There was also a young footman in this room, a subterranean room it was with heavily barred windows, and he was cleaning silver plate with exemplary industry.

" ' So you brought this from the gardens,' said Mr. Petterton with fine irony. ' And may I ask why Mr.—why *Sir John* did not condescend to bring them himself ? '

" ' 'E tole me to bring them,' I said.

" ' And pray who may you be ? '

" ' I'm 'Arry Smith,' I said. ' Mr. Julip, 'e's my uncle.'

" ' Ah ! ' said Mr. Petterton and was struck by a thought. ' That's the son of Smith who's a sort of greengrosher in Cliffstone."

" ' Cherry Gardens, sir, we live at.'

" ' Haven't seen you over here before, my boy. Have you ever visited us before ? '

" ' Not 'ere, sir.'

" ' Not here ! But you come over to the gardens perhaps ? "

" ' Nearly every Sunday, sir.'

" ' Exactly. And usually, I suppose, Master Smith, there's something to carry back ? '

" ' Almost always, sir.'

" ' Something a bit heavy ? '

" ' Not *too* heavy,' I said bravely.

" ' You see, sir ? ' said Mr. Petterton to the foxy little man in tweeds.

" I began to realise that something unpleasant was in the wind when this latter person set himself to cross-examine me in a rapid, snapping manner. What was it I carried ? I became very red about the face and ears and declared I did

not know. Did I ever carry grapes ? I didn't know. Pears ?
I didn't know. Celery ? I didn't know.

" ' Well, *I* know,' said the agent. ' *I* know. So why should
I ask you further ? Get out of here.'

" " I went back to my uncle and said nothing to him of this
very disagreeable conversation, but I knew quite well even then
that I had not heard the last of this matter."

CHAPTER THREE

MISFORTUNES COME UPON THE SMITH FAMILY

§ 1

"A ND now," said Sarnac, " I have to tell of a tornado of
mischances that broke up our precarious little home at
Cherry Gardens altogether.   In that casual, planless
over-populated world there were no such things as security
or social justice as we should understand these words nowadays.
It is hard for us to imagine its universal ramshackle insecurity.
Think of it.   The whole world floated economically upon a
cash-and-credit system that was fundamentally fictitious and
conventional, there were no adequate protections against
greedy abuses of those monetary conventions, no watch kept
over world-production and world-consumption, no knowledge
of the variations of climate year by year, and the fortunes
not only of individuals but of states and nations fluctuated
irrationally and uncontrollably.   It was a world in which life
was still almost as unsafe for men and women as life remains
to-day for a field-mouse or a midge, which is never safe from
one moment to another in a world of cats and owls and swallows
and the like.   People were born haphazard, gladdened, distressed, glorified or killed haphazard, and no one was ready
for either their births or their deaths.   Sudden death there
is still in the world, a bright adventure—that lightning yesterday might have killed all or any of us, but such death is a
rare thing and a clean thing.   There is none of the distressful
bearing-down to death through want, anxiety, and illness ill-
tended and misunderstood, that was the common experience
in the past.   And one death does not devastate a dozen or
more lives as deaths often did in the old days.   A widow in
the old days had lost not only her lover but her ' living.'
Yet life is full of subtle compensations.   We did not feel our
endless dangers in those days.   We had a wonderful power
of disregard until the chances struck us.

" " All children," said Sarnac, " start with an absolute confidence in the permanence of the things they find about them.
Disillusionment about safety postulates clear-headedness.   You
could not realise your dangers unless you were clear-headed,
and if you were clear-headed you had the fortitude to face

your dangers. That old world was essentially a world of muddle-headed sophisticated children, blind to the universal catastrophe of the top-heavy and collapsing civilisation in which they played their parts. They thought that life was generally safe in a world of general insecurity. Misfortune astonished every one in those days, though I cannot understand why they should have been astonished at any misfortune.

"The first blow fell without notice about six weeks after I had come back from Chessing Hanger to my last year of schooling before I became a gardener. It was late afternoon and I was home from school. I was downstairs reading a book and my mother was clearing away tea and grumbling at Fanny who wanted to go out. The lamp was lit, and both I and my father who was having what he called 'a bit of a read at the noosepaper' were as close up to its insufficient light as we could get. We heard the shop-bell jangle overhead.

"'Drat it!' said my father. 'Whaddey want this time o' day?'

"He removed his spectacles. He had bought a pair haphazard at a pawnbroker's shop and always used them when he read. They magnified his large mild eyes very greatly. He regarded us protestingly. What *did* they want? We heard the voice of Uncle John Julip calling down the staircase :—

"'Mort'mer,' he said in a voice that struck me as unusual. I had never heard him call my father anything but Smith before.

"'That you, John?' said my father, standing up.

"'It's me. I want to speak to you.'

"'Come down and 'ave some tea, John,' cried my father at the bottom of the stairs.

"'Somethin' to tell you. You better come up here. Somethin' serious.'

"I speculated if it could be any misdeed of mine he had come over about. But my conscience was fairly clear.

"'Now whatever can it be?' asked my father.

"'You better go up and arst 'im,' my mother suggested.

"My father went.

"I heard my uncle say something about, 'We're busted. We've bin give away and we're busted,' and then the door into the shop closed. We all listened to the movements above. It sounded as though Uncle Julip was walking up and down as he talked. My sister Fanny in her hat and jacket flitted unobtrusively up the stairs and out. After a time Prue came in; she had been helping teacher tidy up, she said, though I knew better. Then after a long interval my father came downstairs alone.

"He went to the hearthrug like one in a trance and stood, staring portentously in order to make my mother ask what was the matter. ' Why hasn't John come down for a bit of tea or something ? Where's he gone, Morty ? '

" ' 'E's gorn for a van,' said my father ; ' that's where 'e's gone. For a van.'

" ' Whatever for ? ' asked my mother.

" ' For removal,' said my father. ' That's what for.'

" ' Removal ? '

" ' We got to put 'em up 'ere for a night or so.'

" ' Put 'em up ! Who ? '

" ' 'Im and Adelaide. He's coming to Cherry Gardens.'

" ' You done mean, Morty, 'e's lost 'is situation ? '

" ' I do. S'Lordship turned against 'im. Mischief 'as been made. Spying. And they managed to get 'im out of it. Turned out 'e is. Tole to go.'

" ' But surely they give 'im notice ! '

" ' Not a bit of it. S'Lordship came down to the gardens 'ot and strong. " 'Ere," 'e said, " get out of it ! " Like that 'e said it. " You thank your lucky stars," 'e said : " I ain't put the 'tecs on to you and your snivellin' brother-in-law." Yes. S'Lordship said that.'

" ' But what did 'e mean by it, Morty ? '

" ' Mean. 'E meant that certain persons who shall be name-less 'ad put a suspicion on John, told lies about 'im and *watched* 'im. Watched 'im they did and me. They've drawed me into it, Martha. They've drawed in young 'Arry. They've made up a tale about us. . . . I always said we was a bit too regular. . . . There it is, 'e ain't a 'ead gardener any more. 'E ain't going to 'ave references give 'im ; 'e ain't ever going to 'ave another regular job. 'E's been betrayed and ruined, and there we are ! '

" ' But they say 'e took sompthing ? my brother John took sompthing ? '

" ' Surplus projuce. What's been a perquisite of every gardener since the world begin.' . . .

" I sat with burning ears and cheeks pretending not to hear this dreadful conversation. No one knew of my own fatal share in my uncle's downfall. But already in my heart, like the singing of a lark after a thunderstorm, was arising a realisation that now I might never become a gardener. My mother expressed her consternation brokenly. She asked incredulous questions which my father dealt with in an oracular manner. Then suddenly my mother pounced savagely on my sister Prue, reproaching her for listening to what didn't concern her instead of washing up."

" This is a very circumstantial scene," said Radiant.

" It was the first great crisis of my dream life," said Sarnac. " It is very vivid in my memory. I can see again that old kitchen in which we lived and the faded table-cloth and the paraffin lamp with its glass container. I think if you gave me time I could tell you everything there was in that room."

" What's a hearthrug ? " asked Firefly suddenly. " What sort of thing was your hearthrug ? "

" Like nothing on earth to-day. A hearthrug was a sort of rug you put in front of a coal-fire, next to the fender, which prevented the ashes creeping into the room. This one my father had made out of old clothes, trousers and suchlike things, bits of flannel and bits of coarse sacking, cut into strips and sewn together. He had made it in the winter evenings as he sat by the fireside, sewing industriously."

" Had it any sort of pattern ? "

" None. But I shall never tell my story, if you ask questions. I remember that my uncle, when he had made his arrangements about the van, came in for a bread-and-cheese supper before he walked back to Chessing Hanger. He was very white and distressed looking, Sir John had all faded away from him ; he was like a man who had been dragged out from some hiding-place, he was a very distressed and pitiful man exposed to the light. I remember my mother asked him, ' 'Ow's Adelaide taking it ? '

" My uncle assumed an expression of profound resignation. ' Starts a new pain,' he said bitterly. ' At a time like this.'

" My father and mother exchanged sympathetic glances.

" ' I tell you——,' said my uncle, but did not say what he told us.

" A storm of weak rage wrung him. ' If I knew who'd done all this,' he said. ' That—that *cat* of a 'ousekeeper—cat I call her—she's got some one what wanted my place. If she and Petterton framed it up——'

" He struck the table, but half-heartedly.

" My father poured him out some beer.

" ' Ugh ! ' said my uncle and emptied the glass.

" ' Got to face it,' said my uncle, feeling better. ' Got to go through with it. I suppose with all these tuppenny-'apenny villa gardens 'ere there's jobbing work to be got. I'll get something all right. . . . Think of it ! Jobbing gardener ! Me—a Jobber ! By the Day ! It'll set up some of these 'ere season-ticket clerks no end to 'ave Lord Bramble's gardener dragging a lawn-mower for them. I can see 'em showing me to their friends out of the window. Bin 'ead-gardener to a Lord, they'll say. Well, well——! '

" ' It's a come-down,' said my father when my uncle had departed. ' Say what you like, it's a come-down.'

" My mother was preoccupied with the question of their accommodation. ' She'll 'ave to 'ave the sofa in the sitting-room I expect, and 'e'll 'ave a bit of a shake-up on the floor. Don't suppose she'll like it. They'll 'ave their own bedding of course. But Adelaide isn't the sort to be comfortable on a sofa.'

" Poor woman ! she was not. Although my uncle and my father and mother all pointed out to her the untimeliness and

inconsiderateness of her conduct she insisted upon suffering
so much that a doctor had to be called in. He ordered a prompt
removal to a hospital for an immediate operation.

"Those were days," said Sarnac, "of the profoundest
ignorance about the body. The ancient Greeks and the Arabs
had done a little anatomy during their brief phases of intellectual activity, but the rest of the world had only been
studying physiology in a scientific way for about three hundred
years. People in general still knew practically nothing of vital
processes. As I have told you they even bore children by
accident. And living the queer lives they did, with abnormal
and ill-prepared food in a world of unchecked infections, they
found the very tissues of the bodies going wrong and breaking
out into the queerest growths. Parts of these bodies would
cease to do anything but change into a sort of fungoid proliferation——"

"Their bodies were like their communities ! " said Radiant.

"The same sort of things. They had tumours and cancers
and suchlike things in their bodies and Cherry Garden urban-
districts on their countrysides. But these growths !—they are
dreadful even to recall."

"But surely," said Willow, " in the face of such a horrible
possibility which might afflict any one, all the world must
have wanted to push on with physiological research."

"Didn't they see," said Sunray, " that all these things were
controllable and curable ? "

"Not a bit of it," said Sarnac. " They didn't positively
like these tumours and cancers, but the community was too
undervitalised to put up a real fight against these miseries.
And every one thought that he or she would escape—until
it had them. There was a general apathy. And the priests
and journalists and so forth, the common opinion-makers,
were jealous of scientific men. They did their best to persuade
people that there was nothing hopeful in scientific research,
they did all they could to discredit its discoveries, to ridicule
its patient workers and set people against them."

"That's what puzzles me most," said Sunray.

"Their mental habits were different. Their minds hadn't
been trained to comprehensive thinking. Their thinking was
all in compartments and patches. The morbid growths in
their bodies were nothing to the morbid growths in their
minds."

§ 2

"My aunt in the hospital, with that lack of consideration
for my uncle that had always distinguished her, would neither
recover nor die. She was a considerable expense to him and
no help ; she added greatly to his distresses. After some days
and at the urgent suggestion of my mother he removed himself
from our sitting-room to a two-roomed lodging in the house

of a bricklayer in an adjacent street ; into this he crowded his furniture from Chessing Hanger, but he frequented my father's shop and showed a deepening attachment to my father's company.

"He was not so successful a jobbing gardener as he had anticipated. His short contemptuous way with his new clients in the villas of Cliffstone failed to produce the respect he designed it to do ; he would speak of their flower-beds as ' two penn'orths of all-sorts ' and compare their gardens to a table-cloth or a window-box ; and instead of welcoming these home-truths, they resented them. But they had not the manliness to clear up this matter by a good straight-forward argument in which they would have had their social position very exactly defined ; they preferred to keep their illusions and just ceased to employ him. Moreover, his disappointment with my aunt produced a certain misogyny which took the form of a refusal to take orders from the wives of his patrons when they were left in sole charge of the house. As many of these wives had a considerable influence over their husbands, this too injured my uncle's prospects. Consequently there were many days when he had nothing to do but stand about our shop to discuss with my father as hearer the defects of Cliffstone villa-residents, the baseness of Mr. Petterton and that cat (' *cat* ' he called her) and the probable unworthiness of any casual customer who strayed into range of comment.

"Nevertheless my uncle was resolved not to be defeated without a struggle. There was a process which he called ' keeping his pecker up,' which necessitated, I could not but perceive, periodic visits to the Wellington public-house at the station corner. From these visits he returned markedly more garrulous, more like Sir John ffrench-Cuthbertson, and exhaling a distinctly courageous smell when he coughed or breathed heavily. After a time, as his business difficulties became more oppressive, my father participated in these heartening excursions. They broadened his philosophical out-look but made it, I fancied, rather less distinct.

"My uncle had some indefinite sum of money in the Post-Office Savings Bank, and in his determination not to be beaten without a struggle he did some courageous betting on what he called ' certs ' at the race-meetings on Byford Downs."

" ' Cert ' beats me altogether," said Radiant.

"A ' cert ' was a horse that was certain to win and never did. A ' dead cert ' was an extreme form of the ' cert.' You cannot imagine how the prospects and quality of the chief race-horses were discussed throughout the land. The English were not a nomadic people, only a minority could ride horses, but everybody could bet on them. The King was, so to speak, head of the racing just as he was head of the army. He went in person to the great race-meetings as if to bless and encourage the betting of his subjects. So that my Uncle John Julip

was upheld by the most loyal and patriotic sentiments when
he wasted his days and his savings on Byford Downs. On
several of these occasions my father went with him and
wrestled with fortune also. They lost generally, finally they
lost most of what they had, but on one or two occasions, as
my uncle put it, they ' struck it rich.' One day they pitched
upon a horse called Rococo, although it was regarded as the
very reverse of a ' cert ' and the odds were heavy against it,
but an inner light seems to have guided my uncle ; it came
in first and they won as much as thirty-five pounds, a very
large sum for them. They returned home in a state of solemn
exaltation, which was only marred by some mechanical
difficulty in pronouncing the name of the winning horse. They
began well but after the first syllable they went on more
like a hen that had laid an egg than like rational souls who
had spotted a winner. ' Rocococo ' they would say or ' Roco-
cococo.' Or they would end in a hiccup. And though each
tried to help the other out, they were not really helpful to
each other. They diffused an unusually powerful odour of
cigars and courage. Never had they smelled so courageous.
My mother made them tea.

" ' *Tea !* ' said my uncle meaningly. He did not actually
refuse the cup she put before him, but he pushed it a little
aside.

" For some moments it seemed doubtful whether he was
going to say something very profound . or whether he was
going to be seriously ill. Mind triumphed over matter. ' Knew
it would come, Marth,' he said. ' Knew all'ong it would come.
Directly I heard name. Roc——' He paused.

" ' Cococo,' clucked my father.

" ' Cocococo—hiccup,' said my uncle. ' I knew our 'our 'ad
come. Some men, Smith, some men 'ave that instink. I would
'ave put my shirt on that 'orse, Marth—only. . . . They
wouldn't 'ave took my shirt.'

" He looked suddenly very hard at me. ' They wouldn't 'ave
took it, 'Arry,' he said. ' They done *take* shirts ! '

" ' No,' he said and became profoundly thoughtful.

" Then he looked up. ' Thirty-six to one against,' he said.
' We'd 'ave 'ad shirts for a lifetime.'

" My father saw it from a wider, more philosophical point of
view. ' Might never 'ave been spared to wear 'em out,' he said.
' Better as it is, John.'

" ' And mind you,' said my uncle ; ' this is only a beginning.
Once I start spotting 'em I go on spotting 'em—mind that.
This Roc——'

" ' Cococo.'

" ' Cocococo—whatever it is, s'only a beginning. S'only the
firs'-rays-sunlight 'v' a glorious day.'

" ' In that case,' said my mother, ' 't'seems to me some of us
might have a share.'

" ' Certainly,' said my uncle, ' certainly, Marth.' And amazingly he handed me a ten-shilling piece—in those days we had gold coins and this was a little disc of gold. Then he handed Prue the same. He gave a whole sovereign, a golden pound, to Fanny and a five-pound Bank of England note to my mother.

" ' Hold on ! ' said my father warningly.

" ' Tha's a' right, Smith,' said my uncle with a gesture of princely generosity. ' *You* share, seventeen pounce ten. Six pounce ten leaves 'leven. Lessee. One 'n' five six—seven—eight —nine—ten—'leven. *Here !* "

" My father took the balance of the money with a puzzled expression. Something eluded him. ' Yers,' he said ; ' but——'

" His mild eye regarded the ten-shilling piece I still held exposed in my hand. I put it away immediately but his gaze followed my hand towards my pocket until it met the table-edge and got into difficulties.

" ' 'Thout the turf, Smith, there wouldn't be such a country as England,' said my Uncle John, and rounded his remarks off with, ' Mark my words.' "

" My father did his best to do so."

§ 3

" But this hour of success was almost the only bright inter-lude in a steady drift to catastrophe. In a little while I gathered from a conversation between my mother and my father that we were ' behind with the rent.' That was a quarterly payment we paid to the enterprising individual who owned our house. I know all that sounds odd to you, but that is the way things were done. If we got behind with our rent the owner could turn us out."

" But where ? " asked Firefly.

" Out of the house. And we weren't allowed to stay in the street. But it is impossible for me to explain everything of that sort in detail. We were behind with the rent and catastrophe impended. And then my sister Fanny ran away from us.

" In no other respect," said Sarnac, " is it so difficult to get realities over to you and make you understand how I thought and felt in that other life than in matters of sex. Nowadays sex is so simple. Here we are free and frank men and women ; we are trained so subtly that we scarcely know we are trained, not to be stupidly competitive, to control jealous impulses, to live generously, to honour the young. Love is the link and flower of our choicest friendships. We take love by the way as we take our food and our holidays, the main thing in our lives is our creative work. But in that dark tormented world in which I passed my dream-life, all the business of love was covered over and netted in by restraints and put in fetters that fretted and tortured. I will tell you

at last how I was killed. Now I want to convey to you something of the reality of this affair of Fanny.

"Even in this world," said Sarnac, "my sister Fanny would
have been a conspicuously lovely girl. Her eyes could be as
blue as heaven, or darken with anger or excitement so that
they seemed black. Her hair had a brave sweep in it always.
Her smile made you ready to do anything for her ; her laughter
made the world clean and brightly clear about her even when
it was touched with scorn. And she was ignorant—— I can
hardly describe her ignorance.

"It was Fanny first made me feel that ignorance was shameful. I have told you the sort of school we had and of our
religious teachers. When I was nine or ten and Fanny was
fifteen, she was already scolding me for fumbling with the
pronunciation of words and particularly with the dropping of
the aspirate.

"'Harry,' she said, 'if you call me Fenny again it's
war and pinching. My name's Fanny and yours is Harry and
don't you forget it. It's not English we talk in this place ;
it's mud.'

"Something had stung her. She had been talking with some
one with a better accent and she had been humiliated. I think
that some one may have mocked her. Some chance acquaintance it must have been, some ill-bred superior boy upon the
Cliffstone promenade. But Fanny was setting out now to talk
good English and make me do the same, with a fury all her
own.

"'If only I could talk French,' she said. 'There's France
in sight over there ; all its lighthouses winking at us, and all
we've got to say is, "Parley vous Francy," and grin as if it was
a joke.' She brought home a sixpenny book which professed
but failed to teach her French. She was reading voraciously,
greedily, to know. She read endless novels but also she was
reading all sorts of books, about the stars, about physiology
(in spite of my mother's wild scoldings at the impropriety of
reading a book 'with pictures of yer insides' in it), about
foreign countries. Her passion that I should learn was even
greater than her own passion for knowledge.

"At fourteen she left school and began to help earn her
living. My mother had wanted her to go into 'service,' but
she had resisted and resented this passionately. While that
proposal was still hanging over her, she went off by herself to
Cliffstone and got a job as assistant book-keeper in a pork-
butcher's shop. Before a year was out she was book-keeper,
for her mind was as neat as it was nimble. She earned enough
money to buy books and drawing-material for me and to get
herself clothes that scandalised all my mother's ideas of what
was becoming. Don't imagine she 'dressed well,' as we used
to say ; she experimented boldly, and some of her experiments
were cheap and tawdry.

" I could lecture to you for an hour," said Sarnac, " of what dress and the money to buy dresses meant for a woman in the Old World.

" A large part of my sister's life was hidden from me ; it would have been hidden altogether but for the shameless tirades of my mother, who seemed to prefer to have an audience while she scolded Fanny. I can see now that my mother was bitterly jealous of Fanny because of her unexhausted youth, but at the time I was distressed and puzzled at the gross hints and suggestions that flew over my head. Fanny had a maddening way of not answering back or answering only by some minor correction. ' It's horrible, mother,' she would say. ' Not 'orrible.'

" Behind her defensive rudenesses, unlit, unguided, poor Fanny was struggling with the whole riddle of life, presented to her with an urgency no man can fully understand. Nothing in her upbringing had ever roused her to the passion for real work in the world ; religion for her had been a grimace and a threat ; the one great reality that had come through to her thoughts was love. The novels she read all told of love, elusively, partially, and an impatience in her imagination and in her body leaped to these hints. Love whispered to her in the light and beauty of things about her ; in the moonlight, in the spring breezes. Fanny could not but know that she was beautiful. But such morality as our world had then was a morality of abject suppression. Love was a disgrace, a leering fraud, a smutty joke. She was not to speak about it, not to look towards it until some good man—the pork-butcher was a widower and seemed likely to be the good man in her case—came and spoke not of love indeed but marriage. He would marry her and hurry home with his prize and tear the wrappings from her loveliness, clumsily, stupidly, in a mood of morbidly inflamed desire."

" Sarnac," said Firefly, " you are horrible."

" No," said Sarnac. " But that world of the past was horrible. Most of the women, your ancestors, suffered such things. And that was only the beginning of the horror. Then came the birth and desecration of the children. Think what a delicate, precious and holy thing a child is ! They were begotten abundantly and abnormally, born reluctantly, and dropped into the squalor and infection of an overcrowded disordered world. Bearing a child was not the jolly wholesome process we know to-day ; in that diseased society it was an illness, it counted as an illness, for nearly every woman. Which the man, her husband, resented—grossly. Five or six children in five or six years and a pretty girl was a cross, worried wreck of a woman, bereft of any shred of spirit or beauty. My poor scolding, worried mother was not fifty when she died. And one saw one's exquisite infants grow up into ill-dressed, under-nourished, ill-educated children. Think of the agony of shamed love that lay beneath my poor mother's slaps and scoldings ! The world has forgotten now the hate and bitterness of disappointed parentage. That was the prospect of the moral life that opened before my sister Fanny ; that was the antistrophe to the siren song of her imagination.

"She could not believe this of life and love. She experimented with love and herself. She was, my mother said, ' a bold, bad girl.' She began, I know, with furtive kissings and huggings in the twilight, with boy schoolfellows, with clerks and errand boys. Some gleam of nastiness came into these adventures of the dusk and made her recoil. At any rate she became prim and aloof to Cherry Gardens, but only because she was drawn to the bands and lights and prosperity of Cliffstone. That was when she began to read and correct her accent. You have heard of our old social stratifications. She wanted to be like a lady ; she wanted to meet a gentleman. She imagined there were gentlemen who were really gentle, generous, wise and delightful, and she imagined that some of the men she saw on the cliff promenade at Cliffstone were gentlemen. She began to dress herself as I have told.

"There were scores of such girls in every town in Europe," said Sarnac, "turning their backs on their dreadful homes. In a sort of desperate hope.

"When you hear about the moral code of the Old World," Sarnac went on, "you are apt to think of it as a rule that every one respected in exactly the same way that you think every one believed the professed religions. We have not so much a moral code now as a moral training, and our religion involves no strain on reason or instincts, and so it is difficult for us to understand the tortuosity and evasions and defiances and general furtiveness and meanness of a world in which nobody really understood and believed the religious creeds, not even the priests, and nobody was really convinced to the bone of the sweetness and justice of the moral code. In that distant age almost everybody was sexually angry or uncomfortable or dishonest ; the restraints we had did not so much restrain as provoke people. It is difficult to imagine it now."

"Not if you read the old literature," said Sunray. "The novels and plays are pathological."

"So you have my pretty sister Fanny, drawn by impulses she did not understand, flitting like a moth out of our dingy home in Cherry Gardens to the lights, bright lights of hope they seemed to her, about the band-stand and promenade of Cliffstone. And there staying in the lodging-houses and boarding-houses and hotels were limited and thwarted people, keeping holiday, craving for bright excitements, seeking casual pleasures. There were wives who had tired of their husbands and husbands long weary of their wives, there were separated people who could not divorce, and young men who could not marry because they could not afford to maintain a family. With their poor hearts full of naughtiness, rebellious suppressions, jealousies resentments. And through this crowd, eager, provocative, and defenceless, flitted my pretty sister Fanny."

§ 4

" On the evening before Fanny ran away, my father and my uncle sat in the kitchen by the fire discoursing of politics and the evils of life. They had both been keeping up their peckers very resolutely during the day and this gave a certain rambling and recurrent quality to their review. Their voices were hoarse, and they drawled and were loud and emphatic and impressive. It was as if they spoke for the benefit of unseen listeners. Often they would both be talking together. My mother was in the scullery washing up the tea-things and I was sitting at the table near the lamp trying to do some homework my teacher had given me, so far as the distraction of this conversation so close to me and occasional appeals to me to ' mark ' this or that, would permit. Prue was reading a book called ' Ministering Children ' to which she was much addicted. Fanny had been helping my mother until she was told she was more a hindrance than a help. Then she came and stood at my side looking over my shoulder at what I was doing.

" ' What's spoiling trade and ruining the country,' said my uncle, ' is these 'ere strikes. These 'ere strikes reg'ler destrushion —destruction for the country.'

" ' Stop everything,' said my father. ' It stands to reason.'

" ' They didn't ought to be allowed. These 'ere miners'r paid and paid 'andsomely. Paid 'andsomely they are. 'Andsomely. Why ! I'd be glad of the pay they get, glad of it. They 'as bulldogs, they 'as pianos. Champagne. Me and you, Smith, me and you and the middle-classes generally ; we don't get pianos. We don't get champagne. Not-tit. . . .'

" ' Ought to be a Middle Classes Union,' said my father, ' keep these 'ere workers in their places. They 'old up the country and stop trade. Trade ! Trade's orful. Why ! people come in now and look at what you got and arst the price of this and that. Think twice they do before they spend a sixpence. . . . And the coal you're expected to sell nowadays ! I tell 'em, if this 'ere strike comes off this 's 'bout the last coal you're likely to see, good *or* bad. Straight out, I tell 'em. . . .'

" ' You're not working, Harry,' said Fanny without troubling to lower her voice. ' Don't see how you *can* work, with all this jawing going on. Come out for a walk.'

" I glanced up at her and rose at once. It wasn't often Fanny asked me to go for a walk with her. I put my books away.

" ' Going out for a bit of fresh air, mother,' said Fanny, taking her hat down from its peg.

" ' No, you don't—not at this time,' cried my mother from the scullery. ' Ain't I said, once and for all——? '

" ' It's all right, mother, Harry's going with me. He'll see no one runs away with me and ruins me. . . . You've said it once and for all—times enough.'

"My mother made no further objection, but she flashed a look of infinite hate at my sister.

"We went up-stairs and out into the street.

"For a time we said nothing, but I had a sense that I was going to be ' told things.'

"' I've had about enough of all this,' Fanny began presently. 'What's going to become of us ? Father and uncle 've been drinking all day ; you can see they're both more than half-screwed. Both of 'em. It's every day now. It's worse and worse and worse. Uncle hasn't had a job these ten days. Father's always with him. The shop's getting filthy. He doesn't sweep it out now for days together.'

"' Uncle seems to have lost 'eart,' I said, ' since he heard that Aunt Adelaide would have to have that second operation.'

"' Lost heart ! He never had any heart to lose.' My sister Fanny said no more of my uncle—by an effort. ' *What* a home ! ' she cried.

"She paused for a moment. ' Harry,' she said, ' I'm going to get out of this. Soon.'

"I asked what she meant by that.

"' Never mind what I mean. I've got a situation. A different sort of situation. . . . Harry, you—you care for me, Harry ? '

"Professions of affection are difficult for boys of thirteen. ' I'd do anything for you, Fanny,' I said after a pause. ' You know I would.'

"' And you wouldn't tell on me ? '

"' Whad you take me for ? '

"' Nohow ? '

"' No'ow.'

"' I knew you wouldn't,' said Fanny. ' You're the only one of the whole crew I'll be sorry to leave. I *do* care for you, Harry. Straight, I do. I used to care for mother. Once. But that's different. She's scolded me and screamed at me till it's gone. Every bit of it. I can't help it—it's gone. I'll think of you, Harry—often.'

"I realised that Fanny was crying. Then when I glanced at her again her tears were over.

"' Look here, Harry,' she said, ' would you do—something for me. Something—not so very much—and not tell ? Not tell afterwards, I mean.'

"' I'd do anything, Fanny.'

"' It's not so very much really. There's that little old port-manteau up-stairs. I've put some things in it. And there's a little bundle. I've put 'em both under the bed at the back where even Prying Prue won't think of looking. And to-morrow —when father's out with uncle like he is now every day, and mother's getting dinner down-stairs and Prue's pretending to help her and sneaking bits of bread—if you'd bring those down to Cliffstone to Crosby's side-door. . . . They aren't so very heavy.'

" ' I ain't afraid of your portmanteau, Fanny. I'd carry it more miles than that for you. But where's this new situation of yours, Fanny ? and why ain't you saying a word about it at home ? '

" ' Suppose I asked you something harder than carrying a portmanteau, Harry ? '

" ' I'd do it, Fanny, if I could do it. You know that, Fanny.'

" ' But if it was just to ask no questions of where I am going and what I am going to do. It's—it's a good situation, Harry. It isn't hard work.'

" She stopped short. I saw her face by the yellow light of a street-lamp and I was astonished to see it radiant with happiness. And yet her eyes were shining with tears. What a Fanny it was, who could pass in a dozen steps from weeping to ecstasy !

" ' Oh ! I wish I could tell you all about it, Harry,' she said. " I wish I could tell you all about it. Don't you worry about me, Harry, or what's going to happen to me. You help me, and after a bit I'll write to you. I will indeed, Harry.'

" ' You aren't going to run away and marry ? ' I asked abruptly. ' It'd be like you, Fanny, to do that.'

" ' I won't say I am ; I won't say I'm not ; I won't say anything, Harry. But I'm as happy as the sunrise, Harry ! I could dance and sing. If only I can do it, Harry.'

" ' There's one thing, Fanny.'

" She stopped dead. ' You're not going back on me, Harry ? '

" ' No. I'll do what I've promised, Fanny. But——' I had a moral mind. I hesitated. ' You're not doing anything wrong, Fanny ? '

" She shook her head and did not answer for some moments. The look of ecstasy returned.

" ' I'm doing the rightest thing that ever I did, Harry, the rightest thing. If only I can do it. And you are a dear to help me, a perfect dear.'

" And suddenly she put her arms about me and drew my face to hers and kissed me and then she pushed me away and danced a step. ' I love all the world to-night,' said Fanny. ' I love all the world. Silly old Cherry Gardens ! You thought you'd got me ! You thought I'd never get away ! '

" She began a sort of chant of escape. ' To-morrow's my last day at Crosby's, my very last day. For ever and ever. Amen. He'll never come too near me again and breathe down my neck. He'll never put his fat hand on my bare arm and shove his face close to mine while he looks at my cash-sheet. When I get to——, wherever I'm going, Harry, I'll want to send him a post-card. Good-bye, Mr. Crosby, good-bye, *dear* Mr. Crosby. For ever and ever. Amen ! ' She made what I knew to be her imitation of Mr. Crosby's voice. ' You're the sort of girl who ought to marry young

and have a steady husband older than yourself, my dear.
Did I ought ? And who said you might call me your dear, dear
Mr. Crosby ? Twenty-five shillings a week and pawings about
and being called *dear*, thrown in. . . . I'm wild to-night,
Harry—wild to-night. I could laugh and scream, and yet
I want to cry, Harry, because I'm leaving you. And leaving
them all ! Though why I care I don't know. Poor boozy
old father ! Poor silly scolding mother ! Some day perhaps
I may help them if only I get away. And you—you've got
to go on learning and improving, Harry, learning, learning.
Learn and get out of Cherry Gardens. Never drink. Never
let drink cross your lips. Don't smoke. For why should any
one smoke ? Take the top side of life, for it's easier up there.
Indeed, it's easier. Work and read, Harry. Learn French—
so that when I come back to see you, we can both talk together.'

" ' You're going to learn French ? You're going to France ? '

" ' Farther than France. But not a word, Harry. Not a
word of it. But I wish I could tell you everything. I can't.
I mustn't. I've given my promise. I've got to keep faith.
All one has to do in the world is to love and keep faith. But
I wish mother had let me help wash-up to-night, my last
night. She hates me. She'll hate me more yet. . . . I wonder
if I'll keep awake all night or cry myself to sleep. Let's race
as far as the goods-station, Harry, and then walk home.' "

§ 5

" The next night Fanny did not come home at all. As
the hours passed and the emotion of my family deepened I
began to realise the full enormity of the disaster that had
come upon our home."

Sarnac paused and smiled. " Never was there so *clinging*
a dream. I am still half Harry Mortimer Smith and only
half myself. I am still not only in memory but half in feeling
also that young English barbarian in the Age of Confusion.
And yet all the time I am looking at my story from our point
of view and telling it in Sarnac's voice. Amidst this sunshine.
. . . Was it really a dream ? . . . I don't believe I am telling
you a dream."

" It isn't a bit like a dream," said Willow. " It is a story—
a real story. Do you think it was a dream ? "

Sunray shook her head. " Go on," she said to Sarnac.
" Whatever it is, tell it. Tell us how your family behaved
when Fanny ran away."

" You must keep in mind that all these poor souls were
living in a world of repressions such as seem almost inconceivable now. You think they had ideas about love and
sex and duty different from our ideas. We are taught that
they had different ideas. But that is not the truth ; the truth
is that they had no clear, thought-out ideas about such things

at all. They had fears and blank prohibitions and ignorances where we have ideas. Love, sex, these were things like the enchanted woods of a fairy-tale. It was forbidden even to go in. And—none of us knew to what extent—Fanny had gone in.

" So that evening was an evening of alarm deepening to a sort of moral panic for the whole household. It seemed to be required of my family that they should all behave irrationally and violently. My mother began to fret about half-past nine. ' I've tole 'er, once for all,' she said, partly to herself but also for my benefit. ' It's got to stop.' She cross-examined me about where Fanny might be. Had she said anything about going on the pier ? I said I didn't know. My mother fumed and fretted. Even if Fanny had gone on the pier she ought to be home by ten. I wasn't sent to bed at the usual hour so that I saw my father and uncle come in after the public-house had closed. I forget now why my uncle came in to us instead of going straight home, but it was not a very unusual thing for him to do so. They were already disposed to despondency and my mother's white face and anxious tidings deepened their gloom.

" ' Mortimer," said my mother, ' that gal of yours 'as gone a bit too far. Sarf-pars' ten and she isn't 'ome yet.'

" ' 'Aven't I tole 'er time after time,' said my father, ' she's got to be in by nine ? '

" ' Not times enough you 'aven't,' said my mother, ' and 'ere's the fruit ! '

" ' I've tole 'er time after time,' said my father. ' Time after time.' And he continued to repeat this at intervals throughout the subsequent discussion until another refrain replaced it.

" My uncle said little at first. He took up his position on the hearthrug my father had made and stood there, swaying slightly, hiccoughing at intervals behind his hand, frowning and scrutinising the faces of the speakers. At last he delivered his judgment. ' Somethin' sappened to that girl,' he said. ' You mark my words.'

" Prue had a mind apt for horrors. ' She's bin in 'naccident per'aps,' she said. ' She may'be bin knocked down.'

" ' I've tole 'er,' said my father, ' time after time.'

" ' If there's bin 'naccident,' said my uncle sagely, ' well . . . 'nything ma've 'appened.' He repeated this statement in a louder, firmer voice. ' 'Nything ma've 'appened.'

" ' 'Stime you went to bed, Prue,' said my mother, ' 'igh time. 'N you too, 'Arry.'

" My sister got up with unusual promptitude and went out of the room. I think she must have had an idea then of looking for Fanny's things. I lingered.

" ' May'be been 'naccident, may not,' said my mother darkly. ' Sworse things than accidents.'

" ' Whaddyoumean by that, Marth ? ' asked my uncle.

" ' Never mind what I mean. That girl worried me times and oft. There's worse things than accidents.'

" I listened thrilled. ' You be orf to bed, 'Arry,' said my mother.

" ' Whaddyou got to do,—simple,' said my uncle, leaning forward on his toes. ' Telephone 'ospitals. Telephone pleece. Old Crow at the Wellington won't 've gone to bed. 'Sgot telephone. Good customers. 'E'll telephone. Mark my words —s'snaccident.'

" And then Prue reappeared at the top of the stairs.

" ' *Mother !* ' she said in a loud whisper.

" ' You be orf to bed, miss,' said my mother. ' 'Aven't I got worries enough ? '

" ' Mother,' said Prue. ' You know that little old portmantle of Fanny's ? '

" Every one faced a new realisation.

" ' Sgorn,' said Prue. ' And her two best 'ats and all 'er undercloe's and 'er other dress—gorn too.'

" ' Then she's took 'em ! ' said my father.

" ' And 'erself ! ' said my mother.

" ' Time after time I tole her,' said my father.

" ' She's run away ! ' said my mother with a scream in her voice. ' She's brought shame and disgrace on us ! She's run away ! '

" ' Some one's got 'old of 'er,' said my father.

" My mother sat down abruptly. ' After all I done for 'er ! ' she cried, beginning to weep. ' With an honest man ready to marry 'er ! Toil and sacrifice, care and warnings, and she's brought us to shame and dishonour ! She's run away ! That I should 'ave lived to see this day ! Fanny ! '

" She jumped up suddenly to go and see with her own eyes that Prue's report was true. I made myself as inconspicuous as possible, for I feared some chance question might reveal my share in our family tragedy. But I didn't want to go to bed ; I wanted to hear things out.

" ' Sany good my going to the p'lice-station for you on my way 'ome ? ' my uncle asked.

" ' P'lice ! ' said my father. ' What good's p'lice ? Gaw ! If I 'ad my 'ands on that villain's throat—I'd p'lice 'im ! Bringing shame on me and mine ! *P'lice !* 'Ere's Fanny, my little daughter Fanny, beguiled and misled and carried away ! . . . I'm 'asty. . . . Yes, John. You go in and tell the p'lice. It's on your way. Tell 'em from me. I won't leave not a single stone unturned so's to bring 'er back.'

" My mother came back whiter than ever. ' It's right enough,' she said. ' She's gorn ! She's off. While we stand 'ere, disgraced and shamed, she's away.'

" ' Who with ? ' said my father. ' That's the question, who with ? 'Arry, 'ave you ever seen any one about with your sister ? Any one 'anging about ? Any suspicious-looking sort of dressed-up fancy man ? 'Ave you ever ? '

" I said I hadn't.

" But Prue had evidence. She became voluble. About a week ago she had seen Fanny and a man coming along from Cliffstone, talking. They hadn't seen her ; they had been too wrapped up in each other. Her description of the man was very vague and was concerned chiefly with his clothes ; he had worn a blue serge suit and a grey felt hat ; he was ' sort of a gentleman-like.' He was a good lot older than Fanny —Prue wasn't sure whether he had a moustache or not.

" My father interrupted Prue's evidence by a tremendous saying which I was to hear him repeat time after time during the next week. ' Sooner'n this sh'd've 'appened,' said my father, ' I'd 've seen 'er lying dead at my feet—*gladly* I'd 've seen 'er lying dead at my feet ! '

" ' Poor girl ! ' said my uncle. ' Sabitter lesson she 'as before 'er. A *bitter* lesson ! Poo' chile ! Poo' little Fanny ! '

" ' Poor Fanny indeed ! ' cried my mother vindictively, seeing it all, I perceived, from an entirely different angle. ' There she is prancin' about with 'er fancy gentleman now in all 'er fallals ; dinners and wine she'll 'ave, flowers she'll 'ave, dresses and everything ! Be took about and shown things ! Shown off and took to theaytres. The shame of it ! And us 'ere shamed and disgraced and not a word to say when the neighbours ask us questions ! 'Ow can I look 'em in the face ? 'Ow can I look Mr. Crosby in the face ? That man was ready to go down on 'is bended knees to 'er and worship 'er. Stout though 'e was. 'E'd 'ave given 'er any-thing she arst for—in reason. What 'e could see in 'er, I could never make out. But see it 'e did. And now I've got to face 'im and tell 'im I've told 'im wrong. Time after time I've said to 'im—" *You wait. You wait, Mr. Crosby.*" And that 'uzzy !—sly and stuck-up and deep ! Gorn ! '

" My father's voice came booming over my mother's shrill outcry. ' Sooner'n this should've 'appened I'd 've seen 'er dead at my feet ! '

" I was moved to protest. But for all my thirteen years I found myself weeping. ' 'Ow d'you *know*,' I blubbered, ' that Fanny 'asn't gone away and got married ? 'Ow d'you know ? '

" ' Married ! ' cried my mother. ' Why should she run away to be married ! If it was merridge, what was to prevent 'er bringing 'im 'ome and having 'im interjuced to us all, right and proper ? Isn't her own father and mother and 'ome good enough for her, that she 'as to run away and get married ? When she could 'ave 'ad it 'ere at St. Jude's nice and respectable with your father and your uncle and all of us and white favours and a carriage and all. I wish I could 'ope she was married ! I wish there was a chance of it ! '

" My uncle shook his head in confirmation.

" ' Sooner'n this should 've 'appened,' boomed my father, ' I'd 'ave seen 'er dead at my feet ! '

" ' Last night,' said Prue, ' she said 'er prayers.'

" ' Didn't she *always* say 'er prayers ? ' asked my uncle, shocked.

" ' Not kneeling down,' said Prue. ' But last night she was kneeling quite a long time. She thought I was asleep but I watched 'er.'

" ' That looks bad,' said my uncle. ' Y'know, Smith ; that looks bad. I don't like that praying. 'Sominous. I don't like it.'

" And then suddenly and violently Prue and I were packed off up-stairs to bed.

" For long the sound of their voices went on ; the three of them came up into the shop and stood at the front door while my uncle gradually took leave. What further things they said I did not hear. But I remember that suddenly I had a brilliant idea, suggested no doubt by Prue's scrap of evidence. I got out of bed and knelt down and said, ' Pray, God, be kind to my Fanny ! Pray, God, not to be hard on Fanny ! I'm sure she means to get married. For ever and ever. Amen.' And after putting Providence upon his honour, so to speak, in this fashion, I felt less mentally distracted and got back into this bed and presently I fell asleep."

Sarnac paused.

" It's all rather puzzling," said Willow.

" It seemed perfectly natural at the time," said Sarnac.

" That pork-butcher was evidently a repulsive creature," said Firefly. " Why didn't they object to him ? "

" Because the importance of the marriage ceremonial was so great in those days as to dominate the entire situation. I knew Crosby quite well ; he was a cunning-faced, oily-mannered humbug with a bald head, fat red ears, a red complexion, and a paunch. There are no such people in the world now ; you must recall some incredible gross Old-World caricature to imagine him. Nowadays you would as soon think of coupling the life of a girl with some gross heavy animal as with such a man. But that mattered nothing to my father or my mother. My mother I suspect rather liked the idea of the physical humiliation of Fanny. She no doubt had had her own humiliations—for the sexual life of this Old World was a tangle of clumsy ignorances and secret shames. Except for my mother's real hostility to Fanny I remember scarcely a scrap of any simple natural feeling, let alone any reasonable thinking, in all that terrible fuss they made. Men and women in those days were so much more complex and artificial than they are now ; in a muddled way they were amazingly intricate. You know that monkeys, even young monkeys, have old and wrinkled faces, and it is equally true that in the Age of Confusion life was so perplexing and irrational that while we were still children our minds were already old and wrinkled. Even to my boyish observation it was clear that my father was acting the whole time ; he was behaving as he imagined he was expected to behave. Never for a moment either when drunk or sober did he even attempt to find out, much less to express, what he was feeling naturally about Fanny. He was afraid to do so. And that night we were all acting—all of us. We were all afraid to do anything but act in what we imagined would be regarded as a virtuous rôle."

" But what were you afraid of ? " asked Radiant. " Why did you act ? "

" I don't know. Afraid of blame. Afraid of the herd. A habit of fear. A habit of inhibition."

" What was the objection to the real lover ? " asked Firefly. " I don't understand all this indignation."

" They guessed rightly enough that he did not intend to marry Fanny."

" What sort of a man was he ? "

" I never saw him until many years afterwards. But I will tell you about that when I come to it."

" Was he—the sort of man one could love ? "

" Fanny loved him. She had every reason to do so. He took care of her. He got her the education she craved for. He gave her a life full of interest. I believe he was an honest and delightful man."

" They stuck to each other ? "

" Yes."

" Then why didn't he marry her—if it was the custom ? "

" He was married already. Marriage had embittered him. It embittered many people. He'd been cheated. He had been married by a woman who pretended love to impose herself upon him and his fortunes and he had found her out."

" Not a very difficult discovery," said Firefly.

" No."

" But why couldn't they divorce ? "

" In those days it took two to make a divorce. She wouldn't let him loose. She just stuck on and lived on his loneliness. If he had been poor he would probably have tried to murder her, but as it happened he had the knack of success and he was rich. Rich people could take liberties with marriage restrictions that were absolutely impossible for the poor. And he was, I should guess, sensitive, affectionate and energetic. Heaven knows what sort of a mind he was in when he came upon Fanny. He ' picked her up,' as people used to say casually. The Old World was full of such pitiful adventures in encounter. Almost always they meant disaster, but this was an exceptional case. Perhaps it was as lucky for him that he met her as it was for her that she met him. Fanny, you know, was one of those people you have to be honest with; she was acute and simple; she cut like a clean sharp knife. They were both in danger and want; the ugliest chances might have happened to her and he was far gone on the way to promiscuity and complete sexual degradation. . . . But I can't go off on Fanny's story. In the end she probably married him. They were going to marry. In some way the other woman did at last make it possible."

" But why don't you know for certain ? "

" Because I was shot before that happened. If it happened at all."

§ 6

" *No !* " cried Sarnac, stopping a question from Willow by a gesture.

" I shall never tell my story," said Sarnac, " if you interrupt with questions. I was telling you of the storm of misfortunes that wrecked our household at Cherry Gardens. . . .

" My father was killed within three weeks of Fanny's elopement. He was killed upon the road between Cherry Gardens and Cliffstone. There was a young gentleman named Wickersham with one of the new petrol-driven motor-cars that were just coming into use; he was hurrying home as fast as possible, he told the coroner, because his brakes were out of order and he was afraid of an accident. My father was walking with my uncle along the pavement, talking. He found the pavement too restricted for his subject and gestures, and he stepped off suddenly into the roadway and was struck by the car from behind and knocked headlong and instantly killed.

" The effect upon my uncle was very profound. For some days he was thoughtful and sober and he missed a race-meeting. He was very helpful over the details of the funeral.

" ' You can't say 'e wasn't prepared, Marth,' he told my mother. ' You can't say 'e wasn't prepared. Very moment 'e was killed, 'e 'ad the name 'v' Providence on 'is lips. 'E'd been saying 'ow sorely 'e'd been tried by this and that.'

" ' E wasn't the only one,' said my mother.

" ' 'E was saying 'e knew it was only to teach 'im some lesson though he couldn't rightly say what the lesson was. 'E was convinced that everything that 'appened to us, good though it seemed or bad though it seemed, was surely for the best. . . .''

" My uncle paused dramatically.

" ' And then the car 'it 'im,' said my mother, trying to picture the scene.

" ' Then the car 'it 'im,' said my uncle."

CHAPTER FOUR

THE WIDOW SMITH MOVES TO LONDON

§ 1

IN those days," said Sarnac, "the great majority of the dead were put into coffins and buried underground. Some few people were burned, but that was an innovation and contrary to the very materialistic religious ideas of the time. This was a world in which you must remember people were still repeating in perfect good faith a creed which included ' the resurrection of the body and the life everlasting.' Intellectually old Egypt and her dreaming mummies still ruled the common people of the European world. The Christian creeds were themselves mummies from Lower Egypt. As my father said on one occasion when he was discussing this question of cremation : ' It might prove a bit orkward at the Resurrection. Like not 'aving a proper wedding-garment so to speak. . . .

" ' Though there's sharks,' said my father, whose mental transitions were sometimes abrupt. ' And them as 'ave been eat by lions. Many of the best Christian martyrs in their time was eat by lions. . . . They'd *certainly* be given bodies. . . .

" ' And if *one* is given a body why not another ? ' said my father, lifting mild and magnified eyes in inquiry.

" ' It's a difficult question,' my father decided.

" At any rate there was no discussion of cremation in his case. We had a sort of hearse-coach with a place for the coffin in front to take him to the cemetery, and in this vehicle my mother and Prue travelled also ; my elder brother Ernest, who had come down from London for the occasion, and my uncle and I walked ahead and waited for it at the cemetery gates and followed the coffin to the grave-side. We were all in black clothes, even black gloves, in spite of the fact that we were wretchedly poor.

" ' Twon't be my last visit to this place this year,' said my uncle despondently, ' not if Adelaide goes on like she's doing.'

" Ernest was silent. He disliked my uncle and was brooding over him. From the moment of his arrival he had shown a deepening objection to my uncle's existence.

" ' There's luck they say in funerals,' said my uncle presently, striking a brighter note. ' 'Fi keep my eye open I dessay I may get a 'int of somethin'.'

" Ernest remained dour.

" We followed the men carrying the coffin towards the cemetery chapel in a little procession led by Mr. Snapes in his clerical robes. He began to read out words that I realised were beautiful and touching and that concerned strange and far-away things : ' I am the Resurrection and the Life. He that believeth in Me though he were dead yet shall he live. . . .'

" ' I know that my Redeemer liveth and that He shall stand at the latter day upon the earth. . . .'

" ' We brought nothing into this world, and it is certain we can carry nothing out. The Lord gave, and the Lord hath taken away ; blessed be the Name of the Lord.'

" Suddenly I forgot the bickerings of my uncle and brother and was overcome with tenderness and grief for my father. A rush from my memory of many clumsy kindlinesses, a realisation of the loss of his companionship came to me. I recalled the happiness of many of my Sunday tramps by his side in springtime, on golden summer evenings, in winter when the frost had picked out every twig in the downland hedgerows. I thought of his endless edifying discourses about flowers and rabbits and hillsides and distant stars. And he was gone. I should never hear his voice again. I should never see again his dear old eyes magnified to an immense wonder through his spectacles. I should never have a chance of telling him how I cared for him. And I had never told him I cared for him. Indeed, I had never realised I cared for him until now. He was lying stiff and still and submissive in that coffin, a rejected man. Life had treated him badly. He had never had a dog's chance. My mind leaped forward beyond my years and I understood what a tissue of petty humiliations and disappointments and degradations his life had been. I saw then as clearly as I see now the immense pity of such a life. Sorrow possessed me. I wept as I stumbled along after him. I had great difficulty in preventing myself from weeping aloud."

§ 2

" After the funeral my brother Ernest and my uncle had a violent wrangle about my mother's future. Seeing that my Aunt Adelaide was for all practical purposes done for, my uncle suggested that he should sell up most of his furniture, ' bring his capital ' into the greengrocery business, and come and live with his sister. But my brother declared that the greengrocery business was a dying concern, and was for my mother moving into a house in Cliffstone where she might let lodgings. Prue would be no end of a 'elp in that. At first this was opposed by my uncle and then he came round to the idea on condition that he participated in the benefits of the scheme, but this Ernest opposed, asking rather rudely what sort of help my uncle supposed he would be in a lodging-house. ' Let alone you're never out of bed before ten,' he said, though how he knew of this fact did not appear.

" Ernest had been living in London, working at a garage ; he drove hired cars by the month or job, and his respect for the upper classes had somehow disappeared. The dignity of Sir John ffrench-Cuthbertson at second-hand left him cold and scornful. ' You ain't going to 'ave *my* mother to work for you and wait on you, now,' he said.

" While this dispute went on my mother with the assistance of Prue was setting out the cold collation which in those days was the redeeming feature of every funeral. There was cold ham and chicken. My uncle abandoned his position of vantage on my father's rag hearthrug and we all sat down to our exceptional meal.

" For some little time the cold ham and chicken made a sort of truce between my brother Ernest and my uncle, but presently my uncle sighed, drank off his beer and reopened the argument. ' You know I think, Marth,' he said, spearing a potato from the dish neatly with his fork, ' *you* ought to 'ave some voice in what is going to become of you. Me and this young man from London 've been 'aving a bit of a difference 'bout what you ought to do.'

" I realised abruptly from the expression of my mother's white face, a sort of white intentness which her widow's cap seemed to emphasise, that she was quite determined to have not only some voice but a decisive voice in this matter, but before she could say anything my brother Ernest had intervened.

" ' It's like this, mother,' he said, ' you got to do something, 'aven't you ? '

" My mother was about to reply when Ernest snatched a sort of assent from her and proceeded : ' Well, naturally I ask, what sort of thing can you do ? and *as* naturally, I answer Lodgings. You carn't expect to go on being a greengrocer, because that ain't natural for a woman, considering the weights and coal that 'as to be lifted.'

" ' And could be lifted easy, with a man to 'elp 'er,' said my uncle.

" ' If 'e *was* a man,' said my brother Ernest with bitter sarcasm.

" ' Meaning——? ' asked my uncle with cold hauteur.

" ' What I say,' said brother Ernest. ' No more, no less. So if you take my advice, mother, what you'll do is this. You go down early to-morrow to Cliffstone to look for a suitable little 'ouse big enough to 'old lodgers and not so big as to break your back, and I'll go and talk to Mr. Bulstrode about ending up your tenancy 'ere. Then we'll be able to see where we are.'

" Again my mother attempted to speak and was overborne.

" ' Fyou think I'm going to be treated as a nonentity,' said my uncle, ' you're making the biggest mistake you ever made in your life. See ? Now you listen to me, Marth——'

" ' You shut up ! ' said my brother. ' Mother's *my* business first and foremost.'

" ' *Shut up !* ' echoed my uncle. ' Wot *manners !* At a funeral. From a chap not a third my age, a mere 'azardous empty boy ! *Shut* up ! You shut up yourself, my boy, and listen to those who know a bit more about life than you do. I've smacked your 'ed before to-day. Not once or twice either

And I warmed your 'ide when you stole them peaches—and much good it did you ! I oughter've took yer skin off ! You and me 'ave never got on much, and unless you keep a civil tongue in your head we ain't going to get on now.'

" ' Seeing which,' said brother Ernest with a dangerous calmness ; ' the sooner you make yourself scarce the better for all concerned.'

" ' Not to leave my on'y sister's affairs in the 'ands of a cub like you.'

" Again my mother essayed to speak, but the angry voices disregarded her.

" ' I tell you you're going to get out, and if you can't get out of your own discretion I warn you I'll 'ave to 'elp you.'

" ' Not when you're in mourning,' said my mother. ' Not wearing your mourning. And besides——'

" But they were both too heated to attend to her.

" ' You're pretty big with your talk,' said my uncle, ' but don't you preshume too far on my forbearance. I've 'ad about enough of this.'

" ' So've I,' said my brother Ernest and stood up.

" My uncle stood up too and they glared at one another.

" ' That's the door,' said my brother darkly.

" My uncle walked back to his wonted place on the hearthrug. ' Now don't let's 'ave any quarrelling on a day like this,' he said. ' If you 'aven't any consideration for your mother you might at least think of 'Im who has passed beyond. My objec' 'ere is simply to try n'range things so's be best for all. And what I say is this, the ideer of your mother going into a lodging-'ouse alone, without a man's 'elp, is ridiculous, perfectly ridiculous, and only a first-class inconsiderate young fool——'

" My brother Ernest went and stood close to my uncle. ' You've said enough,' he remarked. ' This affair's between me and my mother and your motto is Get Out. See ? '

" Again my mother had something to say and again she was silenced. " ' This is man's work, mother,' said Ernest. ' Are you going to shift it, uncle ? '

" My uncle faced up to this threat of Ernest. ' I've a juty to my sister——'

" And then I regret to say my brother laid hands on him. He took him by the collar and by the wrist and for a moment the two black-clad figures swayed.

" ' Lea' go my coat,' said my uncle. ' Lea' go my coat-collar.'

" But a thirst for violence had taken possession of Ernest. My mother and Prue and I stood aghast.

" ' Ernie ! ' cried my mother. ' You forget yourself ! '

" ' 'Sall *right*, mother,' said Ernie, and whirled my uncle violently from the hearthrug to the bottom of the staircase. Then he shifted his grip from my uncle's wrist to the seat of his tight black trousers and partly lifted and partly impelled him up the staircase. My uncle's arms waved wildly as if he clutched at his lost dignity.

" ' John ! ' cried my mother. ' 'Ere's your 'at ! '

" I had a glimpse of my uncle's eyes as he vanished up the staircase. He seemed to be looking for his hat. But he was now offering no serious opposition to my brother Ernest's handling of him.

" ' Give it 'im, 'Arry,' said my mother. ' And there's 'is gloves too.'

" I took the black hat and the black gloves and followed the struggle up-stairs. Astonished and unresisting my uncle was propelled through the front door into the street and stood there panting and regarding my brother. His collar was torn from its stud and his black tie disarranged. Ernest was breathing heavily. ' Now you be orf and mind your own business,' said Ernie.

" Ernie turned with a start as I pushed past him. ' 'Ere's your 'at and gloves, uncle,' I said, handing them to him. He took them mechanically, his eyes still fixed on Ernest.

" ' And you're the boy I trained to be 'onest,' said my uncle to my brother Ernest, very bitterly. ' Leastways I tried to. You're the young worm I fattened up at my gardens and showed such kindness to ! *Grati ood !* '

" He regarded the hat in his hand for a moment as though it was some strange object, and then by a happy inspiration put it on his head.

" ' God 'elp your poor mother,' said my Uncle John Julip. ' God 'elp 'er.'

" He had nothing more to say. He looked up the street and down and then turned as by a sort of necessity in the direction of the Wellington public-house. And in this manner was my Uncle John Julip on the day of my father's funeral cast forth into the streets of Cherry Gardens, a prospective widower and a most pathetic and unhappy little man. That dingy little black figure in retreat still haunts my memory. Even from the back he looked amazed. Never did a man who has not been kicked look so like a man who has been. I never saw him again. I have no doubt that he carried his sorrows down to the Wellington and got himself thoroughly drunk, and I have as little doubt that he missed my father dreadfully all the time he was doing so.

" My brother Ernest returned thoughtfully to the kitchen. He was already a little abashed at his own violence. I followed him respectfully.

" ' You didn't ought t'ave done that,' said my mother.

" ' What right 'as 'e to plant 'imself on you to be kept and waited on ? '

" ' 'E wouldn't 'ave planted 'imself on me,' my mother replied. ' You got 'eated, Ernie, same as you used to do, and you won't listen to anything.'

" ' I never did fancy uncle,' said Ernie.

" ' When you get 'eated, Ernie, you seem to forget every-thing,' said my mother. ' You might've remembered 'e was my brother.'

" ' Fine brother ! ' said Ernie. ' Why !—who started all that stealing ? Who led poor father to drink and bet ? '

" ' All the same,' said my mother, ' you 'adn't no right to 'andle 'im like you did. And your poor father 'ardly cold in 'is grave ! ' she wept. She produced a black-bordered handker-chief and mopped her eyes. ' I did 'ope your poor father would 'ave a nice funeral—all the trouble and expense—and now you've spoiled it. I'll never be able to look back on this day with pleasure, not if I live to be a 'undred years. I'll always remember 'ow you spoiled your own father's funeral—turning on your uncle like this.'

" Ernest had no answer for her reproaches. ' He shouldn't 've argued and said what he did,' he objected.

" ' And all so unnecessary ! All along I've been trying to tell you you needn't worry about me. I don't want no lodging-'ouse in Cliffstone—*with* your uncle or *without* your uncle. I wrote to Matilda Good a week come Tuesday and settled every-thing with 'er—everything. It's settled.'

" ' What d'you mean ? ' asked Ernest.

" ' Why, that 'ouse of hers in Pimlico. She's been wanting trusty 'elp for a long time, what with her varicose veins up and down stairs and one thing 'nother, and directly she got my letter about your poor dear father she wrote orf to me. " You need never want a 'ome," she says, "so long as I got a lodger. You and Prue are welcome," she says, " welcome 'elp, and the boy can easy find work up 'ere—much easier than 'e can in Cliffstone." All the time you was planning lodging-'ouses and things for me I was trying to tell you——'

" ' You mean it's settled ? '

" ' It's settled.'

" ' And what you going to do with your bits of furniture 'ere ? '

" ' Sell some and take some. . . .'

" ' It's feasible,' said Ernest after reflection.

" And so we needn't reely 'ave 'ad that—bit of a' argument ? ' said Ernest after a pause. ' Not me and uncle ? '

" Not on *my* account you needn't,' said my mother.

" ' Well—we *'ad* it,' said Ernest after another pause and without any visible signs of regret."

§ 3

" If my dream was a dream," said Sarnac, " it was a most circumstantial dream. I could tell you a hundred details of our journey to London and how we disposed of the poor belongings that had furnished our home in Cherry Gardens. Every detail would expose some odd and illuminating difference between the ideas of those ancient days and our own ideas. Brother Ernest was helpful, masterful and irascible. He got a week's holiday from his employer to help mother to settle up things, and among other things that were settled up I believe my mother persuaded him and my uncle to ' shake hands,' but I do not know the particulars of that great scene, I did not see it, it was merely mentioned in my hearing during the train journey to London. I would like to tell you also of the man who came round to buy most of our furniture, including that red-and-black sofa I described to you, and how he and my brother had a loud and heated argument about some damage to one of its legs, and how Mr. Crosby produced a bill, that my mother understood he had forgiven us on account of Fanny long ago. There was also some point about something called ' tenant's fixtures ' that led my brother and the landlord, Mr. Bulstrode, to the verge of violence. And Mr. Bulstrode, the landlord, brought accusations of damage done to the fabric of his house that were false, and he made extravagant claims for compensation based thereon and had to be rebutted with warmth. There was also trouble over carting a parcel of our goods to the railway-station, and when we got to the terminus of Victoria in London it was necessary, I gathered, that Ernest should offer to fight a railway-porter—you have read of railway-porters ?—before we received proper attention.

" But I cannot tell you all these curious and typical incidents now because at that rate I should never finish my story before our holidays are over. I must go on now to tell you of this London, this great city, the greatest city it was in the world in those days, to which we had transferred our fates. All the rest of my story, except for nearly two years and a half I spent in the training-camp and in France and Germany during the First World War, is set in the scenery of London. You know already what a vast congestion of human beings London was ; you know that within a radius of fifteen miles a population of seven and a half million people were gathered together, people born out of due time into a world unready for them and born mostly through the sheer ignorance of their procreators, gathered together into an area of not very attractive clay country by an urgent need to earn a living, and you know the terrible fate that at last overwhelmed this sinfully crowded accumulation ; you have read of west-end and slums, and you have seen the cinema-pictures of those days showing crowded streets, crowds gaping at this queer ceremony or that, a vast traffic of clumsy automobiles and distressed horses in narrow unsuitable streets, and I suppose your general impression is a nightmare of multitudes, a suffocating realisation of jostling discomfort and uncleanness and of an unendurable strain on eye and ear and attention.

The history we learn in our childhood enforces that lesson.

" But though the facts are just as we are taught they were, I do not recall anything like the distress at London you would suppose me to have felt, and I do remember vividly the sense of adventure, the intellectual excitement and the discovery of beauty I experienced in going there. You must remember that in this strange dream of mine I had forgotten all our present standards ; I accepted squalor and confusion as being in the nature of things, and the aspects of this city's greatness, the wonder of this limitless place and a certain changing and evanescent beauty, rise out of the sea of struggle and limitation as forgetfully as a silver birch rises out of the swamp that bears it.

" The part of London in which we took up our abode was called Pimlico. It bordered upon the river, and once there had been a wharf there to which ships came across the Atlantic from America. This word Pimlico had come with other trade in these ships ; in my time it was the last word left alive of the language of the Algonquin Red Indians, who had otherwise altogether vanished from the earth. The Pimlico wharf had gone, the American trade was forgotten, and Pimlico was now a great wilderness of streets of dingy grey houses in which people lived and let lodgings. These houses had never been designed for the occupation of lodgers ; they were faced with a lime-plaster called stucco which made a sort of pretence of being stone ; each one had a sunken underground floor originally intended for servants, a door with a portico and several floors above which were reached by a staircase. Beside each portico was a railed pit that admitted light to the front underground room. As you walked along these Pimlico streets these porticos receded in long perspectives and each portico of that endless series represented ten or a dozen misdirected, incomplete and rather unclean inhabitants, infected mentally and morally. Over the grey and dingy architecture rested a mist or a fog, rarely was there a precious outbreak of sunlight ; here and there down the vista a grocer's boy or a greengrocer's boy or a fish-hawker would be handing in food over the railings to the subterranean members of a household, or a cat (there was a multitude of cats) would be peeping out of the railings alert for the danger of a passing dog. There would be a few pedestrians, a passing cab or so, and perhaps in the morning a dust cart collecting refuse-filth—set out for the winds to play with in boxes and tin receptacles at the pavement edge —or a man in a uniform cleaning the streets with a hose. It seems to you that it must have been the most depressing of spectacles. It wasn't, though I doubt if I can make clear to you that it wasn't. I know I went about Pimlico thinking it rather a fine place and endlessly interesting. I assure you that in the early morning and by my poor standards it had a sort of grey spaciousness and dignity. But afterwards I found the thing far better done, that London architectural aquatint, in Belgravia and round about Regent's Park.

" I must admit that I tended to drift out of those roads and squares of lodging-houses either into the streets where there were shops and street-cars or southward to the Embankment along the Thames. It was the shops and glares that drew me at first as the lights began to fail and, strange as it may seem to you, my memories of such times are rich with beauty. We feeble children of that swarming age had I think an almost morbid gregariousness ; we found a subtle pleasure and reassurance in crowds and a real disagreeableness in being alone ; and my impressions of London's strange interest and charm are I confess very often crowded impressions of a kind this world no longer produces, or impressions to which a crowded foreground or background was essential. But they were beautiful.

" For example there was a great railway-station, a terminus, within perhaps half a mile of us. There was a great disorderly yard in front of the station in which hackney automobiles and omnibuses assembled and departed and arrived. In the late twilight of an autumn day this yard was a mass of shifting black shadows and gleams and lamps, across which streamed an incessant succession of bobbing black heads, people on foot hurrying to catch the trains : as they flitted by the lights one saw their faces gleam and vanish again. Above this foreground rose the huge brown-grey shapes of the station-buildings and the façade of a big hotel, reflecting the flares below and pierced here and there by a lit window ; then very sharply came the sky-line and a sky still blue and luminous, tranquil and aloof. And the innumerable sounds of people and vehicles wove into a deep wonderful and continually varying drone. Even to my boyish mind there was an irrational conviction of unity and purpose in this spectacle.

" The streets where there were shops were also very wonderful and lovely to me directly the too-lucid and expository daylight began to fade. The variously coloured lights in the shop-windows which displayed a great diversity of goods for sale splashed the most extraordinary reflections upon the pavements and roadway, and these were particularly gem-like if there had been rain or a mist to wet the reflecting surfaces. One of these streets—it was called Lupus Street, though why it had the name of an abominable skin-disease that has long since vanished from the earth I cannot imagine —was close to our new home and I still remember it as full of romantic effectiveness. By daylight it was an exceedingly sordid street, and late at night empty and echoing, but in the magic hours of London it was a bed of black and luminous flowers, the abounding people became black imps and through it wallowed the great shining omnibuses, the ships of the street, filled with light and reflecting lights.

" There were endless beauties along the river bank. The river was a tidal one held in control by a stone embankment, and the roadway along the embankment was planted at the footway edge with plane-trees and lit by large electric lights on tall standards. These planes were among the few trees that could flourish in the murky London air, but they were unsuitable trees to have in a crowded city because they gave off minute specules that irritated people's throats. That however I did not know ; what I did know was that the shadows of the leaves on the pavements thrown by the electric glares made the most beautiful patternings I had ever seen. I would walk along on a warm night rejoicing in them, more particularly if now and then a light breeze set them dancing and quivering.

" One could walk from Pimlico along this Thames Embankment for some miles towards the east. One passed little black jetties with dangling oil-lamps ; there was a traffic of barges and steamers on the river altogether mysterious and romantic to me ; the frontages of the houses varied incessantly, and ever and again were cleft by crowded roadways that brought a shining and twinkling traffic up to the bridges. Across the river was a coming and going of trains along a railway-viaduct ; it contributed a restless *motif* of clanks and concussion to the general drone of London, and the engines sent puffs of firelit steam and sudden furnace-glows into the night. One came along this embankment to the great buildings at Westminster, by daylight a pile of imitation Gothic dominated by a tall clock-tower with an illuminated dial, a pile which assumed a blue dignity with the twilight and became a noble portent standing at attention, a forest of spears, in the night. This was the Parliament House, and in its chambers a formal King, an ignoble nobility and a fraudulently elected gathering of lawyers, financiers, and adventurers took upon themselves, amidst the general mental obscurity of those days, a semblance of wisdom and empire. As one went on beyond Westminster along the Embankment came great grey-brown palaces and houses set behind green gardens, a railway-bridge and then two huge hotels, standing high and far back, bulging with lit windows ; there was some sort of pit or waste beneath them, I forget what, very black, so that at once they loomed over one and seemed magically remote. There was an Egyptian obelisk here, for all the European capitals of my time, being as honest as magpies and as original as monkeys, had adorned themselves with obelisks stolen from Egypt. And farther along was the best and noblest building in London, St. Paul's Cathedral ; it was invisible by night, but it was exceedingly serene and beautiful on a clear, blue, windy day. And some of the bridges were very lovely with gracious arches of smutty grey stone, though some were so clumsy that only night could redeem them.

" As I talk I remember," said Sarnac. " Before employment robbed me of my days I pushed my boyish explorations far and wide, wandering all day and often going without any meal, or, if I was in pocket, getting a bun and a glass of milk in some small shop for a couple of pennies. The shop-windows of London were an unending marvel to me ; and they would be to you too if you could remember them as I do ; there must have been hundreds of miles of them, possibly thousands of miles. In the poorer parts they were chiefly food-shops and cheap clothing-shops and the like, and one could exhaust their interest, but there were thoroughfares like Regent Street and Piccadilly and narrow Bond Street and Oxford Street crammed with all the furnishings of the life of the lucky minority, the people who could spend freely. You will find it difficult to imagine how important a matter the mere buying of things was in the lives of those people. In their houses there was a vast congestion of objects neither ornamental nor useful ; *purchases* in fact ; and the women spent large portions of every week-day in buying things, clothes, table-litter, floor-litter, wall-litter. They had no work ; they were too ignorant to be interested in any real thing ; they had nothing else to do. That was the world's reward, the substance of success—purchases. Through them you realised your well-being. As a shabby half-grown boy I pushed my way among these spenders, crowds of women dressed, wrapped up rather, in layer after layer of purchases, scented, painted. Most of them were painted to suggest a health-flushed face, the nose powdered a leprous white.

" There is one thing to be said for the old fashion of abundant clothing ; in that crowded jostling world it saved people from actually touching each other.

" I would push through these streets eastward to less prosperous crowds in Oxford Street and to a different multitude in Holborn. As you went eastward the influence of women diminished and that of young men increased. Cheapside gave you all the material for building up a twentieth-century young man from the nude. In the shop-windows he was disarticulated and priced : hat five and sixpence, trousers eighteen shillings, tie one and six ; cigarettes tenpence an ounce ; newspaper a halfpenny, cheap novel sevenpence ; on the pavement outside there he was put together and complete and the cigarette burning, under the impression that he was a unique immortal creature and that the ideas in his head were altogether his own. And beyond Cheapside there was Clerkenwell with curious little shops that sold scarcely anything but old keys or the parts of broken-up watches or the like detached objects. Then there were great food-markets at Leadenhall Street and Smithfield and Covent Garden, incredible accumulations of raw stuff. At Covent Garden they sold fruits and flowers that we should think poor and undeveloped, but which every one in those days regarded as beautiful and delicious. And in Caledonian Market were innumerable barrows where people actually bought and took away every sort of broken and second-hand rubbish, broken ornaments, decaying books with torn pages, second-hand clothing—a wonderland of litter for any boy with curiosity in his blood. . . .

" But I could go on talking endlessly about this old London of mine and you want me to get on with my story. I have tried to give you something of its endless, incessant, multi-tudinous glittering quality and the way in which it yielded a thousand strange and lovely effects to its changing lights and atmosphere. I found even its fogs, those dreaded fogs of which the books tell, romantic. But then I was a boy at the adventurous age. The fog was often very thick in Pimlico. It was normally a soft creamy obscurity that turned even lights close at hand into luminous blurs. People came out of nothingness within six yards of you, were riddles and silhouettes before they became real. One could go out and lose oneself within ten minutes of home and perhaps pick up with a distressed automobile driver and walk by his headlights, signalling to him where the pavement ended. That was one sort of fog, the dry fog. But there were many sorts. There was a sort of yellow darkness, like blackened bronze, that hovered about you and did not embrace you and left a clear nearer world of deep browns and blacks. And there was an unclean wet mist that presently turned to drizzle and made every surface a mirror."

" And there was daylight," said Willow, " sometimes surely there was daylight."

" Yes," Sarnac reflected ; " there was daylight. At times. And sometimes there was quite a kindly and redeeming sunshine in London. In the spring, in early summer or in October. It did not blaze, but it filled the air with a mild warmth, and turned the surfaces it lit not indeed to gold but to amber and topaz. And there were even hot days in London with skies of deep blue above, but they were rare. And sometimes there was daylight without the sun. . . .

" Yes," said Sarnac and paused. " At times there was a daylight that stripped London bare, showed its grime, showed its real ineffectiveness, showed the pitiful poverty of intention in its buildings, showed the many-coloured billstickers' hoardings for the crude and leprous things they were, brought out the shabbiness of unhealthy bodies and misfitting garments. . . .

" These were terrible, veracious, unhappy days. When London no longer fascinated but wearied and offended, when even to an uninstructed boy there came some intimation of the long distressful journey that our race had still to travel before it attained even to such peace and health and wisdom as it has to-day."

§ 4

Sarnac stopped short in his talk and rose with something between a laugh and a sigh. He stood facing westward and Sunray stood beside him.

"This story will go on for ever if I digress like this. See ! the sun will be behind that ridge in another ten minutes. I cannot finish this evening, because most of the story part still remains to be told."

"There are roast fowls with sweet corn and chestnuts," said Firefly. "Trout and various fruits."

"And some of that golden wine ? " said Radiant.

"Some of that golden wine."

Sunray, who had been very still and intent, awoke. "Sarnac, dear," she said, slipping her arm through his. "What became of Uncle John Julip ? "

Sarnac reflected. "I forget," he said.

"Aunt Adelaide Julip died ? " asked Willow.

"She died quite soon after we left Cherry Gardens. My uncle wrote, I remember, and I remember my mother reading the letter at breakfast like a proclamation and saying, ' Seems if she was reely ill after all.' If she had not been ill then surely she had carried malingering to the last extremity. But I forget any particulars about my uncle's departure from this world. He probably outlived my mother, and after her death the news of his end might easily have escaped me."

"You have had the most wonderful dream in the world, Sarnac," said Starlight, "and I want to hear the whole story and not interrupt, but I am sorry not to hear more of your Uncle John Julip."

"He was such a perfect little horror," said Firefly. . . .

Until the knife-edge of the hills cut into the molten globe of the sun, the holiday-makers lingered watching the shadows in their last rush up to the mountain crests, and then, still talking of this particular and that in Sarnac's story, the six made their way down to the guest-house and supper.

"Sarnac was shot," said Radiant. "He hasn't even begun to get shot yet. There is no end of story still to come."

"Sarnac," asked Firefly, "you weren't killed in the Great War, were you ? Suddenly ? In some inconsequent sort of way ? "

"Not a bit of it," said Sarnac. "I am really beginning to be shot in this story though Radiant does not perceive it. But I must tell my story in my own fashion."

At supper what was going on was explained to the master of the guest-house. Like so many of these guest-housekeepers he was a jolly, convivial, simple soul, and he was amused and curious at Sarnac's alleged experience. He laughed at the impatience of the others ; he said they were like childre n in a Children's Garden, agog for their go-to-bed fairy-tale. After they had had coffee they went out for a time to see the moonlight mingle with the ruddy afterglow above the peaks ; and then the guest-master led the way in, made up a blazing pinewood fire and threw cushions before it, set out an after-dinner wine, put out the lights and prepared for a good night's story-telling.

Sarnac remained thoughtful—looking into the flames until Sunray set him off again by whispering : " Pimlico ? "

§ 5

" I will tell you as briefly as I can of the household in Pimlico where we joined forces with my mother's old friend, Matilda Good," said Sarnac ; " but I confess it is hard to be reasonably brief when one's mind is fuller of curious details than this fire is of sparks."

" That's excellent ! " said the master of the guest-house. " That's a perfect story-teller's touch ! " and looked brightly for Sarnac to continue.

" But we are all beginning to believe that he has *been there*," whispered Radiant, laying a restraining hand on the guest-master's knee. " And he "—Radiant spoke behind his hand— " he believes it altogether."

" Not *really* ? " whispered the guest-master. He seemed desirous of asking difficult questions and then subsided into an attention that was at first a little constrained and presently quite involuntary.

" These houses in Pimlico were part of an enormous pro-liferation of houses that occurred between a hundred years and seventy years before the Great War. There was a great amount of unintelligent building enterprise in those decades in London, and all the building, as I have already told you, I think, was done on the supposition that there was an endless supply of fairly rich families capable of occupying a big house and employing three or four domestic servants. There were underground kitchens and servants' rooms, there was a dining-room and master's study at the ground level, there was a ' drawing-room floor ' above, two rooms convertible into one by a device known as folding doors, and above this were bed-rooms on a scale of diminishing importance until one came to attics without fireplaces in which the servants were to sleep. In large areas and particularly in Pimlico, these fairly rich families of the builder's imagination, with servile domestics all complete, never appeared to claim the homes prepared for them, and from the first, poorer people, for whom, of course, no one had troubled to plan houses, adapted these porticoed plaster mansions to their own narrower needs. My mother's friend, Matilda Good, was a quite typical Pimlico householder. She had been the trusted servant of a rich old lady in Cliffstone who had died and left her two or three hundred pounds of money——"

The master of the guest-house was endlessly perplexed and made an interrogative noise.

"Private property," said Radiant very rapidly. "Power of bequest. Two thousand years ago. Made a Will, you know. Go on, Sarnac."

"With that and her savings," said Sarnac, "she was able to become tenant of one of these Pimlico houses and to furnish it with a sort of shabby gentility. She lived herself in the basement below and in the attic above, and all the rest of the house she had hoped to let in pieces, floor by floor or room by room to rich or at least prosperous old ladies, and to busy herself in tending them and supplying their needs and extracting a profit and living out of them, running up and down her staircase as an ant runs up and down a rose-stem tending its aphides. But old ladies of any prosperity did not come into Pimlico. It was low and foggy, the children of its poorer streets were rough and disrespectful, and it was close to the river-embankment over which rich useless old ladies naturally expected to be thrown. So Matilda Good had to console herself with less succulent and manageable lodgers.

"I remember Matilda Good giving us an account of those she had as we sat in her front down-stairs room having a kind of tea supper on the evening of our arrival. Ernest had declined refreshment and departed, his task as travel conductor done, but there were my mother and Prue and myself, all in dingy black and all a little stiff and strange, thawing slowly to tea and hot buttered toast with a poached egg each, our mouths very full and our eyes and ears very attentive to Matilda Good.

"She appeared quite a grand lady to me that night. She was much larger than any lady I had hitherto been accustomed to ; she had a breadth and variety of contour like scenery rather than a human being ; the thought of her veins being varicose, indeed of all her anatomy being varicose and fantastic, seemed a right and proper one. She was dressed in black with outbreaks of soiled lace, a large gold-rimmed brooch fastened her dress at the neck and she had a gold chain about her, and on her head was what was called a 'cap,' an affair like the lower shell of an oyster inverted, made of layers of dingy lace and adorned with a black velvet bow and a gold buckle. Her face had the same landscape unanatomical quality, as her body ; she had a considerable moustache, an overhung slightly mischievous mouth and two different large dark-grey eyes with a slightly vertical cast in them and very marked eyelashes. She sat sideways. One eye looked at you rather sidelong, the other seemed to watch something over your head. She spoke in a whisper which passed very easily into wheezy, not unkindly laughter.

"'You'll get no end of exercise on these stairs, my dear,'

she said to sister Prue, ' no end of exercise. There's times when I'm going up to bed when I start counting 'em, just to make sure that they aren't taking in lodgers like the rest of us. There's no doubt this 'ouse will strengthen your legs, my dear. Mustn't get 'em too big and strong for the rest of you. But you can easy manage that by carrying something, carrying something every time you go up or down. Ugh—ugh. That'll equalise you. There's always something to carry, boots it is, hot water it is, a scuttle of coals or a parcel.'

" ' I expect it's a busy 'ouse,' said my mother, eating her buttered toast like a lady.

" ' It's a toilsome 'ouse,' said Matilda Good. ' I don't want to deceive you, Martha ; it's a toilsome 'ouse.

" ' But it's a 'ouse that keeps full,' said Matilda Good, challenging me with one eye and ignoring me with the other. ' Full I am now, and full I've been since last Michaelmas, full right up ; two permanents I've 'ad three years on end and those my best floors. I've something to be thankful for, all things considered, and now I got 'elp of a sort that won't slide downstairs on a tea-tray or lick the ground floor's sugar lump by lump, knowing the lumps was counted and never thinking that wetness tells, the slut ! we'll get on swimmingly. The sluts I've 'ad, Martha ! These board-schools turn them out a 'orror to God and a danger to men. I can't tell you. It's a comfort to set eyes on any girl as I can see at once 'as been brought up to take a pride in 'erself. 'Ave a little of that watercress with your toast, my dear. It'll do that complexion of yours good.'

" My sister Prue reddened and took some watercress.

" ' The drawing-room floor,' said Matilda Good, ' is a lady. It isn't often you keep a lady three years, what with the things they know and the things they fancy they know, but I've kept her. She's a real lady—born. Bumpus 'er name is—Miss Beatrice Bumpus. I don't know whether you'll like her, Martha, when you set eyes on her, but she's got to be studied. She's a particular sort of Warwickshire Bumpus that hunts. She'll ask you if you want the vote, Martha, directly she sees you're a fresh face. It isn't *a* vote or *any* old vote she asks you to want, it's *the* vote.' The whispering voice grew thicker and richer and a persuasive smile spread far and wide over the face. ' If it's all the same to you, Martha, you better say you do.'

" My mother was sipping her fourth cup of tea. ' I don't know,' she said, ' as I altogether 'old with this vote.'

" Matilda Good's great red hands which had been lying apparently detached in her lap, produced short arms and lace cuffs and waved about in the air, waving my mother's objections away. ' 'Old with it on the drawing-room floor,' wheezed Matilda. ' 'Old with it on the drawing-room floor.'

" ' But if she arsts questions ? '

" ' She won't wait to have them answered. It won't be

difficult, Martha. I wouldn't put you into a position of difficulty,
not if I could 'elp it. You just got to 'old with 'er quietly and
she'll do the rest.'

"'Mother,' said Prue, who was still too overawed by Matilda
Good to address her directly. 'Mother, what *is* this here vote?'

"'Vote for Parliament, my dear,' said Matilda Good.

"'When shall we get it?' asked my mother.

"'You won't get it,' said Matilda Good.

"'But if we did, what should we have to do with it, like?'

"'*Nothing*,' said Matilda Good with bottomless contempt.
'All the same it's a great movement, Martha, and don't you
forget it. And Miss Bumpus she works night and day, Martha,
gets 'it about by policemen, and once she was actually in prison
a night, getting you and me the vote.'

"'Well, it shows a kind nature,' said my mother.

"'My ground floor's a gentleman. The worst of 'im is the
books there are to dust, books *and* books. Not that 'e ever
reads 'em much. . . . Very likely you'll 'ear 'im soon playing
his pianola. You can 'ear it down 'ere almost as if you were
inside it. Mr. Plaice, 'e's an Oxford gentleman and he works
at a firm of publishers, Burrows and Graves they're called ; a
very 'igh-class firm I'm told—don't go in for advertisements or
anything vulgar. He's got photographs of Greek and Latin
statues and ruins round above his bookshelves and shields
with College arms. Naked some of the statues are, but for
all that none of them are anything but quite nice and
genteel, *quite* genteel. You can see at once he's a University
gentleman. And photographs of Switzerland he's got. He goes
up mountains in Switzerland and speaks the language. He's
a smoker ; sits with a pipe writing or reading evening after
evening and marking things with his pencil. Manuscripts he
reads and proofs. Pipes he has with a pipe for every day in the
week, and a smoker's outfit all made with bee-utiful stone,
serpentine they call it, sort of blood-shot green it is ; tobacco-
jar and a pot for feathers to clean his pipes, little places for
each day's pipe, everything all stone ; it's a regular monument.
And when you're dusting it—remember if you drop this here
serpentine it breaks like earthenware. Most of the maids I've
'ad 'ave 'ad a chip at that tobacco-graveyard of 'is. And mind
you——' Matilda Good leaned forward and held out her hand
to arrest any wandering of my mother's attention. ''E don't
'old with Votes for Women !* See?'

"'One's got to be careful,' said my mother.

"'One has. He's got one or two little whims, has Mr. Plaice,
but if you mind about them he don't give you much trouble.
One of 'is whims is to pretend to 'ave a bath every morning.
Every morning he 'as a shallow tin bath put out in his room
and a can of cold water and a sponge, and every morning he
pretends to splash about in it something fearful and makes a
noise like a grampus singing a hymn—calls it 'is Tub, he does ;

though it's a lot more like a canary's saucer. Says he must have it as cold as possible even if there's ice on it. Well——'

" Matilda Good performed a sort of landslide over the arm of her chair, her head nodded, and the whisper became more confidential. ' He *doesn't*,' wheezed Matilda Good.

" ' You mean he doesn't get into the bath ? '

" ' Not-tit,' said Matilda Good. ' You can see when he's really been in by his wet footmarks on the floor. Not 'arf the time does he have that bath. Per'aps 'e used to have it when he was a young man at College. I wonder. But it's always got to be put out and the can always got to be lugged up and poured out and poured away again, and nobody's ever to ask if he'd like the chill taken off. Not the sort of thing you ask a University gentleman. No. All the same,' said Matilda Good, ' all the same I've caught 'im pouring his hand and shaving water into that water-splash in the winter, after he'd been going dirty for a week. But have a can of warm ? Have the chill taken off his water ? Not Tim ! It's curious, ain't it ? But that's one of his whims.

" ' I sometimes think,' said Matilda Good still more extra-vagantly confidential, ' that perhaps he climbs all those mountains in Switzerland same way as he takes his bath. . . .'

" She rolled back large portions of her person into a less symmetrical attitude. ' This Mr. Plaice you must know,' she said, ' has a voice between a clergyman's and a schoolmaster's, sort of hard and superior, and when you say anything to him he's apt to make a noise, " Arrr . . . Arrr . . . Arrr," a sort of slow neighing it is, as though he doesn't think much of you but doesn't want to blame you for that and anyhow can't attend to you properly. You mustn't let it annoy you. It's the way he's been brought up. And he has a habit of using long condescending sort of words to you. And calling you insulting names. He'll think nothing of calling you " My worthy Abigail," or " Come in, my rosy-fingered Aurora," when you knock in the morning. Just as though a girl could keep 'er 'ands pink and clean with all these fires to light ! He'll ask of me, " How's the Good Matilda ? How's honest Matilda Good to-day ? "—sort of fiddling about with your name. Of course he don't mean to be rude ; it's just his idea of being pleasant and humorous, and making you feel you're being made fun of in a gentle sort of way instead of being terrible like he might be, and—seeing he's good pay and very little trouble, Martha—it's no use getting offended with him. All the same I can't help thinking at times of how he'd get on if I answered 'im back, and which of us two would be left alive if we had a fair match of it, making fun of one another. The things—the things I could say ! But that,' said Matilda Good, breaking into an ingratiating smile of extraordinary extent and rolling one eye at me—' is just a dream. It isn't the sort of dream to indulge in in this 'ouse. I've rehearsed it a bit, I admit. Says 'e—but never mind

what 'e says or what I says back to him. . . . Ugh ! Ugh ! . . .
He's good pay and regular, my dear ; he ain't likely to lose his
job and he ain't likely ever to get another, and in this Vale
anyhow we got to put up with 'is whims. And——'

" Matilda Good spoke as one who confesses to a weakness.
' His pianola cheers me up at times. I will say that for 'im.
It's almost the only noise one hears from him. Except when
he takes off his boots.

" ' Well, up above my drawing-room at present is my second
floor front, the Reverend Moggeridge and his good lady. They
been here five months now and they seem like taking root.'

" ' Not a clergyman ? ' said my mother respectfully.

" ' A very poor clergyman,' said Matilda, ' but a clergyman.
So much to our credit, Martha. Oh ! but they're poor old things !
Poor old things ! Been curate or something all his life in some
out-of-the-world place. And lost his job. Somebody had the
heart to turn 'em out. Or something happened. I wonder.
'E's a funny old man. . . .

" ' He dodders off nearly every Saturday on supply, they call
it, to take service somewhere over the Sunday and like as not
he comes back with his cold worse than ever, sniffing. It's
cruel how they treat these poor old parsons on supply, fetch
'em from the station in open traps they do, in the worst of
weather, and often the rectory teetotal without a drop of anything for a cold. Christianity ! I suppose it's *got* to be. . . .
The two of them just potter about upstairs and make shift to
get their meals, such as they are, over the bedroom-fire. She
even does a bit of her own washing. Dragging about. Poor old
things ! Old and forgotten and left about. But they're very
little trouble and there it is. And as I say—anyhow—he's a
clergyman. And in the other room at the back there's a German
lady who teaches—well, anything she can persuade any one to
be taught. She hasn't been here more than a month, and I
don't know whether I like her or not, but she seems straight
enough and she keeps herself pretty much to herself and when
one has a room to let one can't always pick and choose.

" ' And that's the lot, my dear. To-morrow we'll have to
begin. You'll go up presently and settle into your two rooms
at the top. There's a little one for Mortimer and a rather bigger
one for you and Prue. There's pegs and curtains for your things.
I'm next door to you. I'll give you my little old alarum clock
and show you all about it and to-morrow at seven sharp down
we come, you and me and Prue. My Lord, I suppose, has the
privilege of his sex and doesn't come down until half-past !
Oh ! I'm a suffragette, Martha—same as Miss Bumpus. First
thing is this fire, and unless we rake the ashes well forward the
boiler won't heat. Then there's fires and boots, dust the front
rooms and breakfasts : Mr. Plaice at eight sharp and mind it is,
and Miss Bumpus at eight-thirty, and get away with Mr.
Plaice if you can first because of the shortness of tablespoons.

Five I got altogether and before I lost my last third floor back
I 'ad seven. 'E was a nice lot ; 'e was. The old people get their
own breakfast when they want it, and Frau Buchholz has a
tray, just bread and butter and tea, whenever we can manage
it after the drawing-room's been seen to. That's the programme,
Martha.'

" ' I'll do my best, 'Tilda,' said my mother. ' *As* you know.'

" ' Hullo ! ' said Matilda indicating the ceiling, ' the concert's
going to begin. That bump's him letting down the pianola-
pedals.'

" And then suddenly through the ceiling into our subterranean tea-party came a rush of clavier notes—I can't
describe it.

" One of the few really good things of that age was the music.
Mankind perfected some things very early ; I suppose precious
stonework and goldwork have never got very much beyond the
levels it reached under the Seventeenth Dynasty in Egypt, ages
ago, and marble statuary came to a climax at Athens before
the conquests of Alexander. I doubt if there has ever come
very much sweeter music into the world than the tuneful stuff
we had away back there in the Age of Confusion. This music
Mr. Plaice was giving us was some bits of Schumann's *Carnaval*
music ; we hear it still played on the clavier ; and it was almost
the first good music I ever heard. There had been brass bands
on Cliffstone promenade, of course, but they simply made a
glad row. I don't know if you understand what a pianola was.
It was an instrument for playing the clavier with hammers
directed by means of perforated rolls, for the use of those who
lacked the intelligence and dexterity to read music and play
the clavier with their hands. Because every one was frightfully
unhandy in those days. It thumped a little and struck undiscriminating chords, but Mr. Plaice managed it fairly well and
the result came, filtered through the ceiling—As we used to say
in those days, it might have been worse.

" At the thought of that music I recall—and whenever I
hear Schumann as long as I live I shall recall—the picture of
that underground room, the little fireplace with the kettle on a
hob, the kettle-holder and the toasting-fork beside the fireplace
jamb, the steel fender, the ashes, the small blotched looking-
glass over the mantel, the little china figures of dogs in front
of the glass, the gaslight in a frosted glass globe hanging from
the ceiling and lighting the tea-things on the table. (Yes, the
house was lit by coal-gas ; electric light was only just coming
in. . . . My dear Firefly ! can I possibly stop my story to tell
you what coal-gas was ? A good girl would have learned that
long ago.)

" There sat Matilda Good reduced to a sort of imbecile
ecstasy by these butterflies of melody. She nodded her cap, she
rolled her head and smiled ; she made appreciative rhythmic
gestures with her hands ; one eye would meet you in a joyous

search for sympathy while the other contemplated the dingy wall-paper beyond. I too was deeply stirred. But my mother and sister Prue sat in their black with an expression of forced devotion, looking very refined and correct, exactly as they had sat and listened to my father's funeral service five days before.

" ' Sputiful,' whispered my mother, like making a response in church, when the first piece came to an end. . .

" I went to sleep that night in my little attic with fragments of Schumann, Bach, and Beethoven chasing elusively about my brain. I perceived that a new phase of life had come to me. . . .

" Jewels," said Sarnac. " Some sculpture, music—just a few lovely beginnings there were already of what man could do with life. Such things I see now were the seeds of the New World of promise already there in the dark matrix of the Old."

§ 6

" Next morning revealed a new Matilda Good, active and urgent, in a loose and rather unclean mauve cotton wrapper and her head wrapped up in a sort of turban of figured silk. This costume she wore most of the day except that she did her hair and put on a cotton lace cap in the afternoon. (The black dress and the real lace cap and the brooch, I was to learn, were for Sundays and for week-day evenings of distinction.) My mother and Prue were arrayed in rough aprons which Matilda had very thoughtfully bought for them. There was a great bustle in the basement of the house, and Prue a little before eight went up with Matilda to learn how to set out breakfast for Mr. Plaice. I made his acquaintance later in the day when I took up the late edition of *The Evening Standard* to him. I found him a stooping, tall gentleman with a cadaverous face that was mostly profile, and he made great play with my Christian name.

" ' Mortimer,' he said and neighed his neigh. ' Well—it might have been Norfolk-Howard.'

" There was an obscure allusion in that : for once upon a time, ran the popular legend, a certain Mr. Bugg seeking a less entomological name had changed his to Norfolk-Howard, which was in those days a very aristocratic one. . . . Whereupon vulgar people had equalised matters by calling the offensive bed-bugs that abounded in London, ' Norfolk-Howards.'

" Before many weeks were past it became evident that Matilda Good had made an excellent bargain in her annexation of our family. She had secured my mother's services for nothing, and it was manifest that my mother was a born lodging-house woman. She behaved like a partner in the concern, and the only money Matilda ever gave her was to pay her expenses upon some specific errand or to buy some specific thing. Prue, however, with unexpected firmness, insisted upon wages, and enforced her claim by going out and nearly getting employment at a dressmaker's. In a little while Matilda became of the lodgers an unseen power for righteousness in the basement and all the staircase work was left to my mother and Prue. Often Matilda did not go up above the ground level once all day until, as she said, she ' toddled up to bed.'

" Matilda made some ingenuous attempts to utilise me also in the service of the household : I was exhorted to carry up scuttles of coal, clean boots and knives and make myself useful generally. She even put it to me one day whether I wouldn't like a nice suit with buttons—in those days they still used to put small serving boys in tight suits of green or brown cloth, with rows of gilt buttons as close together as possible over their little chests and stomachs. But the very thought of it sent my mind to Chessing Hanger, where I had conceived an intense hatred and dread of ' service ' and ' livery,' and determined me to find some other employment before Matilda Good's large and insidious will enveloped and overcame me. And oddly enough a talk I had with Miss Beatrice Bumpus helped me greatly in my determination.

" Miss Bumpus was a slender young woman of about five-and-twenty I suppose. She had short brown hair, brushed back rather prettily from a broad forehead and she had freckles on her nose and quick red-brown eyes. She generally wore a plaid tweed costume rather short in the skirt and with a coat cut like a man's ; she wore green stockings and brown shoes—I had never seen green stockings before—and she would stand on her hearthrug in exactly the attitude Mr. Plaice adopted on his hearthrug downstairs. Or she would be sitting at a writing-desk against the window, smoking cigarettes. She asked me what sort of man I intended to be, and I said with the sort of modesty I had been taught to assume as becoming my station, that I hadn't thought yet.

" To which Miss Bumpus answered, ' Liar.'

" That was the sort of remark that either kills or cures. I said : ' Well, Miss, I want to get educated and I don't know how to do it. And I don't know what I ought to do.'

" Miss Bumpus held me with a gesture while she showed how nicely she could send out smoke through her nose. Then she said : ' Avoid Blind Alley Occupations.'

" ' Yes, Miss.'

" ' But you don't know what Blind Alley Occupations are ? '

" ' No, Miss.'

" ' Occupations that earn a boy wages and lead nowhere. One of the endless pitfalls of this silly man-made pseudo-civilisation. Never do anything that doesn't lead somewhere. Aim high. I must think your case out, Mr. Harry Mortimer. I might be able to help you. . . .'

" This was the opening of quite a number of conversations between myself and Miss Bumpus. She was a very stimulating influence in my adolescence. She pointed out that although it was now late in the year there were many evening classes of various sorts that I might attend with profit. She told me of all sorts of prominent and successful people who had begun their careers from beginnings as humble and hopeless as mine. She said I was ' unhampered ' by my sex. She asked me if I were interested in the suffrage movement, and gave me tickets for two meetings at which I heard her speak, and she spoke, I thought, very well. She answered some interrupters with extreme effectiveness, and I cheered myself hoarse for her. Something about her light and gallant attitude to life reminded me of Fanny. I said so one day, and found myself, before I knew it, telling her reluctantly and shamefully the story of our family disgrace. Miss Bumpus was much interested.

" ' She wasn't like your sister Prue ? '

" ' No, Miss.'

" ' Prettier ? '

" ' A lot prettier. Of course—you could hardly call Prue *pretty*, Miss.'

" ' I hope she's got on all right,' said Miss Bumpus. ' I don't blame her a bit. But I hope she got the best of it.'

" ' I'd give anything, Miss, to hear Fanny was all right. . . . I did care for Fanny, Miss. . . . I'd give anything almost to see Fanny again. . . . You won't tell my mother, Miss, I told you anything about Fanny ? It kind of slipped out like.'

" ' Mortimer,' said Miss Bumpus, ' you're a sticker. I wish I had a little brother like you. There ! I won't breathe a word.'

" I felt we had sealed a glorious friendship. I adopted Votes for Women as the first plank of my political platform. (No, Firefly, I *won't* explain. I won't explain anything. You must guess what a political platform was and what its planks were.) I followed up her indications and found out about classes in the district where I could learn geology and chemistry and how to speak French and German. Very timidly I mooted the subject of my further education in the basement living-room."

§ 7

Sarnac looked round at the fire-lit faces of his listeners.

" I know how topsy-turvy this story must seem to you, but it is a fact that before I was fourteen I had to plead for education against the ideas and wishes of my own family. And the whole household from top to bottom was brought into the discussion by Matilda or my mother. Except for Miss Bumpus and Frau Buchholz every one was against the idea.

" ' Education,' said Matilda, shaking her head slowly from side to side and smiling deprecatingly. ' Education ! That's all very well for those who have nothing better to do, but *you* want to get on in the world. You've got to be earning, young man.'

" ' But if I have education I'll be able to earn more.'

" Matilda screwed up her mouth in a portentous manner and pointed to the ceiling to indicate Mr. Plaice. ' *That's* what comes of education, young man. A room frowsty with books and just enough salary not to be able to do a blessed thing you want to do. And giving yourself Airs. Business is what you want, young man, not education.'

" ' And who's to pay for all these classes ? ' said my mother. ' That's what *I* want to know.'

" ' That's what we all want to know,' said Matilda Good.

" ' If I can't get education——' I said, and left the desperate sentence unfinished. I am afraid I was near weeping. To learn nothing beyond my present ignorance seemed to me then like a sentence of imprisonment for life. It wasn't I who suffered that alone. Thousands of poor youngsters of fourteen or fifteen in those days knew enough to see clearly that the doors of practical illiteracy were closing in upon them, and yet did not know enough to find a way of escape from this mental extinction.

" ' Look here ! ' I said, ' if I can get some sort of job during the day, may I pay for classes in the evening ? '

" ' If you can earn enough,' said Matilda. ' It's no worse I suppose than going to these new cinema shows or buying sweets for girls.'

" ' You've got to pay in for your room here and your keep, Morty, first,' said my mother. ' It isn't fair on Miss Good if you don't.'

" ' I know,' I said with my heart sinking. ' I'll pay in for my board and lodging. Some'ow. I don't want to be dependent.'

" ' What good you think it will do you,' said Matilda Good, ' I *don't* know. You'll pick up a certain amount of learning perhaps, get a certificate or something and ideas above your station. You'll give all the energy you might use in shoving your way up in some useful employment. You'll get round-shouldered and near-sighted. And just to grow up a discontented misfit. Well—have it your own way if you must. If you earn the money yourself it's yours to spend.'

" Mr. Plaice was no more encouraging. ' Well, my noble Mortimer,' he said, ' they tell me *Arr* that you aspire to university honours.'

" ' I want to learn a little more than I know, sir.'

" ' And join the ranks of the half-educated proletariat ? '

" It sounded bad. ' I hope not, sir,' I said.

" ' And what classes do you propose to attend, Mortimer ? '

" ' Whatever there are.'

" ' No plan ! No aim ! '

" ' I thought they'd know.'

" ' Whatever they give you—eh ? A promiscuous appetite. And while you—while you *Arr* indulge in this mixed feast of learning, this futile rivalry with the children of the leisured classes, somebody I suppose will have to keep *you*. Don't you think it's a bit hard on that kind mother of yours who toils day and night for you, that you shouldn't work and do *your* bit, eh ? One of the things, Mortimer, we used to learn in our much-maligned public schools, was something we called *playing cricket*. Well, I ask you, is this—this disinclination to do a bit of the earning, *Arr*, is it playing cricket ? I could expect such behaviour from an 'Arry, you know, but not from a Mortimer. *Noblesse oblige*. You think it over, my boy. There's such a thing as learning, but there's such a thing as Duty. Many of us have to be content with lives of unassuming labour. Many of us. Men who under happier circumstances might have done great things. . . .'

" The Moggeridges were gently persuasive in the same strain. My mother had put her case to them also. Usually I was indisposed to linger in the Moggeridge atmosphere ; they had old-fashioned ideas about draughts, and there was a peculiar aged flavour about them ; they were, to be plain, a very dirty old couple indeed. With declining strength they had relaxed by imperceptible degrees from the not very exacting standards of their youth. I used to cut into their room and out of it again as quickly as I could.

" But half a century of the clerical life among yielding country-folk had given these bent, decaying, pitiful creatures a wonderful way with their social inferiors. ' Morning, sir and mam,' I said, and put down the coals I had brought and took up the empty scuttle-lining I had replaced.

" Mrs. Moggeridge advanced shakily so as to intercept my retreat. She had silvery hair, a wrinkled face and screwed-up red-rimmed eyes ; she was short-sighted and came peering up very close to me whenever she spoke to me, breathing in my face. She held out a quivering hand to arrest me ; she spoke with a quavering voice, ' And how's Master Morty this morning ? ' she said, with kindly condescending intonations.

" ' Very well thank you, mam,' I said.

" ' I've been hearing rather a sad account of you, Morty, rather a sad account.'

" ' Sorry, mum,' I said, and wished I had the courage to tell her that my life was no business of hers.

" ' They say you're discontented, Morty. They say you complain of God's Mercies.'

" Mr. Moggeridge had been sitting in the arm-chair by the fireplace. He was in his slippers and shirt-sleeves and he had been reading a newspaper. Now he looked at me over his silver-rimmed spectacles and spoke in a rich succulent voice.

" ' I'm sorry you should be giving trouble to that dear mother of yours,' he said. ' Very sorry. She's a devoted saintly woman.'

" ' Yessir,' I said.

" ' Very few boys nowadays have the privilege of such an upbringing as yours. Some day you may understand what you owe her.'

(" ' I begin to,' " interjected Sarnac.)

" ' It seems you want to launch out upon some extravagant plan of classes instead of settling down quietly in your proper sphere. Is that so ? '

" ' I don't feel I know enough yet, sir,' I said. ' I feel I'd like to learn more.'

" ' Knowledge isn't always happiness, Morty,' said Mrs. Moggeridge close to me—much too close to me.

" ' And what may these classes be that are tempting you to forget the honour you owe your dear good mother ? ' said Mr. Moggeridge.

" ' I don't know yet, sir. They say there's classes in geology and French and things like that.'

" Old Mr. Moggeridge waved his hand in front of himself with an expression of face as though it was I who emitted an evil odour. ' Geology ! ' he said. ' French—the language of Voltaire. Let me tell you one thing plainly, my boy, your mother is quite right in objecting to these classes. Geology —geology is—All Wrong. It has done more harm in the last fifty years than any other single influence whatever. It undermines faith. It sows doubt. I do not speak ignorantly, Mortimer. I have seen lives wrecked and destroyed and souls lost by this same geology. I am an old learned man, and I have examined the work of many of these so-called geologists —Huxley, Darwin and the like ; I have examined it very very carefully and very very tolerantly, and I tell you they are all, all of them, *hopelessly mistaken men*. . . . And what good will such knowledge do you ? Will it make you happier ? Will it make you better ? No, my lad. But I know something that will. Something older than geology. Older and better. Sarah dear, give me that book there, please. Yes '—reverentially—' *the* Book.'

" His wife handed him a black-bound Bible, with its cover protected against the rough usage by a metal edge. " Now, my boy,' he said, ' let me give you this—this old familiar book, with an old man's blessing. In that is all the knowledge worth having, all the knowledge you will ever need. You will always find something fresh in it and always something beautiful.' He held it out to me.

" Accepting it seemed the shortest way out of the room, so I took it. ' Thank you, sir,' I said.

" ' Promise me you will read it.'

" ' Oh, yes, sir.'

" I turned to go. But giving was in the air.

" ' Now, Mortimer,' said Mrs. Moggeridge, ' do please promise me to seek strength where strength is to be found and try to be a better son to that dear struggling woman.' And as she spoke she proffered for my acceptance an extremely hard, small, yellow orange.

" ' Thank you, mam,' I said, made shift to stow her gift in my pocket, and with the Bible in one hand and the empty coal-scuttle lining in the other escaped.

" I returned wrathfully to the basement and deposited my presents on the window-sill. Some impulse made me open the Bible and inside the cover I found, imperfectly erased, the shadowy outlines of these words, printed in violet ink : ' Not to be Removed from the Waiting-Room.' I puzzled over the significance of this for some time."

" And what did it signify ? " asked Firefly.

" I do not know to this day," said Sarnac. " But apparently the reverend gentleman had acquired that Book at a railway-station during one of his journeys as a Sunday supply."

" You mean—— ? " said Firefly.

" No more than I say. He was in many ways a peculiar old gentleman, and his piety was I fancy an essential superficial exudation. He was—I will not say ' dishonest,' but ' spas-modically acquisitive.' And like many old people in those days he preferred his refreshment to be stimulating rather than nutritious, and so he may have blurred his ethical perceptions. An odd thing about him—Matilda Good was the first to point it out—was that he rarely took an umbrella away with him when he went on supply and almost always he came back with one—and once he came back with two. But he never kept his umbrellas ; he would take them off for long walks and return without them, looking all the brighter for it. I remember one day I was in the room when he returned from such an expedition, there had been a shower and his coat was wet. Mrs. Moggeridge made him change it and lamented that he had lost his umbrella *again*.

" ' Not *lost*,' I heard the old man say in a voice of infinite gentleness. ' Not lost, dear. Not lost ; but gone before. . . . Gone before the rain came. . . . The Lord gave. . . . Lord hath taken 'way.'

" For a time he was silent, coat in hand. He stood with his shirt-sleeve resting on the mantelshelf, his foot upon the fender, and his venerable hairy face gazing down into the fire. He seemed to be thinking deep, sad things. Then he remarked in a thoughtful, less obituary tone : ' Ten'n-six-pence. A jolly *goo'* 'mbrella.' "

§ 8

" Frau Buchholz was a poor lean distressful woman of five-and-forty or more, with a table littered with the documents of some obscure litigation. She did not altogether discourage my ambitions but she laid great stress on the hopelessness of attempting Kultur without a knowledge of German, and I am inclined to think that her attitude was determined mainly by a vague and desperate hope that I might be induced to take lessons in German from her.

" Brother Ernest was entirely against my ambition. He was shy and vocally inexpressive, and he took me to the Victoria Music Hall and spent a long evening avoiding the subject. It was only as we drew within five minutes of home that he spoke of it.

" ' What's all this about your not being satisfied with your education, 'Arry ? ' he asked. ' I thought you had a pretty decent bit of schooling.'

" ' I don't feel I know anything,' I said. ' I don't know history or geography or anything. I don't even know my own grammar.'

" ' You know enough,' said Ernest. ' You know enough to get a job. Knowing more would only make you stuck-up. We don't want any more stuck-ups in the family. God knows.'

" I knew he referred to Fanny, but of course neither of us mentioned her shameful name.

" ' Anyhow, I suppose I'll have to chuck it,' I said bitterly.

" ' That's about it, 'Arry. I know you're a sensible chap—at bottom. You got to be what you got to be.'

" The only encouragement I got to resist mental extinction was from Miss Beatrice Bumpus, and after a time I found even that source of consolation was being cut off from me. For my mother began to develop the most gross and improbable suspicions about Miss Bumpus. You see I stayed sometimes as long as ten or even twelve minutes in the drawing-room, and it was difficult for so good a woman as my mother, trained in the most elaborate precautions of separation between male and female, to understand that two young people of opposite sex could have any liking for each other's company unless some sort of gross familiarity was involved. The good of those days, living as they did in a state of inflamed restraint, had very exaggerated ideas of the appetites, capacities and un-controllable duplicity of normal human beings. And so my mother began to manœuvre in the most elaborate way to replace me by Prue as a messenger to Miss Bumpus. And when I was actually being talked to—and even talking—in the drawing-room I had an increasing sense of that poor misguided woman hovering upon the landing outside, listening in a mood of anxious curiosity and ripening for a sudden inrush, a disgraceful exposure, wild denunciation of Miss Bumpus, and the rescue of the vestiges of my damaged moral nature. I might never have realised what was going on if it had not been for my mother's direct questionings and warnings. Her conception of a proper upbringing for the young on these matters was a carefully preserved ignorance hedged about by shames and foul terrors. So she was at once extremely urgent and extraordinarily vague with me. What was I up to—staying so long with that woman ? I wasn't to listen to anything she told me. I was to be precious

careful what I got up to up there. I might find myself in more
trouble than I thought. There were women in this world of a
shamelessness it made one blush to think of. She'd always done
her best to keep me from wickedness and nastiness."

" But she was mad ! " said Willow.

" All the countless lunatic asylums of those days wouldn't
have held a tithe of the English people who were as mad in
that way as she was."

" But the whole world was mad ? " said Sunray. " *All*
those people, except perhaps Miss Bumpus, talked about your
education like insane people ! Did none of them understand the
supreme wickedness of hindering the growth of a human mind ? "

" It was a world of suppression and evasion. You cannot
understand anything about it unless you understand that."

" But the whole world ! " said Radiant.

" Most of it. It was still a fear-haunted world. ' Submit,'
said the ancient dread, ' do nothing—lest you offend. And
from the children—*hide*.' What I am telling you about the upbringing of Harry Mortimer Smith was generally true of the
upbringing of the enormous majority of the inhabitants of the
earth. It was not merely that their minds were starved and
poisoned. Their minds were stamped upon and mutilated.
That world was so pitiless and confused, so dirty and diseased
because it was cowed and dared not learn of remedies. In
Europe in those days we used to be told the most extraordinary
stories of the wickedness and cruelty of the Chinese, and one
favourite tale was that little children were made to grow up
inside great porcelain jars in order to distort their bodies to
grotesque shapes so that they could be shown at fairs or sold
to rich men. The Chinese certainly distorted the feet of young
women for some obscure purpose, and this may have been the
origin of this horrible legend. But our children in England were
mentally distorted in exactly the same fashion except that for
porcelain jars we used mental tin-cans and dust-bins. . . . My
dears ! when I talk of this I cease to be Sarnac ! All the rage
and misery of crippled and thwarted Harry Mortimer Smith
comes back to me."

" Did you get to those classes of yours ? " asked Sunray. " I
hope you did."

" Not for a year or two—though Miss Bumpus did what she
could for me. She lent me a lot of books—in spite of much
ignorant censorship on the part of my mother—and I read
voraciously. But, I don't know if you will understand it, my
relations with Miss Bumpus were slowly poisoned by the interpretations my mother was putting upon them. I think you will
see how easy it was for a boy in my position to fall in love, fall
into a deep emotional worship of so bright and friendly a young
woman. Most of us young men nowadays begin by adoring a
woman older than ourselves. Adoring is the word rather than
loving. It's not a mate we need at first but the helpful kindly

goddess who stoops to us. And of course I loved her. But I thought much more of serving her or dying for her than of embracing her. When I was away from her my imagination might go so far as to dream of kissing her hands.

"And then came my mother with this hideous obsession of hers, jealous for something she called my purity, treating this white passion of gratitude and humility as though it was the power that drags a blow-fly to some heap of offal. A deepening shame and ungraciousness came into my relations with Miss Bumpus. I became red-eared and tongue-tied in her presence. Possibilities I might never have thought of but for my mother's suggestions grew disgustingly vivid in my mind. I dreamt about her grotesquely. When presently I found employment for my days my chances of seeing her became infrequent. She receded as a personality and friend, and quite against my will became a symbol of feminity.

"Among the people who called to see her a man of three or four and thirty became frequent. My spirit flamed into an intense and impotent jealousy on account of this man. He would take tea with her and stay for two hours or more. My mother took care to mention his visits in my hearing at every opportunity. She called him Miss Bumpus's ' fancy man,' or alluded to him archly : ' A certain person called again to-day, Prue. When good-lookin' young men are shown in at the door, votes flies out of the winder.' I tried to seem indifferent but my ears and cheeks got red and hot. My jealousy was edged with hate. I avoided seeing Miss Bumpus for weeks together. I sought furiously for some girl, any girl, who would serve to oust her image from my imagination.'

Sarnac stopped abruptly and remained for a time staring intently into the fire. His expression was one of amused regret. "How little and childish it seems now ! " he said ; "and how bitter—oh ! how bitter it was at the time ! "

"Poor little errand-boy ! " said Sunray, stroking his hair. "Poor little errand-boy in love."

"What an uncomfortable distressful world it must have been for all young things ! " said Willow.

"Uncomfortable and pitiless," said Sarnac.

§ 9

"My first employment in London was as an errand-boy—' junior porter ' was the exact phrase—to a draper's shop near Victoria Station : I packed parcels and carried them to their destinations ; my next job was to be boy in general to a chemist named Humberg in a shop beyond Lupus Street. A chemist then was a very different creature from the kind of man or woman we call a chemist to-day ; he was much more like the Apothecary we find in Shakespeare's plays and suchlike old literature ; he was a dealer in drugs, poisons, medicines, a few spices, colouring matters and suchlike odd commodities. I washed

endless bottles, delivered drugs and medicines, cleared up a
sort of backyard, and did anything else that there was to be
done within the measure of my capacity.

" Of all the queer shops one found in the Old World London,
the chemists' shops were I think the queerest. They had come
almost unchanged out of the Middle Ages, as we used to call
them, when western Europe, superstitious, dirty, diseased and
degenerate, thrashed by the Arabs and Mongols and Turks,
afraid to sail the ocean or fight out of armour, cowered behind
the walls of its towns and castles, stole, poisoned, assassinated
and tortured, and pretended to be the Roman Empire still in
being.   Western Europe in those days was ashamed of its
natural varieties of speech and talked bad Latin ; it dared not
look a fact in the face but nosed for knowledge among riddles
and unreadable parchments ; it burned men and women alive
for laughing at the absurdities of its Faith, and it thought the
stars of Heaven were no better than a greasy pack of cards by
which fortunes were to be told. In those days it was that the
tradition of the 'Pothecary was made ; you know him as he
figures in ' Romeo and Juliet ' ; the time in which I lived this
life was barely four centuries and a half from old Shakespeare.
The 'Pothecary was in a conspiracy of pretentiousness with
the almost equally ignorant doctors of his age, and the latter
wrote and he ' made up ' prescriptions in occult phrases and
symbols. In our window there were great glass bottles of red-
and-yellow and blue-tinted water, through which our gas-
lamps within threw a mystical light on the street pavement."

"Was there a stuffed alligator ? " asked Firefly.

" No. We were just out of the age of stuffed alligators, but
below these coloured bottles in the window we had stupendous
china jars with gilt caps mystically inscribed—let me see !
Let me think ! One was *Sem. Coriand.* Another was *Rad.
Sarsap.* Then—what was the fellow in the corner ? *Marant.
Ar.* And opposite him—*C. Cincordif.* And behind the counter
to look the customer in the face were neat little drawers with
golden and precious letters thereon ; *Pil. Rhubarb.* and *Pil.
Antibil.* and many more bottles, *Ol. Amyg.* and *Tinct. Iod.*,
rows and rows of bottles, mystic, wonderful. I do not remember
ever seeing Mr. Humberg take anything, much less sell anything,
from all this array of erudite bottles and drawers ; his normal
trade was done in the bright little packets of an altogether
different character that were piled all over the counter, bright
unblushing little packets that declared themselves to be
Gummidge's Fragrant and Digestive Tooth-Paste, Hooper's
Corn Cure, Luxtone's Lady's Remedy, Tinker's Pills for All
Occasions, and the like. Such things were asked for openly
and loudly by customers ; they were our staple trade. But
also there were many transactions conducted in undertones
which I never fully understood. I would be sent off to the
yard on some specious pretext whenever a customer was

discovered to be of the *sotto voce* variety, and I can only suppose that Mr. Humberg was accustomed at times to go beyond the limits of his professional qualification and to deal out advice and instruction that were legally the privileges of the qualified medical man. You must remember that in those days many things that we teach plainly and simply to every one were tabooed and made to seem occult and mysterious and very very shameful and dirty.

" My first reaction to this chemist's shop was a violent appetite for Latin. I succumbed to its suggestion that Latin was the key to all knowledge, and that indeed statements did not become knowledge until they had passed into the Latin tongue. For a few coppers I bought in a second-hand bookshop an old and worn Latin ' Principia ' written by a namesake Smith ; I attacked it with great determination and found this redoubtable language far more understandable, reasonable, and straightforward than the elusive irritable French and the trampling coughing German I had hitherto attempted. This Latin was a dead language, a skeleton language plainly articulated ; it never moved about and got away from one as a living language did. In a little while I was able to recognise words I knew upon our bottles and drawers and in the epitaphs upon the monuments in Westminster Abbey, and soon I could even construe whole phrases. I dug out Latin books from the second-hand booksellers' boxes, and some I could read and some I could not. There was a war history of that first Cæsar, Julius Cæsar, the adventurer who extinguished the last reek of the decaying Roman Republic, and there was a Latin New Testament ; I got along fairly well with both. But there was a Latin poet, Lucretius, I could not construe ; even with an English verse translation on the opposite page I could not construe him. But I read that English version with intense curiosity. It is an extraordinary thing to note, but that same Lucretius, an old Roman poet who lived and died two thousand years before my time, four thousand years from now, gave an account of the universe and of man's beginnings, far truer and more intelligible than the old Semitic legends I had been taught in my Sunday-school.

" One of the queerest aspects of those days was the mingling of ideas belonging to different ages and phases of human development due to the irregularity and casualness of such educational organisation as we had. In school and church alike, obstinate pedantry darkened the minds of men, Europeans in the twentieth Christian century mixed up the theology of the Pharaohs, the cosmogony of the priest-kings of Sumeria, with the politics of the seventeenth century and the ethics of the cricket-field and prize-ring, and that in a world which had got to aeroplanes and telephones.

" My own case was typical of the limitations of the time. In that age of ceaseless novelty there was I, trying to get back by way of Latin to the half knowledge of the Ancients. Presently I began to struggle with Greek also, but I never got very far with that. I found a chance of going once a week on what was called early-closing night, after my day's work was done, to some evening classes in chemistry. And this chemistry I had discovered had hardly anything in common with the chemistry of a chemist's shop. The story of matter and force that it told belonged to another and a newer age. I was fascinated by these wider revelations of the universe I lived in, I ceased to struggle with Greek and I no longer hunted the dingy book-boxes for Latin classics but for modern scientific works. Lucretius I found was hardly less out of date than Genesis. Among the books that taught me much were one called ' Physiography ' by a writer named Gregory, Clodd's ' Story of Creation ' and Lankester's ' Science from an Easy Chair.' I do not know if they were exceptionally good books ; they were the ones that happened to come to my hand and awaken my mind. But do you realise the amazing conditions under which men were living at that time, when a youngster had to go about as eager and furtive as a mouse seeking food, to get even such knowledge of the universe and himself as then existed ? I still remember how I read first of the differences and resemblances between apes and men and speculations arising thencefrom about the nature of the submen who came before man. It was in the shed in the yard that I sat and read. Mr. Humberg was on the sofa in the parlour behind the shop sleeping off his midday meal with one ear acock for the shop-bell, and I, with one ear acock for the shop-bell and the other for any sounds of movement in the parlour, read for the first time of the forces that had made me what I was—when I ought to have been washing out bottles.

"At one point in the centre of the display behind the counter in the shop was a row of particularly brave and important-looking glass jars wearing about their bellies the gold promises of *Aqua Fortis*, *Amm. Hyd.* and suchlike names, and one day as I was sweeping the floor I observed Mr. Humberg scrutinising these. He held one up to the light and shook his head at its flocculent contents. ' Harry,' he said, ' see this row of bottles ? '

" ' Yessir.'

" ' Pour 'em all out and put in fresh water.'

" I stared, broom in hand, aghast at the waste. ' They won't blow up if I mix 'em ? ' I said.

" ' Blow up ! ' said Mr. Humberg. ' It's only stale water. There's been nothing else in these bottles for a score of years. Stuff I want is behind the dispensary partition—and it's different stuff nowadays. Wash 'em out—and then we'll put in some water from the pump. We just have 'em for the look of 'em. The old women wouldn't be happy if we hadn't got 'em there.' "

Part Two
The Loves and Death of Harry Mortimer Smith

CHAPTER FIVE

FANNY DISCOVERS HERSELF

§ 1

"A<small>ND</small> now," said Sarnac, " I can draw near to the essentials of life and tell you the sort of thing love was in that crowded, dingy fear-ruled world of the London fogs and the amber London sunshine. It was a slender, wild-eyed, scared and daring emotion in a dark forest of cruelties and repressions. It soon grew old and crippled, bitter-spirited and black-hearted, but as it happened, death came early enough for me to die with a living love still in my heart. . . ."

" To live again," said Sunray very softly.

" And love again," said Sarnac, patting her knee. " Let me see. . . ."

He took a stake that had fallen from the fire and thrust it into the bright glow at the centre and watched it burst into a sierra of flames.

" I think that the first person I was in love with was my sister Fanny. When I was a boy of eleven or twelve I was really in love with her. But somehow about that time I was also in love with an undraped plaster nymph who sat very bravely on a spouting dolphin in some public gardens near the middle of Cliffstone. She lifted her chin and smiled and waved one hand and she had the sweetest smile and the dearest little body imaginable. I loved her back particularly, and there was a point where you looked at her from behind and just caught the soft curve of her smiling cheek and her jolly little nose-tip and chin and the soft swell of her breast under her lifted arm. I would sneak round her furtively to-wards this particular view-point, having been too well-soaked in shame about all such lovely things to look openly. But I never seemed to look my fill.

" One day as I was worshipping her in this fashion half-turned to her and half-turned to a bed of flowers and looking at her askance, I became aware of an oldish man with a large white face, seated on a garden-seat and leaning forward and regarding me with an expression of oafish cunning as if he had found me out and knew my secret. He looked like the spirit of lewdness incarnate. Suddenly panic overwhelmed me and I made off—and never went near that garden again. Angels with flaming shames prevented me. Or a terror of again meeting that horrible old man. . . .

" Then with my coming to London Miss Beatrice Bumpus took control of my imagination and was Venus and all the goddesses ; and this increased rather than diminished after she had gone away. For she went away and, I gather, married

the young man I hated ; she went away and gave up her work
for the Vote and was no doubt welcomed back by those Warwickshire Bumpuses (who hunted) with the slaughter of a
fatted fox and every sort of rejoicing. But her jolly frank
and boyish face was the heroine's in a thousand dreams. I
saved her life in adventures in all parts of the world and sometimes she saved mine ; we clung together over the edges of
terrific precipices until I went to sleep, and when I was the
conquering Mahomet after a battle, she stood out among the
captive women and answered back when I said I would never
love her, with two jets of cigarette smoke and the one word,
' Liar ! '

    " I met no girls of my own age at all while I was errand-
boy to Mr. Humberg, my evening classes and my reading
kept me away from the facile encounters of the streets. Sometimes, however, when I could not fix my attention upon my
books, I would slip off to Wilton Street and Victoria Street
where there was a nocturnal promenade under the electric-
lamps. There schoolgirls and little drabs and errand-boys and
soldiers prowled and accosted one another. But though I was
attracted to some of the girlish figures that flitted by me I
was also shy and fastidious. I was drawn by an overpowering
desire for something intense and beautiful that vanished
whenever I drew near to reality."

                              § 2

    " Before a year was over there were several changes in the
Pimlico boarding-house. The poor old Moggeridges caught
influenza, a variable prevalent epidemic of the time, and
succumbed to inflammation of the lungs following the fever
They died within three days of each other, and my mother and
Prue were the only mourners at their dingy little funeral
Frau Buchholz fades out of my story ; I do not remember
clearly when she left the house nor who succeeded her. Miss
Beatrice Bumpus departed, and the second floor was taken
by an extremely intermittent couple who roused my mother's
worst suspicions and led to serious differences of opinion
between her and Matilda Good.

    " You see these newcomers never settled in with any grave
and sober luggage ; they would come and stay for a day or
so and then not reappear for a week or more, and they rarely
arrived or departed together. This roused my mother's mora
observations, and she began hinting that perhaps they were
not properly married after all. She forbade Prue ever to go
to the drawing-room floor, and this precipitated a conflic
with Matilda. ' What's this about Prue and the drawing
room ? ' Matilda asked. ' You're putting ideas into the girl's
head.'

    " ' I'm trying to keep them from 'er,' said my mother
' She's got eyes.'

" ' *And* fingers,' said Matilda witn dark allusiveness. ' What's Prue been seeing now ? '

" ' Marks,' said my mother.

" ' What marks ? ' said Matilda.

" ' Marks enough,' said my mother. ' '*Is* things are marked one name and '*Er's* another, and neither of them Milton, which is the name they've given us. And the way that woman speaks to you, as though she felt you might notice sumpthing —friendly-like and a bit afraid of you. And that ain't all ! By no means all ! I'm not blind and Prue isn't blind. There's kissing and making love going on at all times in the day ! Directly they've got 'ere sometimes. Hardly waiting for one to get out of the room. I'm not a perfect fool, Matilda. I been married.'

" ' What's that got to do with us ? We're a lodging-house, not a set of Nosey Parkers. If Mr. and Mrs. Milton like to have their linen marked a *hundred* different names, what's that to us ? Their book's always marked *paid in advance with thanks, Matilda Good,* and that's married enough for me. See ? You're an uneasy woman to have in a lodging-house, Martha, an uneasy woman. There's no give-and-take about you. No save-your-fare. There was that trouble you made about the boy and Miss Bumpus—ridiculous it was—and now seemingly there's going to be more trouble about Prue and Mrs. Milton—who's a lady, mind you, say what you like, and—what's more—a gentlewoman. I wish you'd mind your own business a bit more, Martha, and let Mr. and Mrs. Milton mind theirs. If they aren't properly married it's they've got to answer for it in the long run, not you. You'll get even with them all right on the Last Great Day. Meanwhile do they do 'arm to any one ? A quieter couple and less trouble to look after I've never had in all my lodging-house days.'

" My mother made no answer.

" ' Well ? ' challenged Matilda.

" ' It's hard to be waiting on a shameless woman,' said my mother, obstinate and white-lipped.

" ' It's harder still to be called a shameless woman because you've still got your maiden name on some of your things.' said Matilda Good. ' Don't talk such Rubbish, Martha.'

" ' I don't see why '*E* should 'ave a maiden name too— on 'is pyjamas,' said my mother rallying after a moment.

" ' You don't know Anything, Martha,' said Matilda, fixing her with one eye of extreme animosity and regarding the question in the abstract with the other. ' I've often thought it of you and now I say it to you. You don't know Anything. I'm going to keep Mr. and Mrs. Milton as long as I can, and if you're too pernikkety to wait on them, there's those who will. I won't have my lodgers insulted. I won't 'ave their underclothes dragged up against them. Why ! Come to think of it ! Of course ! He *borrowed* those pyjamas of 'is ! Or they was given him by a gentleman friend they didn't fit. Or he's been left money and had to change his name sudden-like. It often happens. Often. You see it in the papers. And things get mixed in the wash. Some laundries, they're regular Exchanges. Mr. Plaice, he once had a collar with *Fortescue* on it. Brought it back after his summer holiday. Fortescue ! There's evidence for you. You aren't going to bring up something against Mr. Plaice on account of that, Martha ? You aren't going to say he's been living a double life and isn't properly a bachelor. Do think a little clearer, Martha. And don't think so much evil. There's a hundred ways round before you think evil. But you *like* to think evil, Martha. I've noticed it times and oft. You fairly wallow in it. You haven't the beginnings of a germ of Christian charity.'

" ' One can't help seeing things,' said my mother, rather shattered.

" ' *You* can't,' said Matilda Good. ' There's those who can't see an inch beyond their noses, and yet they see too much. And the more I see of you the more I'm inclined to think you're one of that sort. Anyhow, Mr. and Mrs. Milton stay here—whoever else goes. Whoever else goes. That's plain, I hope, Martha.'

" My mother was stricken speechless. She bridled and subsided and then, except for necessary and unavoidable purposes, remained hurt and silent for some days, speaking only when she was spoken to. Matilda did not seem to mind. But I noticed that when presently Matilda sent Prue upstairs with the Miltons' tea my mother's stiffness grew stiffer, but she made no open protests."

§ 3

" And then suddenly Fanny reappeared in my world.

" It was a mere chance that restored Fanny to me. All our links had been severed when we removed from Cliffstone to London. My brother Ernest was her herald.

" We were at supper in the basement room and supper was usually a pleasant meal. Matilda Good would make it attractive with potatoes roasted in their jackets, or what she called a ' frying-pan ' of potatoes and other vegetables in dripping or suchlike heartening addition to cold bacon and bread and cheese and small beer. And she would read bits out of the newspaper to us and discuss them, having a really very lively intelligence, or she would draw me out to talk of the books I'd been reading. She took a great interest in murders and suchlike cases, and we all became great judges of motive and evidence under her stimulation. ' You may say it's morbid, Martha, if you like,' she said ; ' but there never was a murder yet that wasn't brimful of humanity. Brimful. I doubt sometimes if we know what any one's capable of until they've committed a murder or two.'

" My mother rarely failed to rise to her bait. ' I can't think
'ow you can say such things, Matilda,' she would say. . . .

" We heard the sound of a motor-car in the street above.
Brother Ernest descended by the area-steps and my sister
Prue let him in. He appeared in his chauffeur's uniform, cap
in hand, leather jacket and gaiters.

" ' Got a night off ? ' asked Matilda.

" ' Court Theatre at eleven,' said Ernest. ' So I thought
I'd come in for a bit of a warm and a chat.'

" ' Have a snack ? ' said Matilda. ' Prue, get him a plate
and a knife and fork and a glass. One glass of *this* beer won't
hurt your driving. Why ! we haven't seen you for ages ! '

" ' Thank you, Miss Good,' said Ernest, who was always
very polite to her, ' I *will* 'ave a snack. I bin here, there and
everywhere, but it isn't that I haven't wanted to call on you.'

" Refreshment was administered and converstion hung fire
for awhile. One or two starts were made and came to an early
end. Ernest's manner suggested preoccupation and Matilda
regarded him keenly. ' And what have you got to tell us,
Ernie ? ' she said suddenly.

" ' We-el,' said Ernest, ' it's a curious thing you should
say that, Miss Good, for I 'ave got something to tell you.
Something—well, I don't know 'ow to put it—curious-like.'

" Matilda refilled his glass.

" ' I seen Fanny,' said Ernest, coming to it with violent
abruptness.

" ' *No !* ' gasped my mother, and for a moment no one else
spoke.

" ' So ! ' said Matilda, putting her arms on the table and
billowing forward, ' you've seen Fanny ! Pretty little Fanny
that I used to know. And where did you see her, Ernie ? '

" Ernest had some difficulty in shaping out his story. ' It
was a week last Tuesday,' he said after a pause.

" ' She wasn't—not one of Them—about Victoria Station ? '
panted my mother.

" ' Did you see her first or did she see you ? ' asked Matilda.

" ' A week ago last Tuesday,' my brother repeated.

" ' And did you speak to her ? '

" ' Not at the time I didn't. No.'

" ' Did she speak to you ? '

" ' No.'

" ' Then 'ow d'you know it was our Fanny ? ' asked Prue,
who had been listening intently.

" ' I thought she'd gone to 'er fate in some foreign country
—being so near Boulogne,' my mother said. ' I thought them
White Slave Traders 'ad the decency to carry a girl off right
away from 'er 'ome. . . . Fanny ! On the streets of London !
Near 'ere. I told 'er what it would come to. Time and again
I told 'er. Marry an 'onest man I said, but she was greedy
and 'eadstrong. . . . 'Eadstrong and vain. . . . She didn't try

to follow you, Ernie, to find out where we were or anything like that ? "

"My brother Ernest's face displayed his profound perplexity. ' It wasn't at all like that, mother,' he said. ' It wasn't—that sort of thing. You see——'

"He began a struggle with the breast-pocket of his very tightly fitting leather jacket and at last produced a rather soiled letter. He held it in his hand, neither attempting to read it nor offering it to us. But holding it in his hand seemed to crystallise his very rudimentary narrative powers. ' I better tell you right from the beginning,' he said. ' It isn't at all what you'd suppose. Tuesday week it was ; last Tuesday week.'

"Matilda Good laid a restraining hand on my mother's arm. ' In the evening I suppose ? ' she helped.

"' It was a dinner and fetch,' said my brother. ' Of course you understand I 'adn't set eyes on Fanny for pretty near six years. It was 'er knew me.'

"' You had to take these people to a dinner and fetch them back again ? ' said Matilda.

"' Orders,' said Ernest, ' was to go to one-o-two Brantismore Gardens, Earl's Court top flat, to pick up lady and gentleman for number to be given in Church Row Hampstead and call there ten-thirty and take home as directed. Accordingly I went to Brantismore Gardens and told the porter in the 'all—it was one of these 'ere flat places with a porter in livery—that I was there to time waiting. 'E telephoned up in the usual way. After a bit, lady and gentleman came out of the house and I went to the door of the car as I usually do and held it open. So far nothing out of the ornary. He was a gentleman in evening-dress, like most gentlemen ; she'd got a wrap with fur, and her hair, you know, was done up nice for an evening-party with something that sparkled. Quite the lady.'

"' And it was Fanny ? ' said Prue.

"Ernest struggled mutely with his subject for some moments. ' Not yet, like,' he said.

"' You mean you didn't recognise her then ? ' said Matilda.

"' No. But she just looked up at me and seemed kind of to start and got in. I saw her sort of leaning forward and looking at me as 'E got in. Fact is, I didn't think much of it. I should have forgotten all about it if it 'adn't been for afterwards. But when I took them back something happened. I could see she was looking at me. . . . We went first to one-o-two Brantismore Gardens again and then he got out and says to me, " Just wait a bit here," and then he helped her out. It sort of seemed as though she was 'arf-inclined to speak to me and then she didn't. But this time I thinks to myself : " I seen you before, somewhere, my Lady." Oddly enough I never thought of Fanny then at all. I got as near as thinking

she was a bit like 'Arry 'ere. But it never entered my 'ead
it might be Fanny. Strordinary! They went up the steps to
the door ; one of these open entrances it is to several flats,
and seemed to have a moment's confabulation under the
light, looking towards me. Then they went on up to the
flat.'

" ' You didn't know her even then ? ' said Prue.

" ' 'E came down the steps quarternour after perhaps,
looking thoughtful. White wescoat, 'e 'ad, and coat over 'is
arm. Gave me an address near Sloane Street. Got out and
produced his tip, rather on the large side it was, and stood
still kind of thoughtful. Seemed inclined to speak and didn't
know what to say. " I've an account at the garage," 'e says.
" you'll book the car," and then : " You're not my usual
driver," 'e says. " What's your name ? " " Smith," I says.
" Ernest Smith," he says. " Yes sir," I says, and it was only
as I drove off that I asked myself 'Ow the 'Ell—I reely beg
your pardon, Miss Good.'

" ' Don't mind me,' said Matilda. ' Go on.'

" ' 'Ow the Juice d'e know that my name was Ernest ? I
nearly 'it a taxi at the corner of Sloane Square I was so took
up puzzling over it. And it was only about three o'clock in
the morning, when I was lying awake still puzzling over it,
that it came into my 'ead——'

" Ernest assumed the manner of a narrator who opens out
his culminating surprise. '——that that young lady I'd been
takin' out that evening was——'

" He paused before his climax.

" ' Fenny,' whispered Prue.

" ' Sister Fanny,' said Matilda Good.

" ' Our Fanny,' said my mother.

" ' *No less a person than Fanny!* ' said my brother Ernest
triumphantly and looked round for the amazement proper to
such a surprise.

" ' I thought it was going to be Fenny,' said Prue.

" ' Was she painted up at all ? ' asked Matilda.

" ' Not nearly so much painted as most of 'em are,' said
my brother Ernest. ' Pretty nearly every one paints nowadays.
Titled people. Bishops' ladies. Widows. Every one. She
didn't strike me—well, as belonging to the painted sort particularly, not in the least. Kind of fresh and a little pale—like
Fanny used to be.'

" ' Was she dressed like a lady—quiet-like ? '

" ' Prosperous,' said Ernest. ' Reely prosperous. But
nothing what you might call extravagant.'

" ' And the house you took 'em to—noisy ? Singing and
dancing and the windows open ? '

" ' It was a perfectly respectable quiet sort of 'ouse. Blinds
down and no row whatever. A private 'ouse. The people
who came to the door to say good-night might 'ave been any

gentleman and any lady. I see the butler. 'E came down to
the car. 'E wasn't 'ired for the evening. 'E was a *real* butler.
The other guests had a private limousine with an oldish careful
sort of driver. Whad-you'd speak of as nice people.'

" ' Hardly what you might call being on the streets of
London,' said Matilda, turning to my mother. ' What was the
gentleman like ? '

" ' I don't want to 'ear of 'im,' said my mother.

" ' Dissipated sort of man about town—and a bit screwed ? '
asked Matilda.

" ' 'E was a lot soberer than most dinner fetches,' said
Ernest. ' I see that when 'e 'andled 'is money. Lots of 'em
—oh ! quite 'igh-class people get—'ow shall I say it ?—just
a little bit funny. 'Umerous-like. Bit 'nnacurate with the door.
'E wasn't. That's what I can't make out. . . . And then there's
this letter.'

" ' Then there's this letter,' said Matilda. ' You better
read it, Martha.'

" ' How did you get that letter ? ' asked my mother, not
offering to touch it. ' You don't mean to say she gave you a
letter ! '

" ' It came last Thursday. By post. It was addressed to
me, Ernest Smith, Esq., at the Garage. It's a curious letter
—asking about us. I can't make 'ead or tail of the whole
business. I been thinking about it and thinking about it.
Knowing 'ow set mother was about Fanny—I 'esitated.'

" His voice died away.

" ' Somebody,' said Matilda in the pause that followed,
' had better read that letter.'

" She looked at my mother, smiled queerly with the corners
of her mouth down, and then held out her hand to Ernest."

§ 4

" It was Matilda who read that letter ; my mother's aversion from it was all too evident. I can still remember Matilda's
large red face thrust forward over the supper-things and a
little on one side so as to bring the eye she was using into
focus and get the best light from the feeble little gas-bracket.
Beside her was Prue, with a slack curious face and a restive
glance that went ever and again to my mother's face, as a
bandsman watches the conductor's baton. My mother sat
back with a defensive expression on her white face, and
Ernest was posed, wide and large, in a non-committal attitude,
ostentatiously unable to ' make 'ead or tail ' of the affair.

" ' Let's see,' said Matilda, and took a preliminary survey of
the task before her. . . .

" ' *My dear Ernie*,' she says. . . .

" ' *My dear Ernie :*

" ' *It was wonderful seeing you again. I could hardly believe it was you even after Mr.—Mr.——. She's written it and thought better of it and scratched it out again, Mr. Somebody—Mr. Blank—had asked your name. I was beginning to fear I'd lost you all. Where are you living and how are you getting on ? You know I went to France and Italy for a holiday—lovely, lovely places—and when I came back I slipped off at Cliffstone because I wanted to see you all again and couldn't bear leaving you as I had done without a word.'*

"'She should've thought of that before,' said my mother.

"'*She told me, Mrs. Bradley did, about poor father's accident and death—the first I heard of it. I went to his grave in the cemetery and had a good cry. I couldn't help it. Poor old Daddy ! It was cruel hard luck getting killed as he did. I put a lot of flowers on his grave and arranged with Ropes the Nurseryman about having the grass cut regularly.'*

"'And 'im,' said my mother, 'lying there ! 'E'd 've rather seen 'er lying dead at 'is feet, 'e said, than 'ave 'er the fallen woman she was. And she putting flowers over 'im. 'Nough to make 'im turn in 'is grave.'

"'But very likely he's come to think differently now, Martha,' said Matilda soothingly. 'There's no knowing really, Martha. Perhaps in heaven they aren't so anxious to see people dead at their feet. Perhaps they get sort of kind up there. Let me see,—where was I ? Ah ?—*grass cut regularly.*

"'*Nobody knew where mother and the rest of you were. Nobody had an address. I went on to London very miserable, hating to have lost you. Mrs. Bradley said that mother and Prue and Morty had gone to London to friends, but where she didn't know. And then behold ! after nearly two years, you bob up again ! It's too good to be true. Where are the others ? Is Morty getting educated ? Prue must be quite grown up ? I would love to see them again and help them if I can. Dear Ernie, I do want you to tell mother and all of them that I am quite safe and happy. I am being helped by a friend. The one you saw. I'm not a bit fast or bad. I lead a very quiet life. I have my tiny little flat here and I read a lot and get educated. I work quite hard. I've passed an examination, Ernie, a university examination. I've learned a lot of French and Italian and some German and about music. I've got a pianola and I'd love to play it to you or Morty. He was always the one for music. Often and often I think of you. Tell mother, show her this letter, and let me know soon about you all and don't think unkind things of me. 'Member the good times we had, Ernie, when we dressed up at Christmas and father didn't know us in the shop, and how you made me a doll's house for my birthday. Oh ! and cheese-pies, Ernie ! Cheese-pies !*

"'What were cheese-pies ? ' asked Matilda.

" ' It was a sort of silly game we had—passing people. I forget exactly. But it used to make us laugh—regular roll about we did.'

" ' Then she gets back to you, Morty,' said Matilda.

" ' *I'd love to help Morty if he still wants to be educated. I could now. I could help him a lot. I suppose he's not a boy any longer. Perhaps he's getting educated himself. Give him my love. Give mother my love and tell her not to think too badly of me.*

Fanny.'

" ' Fanny. Embossed address on her note-paper. That's all."

" Matilda dropped the letter on the table. ' Well ? ' she said in a voice that challenged my mother. ' Seems to me that the young woman has struck one of the Right Sort—the one straight man in ten thousand. . . . seems to have taken care of her almost more than an ordinary husband might've done. . . . What'r you going to do about it, Martha ? '

" Matilda collected herself slowly from the table and leaned back in her chair, regarding my mother with an expression of faintly malevolent irony."

§ 5

" I turned from Matilda's quizzical face to my mother's drawn intentness.

" ' Say what you like, Matilda, that girl is living in sin."

" ' Even that isn't absolutely proved,' said Matilda.

" ' Why should 'e—— ? ' my mother began and stopped.

" ' There's such things as feats of generosity,' said Matilda. ' Still—— '

" ' No,' said my mother. ' We don't want 'er 'elp. I'd be ashamed to take it. While she lives with that man—— '

" ' Apparently she doesn't. But go on.'

" ' Stainted money,' said my mother. ' It's money she 'as from 'im. It's the money of a Kep Woman.'

" Her anger kindled. ' I'd sooner die than *touch* 'er money.'

" Her sense of the situation found form and expression. ' She leaves 'er 'ome. She breaks 'er father's 'eart. Kills 'im, she does. 'E was never the same man after she'd gone ; never the same. She goes off to shamelessness and luxury. She makes 'er own brother drive 'er about to 'er shame.'

" ' Hardly—*makes*,' protested Matilda.

" ' 'Ow was '*E* to avoid it ? And then she writes this—this letter. Impudent I call it. Impudent ! Without a word of repentance—not a single word of repentance. Does she 'ave the decency to say she's ashamed of 'erself ? Not a word. Owns she's still living with a fancy man and means to go on doing it, glories in it. And offers us 'er kind assistance—us, what she's disgraced and shamed. Who was it that made us

leave Cherry Gardens to 'iae our 'eads from our neighbours in
London ? *'Er !* And now she's to come 'ere in 'er moty-car
and come dancing down these steps, all dressed up and painted,
to say a kind word to poor mother. 'Aven't we suffered enough
about 'er without 'er coming 'ere to show 'erself off at us ?
It's topsyturvy. Why ! if she comes 'ere at all, which I doubt
—if she comes 'ere at all she ought to come in sackcloth and
ashes and on 'er bended knees.'

" ' She won't do that, Martha,' said Matilda Good.

" ' Then let 'er keep away. We don't want the disgrace of
'er. She's chosen 'er path and let 'er abide by it. But *'ere.*
To come *'ere !* 'Ow'r you going to explain it ? '

" ' *I'd* explain it all right,' said Matilda unheeded.

" ' 'Ow am *I* going to explain it ? And here's Prue ! Here's
this Mr. Pettigrew she met at the Week-day Evening Social
and wants to bring to tea ! 'Ow's she going to explain 'er fine
lady-sister to 'im ? Kep Woman. Yes, Matilda. I say it. It's
the name for it. That's what she is. A Kep Woman ! Nice
things to tell Mr. Pettigrew. 'Ere's my sister, the Kep Woman !
'E'd be off in a jiffy. Shocked 'e'd be out of 'is seven senses.
' Ow would Prue ever 'ave the face to go to the Week-day
Evening Social again after a show-up like that ? And Ernie.
What's 'E going to say about it to the other chaps at the
garage when they throw it up at him that 'is sister's a Kep
Woman ? '

" ' Don't you worry about *that,* mother,' said Ernest gently
but firmly. ' There's nobody ever throws anything up against
me at the garage anyhow—and there won't be. Nohow. Not
unless 'E wants to swaller 'is teeth.'

" ' Well, there's 'Arry. 'E goes to 'is classes, and what if
some one gets 'old of it there ? ' Is sister, a Kep Woman.
They'd 'ardly let 'im go on working after such a disgrace.'

" ' Oh I'd soon—— ' I began, following in my brother's
wake. But Matilda stopped me with a gesture. Her gesture
swept round and held my mother, who was indeed drawing
near the end of what she had to say.

" ' I can see, Martha,' said Matilda, ' just 'ow you feel about
Fanny. I suppose it's all natural. Of course, this letter—— '

" She picked up the letter. She pursed her great mouth and
waggled her clumsy head slowly from side to side. ' For the
life of me I can't believe the girl who wrote this is a bad-
hearted girl,' she said. ' You're bitter with her, Martha.
You're bitter.'

" ' After all—— ' I began, but Matilda's hand stopped me
again.

" ' Bitter ! ' cried my mother. ' I *know* 'er. She can put on
that in'cent air just as though nothing 'ad 'appened and try
and make you feel in the wrong—— '

" Matilda ceased to waggle and began to nod. ' I see,' she
said. ' I see. But why should Fanny take the trouble to write

this letter, if she hadn't a real sort of affection for you all ?
As though she need have bothered herself about the lot of
you ! You're no sort of help to her. There's kindness in the
letter, Martha, and something more than kindness. Are you
going to throw it back at her ? Her and her offers of help ?
Even if she doesn't crawl and repent as she ought to do !
Won't you even answer her letter ? '

" ' I won't be drawn into a correspondence with 'er,' said
my mother. ' No ! So long as she's a Kep Woman, she's no
daughter of mine. I wash my 'ands of 'er. And as for 'er 'Elp !
'Elp indeed ! It's 'Umbug ! If she'd wanted 'elp us she could
have married Mr. Crosby, as fair and honest a man as any
woman could wish for.'

" ' So that's *that*,' said Matilda Good conclusively.

" Abruptly she swivelled her great head round to Ernest.
' And what are you going to do, Ernie ? Are *you* for turning
down Fanny ? And letting the cheese-pies just drop into the
mud of Oblivium, as the saying goes, and be forgotten for
ever and ever and ever ? '

" Ernest sat back, put his hands in his trouser-pockets and
remained thoughtful for some moments. ' It's orkward,' he
said.

" Matilda offered him no assistance.

" ' There's my Young Lady to consider,' said Ernest and
flushed an extreme scarlet.

" My mother turned her head sharply and looked at him.
Ernest with a stony expression did not look at my mother.

" ' O—oh ! ' said Matilda. ' Here's something new. And
who may your Young Lady be, Ernie ? '

" ' Well, I 'adn't proposed to discuss 'er 'ere just yet. So
never mind what 'er name is. She's got a little millinery
business. I'll say that for 'er. And a cleverer nicer girl never
lived. We met at a little dance. Nothing isn't fixed up yet
beyond a sort of engagement. There's been presents. Given
'er a ring and so forth. But naturally I've never told 'er
anything about Fanny. I 'aven't discussed family affairs with
'er much, not so far. Knows we were in business of some
sort and 'ad losses and father died of an accident ; that's
about all. But Fanny—Fanny's certainly going to be orkward to explain. Not that I want to be *'ard* on Fanny ! '

" ' I see,' said Matilda. She glanced a mute interrogation
at Prue and found her answer in Prue's face. Then she picked
up the letter again and read very distinctly : ' One hundred
and two Brantismore Gardens, Earl's Court.' She read this
address slowly as though she wanted to print it on her memory.
' Top flat, you said it was, Ernie ? ' . . .

" She turned to me. ' And what are you going to do, Harry,
about all this ? '

" ' I want to see Fanny for myself,' I said. ' I don't believe——'

" " 'Arry,' said my mother, ' now—once for all—I forbid you to go near 'er. I won't 'ave you corrupted.'

" ' Don't forbid him, Martha,' said Matilda. ' It's no use forbidding him. *Because he will !* Any boy with any heart and spunk in him would go and see her after that letter. One hundred and two, Brantismore Gardens, Earl's Court,'—she was very clear with the address—' it's not very far from here.'

" ' I forbid you to go near 'er, 'Arry,' my mother reiterated. And then realising too late the full importance of Fanny's letter, she picked it up. ' I won't 'ave this answered. I'll burn it as it deserves. And forget about it. Banish it from my mind. *There.*'

" And then my mother stood up and making a curious noise in her throat like the strangulation of a sob, she put Fanny's letter into the fire and took the poker to thrust it into the glow and make it burn. We all stared in silence as the letter curled up and darkened, burst into a swift flame and became in an instant a writhing, agonised, crackling, black cinder. Then she sat down again, remained still for a moment, and then after a fierce struggle with her skirt-pocket dragged out a poor old dirty pocket-handkerchief and began to weep—at first quietly and then with a gathering passion. The rest of us sat aghast at this explosion.

" ' You mustn't go near Fanny, 'Arry ; not if mother forbids,' said Ernest at last, gently but firmly.

" Matilda looked at me in grim inquiry.

" ' I *shall*,'' I said, and was in a terror lest the unmanly tears behind my eyes should overflow.

" ' 'Arry ! ' cried my mother amidst her sobs. ' You'll break—you'll break my heart ! First Fanny ! Then you.'

" ' You see ! ' said Ernest.

" The storm of her weeping paused as though she waited to hear my answer. My silly little face must have been very red by this time and there was something wrong and uncontrollable about my voice, but I said what I meant to say. ' I shall go to Fanny,' I said, ' and I shall just ask her straight out whether she's leading a bad life.'

" ' And suppose she is ? ' asked Matilda.

" ' I shall reason with her,' I said. ' I shall do all I can to save her. Yes—even if I have to find some work that will keep her. . . . She's my sister.' . . .

" I wept for a moment or so. ' I can't help it, mother,' I sobbed. ' I got to see Fanny ! '

" I recovered my composure with an effort.

" ' *So*,' said Matilda, regarding me, I thought, with rather more irony and rather less admiration than I deserved. Then she turned to my mother. ' I don't see that Harry can say fairer than that,' she said. ' I think you'll have to let him see her after that. He'll do all he can to save her, he says. Who knows ? He might bring her to repentance.'

" ' More likely the other way about,' said my mother, wiping her eyes, her brief storm of tears now over.

" ' I can't 'elp feeling it's a mistake,' said Ernest, ' for 'Arry to go and see 'er.'

" ' Well, anyhow don't give it up because you've forgotten the address, Harry,' said Matilda, ' or else you *are* done.   Let it be your own free will and not forgetfulness, if you throw her over.   One hundred and two Brantismore Gardens, Earl's Court.   You'd better write it down."

" ' One hundred and two—Brantismore Gardens.'

" I went over to my books on the corner table to do as she advised sternly and resolutely in a fair round hand on the fly-leaf of Smith's *Principia Latina*.

§ 6

" My first visit to Fanny's flat was quite unlike any of the moving scenes I acted in my mind beforehand.   I went round about half-past eight when shop was done on the evening next but one after Ernest's revelation.   The house seemed to me a very dignified one and I went up a carpeted staircase to her flat.   I rang the bell and she opened the door herself.

" It was quite evident at once that the smiling young woman in the doorway had expected to see some one else instead of the gawky youth who stood before her, and that for some moments she had not the slightest idea who I was.   Her expression of radiant welcome changed to a defensive coldness. ' What do you want, please ? ' she said to my silent stare.

" She had altered very much.   She had grown, though now I was taller than she was, and her wavy brown hair was tied by a band of black velvet with a brooch on one side of it, adorned with clear-cut stones of some sort that shone and twinkled.   Her face and lips had a warmer colour than I remembered.   And she was wearing a light, soft greenish-blue robe with loose sleeves ; it gave glimpses of her pretty neck and throat and revealed her white arms.   She seemed a magically delightful being, soft and luminous and sweet-scented and altogether wonderful to a young barbarian out of the London streets.   Her delicacy overawed me.   I cleared my throat.   ' Fanny ! ' I said hoarsely, ' don't you know me ? '

" She knitted her pretty brows and then came her old delightful smile.   ' Why !   It's Harry ! ' she cried and drew me into the little hall and hugged and kissed me.   ' My little brother Harry, grown as big as I am !   How wonderful ! '

" Then she went by me and shut the door and looked at me doubtfully.   ' But why didn't you write to me first to say you were coming ?   Here am I dying for a talk with you and here's a visitor who's coming to see me.   May come in at any moment.   Now what am I to do.   Let me see ! '

" The little hall in which we stood was bright with white paint and pretty Japanese pictures.   It had cupboards to hide

away coats and hats and an old oak-chest. Several doors
opened into it and two were ajar. Through one I had a glimpse
of a sofa and things set out for coffee, and through the other
I saw a long mirror and a chintz-covered arm-chair. She
seemed to hesitate between these two rooms and then pushed
me into the former one and shut the door behind us.

" ' You should have written to tell me you were coming,'
she said. ' I'm dying to talk to you and here's some one
coming who's dying to talk to *me*. But never mind ! let's talk
all we can. How are you ? *Well*—I can see that. But are you
getting educated ? And mother, how's mother ? What's
happened to Prue ? And is Ernest as hot-tempered as ever ? "

" I attempted to tell her. I tried to give her an impression
of Matilda Good and to hint not too harshly at my mother's
white implacability. I began to tell her of my chemist's shop
and how much Latin and Chemistry I knew, and in the midst
of it she darted away from me and stood listening.

" It was the sound of a latch-key at the door.

" ' My other visitor,' she said, hesitated a moment and was
out of the room, leaving me to study her furniture and the
coffee-machine that bubbled on the table. She had left the
door a little ajar and I heard all too plainly the sound of a
kiss and then a man's voice. I thought it was rather a jolly
voice.

" ' I'm tired, little Fanny ; oh ! I'm tired to death. This
new paper is the devil. We've started all wrong. But I shall
pull it off. Gods ! if I hadn't this sweet pool of rest to plunge
into, I'd go off my head ! I'd have nothing left to me but
head-lines. Take my coat ; there's a dear. I smell coffee.'

" I heard a movement as though Fanny had checked her
visitor almost at the door of the room I was in. I heard her
say something very quickly about a brother.

" ' Oh, *Damn* ! ' said the man very heartily. ' Not another
of 'em ! How many brothers have you got, Fanny ? Send
him away. I've only got an hour altogether, my dear——"

" Then the door closed sharply—Fanny must have discovered it was ajar—and the rest of the talk was inaudible.

" Fanny reappeared, a little flushed and bright-eyed and
withal demure. She had evidently been kissed again.

" ' Harry,' she said, ' I hate to ask you to go and come
again, but that other visitor—I'd promised him first. Do you
mind, Harry ? I'm longing for a good time with you, a good
long talk. You get your Sundays, Harry ? Well, why not
come at three on Sunday when I'll be quite alone and we'll
have a regular good old tea ? Do you mind, Harry ? '

" I said I didn't. In that flat ethical values seemed quite
different to what they were outside.

" ' After all, you did ought to have written first,' said
Fanny, ' instead of just jumping out on me out of the dark.'

" There was no one in the hall when she showed me out

and not even a hat or coat visible. ' Give me a kiss, Harry,' she said and I kissed her very readily. ' Quite sure you don't mind ? ' she said at her door.

" ' Not a bit,' I said. ' I ought to have written.'

" ' Sunday at three,' she said, as I went down the carpeted staircase.

" ' Sunday at three,' I replied at the bend of the stairs.

" Downstairs there was a sort of entrance hall to all the flats with a fire burning in a fireplace and a man ready to call a cab or taxi for any one who wanted one. The prosperity and comfort of it all impressed me greatly, and I was quite proud to be walking out of such a fine place. It was only when I had gone some way along the street that I began to realise how widely my plans for the evening had miscarried.

" I had not asked her whether she was living a bad life or not and I had reasoned with her not at all. The scenes I had rehearsed in my mind beforehand, of a strong and simple and resolute younger brother saving his frail but lovable sister from terrible degradations, had indeed vanished altogether from my mind when her door had opened and she had appeared. And here I was with the evening all before me and nothing to report to my family but the profound difference that lies between romance and reality. I decided not to report to my family at all yet, but to go for a very long walk and think this Fanny business over thoroughly, returning home when it would be too late for my mother to cross-examine me and ' draw me out ' at any length.

" I made for the Thames Embankment, for that afforded uncrowded pavements and the solemnity and incidental beauty appropriate to a meditative promenade.

" It is curious to recall now the phases of my mind that night. At first the bright realities I came from dominated me : Fanny, pretty, and prosperous, kindly and self-assured, in her well-lit, well-furnished flat, and the friendly and confident voice I had heard speaking in the hall, asserted themselves as facts to be accepted and respected. It was delightful after more than two years of ugly imaginations to have the glimpse of my dear sister again so undefeated and loved and cared for and to look forward to a long time with her on Sunday and a long confabulation upon all I had done in the meantime and all I meant to do. Very probably these two people were married after all, but unable for some obscure reason to reveal the fact to the world. Perhaps Fanny would tell me as much in the strictest confidence on Sunday and I could go home and astonish and quell my mother with the whispered secret. And even as I developed and cuddled this idea it grew clear and cold and important in my mind that they were not married at all, and the shades of a long-accumulated disapproval dimmed that first bright impression of Fanny's little nest. I felt a growing dissatisfaction with the part I had played in our

encounter.   I had let myself be handled and thrust out as
though I had been a mere boy instead of a brother full of help
and moral superiority. Surely I ought to have said something,
however brief, to indicate our relative moral position !   I
ought to have faced that man too, the Bad Man, lurking no
doubt in the room with the mirror and of the chintz-covered
chair. He had avoided seeing me—because he could not face
me ! And from these new aspects of the case I began to develop
a whole new dream of reproach and rescue.   What should I
have said to the Bad Man ?   ' And so, sir, at last we meet——'

" Something like that.

" My imagination began to leap and bound and soar with
me.   I pictured the Bad Man, dressed in that ' immaculate
evening-dress ' which my novels told me marked the deeper
and colder depths of male depravity, cowering under my
stream of simple eloquence.   ' You took her,' I would say,
' from our homely but pure and simple home. You broke her
father's heart '—yes, I imagined myself saying that !—' And
what have you made of her ? ' I asked.   ' Your doll, your plaything ! to be pampered while the whim lasts and then to be
cast aside ! '   Or—' tossed aside ' ?

" I decided ' tossed aside ' was better.

" I found myself walking along the Embankment, gesticulating and uttering such things as that."

" But you knew better ? " said Firefly. " Even then."

" I knew better. But that was the way our minds worked
in the ancient days."

§ 7

" But," said Sarnac, " my second visit to Fanny, like my
first, was full of unexpected experiences and unrehearsed
effects. The carpet on the pleasant staircase seemed to deaden
down my moral tramplings, and when the door opened and
I saw my dear Fanny again, friendly and glad, I forgot altogether the stern interrogations with which that second interview was to have opened. She pulled my hair and kissed me,
took my hat and coat, said I had grown tremendously and
measured herself against me, pushed me into her bright little
sitting-room where she had prepared such a tea as I had never
seen before, little ham sandwiches, sandwiches of a delightful
stuff called Gentleman's Relish, strawberry jam, two sorts of
cake, and little biscuits to fill in any odd corners. ' You are
a dear to come and see me, Harry. But I had a sort of feeling
that whatever happened you would come along.'

" ' We two always sort of hung together,' I said.

" ' Always,' she agreed. ' I think mother and Ernie might
have written me a line. Perhaps they will later. Ever seen an
electric kettle, Harry ? This is one. And you put that plug
in there.'

" ' I know,' I said, and did as I was told. ' There's resistances embedded in the coating. I've been doing some electricity and chemistry. Council classes. Six'r seven subjects altogether. And there's a shop window in Tothill Street full of such things.'

" ' I expect you know all about them,' she said. ' I expect you've learned all sorts of sciences,' and so we came to the great topic of what I was learning and what I was going to do.

" It was delightful to talk to some one who really understood the thirst for knowledge that possessed me. I talked of myself and my dreams and ambitions, and meanwhile, being a growing youth, my arm swept like a swarm of locusts over Fanny's wonderful tea. Fanny watched me with a smile on her face and steered me with questions towards the things she most wanted to know. And when we had talked enough for a time she showed me how to play her pianola and I got a roll of Schumann that Mr. Plaice had long ago made familiar to me and had the exquisite delight of playing it over for myself. These pianolas were quite easy things to manage, I found ; in a little while I was already playing with conscious expression.

" Fanny praised me for my quickness, cleared her tea-things away while I played, and then came and sat beside me and listened and talked and we found we had learned quite a lot about music since our parting. We both thought great things of Bach,—whom I found I was calling quite incorrectly Batch—and Mozart, who also had to be pronounced a little differently. And then Fanny began to question me about the work I wanted to do in the world. ' You mustn't stay with that old chemist much longer,' she declared. How would I like to do some sort of work that had to do with books, bookselling or helping in a library or printing and publishing books and magazines ? ' You've never thought of writing things ? ' asked Fanny. ' People do.'

" ' I made some verses once or twice,' I confessed, ' and wrote a letter to *The Daily News* about temperance. But they didn't put it in.'

" ' Have you ever wanted to write ? '

" ' What, books ? Like Arnold Bennett ? *Rather !* '

" ' But you didn't quite know how to set about it.'

" ' It's difficult to begin,' I said, as though that was the only barrier.

" ' You ought to leave that old chemist's shop,' she repeated. ' If I were to ask people I know and found out some better sort of job for you, Harry, would you take it ? '

" ' *Rather !* ' said I."

" Why not altogether ? " interrupted Firefly.

" Oh ! we used to say *Rather*," said Sarnac. " It was artistic understatement. But you realise how dreadfully I lapsed from all my preconceived notions about Fanny and myself. We talked the whole evening away. We had a delightful cold picnic-supper in a pretty little dining-room with a dresser, and Fanny showed me how to make a wonderful salad with onions very finely chopped and white wine and sugar in the dressing. And afterwards came some more of that marvel, the pianola, and then very reluctantly I took my leave. And when I found myself in the streets again I had once more my former sense of having dropped abruptly from one world into another, colder, bleaker, harder, and with entirely different moral values. Again I felt the same reluctance to go straight home and have my evening dimmed and destroyed by a score of pitiless questions. And when at last I did go home I told a lie. ' Fanny's got a pretty place and she's as happy as can be,' I said. ' I'm not quite sure, but from what she said, I believe that man's going to marry her before very long.'

" My cheeks and ears grew hot under my mother's hostile stare.

" ' Did she tell you that ? '

" ' Practically,' I lied. ' I kind of got it out of her.'

" ' But 'e's married already ! ' said my mother.

" ' I believe there is something,' I said.

" ' *Something !* ' said my mother scornfully. ' She's stolen another woman's man. 'E belongs to 'er—for ever. No matter what there is against 'er. " Whomsoever God Hath Joined, Let No Man Put Asunder ! "—that's what I was taught and what I believe. 'E may be older ; 'e may have led her astray, but while she and 'e harbour together the sin is 'ers smutch as 'is. Did you see 'im ? '

" ' He wasn't there.'

" ' A'dn't the face. That's so much to their credit. And are you going there again ? '

" ' I've kind of promised——'

" ' It's against my wishes, 'Arry. Every time you go near Fanny, 'Arry, you disobey me. Mark that. Let's be plain about that, once and for all.'

" I felt mulish. ' She's my sister,' I said.

" ' And I'm your mother. Though nowadays mothers are no more than dirt under their children's feet. Marry 'er indeed ! Why *should* 'e ? Likely. 'E'll marry the next one. Come, Prue, take that bit of coal off the fire and we'll go up to bed.' "

§ 8

" And now," said Sarnac, " I must tell you of the queer business organisation of Thunderstone House and the great firm of Crane & Newberry, for whom, at Fanny's instance, I abandoned Mr. Humberg and his gold-labelled bottles of nothingness. Crane & Newberry were publishers of newspapers, magazines and books, and Thunderstone House was a sort of fountain of printed paper, spouting an unending wash of reading-matter into the lives of the English people.

" I am talking of the world two thousand years ago," said Sarnac. " No doubt you have all been good children and have read your histories duly, but at this distance in time things

appear very much fore-shortened, and changes that occupied
lifetimes and went on amidst dense clouds of doubt, misunderstanding and opposition seem to be the easiest and most
natural of transitions. We were all taught that the scientific
method came into human affairs first of all in the world of
material things, and later on in the matters of psychology and
human relationship, so that the large-scale handling of steel,
and railways, automobiles, telegraphs, flying-machines and
all the broad material foundations of the new age were in
existence two or three generations before social, political and
educational ideas and methods were modified in correspondence
with the new necessities these things had created. There was
a great unanticipated increase in the trade and population of
the world and much confusion and conflict, violent social
stresses and revolutions and great wars, before even the need
of a scientific adjustment of human relationships was recognised. It is easy enough to learn of such things in general
terms but hard to explain just what these processes of blind
readjustment meant in anxiety, suffering and distress to the
countless millions who found themselves born into the swirl
of this phase of change. As I look back to that time in which
I lived my other life I am reminded of a crowd of people in
one of my old Pimlico fogs. No one had any vision of things
as a whole ; everybody was feeling his way slowly and clumsily
from one just perceptible thing to another. And nearly everybody was uneasy and disposed to be angry.

" It is clear beyond question to us now, that the days of
illiterate drudges were already past in the distant nineteenth
century, for power machinery had superseded them. The New
World, so much more complicated and dangerous, so much
richer and ampler, was a world insisting upon an educated
population educated intellectually and morally. But in those
days these things were not at all clear, and it was grudgingly
and insufficiently that access to knowledge and enlightenment
was given by the learned and prosperous classes to the rapidly
accumulating masses of the population. They insisted that
it should be done by special channels and in a new and different
class of school. I have told you of what passed for my education, reading and writing, rudimentary computations, ' jog-
fry ' and so forth. That sort of process, truncated by employment at thirteen or fourteen, when curiosity and interest were
just beginning to awaken, was as far as education had gone
for the bulk of the common men and women in the opening
years of the twentieth century. It had produced a vast multitude of people, just able to read, credulous and uncritical and
pitifully curious to learn about life and things, pitifully wanting to see and know. As a whole the community did nothing
to satisfy the vague aspirations of those half-awakened swarms ;
it was left to ' private enterprise ' to find what profits it could
in their dim desires. A number of great publishing businesses

arose to trade upon the new reading public that this ' elementary ' education, as we called it, had accumulated.

" In all ages people have wanted stories about life. The young have always wanted to be told about the stage on which they are beginning to play their parts, to be shown the chances and possibilities of existence, vividly and dramatically, so that they may imagine and anticipate their own reactions. And even those who are no longer youthful have always been eager to supplement their experiences and widen their judgment by tales and histories and discussions. There has been literature since there has been writing, since indeed there was enough language for story-telling and reciting. And always literature has told people what their minds were prepared to receive, searching for what it should tell rather in the mind and expectation of the hearer or reader—who was the person who paid—than in the unendowed wildernesses of reality. So that the greater part of the literature of every age has been a vulgar and ephemeral thing interesting only to the historian and psychologist of later times because of the light it threw upon the desires and imaginative limitations of its generation. But the popular literature of the age in which Harry Mortimer Smith was living was more abundant, more cynically insincere, lazy, cheap and empty than anything that the world had ever seen before.

" You would accuse me of burlesque if I were to tell you the stories of the various people who built up immense fortunes by catering for the vague needs of the new reading crowds that filled the hypertrophied cities of the Atlantic world. There was a certain Newnes of whom legend related that one day after reading aloud some item of interest to his family he remarked, ' I call that a regular titbit.' From that feat of nomenclature he went on to the idea of a weekly periodical full of scraps of interest, cuttings from books and newspapers and the like. A hungry multitude, eager and curious, was ready to feed greedily on such *hors d'œuvre*. So *Tit-Bits* came into existence, whittled from a thousand sources by an industrious and not too expensive staff, and Newnes became a man of wealth and a baronet. His first experiment upon the new public encouraged him to make a number of others. He gave it a monthly magazine full of short stories drawn from foreign sources. At first its success was uncertain, and then a certain Doctor Conan Doyle rose to fame in it and carried it to success with stories about crime and the detection of crime. Every intelligent person in those days, every one indeed intelligent or not, was curious about the murders and suchlike crimes which still abounded. Indeed, there could have been no more fascinating and desirable subject for us; properly treated such cases illuminated the problems of law, training and control of our social welter as nothing else could have done. The poorest people bought at least a weekly paper in order to quicken their wits over murder mysteries and divorces, driven by an almost instinctive need to probe motives and judge restraints. But Conan Doyle's stories had little of psychology in them ; he tangled a skein of clues in order to disentangle it again, and his readers forgot the interest of the problem in the interest of the puzzle.

" Hard upon the heels of Newnes came a host of other competitors, among others a certain Arthur Pearson and a group of brothers, Harmsworth, who rose to great power and wealth from the beginning of a small weekly paper called *Answers*, inspired originally by the notion that people liked to read other people's letters. You will find in the histories how two of these Harmsworths, men of great thrust and energy, became Lords of England and prominent figures in politics, but I have to tell of them now simply to tell you of the multitude of papers and magazines they created to win the errand-boy's guffaw, the heart of the factory girl, the respect of the aristocracy and the confidence of the *nouveau riche*. It was a roaring factory of hasty printing. Our own firm at Thunderstone House was of an older standing than these Newnes, Pearson, Harmsworth concerns. As early as the eighteenth century the hunger for knowledge had been apparent, and a certain footman turned publisher, named Dodsley, had produced a book of wisdom called the ' Young Man's Companion.' Our founder, Crane, had done the same sort of thing in Early Victorian times. He had won his way to considerable success with a *Home Teacher* in monthly parts and with Crane's ' Circle of the Sciences ' and a weekly magazine and so forth. His chief rivals had been two firms called Cassell's and Routledge's, and for years, though he worked upon a smaller capital, he kept well abreast of them. For a time the onrush of the newer popular publishers had thrust Crane and his contemporaries into the background and then, reconstructed and reinvigorated by a certain Sir Peter Newberry, the old business had won its way back to prosperity, publishing a shoal of novelette magazines and cheap domestic newspapers for women, young girls and children, reviving the *Home Teacher* on modern lines with a memory training system and a ' Guide to Success ' by Sir Peter Newberry thrown in, and even launching out into scientific handbooks of a not too onerous sort.

" It is difficult for you to realise," said Sarnac, " what a frightful lot of printed stuff there was in that old world. It was choked with printed rubbish just as it was choked with human rubbish and a rubbish of furniture and clothing and every sort of rubbish ; there was too much of the inferior grades of everything. And good things incredibly rare ! You cannot imagine how delightful it is for me to sit here again, naked and simple, talking plainly and nakedly in a clear and beautiful room. The sense of escape, of being cleansed of unnecessary adhesions of any sort is exquisite. We read a book

now and then and talk and make love naturally and honestly
and do our work and thought and research with well-aired,
well-fed brains, and we live with all our senses and abilities
taking a firm and easy grip upon life. But stress was in the
air of the twentieth century. Those who had enough courage
fought hard for knowledge and existence, and to them we sold
our not very lucid or helpful *Home Teacher* and our entirely
base ' Guide to Success '; but great multitudes relaxed their
hold upon life in a way that is known now only to our morbid
psychologists. They averted their attention from reality and
gave themselves up to reverie. They went about the world
distraught in a day-dream, a day-dream that they were not
really themselves, but beings far nobler and more romantic,
or that presently things would change about them into a
dramatic scene centering about themselves. These novelette
magazines and popular novels that supplied the chief part of
the income of Crane & Newberry were really helps to reverie
—mental drugs. Sunray, have you ever read any twentieth-
century novelettes ? "

" One or two," said Sunray. " It's as you say. I suppose I
have a dozen or so. Some day you shall see my little collection."

" Very likely *ours*—half of them,—Crane & Newberry's I
mean. It will be amusing to see them again. The great bulk
of this reverie material was written for Crane & Newberry
by girls and women and by a type of slack imaginative men.
These ' authors,' as we called them, lived scattered about
London or in houses on the countryside, and they sent their
writings by post to Thunderstone House, where we edited them
in various ways and put the stuff into our magazines and books.
Thunderstone House was a great rambling warren of a place
opening out of Tottenham Court Road, with a yard into which
huge lorries brought rolls of paper and from which vans departed with our finished products. It was all aquiver with the
roar and thudding of the printing machinery. I remember
very vividly to this day how I went there first, down a narrow
roadway out of the main thoroughfare, past a dingy public-
house and the stage-door of a theatre."

" What were you going to do—pack up books ? Or run
errands ? " asked Radiant.

" I was to do what I could. Very soon I was on the general
editorial staff."

" Editing popular knowledge ? "

" Yes."

" But why did they want an illiterate youngster like yourself at Thunderstone House ? " asked Radiant. " I can understand that this work of instructing and answering the first
crude questions of the new reading-classes was necessarily
a wholesale improvised affair, but surely there were enough
learned men at the ancient universities to do all the editing
and instructing that was needed ! "

Sarnac shook his head. " The amazing thing is that there weren't," he said. " They produced men enough of a sort but they weren't the right sort."

His auditors looked puzzled.

" The rank-and-file of the men they sent out labelled M.A. and so forth from Oxford and Cambridge were exactly like those gilt-lettered jars in Mr. Humberg's shop, that had nothing in them but stale water. The pseudo-educated man of the older order couldn't teach, couldn't write, couldn't explain. He was pompous and patronising and prosy ; timid and indistinct in statement, with no sense of the common need or the common quality. The promoted office-boy, these new magazine and newspaper-people discovered, was brighter and better at the job, comparatively modest and industrious, eager to know things and impart things. The editors of our periodicals, the managers of our part publications and so forth were nearly all of the office-boy class, hardly any of them, in the academic sense, educated. But many of them had a sort of educational enthusiasm and all of them a boldness that the men of the old learning lacked. . . ."

Sarnac reflected. " In Britain at the time I am speaking about—and in America also—there were practically two educational worlds and two traditions of intellectual culture side by side. There was all this vast fermenting hullabaloo of the new publishing, the new press, the cinema-theatres and so forth, a crude mental uproar arising out of the new elementary schools of the nineteenth century, and there was the old aristocratic education of the seventeenth and eighteenth centuries, which had picked up its tradition from the Augustan Age of Rome. They didn't mix. On the one hand were these office-boy fellows with the intellectual courage and vigour— oh ! of Aristotle and Plato, whatever the quality of their intellectual equipment might be ; on the other the academic man, affectedly Grecian, like the bought-and-sold learned man of the days of Roman slavery. He had the gentility of the household-slave ; he had the same abject respect for patron, prince and patrician ; he had the same meticulous care in minor matters, and the same fear of uncharted reality. He criticised like a slave, sneering and hinting, he quarrelled like a slave, despised all he dared despise with the eagerness of a slave. He was incapable of serving the multitude. The new reading-crowd, the working masses, the ' democracy ' as we used to call it, had to get its knowledge and its wisdom without him.

" Crane, our founder, had had in his day some inkling of the educational function such businesses as his were bound to serve in the world, but Sir Peter Newberry had been a hard tradesman, intent only on recovering the prosperity that the newer popular publishers had filched away from our firm. He was a hard driving man ; he drove hard, he paid in niggardly fashion and he succeeded. He had been dead now for some years and the chief shareholder and director of the firm was his son Richard. He was nicknamed the Sun ; I think because some one had quoted Shakespeare about the winter of our discontent being made summer by this Sun of York. He was by contrast a very congenial and warming person. He was acutely alive to the moral responsibility that lay behind the practical irresponsibility of a popular publisher. If anything, he drove harder than his father, but he paid generously ; he tried to keep a little ahead of the new public instead of a little behind ; the times moved in his favour and he succeeded even more than his father had done. I had been employed by Crane & Newberry for many weeks before I saw him, but in the first office I entered in Thunderstone House I saw the evidences of his personality in certain notices upon the wall. They were printed in clear black letters on cards and hung up. It was his device for giving the house a tone of its own.

" I remember ' We lead ; the others imitate,' and ' If you are in any doubt about its being too good put it in '. A third was : ' If a man doesn't know what you know that's no reason for writing as if he was an all-round fool. Rest assured there is something he knows better than you do '."

§ 9

" It took me some time to get from the yard of Thunderstone House to the office in which these inscriptions were displayed. Fanny had told me to ask for Mr. Cheeseman, and when I had discovered and entered the doorway up a flight of steps, which had at first been masked by two large vans, I made this demand of an extremely small young lady inclosed in a kind of glass cage. She had a round face and a bright red button of a nose. She was engaged, I realised slowly, in removing a foreign stamp from a fragment of envelope by licking the back of the paper. She did not desist from this occupation but mutely asked my business with her eyes.

" ' Oran-amoiment ? ' she asked, still licking.

" ' Pardon ? '

" ' Oran-amoiment ? '

" ' I'm sorry,' I said, ' I don't get it quite.'

" ' Mus' be deaf,' she said, putting down the stamp and taking a sufficient breath for slow loud speech. ' 'Ave you gottonappointment ? '

" ' Oh ! ' I said. ' Yes. I was told to come here to-day and see Mr. Cheeseman between ten and twelve.'

She resumed her struggle with the stamp for a time. ' S'pose you don't c'lect stamps ? ' she asked. ' 'Sintresting 'obby. Mr. Cheeseman's written a little 'and-book about it. Looking for a job I suppose ? May 'ave to wait a bit. Will you fill up that bit of paper there ? Formality we 'ave to insist on. Pencil. . . .'

"The paper demanded my name and my business and I wrote that the latter was 'literary employment.'

"'Lordy,' said the young lady when she read it. 'I thought you was in for the ware'ouse. I say, Florence,' she said to another considerably larger girl who had appeared on the staircase, 'look at 'im. 'E's after litry employment.'

"'Cheek!' said the second young lady after one glance at me, and sat down inside the glass box with a piece of chewing-gum and a novelette just published by the firm. The young lady with the button nose resumed her stamp-damping. They kept me ten minutes before the smaller one remarked: 'S'pose I better take this up to Mr. Cheeseman, Flo,' and departed with my form.

"She returned after five minutes or so. 'Mr. Cheeseman says 'e can see you now for *one* minute,' she said, and led the way up a staircase and along a passage that looked with glass windows into a printer's shop and down a staircase and along a dark passage to a small apartment with an office-table, one or two chairs, and book-shelves covered with paper-covered publications. Out of this opened another room, and the door was open. 'You better sit down here,' said the young lady with the button nose.

"'That Smith?' asked a voice. 'Come right in.'

"I went in, and the young lady with the button nose vanished from my world.

"I discovered a gentleman sunken deeply in an arm-chair before a writing-table, and lost in contemplation of a row of vivid drawings which were standing up on a shelf against the wall of the room. He had an intensely earnest, frowning, red face, a large broad mouth intensely compressed, and stiff black hair that stood out from his head in many directions. His head was slightly on one side and he was chewing the end of a lead-pencil. 'Don't see it,' he whispered. 'Don't see it.' I stood awaiting his attention. 'Smith,' he murmured, still not looking at me, 'Harry Mortimer Smith. Smith, were you by any chance educated at a Board-School?'

"'Yessir,' I said.

"'I hear you have literary tastes.'

"'Yessir.'

"'Then come here and stand by me and look at these damned pictures there. Did you ever see such stuff?'

"I stood by his side but remained judiciously silent. The drawings I now perceived were designs for a magazine cover. Upon all of them appeared the words 'The New World' in very conspicuous lettering. One design was all flying-machines and steamships and automobiles; two others insisted upon a flying machine; one showed a kneeling loin-clothed man saluting the rising sun—which however rose behind him. Another showed a planet earth half illuminated, and another was simply a workman going to his work in the dawn.

" ' Smith,' said Mr. Cheeseman ; ' it's you've got to buy this magazine, not me. Which of these covers do you prefer ? It's your decision. *Fiat experimentum in corpore vile.*'

" ' Meaning me, sir ? ' I said brightly.

" His bristle eyebrows displayed a momentary surprise. ' I suppose we're all fitted with the same tags nowadays,' he remarked. ' Which do you find most attractive ? '

" ' Those aeroplane things, sir, seem to me to be shoving it a bit too hard,' I said.

" ' H'm,' said Mr. Cheeseman. ' That's what the Sun says. You wouldn't buy on that ? '

" ' I don't think so, sir. It's been done too much.'

" ' How about that globe ? '

" ' Too like an Atlas, sir.'

" ' Aren't geography and travel interesting ? '

" ' They are, sir, but somehow they aren't attractive.'

" ' Interesting but not attractive. H'm. Out of the mouths of babes and sucklings. . . . So it's going to be that labour chap there in the dawn. You'd buy that, eh ? '

" ' Is this going to be a magazine about inventions and discoveries and progress, sir ? '

" ' Exactly.'

" ' Well, the Dawn's good, sir, but I don't think that sort of Labour Day Cartoon man is going to be very attractive. Looks rheumatic and heavy, sir. Why not cut him out and keep the dawn ? '

" ' Bit too like a slice of ham, Smith—thin pink streaks.'

" I was struck by an idea. ' Suppose, sir, you kept that dawn scene and made it a bit earlier in the year. Buds on the trees, sir. And perhaps snowy mountains, rather cold and far off. And then you put a hand right across it—just a big hand—pointing, sir.'

" ' Pointing up ? ' said Mr. Cheeseman.

" ' No sir, pointing forward and just a little up. It would sort of make one curious.'

" ' It would. A woman's hand.'

" ' Just a hand, I think, sir.'

" ' You'd buy that ? '

" ' I'd jump at it, sir, if I had the money.'

" Mr. Cheeseman reflected for some moments, chewing his pencil serenely. Then he spat out small bits of pencil over his desk and spoke. ' What you say, Smith, is exactly what I've been thinking. Exactly. It's very curious.' He pressed a bell-push on his desk and a messenger-girl appeared. ' Ask Mr. Prelude to come here . . . So you think you'd like to come into Thunderstone House, Smith. I'm told you know a little about science already. Learn more. Our public's moving up to science. I've got some books over there I want you to read and pick out anything you find interesting.'

" ' You'll be able to find me a job, sir ? ' I said.

" ' I've got to find you a job all right. Orders is orders. You'll be able to sit in that room there. . . .''

" We were interrupted by the arrival of Mr. Prelude. He was a tall, thin, cadaverous man with a melancholy expression.

" ' Mr. Prelude,' said Mr. Cheeseman, waving his arm at the cover-sketches ; ' this stuff won't do. It's—it's too banal. We want something fresher, something with a touch of imagination. What I want to see on the cover is—well, say a dawn—a very calm and simple scene, mostly colour, mountain range far away just flushed with sunrise, valley blue and still, high streamer clouds touched with pink. See ? Trees perhaps in the foreground—just budding—spring *motif* and morning *motif*. See ? All a little faint and backgroundy. Then a big hand and wrist across the page pointing at something, something high and far away. See ? '

" He surveyed Mr. Prelude with the glow of creative enthusiasm on his face. Mr. Prelude looked disapproval. ' The Sun will like that,' he said.

" ' It's the goods,' said Mr. Cheeseman.

" ' Why not those flying-machines ? '

" ' Why not midges ? ' asked Mr. Cheeseman.

" Mr. Prelude shrugged his shoulders. ' I've got no use for a magazine on progress without a flying-machine or a Zeppelin,' he said. ' Still—it's your affair.'

" Mr. Cheeseman looked a little dashed by his colleague's doubt, but he held to his idea. ' We'll get a sketch made,' he said. ' How about Wilkinson ? '

" They discussed some unknown Wilkinson as a possible cover-designer. Then Mr. Cheeseman turned to me. ' By the by, here's a youngster we've got to make use of, Prelude. We don't know what he can do, but he seems intelligent. I thought we'd use him to sift some of those scientific books. What he likes, *they*'ll like. *I* can't read that stuff. I'm too busy.'

" Mr. Prelude surveyed me. ' You never know what you can do till you try,' he said. ' Do you know anything of science ? '

" ' Not very much,' I said. ' But I've done some physiography and chemistry and a little geology. And read a lot.'

" ' You don't want to know very much,' said Mr. Prelude. ' You're better without it here. Makes you Highbrow. Highbrow goes to tens of thousands, but Crane & Newberry go to hundreds of thousands. Not that our brows aren't rising some in this establishment. Educational and improving, we're going to be. So far as is consistent with our profits. See that notice, —*We lead* ? All the same, Cheeseman,' said Mr. Prelude, ' the thing that has sold, the thing that sells and the thing that's going to sell, is the magazine with a pretty girl on the cover—and the less costume the better. Consistent with decency. Now here's—what your name ? '

" ' Smith. And here's all these covers on the bookstall. And then I produce *this*. Which does he buy ? '

" *This* was the cover of the summer number of Newberry's Story Magazine, on which two young ladies in skin-tight bathing-dresses disported themselves on a sandy beach.

" ' Smith goes for this,' said Mr. Prelude triumphantly.

" I shook my head.

" ' You mean to say that isn't attractive ? ' said Mr. Cheeseman turning in his chair and pointing with his well-chewed pencil.

" I reflected.

" ' There's never anything about them inside,' I said.

" Got you there, Prelude ! ' said Mr. Cheeseman.

" ' Not a bit. He bought six or seven before he found that out. And most of 'em forget about it when they read inside.' "

§ 10

" I found my introduction to Thunderstone House far less terrifying than I had anticipated. It was gratifying to have come so near to what Mr. Cheeseman had thought about the magazine cover, and there were presently other very reassuring coincidences of the same sort. I was immediately interested in the editorial and publishing work that was going on about me, and my mind took one of those forward strides that are characteristic of adolescence. I was still a boy when I left Mr. Humberg ; I had not been with Crane & Newberry six weeks before I perceived that I was a capable and responsible young man. I began to form opinions rapidly, to write with confidence ; even my handwriting suddenly grew up from a careless or overcareful boyish scrawl to a consistent and characteristic script. I began to think about the clothes I was wearing and of the impression I made upon other people.

" In quite a little time I was writing short contributions to some of our minor weeklies and monthlies and suggesting articles and ' features,' as we called them, to Mr. Cheeseman. The eighteen shillings a week at which I started went up in a series of jerks to three pound, which was quite a big salary in those days for a youngster not yet eighteen. Fanny took the keenest interest in my work and displayed an extraordinary understanding of its conditions. She seemed to know all about Mr. Cheeseman and Mr. Prelude and the rest of my colleagues directly I mentioned them.

" One day I was working in the room next to Mr. Cheeseman's with another youngster called Wilkins at a rather odd little job. One of the authors our firm employed had written a long story for the *Story Reader's Paradise*, and it had been set up by the printers and passed for press before it was discovered that in a careless moment she had given her chief villain the name of a very prominent lawyer who unhappily also had a country-house in a village almost identical in name with the corresponding village in the story. The prominent lawyer might see fit to consider this use of his name as libellous and make trouble for us. So Wilkins and I were going through two sets of proofs, one to check the other, and we were changing the name of the prominent lawyer to an entirely different one whenever it occurred. To brighten the task we had made a game of it. Each one raced down his galley-proof and called the name of ' Reginald Flake ' whenever he found it and scored a point for every name he called first. I was some points up when I heard a voice in the passage that seemed oddly familiar to me. ' They're all spread out on my desk, sir, if you like to come into my room,' I heard Mr. Cheeseman say.

" ' Fay-nits,' said Wilkins. ' It's the Sun.'

" I turned round as the door opened and saw Mr. Cheeseman holding the door open for a good-looking youngish man, with rather handsome regular features and a sort of bang of brown hair over his forehead. He wore a pair of very round large spectacles with glasses tinted a faint yellow colour. He met my eyes and an expression of partial recognition came into his and faded again. Either he recognised me or he recognised a resemblance in me. He followed Mr. Cheeseman across the room. Then he turned sharply.

" ' Of course,' he said smiling and returning a step or two towards me. ' You must be young Smith. How are you getting on here ? '

" ' I'm working for Mr. Cheeseman mostly,' I said standing up.

" He turned to Mr. Cheeseman.

" ' Very satisfactory, sir. Quick, interested ; he'll do well here.'

" ' I'm glad to hear it—very glad. Everyone has a chance here and there's no favours. No favours. The best man does the job. Glad to see you among the directors whenever you care to come up to us, Smith.'

" ' I'll do my best, sir.'

" He hesitated, smiled again in a very friendly way and went into Mr. Cheeseman's room. . . .

" ' Where are we ? ' I said. ' Middle of galley 32 ? Score, 22-29.'

" ' How d'you know 'im ? ' asked Wilkins in a fierce undertone.

" ' I don't know him,' I said, suddenly hot and flushed. ' I've never seen him before.'

" ' Well, he knew you.'

" ' He's heard about me.'

" ' Who from ? '

" ' How the deuce should I know ? ' I asked with needless heat.

" ' Oh ! ' said Wilkins and reflected. ' But——'

" He glanced at my troubled face and said no more.

" But at the game of ' Reginald Flake ' he overhauled me
and beat me at the end of the book, 67-42."

" I concealed altogether from my mother the share that
Fanny had had in getting me my new job and all the opportunities it carried with it in Thunderstone House, and so it was
possible for her to find some pride and satisfaction in my
increasing prosperity. I was presently able to double and then
still further to increase my contribution to the household
expenses, and I exchanged my attic, which was handed over
to Prue for her very own, for the room which had once sheltered
the old Moggeridges. It was rearranged as a bed-sitting-room
for me, and soon I had the first one and then several shelves
full of books and a writing-desk of my own.

" And also I concealed from my mother, for there was no
use in distressing her, the frequency of my visits to Fanny.
We began to make little excursions together, for Fanny, I
discovered, was often very lonely. Newberry was a very busy
man, and often he could not come near her for ten days or a
fortnight, and although she had some women friends, and
classes and lectures, there were gaps often of several days
when she would have had no one to speak to but the servant
who came in daily to her, if it had not been for me. But all
this companioning of Fanny I tried to hide from my mother,
though now and then her suspicions stabbed my falsehoods.
Ernie and Prue, however, were able to follow the calls of
love unhampered by the family shame, and presently they
were both engaged and his young lady and her young man
were brought to a Sunday tea-party in the drawing-room—
through the kind permission of Mr. and Mrs. Milton who were
as usual ' away.' Ernie's Young Lady—I've completely forgotten her name—proved to be a well-dressed self-possessed
young woman with a vast knowledge of people in what we
used to call ' society ' ; she talked freely and fashionably,
taking the larger share of the conversation, of Ascot and Monte
Carlo and the Court. Prue's Mr. Pettigrew was of a more
serious quality, and of the things he said I remember now only
that he expressed a firm conviction that Messages from the
Dead were Bound to Come in a few years' time. He was a
chiropodist and very well thought of in chiropodological
circles."

" Stop ! " cried Radiant. " What is this ? You are talking
nonsense, Sarnac. What is chiropodological—hand—foot—
scientific ? "

" I thought you'd ask me that," said Sarnac smiling.
' Chiropody was corn-cutting."

" Corn-cutting—harvesting," said Starlight. " But where
do the hands and feet come in ? There were machines then,
were there not ? "

" No, this was a different sort of corn. Mr. Humberg's shop was full of corn-salves and corn-cures. Corns were painful and tiresome callosities produced on people's feet by the pressure of ill-fitting boots. We don't know of such things nowadays, but they darkened scores of lives in Pimlico."

" But why did they wear ill-fitting boots ? " demanded Radiant. " Oh !—never mind. Never mind. I know. A mad world which made boots at hazard without looking at the feet that had to wear them ! And wore boots that hurt it when no sane people would dream of wearing boots ! Go on with your story."

" Let me see," said Sarnac. " I was talking of a tea-party, a family tea-party in the drawing-room—in which we talked of everything in the world but my sister Fanny. And quite a little while after that tea-party my mother fell ill and died.

" It was a swift and sudden illness. She caught a cold and would not go to bed. When she did go to bed, she got up after one day of it, because she couldn't bear to think of all that Prue might be doing in the housework down-stairs. And her cold turned to pneumonia, the same sort of inflammation that had carried off the Moggeridges, and she died in three days.

" Now, when the fever came upon her she changed suddenly from something white and hard and unapproachable to something flushed and pitiful. Her face grew smaller and younger-looking, her eyes bright, and something came into them that reminded me of Fanny when Fanny was distressed. And all my habit of sullen resistance to my mother melted when I saw her struggling for breath on her tumbled pillow and realised that she might be near the end of all her hates and drudgeries. Matilda Good became again the old friend who had known her since she was a young woman, and they called each other ' Tilda ' and ' Marty ' instead of Matilda and Martha. Matilda for all her varicose veins was up and down stairs fifty times a day ; and there was much sending out for expensive things, the more expensive the better that Matilda thought my mother might ' fancy.' They stood appealingly untouched upon the table by her bedside. Once or twice towards the end my mother asked for me, and when I came in the evening and bent over her she whispered hoarsely, ' 'Arry boy—promise me ! . . . Promise me ! . . .'

" I sat down and took the hand she held out to me, and so holding to me, she dozed.

" What she wanted me to promise she never said ; and whether it was some last vow she wanted to extract from me that would separate me from Fanny for ever, or whether her thoughts about Fanny had changed under the shadow of death and she had some new message for her, I cannot imagine to this day. Perhaps she herself did not know what I had to promise ; a dying desire for predominance moved her. Wil

stirred in her and faded again to nothing. ' Promise me ! '
Fanny she never mentioned by name and we did not dare
to bring my sister in to her. Ernest came and kissed her and
knelt down by the bedside and suddenly, dreadfully wept aloud
like the child he was and set us all weeping ; he was her first-
born and her dearest, he had known her before her final em-
bitterment, he had always been a dutiful son to her.

" Presently she was lying there very straight and still, as
hushed and still as my father's shop on Sundays, and the
traffics and struggles and angers of life had done with her for
ever. Her face was now neither young nor old, a marble face
of peace. All her peevish resentment was smoothed and wiped
away. It had never occurred to me before that she had or had
not good looks, but now I saw that Fanny's fine regularity of
feature came from her. She was like Fanny, like an immobile,
unhumorous Fanny.

" I stood beside her still body oppressed by a grief too
wide and deep for tears, an immense grief that was not
so much for her as for all that distress of life she had embodied. For now I saw that there was not and there never
had been anything hateful in her ; I saw for the first time the
devotion of her, the misguided passion for right, the mute,
blundering, tormented and tormenting love in her heart. Even
her love of Fanny was a love capsized and inverted ; her
fallen daughter had been to her a detested changeling for the
pretty clever little girl who was to have been a paragon of
feminine virtue. Except for Ernest how bitterly and repeatedly
had we children offended her rigid and implacable standards,
Fanny and I openly and rebelliously and Prue by discovery !
For Prue—I will not tell you the details of Matilda's exposure—
pilfered.

" Long before we children began to thwart my mother there
must have been a still more monstrous disappointment for her.
What sort of dreams of manly piety and decorum had she wrapped
about my poor, maundering, ramshackle, loose-limbed father
when he and she walked out together in their Sunday clothes,
making the best and more than the best of themselves ? He
must have been a tall, good-looking, young man then, and
reassuringly apt, with pious reflections. What shocks had he,
gross, clumsy, wayward, ignorant and incompetent as the
dear man was, inflicted upon her set and limited expectations ?

" And then think of my Uncle John Julip again, that wonderful and adored elder brother with the manners of a sporting
baronet, who had slowly shrivelled down to the figure of a
drunken thief ! Everything had shrivelled for her,—poor
soul ! In our streets in those old days men were permitted to
sell brightly coloured distended bladders to children, the most
apt instruments for acute disappointment you can imagine ;
and the life God had given my mother was very like one of
these bladders. It had burst and shrivelled down to a limp

and empty residue that nothing could ever restore. She had faced her declining days, prematurely wrinkled, weary, laborious and unloved except by one dutiful son. . . .

" Yes, the thought of Ernest was a consolation to me. Surely his loyalty had meant happiness for her."

Sarnac paused. " I find it impossible," he said, " to disentangle my thoughts as I stood by my mother's death-bed from a thousand things that have come to me since about her. I have had to tell of her as an antagonist, as a hard uncharitable soul. That was her rôle in my story. But she was indeed just the creature and victim of that disordered age which had turned her natural tenacity to a blind intolerance and wasted her moral passion upon ugly and barren ends. If Fanny and Ernest and I had shown any stoutness against the disadvantages of our start in life, if we had won for ourselves any knowledge or respect, we inherited that much steadfastness from her ; such honesty as we had was hers. If her moral harshness had overshadowed and embittered our adolescence, her passionate mothering had sheltered our childhood. Our father would have loved us, wondered at us and left us about. But early in her life, that fear, that terror-stricken hatred of sex that over-shadowed the Christian centuries, that frantic resort to the suppressions, subjugations and disciplines of a stereotyped marriage in its harshest form, a marriage as easy to step into and as hard to leave as a steel trap with its teeth hidden by the most elaborate secrecies and misrepresentations, had set its pitiless grip upon my mother's imagination and blackened all the happier impulses in life for her. She was ready, if necessary, to pass all her children through the fires of that Moloch, if by so doing their souls might be saved. She did it the more bitterly because she was doing it against the deeper undeveloped things in her own nature.

" Such things, more dimly appreciated perhaps, passed through the mind of Harry Mortimer Smith, my former self, as he stood beside his dead mother. He was torn—I was torn—by a sense of irrational separation and by the haunting persuasion of lost opportunities. There were things I felt that I might have said, propitious moments I might have seized to make things better between us. I had differed from her so harshly ; I might have been so much kinder to her and still have held my way. She lay there a feeble little old woman, thin, worn and prematurely aged. How often had I struck at her with all my rebel strength, blind to the fact that I could wound her as only a child can wound the mother who bore it. She had been darkened and I also had been darkened, and now—now it was all too late. The door had closed between us. And was closed for ever. For ever. . . ."

§ 12

" The year and a half that intervened between my mother's death and the beginning of the First World War—the War that came before the Poison-Gas War and the Great Desolation —were years of rapid growth for me, mental and physical alike. I remained with Matilda Good because I had come to love that clumsy, wise, friendly creature almost as if she was my second mother, but now I was prosperous enough to occupy the whole of the second floor and to have a sitting-room separate from my bedroom. I still came down to the underground breakfast-room for breakfast or supper or high tea because I liked talking with Matilda. Prue had married Mr. Pettigrew by that time, and in her stead two grey and sedulous women came in—they were sisters, one a spinster and the other the wife of a broken-down prize-fighter—to do the drudgeries Prue and my mother had done.

" My chief companion in those days was my sister Fanny. Our childhood's alliance was renewed and strengthened. We had a need for each other ; we were able to help each other as no one else could help us. I found out very soon that Fanny's life was divided into two very unequal parts ; that she had hours and sometimes days of excitement and happiness with Newberry, who loved her greatly and gave her all the time he could steal away for her and introduced her to such friends as he could trust to respect her and keep their secret, and also she had long stretches of uneventful solitude in which she was terribly left to herself. My sister Fanny was plucky and loyal and devoted, but before we two got together again I think she found those grey intervals of sus-pended animation dreary and dangerous and sometimes almost intolerable. Often she had nothing to live for at all, nothing bright and vital, but the almost daily note, a hasty word or so he scribbled to her. And the better he was, the worse it was for her. The fact that he was pleasant and delight-ful and deeply in love with her, the very brightness of being with him, made those great intervals seem darker and duller."

" Hadn't she work ? " asked Sunray.

" And fellow workers, and other women ? " asked Firefly.

" Not in her position. Not as an unmarried woman—of lowly origins—with a lover."

" But there were others in the same position ? Surely there were many ! "

" A scattered class, a class made to be ashamed of itself. Newberry and Fanny were lovers, such lovers as we are to-day ; they got through with it and at last, I believe, they married according to the custom of the time. But they were the exceptional ones, they knew what they wanted and had stout hearts. Most of these irregular unions succumbed to the boredom in between and to the temptations of separation. Forgetfulness and jealousy played havoc with these insecure couples. The girls in their phases of loneliness picked up with other men and the first lover suspected their infidelities and strayed away. I have a lot to tell you yet about jealousy in the Old World ; it was not regarded as an ugly thing but as a rather high-spirited thing. People let it go and were proud of it. And the majority of these irregular unions were not even love unions in the first place, they were vice unions, dishonest on either side. Drugs and drink crept very easily into lives divided between over-excitement and tedium and darkened by a general disapproval. The defiant pose was the easiest pose. The unmarried lover was made a social outcast and driven towards other sorts of social outcasts, more evil and unhappy. . . . You see perhaps now why my sister Fanny was rather alone and aloof, for all that she belonged to a numerous class.

" I suppose," said Sarnac, " that the object of that rigid legal marriage of the Old World was to keep lovers together. In countless cases it kept the wrong people together and lovers apart. But then you must remember that in those days children were supposed to be providential accidents ; they were indeed accidents of cohabitation and that altered all the conditions of the question. There were no proper schools for children, no sort of refuge if the parents parted and tore the home asunder. We are so secure ; it is hard to imagine now the chancy insecurity of the ancient days. It is hard to imagine the dangers that hung about an unprotected child. In our world nowadays we all seem to get paired ; sooner or later each finds a mate and marriage is a natural and necessary relationship instead of a compulsory device. All the priests of all the religions that have ever been in the world could not bind me to Sunray more firmly than I am bound to-day. Does one get a book and an altar to marry the axe to its handle ? . . .

" None of which does in the least degree affect the fact that my sister Fanny suffered dreadfully from loneliness before she rediscovered me.

" She was full of curiosities and enterprise, and she took possession of my leisure to explore all sorts of shows and resorts in and about old London museums, picture-galleries parks, gardens, and heaths, that I should otherwise never have visited. Indeed she might not have visited them either if I had not been available as her escort, because in that world of crazy suppressions, most of these places were haunted by furtive love-hunters and feeble-minded folk who might have been irritating and tiresome to a solitary girl so pretty as Fanny. They would have followed her about and accosted her when they got her alone, and thrust their disagreeable cravings between her and the beauty and sunshine.

"But together we went gaily to all sorts of interesting things. This old London I am describing to you had a large share of parks and gardens ; there was a pleasing quaintness about all of them and much unpremeditated loveliness. There was a certain Richmond Park, to which we often resorted, with many fine old trees and grassy spaces and wildernesses of bracken, that got very yellow and gay in autumn, and a quantity of deer. You might have been transported from this age to Richmond Park two thousand years ago, and still fancied yourself in the northland parks of to-day. The great trees, like nearly all trees in those days, were, it is true, infested with fungus and partly decayed, but Fanny and I never noticed that. They seemed great healthy trees to us. And there was a view from a hillcrest of the winding Thames, a very delight-ful view. And then there were the oddest old gardens and flower spaces at Kew. I remember a quite good rock-garden and glass houses of flowers ; the brightest flowers the Old World imagined possible. And there were paths through a jungle of rhododendra, primitive small rhododendra, but bright coloured and a great delight to Fanny and me. There was a place where we had tea at little tables in the open air. In that frowsty old germ-saturated world with its dread of draughts and colds and coughs it gave one a bright sense of adventure to eat food in the open air.

"We went to museums and picture-galleries and talked about what the pictures meant and we talked of a thousand things together. There comes back to me one conversation we had at a place called Hampton Court, a queer old red brick palace with a great grape-vine under glass and an ancient garden beside the Thames. There were flower-beds full of half-wild herbaceous flowers, and we walked beside them under trees until we came to a low wall that looked upon the river, and we sat down on a seat and there, after a silence, suddenly Fanny, like one who has been pent up beyond endurance, began talking of love.

"She began by asking questions about the girls I had met and the girls at Thunderstone House. I described one or two of them to her. My chief friend among them was Milly Kimpton from the counting-house ; we had got to the pitch of taking teas together and suchlike friendly acts. 'That's not love,' said Fanny the wise, ' lending each other books. You don't begin to know what love is yet, Harry.

"'But you will, Harry—you will.

"'Don't you be too late about it, Harry. There's nothing in life like loving some one, Harry. People don't talk to you about it and lots of people don't know what they are missing. It's all the difference between being nothing or something. It's all the difference between being dead or alive. When you are really loving some one you're all right and nothing can harm you. And when you aren't, nothing is right, everything is wrong. But love is a queer thing, Harry, and about as dreadful as it is dear. It gets wrong. Sometimes it all goes wrong and it's awful ; it slips from you somehow ; it goes and you're left mean and little—ever so mean !—and you can't get back and it seems you hardly want to get back. You're dead and you're damned and done for, and then again it all comes back again like the sunrise—like being born afresh.'

" And then with a desperate shamelessness she began to talk of Newberry and how much she loved him. She told little irrelevant things about his ' ways.' ' He comes to me whenever he can,' she said, and repeated this presently. ' He's all my life,' she said. ' You don't know what he is to me. . . .'

" Then the constant dread of a separation crept up to the surface of her thoughts.

" ' Perhaps,' she said, ' it will always go on like this. . . . I don't care if it does. I don't care if I never marry him. I wouldn't care—not if at last I'm thrown aside. I'd go through it all again and count myself lucky even if I knew for certain I was to be dropped and cast aside.'

" Queer Fanny ! Her face was flushed and her eyes shining with tears. I asked myself what had been happening.

" ' He'll never throw me aside, Harry. He'll never throw me aside. He can't. He can't. He's half as old again as I am and yet he comes to me in his trouble. Once—— Once he cried to me. Men, all of you, are so strong, and yet so helpless. . . .

" ' You've got to have a woman to come to. . . .

" ' Just a little while ago—— Well—— He was ill. He was very ill. He has pain in his eyes and sometimes he's afraid about them. This time, suddenly he had frightful pains. And he thought he couldn't see. He came straight to me, Harry. He called a cab and came to me, and he came feeling his way up-stairs to me and fumbling at the door ; and I nursed him in my darkened room until the pain had gone. He didn't go home, Harry, where there were servants and nurses to be got and attendants and everything ; he came to me. It was me he came to. Me ! He's my man. He knows I'd give my life for him. I would, Harry. I'd cut my body to pieces bit by bit, if it would make him happy.

" ' It wasn't so much the pain he had, Harry, as the fear. He's not the one to mind a bit of pain or be afraid of many things. But he was afraid and scared. He'd never been afraid before, but he was afraid of going blind—he was too afraid to go to the specialist. It was like a little child, Harry, and him so big and strong—afraid of the dark. He thought they'd get hold of him so that perhaps he'd not be able to come to me. He thought he wouldn't be able to see his beloved magazines and papers any more. And the pain just turned the screw on him. He clung to me.

" ' It was me made him go. I took him there. He wouldn't

have gone if it hadn't been for me. He'd have just let things
drift on and not a soul in the world, for all his money and
power, to mother him. And then he might really have gone
blind if it hadn't been taken in time. I pretended to be his
secretary and I took him and waited in the waiting-room for
him. I dreaded they'd hurt him. I was listening for something
to happen all the time. I had to look at their old *Graphics*
as if I didn't care a rap what they were doing to him. And
then he came out smiling with a green shade on and I had to
stand up stiff and cool and wait to hear what he had to say.
I *was* scared by that shade, Harry. Scared! I held my breath.
I thought it had come. "It isn't so bad as we fancied, Miss
Smith," he said—off-hand. "You kept the taxi? You'll have
to take my arm I'm afraid." "Certainly, sir," I said, mimpsy-
like. I was careful to be awkward taking his arm. There
were people there in the waiting-room and you never know.
Acted respectful. Me!—that has had him in my arms a thousand times.

"'But when we were in the taxi and safe he pushed up the
shade and took me into his arms and he hugged me and he
cried—he cried wet tears. And held me. Because he'd got me
still and his sight still and the work he loves to do. Things
would have to be done to his eyes but he'd keep his sight—
and he has. There's been no trouble now. Not for months.'

"She sat looking away from me over the shining river.

"'How could he ever leave me?' she asked. 'After a
time like that?'

"Stoutly she spoke, but even to my youthful eyes she seemed
little and lonely, sitting there on the old red wall.

"I thought of the busy bustling man with the big tortoise-
shell glasses away from her, and of one or two things I had
heard whispered about him. It seemed to me then that no
men were good enough for the women in the world.

"'When he's tired or in trouble,' said Fanny, sure and still,
'he'll always come back to me.'"

CHAPTER SIX

MARRIAGE IN WAR TIME

§ 1

"AND now," said Sarnac, "comes a change of costume.
You have been thinking of me I suppose, as a gawky
youth of seventeen or eighteen, dressed in those ill-
fitting wholesale clothes we used to call 'ready-mades.' That
youth wore a white collar round his neck and a black jacket
and dark grey trousers of a confused furtive patterning and
his hat was a black hemisphere with a little brim, called a
Bowler. Now he changes into another sort of 'ready-mades,'

even more ill-fitting—the khaki uniform of a young British
soldier in the Great World War against Germany. In 1914
Anno Domini, a magic wand, the wand of political catastrophe,
waved to and fro over Europe, and the aspect of that world
changed, accumulation gave place to destruction and all the
generation of young men I have described as being put together from such shops as those one saw in Cheapside, presently
went into khaki and fell into ranks and tramped off to the
lines of ditches and desolation that had extended themselves
across Europe. It was a war of holes and barbed wire and
bombs and big guns like no war that had ever happened
before. It was a change of phase in the world muddle. It was
like some liquid which has been growing hotter and hotter,
suddenly beginning to boil and very swiftly boiling over. Or
it was like a toboggan-track in the mountains, when after a
long easy almost level run, one comes to a swift drop and a
wild zigzag of downward curves. It was the same old downward run at a dramatic point.

" Change of costume there was and change of atmosphere.
I can still recall the scared excitements of the August days
when the war began and how incredulous we English were
when we heard that our own little army was being driven back
before the German hosts like a spluttering kitten pushed by a
broom, and that the French lines were collapsing. Then came
the rally of September. At the beginning we British youngsters
had been excited spectators, but as the tale of our army's
efforts and losses came home to us we crowded to the recruit-
ing-offices, by thousands and scores of thousands, until at last
our volunteers could be counted by the million. I went with
the crowd.

" It may seem a curious thing to you that I lived through all
the Great World War against Germany, that I was a soldier
in it and fought and was wounded and went back and took
part in the final offensive, that my brother Ernest became a
sergeant and won a medal for gallantry and was killed within
a few weeks of the concluding Armistice, that all the circumstances of my life were revolutionised by the war and that
nevertheless it does not come into the story of my life as a
thing of importance in itself to that story. As I think of it
now, I think of the Great World War as a sort of geographical
or atmospheric fact, like living ten miles from your working-
place or being married in an April shower. One would have
to travel the ten miles every day or put up an umbrella as one
came out of church, but it wouldn't touch what one was intimately, or alter in any essential the living substance of one's
life. Of course the World War killed and tortured millions of
us, impoverished us all and dislocated the whole world. But
that only meant that so many millions went out of life and
that there was a fractional increase in every one's anxiety and
disorder ; it didn't change the nature and passions, the ignor-

ances and bad habits of thought of the millions who remained. The World War arose out of these ignorances and misconceptions and it did nothing to alter them. After it was all over the world was a good deal rattled and much shabbier than before, but it was still the same old mean and haphazard world, acquisitive, divided, cantingly patriotic, idiotically prolific, dirty, diseased, spiteful, and conceited. It has taken two-score centuries of research and teaching, training, thought and work to make any great alteration in that.

" I admit the outbreak of the World War had a really tremendous air of being an end and a beginning. There were great days in it at first, and for us British as much as for any people. We apprehended the thing in splendid terms. We thought quite honestly—I speak of the common people—that the Imperialisms of Central Europe were wholly wrong and that we were wholly right ; hundreds of thousands of us gave ourselves gladly in the sincere belief that a new world was to be won by victory. That spirit was not confined to Britain, nor to either side in this war. I am convinced that the years 1914, 1915, and 1916 saw finer crops of brave and generous deeds and noble sacrifices, of heroic toil and heroic patience, than any years that ever came before in the whole history of mankind or than any of the years that followed for many centuries. The young people were wonderful ; death and honour reaped gloriously among them. And then the inherent unsoundness of the issue began to wear through and that false dawn faded out of men's hearts. By the end of 1917 the whole world was a disillusioned world, with but one hope left, the idealism of the United States of America and the still untested greatness of President Wilson. But of that and what it came to, you read about in the history books and I will not talk about it now. A God in that man's position might have unified the world in the twentieth century and saved it centuries of tragic struggle. President Wilson was not a God. . . .

" And I do not think I need tell you very much of the war itself as I saw it. It was a strange phase in human experience and it was described and painted and photographed and put on record very completely. Most of us have read quite a lot about it—except of course Firefly. You know how human life concentrated for four whole years upon the trenches that stretched across Europe on either front of Germany. You know how thousands of miles of land were turned into wilderness of mud-holes and wire. Nowadays of course nobody reads the books of the generals and admirals and politicians of that time, and all the official war histories sleep the eternal sleep in the vaults of the great libraries, but probably you have all read one or two such human books as Enid Bagnold's ' Diary without Dates ' or Cogswell's ' Ermytage and the Curate ' or Barbusse's ' Le Feu ' or Arthur Green's ' Story of a Prisoner of War ' or that curious anthology, ' The War Stories of Private

Thomas Atkins '; and probably you have seen photographs and films and also pictures painted by such men as Nevinson and Orpen and Muirhead Bone and Will Rothenstein. All of them, I can certify now, are very true books and pictures. They tell of desolation passing like the shadow of an eclipse across the human scene.

" But the mind has the power of reducing and effacing every sort of impression that drags pain with it. I spent great parts out of two years in that noxious, gun-pocked land of haste and hiding, and that time now seems less than many days of my peace-time life. I killed two men with the bayonet in a trench, and it remains as though it was done by some one else and had no significance for me at all. I remember much more clearly that I felt very sick when afterwards I found my sleeve saturated with blood and blood on my hand, and how I tried to get it off by rubbing my arm in the sand because there was no water to be got. In the trenches life was hideously uncomfortable and tedious and while it lasted I was, I know, interminably bored by the drag of the hours, but all those hours are concentrated now into a record of the fact. I remember the shock of the first shell that burst near me and how slowly the smoke and dust unfolded, and how there was a redness in the smoke and how for a time it blotted out the light. That shell burst in a field of yellow-flowering weeds and stubble against the sun, but I do not recall what preceded it nor what followed it ; shell-bursts rattled me more and more as the war went on, but they left weaker and weaker pictures.

" One of my most vivid memories of that time is the excitement of my first leave from the front, and how my party arrived at Victoria Station and were guided in a clattering throng to a sort of transport drain called the Underground Railway by elderly volunteers wearing brassards. I was still muddy from the trenches ; there had been no time for a wash and a brush-up, and I was carrying my rifle and other gear ; we crowded into a brightly lit first-class carriage in which were a number of people in evening dress who were going out to dinner and to the theatre. There could not have been a more vivid contrast if I had seen Firefly there in all her loveliness. There was one young man not much older than myself between two gorgeously dressed women. He had a little white bow under his pink chin and a silk neck-wrap, he had a black cloak with a cape and an opera-hat. I suppose he was an invalid but he looked as fit as I. I felt a momentary impulse to say something humiliating to him. I don't think I did. I do not remember that I did. But I looked at him and then at the brown stain on my sleeve and the wonder of life possessed me.

" No—I said nothing. I was in a state of intense exhilaration. The other fellows were gay and inclined to be noisy, one or two were a little drunk but I was quietly exalted. I seemed to be hearing and seeing and perceiving with such an acuteness as I had never known before. Fanny I should see on the morrow, but that evening I hoped to see Hetty Marcus with whom I was in love. I was in love with her with an intensity that only soldier-boys who had been living in the mud of Flanders for half a year could understand."

§ 2

" How," asked Sarnac, " can I make you see Hetty Marcus, dark-eyed, warm-skinned, wayward, and fragile, who brought me to love and death two thousand years ago ?

" In a way, she was like Sunray here. She was of her type. She had the same darkness in her eyes, the same still bearing. She was like Sunray's hungry sister. With a touch of fire in her blood.

" Yes—and she had those same stumpy little fingers. . . . *Look* at them !

" I met her on those very Downs I used to walk over with my father when I was a boy, to steal the produce from Lord Bramble's gardens. I had a short leave before I was drafted to France and I did not spend it in London with Matilda Good and Fanny, as you may think I should have done, but I went with three other youngsters who had enough money to do so, to Cliffstone. I don't know whether I can make it clear to you why I went to Cliffstone. I was excited at the thought of going into the actual warfare, I meant to do brave and wonderful things over there, but also I was terribly over-shadowed by the thought that I might be killed. I did not think of wounds or suffering, I do not think I feared those things at all, but I had a profound dread and hatred of extinction before ever I had fully lived, before I had ever tasted many of the most alluring things in life. I had always promised myself love and great adventures with women, and I was passionately distressed at the possibility of being cheated of those intensities. All of us young innocents were in the same case. It was I who had thought of Cliffstone, near to our training camp, with its band and promenade and its flitting glancing girls. There, if anywhere, it seemed to me, we must snatch something from life before the great shells splashed us to pieces and the clay of Flanders devoured us. We sneaked off from our families with those fires of protesting romance in our brains and veins.

" You cannot imagine how many millions of lads there were in Europe then, pitifully eager not to miss altogether the secret and magic experiences of love before they died. I cannot tell you of the pot-houses and prostitutes that lay in wait for us or of the gaunt moonlight on the beach. I cannot tell you of temptation and ignorance and disease. It is too ugly to tell you ; such things are passed and done with, and men suffer them no more. We groped in darkness where now men walk in the light. One of my mates had an ugly misadventure ;

all had ugly experiences and I escaped by chance rather than any merit of my own from those slovenly snares. I was for a moment fastidious and I recoiled. And I had not drunken as the others had, because some streak of pride in me had made me habitually wary with drink.

" But I was in a storm of excitements and distresses. I was slipping into the pit though I hated it, and to escape it I set myself to revive my memories of the days when I was a boy. I went to Cherry Gardens to see the old home and then to my father's grave—it was neat and pretty with Fanny's money—and then I determined to walk over the Downs to recall, if I could, something of the wonder that I had felt when first I went over them to Chessing Hanger. And also, if you understand me, I felt love and romance would be there. I hadn't abandoned the quest that had brought me to Cliffstone ; I had only jumped a foul ditch on my way. When I was a child I had supposed Heaven was over the Downs, and certainly the golden summer sunsets were. It seemed natural to turn my back on Cliffstone and go up into the only really lovely country I had ever known, if I wanted to find romance.

" And I found it.

" I was thrilled but not a bit surprised when I saw Hetty appear over the sky-line of the hill and come right over the brow and stand with her hands behind her back and the sun shining on her hair, looking out across the woods and cornfields to Blythe and the distant marshes and the sea. She had taken her hat off and was holding it behind her. She wore an ivory-coloured silk blouse very open at the neck and it was just as though you could see her body through the flimsy stuff.

" She dropped into a sitting position, now looking at her world and now plucking at the little dwarfish flowers in the Downland turf.

" I stood for a time agape at her. Then my whole being was filled with a tremulous resolve to talk to her. My path curved up the slope and carried me over the shoulder of the hill not very far from her. I followed it, stopping ever and again as if to look at the land and sea below, until it brought me as near to her as it could, and then I left it and with a clumsy affectation of carelessness strolled up to the summit until I stood beside her and about six yards away. I pretended not to observe her. I clinched my hands to keep my self-control. She had become aware of me and she was quite motionless now, sitting up and looking at me, but she did not seem in the least dismayed. Your fine face she had, Sunray, and your dark eyes, and I have never known any one, not even you, who could keep a face so still. Not rigid or hard or staring it was, but quietly, profoundly still, like a face in some beautiful picture.

" I was all atremble, my heart was beating fast but I kept my wits about me.

" ' Was there ever a lovelier view ? ' I said. ' I suppose that
bit of blue there that looks like a raft where the water shines,
I suppose that is Denge Ness ? '

" She did not answer for what seemed a long time. She
surveyed me with an unfathomable expression. Then she spoke
and as she spoke she smiled. ' You know that is Denge Ness
as well as I do.'

" I smiled at her smile. Shy pretences were not for her. I
came a step or so nearer with a conversational air. ' I have
known this view,' I said, ' since I was a boy of ten. But I did
not know any one else set any value upon it.'

" ' Nor I,' she said. ' I came to look at it perhaps for the
last time,' she vouchsafed. ' I'm going away.'

" ' I'm going away too.'

" ' Over there ? ' she asked, and nodded her head to where
the land of France hung like a cloud in the sky.

" ' In a week or so.'

" ' I'll get to France too. But not so soon as a week or two.
But I am going into the Women's Auxiliary Army Corps and
I know I shall get over there at last. I join up to-morrow.
How can one stay at home with all you boys out there, get-
ting—— '

" She was going to say getting ' killed.' But she caught the
word back and finished it with, ' Getting into all sorts of danger
and trouble.'

" ' One has to go,' I said.

" She looked at me with her head a little on one side. ' Tell
me,' she said. ' Do you *want* to go ? '

" ' Not a bit. I hate the whole monstrous business. But
there's no way out. The Germans have put it on us and we
have to go through with it.'

" That was how we all saw it in England during the War.
But I won't stop now to argue what really caused a war that
ended two thousand years ago. ' The Germans put it on us.
I hate going. I wanted to go on with the work I was doing.
Now everything is upset.'

" ' Everything,' she said and thought for some moments.
' I hate going too,' she said.

" ' It drags on week after week, month after month,' I
complained. ' The boredom of it ! The drills, the salutes, the
silly little officers ! If only they would take us and raffle us
and kill us and have done with it so that we could either die
or go home and do something sensible ! My life is being wasted.
I have been in the machine a year—and I've only got this far
on my way to France ! When I see a German soldier at last
I shall want to kiss him, I shall be so glad. But either I shall
kill him or he will kill me—and that will be the end of the
story.'

" ' And yet one can't keep out of it,' she said.

" ' And there is something tremendous about it,' she went

on. ' Once or twice I have been up here when there were air-
raids. I live quite close here. These air-raids get more and
more frequent nowadays. I don't know what they are coming
to. You see the search-lights now, every night, waving about
like the arms of a drunken man. All over the sky. But before
that you hear the pheasants in the woods, clucking and crying.
They always hear it first. Other birds take it up. They cry
and twitter. And then far away the guns begin rumbling. At
first a little sound—" *pud-pud*," then like the whoof of a hoarse
dog. And then one gun after another picks it up as the raid
comes nearer. Sometimes you can catch the whirr of the
engines of the Gothas. There's a great gun behind the farm-
house away there and you wait for that and when it fires it
hits you on the chest. Hardly anything is to be seen except the
search-lights. There's a little flicker in the sky—and star-
shells. But the guns—riot. It's mad but it's immense. It
takes you. Either you are wild with fright or you are wild
with excitement. I can't sleep. I walk about my room and
long to be out. Twice I've gone out into the night, into the
moonlight—with everything aquiver. Gone for long walks.
Once sharpnel fell in our orchard with a hiss like rain. It
ripped the bark of the apple-trees and tore off twigs and
branches and killed a hedgehog. I found the little wretch in
the morning, nearly cut in two. Death haphazard ! I don't
mind the death and the danger so much. But it's the quiver
in the world I can't endure. Even in the daytime sometimes,
you can't quite hear them, but you can *feel* the guns, over
beyond there. . . .

" ' Our old servant,' she said, ' believes it is the end of the
world.'

" ' For us it may be,' I said.

" She made no answer.

" I looked at her face and my imagination rioted.

" I began to talk with a bare simplicity such as we rarely
attained in that shy and entangled age. But my heart was
beating fast. ' For years,' I said, ' I have dreamt of the love
of a girl. It was to have been the crown of life. I have saved
myself up for it. I have had a friend or so, but it wasn't love.
And now I am near to going. Out there. It is only a few days
before I go over there—to whatever is waiting for me. And
when it seems beyond hope I come upon some one. . . . Don't
think me mad, please. Don't think I'm lying. I am in love
with you. Indeed I am. You seem altogether beautiful to
me. Your voice, your eyes—everything. I could worship
you. . . .'

" I couldn't say a word more for a moment or so. I rolled
over on the turf and looked her in the face. ' I'm sorry,' I
said. ' I'm a silly young Tommy suddenly in love—oh !
desperately in love.'

" Her grave face regarded me. She did not look frightened

or disconcerted. Perhaps her heart beat faster than I thought. But her voice when she spoke was constrained.

"'Why are you talking like that? You've just met me. . . . How can you love me? It isn't possible people should love like this.'

"'I've seen you long enough——'

"I could not talk. I met her eyes. Hers dropped before mine. The warm colour mounted to her cheeks. She bit her lips.

"'You,' she said in a low voice, 'are just in love with love.'

"'Anyhow, I am in love,' I said.

"She plucked a spray of minute flowers and forgot it in her hand.

"'This is your last day?' she asked, and made my heart beat faster.

"'It may be my last altogether for this sort of thing. Who can tell? . . . For a long time anyhow. Why should it hurt you to let me love you to-day? Why shouldn't you be kind to me? Civil to me—anyhow. I don't ask for so very much. If—suppose—we went for a walk together? Just a long walk. If we spent most of the day together? Somewhere we might get something to eat.' . . .

"She sat considering me gravely.

"'Suppose I did,' she said as if to herself. 'Suppose I did.'

"'What harm could it do you?'

"'What harm could it do?' she repeated with her eyes on mine.

"If I had been older and more experienced I might have known from her warm flushed face and her dark eyes that she too was in love with love that day, and that our encounter was as exciting for her as for me. Suddenly she smiled; she showed herself for an instant as ready as myself. Her constraint had vanished.

"'I'll come,' she decided, and rose with an effortless ease to her feet, and then at my eager movement as I sprang up before her: 'But you'll have to be good, you know. It's just a walk—and a talk. . . . Why shouldn't we? . . . If we keep away from the village.'"

§ 3

"It would seem the queerest story in the world if I told you how we two youngsters spent that day, we who were such strangers that we did not know each other's names and yet who were already drawn so closely together. It was a day of kindly beauty and warmth and we rambled westward until we came to a ridge that dropped steeply to a silvery, tree-bordered canal, and along that ridge we went until we reached a village and a friendly inn, where there were biscuits

and cheese and some apples to make a lunch upon. For a
time a mood of shyness followed our first avowals, then Hetty
talked of her home and of her place in the world. It was only
after we had eaten together that we became easy and familiar
with each other. It was only as the sun was sinking in the
west and our day drew to its golden end that we embraced
suddenly as we sat together on a felled tree in a wood, and
that I learned from her what a sweet and wonderful delight
the kiss of love may be."

§ 4

Sarnac paused.
" It happened two thousand years ago but it seems to me
that it happened just six years from now. Once more I am
back in that wood among the long warm shadows of the
evening and all my dreams and imaginations awake to reality
with Hetty's body in my arms and her lips to mine. I have
been able to tell you my story hitherto with a sort of wonder
and detachment, as though I showed it you through a tele-
scope. But I have been telling you overmuch perhaps of
Fanny and Matilda Good because I have had a sort of reluctance
about Hetty. She is still so fresh in my mind that she seems
as I name her to come even here and to be living still, a perplexity between Sunray, who is so like her and so unlike her,
and myself. I love her again and hate her again as though
I was still that assistant editor, that writer of rubbish, in lost
and forgotten Thunderstone House in dead old London. . . .
" And I can't describe things now," said Sarnac, " as I
have described them up to this. I seem no longer to look back
into past things. My memories are living and suffering ; they
inflame and hurt. I loved Hetty ; she was all the delight of
love to me. I married her. I divorced her, I repented of the
divorce and I was killed for her sake.
" And it seems as if I was killed not a day ago. . . .
" I married while I was in England before I was passed for
active service again after my wound. I was wounded in the
arm―― "
Sarnac stopped and felt his arm. Sunray looked sharply
at it and ran her hand down it from shoulder to elbow as if
to reassure herself. The others burst into laughter at her
manifest anxiety and her expression of relief, the guest-master
being particularly delighted.
" I *was* wounded nevertheless. I was a sitting-up case in
the ambulance. I could tell you stories about the nurses and
the hospital and how we had a panic about a submarine as
we crossed to England. . . . I married Hetty before I went
back because we were now altogether lovers and it was just
possible she might have a child. And moreover there was a
business about allowances if I got killed that was an added
inducement to marry. In those days of haphazard death for

the young there was a world-wide fever of love-making and countless such snatched marriages.

"She had never got to France as she had said she hoped to do. For most of the time she was driving a car for the Ministry of Supplies in London. We spent two days of wild endearment, the only honeymoon we could get, at her mother's farm at Payton Links, a little hamlet near Chessing Hanger. (I do not think I have told you that she was the only daughter of a farmer and that Mrs. Marcus, her mother, was a widow.) Hetty had been a clever girl, an elementary school-teacher and bookish and enterprising for a country-place. She had never mentioned me to her mother until she had written to tell of her approaching marriage.

"When her mother had driven us from the station to the farm and I had helped her to put away the pony, the old lady's non-committal manner relaxed and she said : ' Well, it might have been worse. You've looks and fairish shoulders for one who's town-bred. You can kiss me, my boy, though Smith is a poor exchange for Marcus, and I can't see how any one can ever expect to get a living for man and wife at a fancy trade like publishing. I'd hoped at first she meant a publican. But publishing she says it is. Whether you're properly old enough for Hetty, Time will show.'

"Time did show very rapidly that I was not properly old enough for Hetty, though I resisted the demonstration with passionate vigour.

"In this world of ours we are by comparison very simple and direct. In that old world we should have seemed shockingly simple and direct. It's not only that they wrapped up and hid their bodies in all sorts of queer garments and wrappings but also that they wrapped up and distorted and hid their minds. And while we to-day have the same simple and clean ideas all over the world about sexual restraints and sexual freedoms, people in those days had the most various and complicated codes, half-hidden and half-confessed. And not merely half-hidden but imperfectly realised, subconscious rather than thought out and settled. Few of these codes respected the freedom of other people or set any bounds to the most extravagant developments of jealousy. And while Hetty's thoughts about love and marriage had been nourished on a diet of countryside folk and then of novels and poetry devoured with avidity and had had tremendous releases in the lax atmosphere of war-time London, I, in spite of my love for and faith in Fanny, had almost unwittingly adopted the rigid standards of my mother. As we used to say in those days, Hetty's was a much more artistic temperament than mine. For my part I did not so much think as assume that the worship of a man for a woman gave place to mastery as soon as her love was won, that the problem of absolute fidelity for both lovers was to be facilitated on his side by an absolute submissiveness on hers. And about her, wherever she went, invisible but real, there had to be a sort of cloistered quality. It was implicit, moreover, that she had never thought of love before she met her predestined and triumphant lover. Ridiculous and impossible you will say ! But Sunray has read the old novels and she can witness that that was the code."

Sunray nodded. " That is the spirit of them," she said.

" Well, in fact, Hetty was not only half a year older than I but ages beyond me in the business of love. She was my teacher. While I had been reading about atoms and Darwin and exploration and socialism, she had been sucking the honey of sensuous passion from hints and half-hints in old romances and poems from Shakespeare and the old play-wrights. And not only, I realise now, from books. She took me as one captures and tames an animal and made my senses and my imagination hers. Our honeymoon was magical and wonderful. She delighted in me and made me drunken with delights. And then we parted wonderfully with the taste of her salt tears on my lips, and I went off to the last five months of the War.

" I can see her now, slender as a tall boy in her khaki breeches and driver's uniform, waving to my train as it drew out of Chessing Hanger station.

" She wrote adorable and whimsical love-letters that made me ache to be with her again, and just when we were forcing the great German barrier of the Hindenberg line, came one to tell me we were to have a child. She had not told me of it before, she said, because she had not been quite sure of it. Now she was sure. Would I love her still, now that she would be no longer slim and gracious ? Love her still ! I was filled with monstrous pride.

" I wrote back to tell her how my job at Thunderstone House was being saved for me, how we would certainly get a little house, a ' dear little house,' in some London suburb, how I would worship and cherish her. Her answer was at once tender and unusual. She said I was too good to her, far too good ; she repeated with extraordinary passion that she loved me, had never loved and could never love any one but me, that she hated my absence more than she could tell, and that I was to do everything I could, move heaven and earth to get my discharge and come home to her and be with her and never, never, *never* leave her again. She had never wanted my arms about her as she wanted them now. I read nothing between the lines of that outbreak. It seemed just a new mood amidst the variety of her moods.

" Thunderstone House wanted me back as soon as possible, and the War had done much to increase the power and in-fluence of all magazine-publishers and newspaper-proprietors. I got out of the army within three months of the Armistice and came back to a very soft and tender and submissive

Hetty, a new Hetty more wonderful even than the old. She was evidently more passionately in love with me than ever. We took some furnished rooms in a part of London called Richmond, near the Thames and a great park, and we sought vainly for that bright little house in which our child was to be born. But there were no bright little houses available.

"And slowly a dark shadow fell across the first brightness of our reunion. The seasonable days passed but Hetty's child was not born. It was not born indeed until it was nearly two months too late for it to be my child."

§ 5

"We are trained from earliest childhood in the world, to be tolerant and understanding of others and to be wary and disciplined with our own wayward impulses, we are given from the first a clear knowledge of our entangled nature. It will be hard for you to understand how harsh and how dis- ingenuous the Old World was. You live in a world that is as we used to say 'better bred.' You will find it difficult to im- agine the sudden storm of temptation and excitement and forgetfulness in Hetty's newly aroused being that had betrayed her into disloyalty, and still more difficult will you find the tangle of fear and desperate dishonesty that held her silent from any plain speech with me after my return. But had she spoken instead of leaving it to me to suspect, discover, and accuse, I doubt if she would have found any more mercy in me for her pitiful and abominable lapse.

"I see now that from the day I returned to Hetty she was trying to tell me of her disaster and failing to find a possible way of doing so. But the vague intimations in her words and manner dropped like seeds into my mind and germinated there. She was passionately excited and made happy by my coming back ; our first week together was the happiest week of my old-world life. Fanny came to see us once and we went and had a dinner at her flat, and something had happened to her too, I knew not what, to make her very happy. Fanny liked Hetty. When she kissed me good-night after her dinner, she held me and whispered : ' She's a dear. I thought I'd be jealous of your wife, Harry, but I love her.'

"Yes, we were very happy for that week. We walked along together back to our rooms instead of taking a taxi, for it was better for Hetty to walk. A happy week it was that stretched almost to a happy fortnight. And then the shadows of suspicion gathered and deepened.

"It was in bed in the darkness of the night that I was at last moved to speak plainly to Hetty. I woke up and lay awake for a long time, very still and staring at my bleak realisation of what had happened to us. Then I turned over, sat up in bed and said, ' Hetty. This child is not mine.'

"She answered at once. It was plain she too had been

awake. She answered in a muffled voice as though her face lay against the pillow. ' No.'

" ' You said, no ? '

" She stirred, and her voice came clearer.

" ' I said no. Oh, Husbind-boy, I wish I was dead ! I wish to God I was dead.'

" I sat still and she said no more. We remained like two fear-stricken creatures in the jungle, motionless, in an immense silence and darkness.

" At last she moved. Her hand crept out towards me, seeking me, and at that advance I recoiled. I seemed to hang for a moment between two courses of action, and then I gave myself over to rage. ' You'd *touch* me ! ' I cried, and got out of bed and began to walk about the room.

" ' I knew it ! ' I shouted. ' I knew it ! I felt it. And I have loved you ! You cheat ! You foul thing ! You lying cheat ! ' "

§ 6

" I think I described to you earlier in the story how my family behaved when Fanny left us, how we all seemed to be acting and keeping up a noise of indignation as if we were afraid of some different and disturbing realisations coming through to us should that barrage of make-believe morality fail. And just as my father and my mother behaved in that down-stairs kitchen in Cherry Gardens so now I behaved in that desolating crisis between myself and Hetty. I stormed about the room, I hurled insults at her. I would not let the facts that she was a beaten and weeping thing, that she certainly loved me, and that her pain tortured me, prevail against my hard duty to my outraged pride.

" I lit the gas, I don't remember when, and the scene went on in that watery Victorian light. I began dressing, for never more was I to lie in bed with Hetty. I meant to dress and, having said my say, to go out of the house. So I had to be scornful and loudly indignant, but also I had to find my various garments, pull my shirt over my head and lace up my boots. So that there were interludes in the storm, when Hetty could say something that I had to hear.

" ' It all happened in an evening,' she said. ' It isn't as though I had planned to betray you. It was his last day before he left and he was wretched. It was the thought of you made me go with him. It was just kindness. There were two of our girls going to have dinner with their boys and they asked me to come and that was how I met him. Officers they were all three, and schoolfellows. Londoners. Three boys who were going over—just as you were. It seemed rotten not to make a party for them.'

" I was struggling with my collar stud but I tried to achieve sarcasm. ' I see,' I said, ' under the circumstances mere polite-ness dictated—what you did. . . . Oh, my God ! '

" ' Listen how it happened, Harry. Don't shout at me again for a minute. Afterwards he asked me to come to his rooms. He said the others were coming on. He seemed such a harmless sort ! '

" ' Very ! '

" ' He seemed the sort who'd surely get killed. And I was sorry for him. He was fair like you. Fairer. And it seemed all different that night. And then he got hold of me and kissed me and I struggled, but I didn't seem to have the strength to resist. I didn't realise somehow.'

" ' That's pretty evident. That I *can* believe.'

" ' You've got no pity, Harry. Perhaps it's just. I suppose I ought to have seen the risk. But we aren't all strong like you. Some of us are pulled this way and that. Some of us do the thing we hate. I did what I could. It was like waking up to realise what had happened. He wanted me to stay with him. I ran out from his rooms. I've never seen him since. He's written but I haven't answered.'

" ' He knew you were a soldier's wife.'

" ' He's rotten. He knew it. He planned it while we were at dinner. He prayed and promised and lied. He said he wanted just a kiss, just one kiss for kindness. He began with a kiss. I'd been drinking wine, and I'm not used to wine. Oh, Harry ! Husbind-boy, if I could have died ! But I'd kissed and played about with boys before I met you. It seemed so little—until it was too late.'

" ' And here we are ! ' said I.

" I came and sat down on the bed and stared at Hetty's dishevelled distress. She was suddenly pitiful and pretty. ' I suppose I ought to go and kill this swine,' I said. ' I feel more like killing you.'

" ' Kill me,' she said. ' I wish you would.'

" ' What's his name ? Where is he now ? '

" ' *He* doesn't matter a rap,' said Hetty. ' You may hang for me if you like, but you shan't hang for a thing like that. I tell you he doesn't matter. He's a dirty accident. He happened.'

" ' You're shielding him.'

" ' *Him !* ' she said. ' I'm shielding you.'

" I stared at her. Again came a moment when I seemed to hang undecided at the parting of two courses, and again I decided to explode into rage. ' My *God* ! ' I cried, and then louder and standing up, ' My *God* ! ' Then I ranted at her. ' I suppose I've only got myself to blame for all this. What did I know of what you were before I met you ? I guess I wasn't the first and I guess *he* won't be the last. What do names matter ? I guess you thanked Heaven for a green dud when you met me.' And so on. I paced about the room as I raved.

" She sat up on the bed, her hair disordered and her eyes tearful, regarding me with a still and mournful face. ' Oh,

Harry ! ' she would say ever and again, or ' Oh, Boy ! ' while I let my clumsy fancy rove through a wilderness of coarse reproaches. Ever and again I would come up to her and stand over her. ' Tell me his name,' I would shout and she would shake her head.

" At last I was dressed. I looked at my watch. ' Five.'

" ' What are you going to do ? ' she asked.

" I don't know. Go, I suppose. I can't stay here. I should be sick. I shall get most of my things together and go. I'll find a lodging somewhere. It's nearly dawn. I'll go before you need get up. Meanwhile I'll sit in the other room. I can lie on the sofa for a bit.

" ' But the fire's not lit ! ' she said, ' and it's cold. It's not even laid. And you'll need some coffee ! '

" She stared at me with eyes full of solicitude.

" And forthwith she shuffled out of bed and slipped her feet into her bedroom-slippers and put on a gay dressing-gown that had been a great delight to us—ten days ago. She went meekly by me, moving her poor heavy body rather wearily, and found some fire-lighters in a cupboard and knelt by the fireplace and began to rake out the ashes of the overnight fire. I made no movement to prevent her. I began to collect together various books and small possessions I intended to take with me.

" She was only apprehending the situation very slowly. She turned to me in the middle of her fire-lighting. ' I suppose you'll leave me a little money to go on with ? ' she said.

" That gave me a base opportunity. ' I'll leave you money all right,' I sneered. ' I suppose I've got to keep you until we're free. Then it will be *his* job. Or the next man's.'

" She occupied herself with the fire. She filled a kettle and put it ready. Then she sat down in an armchair by the hearth. Her face was white and drawn but she shed no tears. I went to the window and pulled up the blind and stared at the street outside with its street-lamps still alight ; everything was gaunt and bleak in the colourless cold horror of the earliest dawn.

" ' I shall go to mother,' she said, shivering and pulling her dressing-gown about her shoulders. ' It will be dreadful for her to know what has happened. But she's kind. She'll be kinder than any one. . . . I shall go to her.'

" ' You can do what you like,' I said.

" ' Harry ! ' she said. ' I've never loved any man but you. If I could kill this child—— If it would please you if I killed this child——'

" She spoke with white lips. ' Yes. I tried all I knew. Some things I couldn't bring myself to do. And now it's a thing that's alive. . . .'

" We stared at one another in silence for some moments.

" ' No ! ' I said at last. ' I can't stand it. I can't endure it. Nothing can alter it now. You tell a tale. How do I know ? You've cheated once and you can cheat again. You gave yourself to that swine. If I live to a hundred I'll never forgive that. You gave yourself. How do I know you didn't tempt him ? You gave. You can go. Go where you gave yourself ! They're things no decent man can forgive. Things that are dirty to forgive. He stole you and you let him steal you and he can have you. I wish—If you'd had the beginnings of a sense of honour you'd never have let me come back to you. To think of these last days here. And you—you with this secret next your heart ! The filthiness of it ! You—you, whom I've loved.'

" I was weeping."

Sarnac paused and stared into the fire. " Yes," he said, " I was weeping. And the tears I shed—it is wonderful—the tears I shed were tears of the purest self-pity.

" And all the time I saw the thing from my own standpoint alone, blind to the answering tragedy in Hetty's heart. And the most grotesque thing is that all the time she was getting me coffee and that when it was ready I drank her coffee ! At the end she wanted to kiss me, to kiss me ' good-bye ' she said, and I rebuffed her and struck her when she came near me. I meant only to thrust her back but my hand clenched at the oppor-tunity. ' Harry ! ' she whispered. She stood like a stunned thing watching me go, and then turned suddenly and swiftly and ran back to the bedroom.

" I slammed the outer door and went downstairs into the empty morning Richmond streets ; altogether empty of traffic they were, under the flush of dawn.

" I carried my bag towards the railway-station that would take me to London ; my bag was heavy with the things I had brought away, and it dragged upon my arm, and I felt myself a tragically ill-used but honourably self-vindicated young man."

§ 7

" Oh, poor little things ! " cried Starlight. " Oh ! poor little pitiful pitiless creatures ! This story hurts me. I couldn't endure it, if it were anything more than a dream. Why were they all so hard upon each other and so deaf to the sorrow in each other ? "

" We knew no better. This world now has a tempered air. In this world we breathe mercy with our first fluttering gasp. We are so taught and trained to think of others that their pain is ours. But two thousand years ago men and women were half-way back to crude Nature. Our motives took us unawares. We breathed infections. Our food was poisoned. Our passions were fevers. We were only beginning to learn the art of being human."

" But didn't Fanny——? " began Firefly.

" Yes," said Willow ; " didn't Fanny, who was naturally so wise about love, didn't she take you in hand and send you back to forgive and help your wretched Hetty ? "

" Fanny heard my version of our story first," said Sarnac.

" She never realised the true values of the business until it was too late to stop the divorce. When I told her that Hetty had lived a life of depravity in London while I was in the trenches, she heard me with amazement but never doubted my word.

" ' And she seemed such a dear,' said Fanny. ' She seemed so in love with you. It's wonderful how different women are ! There's women who seem to change into something else directly they get out of sight of you round a corner. I *liked* your Hetty, Harry. There was something sweet about her, be what she may. I never dreamt she'd deceive you and let you down. Fancy !— going about London picking up men ! It's just as though she'd done it to me.'

" Matilda Good too was wonderfully sympathetic. ' No woman goes wrong only just once,' said Matilda. ' You're right to end it.' The Miltons were giving up her drawing-room floor, I could have it, if I cared to take it. I was only too glad to take it and return to my old home.

" Hetty, I suppose, packed up her own belongings as well as she could. She went down from Richmond to her mother's farm at Payton Links, and there it was her child was born.

" Now I want to tell you," said Sarnac, " what is, I believe, the most remarkable thing in all this story I am telling you. I do not remember in all that time right up to and including our divorce, that I felt any impulse of pity or kindliness, much less of love, towards Hetty. And yet in my dream I was very much the same sort of man as I am to-day. I was a man of the same type. But I was driven by storm of amazed and outraged pride and sexual jealousy of the most frantic sort towards acts of spite that are almost inconceivable here and now. I was doing all I could to divorce Hetty in such a way as to force her into marriage with Sumner—for that was the man's name—because I had learned that he was a hopelessly bad character, and because I believed he would make her miserable and mar her life altogether. I wanted to do that to punish her, to fill her with bitter regrets for her treatment of me. But at the same time it drove me to the verge of madness to think that he should ever possess her again. If my wishes could have been given creative force, Hetty would have gone to Sumner disfigured and diseased. They would have come together again amidst circumstances of horrible cruelty ! "

" Sarnac ! " cried Sunray, " that you should even *dream* such things ! "

" Dream ! It is as men were. It is as they are, except for the education and the free happiness that release us. For we are not fourscore generations from the Age of Confusion, and that was but a few thousands more from the hairy ape-men who bayed the moon in the primeval forests of Europe. Then it was the Old Man in lust and anger ruled his herd of women and children and begot us all. And in the Age of Confusion after the Great Wars man was, and he still is, the child of

that hairy Old Ape-Man. Don't I shave myself daily ? And
don't we educate and legislate with our utmost skill and
science to keep the old beast within bounds ? But our schools
in the days of Harry Mortimer Smith were still half-way back
to the cave ; our science was only beginning. We had no
sexual education at all, only concealments and repressions.
Our code was still the code of jealousy—thinly disguised. The
pride and self-respect of a man was still bound up with the
animal possession of women—the pride and self-respect of
most women was by a sort of reflection bound up with the
animal possession of a man. We felt that this possession was
the keystone of life. Any failure in this central business
involved a monstrous abasement, and against that our poor
souls sought blindly for the most extravagant consolations.
We hid things, we perverted and misrepresented things, we
evaded the issue. Man is a creature which under nearly every
sort of stress releases hate and malign action, and we were then
still subjected to the extremest stresses.

" But I will not go on apologising for Harry Mortimer
Smith. He was what the world made him and so are we. And
in my dream I went about that old world, doing my work,
controlling my outward behaviour and spending all the force
of my wounded love for Hetty in scheming for her misery.

" And one thing in particular was of immense importance
to my tormented being. It was that I should get another lover
quickly, that I should dispel the magic of Hetty's embraces,
lay the haunting ghost of my desire for her. I had to persuade
myself that I had never really loved her and replace her in
my heart by some one I could persuade myself was my own
true love.

" So I sought the company of Milly Kimpton again. We
had been close companions before the War, and it was not
difficult to persuade myself that I had always been a little in
love with her. Always she had been more than a little in love
with me. I told her my story of my marriage and she was hurt
for my sake and indignant beyond measure with the Hetty I
presented to her.

" She married me within a week of the completion of my
divorce."

§ 8

" Milly was faithful and Milly was kind ; she was a cooling
refuge from the heat and distresses of my passion. She had
a broad, candid face that never looked either angry or miserable;
she held her countenance high, smiling towards heaven with
a pleasant confidence and self-satisfaction ; she was very fair
and she was broad-shouldered for a woman. She was tender
but not passionate ; she was intelligently interested in things
but without much whim or humour. She was nearly a year
and a half older than I. She had, as people used to say, ' taken

a great fancy ' to me when first I came into the firm, a crude
and inexperienced youngster.   She had seen me rise very
rapidly to Mr. Cheeseman's position on the editorial staff—
he had been transferred to the printing side—and at times she
had helped me greatly. We were both popular in Thunderstone
House, and when we married there was a farewell dinner to
Milly, who gave up her position then in the counting-house ;
there were speeches and a wonderful wedding-present of dinner-
knives and silver forks and spoons in a brass-bound chest of
oak with a flattering inscription on a silver plate.   There had
been a good deal of sympathy with Milly in Thunderstone
House, especially among the girls, and a good deal of indignation at me when my first marriage occurred, and my belated
recognition of my true destiny was considered a very romantic
and satisfactory end to the story.

"We secured a convenient little house in a row of stucco
houses all built together to have one architectural effect,
called Chester Terrace, close to one of the inner parks of
London known as Regent's Park. Milly, I discovered, had a
little fortune of nearly two thousand pounds, and so she was
able to furnish this house very prettily according to current
taste, and in this house in due course she bore me a son.   I
rejoiced very greatly and conspicuously over this youngster's
arrival. I think you will understand how essential it was to
my obsession for defeating and obliterating Hetty that Milly
should bear me a child.

" I worked very hard during that first year of married life
and on the whole I was happy. But it was not a very rich nor
a very deep sort of happiness. It was a happiness made up of
rather hard and rather superficial satisfactions. In a sense
I loved Milly very dearly ; her value was above rubies, she
was honest and sweet and complaisant. She liked me enormously, she was made happy by my attentions ; she helped
me, watched for my comfort, rejoiced at the freshness and
vigour of my work. Yet we did not talk very freely and
easily together. I could not let my mind run on before her ;
I had to shape what I said to her feelings and standards, and
they were very different feelings and standards from my own.
She was everything a wife should be except in one matter ;
she was not for me that particular dear companion for whom
the heart of every human being craves, that dear companion
with whom you are happy and free and safe. That dear
companionship I had met—and I had thrust it from me. Does
it come twice in a life to any one ? "

" How should I know ? " said Sunray.

" We know better than to reject it," said Radiant.

" Perhaps after many years," said Willow, answering
Sarnac's question, " after one has healed and grown and
changed."

" Milly and I were close friends indeed, but we were never

dear companions. I had told Hetty about my sister Fanny
on the evening of our first day together when we walked
over the hills, she was instantly sure that she would love
Fanny.   Fanny had seemed very brave and romantic to
Hetty's imagination ; but I did not tell Milly of Fanny until
close upon our marriage. You will say that it was not Milly's
fault that I was shy with her on Fanny's account, but assuredly
it was a fault in our relationship. And it was clear that Milly
accepted Fanny on my account and refrained from too searching a commentary because of me. Milly believed profoundly
in the institution of marriage and in the obligation upon
women of an unlimited chastity.   ' It is a pity she cannot
marry this man,' said Milly, anticipating perplexities. ' It
must make everything so inconvenient for her—and every
one who knows her. It must be so difficult to introduce her
to people.'

" ' You needn't do that,' I said.

" ' My people are old-fashioned.'

" ' They needn't know,' I said.

" ' That would be the easier way for me, Harry.'

" I found my own declarations of affection for Fanny
considerably chilled by the effort Milly made to be generous
in the matter.

" I found it still more difficult to tell her that Fanny's lover
was Newberry.

" ' Then is that how you got into Thunderstone House ? '
asked Milly when at last I got to that revelation.

" ' It's how I got my chance there,' I admitted.

" ' I didn't think it was like that. I thought you'd made
your way in.'

" ' I've made my way up. I've never been favoured.'

" ' Yes—but—— Do you think people know, Harry ?
They'd say all sorts of things.'

" You perceive that Milly was not a very clever woman
and also that she was very jealous of my honour. ' I don't
think any one knows who matters,' I said. ' Neither I nor
Fanny advertise.'

" But it was clear Milly did not like the situation. She
would have much preferred a world without sister Fanny.
She had no curiosity to see this sister that I loved so dearly
or to find any good in her. On various small but quite valid
scores she put off going to see her for a whole week.   And
always I had to remind her of Fanny and speak of Fanny
first before Fanny could be talked about. In all other matters
Milly was charming and delightful to me, but as far as she could
contrive it she banished Fanny from our world. She could not
see how much of my affection went also into banishment.

" Their meeting when at last it came about was bright
rather than warm.   An invisible athermanous screen had
fallen not only between Milly and Fanny but between Fanny

and myself. Milly had come, resolved to be generous and agreeable in spite of Fanny's disadvantageous status, and I think she was a little disconcerted by Fanny's dress and furniture, for Milly was always very sensitive to furniture and her sensitiveness had been enhanced by our own efforts to equip a delightful home on a sufficient but not too extravagant expenditure. I had always thought Fanny's furnishings very pretty, but it had never occurred to me that they were as Milly put it, ' dreadfully good.' But there was a red lacquer cabinet that Milly said afterwards might be worth as much as a hundred pounds, and she added one of those sentences that came upon one like an unexpected thread of gossamer upon the face : ' It doesn't seem right somehow.'

" Fanny's simple dress I gathered was far too good also. Simple dresses were the costliest in those days of abundant material and insufficient skill.

" But these were subsequent revelations, and at the time I did not understand why there should be an obscure undertone of resentment in Milly's manner, nor why Fanny was displaying a sort of stiff sweetness quite foreign to my impression of her.

" ' It's wonderful to meet you at last,' said Fanny. ' He's talked about you for years. I can remember once long before —long before the War—and everything—at Hampton Court. I can remember sitting on those seats by the river and his talking about you.'

" ' I remember that,' I said, though it wasn't the part about Milly that had stuck in my memory.

" ' We used to go about together no end in those days, said Fanny. ' He was the dearest of brothers.'

" ' I hope he'll still be,' said Milly, very kindly.

" ' A son's a son till he gets a wife,' said Fanny, quoting an old wives' proverb.

" ' You mustn't say that,' said Milly. ' I hope you'll come to see us—quite often.'

" ' I'd love to come,' said Fanny. ' You're lucky to get a house so easily, these days.'

" ' It isn't quite ready yet,' said Milly. ' But as soon as ever it is we must find some day when you are free.'

" ' I'm often free,' said Fanny.

" ' We'll fix a day,' said Milly, obviously quite resolute to insure that we had no unexpected calls from Fanny when other people might be about.

" ' It's nice your having been in the counting-house and understanding all about his work,' said Fanny.

" ' My people didn't like my going into business at all,' said Milly. ' But it's lucky I did.'

" ' Lucky for Harry,' said Fanny. ' Are your—people London people ? '

" ' Dorset,' said Milly. ' They didn't like my coming to

London. They're just a little bit churchy and old-fashioned, you know. But it's college or business, I said, and you don't find me staying at home to dust and put out the flowers. One has to take a firm line with one's people at times. Didn't you find that so ? There was a convenient aunt in Bedford Park to secure the proprieties and head off the otherwise inevitable latch-key, and it was business instead of college because my best uncle, Uncle Hereward—he's the Vicar of Peddlebourne—objects to the higher education of women. And there was also a question of finance.'

" ' It must be interesting for Harry to meet your people,' said Fanny.

" ' He's completely conquered Aunt Rachel,' said Milly. ' Though she started hostile. Naturally, as I'm about the only Kimpton of three generations they pitched their expectations high. They'd like me to have a husband with a pedigree a yard long.'

" I felt Milly was rather over-emphasising the county family side of the Kimptons—her father was a veterinary surgeon near Wimborne—but I did not appreciate the qualities in Fanny's bearing and furniture that were putting Milly into this self-assertive mood.

" They went on to talk with a certain flavour of unreality of the hygienic and social advantages of Regent's Park. ' It's easy to get to for one's friends,' said Milly. 'And quite a lot of interesting people, actors and critics and writers and all that sort of people, live round and about there. Of course Harry will want to know more and more of the artistic and literary world now. I expect we'll have to have a Day for them and give them tea and sandwiches. It's a bore, but it's necessary, you know Harry's got to know people.'

" She smiled at me between pride and patronage.

" ' Harry's going up in the world,' said my sister.

" ' That's what makes it all so wonderful,' said Milly. ' He's a wonderful brother for you.'

" She began to praise the beauty of Fanny's flat, and Fanny offered to show her all over it. They were away some time and I went to the window, wishing stupidly after the manner of a man that they could somehow contrive to be a little different and a little warmer with each other. Didn't they both love me and shouldn't that be a bond of sisterhood between them ?

" Then came tea, one of Fanny's wonderful teas, but I was no longer the indiscriminate devourer of teas that I had been. Milly praised it all like a visiting duchess.

" ' Well,' said Milly at last with the air of one who has many appointments, ' it's time to go I'm afraid.' . . .

" I had been watching Fanny very closely throughout this visit and contrasting her guarded and polished civilities with the natural warmth of her reception of Hetty, half a year before. I felt I could not wait for another occasion before I had a word or two with her. So I kissed her good-bye—even her kiss had changed—and she and Milly hesitated and kissed, and I went down past the landing with Milly and heard the door close above. ' I've left my gloves,' I said suddenly. ' You go on down. I won't be a moment.' And I darted back up-stairs.

" Fanny did not come to the door immediately.

" ' What is it, Harry ? ' she said, when she appeared.

" ' Gloves ! ' said I. ' No ! Here they are in my pocket. Silly of me ! . . . You *do* like her, Fanny ? You think she's all right, don't you ? She's a little shy with you, but she's a dear.'

" Fanny looked at me. I thought her eyes were hard. ' She's all right,' she said. ' Quite all right. You'll never have to divorce *her*, Harry.'

" ' I didn't know. I want you to—like her. I thought— you didn't seem quite warm.'

" ' Silly old Harry ! ' said Fanny, with a sudden return to her old manner. And she took me and kissed me like a loving sister again.

" I went down two steps from the door and turned.

" ' I'd hate it,' I said, ' if you didn't think she was all right.'

" ' She's all right,' said Fanny. ' And it's Good Luck to you, Harry. It's—— You see it's about Good-bye for me. I shan't be seeing very much of you now with that clever wife of yours to take you about. Who's so *well*-connected. But Good Luck, old Brudder ! Oh ! *always* Good Luck ! '

" Her eyes were brimming with tears.

" ' God send you are happy, Harry dear—after your fashion. It's—it's different.' . . .

" She stopped short. She was weeping.

" She banged her door upon me, and I stood puzzled for a moment and then went down to Milly."

CHAPTER SEVEN

LOVE AND DEATH

§ 1

IN the two years that followed I learned to love and trust my stiff-spirited wife more and more. She was very brave in a conscious and deliberate way, very clear-headed, very honest. I saw her fight, and it was not an easy fight, to bring our son into the world, and that sort of crisis was a seal between man and woman in those days even as it is to-day. If she never got to any just intuitions about my thoughts and feelings I did presently arrive at a fairly clear sense of hers. I could feel for her ambitions and humiliations. She worked hard to make our home bright and efficient. She had a taste for

sound and ' solid ' things and temperate harmonies. In that
Old World, encumbered with possessions and with an extreme
household autonomy, servants were a very important matter
indeed and she managed ours with just that measured kindliness and just that avoidance of intimacy that was needed by
the social traditions of the time. She had always been intelligently interested in the internal politics of Thunderstone
House and she showed the keenest desire for my success there.
' I'll see you a director before ten years,' she said. And I
worked very hard indeed and not merely for ambition's sake.
I really understood and believed in the educational importance
of that great slovenly business. Newberry came to recognise
in me a response to his own ideas. He would consult me
about new schemes and the modification of old procedure.
He relied on me more and more and talked with me more
and more frequently. And it is a queer thing to recall that
by a sort of convention between us we never mentioned or
alluded to my sister Fanny in any of our discussions.

" I changed a good deal during my first two and a half
years of married life. I matured and hardened. I became a
man of the world. I was put up for and elected a member
of a good club, and developed my gift for talk. I met a widening variety of people, and some of them were quite distinguished
people, and I found they did not overawe me. I possessed a
gift for caustic commentary that gained me some reputation
as a wit, and I felt a growing interest in the showy and sterile
game of party politics. My ambitions grew. I was active ;
I was self-satisfied. I had largely forgotten my intense sexual
humiliation. But I was not a very happy man. My life was
like a handsome, weel-appointed room with a north light ;
the bowls were full of cut flowers but the sunlight never
came in."

§ 2

" For two years and a half I saw nothing of Hetty and it
was not my fault that I ever saw her again. I did everything
I could to eradicate her from my existence. I destroyed her
photographs and every little vestige of her that might distress
me by its memories. If I caught myself in a reverie in which
she figured I forced my attention to other things. Sometimes
when I made a new success I had a flash of desire that she
should witness it. Ugly, I agree, but is it not what we still
are—except for civilisation ? She came back sometimes in
dreams, but they were anger-soaked dreams. And I cultivated
my pride and love for Milly. With increasing prosperity Milly's
skill in dressing herself developed ; she became a very handsome effective woman ; she gave herself to me with a smiling
sense of temperate and acceptable giving.

" In those days we had not learned to analyse our motives.
We were much less observant of ourselves than men and

women are to-day. I had set my mind upon loving Milly and I did not realise that the essential thing in loving is a thing beyond our wills. Fanny and Hetty I loved by nature and necessity, but my days were now far too completely apportioned between work and Milly for much companionship with Fanny to survive, and Hetty in my heart was like one of those poor shrivelled corpses of offending monks they walled up in the monasteries during the Age of Christendom in Europe. But I found now a curious liveliness in my interest in women in general. I did not ask what these wanderings of attention signified ; I was ashamed of them but I gave way to them. Even when I was in Milly's company I would look at other women and find a vague excitement if the intent of my glances was returned.

" And I began to read novels in a new spirit, though I did not know why I was taking to novels ; I was reading them, I see now, for the sake of the women I found in them. I do not know, Sunray, whether you realise how much the novels and plays of those days served to give men and women love-phantoms with whom they made imaginative excursions. We successful and respectable ones went our dignified and satisfied ways, assuaging the thin protests of our starved possibilities with such unsubstantial refreshment.

" But it was because of that wandering eye for women that I encountered Hetty again. It was in the springtime that I came upon her, either in March or very early April, in some public gardens quite near to Chester Terrace. These gardens were not in my direct way from the underground railway-station, which took me to and fro between home and business and my house, but I was in no hurry for Milly's tea-party and the warmth and sunlight drew me to this place of blossom and budding green. They were what we should call spring gardens nowadays, small but cleverly laid out for display with an abundant use of daffodil, narcissus, hyacinth, almond-blossom and the like, with hard paths and seats placed to command happy patches of colour. On one of these seats a woman was sitting alone with her back to me looking at a patch of scyllas. I was struck by the loveliness of her careless pose. Such discoveries of the dear beauty that hides in the world would stir me like a challenge and then stab me with pain. She was dressed very poorly and simply, but her dingy clothing was no more than the smoked glass one uses to see the brightness of the sun.

" I slackened my pace as I went past and glanced back to see her face. And I saw the still face of Hetty, very grave and sorrowful, Hetty, no longer a girl but a woman, looking at the flowers and quite unheedful of my regard.

" Something greater than pride or jealousy seized me then I went a few steps farther and stopped and turned, as though no other thing was possible.

" At that she became aware of me. She looked up, doubted, and recognised me.

" She watched me with that motionless face of hers as I came and sat down beside her. I spoke in a voice of astonishment on the edge of a storm of emotion. ' Hetty,' I said, ' I couldn't go past you ! '

" She did not answer immediately. ' Are you—— ? ' she began and stopped. ' I suppose we were bound to meet again,' she said, ' sooner or later. You look as if you had grown, Harry. You look well and prosperous.'

" ' Do you live in this part of London ? ' I asked.

" ' Camden Town just now,' she said. ' We move about.'

" ' You married—Sumner ? '

" ' What did you expect me to do ? What else was there to do. I've drunk my cup to the dregs, Harry.'

" ' But—— You had the child ? '

" ' It died—it died all right. Poor little mite. And my mother died a year ago.'

" ' Well, you've got Sumner.'

" ' I've got Sumner.'

" At any time before that meeting I should have exulted over the death of Sumner's child, but in the presence of Hetty's misery that old hatred would not come back for its gratification. I was looking at her face which was so familiar and so changed, and it was as if I woke up again to love for her after two years and a half of insensibility. What a beaten and unhappy thing she was—she whom I had loved and hated so bitterly !

" ' It seems a long way back now to Kent, Harry—and mother's farm,' she said.

" ' You've parted with it ? '

" ' Farm and furniture—and mostly it's gone. Sumner bets. He's betted most of it away. It's hard, you see, to find a job but easy to fancy a winner. Which doesn't win. . . .'

" ' My father used to do that,' I said. ' I'd like to shoot every race-horse in England.'

" ' I hated selling the farm,' she said. ' I sold the farm and came into this dingy old London. Sumner dragged me here and he's dragging me down. It's not his fault ; it's how he's made. But when a spring day comes like this—— ! I think of Kent and the wind on the downs and the blackthorn in the hedges and the little yellow noses of the primroses and the first elder leaves coming out, until I want to cry and scream. But there's no getting out of it. Here I am. I've come to look at these flowers here. What's the good ? They just hurt me.'

" She stared at the flowers.

" ' My God ! ' I said, ' but this hurts me too. I didn't expect——'

" ' What did you expect ? ' she asked, and turned that still face of hers to me and silenced me.

" ' I don't see that it should hurt you,' she said. ' I brought it on myself. You didn't do it. It happened to me. It was my fault. Though why God made me love beautiful things —and then set a trap for me and made me fool enough to fall into it—— ! '

" Silence fell between us.

" ' Meeting you like this,' I began presently, ' makes me see things—so differently. You see—in those old days—in some ways you seemed so much stronger than I was. I didn't understand. . . . I see—— This makes me feel—— I ought to have taken better care of you.'

" ' Or shown me mercy. I was dirty and shameful—yes. All that. But you were merciless, Harry. Men are merciless to women. I did—all through—I loved you, Harry. In a way I've always loved you and I love you now. When I looked up and saw it was you coming back to me—— For a minute you were just like the old Harry. For a moment—— It was like Spring coming real. . . . But it's no good talking like that now, Harry. It's too late.'

" ' Yes,' I agreed. ' Too late. . . .'

" She watched my face through a long pause. I weighed my words when I spoke. ' Up to now,' I said, ' I've never forgiven. Now—— Now I see you here I wish—I wish to God—I had forgiven you. And made a fight for it with you. We might—— Suppose, Hetty, suppose I had forgiven you—— ? '

" ' Harry dear,' she said softly, ' you don't want to be seen here making a woman cry. We won't talk of that. Tell me about yourself. I've heard you married again. A beautiful woman. Sumner saw that I heard of that. Are you happy, Harry ? You look prosperous, and every one isn't prosperous these post-war times.'

" ' That's all so-and-so, Hetty. I work hard. I've got ambitions. I'm still a publisher's assistant at the old place but I'm near to being a director. I'm high up. My wife—— She's a dear and a great help to me. . . . Somehow meeting you . . . My God ! Hetty, what a mess we made of things ! It's all very well, but the second time of marrying isn't like the first. You and I—— I'm a sort of blood-brother to you and nothing can change it. The wood—that little wood where you kissed me ! Why did we smash it up, Hetty ? Why did we do it ? Two fools who'd got so precious a thing ! That's all past. But hate is dead between us. That's past too. If there was anything I could do for you now I would do it.'

" A gleam of the old humour came. ' If you could kill Sumner,' she said, ' and smash the world and destroy the memories of three years. . . . It's no good, Harry. I ought to have kept myself clean. And you—you might have been gentler with me.'

" ' I couldn't, Hetty.'

" ' I knew you couldn't. And I couldn't foresee that my blood would betray me one evening. And here we are ! Like meeting after we are dead. Spring comes now but it comes for other people. All these little crocus trumpets—like a brass band it is—they are trumpeting up the next lot of lovers. Better luck to them ! '

" We sat still for a time. In the background of my mind Milly and her assembled teacups became evident as a faint urgency. ' You're late,' she'd say.

" ' Where are you living, Hetty ? ' I asked. ' What is your address ? '

" She shook her head after a moment's thought. ' Better you shouldn't know.'

" ' But somehow I might help.'

" ' It would only disturb us all. I've got my cup—of dirty water—to drink. I've got to stand what I'm in for. What could you do to help me ? '

" ' Well,' said I, ' my address anyhow is easy to keep in mind. It's just what it was when we—— In the days when we lived—— Thunderstone House it is. Some day there might be something——'

" ' It's good of you.'

" We stood up face to face, and as we stood there a thousand circumstances vanished and nothing remained but our hurt and injured selves. ' Good-bye, Hetty,' I said. ' Good luck.'

" Our hands met. ' Good luck to you, Harry. It's no good, but I'm glad we met like this. And to find you forgive me a little at last.' "

§ 3

" That meeting had a profound effect upon me. It banished much aimless reverie from my mind ; it unlocked the prison in which a whole multitude of forbidden thoughts had been confined. I thought enormously of Hetty. They were vague and impossible thoughts ; they came in the night on the way to business, even during slack moments in business hours ; rehearsals of dramatised encounters, explanations, magic turns of circumstances that suddenly restored our lost world to us. I tried to suppress these cloudy imaginations but with little avail ; they overspread my mental skies in spite of me. I can't tell you how many times I walked through those gardens in Regent's Park ; that détour became my normal route from the station to my home. And I would even go out of my customary way along some side-path because I had caught a glimpse far off, between the tree-branches and the flower-beds, of a solitary woman. But Hetty never came back there.

" In my brooding over Hetty a jealousy and hatred of

Sumner developed steadily. I do not think I had any desire for Hetty myself but I wanted intensely to get her away from him. This hostility to Sumner was the ugly undertow of my remorse and reawakened love of Hetty. He was the evil thing that had deprived me of Hetty. I did not reflect for a moment that it was I with my relentless insistence upon divorce that had forced her back to him.

" And all this dreaming and brooding and futile planning, all this body of desire for something more to happen between Hetty and myself, went on without my breathing a word of it to any living soul. It was on my conscience that it was disloyal to Milly, and I even made a half-hearted attempt to tell Milly that I had met Hetty and been shocked at her poverty and unhappiness. I wanted to bring her into my own state of mind and have her feel as I did. I threw out a remark one day—we had gone to Hampstead Heath for a walk one afternoon— that I had once walked along that ridge by the Round Pond with Hetty during my last leave. ' I wonder how she is living now,' I said.

" Milly did not answer immediately, and when I looked at her face it was flushed and hard. ' I hoped you had forgotten her,' she said in a suffocated voice.

" ' This brought it back to me.'

" ' I try never to think of her. You don't know what that woman meant to me—the humiliation.

" It was not only for myself,' she added. ' It was for you.'

" She said no more but it was manifest how terribly the mere name of Hetty had disturbed her."

" Poor little things ! " cried Firefly. " How insanely jealous you all were ! "

" And I did not go to Fanny and tell her about Hetty for a time. I had misrepresented Hetty to her as a figure of common depravity and I found it difficult to put that right. Nowadays I did not see so much of Fanny as I had formerly done. She was living half-way across London from me. Her relations with Newberry were now much more public than they had been, and she had developed a circle of acquaintances who cared for her. But this publicity made Milly more stiff towards her, because she feared that a scandal would be made about Fanny in relation to my position in the firm of Crane & Newberry. Near Pangbourne, Newberry had taken a bungalow and there Fanny would spend whole weeks at a time, quite out of our range.

" But presently a situation developed which sent me post-haste to Fanny for help and advice."

§ 4

" Suddenly in July when I was beginning to think I should never hear from her again, Hetty appealed to me for help. Would I meet her one evening, she asked, by the fountain in the Park near the Zoological Gardens, and then we would get chairs and she would tell me what she had in mind. She did not want me to write her a letter, Sumner had become very jealous of her, and so would I put an advertisement in *The Daily Express*, with the letters ABCD and giving the hour and date. I made an appointment for the earliest possible evening.

" Instead of the despondent and spiritless Hetty I had met in the spring I found a Hetty high-strung and excited. ' I want some place where we shan't be seen,' she said as I came up to her. She took my arm to turn me about, and led the way towards two green chairs standing apart a little away from the main walk that here traversed the park. I noted that she was still wearing the same shabby dress she had had on our previous encounter. Her manner with me was quite different from the manner of our former meeting. There was something familiar and confident about her as though in between she had met me in imagination a multitude of times—as no doubt she had.

" ' You meant all you said, Harry, when we talked before ? ' she began.

" ' Everything.'

" ' You will help me if you can ? '

" ' Everything I can.'

" ' Suppose I asked you for some money ? '

" ' Naturally.'

" ' I want to get away from Sumner. I have a chance. I could do it.'

" ' Tell me about it, Hetty. All I can do, I will.'

" ' Things have changed, Harry, since that day we met. I'd got into a sort of despairing state. I took whatever came. Seeing you changed me. I don't know why but it did. Perhaps I was going to change anyhow. But I can't stand being with Sumner any longer. And there's a chance now. I shall want a lot of money—sixty or seventy pounds.'

" I thought. ' That's quite possible, Hetty. If you can wait for a week or so. Ten days say.'

" ' You see I have a friend, a girl who married a Canadian. She stayed here to have her child when he went home and now she goes out to him. She's been ill ; she's not very strong and she doesn't want to face the voyage alone. It would be easy for me to get out there with her as her cousin and companion. If I had an outfit—— We've discussed it all. She knows some one who could manage about a passport for me. In my maiden name. That's the scheme. I could have my outfit sent to her place. I could slip away.'

" ' You'd take another name ? Begin again over there ? '

" ' Yes. . . .'

" I sat considering this project. It pleased me. ' There need be no trouble about the money,' I said.

" ' I can't go on living with Sumner. You never saw him. You don't know what he's like.'

" ' I've heard he was good-looking.'

" ' Don't I know that face—flushed and weak! He's a liar and a cheat. He has a conceit he can best every one. And he's begun drinking. God knows why I married him. It seemed the natural thing somehow since you had divorced me. The child had to have a father. . . . But he disgusts me, Harry. He disgusts me. I can't go on. I can't endure it. You can't imagine it—in those little lodgings—in the hot weather. To keep a maudlin drunken man away from one. . . . If I hadn't seen this way out something worse might have happened.'

" ' Can't you come away from him at once ? ' I asked. ' Why should you ever go back to him ? '

" ' No. I must get clear away or there will be mischief. And you mustn't be in it. He'd think of you at once. If he had a hint it was you. That's what you have to do about the money and everything, letters or anything—get it to me without your being mixed up with it. You must get me money, not cheques. We mustn't be seen to meet. Even about here it's risky. He's got into a gang. He's been getting deeper and deeper into a rotten set. They blackmail the bookies. They go about with revolvers. They pass on things to one another. It grew out of betting and now they call it getting a bit of their own back. . . . If they spot you in it, they'll come for you.'

" ' Trench warfare in London. I'll risk it.'

" ' You needn't risk anything—if we are discreet. If there was some one I could see—who'd hand things on.'

" I thought at once of my sister Fanny.

" ' That would be safe,' said Hetty. ' As safe as could be. And I'd love to see her again. I loved her when I met her. . . . But all this is awful good of you, Harry. I don't deserve a moment's kindness.'

" ' Nonsense ! I pushed you into the dirt, Hetty.'

" ' I jumped into it.'

" ' Fell into it. It's nothing very much, Hetty, to give you a hand to get out of it again.'

§ 5

" I went the next day to my sister Fanny to prepare her for Hetty's call. Fanny sat in an armchair and listened and watched my face as I told my story, confessed how I had exaggerated Hetty's offence and asked for help. ' I ought to have seen her, Harry, before I took your word for it,' she said. ' Of course, even now, I can't imagine how a girl who loves one man could ever stand the kiss of another as she did, but then, as you say, she'd been drinking. We women aren't all made alike. There's all sorts make a world. Some girls—the backbone goes out of them when they feel a man's kisses. You and me, Harry, we aren't made like that. I've been thinking while you sat talking there, how like we both are to poor mother really—for all she quarrelled with me. We'll grow hard pre-

sently if we aren't careful. And your Hetty was young and she
didn't know. Only once it was. And all her life's been spoiled
by it ! . . . I didn't know it was like that, Harry.'

" And my sister Fanny began to recall her impressions of
Hetty. She recalled her fine animation and the living interest
of her talk. ' When she left I said to myself, she's got wit ;
that's the first witty woman I've ever met. She's got poetry
in her. Everything she says comes out a little different from
the things most people say. She says things that come like
flowers in a hedgerow. So she did. Does she still ? '

" ' I never thought of it like that before,' I said. ' I suppose
she has a sort of poetry. Only the other day—when I met her
first. What was it she said ? Something.'

" ' It's no good quoting, Harry. Witty things should bloom
where they grow. They're no good as cut-flowers. But you
and I are fairly quick and fairly clever, Harry, but we never
had any of that.'

" ' I've always loved her talk,' I said.

" I began to explain the situation to Fanny more fully and
to show how she could help in it. I was not to see Hetty again ;
Fanny was to see her, pay her the hundred pounds we could put
together for her, communicate with the friends she was to
accompany and get her away. Fanny listened gravely and
agreed.

" Then she reflected.

" ' Why don't you take her to Canada yourself, Harry ? '
she asked abruptly."

§ 6

" I did not answer Fanny for some moments. Then I said :
' I don't want to.'

" ' I can see you love Hetty still.'

" ' Love. But I don't want that.'

" ' You don't want to be with her ? '

" ' It's out of the question. Why ask a painful thing like
that ? All that is dead.'

" ' Isn't a resurrection possible ? Why is it out of the
question ? Pride ? '

" ' No.'

" ' Why then ? '

" ' Milly.'

" ' You don't love Milly.'

" ' I won't have you discuss that, Fanny. I do love her.'

" ' Not as you love Hetty.'

" ' Quite differently. But Milly trusts me. She keeps faith
with me. I'd as soon steal money—from a child's money-box—
as go back on Milly.'

" ' It's wonderful how fine men can be to the wives they
don't love,' said Fanny bitterly.

" ' Newberry's different,' I said. ' I've got my little son.

I've got my work. And though you will never have it, I love Milly.'

" ' In a way. Is she company for you ? Is she fun ? '

" ' I trust and love her. And as for Hetty, you don't understand about Hetty. I love her. I love her enormously. But it's like two ghosts meeting by moonlight. We two are dead to each other and—sorrowful. It isn't as though it was anything like your case over again. I see Hetty in hell and I'd do nearly anything in life to get her out. I don't even want to meet her. I want to get her away out of this filth and stupidity to where she can begin again. That's all I want and that's all she wants. How could she and I ever come together again ? How could we kiss again as lovers kiss ? Poor defiled things we are ! And all my cruelty. You're thinking of something else, Fanny. You're not thinking of Hetty and me.'

" ' Maybe I am,' said Fanny. ' Yes, I think I am. And so she is to go to Canada and begin again—till her health comes back and her courage comes back. It isn't natural for a woman of her temperament to live without a man to love her, Harry.'

" ' Let her live and love,' said I. ' She'll have changed her name. Her friends will stand by her. They won't give her away. Let her forget. Let her begin again.'

" ' With another man ? '

" ' It may be.'

" ' You don't mind the thought of that ? '

" I was stung but I kept my temper. ' Have I any right to mind the thought of that now ? '

" ' But you will. And you will go on living with this wife you trust and respect. Who's dull-spirited—dull as ditch-water.'

" ' No. Who's my son's mother. Who is trustworthy. Whom I'm pledged to. And I've got my work. It may seem nothing to you. It's good enough for me to give myself to it. Can't I love Hetty, can't I help her out of the net she's in, and yet not want to go back to impossible things ? '

" ' Grey Monday mornings,' said Fanny.

" ' As if all life wasn't grey,' I said.

" And then," said Sarnac, " I remember that I made a prophecy. I made it—when did I make it ? Two thousand years ago ? Or two weeks ago ? I sat in Fanny's little sitting-room, an old-world creature amidst her old-world furnishings, and I said that men and women would not always suffer as we were suffering then. I said that we were still poor savages, living only in the bleak dawn of civilisation, and that we suffered because we were underbred, undertrained and darkly ignorant of ourselves, that the mere fact that we knew our own unhappiness was the promise of better things and that a day would come when charity and understanding would light the world so that men and women would no longer hurt themselves and one another as they were doing now everywhere, universally, in law and in restriction, and in jealousy and in hate, all round and about the earth.

" ' It is still too dark for us,' I said, ' to see clearly where we are going, and every one of us blunders and stumbles and does wrong. Every one. It is idle for me to ask now what is the right thing for me to do ? Whatever I do now will be wrong. I ought to go with Hetty and be her lover again —easily I could do that and why should I deny it ?—and I ought to stick to Milly and the work I have found in the world. Right road or left road, both lead to sorrow and remorse, but there is scarcely a soul in all this dark world, Fanny, who has not had to make or who will not presently have to make a choice as hard. I will not pull the skies down upon Milly. I *cannot* because she has put her faith in me. You are my dear sister Fanny and I love you and we have loved each other. Do you remember how you used to take me round to school and hold my hand at the crossings ? Don't make things too hard for me now. Just help me to help Hetty. Don't tear me to pieces. She is still alive and young and— Hetty. Out there she at least can begin again.' "

§ 7

" Nevertheless, I did see Hetty again before she left England. There came a letter for me at Thunderstone House in which she proposed a meeting.

" ' You have been so kind to me,' she wrote. ' It is the next best thing to your never having left me. You have been a generous dear. You've given back happiness to me. I feel excited already at the thought of the great liner and the ocean, and full of hope. We've got a sort of picture of the ship ; it is like a great hotel ; with our cabin marked in it exactly where it is. Canada will be wonderful ; Our Lady of the Snows ; and we are going by way of New York, New York like nothing else on earth, cliffs and crags of windows towering up to the sky. And it's wonderful to have new things again. I sneak off to Fanny's just to finger them over. I'm excited—yes, and grateful—yes, and full of hope—yes. And Harry, Harry, my heart aches and aches. I want to see you again. I don't deserve to but I want to see you again. We began with a walk and why shouldn't we end with a walk ? Thursday and Friday all the gang will be at Leeds. I could get away the whole day either day and it would be a miracle if any one knew. I wish we could have that same old walk again. I suppose it's too far and impossible. We'll save that, Harry, until we're both quite dead and then we'll be two little swirls of breeze in the grass or two bits of thistle-down going side by side. But there was that other walk we had when we went to Shere and right over the North Downs to Leatherhead. We looked across the Weald and saw our own South Downs far, far away. Pinewood and heather there was ; hills beyond hills. And the smoke of rubbish-burning.'

" I was to write to Fanny's address.

" Of course we had that walk, we two half-resuscitated
lovers. We did not make love at all though we kissed when
we met and meant to kiss when we parted. We talked as I
suppose dead souls might talk of the world that had once
been real. We talked of a hundred different things—even of
Sumner. Now that she was so near escape from him her
dread and hatred had evaporated. She said Sumner had a
passionate desire for her and a real need of her and that it
was not fair to him and very bad for him that she despised
him. It wounded his self-respect. It made him violent and
defiant. A woman who cared for him, who would take the
pains to watch him and care for him as a woman should do
for a man might have made something of him. ' But I've
never cared for him, Harry ; though I've tried. But I can see
where things hurt him. I can see they hurt him frightfully
at times. It doesn't hurt him any the less because he does
ugly things.' He was vain, too, and ashamed of his incapacity
to get a sufficient living. He was drifting very rapidly to a
criminal life and she had no power over him to hold him back.

" I can still see Hetty and hear her voice, as we walked
along a broad bridle-path between great rhododendron bushes,
and she talked, grave and balanced and kind she was, of this
rogue who had cheated her and outraged her and beaten her.
It was a new aspect of Hetty and yet at the same time it
was the old dear Hetty I had loved and wasted and lost,
clear-minded and swift, with an understanding better than
her will.

" We sat for a long time on the crest of the Downs above
Shere where the view was at its widest and best, and we
called the old days of happiness in Kent and talked of the
distances before us and of crossing the sea and of France and
so of the whole wide world. ' I feel,' she said, ' as I used to
when I was a child, at the end of the school-quarter. I'm
going away to new things. Put on your frock, put on your hat ;
the big ship is waiting. I am a little frightened about it and
rather happy. . . . I wish—— But never mind that.'

" ' You wish—— ? '

" ' What else could I wish ? '

" ' You mean—— ? '

" ' It's no good wishing.'

" ' I've got to stick the job I've taken. I've got to see it
through. But if you care to know it, Hetty, I wish so too.
My God ?—if wishes could release one ! '

" ' You've got your job here. I wouldn't take you away,
Harry, if I could. Sturdy you are, Harry, and you'll go through
with it and do the work you're made to do—and I'll take
what comes to me. Over there I guess I'll forget a lot about
Sumner and the things that have happened in between—and

think a lot about you and the South Downs and this—how
we sat side by side here.

"'Perhaps,' said Hetty, 'heaven is a place like this. A
great hillside to which you come at last, after all the tugging
and pushing and the hoping and the disappointments and
the spurring and the hungers and the cruel jealousies are
done with and finished for ever. Then here you sit down and
rest. And you aren't alone. Your lover is here and he sits
beside you and you touch shoulder to shoulder, very close
and very still, and your sins are forgiven you ; your blunders
and misunderstandings they matter no longer ; and the beauty
takes you and you dissolve into it, you dissolve into it side
by side and together you forget and fade until at last nothing
remains of all the distresses and anger and sorrow, nothing
remains of you at all but the breeze upon the great hillside
and sunshine and everlasting peace. . . .'

"'All of which,' said Hetty, rising abruptly to her feet
and standing over me, 'is just empty nothingness. Oh Harry !
Harry ! one feels things and when one tries to say them it is
just words and nonsense. We've hardly started on our way
to Leatherhead and you'll have to be back by seven. So get
up, old Harry. Get up and come on. You are the dearest
person alive and it has been sweet of you to come with me
to-day. I was half-afraid you'd think it wasn't wise. . . .'

"In the late afternoon we got to a place called Little Book-
ham and there we had tea. About a mile farther on was a
railway-station and we found a train for London ; it came in
as we got on to the platform.

"Everything had gone well so far and then came the first
gleam of disaster. At Leatherhead we sat looking out on
the station platform and a little ruddy man came trotting
along to get into the compartment next to us, a little common
fellow like an ostler with a cigar under his Hebrew nose, and
as he was about to get in he glanced up at us. Doubt and
then recognition came into his eyes and at the sight of him
Hetty recoiled.

"'Get in,' said the guard, blowing his whistle, and the
little man was hustled out of sight.

"Hetty was very white. 'I know that man,' she said,
'and he knows me. He's named Barnado. What shall I do ? '

"'Nothing. Does he know you very well ? '

"'He's been to our rooms—three or four times.'

"'He may not have been sure it was you.'

"'I think he was. Suppose he were to come to the window
at the next station to make certain. Could I pretend not to
be myself ? Refuse to recognise him or answer to my name ? '

"'But if he was convinced it was you in spite of your
bluff that would instantly make him suspicious and off he'd
go to your husband ! If on the other hand you took it all quite
casually—said I was your cousin or your brother-in-law—he

WIH-D   15*

might think nothing of it and never even mention it to Sumner. But making him suspicious would send him off to Sumner right away. Anyhow, you go to Liverpool to-morrow. I don't see that his recognition of you matters.'

" ' I'm thinking of you,' she said.

" ' But he doesn't know who I am. So far as I know none of that lot has seen me. . . .'

" The train slowed down at the next station. Mr. Barnado appeared, cigar and all, bright-eyed and curious.

" ' Blest if I didn't say to myself that's Hetty Sumner ! ' said Mr. Barnado. ' Wonderful 'ow one meets people ! '

" ' My brother-in-law, Mr. Dyson,' said Hetty, introducing me. ' We've been down to see his little daughter.'

" ' I didn't know you 'ad a sister, Mrs. Sumner.'

" ' I haven't,' said Hetty, with a note of pain in her voice. ' Mr. Dyson is a widower.'

" ' Sorry,' said Mr. Barnado. ' Stupid of me. And what age might the little girl be, Mr. Dyson ? '

" I found myself under the necessity of creating, explaining and discussing an orphan daughter. Mr. Barnado had three and was uncomfortably expert about children and their phases of development. He was evidently a model father. I did as well as I could, I drew out Mr. Barnado's family pride rather than indulged my own but I was immensely relieved when Mr. Barnado exclaimed, ' Gawd ! 'Ere's Epsom already ! Glad to 'ave met you, Mr.——'

" ' Damn ! ' I said to myself. I had forgotten.

" ' Dixon,' said Hetty hastily, and Mr. Barnado, after effusive farewells, proceeded to remove himself from the carriage.

" ' Thank Heaven ! ' said Hetty, ' he didn't come on to London. You're the poorest liar, Harry, I've ever known. As it is—no harm's been done.'

" ' No harm's been done,' said I, but two or three times before we reached the London station where we were to part for ever, we recurred to the encounter and repeated the re-assuring formula that no harm had been done.

" We parted at Victoria Station with very little emotion. Mr. Barnado had brought us back, as it were, to an every-day and incidental atmosphere. We did not kiss each other again. The world about us had become full now of observant eyes. My last words to Hetty were ' Everything's all right ! ' in a business-like, reassuring tone, and the next day she slipped off to join her friends at Liverpool and passed out of my life for ever."

§ 8

" For three or four days I did not feel this second separation from Hetty very greatly. My mind was still busy with the details of her departure. On the third day she sent me a

wireless message, as we used to call it, to Thunderstone House.
'Well away,' she said. 'Fine weather. Endless love and
gratitude.' Then slowly as the days passed my sense of loss
grew upon me, the intimations of an immense loneliness
gathered and spread until they became a cloud that darkened
all my mental sky. I was persuaded now that there was no
human being who could make me altogether happy but Hetty,
and that for the second time I was rejecting the possibility
of companionship with her. I had wanted love, I perceived,
without sacrifice, and in that old world, it seems to me now,
love was only possible at an exorbitant price, sacrifice of
honour, sacrifice of one's proper work in the world, humiliations
and distresses. I had shirked the price of Hetty and she was
going from me, taking out of my life for ever all those sweet
untellable things that were the essence of love, the little
names, the trivial careless caresses, the exquisite gestures of
mind and body, the moments of laughter and pride and
perfect understanding. Day-by-day love went westward from
me. Day and night I was haunted by a more and more vivid
realisation of a great steamship throbbing and heaving its way
across the crests and swelling waves of the Atlantic welter. The
rolling black coal-smoke from its towering funnels poured before
the wind. Now I would see that big ocean-going fabric in the
daylight; now lit brightly from stem to stern, under the stars.

"I was full of unappeasable regret, I indulged in endless
reveries of a flight across the Atlantic in pursuit of Hetty,
of a sudden dramatic appearance before her;—'Hetty, I
can't stand it. I've come'—and all the time I stuck steadfastly
to the course I had chosen. I worked hard and late at Thunderstone House; I did my best to shunt my imagination into
new channels by planning two new quasi-educational publications, and I set myself to take Milly out to restaurants to
dinner and to the theatre and to interesting shows. And in
the midst of some picture-show perhaps I would find my
rebel mind speculating what sort of thing Hetty would have
said of it, had she been there. There was a little show of
landscapes at the Alpine Gallery and several were pictures
of Downland scenery and one showed a sunlit hillside under
drowsy white clouds. It was almost like seeing Hetty.

"It was exactly a week after Hetty's landing in New
York that I first encountered Sumner. It was my usual
time of arrival and I was just turning out of Tottenham
Court Road into the side-street that led to the yard of
Thunderstone House. There was a small public house in this
byway and two men were standing outside it in attitudes of
expectation. One of them stepped out to accost me. He
was a little flushed Jewish man, and for the moment I did
not recognise him at all.

"'Mr. Smith?' said he, and scrutinised me queerly.
"'At your service,' said I.

THE DREAM

" ' Not by any chance Mr. Dyson or Dixon, eh ? ' he asked with a leer.

" ' Barnado ! ' cried my memory and placed him. My instant recognition must have betrayed itself in my face. Our eyes met and there were no secrets between them. ' No. Mr. Barnado,' I said with incredible stupidity ; ' my name's just plain Smith.'

" ' Don't mention it, Mr. Smith, don't mention it,' said Mr. Barnado with extreme politeness. ' I had a sort of fancy I might have met you before.' And turning to his companion and raising his voice a little, he said : ' That's him all right, Sumner—sure as eggs is eggs.'

" Sumner ! I glanced at this man who had given my life so disastrous a turn. He was very much my own height and build, fair with a blotched complexion and wearing a checked grey suit and an experienced-looking grey felt hat. He might have been my unsuccessful half-brother. Our eyes met in curiosity and antagonism. ' I'm afraid I'm not the man you want,' I said to Barnado and went on my way. I didn't see any advantage in an immediate discussion in that place. I perceived that an encounter was inevitable, but I meant it to happen amidst circumstances of my own choice and after I had had time to consider the situation properly. I heard something happen behind me and Barnado said : ' Shut up, you fool ! You've found out what you want to know.' I went through the passages and rooms of Thunderstone House to my own office and there, when I was alone, I sat down in my armchair and swore very heartily. Every day since the departure of Hetty I had been feeling more and more sure that this at least was not going to happen. I had thought that Sumner was very easily and safely and completely out of the story.

" I took my writing-pad and began to sketch out the situation. ' Ends to be secured,' I wrote.

" ' No. 1. Hetty must not be traced.

" ' No. 2. Milly must hear nothing of this.

" ' No. 3. No blackmailing.'

" I considered. ' But if a lump payment,' I began. This I scratched out again.

" I had to scheme out the essential facts. ' What does S. know ? What evidence exists ? Of what ? No clue to lead to Fanny ? There is nothing but that journey in the train. He will have a moral certainty but will it convince any one else ? '

" I wrote a new heading : ' How to handle them ? '

" I began to sketch grotesques and arabesques over my paper as I plotted. Finally I tore it up into very small fragments and dropped it into my waste-paper-basket. A messenger-girl rapped and came in with a paper slip, bearing the names of Fred Sumner and Arthur Barnado.

" ' They've not put the business they want to talk about,' I remarked.

" ' They said you'd know, sir.'

" ' No excuse. I want everybody to fill in that,' I said. ' Just say I'm too busy to see strangers who don't state their business. And ask them to complete the form.'

" Back came the form : ' Inquiry about Mr. Sumner's missing wife.'

" I considered it calmly. ' I don't believe we ever had the manuscript. Say I'm engaged up to half-past twelve. Then I could have a talk of ten minutes with Mr. Sumner alone. Make that clear. I don't see where Mr. Barnado comes in. Make it clear it's a privilege to see me.'

" My messenger did not reappear. I resumed my meditations on the situation. There was time for a lot of aggressive energy to evaporate before half-past twelve. Probably both of the men had come in from the outskirts and would have nowhere to wait but the streets or a public house. Mr. Barnado might want to be back upon his own business at Epsom. He'd played his part in identifying me. Anyhow, I didn't intend to have any talk with Sumner before a witness. If he reappeared with Barnado I should refuse to see them. For Barnado alone I had a plan and for Sumner I had a plan, but not for the two of them together.

" My delaying policy was a good one. At half-past twelve Sumner came alone and was shown up to me.

" ' Sit down there,' I said abruptly and leaned back in my chair and stared at his face and waited in silence for him to begin.

" For some moments he did not speak. He had evidently expected me to open with some sort of question and he had come ready loaded with a reply. To be plumped into a chair and looked at, put him off his game. He tried to glare at me and I looked at his face as if I was looking at a map. As I did so I found my hatred for him shrinking and changing. It wasn't a case for hatred. He had such a poor, mean, silly face, a weak arrangement of plausibly handsome features. Every now and then it was convulsed by a nervous twitch. His straw-coloured moustache was clipped back more on one side than the other, and his rather frayed necktie had slipped down to display his collar-stud and the grubbiness of his collar. He had pulled his mouth a little askew and thrust his face forward in an attempt at fierceness, and his rather watery blue eyes were as open and as protruded as he could manage.

" ' Where's my wife, Smith ? ' he said at last.

" ' Out of my reach, Mr. Sumner, and out of yours.'

" ' Where've you hid her ? '

" ' She's gone,' I said. ' It's no work of mine.'

" ' She's come back to you.'

" I shook my head.

" ' You know where she is ? '

" ' She's gone clear, Sumner. You let her go.'

" ' Let her go! *You* let her go, but I'm not going to. I'm not that sort. Here's this girl you marry and mess about with, and when she comes across a man who's a bit more of a man than you are and handles her as a woman ought to be handled, you go and chuck her out and divorce her, divorce her with her child coming, and then start planning and plotting to get her away from the man she's given her love to——'

" He stopped for want of words or breath. He wanted to exasperate me and start a shouting match. I said nothing.

" ' I want Hetty back,' he said. ' She's my wife and I want her back. She's mine and the sooner this foolery stops the better.'

" I sat up to the desk and put my elbows on it.

" ' You won't get her back,' I said very quietly. ' What are you going to do about it ? '

" ' By God ! I'll have her back—if I swing for it.'

" ' Exactly. And what are you going to do ? '

" ' What *can't* I do ? I'm her husband.'

" ' Well ? '

" ' You've got her.'

" ' Not a scrap of her.'

" ' She's missing. I can go to the police.'

" ' Go to them. What can they do ? '

" ' I can put them on to you.'

" ' Not a bit of it. They won't bother about me. If your wife's missing and you go to the police, they'll clear up all your gang with their inquiries. They'll be only too glad of the chance. Trouble *me* ! They'll dig up the cellars in *your* house and in your previous house to find the body. They'll search you and ransack you. And what they don't do to you, your pals will.'

" Sumner leaned forward and grimaced like a gargoyle to give his words greater emphasis. ' *Yew* were the last man seen with her,' he said.

" ' Not a scrap of evidence.'

" Sumner cursed vigorously. ' He *saw* you.'

" ' I can deny that absolutely. Frowsty little witness your friend Barnado. Don't be too sure he'll stick it. Nasty business if a woman disappears and you find yourself trying to fix something that won't hold water on to some one her husband dislikes. If I were you, Sumner, I wouldn't take that line. Even if he backs you up, what does it prove ? You know of nobody else who pretends to have seen me with Hetty. You won't be able to find anybody.' . . .

" Mr. Sumner extended his hand towards my table. He was too far away to bang it properly so he pulled his chair up closer. The bang when it came was ineffective. ' Look 'ere,' he said, and moistened his lips ' I want my Hetty back and I'm going to have her back. You're precious cool and cucumberish and all that just now, but by God ! I'll warm you up before I've done with you. You think you can get away and bluff me off.

Never made such a mistake in your life. Suppose I *don't* go to the police. Suppose I go for direct action. Suppose I come round to your place, and make a fuss with your wife.'

" ' That would be a nuisance,' I said.

" He followed up his advantage. ' A masterpiece of a nuisance.'

" I considered the forced fierceness of his face.

" ' I shall say I know nothing about your wife's disappearance and that you are a blackmailing liar. People will believe me. My wife will certainly believe me. She'd make herself do so if your story was ten times as possible. Your friend Barnado and you will make a pretty couple of accusers. I shall say you are a crazy jealous fool, and if you keep the game up I shall have you run in. I'd not be altogether sorry to have you run in. There's one or two little things I don't like you for. I'd not be so very sorry to get quits.'

" I had the better of him. He was baffled and angry but I saw now plainly that he had no real fight in him.

" ' And you know where she is ? ' he said.

" I was too full of the spirit of conflict now to be discreet. ' I know where she is. And you don't get her—whatever you do. And as I said before, what can you do about it ? '

" ' My God ! ' he said. ' My own wife.'

" I leaned back with the air of a man who had finished an interview. I looked at my wrist-watch.

" He stood up.

" I looked at him brightly, ' Well ? ' I said.

" Look here ! ' he spluttered. ' I don't stand this. By God ! I tell you I want Hetty. I want her. I want her and I'll do what I like with her. D'you think I'll take *this* ? Me ? She's mine, you dirty thief ! '

" I took up a drawing for an illustration and held it in my hand, regarding him with an expression of mild patience that maddened him.

" ' Didn't I marry her—when I needn't have ? If you wanted her, why the devil didn't you keep her when you had her ? I tell you I won't stand it.'

" ' My dear Sumner, as I said before, What can you do about it ?'

" He leaned over the desk, shook a finger as though it was a pistol-barrel in my face. ' I'll let daylight through you,' he said. ' I'll let daylight through you.'

" ' I'll take my chance of that,' I said.

" He expressed his opinion of me for a bit.

" ' I won't argue your points,' I said. ' I guess we're about through with this interview. Don't shock my clerk, please, when she comes in.' And I rang the bell on my desk.

" His parting shot was feeble. ' You've not heard the last of me. I mean what I told you.'

" ' Mind the step,' said I.

" The door closed and left me strung up and trembling with

excitement but triumphant. I felt I had beaten him and that I could go on beating him. It might be he would shoot. He'd probably got a revolver. But it was ten to one he'd take the trouble to get a fair chance at me and screw himself up to shooting pitch. And with his loose twitching face and shaky hand it was ten to one against his hitting me. He'd aim anyhow. He'd shoot too soon. And if he shot me it was ten to one he only wounded me slightly. Then I'd carry through my story against him. Milly might be shaken for a time, but I'd get the thing right again with her.

" I sat for a long time turning over the possibilities of the case. The more I considered it the more satisfied I was with my position. It was two o'clock and long past my usual lunch-time when I went off to my club. I treated myself to the un-usual luxury of a half-bottle of champagne."

§ 9

" I never believed Sumner would shoot me until I was actually shot.

" He waylaid me in the passage-way to the yard of Thunder-stone House as I was returning from lunch just a week after our first encounter and when I was beginning to hope he had accepted his defeat. He had been drinking, and as soon as I saw his flushed face, half-angry and half-scared, I had an in-timation of what might befall. I remember that I thought then that if anything happened he must get away because otherwise he might be left to tell his tale after I was dead. But I didn't really believe he was man enough to shoot, and even now I do not believe that. He fired through sheer lack of nervous and muscular co-ordination.

" He did not produce his pistol until I was close up to him. ' Now then,' said he, ' you're for it. Where's my wife ? ' and out came the pistol a yard from me.

" I forget my answer. I probably said, ' Put that away ' or something of that sort. And then I may have seemed about to snatch it. The report of the pistol, which sounded very loud to me, came at once, and a feeling as though I'd been kicked in the small of the back. The pistol was one of those that go on firing automatically as long as the trigger is gripped. It fired two other shots, and one got my knee and smashed it. ' Damn the thing ! ' he screamed and threw it down as though it had stung him. ' Get out, you fool. Run ! ' I said as I lurched towards him, and then as I fell I came within a foot of his terrified face as he dashed past me towards the main thorough-fare. He thrust me back with his hand as I reeled upon him.

" I think I rolled over on to my back into a sitting position after I fell, because I have a clear impression of him vanishing like the tail of a bolting rabbit into Tottenham Court Road. I saw a van and an omnibus pass across the space at the end of the street, heedless altogether of the pistol-shots that had sounded so terrible in my ears. A girl and a man passed with equal indifference. He was clear. Poor little beast! I'd stolen his Hetty. And now——

"I was very clear-headed. A little numbed where I had been hit but not in pain. I was chiefly aware of my smashed knee, which looked very silly with its mixture of torn trouser and red stuff and a little splintered pink thing that I supposed was an end of bone.

"People from nowhere were standing about me and saying things to me. They had come out of the yard or from the public house. I made a swift decision. 'Pistol went off in my hand,' I said, and shut my eyes.

"Then a fear of a hospital came upon me. 'My home quite handy,' I said. 'Eight Chester Terrace, Regent's Park. Get me there, please.'

"I heard them repeating the address and I recognised the voice of Crane & Newberry's door-porter. 'That's right,' he was saying. 'It's Mr. Mortimer Smith. Anything I can do for you, Mr. Smith?'

"I do not remember much of the details of what followed. When they moved me there was pain. I seem to have been holding on to what I meant to say and do, and my memory does not seem to have recorded anything else properly. I may have fainted once or twice. Newberry was in it somehow. I think he took me home in his car. 'How did it happen?' he asked. That I remember quite clearly.

"'The thing went off in my hand,' I said.

"One thing I was very certain about. Whatever happened they were not going to hang that poor silly hunted cheat Sumner. Whatever happened, the story of Hetty must not come out. If it did, Milly would think only one thing: that I had been unfaithful to her and that Sumner had killed me on that account. Hetty was all right now. I needn't bother about Hetty any more. I had to think of Milly—and Sumner. It is queer, but I seem to have known I was mortally wounded from the very instant I was shot.

"Milly appeared, full of solicitude.

"'Accident,' I said to her with all my strength. 'Went off in my hand.'

"My own bed.

"Clothes being cut away. Round my knee the cloth had stuck. The new grey suit which I'd meant should last the whole summer.

"Then two strangers became conspicuous, doctors I suppose, whispering, and one of them had his sleeves up and showed a pair of fat pink arms. Sponges and a tinkle of water dripping into a basin. They prodded me about. Damn! That *hurt*! Then stinging stuff. What was the good of it? I was in the body they were prodding, and I knew all about it and I was sure that I was a dead man.

" Milly again.

" ' My dear,' I whispered. ' Dear ! ' and her poor tearful face beamed love upon me.

" Valiant Milly ! Things had never been fair to her.

" Fanny ? Had Newberry gone to fetch her ? Anyhow he had vanished.

" She'd say nothing about Hetty. She was as safe as—safe as what ?—what did one say ?—anything safe.

" Poor dears ! What a fuss they were all in. It seemed almost shameful of me to be glad that I was going out of it all. But I was glad. This pistol-shot had come like the smashing of a window in a stuffy room. My chief desire was to leave kind and comforting impressions on those poor survivors who might still have to stay on in the world of muddle for years and years. Life ! What a muddle and a blundering it had been ! I'd never have to grow old now anyhow. . . .

" There was an irruption. People coming in from the dressing-room. One was a police-inspector in uniform. The other showed policeman through his plain clothes. Now was the time for it ! I was quite clear-headed—quite. I must be careful what I said. If I didn't want to see anything I could just close my eyes.

" ' Bleeding internally,' said some one.

" Then the police-inspector sat down on the bed. What a whale he was !—and asked me questions. I wondered if any one had caught a glimpse of Sumner. Sumner, bolting like a rabbit. I must risk that.

" ' It went off in my hand,' I said.

" ' What was he saying ? How long had I had that revolver ?

" ' Bought it this lunch-time,' I said.

" Did he ask why ? He did. ' Keep up my shooting.'

" Where ? He wanted to know where. ' Highbury.'

" ' What part of Highbury ? ' They wanted to trace the pistol. That wouldn't do. Give Mr. Inspector a paper-chase. ' Near Highbury.'

" ' Not in Highbury ? '

" I decided to be faint and stupid. ' That way,' I said faintly.

" ' A pawn-shop ? '

" Best not to answer. Then as if by an effort, ' Lil' shop.'

" ' Unredeemed pledges ? '

" I said nothing to that. I was thinking of another touch to the picture I was painting.

" I spoke with weak indignation. ' I didn't think it was loaded. How was I to know it was loaded ? It ought not to have been sold—loaded like that. I was just looking at it——'

" I stopped short and shammed exhaustion. Then I felt that I was not shamming exhaustion. I was exhausted. Gods ! but the stuffing was out of me ! I was sinking, sinking, out of the bedroom, out from among this group of people. They were getting little and faint and flimsy. Was there anything more to say ? Too late if there was. I was falling asleep, falling into a sleep, so profound, so fathomless. . . .

" Far away now was the little roomful of people, and infinitely small.

" ' He's going ! ' somebody said in a minute voice.

" I seemed to come back for an instant.

" I heard the rustle of Milly's dress as she came across the room to me.'

" And then, then I heard Hetty's voice again and opened my eyes and saw Hetty bending down over me—in that lovely place upon this mountain side. Only Hetty had become my dear Sunray who is mistress of my life. And the sunshine was on us and on her face, and I stretched because my back was a little stiff and one of my knees was twisted."

" ' Wake up ! I said,' said Sunray. ' Wake up,' and I shook you."

" And then we came and laughed at you," said Radiant. " Firefly and I."

" And you said, ' then there *is* another life,' said Firefly. " And the tale is only a dream ! It has been a good tale, Sarnac, and somehow you have made me think it was true."

" As it is," said Sarnac. " For I am as certain I was Henry Mortimer Smith yesterday, as I am that I am Sarnac here and now."

CHAPTER EIGHT

EPILOGUE

§ 1

THE guest-master poked the sinking fire into a last effort. " So am I," he said, and then with profound conviction, " *That tale is true.*"

" But how could it be true ? " asked Willow.

" I should be readier to believe it true if Sarnac had not brought in Sunray as Hetty," said Radiant. " It was very dream-like, the way Hetty grew more and more like his dear lady and at last dissolved altogether into her."

" But if Smith was a sort of anticipation of Sarnac," said Starlight, " then it was natural for him to choose as his love a sort of anticipation of Sunray."

" But are there any other anticipations in the story ? " asked Willow. " Did you recognise any other people who are intimate with you both. Is there a Fanny in this world ? Is there a Matilda Good or a brother Ernest ? Was Sarnac's mother like Martha Smith ? "

" That tale," said the guest-master, stoutly, " was no dream. It was a memory floating up out of the deep darkness of forgotten things into a living brain—a kindred brain."

Sarnac thought. " What is a personality but a memory ? If the memory of Harry Mortimer Smith is in my brain, then I am Smith. I feel as sure that I was Smith two thousand years ago as that I was Sarnac this morning. Sometimes before this in my dreams I have had a feeling that I lived again forgotten lives. Have none of you felt that ? "

" I dreamt the other day," said Radiant, " that I was a panther that haunted a village of huts in which lived naked children and some very toothsome dogs. And how I was hunted for three years and shot at five times before I was killed. I can remember how I killed an old woman gathering sticks and hid part of her body under the roots of a tree to finish it on the morrow. It was a very vivid dream. And as I dreamt it by no means horrible. But it was not a clear and continuous dream like yours. A panther's mind is not clear and continuous, but passes from flashes of interest to interludes of apathy and utter forgetfulness.

" When children have dreams of terror, of being in the wild with prowling beasts, of long pursuits and hairbreadth escapes, perhaps it is the memory of some dead creature that lives again in them ? " asked Starlight. " What do we know of the stuff of memory that lies on the other side of matter ? What do we know of the relations of consciousness to matter and energy ? For four thousand years men have speculated about these things, and we know no more to-day than they did in Athens when Plato taught and Aristotle studied. Science increases and the power of man grows but only inside the limits of life's conditions. We may conquer space and time, but we shall never conquer the mystery of what we are, and why we can be matter that feels and wills. My brother and I have much to do with animals and more and more do I perceive that what they are I am. They are instruments with twenty strings while we have ten thousand, but they are instruments like ourselves ; what plays upon them plays upon us, and what kills them kills us. Life and death alike are within the crystal sphere that limits us for ever. Life cannot penetrate and death will not penetrate that limitation. What memories are we cannot tell. If I choose to believe that they float away like gossamer nets when we die, and that they float I know not where, and that they can come back presently into touch with other such gossamer nets, who can contradict me ? Maybe life from its very beginning has been spinning threads and webs of memories. Not a thing in the past, it may be, that has not left its memories about us. Some day we may learn to gather in that forgotten gossamer, we may learn to weave its strands together again, until the whole past is restored to us and life becomes one. Then perhaps the crystal sphere will break. And however that may be, and however these things may be explained, I can well believe without any miracles that Sarnac has touched down to the real memory of a human life that lived and suffered two thousand years ago. And I believe that, because of the reality of the story he told. I have felt all along that whatever interrupting question we chose to ask, had we asked what buttons he wore on his jacket or how deep gutters were at the pavement edge or what was the price he had paid for his cigarettes, he would have been ready with an answer, more exact and sure than any historian could have given."

"And I, too, believe that," said Sunray. "I have no memory of being Hetty, but in everything he said and did, even in his harshest and hardest acts, Smith and Sarnac were one character. I do not question for a moment that Sarnac lived that life."

§ 2

"But the hardness of it!" cried Firefly; "the cruelty! The universal heartache!"

"It could have been only a dream," persisted Willow.

"It is not the barbarism I think of," said Firefly; "not the wars and diseases, the shortened, crippled lives, the ugly towns, the narrow countryside, but worse than that the sorrow of the heart, the universal unkindness, the universal failure to understand or care for the thwarted desires and needs of others. As I think of Sarnac's story I cannot think of any one creature in it who was happy—as we are happy. It is all a story of love crossed, imaginations like flies that have fallen into gum, things withheld and things forbidden. And all for nothing. All for pride and spite. Not all that world had a giver who gave with both hands. . . . Poor Milly! Do you think she did not know how coldly you loved her, Sarnac? Do you think her jealousy was not born of a certainty and a fear? . . . A lifetime, a whole young man's lifetime, a quarter of a century, and this poor Hetty Smith never once met a happy soul and came only once within sight of happiness! And he was just one of scores and hundreds of millions! They went heavily and clumsily and painfully, oppressing and obstructing each other, from the cradle to the grave."

This was too much for the guest-master, who almost wailed aloud. "But surely there was happiness! Surely there were moods at least of happiness!"

"In gleams and flashes," said Sarnac. "But I verily believe that what Firefly says is true. In all my world there were no happy lives."

"Not even children?"

"Lives, I said, not parts of lives. Children would laugh and dance for a while if they were born in Hell."

"And out of that darkness," said Radiant; "in twenty short centuries our race has come to the light and tolerance the sweet freedoms and charities of our lives to-day."

" Which is no sort of comfort to me," said Firefly, " when I think of the lives that *have* been."

" Unless this is the solution," the guest-master cried, " that every one is presently to dream back the lives that have gone. Unless the poor memory-ghosts of all those sad lives that have been are to be brought into the consolation of our happiness. Here, poor souls, for your comfort is the land of heart's desire and all your hopes come true. Here you live again in your ampler selves. Here lovers are not parted for loving and your loves are not your torment. . . . Now I see why men must be immortal, for otherwise the story of man's martyrdom is too pitiful to tell. Many good men there were like me, jolly men with a certain plumpness, men with an excellent taste for wine and cookery, who loved men almost as much as they loved the food and drink that made men, and they could not do the jolly work I do and make comfort and happiness every day for fresh couples of holiday friends. Surely presently I shall find the memories of the poor licensed innkeeper I was in those ancient days, the poor, overruled, ill-paid publican, handing out bad stuff in wrath and shame, I shall find all his troubles welling up again in me. Consoled in this good inn. If it was I who suffered in those days, I am content ; but if it was some other good fellow who died and never came to this, then there is no justice in the heart of God. So I swear by immortality now and henceforth—not for greed of the future but in the name of the wasted dead.

" Look ! " the guest-master continued. " Morning comes and the cracks at the edge of the door-curtain grow brighter than the light within. Go all of you and watch the mountain-glow. I will mix you a bowl of warm drink and then we will sleep for an hour or so before you breakfast and go your way."

§ 3

" It was a life," said Sarnac, " and it was a dream, a dream within this life ; and this life too is a dream. Dreams within dreams, dreams containing dreams, until we come at last, maybe, to the Dreamer of all dreams, the Being who is all beings. Nothing is too wonderful for life and nothing is too beautiful."

He got up and thrust back the great curtain of the guest-house room. " All night we have been talking and living in the Dark Ages of Confusion and now the sunrise is close at hand."

He went out upon the portico of the guest-house and stood still, surveying the great mountains that rose out of cloud and haze, dark blue and mysterious in their recesses and soaring up at last into the flush of dawn.

He stood quite still and all the world seemed still, except that, far away and far below, a mist of sound beneath the mountain-mists, a confusion of birds was singing.

MISS WINCHELSEA'S HEART

MISS WINCHELSEA'S HEART

MISS WINCHELSEA was going to Rome. The matter had filled her mind for a month or more, and had overflowed so abundantly into her conversation that quite a number of people who were not going to Rome, and who were not likely to go to Rome, had made it a personal grievance against her. Some indeed had attempted quite unavailingly to convince her that Rome was not nearly such a desirable place as it was reported to be, and others had gone so far as to suggest behind her back that she was dreadfully " stuck up " about " that Rome of hers ". And little Lily Hardhurst had told her friend Mr. Binns that so far as she was concerned Miss Winchelsea might " go to her old Rome and stop there ; *she* (Miss Lily Hardhurst) wouldn't grieve ". And the way in which Miss Winchelsea put herself upon terms of personal tenderness with Horace and Benvenuto Cellini and Raphael and Shelley and Keats—if she had been Shelley's widow she could not have professed a keener interest in his grave—was a matter of universal astonishment. Her dress was a triumph of tactful discretion, sensible but not too " touristy "—Miss Winchelsea had a great dread of being " touristy "—and her Baedeker was carried in a cover of grey to hide its glaring red. She made a prim and pleasant little figure on the Charing Cross platform, in spite of her swelling pride, when at last the great day dawned and she could start for Rome. The day was bright, the Channel passage would be pleasant, and all the omens promised well. There was the gayest sense of adventure in this unprecedented departure.

She was going with two friends who had been fellow-students with her at the training college, nice honest girls both, though not so good at history and literature as Miss Winchelsea. They both looked up to her immensely, though physically they had to look down, and she anticipated some pleasant times to be spent in "stirring them up" to her own pitch of æsthetic and historical enthusiasm. They had secured seats already, and welcomed her effusively at the carriage door. In the instant criticism of the encounter she noted that Fanny had a slightly " touristy " leather strap, and that Helen had succumbed to a serge jacket with side pockets, into which her hands were thrust. But they were much too happy with themselves and the expedition for their friend to attempt any hint at the moment about these things. As soon as the first ecstasies were over—Fanny's enthusiasm was a little noisy and crude, and consisted mainly in emphatic repetitions of " Just *fancy!* we're going to Rome, my dear !—Rome ! "—they gave their attention to their fellow-travellers. Helen was anxious to secure a compartment to themselves, and, in order to discourage intruders, got out and planted herself firmly on the step. Miss Winchelsea peeped out over her shoulder, and made sly little remarks about the accumulating people on the platform, at which Fanny laughed gleefully.

They were travelling with one of Mr. Thomas Gunn's parties —fourteen days in Rome for fourteen pounds. They did not belon to the personally conducted party of course—Miss Winchelsea had seen to that—but they travelled with it because of the convenience of that arrangement. The people were the oddest mixture, and wonderfully amusing. There was a vociferous red-faced polyglot personal conductor in a pepper and salt suit, very long in the arms and legs and very active. He shouted proclamations. When he wanted to speak to people he stretched out an arm and held them until his purpose was accomplished. One hand was full of papers, tickets, counterfoils of tourists. The people of the personally conducted party were, it seemed, of two sorts ; people the conductor wanted and could not find, and people he did not want and who followed him in a steadily growing tail up and down the platform. These people seemed, indeed, to think that their one chance of reaching Rome lay in keeping close to him. Three little old ladies were particularly energetic in his pursuit, and at last maddened him to the pitch of clapping them into a carriage and daring them to emerge again. For the rest of the time, one, two, or three of their heads protruded from the window wailing enquiries about " a little wickerwork box " whenever he drew near. There was a very stout man with a very stout wife in shiny black ; there was a little old man like an aged ostler.

" What *can* such people want in Rome ? " asked Miss Winchelsea. " What can it mean to them ? " There was a tall curate in a very small straw hat, and a short curate encumbered by a long camera stand. The contrast amused Fanny very much. Once they heard someone calling for " Snooks." " I always thought that name was invented by novelists," said Miss Winchelsea. " Fancy ! Snooks. I wonder which *is* Mr. Snooks." Finally they picked out a stout and resolute little man in a large check suit. " If he isn't Snooks, he ought to be," said Miss Winchelsea.

Presently the conductor discovered Helen's attempt at a corner in carriages. " Room for five," he bawled with a parallel translation on his fingers. A party of four together—mother, father, and two daughters—blundered in, all greatly excited. " It's all right, Ma—you let *me*," said one of the daughters, hitting her mother's bonnet with a handbag she struggled to put in the rack. Miss Winchelsea detested people who banged about and called their mother " Ma." A young man travelling alone followed. He was not at all " touristy " in his costume, Miss Winchelsea observed ; his Gladstone bag was of good pleasant leather with labels reminiscent of Luxembourg and

Ostend, and his boots, though brown, were not vulgar. He carried an overcoat on his arm. Before these people had properly settled in their places, came an inspection of tickets and a slamming of doors, and behold ! they were gliding out of Charing Cross station on their way to Rome.

" Fancy ! " cried Fanny, " we are going to Rome, my dear ! Rome ! I don't seem to believe it, even now."

Miss Winchelsea suppressed Fanny's emotions with a little smile, and the lady who was called " Ma " explained to people in general why they had " cut it so close " at the station. The two daughters called her " Ma " several times, toned her down in a tactless effective way, and drove her at last to the muttered inventory of a basket of travelling requisites. Presently she looked up. " Lor ! " she said, " I didn't bring *them !* " Both the daughters said " Oh, Ma ! " but what " them " was did not appear. Presently Fanny produced Hare's *Walks in Rome,* a sort of mitigated guide-book very popular among Roman visitors ; and the father of the two daughters began to ex- amine his books of tickets minutely, apparently in a search after English words. When he had looked at the tickets for a long time right way up, he turned them upside down. Then he produced a fountain pen and dated them with considerable care. The young man having completed an unostentatious survey of his fellow travellers produced a book and fell to reading. When Helen and Fanny were looking out of the window at Chislehurst—the place interested Fanny because the poor dear Empress of the French used to live there—Miss Winchelsea took the opportunity to observe the book the young man held. It was not a guide-book but a thin volume of poetry—*bound.* She glanced at his face—it seemed a refined pleasant face to her hasty glance. He wore a gilt *pince-nez.* " Do you think she lives there now ? " said Fanny, and Miss Winchelsea's inspection came to an end.

For the rest of the journey Miss Winchelsea talked little, and what she said was as pleasant and as stamped with re- finement as she could make it. Her voice was always low and clear and pleasant, and she took care that on this occasion it was particularly low and clear and pleasant. As they came under the white cliffs the young man put his book of poetry away, and when at last the train stopped beside the boat, he displayed a graceful alacrity with the impedimenta of Miss Winchelsea and her friends. Miss Winchelsea " hated non- sense," but she was pleased to see the young man perceived at once that they were ladies, and helped them without any violent geniality ; and how nicely he showed that his civilities were to be no excuse for further intrusions. None of her party had been out of England before, and they were all excited and nervous at the Channel passage. They stood in a little group in a good place near the middle of the boat—the young man had taken Miss Winchelsea's hold-all there and had told her it was a good place—and they watched the white shores of Albion recede and quoted Shakespeare and made quiet fun of their fellow travellers in the English way.

They were particularly amused at the precautions the bigger-sized people had taken against the waves—cut lemons and flasks prevailed, one lady lay full length in a deck chair with a handkerchief over her face, and a very broad resolute man in a bright brown " touristy " suit walked all the way from England to France along the deck, with his legs as widely apart as Providence permitted. These were all excellent precautions, and nobody was ill. The personally conducted party pursued the conductor about the deck with enquiries, in a manner that suggested to Helen's mind the rather vulgar image of hens with a piece of bacon peel, until at last he went into hiding below. And the young man with the thin volume of poetry stood in the stern watching England receding, looking, to Miss Winchelsea's eye, rather lonely and sad.

And then came Calais and tumultuous novelties, and the young man had not forgotten Miss Winchelsea's hold-all and the other little things. All three girls, though they had passed government examinations in French to an extent, were stricken with a dumb shame of their accents, and the young man was very useful. And he did not intrude. He put them in a comfortable carriage and raised his hat and went away. Miss Winchelsea thanked him in her best manner—a pleasing cultivated manner—and Fanny said he was " nice " almost before he was out of earshot. " I wonder what he can be," said Helen. " He's going to Italy, because I noticed green tickets in his book." Miss Winchelsea almost told them of the poetry, and decided not to do so. And presently the carriage windows seized hold upon them and the young man was forgotten. It made them feel that they were doing an educated sort of thing to travel through a country whose commonest advertisements were in idiomatic French, and Miss Winchelsea made unpatriotic comparisons because there were weedy little sign-board advertisements by the rail side instead of the broad hoardings that deface the landscape in our land. But the north of France is really uninteresting country, and after a time Fanny reverted to Hare's *Walks* and Helen initiated lunch. Miss Winchelsea awoke out of a happy reverie ; she had been trying to realise, she said, that she was actually going to Rome, but she perceived at Helen's suggestion that she was hungry, and they lunched out of their baskets very cheerfully. In the afternoon they were tired and silent until Helen made tea. Miss Winchelsea might have dozed, only she knew Fanny slept with her mouth open ; and as their fellow passengers were two rather nice critical-looking ladies of uncertain age—who knew French well enough to talk it— she employed herself in keeping Fanny awake. The rhythm of the train became insistent, and the streaming landscape

outside at last quite painful to the eye. Before their night's
stoppage came they were already dreadfully tired of travelling.

The stoppage for the night was brightened by the appearance
of the young man, and his manners were all that could be
desired and his French quite serviceable. His coupons availed
for the same hotel as theirs, and by chance as it seemed he
sat next Miss Winchelsea at the *table d'hôte*. In spite of her
enthusiasm for Rome, she had thought out some such possibility very thoroughly, and when he ventured to make a remark upon the tediousness of travelling—he let the soup and
fish go by before he did this—she did not simply assent to
his proposition, but responded with another. They were soon
comparing their journeys, and Helen and Fanny were cruelly
overlooked in the conversation. It was to be the same journey,
they found ; one day for the galleries at Florence—" from
what I hear," said the young man, " it is barely enough,"—
and the rest at Rome. He talked of Rome very pleasantly ;
he was evidently quite well read, and he quoted Horace about
Soracte. Miss Winchelsea had " done " that book of Horace
for her matriculation, and was delighted to cap his quotation.
It gave a sort of tone to things, this incident—a touch of
refinement to mere chatting. Fanny expressed a few emotions,
and Helen interpolated a few sensible remarks, but the bulk
of the talk on the girls' side fell naturally to Miss Winchelsea.

Before they reached Rome this young man was tacitly of
their party. They did not know his name nor what he was,
but it seemed he taught, and Miss Winchelsea had a shrewd
idea he was an extension lecturer. At any rate he was something of that sort, something gentlemanly and refined without
being opulent and impossible. She tried once or twice to ascer-
tain whether he came from Oxford or Cambridge, but he
missed her timid opportunities. She tried to get him to make
remarks about those places to see if he would say " go up "
to them instead of " go down "—she knew that was how you
told a 'Varsity man. He used the word " 'Varsity "—not
university—in quite the proper way.

They saw as much of Mr. Ruskin's Florence as their brief
time permitted ; the young man met them in the Pitti Gallery
and went round with them, chatting brightly, and evidently
very grateful for their recognition. He knew a great deal
about art, and all four enjoyed the morning immensely. It
was fine to go round recognising old favourites and finding
new beauties, especially while so many people fumbled helplessly with Baedeker. Nor was he a bit of a prig, Miss Winchelsea said, and indeed she detested prigs. He had a distinct
undertow of humour, and was funny, for example, without
being vulgar, at the expense of the quaint work of Beato
Angelico. He had a grave seriousness beneath it all, and was
quick to seize the moral lessons of the pictures. Fanny went
softly among these masterpieces ; she admitted " she knew

so little about them ", and she confessed that to her they were
" all beautiful ". Fanny's " beautiful " inclined to be a little
monotonous, Miss Winchelsea thought. She had been quite
glad when the last sunny Alp had vanished, because of the
staccato of Fanny's admiration. Helen said little, but Miss
Winchelsea had found her a little wanting on the æsthetic
side in the old days and was not surprised ; sometimes she
laughed at the young man's hesitating delicate little jests and
sometimes she didn't, and sometimes she seemed quite lost
to the art about them in the contemplation of the dresses of
the other visitors.

At Rome the young man was with them intermittently.
A rather " touristy " friend of his took him away at times.
He complained comically to Miss Winchelsea. " I have only
two short weeks in Rome," he said, " and my friend Leonard
wants to spend a whole day at Tivoli looking at a waterfall."

" What is your friend Leonard ? " asked Miss Winchelsea
abruptly.

" He's the most enthusiastic pedestrian I ever met," the
young man replied—amusingly, but a little unsatisfactorily,
Miss Winchelsea thought.

They had some glorious times, and Fanny could not think
what they would have done without him. Miss Winchelsea's
interest and Fanny's enormous capacity for admiration were
insatiable. They never flagged—through pictures and sculpture galleries, immense crowded churches, ruins and museums,
Judas trees and prickly pears, wine carts and palaces, they
admired their way unflinchingly. They never saw a stone
pine nor a eucalyptus but they named and admired it ; they
never glimpsed Soracte but they exclaimed. Their common
ways were made wonderful by imaginative play. " Here
Cæsar may have walked," they would say. " Raphael may
have seen Soracte from this very point." They happened on
the tomb of Bibulus. " Old Bibulus," said the young man.
" The oldest monument of Republican Rome ! " said Miss
Winchelsea.

" I'm dreadfully stupid," said Fanny, " but who *was* Bibulus ? "

There was a curious little pause.

" Wasn't he the person who built the wall ? " said Helen.

The young man glanced quickly at her and laughed. " That
was Balbus," he said. Helen reddened, but neither he nor
Miss Winchelsea threw any light upon Fanny's ignorance
about Bibulus.

Helen was more taciturn than the other three, but then
she was always taciturn ; and usually she took care of the
tram tickets and things like that, or kept her eye on them if
the young man took them, and told him where they were
when he wanted them. Glorious times they had, these young
people, in that pale brown cleanly city of memories that was

once the world. Their only sorrow was the shortness of the time. They said indeed that the electric trams and the '70 buildings, and that criminal advertisement that glares upon the Forum, outraged their æsthetic feelings unspeakably; but that was only part of the fun. And indeed Rome is such a wonderful place that at times it made Miss Winchelsea forget some of her most carefully prepared enthusiasms, and Helen, taken unawares, would suddenly admit the beauty of unexpected things. Yet Fanny and Helen would have liked a shop window or so in the English quarter if Miss Winchelsea's uncompromising hostility to all other English visitors had not rendered that district impossible.

The intellectual and æsthetic fellowship of Miss Winchelsea and the scholarly young man passed insensibly towards a deeper feeling. The exuberant Fanny did her best to keep pace with their recondite admiration by playing her " beautiful " with vigour, and saying " Oh ! *let's* go," with enormous appetite whenever a new place of interest was mentioned. But Helen towards the end developed a certain want of sympathy, that disappointed Miss Winchelsea a little. She refused to " see anything " in the face of Beatrice Cenci—Shelley's Beatrice Cenci !—in the Barberini gallery ; and one day, when they were deploring the electric trams, she said rather snappishly that " people must get about somehow, and it's better than torturing horses up these horrid little hills." She spoke of the Seven Hills of Rome as " horrid little hills ! "

And the day they went on the Palatine—though Miss Winchelsea did not know of this—she remarked suddenly to Fanny, " Don't hurry like that, my dear ; *they* don't want us to overtake them. And we don't say the right things for them when we *do* get near."

" I wasn't trying to overtake them," said Fanny, slackening her excessive pace ; " I wasn't indeed." And for a minute she was short of breath.

But Miss Winchelsea had come upon happiness. It was only when she came to look back across an intervening tragedy that she quite realised how happy she had been, pacing among the cypress-shadowed ruins, and exchanging the very highest class of information the human mind can possess, the most refined impressions it is possible to convey. Insensibly emotion crept into their intercourse, sunning itself openly and pleasantly at last when Helen's modernity was not too near. Insensibly their interest drifted from the wonderful associations about them to their more intimate and personal feelings. In a tentative way information was supplied ; she spoke allusively of her school, of her examination successes, of her gladness that the days of " Cram " were over. He made it quite clear that he also was a teacher. They spoke of the greatness of their calling, of the necessity of sympathy to face its irksome details, of a certain loneliness they sometimes felt.

That was in the Colosseum, and it was as far as they got that day, because Helen returned with Fanny—she had taken her into the upper galleries. Yet the private dreams of Miss Winchelsea, already vivid and concrete enough, became now realistic in the highest degree. She figured that pleasant young man, lecturing in the most edifying way to his students, herself modestly prominent as his intellectual mate and helper ; she figured a refined little home, with two bureaus, with white shelves of high-class books, and autotypes of the pictures of Rossetti and Burne-Jones, with Morris's wall papers and flowers in pots of beaten copper. Indeed she figured many things. On the Pincio the two had a few precious moments together, while Helen marched Fanny off to see the *muro Torto*, and he spoke at once plainly. He said he hoped their friendship was only beginning, that he already found her company very precious to him, that indeed it was more than that.

He became nervous, thrusting at his glasses with trembling fingers as though he fancied his emotions made them unstable. " I should of course," he said, " tell you things about myself. I know it is rather unusual my speaking to you like this. Only our meeting has been so accidental—or providential—and I am snatching at things. I came to Rome expecting a lonely tour . . . and I have been so very happy, so very happy. Quite recently I have found myself in a position —I have dared to think—— And——"

He glanced over his shoulder and stopped. He said " Demn!" quite distinctly—and she did not condemn him for that manly lapse into profanity. She looked and saw his friend Leonard advancing. He drew nearer ; he raised his hat to Miss Winchelsea, and his smile was almost a grin. " I've been looking for you everywhere, Snooks," he said. " You promised to be on the Piazza steps half an hour ago."

Snooks! The name struck Miss Winchelsea like a blow in the face. She did not hear his reply. She thought afterwards that Leonard must have considered her the vaguest-minded person. To this day she is not sure whether she was introduced to Leonard or not, nor what she said to him. A sort of mental paralysis was upon her. Of all offensive surnames— Snooks !

Helen and Fanny were returning, there were civilities and the young men were receding. By a great effort she controlled herself to face the inquiring eyes of her friends. All that afternoon she lived the life of a heroine under the indescribable outrage of that name, chatting, observing, with " Snooks " gnawing at her heart. From the moment that it first rang upon her ears, the dream of her happiness was prostrate in the dust. All the refinement she had figured was ruined and defaced by that cognomen's inexorable vulgarity.

What was that refined little home to her now, spite of

autotypes, Morris papers, and bureaus? Athwart it in letters of fire ran an incredible inscription: "Mrs. Snooks." That may seem a small thing to the reader, but consider the delicate refinement of Miss Winchelsea's mind. Be as refined as you can and then think of writing yourself down: "Snooks." She conceived herself being addressed as Mrs. Snooks by all the people she liked least, conceived the patronymic touched with a vague quality of insult. She figured a card of grey and silver bearing "Winchelsea" triumphantly effaced by an arrow, Cupid's arrow, in favour of "Snooks." Degrading confession of feminine weakness! She imagined the terrible rejoicings of certain girl friends, of certain grocer cousins from whom her growing refinement had long since estranged her. How they would make it sprawl across the envelope that would bring their sarcastic congratulations. Would even his pleasant company compensate her for that? "It is impossible," she muttered; "impossible! *Snooks!*"

She was sorry for him, but not so sorry as she was for herself. For him she had a touch of indignation. To be so nice, so refined, while all the time he was "Snooks," to hide under a pretentious gentility of demeanour the badge sinister of of his surname seemed a sort of treachery. To put it in the language of sentimental science she felt he had "led her on."

There were of course moments of terrible vacillation, a period even when something almost like passion bid her throw refinement to the winds. And there was something in her, an unexpurgated vestige of vulgarity that made a strenuous attempt at proving that Snooks was not so very bad a name after all. Any hovering hesitation flew before Fanny's manner, when Fanny came with an air of catastrophe to tell that she also knew the horror. Fanny's voice fell to a whisper when she said *Snooks*. Miss Winchelsea would not give him any answer when at last, in the Borghese, she could have a minute with him; but she promised him a note.

She handed him that note in the little book of poetry he had lent her, the little book that had first drawn them together. Her refusal was ambiguous, allusive. She could no more tell him why she rejected him than she could have told a cripple of his hump. He too must feel something of the unspeakable quality of his name. Indeed he had avoided a dozen chances of telling it, she now perceived. So she spoke of "obstacles she could not reveal"—"reasons why the thing he spoke of was impossible." She addressed the note with a shiver, "E. K. Snooks."

Things were worse than she had dreaded; he asked her to explain. How *could* she explain? Those last two days in Rome were dreadful. She was haunted by his air of astonished perplexity. She knew she had given him intimate hopes, she had not the courage to examine her mind thoroughly for the extent of her encouragement. She knew he must think her the most changeable of beings. Now that she was in full retreat, she would not even perceive his hints of a possible correspondence. But in that matter he did a thing that seemed to her at once delicate and romantic. He made a go-between of Fanny. Fanny could not keep the secret, and came and told her that night under a transparent pretext of needed advice. " Mr. Snooks," said Fanny, " wants to write to me. Fancy ! I had no idea. But should I let him ? " They talked it over long and earnestly, and Miss Winchelsea was careful to keep the veil over her heart. She was already repenting his disregarded hints. Why should she not hear of him sometimes —painful though his name must be to her ? Miss Winchelsea decided it might be permitted, and Fanny kissed her good-night with unusual emotion. After she had gone Miss Winchelsea sat for a long time at the window of her little room. It was moonlight, and down the street a man sang " Santa Lucia " with almost heart-dissolving tenderness. . . . She sat very still.

She breathed a word very softly to herself. The word was " Snooks." Then she got up with a profound sigh, and went to bed. The next morning he said to her meaningly, " I shall hear of you through your friend."

Mr. Snooks saw them off from Rome with that pathetic interrogative perplexity still on his face, and if it had not been for Helen he would have retained Miss Winchelsea's hold-all in his hand as a sort of encyclopædic keepsake. On their way back to England Miss Winchelsea on six separate occasions made Fanny promise to write to her the longest of long letters. Fanny, it seemed, would be quite near Mr. Snooks. Her new school—she was always going to new schools—would be only five miles from Steely Bank, and it was in the Steely Bank Polytechnic, and one or two first-class schools, that Mr. Snooks did his teaching. He might even see her at times. They could not talk much of him—she and Fanny always spoke of " him," never of Mr. Snooks—because Helen was apt to say unsympathetic things about him. Her nature had coarsened very much, Miss Winchelsea perceived, since the old Training College days ; she had become hard and cynical. She thought he had a weak face, mistaking refinement for weakness as people of her stamp are apt to do, and when she heard his name was Snooks, she said she had expected something of the sort. Miss Winchelsea was careful to spare her own feelings after that, but Fanny was less circumspect.

The girls parted in London, and Miss Winchelsea returned, with a new interest in life, to the Girls' High School in which she had been an increasingly valuable assistant for the last three years. Her new interest in life was Fanny as a correspondent, and to give her a lead she wrote her a lengthy descriptive letter within a fortnight of her return. Fanny answered very disappointingly. Fanny indeed had no literary

gift, but it was new to Miss Winchelsea to find herself deploring the want of gifts in a friend. That letter was even
criticised aloud in the safe solitude of Miss Winchelsea's study,
and her criticism, spoken with great bitterness, was "Twaddle!"
It was full of just the things Miss Winchelsea's letter had been
full of, particulars of the school. And of Mr. Snooks, only this
much : " I have had a letter from Mr. Snooks, and he has
been over to see me on two Saturday afternoons running. He
talked about Rome and you ; we both talked about you.
Your ears must have burnt, my dear. . . ."

Miss Winchelsea repressed a desire to demand more explicit
information, and wrote the sweetest long letter again. "Tell
me all about yourself, dear. That journey has quite refreshed
our ancient friendship, and I do so want to keep in touch with
you." About Mr. Snooks she simply wrote on the fifth page
that she was glad Fanny had seen him, and that if he *should*
ask after her, she was to be remembered to him *very kindly*
(underlined). And Fanny replied most obtusely in the key of
that " ancient friendship," reminding Miss Winchelsea of a
dozen foolish things of those old schoolgirl days at the training college, and saying not a word about Mr. Snooks !

For nearly a week Miss Winchelsea was so angry at the
failure of Fanny as a go-between that she could not write to
her. And then she wrote less effusively, and in her letter she
asked point blank, " Have you seen Mr. Snooks ? " Fanny's
letter was unexpectedly satisfactory. " I *have* seen Mr. Snooks,"
she wrote, and having once named him she kept on about him ;
it was all Snooks—Snooks this and Snooks that. He was to
give a public lecture, said Fanny, among other things. Yet
Miss Winchelsea, after the first glow of gratification, still
found this letter a little unsatisfactory. Fanny did not report
Mr. Snooks as saying anything about Miss Winchelsea, nor as
looking white and worn, as he ought to have been doing. And
behold ! before she had replied, came a second letter from
Fanny on the same theme, quite a gushing letter, and covering six sheets with her loose feminine hand.

And about this second letter was a rather odd little thing
that Miss Winchelsea only noticed as she re-read it the third
time. Fanny's natural femininity had prevailed even against
the round and clear traditions of the training college ; she
was one of those she-creatures born to make all her *m*'s and
n's and *u*'s and *r*'s and *e*'s alike, and to leave her *o*'s and *a*'s
open and her *i*'s undotted. So that it was only after an elaborate
comparison of word with word that Miss Winchelsea felt
assured Mr. Snooks was not really " Mr. Snooks " at all !
In Fanny's first letter of gush he was Mr. " Snooks," in her
second the spelling was changed to Mr. " Senoks." Miss
Winchelsea's hand positively trembled as she turned the sheet
over—it meant so much to her. For it had already begun to
seem to her that even the name of Mrs. Snooks might be

avoided at too great a price, and suddenly—this possibility!
She turned over the six sheets, all dappled with that critical
name, and everywhere the first letter had the form of an *e*!
For a time she walked the room with a hand pressed upon her
heart.

She spent a whole day pondering this change, weighing a
letter of inquiry that should be at once discreet and effectual,
weighing too what action she should take after the answer
came. She was resolved that if this altered spelling was anything more than a quaint fancy of Fanny's, she would write
forthwith to Mr. Snooks. She had now reached a stage when
the minor refinements of behaviour disappear. Her excuse
remained uninvented but she had the subject of her letter
clear in her mind, even to the hint that " circumstances in
my life have changed very greatly since we talked together."
But she never gave that hint. There came a third letter from
that fitful correspondent Fanny. The first line proclaimed
her " the happiest girl alive."

Miss Winchelsea crushed the letter in her hand—the rest
unread—and sat with her face suddenly very still. She had
received it just before morning school, and had opened it
when the junior mathematicians were well under way. Presently she resumed reading with an appearance of great calm.
But after the first sheet she went on reading the third without
discovering the error : " told him frankly I did not like his
name," the third sheet began. " He told me he did not like
it himself—you know that sort of sudden frank way he has "
—Miss Winchelsea did know. " So I said, ' Couldn't you change
it ? ' He didn't see it at first. Well, you know, dear, he had
told me what it really meant ; it means Sevenoaks, only it
has got down to Snooks—both Snooks and Noaks, dreadfully
vulgar surnames though they be, are really worn forms of
Sevenoaks. So I said — even I have my bright ideas at
times—' if it got down from Sevenoaks to Snooks, why not
get it back from Snooks to Sevenoaks ? ' And the long and
the short of it is, dear, he couldn't refuse me, and he changed
his spelling there and then to Senoks for the bills of the new
lecture. And afterwards, when we are married, we shall put
in the apostrophe and make it Se'noks. Wasn't it kind of him
to mind that fancy of mine, when many men would have taken
offence ? But it is just like him all over ; he is as kind as he
is clever. Because he knew as well as I did that I would have
had him in spite of it, had he been ten times Snooks. But he
did it all the same."

The class was startled by the sound of paper being viciously
torn, and looked up to see Miss Winchelsea white in the face,
and with some very small pieces of paper clenched in one
hand. For a few seconds they stared at her stare, and then
her expression changed back to a more familiar one. " Has
anyone finished number three ? " she asked in an even tone.

She remained calm after that. But impositions ruled high that day. And she spent two laborious evenings writing letters of various sorts to Fanny, before she found a decent congratulatory vein. Her reason struggled hopelessly against the persuasion that Fanny had behaved in an exceedingly treacherous manner.

One may be extremely refined and still capable of a very sore heart. Certainly Miss Winchelsea's heart was very sore. She had moods of sexual hostility, in which she generalised uncharitably about mankind. "He forgot himself with me," she said. "But Fanny is pink and pretty and soft and a fool —a very excellent match for a Man." And by way of a wedding present she sent Fanny a gracefully bound volume of poetry by George Meredith, and Fanny wrote back a grossly happy letter to say that it was "*all* beautiful." Miss Winchelsea hoped that some day Mr. Senoks might take up that slim book and think for a moment of the donor. Fanny wrote several times before and about her marriage, pursuing that fond legend of their "ancient friendship," and giving her happiness in the fullest detail. And Miss Winchelsea wrote to Helen for the first time after the Roman journey, saying nothing about the marriage, but expressing very cordial feelings.

They had been in Rome at Easter, and Fanny was married in the August vacation. She wrote a garrulous letter to Miss Winchelsea, describing her home-coming, and the astonishing arrangements of their "teeny weeny" little house. Mr. Se'noks was now beginning to assume a refinement in Miss Winchelsea's memory out of all proportion to the facts of the case, and she tried in vain to imagine his cultured greatness in a "teeny weeny" little house. "Am busy enamelling a cosy corner," said Fanny, sprawling to the end of her third sheet, "so excuse more." Miss Winchelsea answered in her best style, gently poking fun at Fanny's arrangements, and hoping intensely that Mr. Se'noks might see the letter. Only this hope enabled her to write at all, answering not only that letter but one in November and one at Christmas.

The two latter communications contained urgent invitations for her to come to Steely Bank on a visit during the Christmas holidays. She tried to think that *he* had told her to ask that, but it was too much like Fanny's opulent good-nature. She could not but believe that he must be sick of his blunder by this time ; and she had more than a hope that he would presently write her a letter beginning "Dear Friend." Something subtly tragic in the separation was a great support to her, a sad misunderstanding. To have been jilted would have been intolerable. But he never wrote that letter beginning "Dear Friend."

For two years Miss Winchelsea could not go to Steely Bank, in spite of the reiterated invitations of Mrs. Sevenoaks—it became full Sevenoaks in the second year. Then one day near the Easter rest she felt lonely and without a soul to understand her in the world, and her mind ran once more on what is called Platonic friendship. Fanny was clearly happy and busy in her new sphere of domesticity, but no doubt *he* had his lonely hours. Did he ever think of those days in Rome— gone now beyond recalling. No one had understood her as he had done ; no one in all the world. It would be a sort of melancholy pleasure to talk to him again, and what harm could it do ? Why should she deny herself ? That night she wrote a sonnet, all but the last two lines of the octave—which would not come, and the next day she composed a graceful little note to tell Fanny she was coming down.

And so she saw him again.

Even at the first encounter it was evident he had changed ; he seemed stouter and less nervous, and it speedily appeared that his conversation had already lost much of its old delicacy. There even seemed a justification for Helen's discovery of weakness in his face—in certain lights it *was* weak. He seemed busy and preoccupied about his affairs, and almost under the impression that Miss Winchelsea had come for the sake of Fanny. He discussed his dinner with Fanny in an intelligent way. They only had one good long talk together, and that came to nothing. He did not refer to Rome, and spent some time abusing a man who had stolen an idea he had had for a text-book. It did not seem a very wonderful idea to Miss Winchelsea. She discovered he had forgotten the names of more than half the painters whose work they had rejoiced over in Florence.

It was a sadly disappointing week, and Miss Winchelsea was glad when it came to an end. Under various excuses she avoided visiting them again. After a time the visitor's room was occupied by their two little boys, and Fanny's invitations ceased. The intimacy of her letters had long since faded away.

THE STOLEN BACILLUS

THE STOLEN BACILLUS

This again," said the Bacteriologist, slipping a glass slide under the microscope, " is a preparation of the celebrated Bacillus of cholera—the cholera germ."

The pale-faced man peered down the microscope. He was evidently not accustomed to that kind of thing, and held a limp white hand over his disengaged eye. " I see very little," he said.

" Touch this screw," said the Bacteriologist ; " perhaps the microscope is out of focus for you. Eyes vary so much. Just the fraction of a turn this way or that."

" Ah ! now I see," said the visitor. " Not so very much to see after all. Little streaks and shreds of pink. And yet those little particles, those mere atomies, might multiply and devastate a city ! Wonderful ! "

He stood up, and releasing the glass slip from the microscope, held it in his hand towards the window. " Scarcely visible," he said, scrutinising the preparation. He hesitated. " Are these—alive ? Are they dangerous now ? "

" Those have been stained and killed," said the Bacteriologist. " I wish, for my own part, we could kill and stain every one of them in the universe."

" I suppose," the pale man said with a slight smile, " that you scarcely care to have such things about you in the living —in the active state ? "

" On the contrary, we are obliged to," said the Bacteriologist. " Here, for instance——" He walked across the room and took up one of several sealed tubes. " Here is the living thing. This is a cultivation of the actual living disease bacteria." He hesitated. " Bottled cholera, so to speak."

A slight gleam of satisfaction appeared momentarily in the face of the pale man. " It's a deadly thing to have in your possession," he said, devouring the little tube with his eyes. The Bacteriologist watched the morbid pleasure in his visitor's expression. This man, who had visited him that afternoon with a note of introduction from an old friend, interested him from the very contrast of their dispositions. The lank black hair and deep grey eyes, the haggard expression and nervous manner, the fitful yet keen interest of his visitor were a novel change from the phlegmatic deliberations of the ordinary scientific worker with whom the Bacteriologist chiefly associated. It was perhaps natural, with a hearer evidently so impressionable to the lethal nature of his topic, to take the most effective aspect of the matter.

He held the tube in his hand thoughtfully. " Yes, here is the pestilence imprisoned. Only break such a little tube as this into a supply of drinking-water, say to these minute particles of life that one must needs stain and examine with the highest powers of the microscope even to see, and that one can neither smell nor taste—say to them, ' Go forth, increase and multiply, and replenish the cisterns,' and death—mysterious, untraceable death, death swift and terrible, death full of pain and indignity—would be released upon this city, and go hither and thither seeking his victims. Here he would take the husband from the wife, here the child from its mother, here the statesman from his duty, and here the toiler from his trouble. He would follow the water-mains, creeping along streets, picking out and punishing a house here and a house there where they did not boil their drinking-water, creeping into the wells of the mineral-water makers, getting washed into salad, and lying dormant in ices. He would wait ready to be drunk in the horse-troughs, and by unwary children in the public fountains. He would soak into the soil, to reappear in springs and wells at a thousand unexpected places. Once start him at the water supply, and before we could ring him in, and catch him again, he would have decimated the metropolis."

He stopped abruptly. He had been told rhetoric was his weakness.

" But he is quite safe here, you know—quite safe."

The pale-faced man nodded. His eyes shone. He cleared his throat. " These Anarchist—rascals," said he, " are fools, blind fools—to use bombs when this kind of thing is attainable. I think——"

A gentle rap, a mere light touch of the finger-nails was heard at the door. The Baceriologist opened it. " Just a minute, dear," whispered his wife.

When he re-entered the laboratory his visitor was looking at his watch. " I had no idea I had wasted an hour of your time," he said. " Twelve minutes to four. I ought to have left here by half-past three. But your things were really too interesting. No, positively I cannot stop a moment longer. I have an engagement at four."

He passed out of the room reiterating his thanks, and the Bacteriologist accompanied him to the door, and then returned thoughtfully along the passage to his laboratory. He was musing on the ethnology of his visitor. Certainly the man was not a Teutonic type nor a common Latin one. " A morbid product, anyhow, I am afraid," said the Bacteriologist to himself. " How he gloated on those cultivations of disease germs ! " A disturbing thought struck him. He turned to the bench by the vapour-bath, and then very quickly to his writing-table. Then he felt hastily in his pockets, and then rushed to the door. " I may have put it down on the hall table," he said.

" Minnie ! " he shouted hoarsely in the hall.

" Yes, dear," came a remote voice.

" Had I anything in my hand when I spoke to you, dear, just now ? "

Pause.

" Nothing, dear, because I remember——"

" Blue ruin ! " cried the Bacteriologist, and incontinently ran to the front door and down the steps of his house to the street.

Minnie, hearing the door slam violently, ran in alarm to the window. Down the street a slender man was getting into a cab. The Bacteriologist, hatless, and in his carpet slippers, was running and gesticulating wildly towards this group. One slipper came off, but he did not wait for it. " He has gone *mad !* " said Minnie ; " it's that horrid science of his ; " and, opening the window, would have called after him. The slender man, suddenly glancing round, seemed struck with the same idea of mental disorder. He pointed hastily to the Bacteriologist, said something to the cabman, the apron of the cab slammed, the whip swished, the horse's feet clattered, and in a moment cab, and Bacteriologist hotly in pursuit, had receded up the vista of the roadway and disappeared round the corner.

Minnie remained straining out of the window for a minute. Then she drew her head back into the room again. She was dumbfounded. " Of course he is eccentric," she meditated. " But running about London—in the height of the season, too—in his socks ! " A happy thought struck her. She hastily put her bonnet on, seized his shoes, went into the hall, took down his hat and light overcoat from the pegs, emerged upon the doorstep, and hailed a cab that opportunely crawled by. " Drive me up the road and round Havelock Cresent, and see if we can find a gentleman running about in a velveteen coat and no hat."

" Velveteen coat, ma'am, and no 'at. Very good, ma'am." And the cabman whipped up at once in the most matter-of-fact way, as if he drove to this address every day in his life.

Some few minutes later the little group of cabmen and loafers that collects round the cabmen's shelter at Haverstock Hill were startled by the passing of a cab with a ginger-coloured screw of a horse, driven furiously.

They were silent as it went by, and then as it receded— " That's 'Arry 'Icks. Wot's *he* got ? " said the stout gentleman known as Old Tootles.

" He's a-using his whip, he is, *to* rights," said the ostler boy.

" Hullo ! " said poor old Tommy Byles ; " here's another bloomin' loonatic. Blowed if there ain't."

" It's old George," said Old Tootles, " and he's drivin' a loonatic, *as* you say. Ain't he a-clawin' out of the keb ? Wonder if he's after 'Arry 'Icks ? "

The group round the cabmen's shelter became animated.

Chorus: " Go it, George ! " " It's a race." " You'll ketch 'em ! " " Whip up ! "

" She's a goer, she is ! " said the ostler boy.

" Strike me giddy ! " cried Old Tootles. " Here ! *I'm* a-goin' to begin in a minute. Here's another comin'. If all the kebs in Hampstead ain't gone mad this morning ! "

" It's a fieldmale this time," said the ostler boy.

" She's a followin' *him*," said Old Tootles. " Usually the other way about."

" What's she got in her 'and ? "

" Looks like a 'igh 'at."

" What a bloomin' lark it is ! Three to one on old George," said the ostler boy. " Nexst ! "

Minnie went by in a perfect roar of applause. She did not like it but she felt that she was doing her duty, and whirled on down Haverstock Hill and Camden Town High Street with her eyes ever intent on the animated back view of old George, who was driving her vagrant husband so incomprehensively away from her.

The man in the foremost cab sat crouched in the corner, his arms tightly folded, and the little tube that contained such vast possibilities of destruction gripped in his hand. His mood was a singular mixture of fear and exultation. Chiefly he was afraid of being caught before he could accomplish his purpose, but behind this was a vaguer but larger fear of the awfulness of his crime. But his exultation far exceeded his fear. No Anarchist before him had ever approached this conception of his. Ravachol, Vaillant, all those distinguished persons whose fame he had envied dwindled into insignificance beside him. He had only to make sure of the water supply, and break the little tube into a reservoir. How brilliantly he had planned it, forged the letter of introduction and got into the laboratory, and how brilliantly he had seized his opportunity ! The world should hear of him at last. All those people who had sneered at him, neglected him, preferred other people to him, found his company undesirable, should consider him at last. Death, death, death ! They had always treated him as a man of no importance. All the world had been in a conspiracy to keep him under. He would teach them yet what it is to isolate a man. What was this familiar street ? Great Saint Andrew's Street, of course ! How fared the chase ? He craned out of the cab. The Bacteriologist was scarcely fifty yards behind. That was bad. He would be caught and stopped yet. He felt in his pocket for money, and found half-a-sovereign. This he thrust up through the trap in the top of the cab into the man's face. " More," he shouted, " if only we get away."

The money was snatched out of his hand. " Right you are," said the cabman, and the trap slammed, and the lash lay along the glistening side of the horse. The cab swayed, and the Anarchist, half-standing under the trap, put the hand con-

taining the little glass tube upon the apron to preserve his
balance. He felt the brittle thing crack, and the broken half
of it rang upon the floor of the cab. He fell back into the seat
with a curse, and stared dismally at the two or three drops of
moisture on the apron.

He shuddered.

" Well ! I suppose I shall be the first. *Phew !* Anyhow,
I shall be a Martyr. That's something. But it is a filthy death,
nevertheless. I wonder if it hurts as much as they say."

Presently a thought occurred to him—he groped between
his feet. A little drop was still in the broken end of the tube,
and he drank that to make sure. It was better to make sure.
At any rate, he would not fail.

Then it dawned upon him that there was no further need
to escape the Bacteriologist. In Wellington Street he told the
cabman to stop, and got out. He slipped on the step, and his
head felt queer. It was rapid stuff this cholera poison. He
waved his cabman out of existence, so to speak, and stood on
the pavement with his arms folded upon his breast awaiting
the arrival of the Bacteriologist. There was something tragic
in his pose. The sense of imminent death gave him a certain
dignity. He greeted his pursuer with a defiant laugh.

" Vive l'Anarchie ! You are too late, my friend. I have
drunk it. The cholera is abroad ! "

The Bacteriologist from his cab beamed curiously at him
through his spectacles. " You have drunk it ! An Anarchist !
I see now." He was about to say something more, and then
checked himself. A smile hung in the corner of his mouth.
He opened the apron of his cab as if to descend, at which the
Anarchist waved him a dramatic farewell and strode off
towards Waterloo Bridge, carefully jostling his infected body
against as many people as possible. The Bacteriologist was so
preoccupied with the vision of him that he scarcely manifested
the slightest surprise at the appearance of Minnie upon the
pavement with his hat and shoes and overcoat. " Very good
of you to bring my things," he said, and remained lost in contemplation of the receding figure of the Anarchist.

" You had better get in," he said, still staring. Minnie felt
absolutely convinced now that he was mad, and directed the
cabman home on her own responsibility. " Put on my shoes ?
Certainly, dear," said he, as the cab began to turn, and hid
the strutting black figure, now small in the distance, from his
eyes. Then suddenly something grotesque struck him, and
he laughed. Then he remarked, " It is really very serious
though.

" You see, that man came to my house to see me, and he is
an Anarchist. No—don't faint, or I cannot possibly tell you
the rest. And I wanted to astonish him, not knowing he was
an Anarchist, and took up a cultivation of that new species
of Bacterium I was telling you of, that infest, and I think

cause, the blue patches upon various monkeys; and like a fool, I said it was Asiatic cholera. And he ran away with it to poison the water of London, and he certainly might have made things look blue for this civilised city. And now he has swallowed it. Of course, I cannot say what will happen, but you know it turned that kitten blue, and the three puppies—in patches, and the sparrow—bright blue. But the bother is, I shall have all the trouble and expense of preparing some more.

"Put on my coat on this hot day! Why? Because we might meet Mrs. Jabber. My dear, Mrs. Jabber is not a draught. But why should I wear a coat on a hot day because of Mrs.——? Oh! *very* well."

THE GRISLY FOLK

THE GRISLY FOLK

"CAN these bones live ? "

Could anything be more dead, more mute and inexpressive to the inexpert eye than the ochreous fragments of bone and the fractured lumps of flint that constitute the first traces of something human in the world ? We see them in the museum cases, sorted out in accordance with principles we do not understand, labelled with strange names. Chellean, Mousterian, Solutrian and the like, taken mostly from the places Chelles, La Moustier, Solutre, and so forth where the first specimens were found. Most of us stare through the glass at them, wonder vaguely for a moment at that half-savage, half-animal past of our race, and pass on. "Primitive man," we say. "Flint implements. The mammoth used to chase him." Few of us realize yet how much the subtle indefatigable cross-examination of the scientific worker has been extracting from the evidence of these rusty and obstinate witnesses during the last few years.

One of the most startling results of this recent work is the gradual realisation that great quantities of these flint implements and some of the earlier fragments of bone that used to be ascribed to humanity are the vestiges of creatures, very manlike in many respects, but not, strictly speaking, belonging to the human species. Scientific men call these vanished races man (*Homo*), just as they call lions and tigers cats (*Felis*), but there are the soundest reasons for believing that these earlier so-called men were not of our blood, not our ancestors, but a strange and vanished animal, like us, akin to us, but different from us, as the mammoth was like, and akin to, and yet different from, the elephant. Flint and bone implements are found in deposits of very considerable antiquity ; some in our museums may be a million years old or more, but the traces of really human creatures, mentally and anatomically like ourselves, do not go back much earlier than twenty or thirty thousand years ago. True men appeared in Europe then, and we do not know whence they came. These other tool-using, fire-making animals, the things that were like men and yet were not men, passed away before the faces of the true men.

Scientific authorities already distinguish four species of these pseudo-men, and it is probable that we shall learn from time to time of other species. One strange breed made the implements called Chellean. These are chiefly sole-shaped blades of stone found in deposits of perhaps 300,000 or 400,000 years ago. Chellean implements are to be seen in any great museum. They are huge implements, *four or five times as big as those made by any known race of true men*, and they are not

ill made. Certainly some creature with an intelligent brain
made them. Big clumsy hands must have gripped and used these
rocky chunks. But so far only one small fragment of a skeleton
of this age has been found, a very massive chinless lower jaw-
bone, with teeth rather *more* specialised than those of men
to-day. We can only guess what strange foreshadowing of the
human form once ate with that jaw, and struck at its enemies
with those big but not unhandy flint blades. It may have been
a tremendous fellow, probably much bigger in the body than a
man. It may have been able to take bears by the scruff and the
sabre-toothed lion by the throat. We do not know. We have
just these great stone blades and that bit of a massive jaw
and—the liberty to wonder.

Most fascinating riddle of all these riddles of the ages of ice
and hardship, before the coming of the true men, is the riddle
of the Mousterian men, because they were perhaps still living
in the world when the true men came wandering into Europe.
They lived much later than those unknown Chellean giants.
They lived thirty or forty thousand years ago—a yesterday
compared with the Chellean time. These Mousterians are also
called Neandertalers. Until quite recently it was supposed
that they were true men like ourselves. But now we begin to
realise that they were different, so different that it is impossible
that they can be very close relations of ours. They walked or
shambled along with a peculiar slouch, they could not turn
their heads up to the sky, and their teeth were very different
from those of true men. One oddity about them is that in one
or two points they were less like apes than we are. The dog
tooth, the third tooth from the middle, which is so big in the
gorilla, and which in man is pointed and still quite distinct
from the other teeth, is not distinct at all in the Neandertaler.
He had a very even row of teeth, and his cheek teeth also
were very unlike ours, and less like the apes' than ours. He
had more face and less brow than true men, but that is not
because he had a lesser brain; his brain was as big as a modern
man's but it was different, bigger behind and smaller in front, so
that probably he thought and behaved differently from us. Perhaps he had a better memory and less reasoning power than
real men, or perhaps he had more nervous energy and less
intelligence. He had no chin, and the way his jawbones come
together below make it very doubtful if he could have used
any such sounds in speech as we employ. Probably he did not
talk at all. He could not hold a pin between his finger and
thumb. The more we learn about this beast-man the stranger
he becomes to us and the less like the Australoid savage he was
once supposed to be.

And as we realise the want of any close relationship between this ugly, strong, ungainly, manlike animal and mankind, the less likely it becomes that he had a naked skin and
hair like ours and the more probable that he was different

and perhaps bristly or hairy in some queer inhuman fashion like the hairy elephant and the woolly rhinoceros who were his contemporaries. Like them he lived in a bleak land on the edge of the snows and glaciers that were even then receding northward. Hairy or grisly, with a big face like a mask, great brow ridges and no forehead, clutching an enormous flint, and running like a baboon with his head forward and not, like a man, with his head up, he must have been a fearsome creature for our forefathers to come upon.

Almost certainly they met, these grisly men and the true men. The true man must have come into the habitat of the Neandertaler, and the two must have met and fought. Some day we may come upon the evidences of this warfare.

Western Europe, which is the only part of the world that has yet been searched with any thoroughness for the remains of early men, was slowly growing warmer age by age ; the glaciers that had once covered half the continent were receding, and wide stretches of summer pasture and thin woods of pine and birch were spreading slowly over the once icy land. South Europe then was like northern Labrador to-day. A few hardy beasts held out amidst the snows ; the bears hibernated. With the spring grass and foliage came great herds of reindeer, wild horses, mammoth, elephant, and rhinoceros, drifting northward from the slopes of the great warm valley that is now filled up with water—the Mediterranean Sea. It was in those days before the ocean waters broke into the Mediterranean that the swallows and a multitude of other birds acquired the habit of coming north, a habit that nowadays impels them to brave the passage of the perilous seas that flow over and hide the lost secrets of the ancient Mediterranean valleys. The grisly men rejoiced at the return of life, came out of the caves in which they had lurked during the winter, and took their toll of the beasts.

These grisly men must have been almost solitary creatures. The winter food was too scanty for communities. A male may have gone with a female or so ; perhaps they parted in the winter and came together in the summer ; when his sons grew big enough to annoy him, the grisly man killed them or drove them off. If he killed them he may have eaten them. If they escaped him they may have returned to kill him. The grisly folk may have had long unreasoning memories and very set purposes.

The true men came into Europe, we know not whence, out of the South. When they appeared in Europe their hands were as clever as ours ; they could draw pictures we still admire, they could paint and carve ; the implements they made were smaller than the Mousterian ones, far smaller than the Chellean, but better made and more various. They wore no clothes worth speaking of, but they painted themselves and probably they talked. And they came in little bands. They

were already more social than the Neandertaler; they had laws
and self-restraints; their minds had travelled a long way along
that path of adaptation and self-suppression which has led to
the intricate mind of man to-day with its concealed wishes,
its confusions, and laughter and the fantasies and reveries and
dreams. They were already held together, these men, and kept
in order by the strange limitations of tabu.

They were still savages, very prone to violence and convulsive in their lusts and desires; but to the best of their poor
ability they obeyed laws and customs already immemorably
ancient, and they feared the penalties of wrong-doing. We
can understand something of what was going on in their minds,
those of us who can remember the fears, desires, fancies and
superstitions of our childhood. Their moral struggles were
ours—in cruder forms. They were our kind. But the grisly
folk we cannot begin to understand. We cannot conceive in
our different minds the strange ideas that chased one another
through those queerly shaped brains. As well might we try
to dream and feel as a gorilla dreams and feels.

We can understand how the true men drifted northward
from the lost lands of the Mediterranean valley into the high
Spanish valleys and the south and centre of France, and so
on to what is now England—for there was no Channel then
between England and France—and eastward to the Rhineland
and over the broad wilderness which is now the North Sea,
and the German plain. They would leave the snowy wilderness of the Alps, far higher then and covered with great glaciers,
away on their right. These people drifted northward for the
very good reason that their kind was multiplying and food
diminishing. They would be oppressed by feuds and wars.
They had no settled homes; they were accustomed to drift
with the seasons, every now and then some band would be
pushed by hunger and fear a little farther northward into the
unknown.

We can imagine the appearance of a little group of these
wanderers, our ancestors, coming over some grassy crest into
these northern lands. The time would be late spring or early
summer, and they would probably be following up some grazing beasts, a reindeer herd or horses.

By a score of different means our anthropologists have been
able to reconstruct the particulars of the appearance and
habits of these early pilgrim fathers of mankind.

They would not be a very numerous band, because if they
were there would be no reason why they should have been
driven northward out of their former roving grounds. Two
or three older men of thirty or so, eight or ten women and
girls with a few young children, a few lads between fourteen
and twenty, might make up the whole community. They
would be a brownish brown-eyed people with wavy dark hair;
the fairness of the European and the straight blue-black hair

of the Chinaman had still to be evolved in the world. The older men would probably lead the band, the women and children would keep apart from the youths and men, fenced off by complex and definite tabus from any close companionship. The leaders would be tracking the herd they were following. Tracking was then the supreme accomplishment of mankind. By signs and traces that would be invisible to any modern civilised eye, they would be reading the story of the previous day's trek of the herd of sturdy little horses ahead of them. They would be so expert that they would go on from one faint sign to another with as little delay as a dog who follows a scent.

The horses they were following were only a little way ahead —so the trackers read the signs—they were numerous and nothing had alarmed them. They were grazing and moving only very slowly. There were no traces of wild dog or other animals to stampede them. Some elephants were also going north, and twice our human tribe had crossed the spoor of woolly rhinoceros roaming westward.

The tribe travelled light. They were mainly naked, but all of them were painted with white and black and red and yellow ochre. At this distance of time it is difficult to see whether they were tattooed. Probably they were not. The babies and small children were carried by the women on their backs in slings or bags made of animal skins, and perhaps some or all of them wore mantles and loin bands of skin and had pouches and belts of leather. The men had stone-pointed spears, and carried sharpened flints in their hands.

There was no Old Man who was lord and master and father of this particular crowd. Weeks ago the Old Man had been charged and trampled to a jelly by a great bull in the swamp far away. Then two of the girls had been waylaid and carried off by the young men of another larger tribe. It was because of these losses that this remnant was now seeking new hunting grounds.

The landscape that spread before the eyes of this little band as they crested the hills was a bleaker, more desolate and altogether unkempt versio of the landscape of western Europe to-day. About them was a grassy down athwart which a peewit flew with its melancholy cry. Before them stretched a great valley ridged with transverse purple hills over which the April cloud-shadows chased one another. Pinewoods and black heather showed where these hills became sandy, and the valleys were full of brown brushwood, and down their undrained troughs ran a bright green band of peaty swamps and long pools of weedy water. In the valley thickets many beasts lurked unseen, and where the winding streams had cut into the soil there were cliffs and caves. Far away along the northern slopes of the ridge that were now revealed, the wild onies were to be seen grazing.

At a sign from the two leaders the little straggle of menfolk
halted, and a woman who had been chattering in subdued
tones to a little girl became silent. The brothers surveyed the
wide prospect earnestly.

" Ugh ! " said one abruptly and pointed.

" Ugh ! " cried his brother.

The eyes of the whole tribe swung round to the pointing
finger.

The group became one rigid stare.

Every soul of them stood still, astonishment had turned
them into a tense group of statuettes.

Far away down the slope with his body in profile and his
head turned towards them, frozen by an equal amazement,
stood a hunched grey figure, bigger but shorter than a man.
He had been creeping up behind a fold in the ground to peer
at the ponies, and suddenly he had turned his eyes and seen
the tribe. His head projected like a baboon's. In his hand he
carried what seemed to the menfolk a great rock.

For a little while this animal scrutiny held discoverers and
discovered motionless. Then some of the women and children
began to stir and line out to see the strange creature better.
" Man ! " said an old crone of forty. " *Man !* " At the movement of the women the grisly man turned, ran clumsily for a
score of yards or so towards a thicket of birch and budding
thorn. Then he halted again for a moment to look at the newcomers, waved an arm strangely, and then dashed into cover.

The shadows of the thicket swallowed him up, and by hiding
him seemed to make him enormous. It identified itself with
him, and watched them with his eyes. Its tree stems became
long silvery limbs, and a fallen trunk crouched and stared.

It was still early in the morning, and the leaders of the tribe
had hoped to come up with the wild ponies as the day advanced
and perhaps cut one off and drive it into difficulties among the
bushes and swampy places below, and wound it and follow it
up and kill it. Then they would have made a feast, and somewhere down in the valley they would have found water and
dry bracken for litter and a fire before night. It had seemed a
pleasant and hopeful morning to them until this moment.
Now they were disconcerted. This grey figure was as if the
sunny morning had suddenly made a horrible and inexplicable
grimace.

The whole expedition stood gazing for a time, and then the
two leaders exchanged a few words. Waugh, the elder, pointed.
Click, his brother, nodded his head. They would go on, but
instead of slanting down the slopes towards the thickets they
would keep round the ridge.

" Come," said Waugh, and the little band began to move
again. But now it marched in silence. When presently a little
boy began a question his mother silenced him by a threat.
Everybody kept glancing at the thickets below.

Presently a girl cried out sharply and pointed. All started and stopped short.

There was the grisly thing again. It was running across an open space, running almost on all fours, in joltering leaps. It was hunchbacked and very big and low, a grey hairy wolf-like monster. At times its long arms nearly touched the ground. It was nearer than it had been before. It vanished amidst the bushes again. It seemed to throw itself down among some red dead bracken. . . .

Waugh and Click took counsel.

A mile away was the head of the valley where the thickets had their beginning. Beyond stretched the woldy hills, bare of cover. The horses were grazing up towards the sun, and away to the north the backs of a herd of woolly rhinoceros were now visible on a crest—just the ridges of their backs showing like a string of black beads.

If the tribe struck across those grassy spaces, then the lurking prowler would have either to stay behind or come into the open. If he came into the open the dozen youths and men of the tribe would know how to deal with him.

So they struck across the grass. The little band worked round to the head of the valley, and there the menfolk stayed at the crest while the women and children pushed on ahead across the open.

For a time the watchers remained motionless, and then Waugh was moved to gestures of defiance. Click was not to be outdone. There were shouts at the hidden watcher, and then one lad, who was something of a clown, after certain grimaces and unpleasant gestures, obliged with an excellent imitation of the grey thing's lumbering run. At that scare gave place to hilarity.

In those days laughter was a social embrace. Men could laugh, but there was no laughter in the grisly pre-man who watched and wondered in the shadow. He marvelled. The men rolled about and guffawed and slapped their thighs and one another. Tears ran down their faces.

Never a sign came from the thickets.

" Yahah," said the menfolk. " Yahah ! Bzzzz, Yahah ! Yah ! "

They forgot altogether how frightened they had been.

And when Waugh thought the women and children had gone on a sufficient distance, he gave the word for the men to follow them.

In such fashion it was that men, our ancestors, had their first glimpse of the pre-men of the wilderness of western Europe. . . .

The two breeds were soon to come to closer quarters.

The newcomers were pushing their way into the country of these grisly men. Presently came other glimpses of lurking semi-human shapes and grey forms that ran in the twilight.

In the morning Click found long narrow footprints round the camp. . . .

Then one day one of the children, eating those little green thorn-buds that rustic English children speak of as bread and cheese, ventured too far from the others. There was a squeal and a scuffle and a thud, and something grey and hairy made off through the thickets carrying its victim, with Waugh and three of the younger men in hot pursuit. They chased the enemy into a dark gully, very much overgrown. This time it was not a solitary Neandertaler they had to deal with. Out of the bushes a big male came at them to cover the retreat of his mate, and hurled a rock that bowled over the youth it hit like a nine-pin, so that thereafter he limped always. But Waugh with his throwing spear got the grey monster in the shoulder, and he halted snarling.

No further sound came from the stolen child.

The female showed herself for a moment up the gully, snarling, bloodstained, and horrible, and the menfolk stood about afraid to continue their pursuit, and yet not caring to desist from it. One of them was already hobbling off with his hand to his knee.

How did that first fight go ?

Perhaps it went against the men of our race. Perhaps the big Neandertaler male, his mane and beard bristling horribly, came down the gully with a thunderous roar, with a great rock in either hand. We do not know whether he threw those big discs of flint or whether he smote with them. Perhaps it was then that Waugh was killed in the act of running away. Perhaps it was bleak disaster then for the little tribe. Short of two of its members it presently made off over the hills as fast as it could go, keeping together for safety, and leaving the wounded youth far behind to limp along its tracks in lonely terror.

Let us suppose that he got back to the tribe at last—after nightmare hours.

Now that Waugh had gone, Click would become Old Man, and he made the tribe camp that night and build their fire on the high ridges among the heather far away from the thickets in which the grisly folk might be lurking.

The grisly folk thought we knew not how about the menfolk, and the men thought about the grisly folk in such ways as we can understand ; they imagined how their enemies might act in this fashion or that, and schemed to circumvent them. It may have been Click who had the first dim idea of getting at the gorge in which the Neandertalers had their lair, from above. For as we have said, the Neandertaler did not look up. Then the menfolk could roll a great rock upon him or pelt him with burning brands and set the dry bracken alight.

One likes to think of a victory for the human side. This Click we have conjured up had run in panic from the first onset of the grisly male, but as he brooded by the fire that night he heard again in imagination the cry of the lost girl, and he was filled with rage. In his sleep the grisly male came to him and Click fought in his dreams and started awake stiff with fury. There was a fascination for him in that gorge in which Waugh had been killed. He was compelled to go back and look again for the grisly beasts, to waylay them in their tracks, and watch them from an ambush. He perceived that the Neandertalers could not climb as easily as the menfolk could climb, nor hear so quickly, nor dodge with the same unexpectedness. These grisly men were to be dealt with as the bears were dealt with, the bears before whom you run and scatter, and then come at again from behind.

But one may doubt if the first human group to come into the grisly land was clever enough to solve the problems of the new warfare. Maybe they turned southward again to the gentler regions from which they had come, and were killed by or mingled with their own brethren again. Maybe they perished altogether in that new land of the grisly folk into which they had intruded. Yet the truth may be that they even held their own and increased. If they died there were others of their kind to follow them and achieve a better fate.

That was the beginning of a nightmare age for the little children of the human tribe. They knew they were watched.

Their steps were dogged. The legends of ogres and man-eating giants that haunt the childhood of the world may descend to us from those ancient days of fear. And for the Neandertalers it was the beginning of an incessant war that could end only in extermination.

The Neandertalers, albeit not so erect and tall as men, were the heavier, stronger creatures, but they were stupid, and they went alone or in twos and threes ; the menfolk were swifter, quicker-witted, and more social—when they fought they fought in combination. They lined out and surrounded and pestered and pelted their antagonists from every side. They fought the men of that grisly race as dogs might fight a bear. They shouted to one another what each should do, and the Neandertaler had no speech ; he did not understand. They moved too quickly for him and fought too cunningly.

Many and obstinate were the duels and battles these two sorts of men fought for this world in that bleak age of the windy steppes, thirty or forty thousand years ago. The two races were intolerable to each other. They both wanted the caves and the banks by the rivers where the big flints were got. They fought over the dead mammoths that had been bogged in the marshes, and over the reindeer stags that had been killed in the rutting season. When a human tribe found signs of the grisly folk near their cave and squatting place, they had perforce to track them down and kill them ; their own safety and the safety of their little ones was only to be

secured by that killing. The Neandertalers thought the little
children of men fair game and pleasant eating.

How long the grisly folk lived on in that chill world of pines
and silver birch between the steppes and the glaciers, after
the true menfolk came, we do not know. For ages they may
have held out, growing more cunning and dangerous as they
became rare. The true men hunted them down by their spoor
and by their tracks, and watched for the smoke of their fires,
and made food scarce for them.

Great Paladins arose in that forgotten world, men who
stood forth and smote the grey man-beast face to face and
slew him. They made long spears of wood, hardened by fire
at the tips ; they raised shields of skin against his mighty
blows. They struck at him with stones on cords, and slung
them at him with slings. And it was not simply men who
withstood the grisly beast but women. They stood over their
children ; they stood by their men against this eerie thing
that was like and yet not like mankind. Unless the *savants*
read all the signs awry, it was the women who were the makers
of the larger tribes into which human families were already
growing in those ancient times. It was the woman's subtle,
love-guided wits which protected her sons from the fierce anger
of the Old Man, and taught them to avoid his jealousy and
wrath, and persuaded him to tolerate them and so have their
help against the grisly enemy. It was woman, says Atkinson,
in the beginning of things human, who taught the primary
tabus, that a son must go aside out of the way of his step-
mother, and get himself a wife from another tribe, so as to
keep the peace within the family. She came between the
fratricides, and was the first peacemaker. Human societies in
their beginnings were her work, done against the greater
solitariness, the lonely fierceness of the adult male. Through
her, men learnt the primary co-operation of sonship and
brotherhood. The grisly folk had not learnt even the rudest
elements of co-operation, and mankind had already spelt out
the alphabet of a unity that may some day comprehend the
whole earth. The menfolk kept together by the dozen and by
the score. By ones and twos and threes therefore the grisly
folk were beset and slain, until there were no more of them left
in the world.

Generation after generation, age after age, that long struggle
for existence went on between these men who were not quite
men and the men, our ancestors, who came out of the south
into western Europe. Thousands of fights and hunts, sudden
murders and headlong escapes there were amidst the caves
and thickets of that chill and windy world between the last
age of glaciers and our own warmer time. Until at length the
last poor grisly was brought to bay and faced the spears of his
pursuers in anger and despair.

What leapings of the heart were there not throughout that

long warfare ! What moments of terror and triumph ! What acts of devotion and desperate wonders of courage ! And the strain of the victors was our strain ; we are lineally identical with those sun-brown painted beings who ran and fought and helped one another, the blood in our veins glowed in those fights and chilled in those fears of the forgotten past. For it was forgotten. Except perhaps for some vague terrors in our dreaming life and for some lurking element of tradition in the legends and warnings of the nursery, it has gone altogether out of the memory of our race. But nothing is ever completely lost. Seventy or eighty years ago a few curious *savants* began to suspect that there were hidden memories in certain big chipped flints and scraps of bone they found in ancient gravels. Much more recently others have begun to find hints of remote strange experiences in the dreams and odd kinks in modern minds. By degrees these dry bones begin to live again.

This restoration of the past is one of the most astonishing adventures of the human mind. As humanity follows the gropings of scientific men among these ancient vestiges, it is like a man who turns over the yellow pages of some long-forgotten diary, some engagement book of his adolescence. His dead youth lives again. Once more the old excitements stir him, the old happiness returns. But the old passions that once burnt, only warm him now, and the old fears and distresses signify nothing.

A day may come when these recovered memories may grow as if we in our own persons had been there and shared the thrill and the fear of those primordial days ; a day may come when the great beasts of the past will leap to life again in our imaginations, when we shall walk again in vanished scenes, stretch painted limbs we thought were dust, and feel again the sunshine of a million years ago.

Printed by H. Henderson at the Villafield Press, Bishopbriggs